THE DRAGON AZHDEEN ROUSED IN SURPRISE—

and a picture appeared in the air. Dragon-conjured before Pol was a strange sight: dragons floating on the sea. Not living dragons, but stiff, motionless, with uplifted wings frozen in place. Like sails, Pol thought, tracing with his gaze the raised necks with their sightless heads dipping to the rise and fall of the waves. Ships, of course, built of wood and not dragon bones and hide, but Azhdeen couldn't know that. He evidently thought dragons had been killed and made to float on water.

Pol wove his colors into the picture, altering it to reflect what he knew was the reality. Wings became sails; bones changed to masts and rigging. He had never seen such a vessel himself, but his years as a squire at Graypearl had familiarized him with ships. He added people on what was now a wooden deck.

It's nothing more than that, he told Azhdeen, conveying reassurance.

The reaction felled him. The dragon threw back his head with a roar. Pol was knocked off his feet and out of the intricate weave of color. His wits spun and for a time he could barely see. When Pol could stand again, Azhdeen was rearing back on his hind legs, wings unfurled, bellowing his rage.

Pol again offered his colors to the dragon. *What is it? What have I done?*

Azhdeen glared. Again the picture formed. *Believe!* was the emotion whirling on sunlight. . . .

Melanie Rawn's magnificent saga of love and war, of sunweaving magic and princes' honor—and of the dragons, deadly dangerous yet holding the secret of power beyond imagining. . . .

DRAGON PRINCE:

DRAGON PRINCE
(*Book One*)

THE STAR SCROLL
(*Book Two*)

SUNRUNNER'S FIRE
(*Book Three*)

DRAGON STAR:

STRONGHOLD
(*Book One*)

THE DRAGON TOKEN
(*Book Two*)
(*available in hardcover in February 1992*)

DAW BOOKS, INC.
DONALD A. WOLLHEIM, FOUNDER
375 Hudson Street, New York, N.Y 10014
ELIZABETH R. WOLLHEIM
SHEILA E. GILBERT
PUBLISHERS

Cover art by Michael Whelan.

For color prints of Michael Whelan paintings, please contact:
Glass Onion Graphics
P.O. Box 88
Brookfield, CT 06804

Map by Marty Siegrist.

DAW Book Collectors No. 832.

DAW Books are distributed by Penguin U.S.A.

First Paperback Printing, September 1991

1 2 3 4 5 6 7 8 9

PRINTED IN THE U.S.A.

For all the teachers who figured there must be
something going on with this kid—
but never suspected it would be anything like this.

N
W
E
S
TIRON
BALARAT
TESSENDEN
Dark Water
Ush River
CASTLE CRAG
PRINCEMARCH
ISEL
Brochwell Bay
WAES
KIERST
GRIB
L. Kadar
Goddess Keep
OSSETIA
Far Islands

CUNAXA
Tuath Castle
Tiglath
Sunrise Water
Feruche
DESERT
Skybowl
Remagev
Stronghold
Vere Hills
The Long Sand
DORVAL
Radzyn Keep
Graypearl
Faolain River
SYR
Catha River
Catha Hills
Small Islands
South Water

PART ONE

Chapter One

Rohan squinted into the Desert sky, watching his circling hawk. All at once the bird plummeted to the rough scrub of the Vere Hills. Rohan held his breath. A few moments later the hawk soared upward, a greentail clutched in her talons. She spiraled on a thermal, then swooped down to deposit the plump bird neatly at Rohan's feet. When she balanced on his arm again, he whistled appreciatively; she replied with a grating coo of affection.

"She's flirting with you again," Sioned observed.

"I have that effect on ladies of taste and perception." He fed the bird a morsel of raw meat, whistled the flight command again, and flung her smoothly into the air. The hawk flew off to seek her own dinner.

Sioned sat down on a rock. "I assume that means Avaly of Rezeld would've had more luck if she'd batted her lashes?"

"So *that's* what's been bothering you all day." Unhooking the water skin from his belt, he took a swig and offered her some.

"It was embarrassing to watch." She drank and stoppered the skin.

"All I could think about was getting her off her knees and out of my sight as fast as possible."

"Why did she wait nine years? It couldn't have taken that long to think up that tale about her father's being under a *diarmadhi* spell like Chiana."

"Her proposed husband evidently inspired her. He wants the holding and the title along with her highborn blood. That's the only dowry a merchant that wealthy would care about."

"Well, he can't have them. Morlen was just waiting for a chance to betray you and Pol, and I see no reason to reward his daughter for it. And anyway, how could she think of marrying a man who forced her to that performance?"

"Sioned! Wouldn't you plead on your knees for me?"

"With *my* aching joints? Certainly not."

He grinned down at her. "Well, I suppose you *are* getting old and crippled and decrepit."

"Half a season your senior, young fellow, and don't you forget it!" She wagged a finger at him, laughing.

He caught her hand and was about to pull her up into his arms when a screech and a feather-rush warned him. He turned just in time to extend his right arm to his hawk, who dug her talons into protective leather and preened.

"Jealous, too," Sioned remarked. "Goddess, doesn't she look pleased with herself!"

They walked back through the late afternoon haze to Stronghold, entering by the grotto passage—once secret, but not anymore. Sioned lingered by the waterfall to bathe her face and arms while Rohan returned his hawk to the mews. This autumn, her thirty-ninth in the Desert, was the hottest she could recall. She and Rohan had avoided summer completely this year by indulging in a lengthy journey through Syr before going up to Dragon's Rest for the *Rialla*. She'd shown him her childhood home of River Run, taken a side trip into the Catha Hills to investigate the dragons' winter lairs, and stopped in at High Kirat to visit her nephew Prince Kostas and his family. Many times they'd left their small retinue behind and slept in the open, hunted or hawked as fancy dictated, and forgotten for days at a time that there were titles and responsibilities attached to their names.

But having escaped the summer heat, they returned after the *Rialla* to find their princedom had taken on all the soothing qualities of a smelting furnace. The sun blazed, the dunes burned with shimmer-visions, and heat clung to every stone. Rohan shrugged off the brutal climate, being Desert born and bred, but even though she'd spent two-thirds of her life here, Sioned felt the heat more as she grew older.

She settled on a mossy rock and hauled off her boots. Gasping with the shock as she plunged her feet into cool water, she closed her eyes and tried to dream herself back at River Run. No use. If Avaly hadn't arrived yesterday with her foredoomed plea, she could have been at Radzyn by now, enjoying its crisp sea breezes, visiting Maarken and Hollis at Whitecliff—

"Don't get too comfortable," advised Rohan from behind her. "We've just been graced with an emissary from Prince Velden of Grib."

"Damn it, what's wrong with these people? Why couldn't they have talked to us at the *Rialla*?"

"Doubtless they had their reasons."

"Whatever they are, I don't like them."

"Come on, High Princess—we played all summer. Time to get back to work."

She kicked water at him across the little pool. "I don't want to."

"Now you sound like Jihan."

"Well, you have to admit people make things difficult. You can hardly pretend to be reluctant with your power when they're always handing you chances to use it."

"Pretend?" He frowned.

"Demanding that you use it, actually. At least Pol's honest about it. He *loves* to fix things and makes no pretense of—"

"Just be grateful that someone still finds it worthwhile to consult us old folks," he drawled.

That silenced her. She followed him back through the gardens and upstairs, gnawing over his implication. It was amusing to tease each other about oncoming old age—especially when neither believed the other had aged at all—but at times they were forcibly reminded that the years were indeed accumulating.

The knowledge had sneaked up on them at first. Perhaps it had started at the *Rialla* of 731, Pol's first as husband and father as well as prince. He had spoken for Princemarch before, of course, but with his new family had come new awarenesses. The terms he gained, independent of anything Rohan won for the Desert, were highly advantageous and gave subtle hints about his plans for his daughters' future. Rohan and Sioned had congratulated themselves on their success—after all, they had taught Pol everything he knew.

But more leisurely reflection, and repetition of the experience in 734 and again this very summer, had shown them a hard truth. While the princes still looked to them, they also looked to Pol. The next High Prince.

Rohan and Sioned had given him the world in which he exercised his share of the family cunning. The peace they'd established had lasted with only minor lapses since 704.

They'd founded a school for physicians and a scriptorium. Specific borders agreed to by all princes ensured that no more wars were fought over a few square measures of land. Arts and sciences thrived. Interwoven trade made the princedoms economically dependent on each other. Most importantly, Rohan had nudged the other rulers into standardizing much of the legal code. Over the years this had come to be known as the High Prince's Writ, and it would be his most lasting achievement. It was more than any other High Prince had done before him, more than anyone else could have hoped to do in a lifetime—even if anyone else had been the dreamer Rohan was. But because he did have dreams, leavened with vast patience and ruthless practicality, there was so much more that he wanted to accomplish.

It was a proud thing to watch Pol fulfill their hopes. And Meiglan had surprised them all with her adjustments to her role as his wife. Though she would never be the kind of High Princess Sioned was, she had grown into her own sort of wisdom. People didn't confide in Meiglan, or consult her about matters of state. They merely did not guard their tongues around her. It was an opportunity not open to Sioned, whose intelligence was well known and often feared. She learned more from what people didn't tell her than from what they did. But Meiglan was so quiet, so unobtrusive, that most of the time one forgot she was there. What she reported was colored by her personal prejudices—she loathed Pirro of Fessenden, for instance, and was terrified of Chiana. But she had learned to weed out what was important and present it with an eye to Pol's needs. Her methods differed from Sioned's, but she got the job done.

This past *Rialla* Rohan and Sioned had mostly watched the young couple's work, giving private advice here and there. It was time for them to move into the background; eventually Pol and Meiglan would take their places. The other princes must accustom themselves to the next generation. Eminently practical—but a little depressing.

Sioned wondered if Zehava had experienced the same thing when Rohan had been the one young and strong and full of impatient energy. She understood Pol's eagerness—the young dragon exhilarated by the strength of his wings. Perhaps Zehava had watched with the same smile she saw sometimes on Rohan's face, a look of pride and rueful regret.

She sat at her dressing table, brushing out her hair, watching him covertly in the mirror. The hot misted light of sunset drifting through open windows turned his hair as gold as it had been in his youth. Looking at him as he shrugged out of his sweat-stained shirt, it was impossible to convince herself that this coming winter would be his sixty-first. That it would be forty years next spring since she'd first seen him on the road to Stronghold, bloodied and exhausted after killing the dragon that had killed his father. That they were not just growing older, but growing old. That not only had she never fallen out of love with him, but had, in fact, fallen in love with him all over again many times—most recently this very summer.

Preposterous. The product of an overactive imagination that insisted on picturing him at River Run, enchanted with the greenness, lazing back in flower-strewn grass, making love to her in a hayloft, racing for shelter during a sudden thundershower. Or at Dragon's Rest: long walks in the forest or through Pol's beloved gardens, nights on their own in Meiglan's little hillside cottage, a memorable evening when she took him on a tasting tour of the wine cellar she'd personally assembled for their son.

Yet there had been reminders of age, too, most obviously in the form of twin seven-year-old granddaughters. Rohan didn't *look* like a grandsire. But Jihan had not only half his name but his blue eyes as well, and the cleft in Rislyn's dainty chin could have come from no one else. He gleefully indulged them with endless games of dragon slaying, and earned the supreme accolade that Grandsir was *much* better at it than Papa. Jihan usually won; she was the dominant twin, running riot around the palace, trailing mischief in her wake. Rislyn was quieter, gentler, more like her shy mother. Everyone adored Jihan, but everyone's favorite was Rislyn.

They even said that Rislyn looked very like Sioned.

Gentle fingers clasped her shoulders, and she gave a start. "I didn't mean that, you know," Rohan said. "About being old."

"I know you didn't, but it's true." She met his gaze in the mirror. "Though it's hard to believe, looking at you. You've gone all silvery instead of golden—that's the only difference."

"Liar. My bones creak and my right shoulder aches in the cold and my arms aren't long enough to hold parchments where I can read them."

"And last night all you could do in bed was sleep."

He grinned. "Well, I do seem to have a soft spot for elderly ladies."

"My dear decrepit *azhrei*, right now I haven't the slightest interest in your *soft* spots."

Quite some time later, he stretched and dug his toes into the cool silk of bunched sheets at the end of the bed. Using a strand of Sioned's long hair to tickle her shoulder, he whispered, "I think I saw it that time."

"Hmm?" she asked drowsily. "Saw what?"

"The colors."

She quivered with silent laughter. "Now we have the truth at last. He only makes love to the Sunrunner witch for the sake of intellectual curiosity."

"Certainly," he agreed. "You should never have told me what you see. I've been trying to catch a glimpse ever since."

"And did you?"

"Why don't we try it again and I'll let you know?"

* * *

The Gribains were growing impatient by the time Rohan and Sioned finally came downstairs for dinner in the Great Hall. Casual pleasantries were the order of conversation; the Gribains were firmly steered away from any formal discussion during the meal. Rohan knew why they were here. According to his habit, he had made no decision and would not until one presented itself. Though open discussion was prevented by Sioned's tact and Rohan's sporadic deafness whenever the subject was hinted at, he had not counted on the artless innocence of the squire who was serving at dinner.

Isriam was the only child of Sabriam of Einar and Isaura of Meadowlord, Prince Halian's niece. With his family connections and the wealth of his father's city, one day Isriam would be an important man. At sixteen he was a dark-eyed, dark-haired, gawky adolescent possessed of not the slightest hint of subtlety. Rohan kept telling himself the boy would grow out of his awkwardness, but despaired of ever teaching him how to keep his every thought from his face and his every idea from spilling over into speech. As he served taze and cakes to the high table, Isriam asked, "Will your grace desire the Summer Room made ready for a conference with the Gribain ambassadors this evening?"

This was the perfect opening, and the courtier who had been sent by Prince Velden took advantage of it with practiced smoothness. "It is extremely wise of your grace to wish this unhappy matter settled as quickly as possible. We will, of course, make ourselves available to your grace immediately after dinner."

Rohan considered answering Isriam in the negative, then chided himself. He had spent most of the spring and all summer at play. He planned a trip to Radzyn in a few days that would extend the holiday well into autumn. He really ought to do a little work and earn the privilege of being bowed to and gossiped about behind his back. Deciding to give in, he replied with a smile, "That's very kind of you, Master Eschur. The journey from Grib is a tiring one. But if it suits, then yes, we'll meet in a little while."

"As your grace wishes," Eschur said with a slight bow. Rohan reflected that his name suited him; eyes with a "wolf's sight" he truly had, yellowish and sharp. The High Prince did not anticipate a fun evening.

He was right. With Sioned at his side and Isriam attending them—one could only hope he would learn something—Rohan listened as the Gribains presented their prince's views. The problem outlined to him was a reminder that whatever he had accomplished by way of codifying laws, he hadn't thought of everything. Not by any means.

The difficulty was one of inheritance. An Ossetian younger brother had married the heiress of a neighboring *athri* in Grib. It was agreed all around that the young man would forswear his allegiance to Prince Tilal and commit himself instead to Prince Velden. The *athri* had died this spring and the daughter and her husband had inherited. But the elder brother had recently suffered a serious head injury; he recognized no one and was subject to intermittent fits of violence. His heartbroken brother had reluctantly ordered him confined for his own safety and that of his people.

With the elder brother incapable of rule, the younger was the heir. But this would leave the young man with two holdings in two different princedoms—with two sets of loyalties. Should the lands be combined under one princedom? If so, which? Should they be kept separate against the day when sons would be born to take one holding each? Or should the man inherit only his own father's land, with the Gribain holding reverting to Prince Velden and being bestowed at his pleasure to someone else?

Tilal sent no emissary; nor had he come to Stronghold from Dragon's Rest, where he and his wife Gemma lingered to see their daughter Sioneva settled in for a long visit. Tilal had merely conveyed to Sioned through Pol that whatever was decided would be fine with him. Rohan thanked the Goddess for providing him with at least one prince who trusted him completely. Of course, Tilal was Sioned's nephew and had been Rohan's squire. His faith in the High Prince was a very personal thing, not to be confused with the sometimes wary acquiescence of others.

Fifty years ago, the two princedoms would have mustered armies by now and tested each other's commitment through a few skirmishes, consulting the High Prince only if neither force left the field—and the holding—to the other. Roelstra would have been called on to stop a war already half begun. This time no one had even considered battle. Rohan was being asked to settle a difficulty of law. But he did not congratulate himself yet on the happy progress of civilization. If the High Prince's Writ could not provide a satisfactory solution, things could still degenerate into open conflict.

Still, at least they were talking about it instead of fighting. However often he accused himself of throwing words at a problem until it collapsed under their sheer weight, he was always reminded of something Chay had told him long ago: that those words were his armies, fighting battles without bloodshed, more effective than any swords or arrows. Rohan supposed this was true; he felt like a battleground often enough.

As anticipated, Velden wanted the property to revert to himself. This was couched in much flowery sympathy for the family and regret for not continuing a holding in the line that had held it so long. But the meaning was plain: Velden wanted those valuable square measures, and he intended Rohan to take his side.

"We thank you for your statements," Rohan said when they were finished. "We will, of course, consider them very carefully."

Sioned coughed to hide what he knew was amusement at a speech she had heard a million times. Then she said, "I gather there is no objection to the young man's qualifications?"

"None, your grace," Eschur said. "He is honest, capable, and well-liked."

"I'm glad to hear it," she replied warmly. "We must be careful that no insult is implied to his abilities. No matter what is decided, he will still be an *athri* and conscious of his honor as such." She paused, frowning slightly. "If our cousin of Grib *did* have the giving of this holding, who do you think it would go to, Master Eschur? Just to satisfy my curiosity, you understand."

Rohan wondered what she knew, or thought she knew. Eschur's wolfish eyes narrowed in a flash of some powerful emotion and a corner of his mouth twitched downward. He said, "I am not sufficiently in Prince Velden's confidence to know, your grace."

Sioned smiled in sweet sympathy. "Ah, yes, we princes must have our little secrets, mustn't we? How irritating it must be sometimes!"

"The ways of princes, your grace, are not to be questioned by mere common folk like myself."

A proper answer, delivered with the proper humility, but the whole byplay told Rohan what Sioned had guessed: Eschur himself coveted the holding and the title that went with it. Crafty of Velden, sending a man who wanted the lands to argue for them. If he gained them for his prince, they would be his reward.

But Master Eschur had something else to say. "His grace has, however, instructed me to make known to your royal highnesses that he would appreciate a consultation with Lord Andry."

Rohan kept startlement from his face. "To what purpose?"

"It is said that certain powerful *faradh'im* can see the future in a flame. Prince Velden considers that this might be a useful—" Eschur's yellow gaze strayed to Sioned: a mistake. The look in her eyes deprived him of the power of speech.

She asked very softly, "And did Lord Andry volunteer his personal services for this little experiment in oracle reading? Or will any Sunrunner do?"

He swallowed hard, rallied, and managed, "Lord Andry reacted favorably to the suggestion. I meant no offense, your grace."

"We know precisely what you meant."

There were levels to Sioned's rage; Rohan had rarely seen

this one. Tobin vented her wrath with the same vehemence whatever the weight of the matter. Sioned's responses varied—and in her green eyes now was the lethal fury that paralyzed its object the way legend said a dragon's gaze turned men to stone.

"Convenient to have a fortune-teller ready to hand, isn't it?" she said in that same silken voice. Extending both her hands, the single great emerald flashing in bright candle-light, she added, "But perhaps we do not meet the current standard. Do you think our lack of Sunrunner's rings disqualifies us?"

That lack had caused many to forget what Sioned truly was: Sunrunner as well as High Princess. Eschur's face turned white. "Your g-grace, I—"

"Or perhaps," Sioned went on inexorably, "our training at Goddess Keep under Lady Andrade was so long ago that we are not fully conversant with the rituals now considered necessary by Lord Andry."

Eschur gulped again and flung a look of appeal at Rohan.

"We suggest you withdraw your proposal," the High Prince said mildly.

After several tries he stammered out, "I—I will so inform Prince Velden." He and his companion departed the Summer Room with indecent haste.

Rohan gestured to the slack-jawed Isriam. Sioned saw it and snapped, "I don't need any wine. I need a few moments in private with the Prince of Goddess Keep!"

"Drink it anyway." When Isriam had provided full goblets for them both, Rohan waited until Sioned had downed a good half of hers and was seething in silence before saying, "I understand how you feel."

"No, you don't," she stated flatly. "You're not a Sunrunner."

Aware that they ought not discuss this around Isriam, he turned from her and beckoned the squire forward. "Well? What do you think?" he asked.

"Me, my lord?" Isriam turned red and stared.

"You, my lord," Rohan replied, wishing the boy would cease his imitation of an astonished lobster, all red face and blinking eyes. "You heard Master Eschur explain the problem. You know the circumstances. What is your opinion?" Isriam continued to gape, and Rohan sighed. Goddess help Einar if her future ruler didn't learn to see people with his mind as well as his eyes.

Sioned had made the effort and recovered her balance by now. She entered into a conversation designed to instruct the squire in statecraft—as well as to clarify the available options. Rohan's other purpose was to distract her from her anger; that she knew it was clear in the glance she gave him before asking, "What do you think of Prince Velden's claim, Isriam?"

"It sounds valid, my lady," he ventured.

"It does indeed. Did you draw any conclusions from Master Eschur's reply when I asked about who might receive the holding?"

Isriam's brow furrowed. At length he said, "I—I'm not sure, my lady. But I think perhaps he knows who wants it, even if he doesn't know who'll get it."

"Absolutely true. He does know who wants it. And so do I."

"Really? Who?"

"He does. Think about it. If you had a case to present to the High Prince, who would you send to do it? Who would argue most strongly?"

Isriam considered with an even mightier frown. Then sunlight broke across his face. "Master Eschur himself!"

Rohan felt like applauding. Instead he drawled, "If you two are finished being brilliant. . . ."

"Isriam and I are doing very nicely without you. Run away and play while we solve all your problems."

Emboldened by his success, Isriam actually grinned. Rohan chuckled; there might be hope for the boy after all.

"All right, then," he said, "consider this. The two holdings lie on the coast and command a nice little harbor. The only reason no substantial town has grown up there before is that the place is held by two princes, not one. They do a minor shipping business, but most goods go to port at Waes—or Einar." He let Isriam ruminate on this for a moment, and saw the dark eyes go wide. Sioned gave him a disgusted look that told him he was being unfair.

"My father wouldn't half like it if the two combined and a port was built," Isriam said worriedly.

"No, he wouldn't. But I'm not Lord of Einar, I'm High Prince. More and easier trade is always profitable and therefore desirable. It's part of my duty to foster such. So again I ask: what would you recommend?"

The boy looked miserably unhappy. "My lord . . . I don't think I'm able to say. I am my father's son."

Sioned took pity on him. "Isriam, that is exactly the right answer for you to give. It's not your decision and you're correct to remind his grace of that. As an *athri*, your duty is to look to your own interests first and foremost."

Isriam's brows knotted over his nose. "But—but still I have to think about what might happen to everyone else."

Rohan was pleased. "That's very wise of you. You're fortunate. You can consider possibilities and choose the most personally advantageous with a clear conscience. I have to pick what's best for everyone."

Sioned added in dry tones, "His grace's conscience does not bear close scrutiny, Isriam."

A tentative smile curved the squire's mouth, and Rohan laughed softly. "Which is why I'm going to delay a decision for a few days."

Shaking her head, Sioned confided, "He's a cruel man. After a few days in this heat the Gribains will agree to anything he says, just to go home!"

Rohan dismissed the squire for the night and took his wife for a stroll in the gardens. The moons were down and the sky was alive with stars, their silvery light almost bright enough to read by.

"You handled Isriam very nicely," Rohan commented.

"*You* certainly didn't," she scolded. "He's not like Daniv or any of your other squires. He needs to be led—gently enough so his pride isn't hurt, but firmly enough so he understands. He's not unintelligent. Just young and shy."

They came to his mother's fountain, which trickled feebly as it always did at this time of year. When rain came to the northern hills and flowed down to swell the spring that was Stronghold's life, the water would again play as Milar had intended, a joyous patter dancing to the rhythm of the wind.

Sioned bent to rinse her hands in the pool, then straightened. "You weren't very subtle about diverting me from things too dangerous for Isriam to know," she accused.

"He didn't notice. I knew you would. I save subtlety for those who need or earn it." Seating himself on the fountain's tiled rim, he went on, "Not that you spared Eschur your talons, my love."

She shrugged irritably. "You can't understand," she repeated. "You're not a Sunrunner."

"You're right, I'm not. But I *am* the High Prince. I don't like Andry's interference any more than you do."

She paced the summer-sere grass. "Prince I called him, and prince he's trying to become—in function if not title. Prince of Concocted Mysteries! I would never have believed it of a son of Tobin and Chay!"

"Andrade had the making of the Sunrunner he became," he reminded her. "Just like you."

Sioned rounded on him. "And I took to princely rule like a sorcerer to *dranath*, is that it?"

"Partly. I think Lady Merisel had the right idea long ago—strongly discouraging trained Sunrunners from marrying princes or *athr'im*."

"I wasn't the first."

"No. But your grandmother Siona was."

"That only gave Andrade the idea. *You* were the great experiment."

"One that failed," he said lightly.

"This is different, Rohan. Andrade's ambitions were for you, not for herself. And whatever your disagreements with her—caused mostly by me—" She held up a hand to stop his interruption. "By me," she repeated. "I'm the one who defied her by becoming a princess first and a Sunrunner second. But you and she were always working toward the same thing. The power of the High Prince working together with the power of a *faradhi*. Andry, on the other hand, is ambitious for himself."

"It infuriates you, doesn't it?" he asked softly. "All the ceremony. The ritual."

"Andrade would have cut the rings from her fingers before she'd countenance half of what he's done 'in the Name of the Goddess.' "

Rohan stood and put his arm around her waist. He drew her along the paths to the grotto, speaking only when they stood beside the thin waterfall. "There isn't a way to stop him. All we can do is live with it and hope most people have more sense than to believe in superstition."

She kicked a loose rock into the pond. "He knows what's seen in Fire and Water isn't the destiny of princedoms, it's personal. And it's only what *might* be. Andrade always said that the future isn't carved in stone—and even if it were, stone can be broken."

"If it were a truly reliable skill, it would have become

widespread long before this. This is the first time Andry's suggested it. I think he knew all along that he wouldn't have to do it. He just wanted to give the impression that he could."

"That makes it even worse."

He should have known what she would do next, but still was startled when a trickle of Fire crossed the pond, brilliant with color and sternly controlled. He had learned over the years to recognize the elusive response of his own *faradhi* blood when she worked this way; it was a fragile quiver deep within him, something he could never touch, never use.

She conjured what she had shown him a very long time ago, when they'd both been young and untried, when they'd felt the Fire but were unable to trust that it wouldn't burn their hearts to ashes. Two faces appeared in Fire and Water, poignantly young and solemn, foreheads circled by thin gold crowns like living flame.

"I saw this first when I was barely sixteen," Sioned murmured. "It's what I've seen all my life."

"You *are* my life," he replied simply.

She rested her head on his shoulder and allowed the vision to fade. "Were we ever that young?"

"I thought we'd already agreed that we're both elderly and decrepit." He held her closer, burying his lips in her hair.

"Oh, yes . . . I'd forgotten."

"So," he said, "had I."

Chapter Two

To the Sunrunners standing on the battlements of Goddess Keep, the ocean was as vast a wilderness as the Desert, and more threatening. They could at least retain their wits if forced to traverse the Long Sand; setting sail across Water meant incapacitating sickness which, though it wouldn't kill them, would surely make them wish they were dead. A *faradhi* on water was as helpless as a dragon without wings. Andry sometimes wondered how Lady Merisel had convinced her people to leave Dorval for the continent.

And why had they come here, of all places? he asked himself as Valeda chanted the day's end. Goddess Keep had several advantages—rich farmland that made it self-sufficient, comforting isolation, a defensible approach on one side and forbidding cliffs on the other, no mountains to block the sunlight, and a far southwesterly location that gave it a maximum-length day even in winter. But rain and thick fog walled up the castle every year, rendering the light of sun and moons inaccessible. Was this the best Merisel could find? Or had there been some unknown but compelling reason to build here?

He chided himself for letting his attention stray from the ritual. He'd already missed half of it; Torien's deep voice, representing Earth, alternated now with his wife Jolan's ringing words as she personified Fire. The two aspects of the Goddess were thus invoked—male and female, Earth and Fire. Deniker then took over the male's part, speaking for that aspect of the Storm God that was Air. Ulwis assumed the voice of Water, sweetly melodic as a mountain stream as she recited the counterpoint to her husband's words. Andry let the chant wash over him. Not the best poetry, but adequate to the purpose. It got the idea across.

All four voices invoked protection over the times between sunset and moonrise, moonset and sunrise, when there was no light for a *faradhi* to use. Andry found the cadences more powerful in the old language, with its terse nouns and spare verbs. But the majority of *faradh'im* knew little of it, so perforce the rituals were in modern speech. He often wondered why Merisel had forbidden the use of the continent's original language. And how had she managed to all but obliterate it, except for remote places in the northern princedoms, in a mere few hundred years? It was the language of sorcery, and that might have been the reason for her adamant eradication. Andry suspected, though, that she had decided to emphasize the establishment of a new order of things by establishing another tongue. But on this, as on many other things, her histories were frustratingly silent.

Only magical terms and personal names were still as they had been. Logical enough; the terms were evocative of power in and of themselves, and a Naming was a very solemn ceremony—also magic. Many places retained their old names in sometimes corrupted forms. Veresch translated into "silent wolf"—appropriate to those mountains. Dorval, home of the Sunrunners before their arrival on the continent, meant "loyal sword"; Catha was a particularly potent word combining Water and breath, or Air. But it was anybody's guess what Ossetia or Zaldivar or Ussh had originally been. Even some personal names were puzzling. Jolan, the scholar among his *devr'im,* often spent whole nights working on a single term. Intellectual puzzles appealed to her.

Andry translated the last lines back and forth from one language to the other, enjoying the unison of four differing voices.

Protect us from the dark time of night
(Vis-tiel wis'im se'eltan la bellia)
Until the Sun brings light and life.
(Josclen dev edeva.)

He and his *devr'im* had no reason to feel helpless without sun or moons. But common Sunrunners were not taught to use the stars. Gathered down below in the courtyard, they found great meaning in this daily ritual conducted by their superiors.

He and Jolan had spent a whole winter and spring working out the specifics of the Elements. No one had ever codified belief before. This amazed Andry—for there was much satisfaction to be had from organized, definitive tenets. Surely Merisel had known that. But she had allowed no formalization of the attributes of the Goddess and the Father of Storms, and no rituals other than the ancient ones of Naming, Choosing, and Burning. Faith was a casual thing, casually observed. Andry suspected she had overreacted to the complex ceremonies of the *diarmadh'im*; this "Nameless One" he had heard sorcerers swear by had evidently demanded elaborate rites. Andry did not propose the same. What he was doing he likened to what Rohan had done at his first *Rialla* as ruling prince. Just as Rohan had used ancient maps and treaties to clarify borders and set every princedom's boundaries so everyone would know literally where he stood, Andry found clues in the histories and the Star Scroll to set the boundaries of belief.

The four voices rose in unison for the final verse, praising the Goddess and the Storm God. Air and Water were obviously Elements of the latter, each capable of bringing both life and destruction—but not to each other. Fire, the most sacred, could scorch Earth to ashes. This was the source of tension and thus of power, for it was the Goddess' strength that kept her two aspects under control. Sunrunners were first and foremost servants of the Goddess, drawing their power from her.

All persons were made of all four Elements: the Air of breath, the Water of blood, the Earth of bones and flesh, and the Fire that was the life of the mind and heart. Their tensions were reflected in everyone. It was a tidy system, and appealed to Andry's sense of order.

For example, Sunrunner physicians now knew exactly where to direct their energies to effect a cure. A broken bone required no Water-rich potions, nor cauterizing Fire, nor inhalations of herbs on Air, but rather splints made of Earth-born wood. Likewise a poisoning of the blood's crimson Water could be helped only by certain plants that grew in rivers and lakes. It was entirely fitting and logical that *dranath*, the herb of the mind, should require baking in hot ovens or drying in the sun's Fire to reach its full effectiveness. These remedies had been known before, but now physicians knew the why of them.

Andry was not responsible for the medicinal aspect of belief. For that he credited a young man who had come to Goddess Keep two years ago after training in Gilad. Evarin had been only nineteen, the most brilliant student ever known at the school for physicians. But he was also *faradhi* gifted, and knew it, and had left Gilad before receiving his certificate.

"I won't waste a weary year as a drudge for some idiot who couldn't soothe a skinned knee, and then pay over part of my earnings for three more years to support the school. Especially when I've known what I really am since the first time I set foot in a fishing boat! And besides that, my Lord, you need me."

Evarin offended many with what they saw as arrogance. Andry knew it was the supreme confidence of someone born to a specific work; after all, *he* was called arrogant, too. Valeda had had Evarin's man-making night, reporting with amusement that the boy's pride had suffered a serious hurt remedied just before dawn. This secretly increased Andry's liking for him—his own first night had not been a resounding success. He'd made up for it since. So had Evarin, if rumors were to be believed. He now wore eight rings, and it was for him and at his suggestion that the eighth was reserved hereafter for Master Physicians. Andry alone kept that ring without having to qualify for it; his *devr'im*, who wore nine, had mostly chosen to give it up. Deniker, Oclel, and Nialdan had no talent for healing; Jolan and Rusina couldn't be bothered. Ulwis attended Evarin's classes every so often, halfheartedly. Torien, as chief steward and senior *devri*, felt it incumbent upon himself to earn the Master Physician's ring. But Valeda showed a true gift for advanced medicine, and the eighth ring was back on her left thumb before Evarin had been at Goddess Keep a year.

Utterly self-confident, convinced that only Sunrunners should treat the sick and injured, Evarin might have become Andry's rival within and without Goddess Keep. A physician's power was formidable and Evarin was prodigiously gifted. But Andry was not only Lord here and grandson of a prince, but had possession of that which earned Evarin's instant respect: the Star Scroll. In it were encoded the spells and potions of the *diarmadh'im,* lost for hundreds of years—even to them. The sorcerer Mireva had sent one of her own to steal it if possible, and had failed. It was never read except in a closed, windowless, hearthless room, so that no conjuring by light could gain a glimpse of it. Urival had given Sioned a translated copy, which infuriated Andry even at this late date. But she was afraid of using power—like her husband and like the man she called her son.

Knowledge of Pol's true birth was a power Andry had not yet decided how to use. He had come to believe that the Goddess would not have allowed him to know if there was no purpose for the information. He had not yet found one. He would not reveal it for childish spite; there was no point in that except his own satisfaction.

He had almost revealed it once, during an ugly confrontation at the *Rialla* of 731. Three years earlier, Andry had gone secretly into the Veresch to kill any *diarmadh'im* he could find. Gloves had hidden *faradhi* rings; he and Valeda and Nialdan had been careful to draw no attention to themselves, posing as simple travelers. The mountain folk knew only that certain people who had lived among them vanished without trace, the doors of their homes marked with a sunburst pattern burned into the wood. The mark of the Goddess, it came to be called. No one ever connected them with the executions.

But somehow Pol found out. He had waited through the first days of the *Rialla,* treating Andry with a cool, distant respect. Then, on the morning of the races, while Andry stood at a paddock fence admiring his father's horses, there came a flash of colors so blindingly intense that if not for the wooden rail at his chest, he would have collapsed.

Surprised, cousin? said a coldly furious voice in his mind. *I ought to do to you what I did to Ruval three years ago. How would you like a Star Scroll spell used on you, cousin? How about the same one you used to kill citizens of my princedom?*

He saw nothing but the angry swirl of Pol's colors imprisoning his senses. He tasted acid emerald edged in black, felt the slice of diamond brightness, smelled stinging topaz-gold smoke. Pol's power staggered him.

Oh, yes, I know all about it. I know how you came into my lands in defiance of the edict against you and murdered my people. "In the Name of the Goddess," you'd say, wouldn't you? Justified because they were sorcerers, and therefore evil. Why didn't you go after Riyan? Or Ruala? Why don't you kill Princess Naydra—she's the last living daughter of High

Princess Lallante. Or is it only the obscure and nameless you have the courage to kill?

They merited killing, he managed, and Pol's grip on him increased until he felt his head would split like a ripe apple in a clenched fist.

That was for me to decide. Not you. I am the law in Princemarch. Not you.

He had almost revealed it then. Almost flung the damning words at Pol: I know about you, I know whose son you really are. But he had not.

I won't warn you again, cousin. If any more die, if any more of those ludicrous sun patterns are found, I *will come after* you.

There was a cruel, deliberate wrench at his senses, and then his mind was his own again. He discovered that his fingers had clawed so deeply into the wood that splinters were embedded in his palms and under his nails. When sight returned to his aching eyes, he turned his head, seeking Pol. Standing far away across the paddocks and the track was the tall figure, blond hair glowing in the sunlight. Pol was looking straight at him and even at a distance Andry saw rage in every line of him.

He should have told Pol then, should have shattered that insufferable insolence. But he had not. It was not yet time. It would have served no purpose but to vent his own anger, soothe his own pride.

It suited him that Pol ruled Princemarch and would be the next High Prince. Better him than Rinhoel of Meadowlord or Daniv of Syr, who were also grandsons of Roelstra. But the right moment had not yet come to reveal what he knew. Whether he would tell only Pol in private or proclaim it to all the princedoms, he did not know. But someday. . . .

The ceremony ended with the day itself. Andry leaned one shoulder against the crenellated wall as the *faradh'im* left the battlements. Torien approached, murmuring something about meeting to plan the harvest, but Andry shook his head and smiled.

"No, not tonight, my friend. Jolan wouldn't thank me for depriving her of your company this evening, if her eyes are any indication." He laughed as Torien looked flustered, and slapped his friend's back. Deniker and Ulwis came to Andry soon after to ask if he would join them for a little music later on. He politely declined this offer as well. Not that he would spend the night alone. He would share it with Brenlis.

Of the five women who had given him children, Brenlis was the only one who held more than a small piece of his heart. The daughter she had borne him of her first night was three this year, and bid fair to becoming the enchantress her mother was. From the moment Brenlis had come to Goddess Keep, everything about her had captivated him. Her beauty was unusual and compelling—golden-brown hair framed eyes that changed from gray to turquoise depending on her mood, and her face was as delicately perfect as her body. But more fascinating was her strangeness. He had never met anyone quite like her. Even the memory of Alasen faded when he was with Brenlis.

She was the daughter of a Syrene farmer, born within sight of the sea. She had been fostered for a short time at Stronghold, where Sioned had detected her gifts. Andry still remembered the morning Brenlis had arrived, appearing before him like a conjured vision, sunlight making her long braids twin rivers of shadowed gold. She had given the stunned Andry a letter from Sioned—the two of them never communicated through *faradhi* means anymore—and waited for his verdict.

I ask that you take her in and teach her Sunrunner ways, my Lord, Sioned had written in a formal style that betokened their estrangement, going on to detail the signs that meant possession of great gifts. But then she had added a personal note; he could hear her voice in the words, wistful with memory. *When I look at her, I see myself as I was when even younger than she—called "fey" and looked on askance by my brother's wife, who did not wish so strange a girl in her household. But in Brenlis there is something else, something deeper. I have taught her only how to call Fire—I am not qualified to nurture such gifts as she possesses. They are not easily explained, but within a few days of meeting her you will see.*

He had seen the instant those blue eyes met his own. She had been only fifteen. A year later Merisel was born. But if Andry had expected his feelings for Brenlis to settle into the same comfortable friendship he had with Valeda and Rusina and Ulwis, who had also borne his children, he was mistaken. The girl bewitched him. He had not felt this even with Alasen in his youth.

Andry sometimes feared he made himself foolish with this passion for a girl half his age. But none questioned or gossiped—not only due to respect for him, though he commanded vast reverence, but because the gifts Brenlis evidenced were so awesome. Her talents as a conventional Sunrunner were negligible—she had earned but two rings in the four years of her training, where most wore a fourth and often a fifth. She could call Fire and Air, and go Sunrunning with difficulty, and that was all.

But she needed no flame to see what would be. She warned of oncoming storms before the most careful Sunrunner observations could discern them. She saw Milosh of Fessenden's wife die days in advance of that lady's fatal accident. She knew when Sionell of Tiglath would be brought to bed of a child, and that it would be a son Named Meig. She *knew* things, as if the Goddess and Father of Storms, having decided an event, shared knowledge of it with her.

During her first year here, people had come to her with all manner of questions about their futures. The farmers who served Goddess Keep had consulted her about the best days for planting and harvest. To such questions she could reply only with a helpless shrug.

"I don't see simple things," she had told Andry. "I see what happens to princes and lords, or storms and winds that affect many people. I suppose it's like dreams sent by the Goddess—only my dreams come when I'm awake. Nothing I've ever seen is more than a few days into the future. My Lord, please tell them that if I could see in response to their needs, that if I could look far into the future, I'd do it. But I can't."

Andry had forbidden people to bother her with questions she could not answer. Some grumbled that what use was such seeing, but the rest knew that Brenlis' gift was something out of the ordinary, understanding that the small doings of everyday life were not the stuff of which the Goddess' visions were made. Was there not a circle of mighty trees in the forest for such questions—who would one marry, how many children, what would old age be like? Visions were reserved for great matters and great warnings.

The sky darkened as the first stars appeared. Andry had no fear of being powerless under a night sky all dazzled with distant light; he had learned from the Star Scroll how to use that brilliance, so different from sun and moons. The *diarmadh'im* might consider the stars to be a Fire different from that of the Goddess, coming instead under the power of their Nameless One. Andry knew that Fire was Fire, but just the same there was something different about the stars. More subtle than other light, they burned not with the white-hot intensity of noon sun or the cool silvery glow of the moons, but with a fierce, icy brightness. All his dreams of war and terror and destruction had come when stars alone ruled the night.

He had not had such a dream in several years. Someone less wise would have believed that the danger was no longer imminent, and having done everything possible to prepare against disaster, could now relax the vigil. Andry did not fool himself. War was coming as surely as the sun would rise tomorrow. And it would come in autumn, when hatchling dragons darkened the sky.

He had seen them in the last dream. While funeral ships were sent out to sea, there to burn with their sails like great flaming dragon wings, the dragons themselves flew over Radzyn, shrieking. The invaders, gold beads glinting in their long beards, fell on their faces in the sand. All groveled but one—a tall, dark, regal man, a prince among these savages, who grabbed up a bow and shot a defiant arrow at the hatchlings. One was wounded, and screamed as she fell from the sky. Andry woke thinking, *Rohan will be furious that someone killed one of his dragons.*

No dreams had come to him since, but the ones he'd already had were burned into his brain. Each expanded on the first—Radzyn and its port town sacked, ruined, ablaze. Next had come sight of the looting, then the loading of dead warriors and living captives onto ships to be burned at sea, and finally the hatchling dragons. Autumn, unmistakably autumn, in a Dragon Year of mating when the young tried out the strength of new wings.

"My Lord? The evening is soft, but you look like thunder."

Andry turned and the heavy dread left him at beholding Brenlis. She was dressed in white silk, her hair lighter than usual after a long summer of sun, her skin glowing like moonlight on thick cream. Her lashes and brows and the rich wine-colored curve of her lips defined her face; otherwise she was all pale shadows as she drifted toward him across the stones. Sometimes, when the dusk touched her the way it did now or a single candle lit her face, and she tilted her head in a certain manner, he could almost believe she was Alasen. But it was not the poignant pain of recognizing another in her that stopped his breath; it was her beauty, hers alone, as if Alasen had been a mere foreshadowing of this woman.

He smiled and held out his hands. "No thunder. Although in that gown you make my blood roar so I can hardly hear. Do you think it's quite fair of you, my lady, to grow more lovely every instant?"

She shrugged, embarrassed. She didn't like compliments, no matter how sincere. He gave them anyway. He couldn't help himself. She was so exquisite—and so elusive. Words about her beauty made her seem more . . . *here*. If only she would blush, giggle, arch a brow, tease, or any of the other things women did when complimented—but then, if she did those things, she would not be Brenlis.

And despite the elusive quality of her mind and heart, she always came to him. Sometimes he wondered if this was because she wished to, or because she understood that his position would never allow him to be the one to come to her. Was it her own desire or her care of his pride that brought her?

Such thoughts left him as he turned her face to the stars with a gentle finger under her chin, intending to kiss her. But there was that in her eyes he knew meant seeing. "What is it, dear heart?"

"I—I'm not sure," she said, frowning. "It was very quick. I saw myself standing on the cliffs at my parents' farm."

It was a six-day journey to her home in coastal Syr. That was a long time in comparison to her other visions. But this concerned him less than the other aspect of her sight. No simple, everyday occurrences, but major events—or things that would become so in time. He had tried to puzzle out why she had seen the birth of Sionell's son; there had been no visions when the children of other *athr'im* were born. He could only wonder what role the boy would play when he was grown. The death of Milosh's wife had shown its significance quickly: grief-stricken, he stayed at his estates long enough to see her ashes blow away on the wind, then rode off into the hills. Pirro of Fessenden pleaded with Andry through his court Sunrunner to find his brother before he did himself some injury in his mad flight. Andry obliged—and worked *devri* spells at a great distance when it was seen that Milosh was in the hands of a sorcerer with a grudge against Pirro. Milosh had escaped with his life and a loathing of *diarmadh'im* that rivaled Chiana's—she who had also been used by a sorcerer. Andry had been able to rid the continent of one more enemy—and not in Princemarch, where Pol could make self-righteous objections. The death of Milosh's wife had been the catalyst.

Now, however, he could not fathom why Brenlis should have seen herself on the shores near her home. "Perhaps it was only a wish, a memory," he suggested.

"That's possible," she said, and seemed relieved.

But he couldn't make himself believe it. "Brenlis, if you want to go home and see your family. . . ."

She smiled and shook her head. "I miss them sometimes, especially my little brother. But my home is here, at Goddess Keep."

He waited for her to add, *With you.* He was a fool to expect it, but couldn't help hoping. "Come inside. It's getting chilly."

He read to her while she sewed a new dress for their daughter, Merisel, thinking with amusement how astounded the others would be to see them. Just like an old married couple. Sometimes she asked for stories of his childhood or Desert legends, but most of all she loved to have him read to her. She was as mind-hungry as he had been in his youth, but with a tragic difference: she could not read. It had not been thought necessary for the child of a farmer, so she had never been taught. In her four years here she had tried again and again to learn, but without success. She confused letters, her mind making them into so many meaningless ink squiggles on a page. It was Jolan's opinion that the Goddess had given her one gift in exchange for another. Brenlis could write her name, and that was all.

Andry read to her that night from a book recently sent from the scriptorium on Kierst. The story dated back hundreds of years before Sunrunners and *diarmadh'im* had battled for the continent, a thrilling and unlikely tale of a quest for a lost crown called a *selej*. It took until midnight to finish it, and he was dry-voiced and hoarse by the time he was done, but he had enjoyed the story and Brenlis had begged him to keep reading. He supposed that tales of the past must soothe a mind that so often saw the future.

Perhaps that was why she came to him: for refuge, quiet

companionship. She never spoke of her own people or her home, or shared any of her thoughts or feelings unless he specifically asked. He had learned not to ask, schooling himself to patience. The night she spoke freely was the night he would know he had won her.

Whatever her elusiveness, it did not extend to rejection of physical pleasure. She had had no lover but him, ever since her first night when he had worn the Goddess' illusion—and she had seen right through it. But tonight, even as she cried out in his arms, shuddering and clasping him ever closer, he knew he had not reached her heart. He never had. But someday, he promised himself, nestling her in his arms to sleep, someday. . . .

When he woke just before dawn, he was alone. Brenlis rarely stayed with him until morning. He buried his face for a moment in her pillow, scenting her in the silk, and wondered yet again if he ought to marry her. He was often near to asking, but supposed he was afraid she would refuse him—or, worse, accept for the wrong reasons.

It was Valeda who brought his breakfast, instead of the boy who usually waited on him. She obviously had something to discuss in private. In a single glance she took in the evidence of Brenlis' presence the night before: rumpled sheets, the impression left in the second pillow, stray hairpins on the carpet. Valeda tended to take a rather proprietary interest in his bed life, though she was never so foolish as to display jealousy. She knew better, having observed Othanel, long-dead mother of his son Andrev, who had been tediously possessive.

"How are the children this morning?" he asked. Valeda looked after his three daughters and two sons as devotedly as if all of them, not just Chayly, were hers. To the two eldest in particular—Andrev, Othanel's son, and Tobren, whom Rusina had never wanted—Valeda was the only mother they had ever known. Ulwis and Brenlis were more like fond aunts to Joscev and Merisel than mothers.

"They're all quite well, my Lord."

"Are they used to Tobren's being gone yet?" He had sent his eldest girl, aged twelve, to foster with his brother Maarken—a calculated move on Andry's part, and they all knew it.

"Tobren?" Valeda looked blank for a moment, then nodded. "Oh—they miss her very much, my Lord."

"You're formal today. What's wrong?"

"Nothing. Just a little nervous, perhaps. Today we test Evarin's idea, after all." She paused. "Brenlis rode out at dawn. Alone."

"She did? Why?" He sat straighter, frowning.

"Word came on first light that her brother is ill. Torien gave permission. She was frantic, poor thing."

"Why didn't she take one of the physicians with her?"

"The Sunrunner who sent the message is a Master Physician. Thelyn—you remember him, the itinerant *faradhi* who rides Syr and Gilad."

So Brenlis had been correct in her seeing; within days she would in truth be standing on the grassy bluffs of her home. "Very well. I wish she'd taken an escort, though."

Valeda's lips quirked in an almost-smile. "Young she may be, and with only two rings—but none could mistake those rings and none would dare even *think* wickedness toward a Sunrunner. Your doing, my Lord."

"Not entirely."

"Don't worry about her. They know she's coming, and will probably send someone to meet her. Besides, consider the country she'll be traveling in."

Not all *diarmadh'im* had fled to the Veresch all those years ago after defeat at Lady Merisel's hands. While most had sought refuge in Princemarch, some had blended into the populations of the other lands. Only last winter Thelyn had found a tiny community living in the Catha Hills, and a year earlier a pair had been discovered in Gilad. Their homes now stood empty, marked on the doors with the sunburst that had become the Goddess' sign.

"I suppose you're right, and I shouldn't be concerned for her safety," Andry said. "They have a healthy respect for Sunrunners in the south. Besides, she saw this last night—or at least herself at her parents' home."

"Did she? An odd talent, this sight. I don't think I'd choose to have it."

"At times I don't think Brenlis likes it, either."

"Her absence won't affect the problem in Grib, will it?"

A slow smile spread over his face. "Not at all. I don't have to promise that the future *will* be foreseen—I only have to hint that it *might*."

"You enjoy tweaking the High Prince's nose, don't you?"

"Not his, and not the nose. Pol's pride. And don't tell me again that it may get me in trouble one day."

"I wouldn't presume," Valeda said. "You always know what you're doing—and how far to take it."

"Your faith warms me," he drawled. Then more briskly, "Well, shall we go over the working Evarin proposes?"

A broad grin lit her face, uncharacteristic in its almost malicious glee. "I don't think that's necessary. It's already been done," Valeda said in Rusina's voice.

Andry sat straight up in bed, gaping.

She called out, "You can come in now," and the bedchamber door opened to admit Evarin—looking indecently pleased with himself—Oclel, and a second Valeda. The real one. Andry was thunderstruck. The dark blonde hair, blue-gray eyes, and sturdy build of the woman seated nearby changed. Dark curls clustered around a high, polished forehead, and the figure fined down to dainty elegance.

Rusina laughed as he greeted the change with a gasp, then rose and went to her husband. "Perhaps I should try it out on you some night, now that I'm good enough to fool even Andry!"

Oclel made a face at her. "You're enjoying this, aren't you?"

Andry closed his jaw and felt his lips thin angrily at the trick played on him—her vengeance at last for fathering Tobren on her during her first night. She'd even forgotten that the girl was at Whitecliff—which Valeda never would have done. That ought to have told him something was wrong. Rusina cared nothing for the daughter he'd given her. It had been her own damned fault, he reminded himself sharply; if she hadn't been silent about her feelings for Oclel, if she hadn't hesitated so long to Choose him publicly, Andry would never have given her a child.

The others were laughing, too: Evarin at his own cleverness, Oclel at his wife's impudence, Valeda at Andry. He realized that he would have to join in or look even more of a fool. Forcing a rather weak chuckle, he shook his head.

"I ought to toss the lot of you on the next ship to Kierst! How dare you!"

"Don't blame me," Oclel said. "It was Evarin's idea."

"And you gladly volunteered, didn't you?" he asked Rusina, who grinned again and nodded. "Congratulations. I never suspected a thing. I want a complete explanation after I've—"

"Soothed your pride?" Valeda offered, smiling. "Poor Andry! It really was rotten to do it this way, but Evarin insisted on a graphic demonstration of success."

"Nonsense," Andry growled. "You did it to humiliate me. Now, get out before I change my mind and ask Prince Tilal to lend me his oldest, smallest, leakiest ship and send you all on a long ocean voyage. Out!"

All but Valeda left him. "I'll help you bathe. The best cure I know for injured pride is a nice, hot soak."

He followed her into the bathroom. "You're a miserable, disrespectful, incorrigible group and I don't know why I put up with you."

"Yes, my Lord," she agreed, and twisted the faucets. The silver spigot gushed forth steaming water from the closed cistern on the roof, heated by the sun in summer and by fire the rest of the year. The tub drain connected to the pipes of the middens, flushing them out every time someone took a bath. Modern plumbing was Andry's contribution to comfort at Goddess Keep—grossly expensive, but worth it.

Valeda tested his bath water and gestured for him to get in. She scooped up a cake of herb-scented soap, a soft brush, and a razor, obviously intending to give him a thorough bath and shave.

"I'm quite capable of washing myself," he said.

"Don't sulk. And it's always wise to be nice to the lady with the razor."

He grinned and submitted to her ministrations. She rubbed soap down his back and he leaned into her strong, massaging hands. "I consider myself warned. But I refuse to be placated by pampering. You're all going to Kierst as soon as I can find a boat."

"Yes, my Lord."

"And don't think you can get around me by being sweet to me."

"Of course not, my Lord. Although I'd be more inclined to believe you if you weren't purring like a hunting cat in the sun."

He chuckled unwillingly. After a few moments' silence, he said, "Rusina really enjoyed fooling me."

Valeda shrugged. "She's always held a grudge."

"It wasn't my fault."

"Not your fault she got pregnant?"

"You know what I mean."

"Yes. But the mistake was made just the same."

He was quiet for a moment, then burst out, "How in all Hells did she and Evarin *do* this, anyway? I thought it was only in the planning stages."

"If I tell you, will you promise not to shout at them?"

"Well. . . ."

"Promise, Andry."

He sighed. "Just keep rubbing my back."

She walked her thumbs down either side of his spine. "They used *dranath*."

"They *what?*"

"Oh, come now. We've all experimented with it. If it makes you feel better about Rusina, consider the headache she'll have for the rest of the day."

Andry jerked away and turned to grab her wrist. "She used it *without my permission*. How dare any of you—"

Valeda responded by dumping a pitcher of cool water over his head to rinse him off. "Stop being so damned self-righteous!" she snapped. "As if you had a lock and key on power!"

Letting her go, he snatched up a towel and got out of the tub. "Don't you understand how dangerous this is?"

"That's never stopped *you*. And it's from you that we all take our example, my Lord," she said acidly. "In case it had escaped your notice."

He scrubbed himself vigorously with the towel, glaring at her. "Tell me the rest."

"Not while you're yelling at me."

"I promised to spare *them*, not you. By the Goddess, Valeda, you of all people should know better than to countenance this!"

"Who said I did?" She stalked out of the bathroom and into his bedchamber. Andry followed, the towel wrapped around his waist.

"Explain yourself," he ordered.

Valeda whirled, blue-gray eyes flashing. Yet her voice was tightly controlled, her words clipped. "How would *you* react, my Lord, if you opened your chamber door one morning and looked into your own face?"

* * *

The four culprits sat in chairs before Andry's huge desk. Subdued now, uneasy at his silence, they did not look like children brought up before their schoolmaster after some transgression, but instead like adults caught playing like children with something much too dangerous.

Andry let them wait. He sat straight-spined and unmoving in his chair, his hands with their ten gleaming rings flat on the polished wood before him. Four rings were set with tiny rubies or diamonds, tokens of his lineage in the colors of his father's holding. The rest were plain gold or silver, connected by chains as fine as woven hairs to bracelets clasping his wrists. The left cuff was gold, set with a huge, irregular cabochon lump of darkest blue sapphire. There was a similarly sized moonstone, smooth and milky and glowing, in the silver encircling his right wrist. He had chosen the gems and bracelets himself some years ago when he felt himself to be truly the Lord of Goddess Keep. The sapphire represented truth; the moonstone, wisdom; together with the virtue signified by rubies and the cunning of diamonds, they were the jewels he considered most symbolic of his aspirations. That rubies also meant success in war afforded him a grim private smile. Andrade had worn a different gem on each finger, taking unto herself all the traditional symbolism. Andry had not done the same—not because he was more modest than Andrade, or less ambitious, but because his ambitions were more keenly focused.

There were no windows in this room to spill the day's sunlight onto the jewels, but by candlelight they danced and sparkled just the same. Andry had made this chamber his office primarily because no outside light ever shone in it. He wanted no prying eyes, either Sunrunner directed by Pol or Sioned, or sorcerer directed by persons unknown. He eliminated the risk of flames lit here by hand, fire that might be used by someone else to watch him, by igniting candles only with his own Sunrunner's Fire. Today, if any *diarmadh'im* attempted observation by unfamiliar means, Torien would sense it: he had the Old Blood in his veins, and in the presence of sorcery his *faradhi* rings would burn as if to sear the flesh from his bones.

So Andry felt perfectly safe in discussing this new and dangerous working here—one of the few places in Goddess Keep that was indeed secure. But discuss he did not, and would not until his people had had the chance to appreciate the fine points of the morning's trick.

He kept his gaze on them, waiting for the moment when none of them had the temerity to look at him. As expected, Rusina was the last to submit. The others—Oclel, Torien, even the usually irrepressible Evarin—had been staring at their folded hands for a long while now. But Rusina kept stealing small glances at him, smug amusement slowly becoming resentment. When her gaze finally lowered for good, Andry spoke.

"Now," he said softly, "since you've all had the chance to consider your actions—would one of you care to tell me how in all Hells you did it?"

Evarin cleared his throat. "We didn't mean—my Lord, it was just—"

"—too good to pass up," Andry finished. "I understand. I even forgive you for startling me out of five years of my life. You'll have to make your own peace with poor Valeda for showing up at her door like that this morning." He grinned. "Start explaining or I really *will* find that ship."

Evarin exhaled in relief and began. Andry listened, and remembered another experiment when another ruler of Goddess Keep had received a shock and another arrogant youth had done the shocking.

"—and so when I realized the working done for a first night could be adapted, I asked Rusina to help. She's familiar with it and was willing to try the variation. A few days ago we succeeded in changing her enough to make her unrecognizable as Rusina. But we couldn't get her to look like another specific person. That's when we went to Torien and came up with the *dranath* idea."

The chief steward nodded. "We know that it augments power. But there's nothing in the Star Scroll about shapechanging. We've had to go about it on our own. This seemed the logical approach—especially considering that Mireva certainly and Princess Ianthe's sons probably were addicted to *dranath*."

"One dose isn't enough to cause any serious harm," Rusina said. "I've taken it before, as part of the *devri* training." She gave a resigned sigh. "But I can already feel the headache beginning."

"Serves you right," Andry said "Tell me what you had to do to look exactly like Valeda."

She pursed her lips, frowning, then shrugged. "Making changes at random, the way I did the other day—that was hard. I didn't have a specific picture in my head of what I wanted to look like. And, of course, there was no *dranath*. This morning it was difficult in another way. I had a model to base the changes on, and I had the *dranath*, but—" She stopped, frustrated. "I don't really change, you see. I project an illusion. When I wear the guise of the Goddess on a man-making night, I conjure a haze to obscure my identity. Coloring, voice, size—I don't assume some other shape, I just hide my own. When I was making random changes, it was just four or five things—the color of my hair—"

"Blonde," Oclel interrupted in a casual drawl. "I rather liked it."

Andry was grateful for the teasing that lightened the atmosphere and took some of the tension from Rusina's face.

"Oh?" she asked. "And what did you think of my hands?"

Oclel shuddered. "If I wanted to be clawed by a dragon, I'd go live in the Desert." To Andry he said, "Fingernails like talons!"

"Was it difficult to sustain?"

"Yes. I didn't have any specific image in mind. Just vague things, like the hair. But when I became Valeda, it was both easier and more difficult." She paused, searching for words. "It's a set pattern, you see. Like our own colors. We know them and they don't change. I know what Valeda looks like and it was simply a matter of repatterning myself—making a conjured illusion much the same way as we conjure in Fire." Rusina hesitated again. "It felt odd. It was—*uncomfortable.* She didn't fit. I can't think how to explain it. Beneath it, I was still me. But it was like—like I was trying to wear someone else's skin."

Evarin leaned forward and said, "I have an idea about that. Subtle changes superimposed on our own bodies are one thing. Creating an illusion to fit around ourselves is quite another."

"I see," Andry said, although he didn't, quite. "Will this be a problem?"

"Not once we get used to it. I think." He gave a rueful smile. "Rusina was Valeda for only a short while. She didn't have time to learn how to move comfortably inside the illusion."

"Do you think you could get used to it?" Andry asked her.

"How'd you like to be wearing someone else's clothes?" She thought for a moment, then added, "Underwater."

Andry tried to imagine it, could not, and said so. Evarin shrugged.

"It's only a curiosity, after all, my Lord," the physician said. "It's like that mirror you found in Princemarch years ago. No real use for it. But we all wanted to figure out how the sorcerers do it, and now we know."

"No, it's not like the mirror," Torien said suddenly. "The mirror simply *is*. This could be mischief if the wrong people learn it."

"Well, they won't," Evarin stated. "Besides, it takes *dranath* to accomplish it, and that's strictly controlled."

"But not by us," Oclel reminded him. "Prince Pol owns its source. We take what we can in secret, but he harvests most of it against the day when there might be another Plague. How well does he guard it, Andry?"

"Very—if only to keep me from getting my hands on it." Andry leaned back in his chair and folded his arms over his chest. "My cousin is as possessive of his power as I am of mine. We are worthy adversaries."

"I don't see why you have to be," Rusina said. "He has his area of influence, and you have yours."

"You truly don't understand?" Oclel stared at his wife in amazement. "Don't you see that those areas overlap—to our detriment? He's a Sunrunner, not just a prince."

"He should have been truly one of us," Torien mused. "But his parents had other ideas—prompted by his all-too-talented mother, who taught him everything she knows."

"Don't forget the lessons Urival gave him in his so-called 'retirement,' " Oclel said. "And Morwenna. They went to Stronghold to train him in things Sioned didn't know."

"Which wasn't much." Andry gave an annoyed shrug. "What's done is done, and cannot be undone. I won't waste time or energy on it at this late date."

"But can't you make him see that he shouldn't be at odds with you?" Rusina clung to her absurd objections. "If you worked together—"

Andry laughed harshly. "We're both far too old to change now. He'd never submit to my rule, and I would betray the Goddess and everything we *faradh'im* are if I bowed to him." Pol would find out soon enough how much he needed Andry. When the ships came and the battles began, he would call out for help. Andry knew he would give whatever help he could—considerable help, with his *devr'im*. But Pol would pay for that help. Dearly.

"It's a pity things can't be different," Rusina said.

"It's really no different from the days when Andrade contended against Roelstra. Perhaps it's meant to be that way." Andry got to his feet. "As it happens, I agree with Torien. There's potential danger if the wrong people learn this. Write nothing down, and discuss it nowhere but in a room as secure as this one. I needn't add that only the *devr'im* and Evarin should know this exists at all. I want all of you to consider for a few days, and then we'll meet here and talk in more depth. For now, however, we've heard enough to keep us busy." He pointed a stern finger at them and added, "But if you ever, and I do mean *ever*, give me such a fright again, drowning will be too good for you."

They wore properly guilty expressions—Rusina's still tinged with smugness—as they filed out. Andry grinned, shook his head, and decided that the very thing to get the taste of words about Pol out of his mouth was a morning spent with his children. He whistled as he made his way to the nursery, and earned an exasperated scowl from Valeda when he disrupted routine, declared a holiday, and took the four of them—even little Merisel—outside to play dragons.

Chapter Three

After all the years it had taken Walvis to transform a broken-down castle into one of the most prosperous in the Desert, he might have been expected to sit back and enjoy life. By any standard, he was a successful, powerful man. He adored his wife. His son and daughter had married well, and given him five grandchildren. Former squire to the High Prince, he was honored with Rohan's friendship; victor of the Battle of Tiglath and the canny ruler of a difficult holding, he had earned the respect of his peers. After more than thirty years of concentrated toil, Remagev now produced the finest glass ingots in the Desert, and in the last few years Walvis had gotten rich on, of all things, cactus seeds coveted for their incomparable aroma in taze. No one had to lift a finger to grow *pemric* plants; harvest was simply a matter of getting a good hold on the cactus—avoiding the dagger-long needles—and shaking.

But for all his sleek prosperity at the age of fifty-two, he did not equip a cool room in his keep with a cozy chair and a few good books. Instead, every autumn he conducted a minor war.

Walvis sat his stallion as easily as he had at nineteen, watching a spectacle not unlike the one over which he had presided at Tiglath at that young age. The two armies were much smaller, of course, and both were under his command this time, and there were no chin-scarred Merida to be killed. But the battle cries and the flash of swords and the thunder of hooves were all the same. The young men—and even a few highborn young women—who came to him hoping to learn pretty tricks of riding and swordplay were always in for a shock. End-of-training exercises were no genteel final examinations of horsemanship and of skill with blades and bow.

Despite emphasis on military matters, a year spent at Remagev was not for the purpose of creating warriors eager to prove their prowess by doing battle with neighbors at home. Chay had established the school with the idea of educating all that out of them. It was his belief, eventually supported with reluctance by Rohan, that if everyone had everyone else's measure as a soldier, there could be no wars to test skills and wits. Naturally, not all the youths were of equal accomplishment—but they all knew the basics of battle and tactics, and how to work with their own limitations. They might discover each other's weaknesses, but they also knew each other's strengths.

This was the cynical, practical reason Chay had originally given. Rohan would have preferred that the use of sword and bow be confined to the hunt, but had agreed to Chay's plan after realizing something else. Comradeship and mutual respect were the major results of a year spent in such training. Even sons and daughters of hereditary enemies learned to work together at Remagev. The companionship of training field and barrack went a long way toward negating traditional rivalries. Walvis had seen it happen a dozen times, most notably between two young men from Syr.

Their families had sparred since time's beginning over precisely five and one-half square measures of pastureland. Kostas, weary of seeing them in his law court, took his brother Tilal's advice and sent a son from each holding to Walvis. Bloody noses and black eyes were shared pretty equally between them during the first season of their residence. Walvis then used the oldest trick in anyone's book and sent them off on a six-day survival trek through the Desert. They returned exhausted, filthy, and with still more bruises, but also with the beginnings of respect for each other. By the end of their year at Remagev, they fought on the same side in the mock war and returned home friends. One of them had even married the other's sister.

Walvis grinned beneath his beard to remember the ironic end of their story. No longer fighting each other, the families united to turn on a neighbor who had long been a source of irritation to both. A thoroughly exasperated Kostas had gritted his teeth, descended on them with fifty of his household guard, and told them to behave or be gone from his princedom. On the ride back to High Kirat, he'd laughed himself out of breath.

Despite the absurd comedy of that particular incident, the school was an overall success. It had the same foundation as Rohan's carefully slow insistence that squires not be fostered exclusively with those princes and lords with whom their fathers were on good terms. People who knew each other, who had ties of respect and affection, were reluctant to make war.

He stroked Pashtul's glossy neck and from a tall dune watched his little war unfold before him down on the plain. He had chosen a simple strategy today—cavalry only, no bows. Each side was split into two wings with instructions for an orderly fight. Order had long since vanished in the excitement of battle. Walvis shook his head, wondering when and if anyone would have the sense to withdraw and regroup. The instant any action disintegrated into chaos, it was usually problematical which side would lose. Discipline brought victory. He had proved that himself at Tiglath.

Discipline learned here helped these youngsters in later life. When some hardship or difficulty faced them, they always looked back to their year at Remagev—with its searing heat and glare, days away from cool shade and water, let alone anything that could honestly be called a tree—and thought, "I did that, therefore I can do this." Walvis often had the same reaction. He'd won the Battle of Tiglath at only nineteen; not much had given him pause since.

He heard hoofbeats behind him and turned in his saddle. Another grin lit his face, and this time his eyes kindled as well, for it was his wife who rode up the dune on a gray gelding. He didn't know who had first called Feylin "Lady *Azhben*"—mainly behind her back, sometimes to her face—but today especially it fit her. The folds of her cloak blew back from her shoulders like dragon wings, pale green lined with yellow. A daughter of the northern Desert, up near the border with Cunaxa that had seen more skirmishes against the Merida than any other area of the princedom, she had been with him at Tiglath all those years ago and was a discerning critic of his annual war.

"What a mess!" she pronounced as she drew rein beside him and surveyed the field. "Are you sure you told them what to do? Or did you just saddle them up and turn them loose?"

"They'll learn," he replied complacently. "I'm going to try out your maneuver tomorrow. What did you call it? 'Dragon Claw'?"

" 'Winged Dragon.' If it doesn't work, I'll let you take the credit."

They observed the disaster below for a while. Swords were blunted and no one was ever seriously injured, but when the discipline of ranks was forgotten, the combatants tended to forget the niceties of not wounding their fellows. Happily, Feylin's mother had been a physician and had taught her daughter most of what she knew. Walvis suspected that part of the reason they called his wife Lady Dragon-woman came from the scant sympathy she gave to the wounded.

Walvis sighed and waited out the chaos, wondering if the masters at the physicians school in Gilad and the scriptorium on Kierst-Isel had similar problems. Andry didn't, of that he was sure. No one would dare defy a man who did not discourage the notion that he enjoyed the constant and favorable attention of the Goddess.

"Ah, look," Feylin said. "Sethric has rallied some of them."

"Perhaps I'll put him in charge of one of your wings tomorrow." Walvis squinted at the sunlit plain, seeing the blazing red pennant Sethric had raised to signal his leadership. It was difficult to follow the battle for the sand kicked up by the horses, but many on the red team were wheeling around, gathering near Sethric, massing for a thrust through the thick of the fray.

"A pity he's the younger son of a younger son," Feylin mused. "He's shown some initiative now that he's out from the shadow of his father and brothers."

That was the dilemma faced by many young men: what to do with themslves. Heirs presented certain problems of their own—and he frowned as he remembered the scant summer Rinhoel of Meadowlord had spent here—but those without expectation of place or property beyond what they might marry troubled Walvis considerably. A year's training here provided occupation for youths who would otherwise have almost nothing to do. But though most families were pleased to send out boys and receive back men, what was there to occupy the lives of extraneous sons?

Before giving final approval to the school, Rohan had told Chay and Walvis either to come up with a plan for helping such landless young men after training at Remagev was completed, or to scrap the idea altogether. Three things were recommended. First, that wealthier fathers with lands to spare should be persuaded to give their younger sons manors or other responsibilities to keep them busy. Second, those youths from poorer places should be offered positions in their prince's guard. Third, if neither of these was appropriate or acceptable, they could join a company which, from its base here at Remagev, ranged out through the Desert, keeping order and settling disputes.

This idea was completely new. Walvis had had the rare satisfaction of seeing Rohan's jaw actually drop open in astonishment when he and Chay had proposed it. The concept of representatives of the High Prince, armed but traveling in unthreatening groups of five, riding the land to keep the peace was so compellingly outrageous that it had taken Rohan only enough time to recover his powers of speech before he agreed to it.

"But not one of them sets foot out of Remagev until fully versed in the law," he warned. "If they're going to uphold it, they're damned well going to know what it is."

The first six of these groups had been sent out as an experiment in the spring of 734. They had ridden Princemarch as well as the Desert, returning in time for the *Rialla* at Dragon's Rest that year. Pol reported himself and his vassals pleased with the results—Kerluthan of River Ussh especially, who told the princes that outlaws who had eluded his own punitive expeditions had been caught at last by the High Prince's men.

The other princes, even Rohan's allies, greeted this novel idea with skepticism. Their obvious fear was that he would propose to send these *Medr'im*, as Chay named them—"the Fives"—into their lands as well to uphold the High Prince's laws. Something else troubled Tilal, however, which he told Rohan in private. If each prince established his own corps of *Medr'im*, he might end up with a small but very well-trained army that could become bored, restless, and dangerous. Twenty armed horsemen could easily seize and hold a fair-sized manor; sixty could lay successful siege to a keep. Once a princely army took the field, they would not retain a conquest long—but why tempt fate?

Rohan's response was that the *Medr'im* were not to be copied by other princes, and for one of the few times in his long rule as High Prince he issued a summary decree to that effect.

"I'm not going to use my money in pursuit of your justice," he told the princes, thus allaying their fears that he would expand the *Medr'im*'s sphere of influence. "I have no objection to giving these young men something to do for a few years, until they marry or settle to some occupation. By taking them off your hands and out of their families' hair, I'm doing you a favor and we all know it." He grinned briefly, then shrugged. "But my investment is in the Desert and Princemarch. I claim the right of the High Prince to exclusivity on this matter—just as Volog has sole rights over the scriptorium and Cabar over the physicians school. The *Medr'im* are my solution to a problem faced by us all, but they are my resource—no one else's."

No one argued with him. They were too busy congratulating themselves that the High Prince's people would not be riding their lands and superceding their laws with his own.

The *Medr'im* had proved a resounding success. They made sure that criminals were taken to the proper authority for justice—whether it be the local *athri* or the High Prince. Walvis chose them with great attention to their maturity, character, and understanding of the law as well as their prowess at arms. Fifteen groups rode the two princedoms, seventy-five men total, but he could have fielded twice that many. He dreaded the day he would be faced with a mistake in his own judgment, but tried not to worry overmuch about it. The beginning had been made.

He had spotted a few likely candidates in this year's collection of young blades, but two had been promised manors on their return home and one was needed to succeed his brother, who had died that summer without an heir. But Lord Sethric of Grib, youngest son of Prince Velden's youngest brother, was showing himself an effective leader today. Remagev had taught him he had much of value to offer; he might make a very effective *Medri*.

Currently he was rallying troops to the red banner. He took them into a retreat, regrouped, and charged. The blue forces split neatly down the middle—neat not because of any tactical plan, but because Sethric's riders sliced through them like a knife through a ripe apple. The reds pivoted in good order, trapped the blues, and pushed them across the field in a frantic retreat.

"Nicely done," Feylin said. "But I'll be busy tonight stitching up their foolish hides."

"Do try to be a little sweeter to them, my love," he urged, laughing. "They have their pride, after all."

"I'm *very* sweet to them. I rate their scars on a scale of probable allurement to young ladies."

"How comforting. They get no sympathy from Chayla, either."

"She's perfectly nice to them—as long as they don't flirt too much," Feylin laughed. "And she's an excellent pupil. Maarken and Hollis will have a hard time deciding whether to send her to Goddess Keep or Gilad."

Chayla was fifteen, and had been renewing memories of her great-grandmother Princess Milar's golden loveliness practically since her cradle. Her mother was tawny as a topaz, but Chayla was all the colors of dawn, like Milar: pale gold, soft blue, rose pink, cream white. Her beauty was matched by her instinctive feel for medicine—and her *faradhi* gifts. Her Sunrunner parents had acceded to her plea to spend this year learning the basics of healing from Feylin. But a decision would have to be made soon about her future. Goddess Keep, for training as Sunrunner and physician? Stronghold, to learn *faradhi* skills from Sioned as Pol had done, and then Gilad for medical schooling? It hinged on Maarken's evaluation of Andry's intent.

Being unable to trust his only living brother rent Maarken's soul. He'd spoken of it when he brought Chayla to Remagev this spring, and from certain clues, Walvis guessed that Maarken would send her to Andry if only to prove that his fears were unfounded. After all, had not Andry given his eldest daughter Tobren into Maarken's care at this year's *Rialla*? Surely this was a sign of love and trust between them. Surely that was what it meant—to anyone who did not know him.

It was Maarken's undeserved Hell that he must always doubt his own brother. Walvis gave grateful thanks that his own loyalties were so simple. He had been Rohan's man all his life and would be until one of them died.

Sethric was about to claim victory for the reds over the blues. Walvis chuckled as his horse blew out a long sigh; Pashtul fretted when not allowed to join in the fun. Grandson of Rohan's own great war stallion out of one of Chay's best mares, Pashtul liked nothing better than to show off his training by lashing out with hooves and teeth in the annual mock war. Tomorrow he might get his chance when Walvis experimented with Feylin's new tactic.

All at once the stallion bellowed a challenge. Walvis hung on hard to keep Pashtul from bolting down into the cloud of sand on the field. A second cloud rose in the north, a charge accompanied by the most bloodcurdling howls this side of a battle between dragonsires.

Walvis laughed so hard he nearly fell from his saddle. Feylin whooped with glee beside him as fifty men mounted on fifty identical gray horses swept across the sand and surrounded the thunderstruck young warriors as easily as a wedding necklet clasps the throat of a happy bride. When red and blue banners had been confiscated to the accompaniment of more savage shrieks, one of the gray horses galloped up to where the Lord and Lady of Remagev were trying without success to regain their composure.

The young man was tall and lean, his brown eyes snapping with excitement in a sun-darkened face, his white teeth gleaming in a broad grin beneath a hawk's beak of a nose and a fierce black mustache. His head was covered by a white cloth held in place by a band of beaten gold set with white jade, and a white cloak billowed back from broad shoulders. He reined in ten paces from Walvis, planted red and blue banners in the sand, and touched the fingers of his right hand to his eyelids, his lips, and his heart.

"I have the honor to spit in your face after my great victory, once-mighty *athri*, former lord of all you survey!" he announced.

"Kazander! You simpering goat-footed idiot!" Feylin laughed in delight. "Trust you to make a grand entrance!"

"And scare those poor children out of a year's growth," Walvis added. "I didn't expect you until tomorrow evening. Rude as usual, coming early when the wine hasn't been poisoned for you yet! Not that anything could possibly be more lethal than that sheep-piss you had the gall to serve me. How are you?"

"Refreshed by my victory, renewed by your regard, and resentful at the sight of the Lady Feylin's loveliness." He grinned. "She has not yet seen fit to leave you, you pathetic excuse for a goat's backside, for the obvious charms of my person."

"Stop flirting with my wife, or I'll tell the three you already have," Walvis chided. "You didn't bring the lovely ladies with you, by any chance?"

"So that you might seduce them? May the Goddess in her wisdom dry up my seed if I was ever so foolish as that!" He settled into his saddle, pleased with the exchange of insults, and looked mournful. "But my heart is wounded, I may die of it. You are holding a war and didn't invite me!"

"A thousand apologies, Kazander. Would you like to play tomorrow? My eighty against your fifty. You always said one of your warriors unarmed is worth two of mine with sword and bow, so the odds are in your favor."

Kazander's dark eyes narrowed. "Your words are silk covering a stinking corpse. What are you planning to shame me with now, mighty *athri*?"

"Don't ask me, ask my lady wife. It was her idea."

The man moaned and rolled his eyes skyward. "Goddess witness it, a woman with a brain is more dangerous than a whole army!" He waggled a long finger at Feylin. "And it is your fault I have wives with more between their ears than praises of my name! Association with you in my boyhood caused me to value women with wits. Why did I never realize that when that sort of woman belongs to another man, she is a delight—but when she is your own, you live in misery?"

Feylin gave him her sweetest smile. "Oh, yes, you seem desperately miserable, Kazander—complacent as a dragonsire watching his get, and looking as if you'd said farewell to your wives so fondly that you rubbed all the skin off your—"

"Feylin!" Walvis exclaimed.

Kazander was roaring with laughter. "I adore you! Come away with me, Lady of the Dragons, I will make you first among my wives!"

"Make me the only one and I'll consider it."

"But what would I do with the others?" he wailed. "They would surely die if deprived of my presence!"

"That's the bargain, you honey-tongued devil," she purred.

"You think it over while you sleep in the stables tonight. You really are the most inconvenient and inconsiderate guest," she went on in disgruntled tones. "There's nothing ready for you yet." This was a bald-faced lie and they all knew it. Remagev was ready at all times for visitors, and twice the fifty Kazander had brought could be housed in luxurious comfort.

"To be within seeing distance of your splendor, even the *korrus* would sleep in a dung heap," Kazander replied, hand once more over his heart.

Feylin gave an appreciative giggle, then resumed her role. "It offends me to honor you with even that much. You've deliberately shamed me, and for the insult you'll bed down with your horse tonight."

Walvis grinned. "That's no hardship, Feylin—he *prefers* his horse."

He rode down the hill to reorganize his troops before Kazander could frame a reply. He greeted those among the Isulk'im he knew, told his fuming young warriors to escort their guests back to Remagev, and waited for Feylin and Kazander to join him.

Walvis always looked forward to these encounters with the young man he'd fostered during boyhood. The same age as Walvis' son Jahnavi, Kazander was the *korrus*—"battle leader"—of the agglomeration of Desert nomads known as the Isulk'im. Although Zehava's line had sprung from them and fifteen generations ago they had seized Stronghold and made it their capital, the original prince's brother had had no taste for politics and settled living. He had taken those of their people who longed for the old life and returned to the vast wastes of the Long Sand, there to herd goats and relish their freedom. They were, as Walvis' teasing implied, mad about horses, some of which looked very like certain Radzyn stallions that had vanished mysteriously over the years. Isulki raiders sometimes stole a particularly fine stud from Chay's very stables and then, once their own mares had been serviced, sent the stallion home. They were never caught; the name did not mean "swift ones" for nothing. But neither was there any retaliation for these occasional thieveries; it was longstanding tradition that Radzyn supplied its ruling family with the finest horses, and the Isulk'im were only claiming their share.

Inevitably, the Isulki population had split into factions as it grew. With equal inevitability, they warred over who had rights to which endless ranks of sand dunes. But ever since 695, when Zehava had been helped by his distant kin to victory over the Merida, they had organized into a loose confederation of tribes. Kazander's great-grandsire had become their *korrus*. Though formally submitting to Zehava's leadership and sovereignty, he and his people kept to themselves in the vastness of the Long Sand, an isolation that had spared them the Plague of 701. They sent several warriors to fight with Rohan against Roelstra in 704, and every so often an emissary arrived at Stronghold or Radzyn or Remagev with a gift of gorgeous blankets or carved jade.

"Just to let the High Prince know we're still out here," Kazander's father had said once, blithely, when presenting Walvis with a fabulous necklace for Feylin in celebration of Jahnavi's birth. "I have a new son myself, by my favorite wife. She is as wild as a she-dragon, so I worry about the boy's capacity for civilization. Perhaps when he is of an age for it and has learned what manners I can beat into him, you might consent to receive him here."

Thus, casually, they had agreed to Kazander's sojourn at Remagev. He had arrived ten winters ago, a lanky, wide-eyed boy of sixteen who had learned to ride before he had learned to walk. In him were embodied the things Walvis liked best about the Isulk'im: their mastery of the affectionate insult, their fierce pride, and their humor. To that list Feylin always added their love of dragons and their hatred of the Merida. She was from the north, where the descendants of the assassins' league were more familiar enemies than here in the south. But her undying loathing paled beside the rage mere mention of the Merida could excite in the Isulk'im. Their songs and tales told of shocking atrocities and it was the sworn duty of the tribes to butcher any Merida unlucky enough to encounter them.

Kazander had stayed at Remagev through the autumn of 729, and despite his youth had insisted on being trained in the ways of battle. The annual little war had seen him fight all day long with a broken collarbone and two cracked ribs; Walvis had been given undeniable proof that claims of Isulki valor were not in the least exaggerated. Since then, Kazander had appeared at Remagev every so often, sometimes alone and sometimes, as now, with an escort—just to let the High Prince know the Isulk'im were still out there.

He had succeeded his father two years ago. Walvis had not seen him since that time, though he received news occasionally. As they rode back to the castle, he looked the young man over and nodded to himself. "Marriage and new fatherhood agree with you," he commented.

"How did you know I am a father again?"

"Because if you didn't keep fathering children, you wouldn't still be *korrus*," Walvis replied with irrefutable logic. "How many is it now?"

"Three sons, two daughters," came the proud answer. "Another will be born next spring."

"However do you manage it?" Feylin asked indelicately, then made a face as Kazander gave her a long, slow smile. "I didn't mean *that!* And don't you dare offer to teach me, you wicked boy. I meant, why is it that your women bear so many children? I can't think of anyone who's had more than four."

"The late unlamented Lady Palila birthed six," Walvis reminded her.

"One of whom inflicts herself on us as Princess of Meadowlord," she agreed. "But she only has two."

"It's quite simple," Kazander said. "Our women have more children because our men prove the strength of their siring. The more children, the more wives—if he earns them in battle and in bed. Sometimes I wonder which can be the most dangerous." Then he grinned. "But I have a special secret. My girls are twins!"

Twins were uncommon among the Isulk'im. Walvis congratulated his young friend warmly. "Tell my wife you named one of them after her or she'll be heartbroken."

"One? Both! Feylani and Feylina I called them, and alike as dragons hatched from the same shell." Kazander shook his head sadly. "If I cannot have you, then at least I can torment my soul with hearing the echoes of your name."

"I truly am honored, Kazander," she said sincerely. "And for that, you'll get a decent bed after all. How old are they now? And what about the boys?"

Discussion of his growing family took them all the way to the walls of Remagev. As ever, Walvis felt his heart lift at the sight. He had first come here in the spring of 704 with Rohan. That royal progress had ended near Skybowl when

Ianthe's men had kidnapped the prince to Feruche. But before the horror of Rohan's imprisonment, they had spent several days with his distant cousin Hadaan—a fiery old warrior whose many battles with the Merida had cost him an eye. Hadaan had no children, and although Walvis had not known it at the time, the old man had a mind to making him the heir. In early 705 Walvis had been named the future Lord of Remagev and, once it had been made clear to him that he was going to marry Feylin, had done just that and taken up residence.

The keep had been built in days long past by Zehava's ancestors. It was one of what had once been a string of castles reaching all the way to the Sunrise Water. The encroaching Desert had gradually made all of them but Remagev insupportable. But it had been in terrible shape, for Hadaan was more warrior than *athri*.

"I'm no good at peace," Hadaan had said frankly. "Give me a sword and I'm a happy man, but this business of glass and smelters—bah! Rohan's taught you the trick of it, and welcome. You're *athri* here from this moment on, boy. Just send your pretty wife to flirt with me sometimes, and otherwise forget I'm here."

They had done no such thing—though Feylin flirted with great enjoyment. For all his professed lack of interest in peaceful pursuits, what Hadaan didn't know about Remagev and the surrounding sands wasn't worth knowing. In the years remaining to him he involved himself in rebuilding the keep, supervising improvements, cheerfully harassing everyone, and watching proudly with his one good eye as Remagev turned into a thriving castle. His death, when Sionell was six and Jahnavi three, had been deeply mourned.

Remagev was and always would be only a minor keep on the fringes of Desert civilization. It had no fine, proud towers like Radzyn, no bustling town like Tiglath, no elegance of design like Feruche. It was a squat, square defensive castle, hunkered atop one rocky hill and abutting another like a huge sandy dragon. But it belonged to Walvis, and he loved it fiercely.

His eighty men and Kazander's fifty lined the road to the main gates, each faction taking one side, to honor the two lords and the lady who rode past. Walvis met his guards commander at the gate and gave instructions for the comfort and housing of their guests. Feylin promised to make short work of tending the wounds acquired in today's battle and join them later.

Remagev did boast one architectural excellence. The double staircase branching up from the main hall was a miracle of grace in this otherwise undistinguished keep. Steps rose in wide arcs that met on a broad landing, whence five more steps led to the second floor. Walvis and Kazander mounted the right-hand stairs just as a girl ran down the left side, frantically pinning up her long golden braids. Walvis grinned as his guest frankly stared.

"Gentle Goddess, Mother of Dragons," Kazander whispered as he turned to watch the girl vanish through the main doors.

"I see the Lady Chayla has supplanted my wife in your affections," Walvis murmured.

"The Lady Chayla would blind a sighted man and cause the sightless to see! Who is she? Who is her father? When may I beg him for her hand?"

"You don't change, do you? Even at sixteen years old you tried to seduce every woman within a hundred measures! Don't waste your time with this one, my friend. She's the daughter of Lord Maarken, the granddaughter of Lord Chaynal, and the great-granddaughter of Prince Zehava. Not to mention the niece of the Lord of Goddess Keep and the grand-niece of the High Prince himself."

Kazander's face grew longer with each addition to the list of Chayla's exalted kin. "I obey, mighty *athri*. I will not touch. I would not dare! But you wouldn't be so cruel as to forbid me to look, would you?"

"Go right ahead. Not that she'll notice you looking. Come, let's take our ease in Feylin's chambers. I recently had a shipment of a rather good mossberry wine from the High Princess' own home of River Run."

"You *are* planning to poison me!"

Soon they were alone in the solar, with full goblets and a selection of fruit and cheese to hand. Kazander complained for a few moments about gutless Syrene wines, but Walvis saw that his heart wasn't in it. And suddenly the young man became too serious for Walvis' peace of mind.

"There are signs," he said in answer to Walvis' inquiry, "and though I know you hold little with magic other than that of Sunrunners, I know you will hear me. A three-legged goat was born at New Year. It bleated three times and died. A cloud was seen like a sail over the Sunrise Water, all afire. It advanced over the cliffs and swallowed them up in flames. From Dorval came a great gust of wind that blew down a hundred tents, killing eight people. Shimmer-visions in the Desert have been not of the usual water or green grass, but of blood."

Walvis knew he ought not smile at Isulki superstitions. He had witnessed Sunrunners and sorcerers do too many incredible things to joke at other beliefs. Still, he had always heard these portents of the Desert tribes with a certain degree of amusement. Kazander's dark solemnity was something new in his experience.

"And to your wisest ones, all this means . . . ?" he asked.

"The goat—that terrible things await, and will last three seasons or three years, depending on who one consults. The cloud is interpreted as disaster descending upon the Desert in the form of fire." He paused, and a hint of a smile touched his mouth. "Although I remember that ten springs ago, Sunrunner's Fire very nearly incinerated us all!"

Walvis smiled back, remembering how Pol had ignited the very sands in his battle against Ianthe's son Ruval. The young prince had been teased ever since about a tendency toward arson. In fact, it had been this inconceivable occurrence that had brought Kazander and his father to Remagev to find out just what in Hells had caused it.

Kazander went on, "The great wind tells us that the danger and death will come from Dorval."

"Impossible, Kazander."

"The noble Prince Chadric can have no possible quarrel with us here. Unless the mighty *athri*, husband to the legendary Princess Tobin, has been cheating him on the silk revenues again." They both smiled at the old joke, but Walvis saw that Kazander was only going through the expected motions. "The final sign, that of blood-visions, I have seen myself. I am not ashamed to admit that while any one of these might be dismissed, taken all together they frighten me."

"Only a fool ignores the warnings of the Goddess. Is it your wish that I inform the High Prince?"

The *korrus* nodded. "Yes. There is one other thing. A star was seen rising—not falling, mind you, rising—into the constellation of the Father of Dragons. This can mean only one thing."

"Pol."

"None other."

"So despite these horrors to come, Pol will prevail."

Kazander hesitated, then shrugged. "I would be serving him and you badly if I did not repeat the caution our wisest ones gave me. Whereas most are agreed that this star means ascendency, there are some who warn that it may mean the opposite. That Prince Pol will indeed ascend—but on Desert winds, his ashes to join with those of his *azhrei* ancestors."

Walvis took a long swallow of wine. "This is not an interpretation I favor, Kazander. And I don't believe the High Prince will like it much, either."

* * *

There was no banquet that night. One had been planned for the following evening to celebrate the conclusion of the annual little war, and Feylin declined to upset her household by destroying their careful arrangements. The Isulk'im ate in the mess, their *korrus* with Walvis, Feylin, and Chayla. Kazander was as flamboyant in his praise and as outrageous in his suggestions to Feylin as ever, but hardly addressed a word to Chayla. He did, however, look. Constantly.

After he left to check on his men and horses, Chayla asked Walvis, "What in the world is his problem?"

"What do you mean?"

"Have my teeth turned green? Doesn't he like me? He wouldn't talk to me at all—just stared!"

Feylin covered laughter with a fit of coughing. Her preemption of that ploy—it would have seemed odd if they'd both choked on wine simultaneously—left the time-honored "I dropped something on the floor" for Walvis. He searched the carpet beneath his chair until he could control his features, then sat up again and smiled, the deliberately jettisoned spoon in his hand.

"Believe it or not, Kazander is rather shy around young ladies."

This brought another spasm from Feylin. Chayla turned to her. "Are you all right, my lady?"

"Swallowed—the wrong way—" she gasped, covering her mouth with a napkin while tears streamed from her eyes.

"I don't know much about the Isulk'im," Chayla went on.

"We never see them at Whitecliff. The *korrus* seems nice enough, if a little. . . ."

"Overly eloquent?" Walvis suggested. "Something you have to understand about them is that while other men's wives and girls under twelve or so are fair game for their flattery, an unmarried woman is left strictly alone until one has approached her father for permission to speak to her. You're not a child, and your father isn't here, so—" He finished with a shrug.

Feylin had recovered. "You should have heard Kazander's father when Sionell was little. He swore up canyons and down dunes that when she was old enough, he'd carry her off on his saddle to become his sixth wife—or was it the seventh?"

"Seven wives?" Chayla's blue eyes widened. "I don't like that much!"

"Neither did Sionell." Feylin was at last able to indulge herself freely in laughter. "I can still see her, planting both feet in the sand with her fists on her hips, telling him that while she was very honored to be considered, no woman but herself would rule in her home—be it castle, cottage, or tent!"

After Chayla bid them good night, they conducted a little business with their steward in the cool of the evening, then went for a stroll around the upper walls of the castle to watch for dragons. The creatures seldom ventured this far into the Long Sand, which Walvis regretted but which was just fine with his wife. She loved them—but at a safe distance. This was the time of year for it, though, if they were to see dragons at all. After the triennial mating in the Desert, after the caves had been walled up with eggs inside to bake through the summer, after the hatchlings had flown, dragons lingered for a while before flying south to the Catha Hills and their wintering grounds. They sometimes ranged east to Remagev and west to the city of Waes. Every summer except mating years, they were a common sight from Syr to Fessenden, with their main precincts in the Veresch. Now that they were no longer hunted as adults or butchered as hatchlings, and the caves at Rivenrock Canyon were in use once more, the dragon population had increased to a number Feylin considered safe. This year more than eight hundred dragons—sires, mature females, three-year-olds and new hatchlings—had been seen in flight.

The Lord and Lady of Remagev watched the skies until night was full upon them, but they saw no dragons. "Perhaps we should have asked Chayla if there are any in our area tonight," Feylin mused.

"I don't think she's picked up the knack of it yet. Pol came to it late, though, so I suppose she might, too."

Chayla had not yet shown signs of having inherited the odd family trick of sensing dragons before they could be seen. Rohan had it, and Tobin, and Pol and Maarken and Andry. It was said of old Prince Zehava that he could tell merely by glancing at the clouds when the dragons would appear on the wind. Walvis hoped the trait would not be lost; it was always amusing to watch outsiders blanch and stare when Zehava's descendants turned their faces as one toward the sky. It was almost as much fun as observing the reactions of those who had never before seen a Sunrunner at work.

"Busy day tomorrow," Feylin said at length. "Will you explain Kazander's part to him in the morning?"

"Yes—to give him as little time as possible to work out his own variations on it. You know how he is."

"Scamp," she grumbled fondly. "Speaking of which, you didn't have to make me laugh so hard! I nearly choked to death when you told Chayla that Kazander is shy!"

"Except, you know, I think he really *was* shy around her." He slipped one arm around her waist and they started back to the inner stairs. Torches in iron holders along the parapets lit their way. Walvis occasionally came home from a hunt after dark, and the sight of Remagev with its glowing crown of light was always an impressive one. He nodded to the sentry on duty and continued to his wife, "He hasn't met any highborn young ladies now that he's of an age to appreciate them. Ell was always just that bit too much older than he."

"Oh, don't be silly! Chayla's barely fifteen!" She laughed and ducked around the door he held open for her. "Can't you just see her living out on the Long Sand in a tent?"

"Now that you mention it, no. But I'll keep an eye on him just the same. He's still young enough to be dealt quite a wallop by a pretty girl."

Feylin gave him one of her patient looks. "The man is thrice a husband and five times a father. Really, Walvis, you can be absurd at times."

* * *

"Attack," Kazander had been bidden. "Attack—but don't damage my younglings unnecessarily. They may get irritated and forget to check their own blows. Goddess forfend that any of your great warriors go home to their mothers with so much as a bloody nose."

He almost wished this could be a real battle. The Lady Chayla—to whom, in the way of his people, he had already given a secret name to be whispered only when her body graced his sleeping silks in the marriage tent—was watching from the crest of a dune nearby. He wished he could show her all his prowess, all his strength and cunning. Failing that, he could almost hope to take some small wound of valor, so that he might know the touch of her hands healing him.

Kazander knew how preposterous—not to mention dangerous—such thoughts were when excited by the granddaughter of Chaynal of Radzyn. But the girl enchanted him. It was not that he didn't cherish his wives. All three of them were strong, beautiful, intelligent women. But Chayla—young as she was, he had found in her the proverbial *ricsina*, the knife that pierces the heart. He had no hope that time and knowledge of him might allow the same to happen to her.

Her life would be elsewhere. Sunrunner, physician, wife to some great lord with a castle and a hundred servants, bedecked in silks and jewels, an important force in the princedoms. The Isulk'im had rejected that sort of life many generations ago, when the *faradh'im* had come and sorcerers had been banished. It was too much to hope that somewhere in Chayla there lingered a few drops of ancestral blood that might cause her to hear the Desert's call of passion and freedom.

However futile Kazander knew his desires to be, still he wanted to impress her. So he bade his warriors attack as the *athri* had commanded—mentioning that any man who disappointed him would be taken back to the Long Sand flung across his saddle like a sack of grain.

Kazander's fifty would defend the red flag against Remagev's eighty and attempt to seize their blue banner. Simple enough, but Kazander knew the mischievous workings of Lady Feylin's mind and understood that whatever move the blues made was to be countered at once, spontaneously, as in the heat of real battle. That was the lesson she intended him to provide these children.

Only the blue center charged. Kazander yelled and swung his sword—careful to bruise, not break—and urged his gray stallion deeper into the fray, keeping an eye on the two flanks that waited for some signal to attack. The blues fell back to regroup. Kazander sighed, knowing he was supposed to pursue and let the flanks set upon him from either side—Feylin's "dragon wings." He gave the order, but with a variation. The Isulk'im shrieked battle cries like enraged dragons, cloaks streaming behind them, as the west flank of the Remagev forces descended on them. But the blues found a third of their prey taking off at a full gallop across the plain. As he fought, Kazander snatched glances at the merry chase his horsemen led the frustrated blues, and grinned.

All at once the eastern cavalry began driving the Isulk'im back. The blue center pushed forward, led by a tall youth who bellowed *"Eztiel Grib!"*—"All victory to Grib." Kazander shouted a warning at his youngest wife's brother, who carried the red banner. But it was too late. Sethric of Grib grabbed the pennant and galloped away with it behind the lines.

The rules said Kazander should give in, for his flag had been seized. He only smiled. Battles were not fought over trophies. He turned in his saddle as a youth challenged him from the right, and casually unhorsed the boy with a thrust of blunted sword against armored chest. A sore backside and a shallow pinprick would be humiliating but not fatal souvenirs.

Kazander broke free of the battle and called to his galloping warriors. They wheeled their horses with instant obedience and followed the sound of the *korrus*' voice. Sixteen riders were not quite enough for this, but they would have to do. In a variation of the maneuver used the previous day, the Isulk'im escaped their pursuers in a blinding whirl of sand and formed a half-circle outside the blue half-circle. Now the Remagev troops had to fight both forward and backward. Kazander hoped Feylin would forgive him for ruining her little demonstration, but the lesson *he* intended to teach was the more important one. Capturing a banner had nothing to do with winning a battle.

His smugness evaporated as he heard thunder on the ground behind him. Sethric had come back. Cursing, Kazander assessed the situation once more while chewing on his mustache and fending off a determined young man who seemed to have forgotten that his thrusts should not have lethal intent. Growling, Kazander taught him a painful lesson with the flat of his sword and shouted another order. The Isulki half-circle split in the middle, creating a pathway for their beleaguered comrades. All Kazander's men were soon free. They regrouped, turned, and waited for the blues to charge them once more.

Exhilarated by the return of Sethric's wing, the Remagev forces did not pause to organize themselves but instead rode whooping and cheering toward the Isulk'im at top speed. Kazander exchanged a grin with his brother-by-marriage.

"The girl is mine, Visian," he cautioned—and then led his men in a single line through the oncoming blues and up the slope of the dune. Before Walvis or Feylin or Chayla could react with more than disbelief, all three were lifted from their saddles and clutched to the chests of Isulk'im.

"Put me down!" Feylin raged. "Kazander! How dare you!" But Walvis was laughing uproariously as they were carried away.

Kazander had plucked the Lady Chayla from her horse with exquisite care. She did not struggle the way that spitfire Feylin was doing, merely settled on his thigh, supported by his arm around her waist. Otherwise he kept his hands to himself. Her coiled golden braids were at his shoulder, within easy reach of his lips; he could smell the fresh scents of herb soap and Desert wind in her hair. Her buttocks were surprisingly well-muscled against his thigh, but he supposed that was to be expected; after all, as the granddaughter of Radzyn's lord, she would have been in the saddle from early childhood. It was a sweet, firm, supple armful he held, and he wondered if he could persuade Walvis to persuade Lord Maarken not to slay him for daring to touch her.

He slowed his horse and finally stopped. Chayla was still relaxed against him. He turned to Visian, who was losing his grip on the taller, heavier *athri.* With a grin Kazander was about to claim victory—for he had stolen the real prizes of this little war.

All at once the air left his lungs in a painful gasp, propelled out of him by Chayla's elbow in his stomach. She slid neatly down to the sand, glaring up at this man who had been the first in her life ever to lay hands on her. She said nothing. She didn't have to. It was all in her eyes. He was incapable of responding in any case; he was too busy remembering how to breathe. But once his lungs had filled and there was only a dull ache in his belly, he could not help grinning down at her. Goddess, what a woman!

Late that night, after the banquet had been devoured and the battle analyzed a dozen times and the Isulk'im had taught Remagev's youthful warriors the steps of a traditional victory dance—and enough wine had flowed to make everyone feel very brotherly—Walvis and Kazander took a tour of the walls.

"You went to a lot of trouble to get your hands on her," the *athri* scolded, laughing. "And after you swore not to touch!"

Kazander, knowing he'd been forgiven and greatly relieved that he would not be facing Lord Maarken across the latter's sword, gave a deep sigh. "For those sweet moments, I knew all the glories of the world. Although she may never forgive me."

"That's what the High Princess would call an absolutely certain bet—the kind she wagers the whole princedom on." Walvis chuckled, leaning his elbows on the stone and looking out over the Desert night. "I hear you put yourself in the way of being treated by Chayla, not Feylin, afterward."

"A trifling cut that I didn't even feel until later. Not even a scar will be left—but no gratitude to her for it! I swear to you, she pummeled my bruised and bleeding leg as if I were made of bread dough!"

"Well, let that be a lesson to behave yourself. Actually, I'm surprised she didn't pull a knife on you. Like all her family, she takes her cue from the High Prince and carries one in each boot. She knows how to use them, too."

He smote his forehead with the flat of his palm. "With her temper, I would sing like a virgin girl for the rest of my life!"

"Her restraint in the matter may indicate that she likes you—either that or she hesitated to geld a friend of mine."

"She-dragon," Kazander muttered.

"Unlike her sweet and ladylike mother, but entirely reminiscent of Princess Tobin. I was proud of her—if she'd gotten free while you were still at a gallop, she might have hurt herself in the fall. Why did you pull such a stunt? Aside from getting around your promise not to touch her, I mean."

"The red pennant was taken—and these children thought this was all there is to war," he answered forthrightly. "If prizes are the goal, then one should go for the most essential ones. But prizes are not the goal in battle. They should think about that over the next few days."

"That's so." Walvis put a hand on his shoulder. "And you're right to have taught that lesson. But my little wars are just skirmishes, Kazander. I never expect them to fight the real thing. No one does. That's what Rohan's being High Prince is all about."

The younger man nodded. "He is greatly revered among us, even more than his father who drove the Merida from Stronghold." Kazander hesitated. "But—and I would say this to no one but you, mighty *athri*—it surpasses my understanding and that of our wisest ones why Prince Pol should take to wife the daughter of the snake who has given shelter to the Merida these many years."

"I would say this to no one but you, mighty *korrus*—but I've never understood it, myself. Princess Meiglan is beautiful and gentle and innocent of her father's wickedness. And marriage to bring alliances and peace is not uncommon. Still. . . ."

"The vermin still raid in the north. My great-grandfather fought them and killed many. My grandfather fought them and killed many more. My father was young but remembers your victory at Tiglath, where you killed hundreds. And yet they still raid in the north." Aware that his temper was seething, as always at the mere mention of the ancient enemy, he made an effort and said, "But perhaps it is as you say, and this alliance will bring peace one day."

"Is it true, do you suppose, that Prince Miyon has no sons to follow him?"

"That is the rumor. It's said there are bastards, but he keeps none of them at his court. If he dies without naming an heir, there will be war."

"Not if Pol claims Cunaxa on his wife's behalf," Walvis said musingly. "Rohan once told me that her marriage to Pol was a stroke of genius. But he never said *whose*."

"It is beyond my poor powers of understanding," Kazander sighed.

Walvis changed the subject. "How long can you stay this time?"

"As long as it takes the Lady Chayla to forgive me." He grinned.

"I thought we agreed that would take forever! I'm not contributing my substance to feed your ravenous hordes or your flea-bitten horses while you make large eyes at her! You have ten days, and then I'm packing you back to your long-suffering wives."

"As you command, mighty *athri*." Kazander gave him the eyes-lips-heart salute once again, with a low bow.

Walvis snorted. "I thought I told you to stop calling me that."

Chapter Four

Precisely one step into his wife's solar, Pol was accosted by a child who climbed him like a tree and demanded a lengthy list of indulgences at the top of her lungs. Making sure a thick carpet was under him, Pol collapsed onto it, howling for mercy.

"Jihan!" Meiglan clapped her hands sharply. "Stop that at once!"

"*He* did it on purpose," Jihan asserted, immobilizing the paternal right arm through the simple expedient of sitting on it. "Please, Papa, please can we go to the lake? And ride our new ponies and will you be our dragon and I'll even let Rislyn win this time, please?"

Pol eyed his offspring with the mixture of exasperation and affection that usually meant Jihan got whatever she wanted. "If you want to play dragons, then don't break my wing!"

Instant cooperation. Pol levered himself up from the rug and secured Jihan under one arm. He grabbed Rislyn up in the other and growled. Shrieks became giggles as he tickled; they attacked; he eventually surrendered; Meiglan watched the entire performance with a resigned sigh.

At last order was restored. Pol gave his wife a belated good-morning kiss and shook his head at her offer of breakfast.

"Not today, I'm afraid. My steward awaits. By the way, Jihan, if you're set on a swim, why don't you take my squires with you? I won't need them this morning, and they could do with some fun."

"Do I have to? Kierun never says anything and Dannar makes me sick."

"Jihan!" exclaimed Meiglan.

"Well, it's true, Mama. Do I *have* to ask them?"

Pol kept a straight face. "It's a princess' duty to get along with her father's squires."

"Oh, all right. May I be excused now, Mama?"

"Fold your napkin," Meiglan instructed, "and change out of your new dress before you ruin it—" But Jihan was already out the door. "Pol, I despair of that child! She simply must learn some manners. I won't have her disgracing us by being so ungovernable."

"Don't worry," he soothed. "She has Rislyn's gentle example, doesn't she, little one?" He smiled at his other daughter. Like Jihan, she was small for her age, but almost frail where her sister was quick and wiry. No one who knew the truth of Pol's ancestry ever said it aloud, but it had not gone unnoticed that Rislyn's eyes were as limpid a green as Roelstra's, while Jihan's were Rohan's startling blue. It was convenient that Pol's own eyes were a changeable combination of both. But the real distinction between the twins was signaled by the fact that Jihan swam like a fish and Rislyn paled at the sight of water. She had inherited Pol's Sunrunner gifts; Jihan was pure *diarmadhi.*

"Shall we really ride our new ponies today, Papa?" Rislyn asked hesitantly.

"We shall," he confirmed. "Give me a kiss, ladies, I'm off to my daily ordeal. Pity your poor prince, who has to work so hard on such a lovely day!"

The morning beckoned to him through the hallway windows as he strode resolutely to his office. Infinitely more pleasant to conduct business in the open air—but also unconducive to getting any real work done. Except for pruning the roses, redesigning a flowerbed, or coaxing a shy herb to grow. He ordered himself to attend to the affairs of his princedom—and stopped to look wistfully out at the gardens anyway.

Pride of ownership sang in him. Much as he loved Stronghold, it had belonged to his family for generations. Dragon's Rest was *his* creation. Every stone of it, every tree and fountain and carpet and tapestry and tile. Here, the generations would be counted from *him*.

Footsteps down the corrider alerted him to the arrival of his steward. Suppressing a sigh, he greeted the man and invited him into his office. By noon he'd heard the reports submitted by his masters of horse, hawk, and guard; decided the inheritance of eleven disputed farms; discussed the number of wolves to be hunted that winter (enough to decrease the threat to herds but not enough to overpopulate mountain elk and deer); chosen an official gift for his father-by-marriage's birthday; signed multiple copies of documents needed to authorize various shipments to various princedoms; and settled how many people would be needed from the surrounding countryside to help with the harvest. A tidy morning's work—but he hadn't taken a breath of air outside since waking.

Before his marriage, he'd done pretty much as he liked. He ate when he was hungry, slept when he was tired, and took care of his princedom in between building Dragon's Rest. Rialt had done most of the work Pol loathed, the kind that involved sitting at a desk with piles of parchments. But for the past few years Rialt had been regent of Waes. Halian had forfeited the city and all its revenues—a mere slap on the wrist for Chiana's raising an army, sorcerer-inspired or not. Charged with making Waes a model of profit and efficiency, Rialt had succeeded admirably; his administrative talents were perfectly suited to the task. Still, in losing him, Pol had lost his own comparative freedom and gained long days at this damned desk.

His stomach started growling halfway through a review of the upcoming law court. The steward politely pretended not to notice. Pol drank some water. The growl became a gurgle. He coughed to hide the sound. When a second cup of water sloshed inside him like wine in a half-empty barrel, he gave up and grinned.

"My brain is fascinated by the prospect of deciding who has the better claim to which plow-elk, but my stomach has other ideas. Shall we continue later?"

"As you wish, my lord," the steward said. "If it's convenient, the winemaster begs a few words sometime today."

"Fine." Pol hid his eagerness; consultation with Master Irul might include a long walk through the vineyards—precisely what he needed.

The steward shuffled parchments and ceremoniously bowed himself out. Pol sighed for the old days, when Rialt had run palace and princedom by consulting him and then writing appropriate orders. All Pol ever had to do then was read, sign, seal—and return to his horses, his gardens, his crops, or his architects.

He would have been entirely happy with only those things to occupy him. Uninterrupted enjoyment of the gentle arts of peace was just what Rohan had wanted to accomplish. Rich crops and fat cattle were impossible in the Desert; Dragon's Rest was as much Rohan's dream as Pol's. Long, tranquil seasons of growth and plenty, the simple life of a farmer—

Pol heard his breath exhale in an absurdly wistful sigh and burst out laughing. Some simple farmer it was who held conversations with a dragon.

Not that *that* art was anywhere near perfected. Yet. But Pol now communicated easily with Azhdeen, in a strange combination of emotion and Sunrunner conjurings. He thought of the dragon as his, just as Elisel was Sioned's. But the dragons saw it the other way around.

Three years ago, Riyan had learned to "speak" with Sadalian, a young green-bronze sire—and not by choice. The dragon had simply landed in front of him one afternoon outside Skybowl and established contact in a swirl of brilliant colors. This summer Morwenna's trepidation had succumbed to a dainty little blue-gray female she named Elidi. It was six years this spring since Hollis had approached her dragon, though she couldn't explain what process had led to the selection. "I just *knew*," Hollis had said. "Abisel isn't the biggest sire or the most beautiful—but there's something about him. . . ." The bemusement in her smile made Maarken and Ruala nod with perfect understanding; they had picked their dragons the same way. Friendships with seven dragons out of the hundreds that flew Desert skies was promising, but the exclusivity of such contact frustrated Pol. Dragons were intrigued by their humans, always treated them with care—and never deigned to speak with any others. When Maarken tried to discover the reason for this, Pavisel reacted with a snort, a toss of her black head, and a scornful conjure of other dragons tripping over their own wings.

"I think she's saying the others are too stupid," Maarken reported. "But you know something else? I think they're jealous. We belong to them—one person, one dragon. They don't object to talks between other humans and other dragons, but. . . ." And he gave that bewildered shrug that was fast becoming characteristic of someone who talked with a dragon.

It gnawed at Pol sometimes that the one person who

should have been able to was incapable of it. Of them all, Rohan should know communion with a dragon.

"Ah, but I have my dragons, Pol," he smiled when Pol complained about how unfair it was. "Hundreds of them—every dragon that ever flew across the Long Sand. I belong to all of them."

Pol met his new winemaster in the lower garden. Sioned had coaxed and cajoled and finally pried Master Irul loose from the vineyards at Catha Freehold this summer. Dragon's Rest had potential that she was determined to see—or perhaps "taste" was the more appropriate term—fulfilled. Having spent the summer inspecting every aspect of the winemaking from the trellises to the shape of the bottles, the master now gave Pol his succinct verdict:

"Pig swill."

Pol blinked. "I beg your pardon?"

"Grapes left too long on the vine. First fermentation vats a disaster. Too much resin in the wood. Aging barrels all wrong. Porous, bad design, aftertaste like rotted wood."

"That's quite a condemnation," Pol said, amused.

Irul shrugged. He was a short, burly, sun-weathered man who took two steps to Pol's one as they walked the vineyards. "Drinkable, I suppose. To anyone lacking a tongue. Dump it. Serve it to unwanted guests." Stopping beside a row of vines, he plucked a single fat grape. A slight pressure of thick fingers split the skin. Irul sniffed, then licked his fingers. "Juice, skin, no pulp, just enough sugar. We harvest tomorrow. There *might* be enough decent wine for the next *Rialla*."

"So my mother hopes."

"Best nose in the princedoms—except mine." Irul rubbed a leaf between his fingers. "Good climate, this. Cool mornings, hot afternoons. I've cost you a fortune in new vats, but worth it."

"I'll hold you to that, Master Irul. And I expect something worth drinking by next summer. The lighter wines should be ready by then, yes?"

"Perhaps," he conceded with a grunt.

Pol thanked him and continued up the hill. From the cool shade of the woods crowning the rise, he could see most of the valley, but not the shimmering lake to the north or the sheep kept penned there for the dragons' refreshment. Pol lazed back on his elbows to observe his little world, smiling.

Irul was dictating harvest orders to the farmers; down the valley, the master of horse supervised saddle-breaking. The tall, skinny figure of the cook proceeded in state to the vegetable garden, trailed by a small troop of kitchen servants whom he set to picking produce for dinner. The chief steward crossed the garden on his daily inspection, and stopped to argue with the head groundskeeper—also a daily occurrence. The chamberlain ran out of the Princes Hall, waving her arms madly at the men washing the windows; the guardmaster set up archery practice in a newly shorn wheatfield; and from the wooden village hall that also served as a schoolhouse, dozens of children were being shooed back inside after their games.

Pol laughed softly at all this industrious activity that enabled their prince to lounge in idle repose. Despite the time he put in on management and governance, he had no illusions about who really ruled Dragon's Rest. He was surrounded by despots who did all the work for him—the secret to being a successful prince, according to his father.

"Find people who know what they're doing, and let them do it. It leaves one free to think great thoughts—which is frequently best done with one's eyes closed."

Aware that his lids were indeed drooping, Pol pushed himself to his feet. He had a game of dragons to play—and a warning to give Jihan not to break the chamberlain's heart by riding *this* pony across the flawless polished floor of the Princes Hall.

* * *

"I know Gemma and I have outstayed our welcome—" Tilal began, and Pol laughed.

"According to whom? Not me, and not Meggie."

"According to my daughter!" Tilal grinned and kicked at the pebbled pathway of the water garden. "I know—she's sixteen, not six. As she informs me at least once a day. But I still can't help thinking of her—"

"As your little girl?" Pol suggested.

"Go on, laugh—but remember this when your own hatchlings try their wings!"

Pol couldn't imagine Dragon's Rest without Jihan and Rislyn, and said so. Tilal's turn to laugh.

"Now you've got some idea of how I feel. First Rihani

went off to become a squire, and now Sioneva's going to be here with you—Sorin's only nine, but in a few years he'll be fostered, too. I tell you, Pol, it's depressing."

"Then let's change the subject. How long will it take Kolya to rebuild his fishing boats? The storms on Lake Kadar this winter were pretty vicious, judging by the wood you skinned me out of this year."

"Actually, I keep telling myself that's the main reason I'm staying on. Laric's helping with a new design so Kolya can get as many boats as possible from your timber. Goddess knows you were stingy enough with it!"

They continued trading affectionate accusations as they left the water garden for the front lawns. Tilal and Gemma could stay all winter if they liked; Pol enjoyed filling Dragon's Rest with his friends and family. Sioneva, another in the ranks of Sioned's namesakes, would be living here for the odd year or so under Meiglan's care. The custom of fostering young highborn boys to other courts had expanded recently to include their sisters—Meggie's idea, for she had grown up totally ignorant of anything outside her home manor of Gracine and her father's Castle Pine. Her object was to give the girls wider experience—but Pol embraced the plan because the exchange of sons and daughters forged alliances. What she did through kind concern that others would not suffer her agonies of inadequacy, he approved for political reasons.

"Any quiver of dragons yet, *azhri*?" Tilal asked suddenly.

Pol arched a brow. "I note the distinction between *azhri* and *azhrei*!"

"Only one Dragon Prince. Back when I was his squire, I learned to recognize the signs in him, but I never did figure out how he did it."

"One of life's mysteries."

"Like the ones Andry's weaving around the Goddess?" Tilal made a face. "Tell me, Pol, wasn't it nicer when she was simply *here*, and we could chat with her without all these ritual mumblings?"

This was a sore point, but Pol kept hold of his temper. "Doubtless Andry uses what words he sees fit. I'm no more qualified to advise him in such things than he is to make recommendations about Princemarch."

"That will come." The Kierstian green eyes were dark

with warning. "I've noticed a few signs, myself. Like people wearing little medallions carved with that sunburst crest."

"Charming," he rasped.

"And there's not a damned thing we can do, is there?"

"Except trust to people's sense."

"When Sunrunner physicians are more and more sought after? They aren't any better trained and they use the same remedies—with the same rate of success. But a *Sunrunner* has a direct link to the Goddess," Tilal finished angrily.

"I really don't want to discuss this, Tilal."

"No, nobody does. That's the problem. We complain in private—and let Andry do as he likes. I knew him when he was little, Pol. What happened to him? Power? Is that the explanation?"

"Among other things." He greeted the arrival of his daughters with relief. But taking them to the paddocks, lifting them to their new ponies, watching them put the animals through their paces—both girls were splendid riders even at seven years old—served as only a minor distraction. He kept remembering a conversation he'd had with his parents this summer.

* * *

"It's my fault," Rohan sighed when Sioned stormed into the Tapestry Room with news that Pirro of Fessenden had dismissed his court physician in favor of a Sunrunner. "If I hadn't set up the school in Gilad to rival Goddess Keep. . . ."

In 728, a young *faradhi* trained but not perfected in medical arts had failed to cure a Giladan master weaver. Had Andry paid the death-price according to Giladan law, the whole unfortunate business could have been forgotten. But he had insisted that the woman had been acting as a Sunrunner, under no jurisdiction but that of the Lord of Goddess Keep.

Cabar of Gilad had been furious. Rohan had been forced to decide between essentially equal claims. He chose neither, citing ancient law that Goddess Keep was held of the High Prince; thus ultimate authority over Sunrunners was his. Andry's rage was beyond repairing. Cabar had been placated—barely—by establishment in Gilad of a school for physicians, whose training until then had been unregulated. Sunrunners received basic medical education, but could not be expected to see to the needs of the whole continent. Physicians took on apprentices, as in any other trade, but there were vast differences in skills and methods. Rohan had hoped to remedy this by creating a school where learning could be shared, new techniques devised, and training standardized to provide a higher degree of competence.

In large part, it worked. Medical care improved. Those who lacked apprentice fees paid for the education with a year's service to an established master and a tax on earnings for the first three years of practice. Tobin had forbidden Rohan to pay all expenses himself; such blatant use of dragon wealth was unwise and, practically speaking, the school must be self-supporting.

At first the older physicians balked. But then they began to receive assistants who, already well trained, worked for room and board and moreover knew the very latest treatments. It became a matter of prestige to have such an assistant—as long as he or she decently deferred in public to the opinions of the senior physician—and to boast that one had been sought out for training that not even the Giladan school could provide.

Then Andry decreed that the eighth *faradhi* ring would signify a Master Physician. Sunrunners who had earned it prior to this rule had three choices: qualify for it, give it up, or break with Goddess Keep. Very few had the courage for the last.

"It is *not* your fault!" Sioned fumed that summer morning. "Competition was never the idea, damn it! This is Andry's doing. All these rituals and—and *incantations!*—they use Sunrunner's Fire to light a sickroom candle!"

Rohan shrugged. "Which of us, when we're ill, won't try almost anything to recover? If a few rituals could have eased the pain in my back tooth last year, I might've called in a Sunrunner physician myself." He grinned at his furious wife. "Instead, my Sunrunner witch insisted I have the damned thing pulled."

"And you howled like a wounded dragon, too. Disgusting."

Pol gestured impatiently. "But what Andry's doing is a fake. The cures are the same and they either work or they don't—but people think they're more effective because of the show that goes along with them."

"Appearances can be *most* effective," Rohan murmured.

"I've indulged in a few manipulations myself from time to time."

"That's different," Sioned snapped.

"Why? Because I'm a dear, sweet, charming, nice man?" He laughed, but Pol heard a bitter undertone. "Or because you happen to agree with what I do, but not with Andry?"

"Superstition is wrong," Pol said flatly.

"And it's not just the medicine," Sioned agreed. "It's *all* Sunrunner things. I talk every so often with a friend at Goddess Keep—"

"Who obliges you with information on the sly," Pol interpreted.

"Of course. I'm told of ceremonies and a great deal of formality—even when no envoys or ambassadors are there to impress."

"Which they seem to be more and more often." Pol frowned. "Does your friend let you know who sends ranking representatives to Andry these days?"

"As faithfully as Andry's eyes and ears at Stronghold advise him of our doings. Although I flatter myself that what Andry knows of us is only what we wish him to know. More or less."

"Mother!"

Rohan laughed again at Pol's shock. "The game dictates that we all spy on each other. The zest of playing is making sure you control information. How can you have ruled this long without realizing so simple a truth? Your dealings with fellow princes demand accuracy in what you know about them and inaccuracy in what they think they know about you."

"It shouldn't be like that," Pol said stubbornly.

"Of course it shouldn't. We all ought to be honest with each other—in an ideal world. But do you trust, say, Velden of Grib?"

"Not past spitting distance," Pol admitted. "But it's demeaning to live like this."

"I have two answers for you," Rohan replied more seriously. "The first is that I agree. It's a waste of time, energy, and resources to worry about managing information. What to believe, what to make others believe—it's not my pride that twinges, it's my conscience. And yet—how else do you think I've managed to keep peace all these years? With your mother's invaluable help, of course," he added, nodding to Sioned.

"Nice to know I'm appreciated. Pol, when I married your father, Sunrunners were cast into politics as never before. Andrade wanted me to represent the *faradhi* point of view, and advance her notions of how the world should be run."

"But you didn't," Rohan said softly, and smiled.

"I was a vast disappointment to her," she acknowledged, not sounding at all unhappy about it. "But when Andrade chose us against Roelstra, a partnership of Sunrunners and High Prince was established—"

"Which might exist today if Andry and I hadn't started loathing each other," Pol finished.

"It's far more complex than personal feelings." Rohan sighed. "We've gone back to what used to be before our marriage—a network of Sunrunners reporting exclusively to Goddess Keep. But this Goddess Keep behaves much as if it, too, were a seat of government." He brooded over this for a moment. "Andry's an able man. If he'd stayed in the Desert to rule a small holding, or even married a girl with a large one, I doubt he would've been content. Limited scope."

"Yes," Sioned drawled, "one can hardly weave mysteries when one is worried about the goats."

"What about your other answer?" Pol prompted.

"What? Oh. My first being that I find spying an exercise in irritation, the second is that it's a necessary part of civilized life."

Even Sioned stared at him. "You'll have to explain that one."

He gave them a patient look. "If I am a barbarian, I make war. That kind of information is easy. How many horses and swords does my enemy have? Will he use them against me before I can use mine against him? Very simple. Very direct."

Pol sat forward, intrigued. "But if what you're trying to do is live in peace so the crops can grow—"

"—you need much more complex information."

"My clever *azhrei*," Sioned observed sardonically. "So intricate spying is one of the privileges of civilization, is it? Such a comfort to know I'm contributing to ongoing enlightenment."

"But Andry isn't, and that's just the point," Pol said.

"He's creating mysteries around things that aren't mysterious at all."

"Not to you, perhaps," Rohan answered. "But I've lived with a Sunrunner most of my life and I don't even pretend to comprehend what it is she does. People believe what those powerful enough to affect belief demonstrate is believable. Convoluted, but it's the idea that counts," he smiled.

"But what Andry's doing is wrong!" Pol insisted.

"Anything that promotes superstition instead of truth is wrong. Yet how do you explain the way you talk to your dragon? How do you make Sunrunner skills comprehensible? Your mother hasn't been able to make it clear to me in almost forty years, and I've even got the—what's Andry calling it now? The 'halfling gift.' What amazes me is that all this hasn't appeared before now."

"Andrade would never have allowed it," Sioned told him. "None of the other rulers of Goddess Keep would have, either. But Andry's cultivating it."

"An apt description, Mother," Pol remarked. "Seeing as how what he spreads on it to make it grow stinks to the high Veresch."

* * *

"Papa! Papa, come be the dragon!"

He abandoned memories of a conversation that had yielded no solution. Pol liked solutions. He had limitless faith in his parents' ability to provide them—one way or another. But where Andry was concerned, Tilal was right: everyone complained in private, but no one did anything. What was there to do?

He forgot his impatience with his cousin and his nagging wish that Rohan would do something, *anything*, about Andry, and dutifully donned a sweeping cloak for his performance. He had been vanquished three times—twice by Jihan, once by Rislyn—and was filthy from head to heels when their tutor arrived to collect them for afternoon lessons. Catallen had been sent by Miyon, and everyone knew he was a spy. Pol instinctively put Rohan's principles into practice: he chatted with the tutor every so often, dropping half-truths here and there to keep Miyon contented—so he wouldn't send someone Pol might not recognize as being in his father-by-marriage's pay.

Tilal had called out encouragement and tactics based on many similar games with Walvis or Rohan himself as the dragon. Now, as the children accompanied Catallen back to the palace, the older prince grinned at the younger.

"Not bad. Nice flourish to the wings, but I'd work on the death flutter. Go relax, Pol. You look frayed around the edges—like a cloth that's mopped up one too many spills."

"After my hellions mopped up the paddock with *me,* you mean?" He laughed and went to his chambers to wash, reflecting that a wrung-out rag was exactly what he felt like after a *Rialla*, no matter what his triumphs. Maneuvering the other princes into doing what he wanted while making sure they thought it was all their own idea; scrupulous attention to their privileges and personal conceits; the jaw-grinding he had to hide when what was perfectly obvious to him remained perfectly obscure to them—no wonder his father had turned the bulk of the work over to him. He cleaned up messes and polished self-images and soaked up any spills of ill-feeling among the princes, and sent them home convinced that they alone were responsible for all this peace and good will.

At times he longed to tell them exactly what he thought of them—and to show them the path he had chosen and tell them to start marching. But he suspected that if they allowed him to do such a thing, he would have even more contempt for them than he did now.

Not all of them, of course. In fact, he liked most of the men he worked with. Tilal, Volog, Arlis—not surprisingly, they were his mother's kin and in theory his own as well. Laric of Firon and his father, Chadric of Dorval, were two others he liked and respected; they really were kin to him through Rohan.

But he hadn't his father's patience with the others. Cabar, Velden, Halian, Pirro, especially Miyon and even at times Kostas of Syr, Tilal's brother—the difficulties they often presented were annoyances that Rohan saw as creative opportunities. He listened, considered, consulted, and suggested solutions agreeable to all. Pol's impulses were either to tell them to stop bothering him or to settle the whole thing himself with a single command.

"You're too direct," Sioned had lectured. "You don't think things all the way through. You want to act too fast."

"And who'd I learn *that* from, Mother mine?" he'd countered, grinning, and she'd had the grace to blush.

At times he despaired of ever being half the prince his father was. Then again, Rohan had had nearly forty years of practice; Pol, only a little over ten. Well, he was learning. He'd watched his father carefully at the past six *Riall'im*, trying to adapt Rohan's style and methods to his own character. He'd done very good work this summer, work to be proud of. He was learning his father's techniques; eventually he'd learn Rohan's patience as well.

* * *

Pol stood obediently still as his squires scrutinized him. He never cared what he wore. His father had the knack of impressive personal adornment—probably because at first glance he was physically rather unprepossessing—and had been known to take a whole afternoon dressing for a banquet. Pol put on his back whatever was handed to him. That he was always elegantly clothed was a tribute to a succession of servants and squires much more concerned with their prince's appearance than he was. Rialt had trained Edrel, who had trained Amiel, who had recently laid down the law to Dannar and Kierun. Privately, Pol suspected Amiel of having given them an instructional treatise. It amused him endlessly.

He'd had the pleasure of knighting Amiel at this year's *Rialla*, and giving him the black elkhoof cup rimmed in gold that was Princemarch's gift to a new-made knight. The choice of the Giladan heir to join Edrel of River Ussh as his squire in 729 had been a frankly political one. After Edrel's knighting in 735, Amiel stayed on for two years' further training in statecraft.

Though politics had brought him to Dragon's Rest, he also found a wife. People were shocked when Cabar's heir threw himself away on a nobody. Granted, Princess Meiglan had fostered her for a year, which was how the unsuitable attachment had begun, but Nyr was barely highborn and came from someplace in Fessenden no one had ever heard of. Amiel married his bronze-haired lady in a double ritual with Edrel and his Chosen—even more shocking, for though fast friends, one was a prince, the other a mere younger son.

This younger son had won one of the finest prizes in the princedoms. Norian of Grib was blithe, blonde, and as besotted with Edrel as he was with her. That she should waste herself on him was the talk of the *Rialla*. Her father, Prince Velden, threatened to forbid the marriage. Norian announced publicly that she would wed Edrel or no one. Pol chose a more private moment to hint that the young man would one day rule an important holding in Princemarch; this had almost reconciled Velden to the match. Thus Pol discovered the fun of being powerful enough to make a future for a deserving friend.

He liked arranging things. It was his mother's opinion that in *this* he took after Andrade. But, unlike her, he would never have maneuvered anyone into so important a Choice for political aims. People met, fell in love, married, had children. That was life, from cottage to castle. For highborns with wealth, property, and titles to pass along, the process often overwhelmed the personal. Fosterings were politics enough for Pol, and he frankly distrusted people who married for anything but love.

His selection of two new squires this year had nothing to do with politics at all. One of them, in fact, he accepted out of curiosity. Kierun was the son of Allun of Lower Pyrme, a man Pol wryly admired for being committed to his own square measures and absolutely nothing else. He had attended only two *Riall'im* in his life: one to find a wife and the other to deliver his heir to Pol. Otherwise he never set foot off his own property. Allun intended a more active part for Kierun in the affairs of the continent, however, and to this end gave the boy into Pol's care. Kierun was black-haired, gray-eyed, barely twelve, and unable to believe he was squire to the next High Prince. He had lived in a state of perpetual wonderment since the *Rialla* and barely dared to breathe.

Pol's second squire was a choice of pure affection. Dannar of Castle Crag was Ostvel and Alasen's son. Though a year Kierun's junior, he was perfectly relaxed around Pol. They knew each other very well. From his mother, Dannar inherited the Kierstian green eyes—like Sioned's and Tilal's—and his red hair came from that side of the family as well. But his features and strong build were Ostvel's. Except for the difference in coloring, Dannar and his much older half-brother Riyan looked quite a bit alike.

The pair conducted their inspection as if the fate of princedoms hung on the color and cut of Pol's tunic. Amiel must have been incredibly stern with them. Pol sighed and kept his impatience to himself, knowing Kierun would look like a startled kitten if he said anything. The child was completely overawed and it made him nervous.

"It wants something, my lord," Dannar said at last. "What do you think, Kier? Something black, to offset the boots?"

"A belt?" the other boy ventured.

"Exactly! Remind me to add it to Prince Amiel's list."

Pol laughed so hard he had to sit down.

The belt was produced—a bit tight in its usual notch, due to lavish *Rialla* meals—and an onyx earring for good measure. Finally Pol was pronounced presentable. As the squires accompanied him down the hall to the stairs, he asked about their morning swim.

Dannar shrugged. "Jihan got mad when I dunked her, my lord."

"*Princess* Jihan!" Kierun exclaimed, shocked out of his usual shyness.

Pol grinned. "So she's made that clear, has she? Let me tell you something, Kierun. Jihan is a miserable little brat, as Dannar knows very well. Next time she pesters you, you have my permission to remind her that though she may be a princess, one day *you* will be Lord of Lower Pyrme with two fine castles, four rich manors, and four hundred square measures of the best farmland on the continent."

"Oh, she won't let on she's impressed by that, my lord," Dannar told him. "Kier, just let her know that when you grow up, your wife will be *much* prettier than she is. Worked for me."

Pol heroically kept a straight face. It was more difficult to keep the suspicious quiver from his voice as he said, "You'd better go get ready to serve. And by the way, tell that madman in the kitchen that if he so much as *thinks* a dessert in my direction, I'll have him trussed up and thrown in with the sheep to feed the dragons."

Kierun cast a startled look at Dannar, whose grin reassured him. The boys ran off to their duties—leaving Pol free to laugh himself out of breath.

* * *

"Meiglan, won't you play for us this evening? Please?" Gemma's smile was warmly cajoling, and Pol leaned over to whisper, "For me?"

She rose from his side to a smattering of excited applause. There were just friends here, she told herself as she approached the *fenath*, people she knew, not the hordes of strangers her father had ordered her to play for at Castle Pine.

Miyon had tricked her at the *Rialla,* offering her up for public view at a banquet by presenting her with a new instrument. She had trembled all the way down the long white floor of the Princes Hall. As the first notes echoed through the huge chamber, his sleek malicious smile had practically paralyzed her. Out of tune. Purposely out of tune, at her father's order, so that she must test strings and twist pegs until she thought she'd die of humiliation.

But tonight she would play for friends in the gentle intimacy of the Tapestry Room. None but kind, fond people here, people she knew and liked—even if she would never understand them, never be like them.

The new *fenath* was a spectacular instrument—carved, inlaid, jeweled, each of its fifty strings having pearl-headed anchor- and tuning-pegs. Even the little wooden hammers were decorated, a different gem sparkling from each so that while she played, the motions of her hands traced colors through the air.

Meiglan slid the hammers between her curled fingers and flexed her wrists. The first song she played was one she had heard Gemma humming yesterday; the princess smiled in delight. As Meiglan glanced through the strings at her audience, she savored the joy of bringing such pleasure. It had never been so at her childhood home of Gracine Manor, nor during the two years she had lived with Miyon. Back then she played only for herself, mercifully losing all consciousness of where and who she was in the ripple of the strings.

Pol had changed all that. She could not fade into the music when he was here to listen and sometimes add his rich voice to the songs her *fenath* wove. When she played for him alone, she knew only the movements of her hands and the glow in his blue-green eyes—so different from the self-absorption of her girlhood music. Gradually she had acquired the courage to play for small groups in private. The best times were when Lord Ostvel was here to accompany her with his lute and his voice that so perfectly blended with Pol's. But though it was difficult to play at the *Rialla*—it reminded her of her father's demands—she always did. She could deny Pol nothing and he was so proud of her music.

Tilal asked for a Syrene ballad remembered from his youth at River Run. She put the sticks down, rubbed her fingers back to suppleness, then plucked the strings with a rapidity that always startled onlookers. The width of the *fenath* had defeated her before she'd learned how to sway lightly back and forth, moving her feet only a little. Rohan had once told her she looked like a flower floating on a breeze and watching her was almost as lovely as listening to her.

It was a distinguished company of listeners tonight. Laric and Lisiel of Firon had lingered after the *Rialla* to await the birth of their second child, conceived last winter before a visit to Graypearl. Not sure of her pregnancy until early spring, they had hoped she would be able to travel after the *Rialla*. But thirty-eight was a risky age for childbearing. So they stayed at Dragon's Rest while her brother, Yarin of Snowcoves, tended their princedom from his holding.

Edrel and Norian had also delayed departure, intending to escort Laric and Lisiel as far as Edrel's home of River Ussh after the birth. It was thus almost exclusively a family party—Laric and Tilal were Pol's kin, Edrel had been his squire, and Norian was distantly related to Gemma. Meiglan, who had no family but her father and a few half-brothers she'd never met, was constantly amazed by the complex web of kinships that had Rohan, Sioned, and Pol at its center.

Kierst, Isel, Dorval, Syr, Firon, Ossetia—six of thirteen princedoms were tied by blood to Pol. His father was High Prince; his cousin, Lord of Goddess Keep. Other relations or close friends were important *ath'rim*. Between them, Rohan and Pol directly controlled or strongly influenced most of the continent. But Meiglan didn't let herself think too often about the power she'd married. She'd learned to hide her nervousness and behave like other highborn ladies. Sionell was her idol and mentor for many things she was too shy to ask anyone else about. Kostas' wife, Danladi, was another model for behavior—and much easier to emulate, being nearly as quiet and self-effacing as Meiglan herself. But Meiglan was never sure if she truly succeeded at impersonating a great lady or if people merely acted as if she did because of Pol.

Yet this summer something astonishing had happened. Sioned—who wore her two kinds of power, princely and Sunrunner, with authority that Meiglan never dared dream of attaining—had asked, "Meggie, what's your opinion?"

At face value it was a request for information. But Sioned had never used her nickname before. Though that was startling enough, the real shock had been that Sioned—vibrant, brilliant, beautiful even at sixty—*Sioned* had paid her the ultimate compliment of asking her thoughts without first saying that her thoughts were valuable. Among these powerful people, compliments were in fact thinly veiled sarcasm; everyone expected everyone else to have wits and to use them. Praise for one's person was eagerly sought and smugly received, but intelligence was expected, and compliments on it usually implied its lack.

Because of that one question, Meiglan had begun to believe that she might become the kind of princess Pol needed. Someone poised and self-assured and clever. Someone like Sionell.

Thinking of her friend, Meiglan plucked a song Sionell had taught her. They were friends—despite the awkward revelations that had occurred when Meiglan asked Pol if it would be proper to ask Sionell to stand with her at their marriage.

"She's been so kind to me, and—I don't have anybody but my father to be with me, and I so much want a friend there as well—but if it's not suitable—"

He looked dismayed for a moment, then smiled and shrugged. "I'm sure she'd be glad to stand with you, Meggie."

His expression was such that she had not asked. That evening she found out from her servant that Sionell had been in love with Pol since childhood.

"It's been over a long time," Thanys reported. "Since before she married Lord Tallain, they say. But don't distinguish her, my lady. She could be a threat to you."

Never. Absurd. Still, looking back over certain things which had been incomprehensible at the time, there had been an unspoken tension between Pol and Sionell, as if things had been said that could never be forgotten. Or forgiven.

Meiglan attributed it all to some mystery in the past that

she had no right to ask about. She had no right to jealousy, either; Pol so obviously loved her. Everyone remarked on it, even loathsome Princess Chiana in that nasty-sweet way of hers: "My dear, I declare that if you took a fancy to a certain star in the night sky, he'd pull it down for you to wear around your pretty throat." Pol and Sionell shared the affection of lifelong friends. The two families saw each other often at Dragon's Rest and Stronghold. Letters were frequent. Sionell had Named her second son Meig. She was one of the few people Meiglan trusted.

On Pol's love Meiglan's life was built. She saw him smiling at her and decided to play a familiar song, hoping Edrel would nudge him into singing it.

The lyric was about the *faradhi* who had married a Prince of Kierst. It had been a great scandal at the time, for no highborn had ever wed a trained Sunrunner. Their marriage at a *Rialla* was ostensibly the song's subject, but everyone knew it was really about Rohan and Sioned.

Pol laughed as she began, and, sure enough, Edrel coaxed him to sing. He rose and walked toward her, his clear, firm voice carrying the melody while her fingers danced over the *fenath*. Ostvel was strongly suspected of having written the words, but he always denied all responsibility.

Faradh'im *whispered on the light, and merchants gossiped at the Fair,*
And Princes frowned in warning dire at Kierst's colossal dare:
A Sunrunner, with rings of gold and rings of silver shining,
Kierst's Princess she would surely be, her powers his entwining.
It's said it happened with a look, a touch of fated hands—
But I attest Sunrunner's Fire, as hot as Desert sands.
The voices rose like Storm God's wind—the High Prince—

Meiglan faltered as Pol stopped singing. He turned to the windows, his body tense and his eyes lit with excitement. Meiglan hid her trembling as best she could. She knew what that look meant.

"Hear me well, daughter. I don't give a damn how much dragons frighten you. Don't ever *show it or say so aloud—not to him, not to your dearest friend, not to your most trusted servant, not even to yourself when you're alone!"*

Meiglan stood still, hoping no one would look at her, or that her frozen stance would be taken for surprise. The trumpeting of the dragons echoed and shuddered through the room, rattling crystal goblets like glass bones. Pol had explained their habits, their differing calls, their brilliant colors, their intelligence. She had stood at his side to watch and listen, ridden with him headlong down the valley to greet them while he laughed with the joy of being nearly airborne himself on a golden stallion. She said and did all the right things. No one ever guessed that she feared dragons to the depths of her soul.

Startled silence gave way to excited shouts; stillness became a riotous scramble toward the windows.

"You see?" Tilal laughed at Gemma. "We've been watching for them in vain for two days, but he knew they were here even before they called out!"

Jihan and Rislyn darted to the windows where their father lifted them up to see the dragons. Meiglan stayed where she was and tried to recover her senses.

"Look!" Rislyn cried. "Is that Azhdeen, Papa?"

She could never reveal her fear. Who could she tell? None of these people would understand, and certainly not Pol. His laughter rang out as if greeting old friends—which, to him, they were. Especially his own dragon, Azhdeen. Pol would be disappointed by her fear, hurt that she had lied to him for so long.

"Can we ride out to see them tonight, my lord?" This from Sioneva, her new fosterling—descended from the royalty of five princedoms—what could Meiglan possibly teach this girl about being a princess?

"We'll go up to the lake tomorrow and watch them," Pol replied.

"Why don't you take your sketchbook along, darling?" Gemma said. "I know Dani would love to see a drawing of so many dragons."

Gemma had grown up with Danladi, second-youngest of Roelstra's daughters, and the two were as close as sisters. Meiglan thought of her own dearest friend, almost a sister, but she could never let Sionell know her fear either. Sionell loved dragons as much as Pol did. They shared so many things: a Desert childhood, the same friends and family, a love for dragons, a quickness of mind and toughness of spirit—and neither of them would ever comprehend her terror.

"I assume you're going to have a little chat with Azhdeen?" Laric asked Pol, his amusement tinged with envy.

"If he's in an expansive mood—and finds sheep to his taste! He's like a cat, that one, picking over the best until one tempts his appetite."

Thanys sidled up to Meiglan and took her elbow, guiding her unobtrusively away from the *fenath*. She gave the servant a grateful look for the prompting and the support. The others must never guess at the sick weakness in her limbs. Thanys always looked out for her, always protected her—a trusted servant who knew what the sound and sight of dragons did to her. But Thanys had been the one who had brought the sorcerer Mireva to Stronghold in Meiglan's suite. How could she trust Thanys?

She gathered her courage and approached Pol. He turned from the twilight view of dragons in flight and smiled down at her. "I'm sorry, sweet. We've crowded you out. Here, come stand by the window. Aren't they magnificent?"

She nodded, lying to him with the gesture. There were so many dragons that the soft blue of the day-fading sky was shadowed by wings like dark clouds descending. The people around her pressed close; she could barely breathe for the crush and the fear.

" . . .*not even to yourself when you're alone!*" That was the real irony. She was never and always alone. She was both surrounded by people and encased in solitude. Like a winter-iced pine, she lived in a forest and was separated from it by a thin layer of crystal that allowed others to see but never to touch her. Except for Pol, except for his warmth like the heart of the sun itself, nothing and no one touched her. Not even her children. She lived in fear of shattering, of watching the icy glass splinter around her to leave her naked and trembling with cold.

* * *

Everyone rode to the lake the next day except Lisiel, big with child, and Meiglan, who kept her company. Pol left them in his wife's chambers, placidly sewing baby clothes and listening to Catallen, who also had bardic pretensions, read his latest work. Personally, Pol had no use for poetry unless he could sing it, but it was incumbent upon a prince to have a bard in residence; that was why Miyon had known he could not refuse Catallen's services.

It was a relief to see Meiglan pleasantly occupied while he went chasing dragons. She was a gallant darling to hide it, but he knew how they frightened her. Lisiel provided the perfect excuse for her to stay home. He need not worry about her and she need not wear her nerves raw pretending to be unafraid.

So he rode out with a clear conscience. The horse beneath him was nearly as eager as he. Azhenel—"dragon horse"—was the finest of the golden breed at Dragon's Rest. The name had come from an incident four years ago, when the yearling escaped the paddock and galloped up the valley to the lake. Amazingly, the dragons' meal had not included the colt. Perhaps it was because they had already dined on fat sheep, or perhaps it was as the awed Master of Horse said—that a mysterious affinity for dragons allowed the colt to gambol about among them with perfect unconcern. Pol arrived to find him actually *playing* with immature dragons five times his size, for all the world like children from neighboring farms come together for a holiday.

When dragons came each year on their migrations, Azhenel called out in welcome instead of fretting with the high, nervous whinny of more skittish stablemates. Horses could be trained not to fear dragons, but Azhenel was the only one in Pol's experience—or anybody else's—that genuinely liked them. Chay often ascribed human characteristics to horses, but even he was taken aback by Azhenel's behavior.

"Damned animal's making fun of us," he growled the first time he saw the young stallion, well-grown and with a cascade of snowy white mane and tail, cavort with dragons. "Look at him! As if those talons weren't half as long as his legs!" Then, eyeing Pol with amusement sparkling in his gray eyes: "Have you learned how to talk to horses, too? Whispered a word or two in his ear that as long as they're well-fed, they won't be interested in him?"

In his more whimsical moments Pol sometimes thought that Azhenel was the one who'd learned how to talk, and his conversations were with dragons. Certainly when they reached the lake and he dismounted to let the stallion greet his winged friends, Azhenel delighted in nudging dragons with his nose, whinnying, flicking his tail playfully in their faces, and gently nipping his favorites. The older dragons reacted with genial grunts. The hatchlings fluttered and called out in bewilderment at this strange, hooved, unwinged thing, nearly their own size, that invited them to play. But soon they were chasing Azhenel, screeching gleefully as they flew to catch up with him.

"That's the most incredible thing I've ever seen," Tilal breathed. "You'd think they'd rip him to shreds!"

Gemma stared with wide brown eyes. "And you say he's been doing this all his life?"

Pol nodded. "I've known a few cats who thought they were people, but this is the only horse I ever heard of who thinks he's a dragon!"

"Why is that, my lord?" Dannar asked. He was off his own horse and standing beside Rislyn's pony, a gentling hand on the little mare's neck as she danced nervously in the presence of dragons.

"Because Papa's *azhrei*, just like Grandsir," Jihan responded. "Kierun, you don't have to hold my reins. Thank you very much, but I can handle a horse."

The squire turned crimson and started to back away.

"Stay put, Kierun," Pol ordered. "Jihan, your new pony hasn't seen dragons before and might bolt. A few broken bones would probably benefit your temper, but I don't feel like explaining to your mother how you got them."

Laric slid from his saddle and joined Pol. "Good Goddess, there's enough of them to drink the lake dry. And the sheep must be half gone."

"There's not much to eat in the Desert," Sioneva said. "They must have been hungry, poor darlings."

Tilal glanced sidelong at his daughter, brows arching. "*Azhwis,*" was all he said, but those who understood bits of the old language began to laugh.

"My girls, too," Pol grinned at him. "Daughters of dragons, all of them!'

"I swear to you, the first thing she said may have been 'mama,' but the second was 'Take me to see dragons'!"

"Is that Azhdeen, Pol?" Laric asked all at once.

His heart skipped with excitement as the huge sire called out, paced in elegant state to the water's edge, and with a single wingstroke leaped into the air. Horses neighed as the dragon sailed across the lake and landed with breathtaking precision a few lengths from Pol.

Azhdeen was gorgeous and knew it. His blue-gray hide was marked by the fewest battle scars of any sire there—sign of his supremacy—and rippled with the strength of massive muscles. He rose up on hind legs and spread his wings to show their silver undersides. It was his usual greeting to Pol, who went forward and lifted his own arms wide as if to embrace the dragon. *His* dragon.

Into the space between them swirled a riot of color. Pol expanded his own colors to meet and merge with those of the dragon. Instantly he was surrounded, absorbed, engulfed—ecstatic.

Emotions first—pleasure at seeing Pol; satisfaction at thirst assuaged and plump sheep devoured; smugness at the number and quality of females who'd chosen him for mating at Rivenrock; pride in his many new offspring. Curiosity about Pol's own mate and hatchlings; amazement tinged with scornful superiority that the little females had grown no bigger and there were no new ones despite the fact that this was a mating year.

Pol laughed and apologized for his lack, reveling in Azhdeen's matter-of-fact arrogance. *You great lumbering beautiful beast*, he thought, knowing the words were meaningless to the dragon but that the affection would be clear as crystal, *I have only one mate and you spread your favors among scores! Of course you have more hatchlings than I do!*

Azhdeen settled into an easy crouch on the shore, his tail lashing softly in cool water. This was the sign Pol had been waiting for. He would now be allowed to approach the dragon. He never lost the wonder of it, of walking slowly toward that huge head with its large, dark, shrewd eyes and jawful of dagger-sharp teeth. Once, Azhdeen had batted playfully at him with what was for him a gentle hand. Pol had toppled, nearly unconscious. Since then the dragon had restrained himself from touching the puny, fragile human.

But Pol could touch the dragon. He stood beside Azhdeen's lowered head and scratched the smooth hide between the eyes, careful to avoid the bony spines streaking back from the brow. He ran the flats of his palms down the dragon's face to the ridges of the nostrils, tickling the sensitive skin there. Azhdeen hummed low in his throat with pleasure. Pol rubbed along the closed jaw to the dragon's eyes, and lids drifted lazily shut as he luxuriated in the petting.

Glutton, Pol accused fondly, scratching Azhdeen's throat. When he was close to the dragon this way, it was easy to think of him as a kind of gigantic, furless, winged cat: the predator that purred. Dragons had no enemy but man. It had been nearly forty years since the last Hatching Hunt, but only nine since Pol's half-brother Ruval had slaughtered two adult dragons near Elktrap Manor. He had used sorcery to pull the mighty creatures down from the sky and then dealt them a slow, agonizing death. Memory caused Pol's colors to darken, and Azhdeen opened one eye in surprise.

A picture appeared in the air, accompanied by the emotional equivalent of a loud demand: *How did you know?* Conjured before Pol was a strange sight: dragons floating on the sea. Not living dragons, but stiff, motionless, with uplifted wings frozen in place. Like sails, Pol thought, tracing with his gaze the raised necks with their sightless heads dipping to the rise and fall of the waves. Ships, of course, built of wood and not dragon bones and hide, but Azhdeen couldn't know that. He evidently thought dragons had been killed and somehow made to float on water with spread wings. Perhaps he had seen ships with wary watchers on the prows carved in the shape of dragon heads; sails naturally reminded him of wings. So to him it was an obvious conclusion.

Pol wove his colors into the picture, altering it to reflect what he knew was the reality. Wings became sails; bones changed to masts and rigging. The contours of dragon bodies he amended to wooden keels. He had never seen such a vessel himself, but his years as a squire at Graypearl had familiarized him with ships. He elaborated on the picture, adding people on the decks and in the dragon's nest from which they watched for land when sailing far from shore.

It's nothing more than that, he told Azhdeen, conveying reassurance.

The reaction felled him. The dagon threw back his head with a roar that brought whines from other dragons and terrified screams from the horses. Pol was knocked off his feet and out of the intricate weave of color. His wits spun and for a time he could barely see. When he could stand again, Azhdeen was rearing back on his hind legs, wings unfurled, bellowing his rage.

Pol again offered his colors to the dragon. *What is it? What have I done?* Azhdeen glared. Again the picture formed. *Believe!* was the emotion whirling on sunlight.

Then the colors vanished brutally. Pol gasped with the loss, his head nearly splitting in two. The dragon leaped into the air and circled the lake before coming to rest on the opposite shore, where he snapped at those around him and cuffed a few who didn't move out of his way fast enough.

Pol had never seen the like. He stood stunned and incredulous, unable to think what he had done wrong.

"Papa?"

He looked down. He might have expected Jihan to be the one tugging at his hand. Instead it was Rislyn—green eyes huge with worry but unafraid. He grasped her small fingers gently.

"It's all right, hatchling," he said. "I was unwise enough to contradict my high and mighty friend over there, and he took exception to it."

She squeezed his hand, relieved. But he could not reassure himself that he understood the cause of Azhdeen's fury. Never had he known such violence in the dragon. Never had Azhdeen been other than gentle in ending their contact.

Azhenel trotted up, ears laid back; he had been frightened by the dragon, too. As Pol mounted to ride back to the palace, he reflected that it was just as well it was a short way. He was going to have the great-great-grandsire of all headaches for the next two days.

Chapter Five

Andry had been fourteen when he made the ceremonial walk through Goddess Keep's long, light-filled refectory to the place where Lady Andrade sat. Caught between pride and humility, violent trembling and a terror of total paralysis, his steps had been like those of a drunkard. He had worn his father's colors as a reminder to all of who he was, but all he could think of was what he wanted to become. What he must become, or his life would be meaningless.

One woman, familiar to him from childhood, had the power to decide. But he had not met Andrade as her kinsman. There had been no family fondness in her eyes, only the cool, shrewd, judging look she sometimes gave Sioned.

Sudden thought of Sioned and all he owed her had straightened Andry's back, firmed his steps. When his parents insisted he be fostered as a squire, Sioned had arranged for him to go to her brother, Prince Davvi of Syr, with the understanding that he might leave at any time. Davvi knew as well as Sioned that Andry was not meant to be like Maarken, Sunrunner and great lord both. So when permission was finally wrung from Chay, the prince wished him well, gave him a jeweled knife in token of friendship and service, and sent an escort of honor with him to Goddess Keep.

Andry still had the knife. He toyed with it when young hopefuls came into his presence, just as Andrade in the same circumstances had toyed with a little gold medallion given her by her sister Milar. He could still see it in her hand, could still feel the hilt of Davvi's gift clenched in his own fist as he took that long, long walk. All Goddess Keep had watched—some of them highborn but few of such exalted blood and fewer still who could claim royal descent.

Only his brother had matched him that way. He'd caught sight of Maarken in the crowd, glowing with pride in his little brother. It had helped, but as he'd approached Andrade he had still felt a short gulp of air away from panic.

Andrade was then in her sixty-fourth year, severely elegant, a sharper version of the grandmother he hardly remembered. As expected, there was no acknowledgment of kinship in her wintry blue eyes. If anything, she looked with greater skepticism at the proud red-and-white of his heritage and the jeweled knife given by a prince. Dressed plainly as always, her rings and bracelets gleamed with both promise and warning. The medallion of Desert gold turned over and over in her long fingers, a wink and a shadow. Under Andrade's stern gaze he lost all consciousness of himself as his parents' son, but some spark of defiant pride asserted that if he was nothing more than anyone else who had ever stood before her, neither was he anything less.

As it turned out, he was considerably more. For now it was Andry who waited for prospective Sunrunners to come to him; Andry who sat in a large chair with a sunburst carved into its back; Andry who watched as faces paled and knees quivered and eyes were caught by his own inexorable gaze. But where Andrade had presided over an appearance before the whole community of Goddess Keep, he administered a private ritual. She would not have approved. He had never let that worry him. Her goal had been to create a world; his was to ensure that world's survival.

The youth standing before him now—so white-cheeked and wide-eyed that it was hard not to feel sympathy—looked ready to prostrate himself before the three great ones of Goddess Keep. Andry sensed Torien's amusement, wondering if his chief steward was remembering as he himself remembered. Jolan stood on his other side, ready to analyze responses—but not in the manner young Kov probably anticipated.

"So you wish to become a Sunrunner," Andry said all at once, and the boy flinched at the sound of his voice.

"Yes, my Lord," he managed breathlessly.

"Why?"

"To s-serve the Goddess."

"And what do you believe to be the nature of the Goddess?"

The question used to evoke vastly different answers. Nowadays there were only small variations, usually reflecting the personality and aspirations of the respondent. Jolan found the differences fascinating; they were excellent indications of success in spreading a unified philosophy.

"The Goddess is the Lady of Light, all-knowing, all-seeing, and all-powerful, my Lord," Kov recited, secure now. "Sunrunners are her servants who command light, and through it may see and know as she does. She has given Sunrunners the gift of light."

So far by rote. "What shall Sunrunners do with this gift?"

"Use it in her service, my Lord, to let all people know her intentions for them, and so that they may come to honor her as Sunrunners do."

"How may we know her intentions?" Andry asked.

"Through the visions and conjurings of the powerful." The boy bent his head shyly in the presence of the powerful.

"Do you expect to see such visions?"

"If it is the Goddess' will that I should be so honored, my Lord."

"And if it is not?"

"I shall serve her all my days." There was a pause, and then Kov rushed on to finish what he'd forgotten: "And—and with all my heart and mind, my Lord."

How predictable the answers were becoming. Andry fingered Davvi's knife and began the more difficult questions. "If she is all-powerful, why isn't the world perfect?"

Kov glanced up and frowned with the innocence of the very young. "I don't understand, my Lord. I have been taught that it *is* perfect."

Andry envied him his simplicity. "Perhaps *your* portion of the world is. That's not so for everyone."

"Then they have not yet learned to honor the Goddess, my Lord."

"If she is all-powerful, why does she require us to honor and serve her?"

"To turn hearts away from wickedness and sorcery, my Lord."

Andry arched a brow fractionally. He'd heard the part about sorcery only a few times, and was intrigued. Leaning forward, he caught the boy with his gaze. "And what is sorcery, Kov?"

"I—I'm not sure, my Lord." Kov's desperate desire to fidget was in his dark eyes; Andry's hold on him prevented movement. All at once he blurted out, "Wickedness is hurting others on purpose, and sorcery is using magic to do it."

"But there are some very wicked people who flourish like weeds, and plenty of sorcerers left. One might think the Goddess would punish them."

Kov's whole face wrinkled with the effort of thought. "People do bad things to each other, and—that's what the High Prince's Writ is for, to punish people who hurt others. Sorcerers go against the Goddess herself, and—and—" He stumbled to a halt, confused.

"How should sorcerers be punished, do you think?"

"The Goddess must have a way of—" Suddenly Kov's eyes lit. "Oh, my Lord, she does it through Sunrunners, who are her servants, with her gift of Light!"

"Why should this all-knowing, all-seeing, all-powerful Goddess have the slightest interest in being served by such pathetic creatures as we?"

"I—I don't know, my Lord."

Jolan spoke for the first time. "Surely you have an opinion. Why should she be pleased that we honor her, that we are present at courts great and small, that we ride the light of sun and moons to see what she already sees and know what she already knows? What possible use are we to her? Couldn't she rid the world of evil and sorcery all on her own? Why does she need us?"

"I—" The boy bit his lip in anguish.

Andry had pity on him; Jolan could be a pedantic witch when it suited her. "Could it be because we may speak to our fellows in ways they can understand? And that they will listen because we can also speak the language of light that is the Goddess' gift to us? And because we are the only ones who can do so?"

Relief broke over the young face like waves sweeping sand smooth. "Oh, yes, my Lord. That must be it. Thank you for explaining it to me."

"Put it in your own words," Jolan instructed.

Another hesitation, and then Kov replied, "Sunrunners are the only ones who understand light, the language of the Goddess. She speaks through Sunrunners and—and shows her power, and punishes sorcerers." He looked up anxiously. "Is that right, my Lord?"

"Very good," Andry said. "Now listen carefully. Today you will be assigned a bed in the dormitory, a seat at table, and a desk in the schoolroom. You'll be told about everyday life here, what's expected of you. Within a few days you'll be tested and we'll know for certain whether or not you can become a Sunrunner. If you cannot, you will be sent back home and—"

"Oh, please, my Lord! I want to stay here!"

"We'll see. Leave us now." He concealed a smile and waited until the boy was halfway to the door before calling out, "Kov!'

He turned awkwardly, his knees as tentative as Andry's had been all those years ago. "My Lord?"

"The Sunrunner who sent you to us thinks highly of your potential."

Adoration lit the young face. "Oh, thank you, my Lord! I won't disappoint you, I swear!"

When he was gone, Andry leaned back in his chair. The sunburst was lumpy against his spine and he squirmed. "I suppose this thing *had* to be carved so I can't get comfortable in it," he commented.

"Think of it as a reminder not to slouch," Torien said, grinning.

"You sound like my mother. Well, what do you think of the boy?"

Jolan shrugged. "Potential, certainly. They don't make it this far unless they've got that. But I doubt he'll set the world on fire."

Andry grimaced. "My beloved cousin Pol has already demonstrated that little trick, thank you. What did you make of Kov's answers?"

"I assume you're talking about the sorcery. I'm pleased, of course. I've worked very hard to instill that in the responses."

"With so lovely a face, who would ever suspect such deviousness?" Andry looked over at Torien. "The women around here are showing alarming tendencies. First the shape-changing, and now—"

Torien cleared his throat and said, "I was surprised when Kov mentioned sorcery. I hadn't thought the idea of Sunrunners being designated by the Goddess to punish *diarmadh'im* would root so quickly. It's taken years to get the rest of it right." Years of planting the chosen words here and there, watching them grow to cover most of the continent like an invisible, interlacing vine weaving belief into a coherent whole.

Jolan shrugged again. "Kov's Fironese."

"Ah. Of course. Might he be of the Old Blood?"

Torien shifted uneasily. "Half the Sunrunners who come from Firon are."

Andry laid a hand on Torien's arm. "When are you going to stop being so sensitive about it? I've never doubted you."

"Doubting yourself is worse than anything anyone else can do to you."

"Torien," Jolan said impatiently, "don't be a fool. I trust you and Andry trusts you. Would I have stayed married to you otherwise? Would you still hold the honor of chief steward?"

"Wise as well as devious," Andry smiled. But after they had left him, he reflected that not every man was so trusted by the woman he loved. Alasen had never trusted him. He wondered sometimes if he even loved her anymore, or whether it had simply become habit to think of her with that dull ache of longing. Certainly he forgot Alasen when he was with Brenlis, when he even thought of that lovely, fey, fascinating girl who so captivated him.

Turning his thoughts from her with an effort, he considered Torien's *diarmadhi* blood. Cold as it might sound, it suited him very well that his friend was ashamed of that heritage. It made Torien all the more devoted to Sunrunner ways and to eradicating sorcerers. It also made him useful, for his rings burned in fiery warning in the presence of such spells.

Jolan's introduction of the right of *faradh'im* to punish sorcerers fit in neatly with one Andry himself had recently disseminated in secret. It was a new idea, something he wasn't sure would work. He had yet to hear it echoed by any of the young girls and boys who came to him here. But soon it would be.

Punishment of evil done by people to each other was the responsibility of princes. Punishment of evil done by sorcerers was the province of Sunrunners. But there had to be a law that embraced everyone. Rohan would have it that his own writ was this law—and had demonstrated it years ago by claiming jurisdiction over that wretched *faradhi* who had, in attempting to heal, accidentally killed instead. Andry had searched ever since for a way to get around the High Prince's Writ. He had found it at last in the concept of sin.

The prohibition given by Lady Merisel about use of Sunrunner gifts in battle had given him the clue. She had not referred to it in terms of breaking a law or doing evil. Instead she had written, "Use of the gifts in battle will be punished by the Lady or Lord of Goddess Keep, as being willful disobedience, a sin against the generosity of the Goddess in sharing Fire with *faradh'im*." It had taken him a long time to translate "sin" adequately; there was no word for it in the language used now. It had taken him even longer to understand her meaning: that such disobedience was not an offense against the law or even the natural order of things. Either of these he could readily have comprehended. To steal, to cheat, to kill, all were unlawful and must be punished. To eradicate wolves in order to protect herds, to harvest all the pearl-bearing oysters to gain maximum profit, to strip whole hillsides clean of trees—people had learned through bitter experience that such things were sheer stupidity. But "sin" was something else. It meant to offend against the Goddess herself.

And yet . . . who was to know what she desired? Lady Merisel had not. She had admitted as much in her private writings. She had established use of the gifts in battle as a sin—but only *after* the Sunrunners had defeated the *diarmadh'im* and chased them into exile. Andry had not failed to note this. A practical, pragmatic lady. What Merisel had not mentioned, and what he had had to learn through example, was that if iron pierced a Sunrunner's flesh during a working, that Sunrunner died. Sorcerers were not as vulnerable, though spells were more difficult and less effective when woven while the metal drew blood. He surmised that Pol and Riyan had this strength in relation to iron, and it galled him. But Merisel's reason for establishing the sin clarified the whole concept for Andry. Sin was nothing more than the codification of practical necessity.

It opened up whole realms of possibility.

He would have to use it carefully. His first thought had been to call it sin when anyone gifted with Sunrunner abilities was not allowed to be trained. But—too mild. Practical, but not necessary to the growth of Goddess Keep's population. So he had ruminated for a very long time, picking and choosing among things he wished to accomplish, and had finally invented the perfect sin.

It was this: Anyone who hindered a *faradhi* in the search for or execution of *diarmadh'im* committed a sin against the Goddess.

Only a fool would fail to discern whose right it was to punish that sin.

It was something not even Rohan would dare protest. How could he, when his own son had nearly been killed by a sorcerer? Besides, as Kov's answers had indicated, it was a Sunrunner's right and duty to punish *diarmadh'im*. And it was so small and elegant a step to condemnation of anyone who interfered with that right. Even the High Prince.

Altogether a very satisfactory sin—simple, yet subtle; specific, yet encompassing. Very, very practical, and necessary for reasons beyond the destruction of sorcerers. He had spread word of it through trusted Sunrunners in all princedoms, and while none of the young people had spoken of it yet on arrival at Goddess Keep, he had faith that they soon would. The only thing that traveled faster than a *faradhi*'s thoughts on light was the unfathomable communication amongst the common folk.

When disaster struck, as Andry knew it must, the sin would already be there to assist him and his *devr'im* in destroying their enemies. Neither Rohan nor Pol would be able to protest—indeed, they would welcome a Goddess-given right to slaughter.

Sometimes it amused him and sometimes it appalled him to think that he could even invoke the sin against Pol himself.

He sat back and immediately grimaced; he always forgot the uncomfortable carving until it bruised his spine. Rising, he went outside on a long walk to the sea cliffs. Mellow autumn sunshine hazed the distance, and his steps brought up tiny puffs of dry dust from ground thirsting for rain. The pines rose in silent majesty to his right, and he started for them, intending to consult the small pool in the tree circle for guidance. The Goddess had not favored him with a vision in a long time, but he never gave up hoping. He needed the reassurance of a conjuring in Fire and Water today. The countryside around him, the crashing sea, the clear blue sky, the stubbled fields after a good harvest—everything was as it should be, and so beautiful that his

Desert-bred senses ached with its richness. Yet the threat of its loss weighed on his heart. Despite his preparations, despite sure knowledge that he was doing all he could to avert destruction, he needed to look into a future only the Goddess could show him. He needed to see that it had changed.

Andry? Andry!

He nearly stumbled in the sunlight, the voice catching him unawares. He was caught up in a weave of light such as no one ever had the temerity to use on him anymore. Sunrunners approached him with respect and waited for him to make the initial contact. But he could not be angry, not when he recognized the woman's voice and the swirl of her colors.

Brenlis! It's sweet to touch you, my dear. You honor me.

I've missed you, my Lord. Forgive me for startling you.

The most wonderful of surprises. But rather an unsubtle technique, you know. You need practice! he teased lovingly.

I'm sorry, Andry. But I heard something today that I must tell you. There's word from Radzyn Keep that a highly trained physician is needed there.

His heart seem to stop in his chest. *Is it Tobren? Is my daughter ill?*

No, my Lord. She is well. It's your mother. They say she had an accident of some kind and lies in her bed unable to move. I heard this today from some travelers we met on the road, and I thought at once of Evarin. It would take him some time to ride to Radzyn, but—

You thought exactly right, my darling. I'll send him at once. But is there no specific word of what happened?

None. I'm sorry to have to tell you such painful news, but I'd hoped you'd already heard it.

He had not; and for this he would never forgive his family. He hid the emotion from Brenlis and told her, *You did well to send to me in such haste. How goes it with you?*

We're not far from my parents' holding. I'd forgotten how beautiful Ossetia and Gilad and Syr can be. The best of harvests this year, and perfect apples. I'll bring back crates and crates for you!

He smiled and caressed her with his thoughts. *Then come back to me soon, my lady, for I've a hunger for fresh ripe apples—and for you.*

There was an impression of embarrassed laughter, and then he gently let her go. Almost immediately he wove other strands of sunlight, casting them far to the east and the eight massive towers of Radzyn Keep. He had not seen it except this way, on light, for years. Every time he looked upon it, the fear shuddered in him at memory of the dream in which Radzyn was a smoking ruin.

He sought the tower where his parents' apartments were, and gave thanks for the afternoon sun shining in the windows. Stealthily he entered, able to go only as far as the light—to the middle of the spacious state bedroom in which he and all his brothers, his father and Radzyn's lords back ten generations had been conceived and born. It was a beautiful room, rich with tapestries and embroidered bed-hangings and thick Cunaxan and Giladan rugs, furnished in aged, sun-faded wood. Andry hovered, cautious lest someone be near who might walk into the light and disrupt it, but everyone was gathered on the far side of the bed, gazing in anguish down at his mother.

White and delicate as winter roses, she lay in an ocean of pale blue sheets frothed with lace. His father knelt beside the bed, holding her hand carefully in his two trembling ones. Andry was shocked at how much silver shone in Chay's hair. A physician stood nearby, speaking to Maarken and Hollis and Betheyn, the woman who would have been his brother Sorin's wife. The helpless misery on all their faces struck him to the soul.

Gentle Goddess, what had happened? Why was Tobin so pale, so motionless? He had never seen his mother at rest for more time than it took to eat a meal; her vitality was legend and her energy prodigious. Even during the battle for Stronghold when he was a little boy, when she had taken an arrow in her thigh that had left a lifelong limp, she had ignored the wound and fought on like the warrior princess she was. To see her thus was to imagine her in death.

But she breathed still. The thick, carved bedpost interfered with his view of her, but he could see her chest rise and fall—slowly, so slowly.

Andry withdrew down the sunlight and discovered he was on his knees in the dirt. A cry clawed its way from his throat and he clamped his jaw tight shut around it, not knowing if he was more frightened by his mother's illness, or furious that he had not been told of it.

Brenlis was right. Evarin must go to Radzyn and give Tobin the best care available in all the princedoms. He began to run toward the keep, and along the way a resolve hardened in him: not just Evarin but Andry himself would travel to Radzyn. To hell with Rohan's decree of exile from the Desert. His own father could forbid him, and he would still go.

And if this put Chay in an impossible position—allowing a son into his castle who had been banished from his prince's lands—then too damned bad. Not even Rohan could be such a monster as to keep him from his mother's side.

* * *

Pol made it up with Azhdeen, more or less. Dealing with dragons was a good exercise in humility for prince and Sunrunner alike. A cautious approach the next morning, and this despite the headache which was still very much with him; a tentative offering of his colors; a shake of wings and an annoyed snort—and they were friends again.

Pol created pictures for Azhdeen of the summer's *Rialla* (the dragon was always curious about the strange doings of humans, especially in groups), and laughed as pride enwrapped him when he showed Azhdeen the splendor of the Lastday banquet over which Pol had presided. The dragon's proprietary interest in Pol's consequence was that of a parent for a particularly promising child. In return, Azhdeen presented the picture of new caves he'd discovered on a lazy flight through the Vere Hills—caves long abandoned by dragons for one reason or another, but which Azhdeen thought might make reasonably adequate mating areas. For lesser dragonsires, of course; *he* ruled Rivenrock Canyon, and to see him visualize it, every one of its hundred and seven caves had been filled with females he himself had won this year.

Pol didn't laugh; he didn't dare offend the dragon again. But he was unable to hide amazement that Azhdeen had actually gone out looking for new caves. It suggested a capacity for thought which, for all their intelligence, dragons weren't considered capable of. But then, people had been underestimating dragons forever.

Pol managed to convey a question about why Azhdeen had gone out looking for new caves. The reply was a series of flashing images illustrating an impressively logical turn of mind. Rivenrock with dragon corpses during the Plague of 701; Rivenrock deserted; Rivenrock the night Pol had lit the

Desert with Fire and broken Ruval's hold over Azhdeen himself. He had never been shown the rest of what had happened that night—but now he saw from the dragon's vantage point. The human enemy dangled from his talons as he flew over the Long Sand, finding at last a nicely desolate spot to shred Ruval uninterrupted. The death was a righteous one as far as Azhdeen was concerned; Ruval had ensnared him, Pol had freed him, and he was doing himself and Pol a favor. Pol learned then that no dragon would eat human flesh; Azhdeen had simply enjoyed tearing Ruval limb from limb at his leisure and leaving him as a present for the Desert scavengers. Remembering the scattered, incomplete pile of bleached bones found days later, Pol felt a little queasy.

Finally Azhdeen showed him Rivenrock, alive again with hatchlings that flew joyously from the caves, exhaling fire. Pol had long suspected that the flames he called that night had cleansed the canyon in dragon minds. But he hadn't known Azhdeen would make the connection between an increase in the number of caves and an increase in the dragon population. A picture formed of egg-heavy females dying in the sand without caves in which to mate, and then a view of the new/old caves in the Vere Hills. Hatchlings flew from those caves, too, and Pol was struck by the ease with which the dragon projected events into the future. He would have to tell Feylin about those caves as soon as possible.

All this took place in under fifty heartbeats. Then, with a final whirl of colors that all but blinded Pol, Azhdeen withdrew with courteous gentleness and called to his flight of dragons. Soon they were airborne, females nipping at slow-flying hatchlings, and after a last turn around the lake, they were gone.

Pol spent the rest of the day recovering—even the least demanding exchanges with his dragon left him with a grotesque headache—and the following morning he set out on sunlight to find Walvis' resident Sunrunner at Remagev. There was much to relay to Feylin about this year's count of hatchlings and especially about the new caves. He spent a pleasant time conferring with Relnaya, conveying his news and learning all about this year's mock battle and how the Isulk'im had enjoyed themselves. On hearing that his parents hadn't yet been told of Kazander's part in Walvis' little war, he came back by way of Stronghold to give them a good laugh.

He found the keep in the controlled uproar that meant preparation for a hasty journey. His mother was nowhere to be seen, but he spied his father testing saddle girths and bridles in the courtyard, a grim expression on his face. Unable to speak to Rohan, he cast about for someone he *could* talk to, and found Morwenna.

Goddess greeting, Sunrunner, he told her cheerfully. *What's all the fuss?*

Pol! I was going to come look for you at Dragon's Rest in a little while. You're a considerate child to spare me the bother. It's Princess Tobin. She's taken ill and your parents are going to her at once.

Tobin? What's wrong?

Yesterday morning Chay found her unconscious by a paddock fence and they haven't been able to waken her. By the sound of it—and poor Hollis was nearly beside herself—it's some sort of seizure.

I'll start for Radzyn at once.

You'll do no such thing!

I can be there in three days. He paused. *Has Andry been told?*

Not that I know of.

Merciful Mother of All! Hasn't anyone got any sense? He's her *son! Somebody's got to let him know at once!*

Who did you have in mind? she asked dryly. *No one but your parents can give him permission to cross Desert borders. Rohan's frantic with worry for his sister, and Sioned is nearly as upset.*

I'll do it myself. I doubt they'll argue the point.

That's exactly what I was hoping you'd say. Now all that's left is for you to command me not to tell them you're on your way to Radzyn, and my conscience will be as pure as a virgin bride's.

Morwenna, I order you to say nothing of my plans, I adore your devious Fironese mind, and I know exactly in what esteem you hold virginity—let alone marriage!

A few moments later, after he had paused to direct a servant to find his squires and see to saddling Azhenel for a journey, he drew in a deep breath and wove light yet again. This time he turned west for Goddess Keep.

He didn't relish the thought of sharing the sun with his

cousin. He saw Andry only at *Riall'im* now, and while they were always exquisitely polite to each other, the underlying tension was obvious to all. They were long past the point at which they might sit down alone and discuss their differences. Each was too entrenched in dislike, suspicion, and jealousy of the other's power. Pol's adult brain grieved for the waste and decried the uselessness of conflict between them, they two who ought to have been allies for the greater good. But the stronger emotions remained disgustingly childish and he would never trust Andry as long as either of them drew breath. Boyhood memories of friendship evoked a deep sense of betrayal combined with angry bewilderment that things had turned out so harshly between them.

He came upon Goddess Keep from a great height. The only time he'd ever seen the Sunrunners' castle was this way, descending over its battlements like a swooping dragon. Childish, too, his determination that Andry would never learn how to speak with a dragon.

This courtyard swarmed with activity just as Stronghold's did. Pol hesitated, watching as four horses were saddled and another laden with provisions. Enough for a journey as far as Radzyn? He had his answer when a young man hurried from the keep and strapped the bags he carried on the pack horse. The ring of a Master Physician was on his hand. Pol's surmise was confirmed as Andry strode down the steps, nodded curtly to the groom holding his horse, and mounted in a swirl of white cloak. Sunrunners perforce became competent at reading lips; no one admitted it but everyone did it. Pol saw the physician say, "I have everything Princess Tobin might need, my Lord."

So Andry knew. Pol couldn't guess how, but he knew. He felt guilty relief that he wouldn't have to contact his cousin, then berated himself for the cowardice.

Goddess greeting, my Lord, he said respectfully. *You've heard about your mother, I see. I thought to tell you myself, but—*

Go away, Pol, came the weary answer, not the bitter rancor he'd expected. *I don't have time for you.*

I'll see you at Radzyn—and I hope we both see Tobin recovered.

Spare me your soothings. I had to learn by chance that she's ill. And I warn you, Pol, I don't give the slightest damn for—

Before he could finish, Pol said quickly, *You'll cross into the Desert on my authority, Andry. No one will stop or question you. I promise.*

As if I need, want, or care about your safe-conduct!

Andry—

But the contact was broken. Pol watched his cousin ride out the gates, the physician beside him leading the packhorse. Perhaps he'd been stupid and arrogant to make the attempt to speak with Andry now, but at least he'd tried. A feeble sop to his conscience: *I was willing, and you rebuffed me.* What timing. What impeccable timing.

Back at Dragon's Rest, Dannar was waiting for him, maintaining that rapt silence adopted by those who watched a Sunrunner at work. Pol put a hand on the boy's shoulder. "How soon can I leave?"

"As soon as cook finishes wrapping food and wine for three days, plus a few things to nibble in the saddle, my lord. I'm to ask who's riding with you."

"Who said to ask that?"

"His grace of Ossetia."

"I have such solicitous relatives, all of whom think I'm still ten winters old," he commented, and started for the steps leading to his wife's chambers. "You may tell his grace I'm taking one guard and one squire. You." He tightened his fingers on Dannar's shoulder as the boy exclaimed with excitement. "Not a word to Kierun. I'll tell him myself."

"Of course, my lord. Thank you."

"Go out to the stables and make sure everything's ready. And if the food isn't in the saddlebags by the time I get there, we'll just have to starve. I'm not waiting for that shattershell in the kitchens to roast a suitable haunch for my grace to dine from."

To his relief, Kierun was attending Meiglan in her solar, helping move furniture. Pol gestured the boy and Thanys out of the room and went to take his wife in his arms.

"I have to go to Radzyn right away," he began, and told her why. Her velvet dark eyes, so astonishing a contrast to her pale golden hair and skin, filled with tears at hearing of Tobin's illness. "You'll be regent in my absence, but don't work too hard. Dragon's Rest runs itself."

"Yes, Pol. Don't worry." She stood on tiptoe to kiss him. "I'll manage on my own. I promise."

They had not been separated since the day she'd first

ridden into Stronghold. He took her with him on all his progresses through his lands, on visits to other courts; he could not conceive of not having her beside him. "I'll miss you, Meggie."

"And I you, my lord." She held tight to him, trembling for an instant, then pulled away. "I don't want you to go, but I feel you must hurry. Please tell Princess Tobin I think of her."

"I will." Tracing the sweet curve of her cheek with one finger, he said, "I don't like leaving—but with Gemma and Lisiel and Sioneva here you won't be too lonely, I hope."

"Of course I won't."

He smiled and lifted her off her feet to kiss her again, his hands circling her tiny waist. "Have a care to yourself, my love."

Meiglan kept her feet until he went into the next room to speak with Kierun, then sank into a chair with a shudder. Leaving her, he was leaving her all alone here—but he would not be doing so if he did not believe that she was capable—but she had never been apart from him, never—

"Kierun, I'm taking Dannar with me to Radzyn. You're staying here for a very important reason. I depend on you to see to her grace's comfort and safety—and to look after the princesses."

The whole of Dragon's Rest to supervise—any problems that came up in Pol's absence—and what if something happened to do with all Princemarch? He would be far away and she would be alone—

"You'll be guarding that which I hold most dear—even if Jihan is an impossible pest at times."

"Yes, my lord—I mean, no, my lord—"

Pol laughed. "I understand, Kierun. Now, if you would, please go find the princesses so I can bid them good-bye."

She heard his footsteps fade, panic racing and then slowing her heart. She must show everyone the face she had just shown him—calm, dutiful, competent. It was true that Gemma and Lisiel were here to guide her, but she had been princess here for nine years and she could never admit to them that she was not a princess in the way they were. She should not be so frightened of being without Pol. It was childish and absurd and she loathed herself for it.

She forced herself to rise and go downstairs. Kierun, solemn with his new responsibility, escorted Jihan and Rislyn to her side. Pol rode out of the stableyard with Dannar beside him, and cantered to the front of the Princes Hall where his ladies waited.

For once, Jihan behaved herself. She adored her Aunt Tobin and was deeply upset by news of her illness. Rislyn was pale and withdrawn. They, too, had never been separated from their father. Meiglan stood dry-eyed and silent as Pol lifted each little girl in turn up to be kissed. All at once she ran toward him and clung to his hand. The great amethyst and topaz ring felt very hard and cold on his finger. He leaned down and kissed her upturned brow.

"I'll be home sooner than you think, sweet Meggie," he assured her. And rode away.

Chapter Six

Rohan and Sioned made the trip from Stronghold to Radzyn in a little over one day, and nearly killed their horses doing it. With them rode two guards and Rohan's senior squire, Daniv. Isriam had been left behind at Stronghold.

Sioned's nephew Daniv was Kostas' son and heir. A tall, well-built boy of sixteen, his long-lidded eyes were the deep turquoise of a summer dawn, almost a perfect match to the color of his father's banner, and their effect was even more striking in combination with his dark hair and tanned skin. He had strong, rugged good looks that no one ever mentioned were reminiscent of his grandsire Roelstra in his youth.

As the last dunes fell away behind them in the afternoon sun, Daniv said what they were all thinking: it was impossible to believe there was anything amiss here. Blooded horses, the pride and profit of Chay's family for generations, cropped what was left of the summer grass. Geldings meandered placidly among the well-grown colts and fillies racing around their mothers, while dozens of mares heavy with foal plodded the sun-baked paths back to the stables. The paddocks and barns were scrupulously cared for, as were the buildings of the small port beyond the keep. Ships at anchor bobbed on the waves, sails furled in winter harborage after the last voyage of the season laden with silks from Dorval or foodstuffs and other goods from far princedoms.

The castle itself was an awesome sight. Eight towers stood dignified sentry between pastures and sea cliffs, lit from the west with a rosy-gold light that gentled the rough-hewn stone. In appearance and activity Radzyn was as it had always been: strong, prosperous, secure in its wealth and power. It was impossible to believe that its mistress might be dying.

The red-and-white pennant flew from the main tower, soon to be joined by Rohan's crowned golden dragon. Chay's was an honor shared only by Ostvel in all the princedoms: the right to display a symbol just as princes did on their banners. Castle Crag enjoyed the distinction as the former seat of Princemarch and at Rohan's pleasure, but it had been his first pleasure to give Radzyn a silver sword on a red field, bound in Desert blue. It signified that the Lord of Radzyn Keep was also Battle Commander of the Desert. The pennant rippled on a cooling ocean breeze, as if the sword upon it thrust against any and all enemies, reminding those who saw it that while Rohan believed in the rule of law, there was yet a powerful sword at his command.

The gates opened for them, and it suddenly became obvious that things at Radzyn were very wrong. At any other time the High Prince and High Princess rode in, the courtyard would have been packed with people come from their duties to cheer an enthusiastic greeting. Cool wine would be offered and friendly banter exchanged between highborns and servants; Stronghold guards would be greeted with laughing insults by those of Radzyn while children of all stations clamored for attention; mothers would show off new babies and grooms the best foals—and Chay and Tobin would arrive at last into the chaos, good-naturedly berating their people for making such a fuss over such unimportant guests.

This time it was different. The courtyard was nearly empty. Grooms took charge of the winded horses quietly, eyes lowered as they murmured greetings. There was no bustle of welcome, no crowd glad to see them, no laughter and no joy. And only Maarken came to meet them, his handsome face strained and afraid.

"Thank the Goddess you're here," he said, kissing Sioned and grasping Rohan's arm tightly. "It's been a nightmare."

"Is she any better?" Rohan took the steps two at a time; only his weariness after the long, hard ride prevented him from making it three.

"The same. She woke up for a few moments last night, but. . . ."

Nothing more was said. They hurried through the high-ceilinged foyer and turned for the stairs leading to the family's tower. Daniv could barely keep up with them.

Sioned paused to send him to the suite kept for her and Rohan, finishing the order just as Hollis called out from above.

"Maarken!"

They raced up the remaining stairs and arrived at the door to Chay and Tobin's suite. Hollis stood there, her dark-gold hair streaming around her as if she hadn't had time or thought to tend it in two days. She had no greeting beyond a glance for Rohan and Sioned as she clasped her husband's hands.

"She's awake now, she recognizes us, I know she does! But she can't move her right arm or leg, and she's so weak she can barely move the left." Hollis turned to Sioned. "The physician from Radzyn port feels as helpless as I do. Please tell me you'll be able to do something for her."

Sioned had begun to get an idea of what was wrong with Tobin, but would say nothing until she saw her. She accompanied Rohan into the anteroom after a soothing word for Hollis. The bedchamber doorway was abruptly filled with Chay's tall form. He looked a hundred years old. There was an emotional battle raging across his face more rending than any he had ever fought in the field—terror for his wife, relief that she was awake, helpless agony at her illness, gratitude that Rohan and Sioned had come so swiftly. Rohan put an arm around him and for an instant he sagged against his brother-by-marriage's slight frame. Then he led them into the large, airy room.

Tobin lay in bed, propped up by pillows. Her long hair, tenderly cared for, flowed in a single braid all the way to her hip. It shone black and silver like night sky plaited with moonlight. She might have just wakened from an afternoon nap, but for the tragic alteration in her face.

Sioned allowed none of her feelings to disturb her expression at the sight of the slurred features. She was sure now what had happened. The left side of Tobin's face was the same as always, but the right half dragged down at eyelid, mouth, and cheek. It was as if someone had copied her delicate face in soft clay, then passed a hand over one side to blur the fineness. Sioned touched Rohan's arm, a warning to hide his shock, and went forward to the bed.

Tobin's eyes were open, the left fully and the right only halfway. Chay caught his breath as her left hand raised slightly, thin and bony. Sioned lifted the hand to her cheek.

The tears gathering at the corner of the drooping right lid nearly shattered her composure. Black eyes fixed on her for a moment, then flickered to where Chay and Rohan stood. Sioned glanced around. A husband's mute agony, a brother's stricken silence; and behind them Maarken and Hollis close together, equally quiet. It was as if Tobin's enforced silence held them, too, in thrall.

Sioned broke it with deliberate harshness. "What can you be thinking of, all of you? Maarken, Hollis, I forgive Chay for not realizing, but you two should have known!" She stripped off her riding gloves and threw them onto the bedside table. "Well? What are you waiting for? Maarken, come here at once and put a chair next to the window. Rohan, take the blanket. Chay, carry her. Don't stand there like hothouse plants! Get moving!"

If she ordered them like servants, they were even more surprised at the content of those orders—and hurried to do as bidden. But Tobin understood, and as Chay lifted her in strong arms, more tears slipped out, the desolation gone from her eyes.

Placed gently in the chair with a blanket across her knees, Tobin gave a long sigh as afternoon sun flowed over her face and body. Sioned knelt beside her, taking her left hand again. "Now," she murmured, gazing up into the beautiful eyes.

Colors merged, woven into the sunlight. *Sioned—oh, thank you! I couldn't speak, I couldn't tell Chay to put me in the sun—*

You're going to get well. I give you my word. She smiled and the corner of Tobin's mouth lifted in half of her usual warm, brilliant smile. *Tell me what happened, if you remember.*

I was out by the paddocks looking over the new foals. Suddenly I fell—I couldn't break my fall. Nothing would work! I tried to cry out, but I couldn't. I couldn't even reach the sunlight—Sioned, I lay there forever, trapped inside my body—

You're a Sunrunner. You're not trapped anymore.

I was so frightened—it was like being smothered and bound and I was so helpless—they finally found me and carried me up here. At first I couldn't feel anything, but feeling has come back to my left side. I think I could move my hand and my leg if I tried hard enough—

Not yet. Give it time. You only just woke up.

Tobin's colors—rich amber and sapphire and amethyst—trembled with the trembling of her body. Then she gave a deep sigh and relaxed. *I can't seem to get my arm to do much,* she told Sioned, sounding almost like her old self. *But I suppose that will come back in time,* she added, more confident now that she was no longer a prisoner in her own mind. *I can't talk, though, and it hurts to try. And my right side is gone. I can't feel it and I can't move anything.*

I'm betting that feeling will come back—and you know I never make a wager I can't win. It'll take a while, but you'll be all right, Tobin. I know what this is. You're going to recover. I promise.

"Sioned?" Rohan's voice: hushed, not daring to hope. Chay's face was as pale as Tobin's. Both men appeared stunned, uncomprehending. But Maarken and Hollis understood.

"Forgive me, Mother," Maarken whispered. "I didn't think."

"She needed the sunlight," Hollis said. "Just sunlight. . . ."

Sioned!

What is it, Tobin? Are you in pain?

Tell Chay—tell him I love him. It's all I could think about while I was helpless—

Sioned unlaced the sunlight, pressed Tobin's hand, and looked anywhere but at Chay. "She wants you to know—how much she loves you."

"Tobin—" He knelt and buried his face in her lap. Her left hand fell gently on his gray hair.

* * *

A little while later they gathered in the antechamber, all eyes on Sioned. She sipped wine to ease her dry throat, and held Chay's haggard gaze with her own as she spoke, willing him to believe her.

"What I think happened is this. A part of her brain was affected by a seizure that impaired the right side of her body. If it had been her left, she wouldn't be able to use sunlight."

"Why? And where did you learn this?" Maarken asked.

"You didn't do as much medicine at Goddess Keep as most of us," Hollis said slowly. "I remember reading about such things. If I'd been thinking clearly, I would have recognized it earlier. I'm sorry, Chay."

He shook his head. "No need, daughter. Tell me what it is."

Hollis glanced at Sioned, who nodded for her to continue. "Some think a poison in the blood affects only the brain. Others think the brain just wears out. It may run in families—and then again, it may not. There's evidence that very fat people have seizures like this more often than thin people do. Obviously that doesn't apply to Tobin, and I don't have any idea why this happened to her. But unless it kills within the first day, or unless more occur after the first, the victims often recover most of their strength."

"And Tobin's the strongest woman I know," Sioned finished. Sipping again from her goblet, she went on, "It happened to a Sunrunner at Goddess Keep when I was a girl. He was extremely gifted, but after this seizure, he was helpless. He couldn't even *feel* colors, let alone use light. It was horrible. A friend of mine told me he begged her to help him die." She paused thoughtfully. "It was the *left* side of his body that was affected."

"But how does that—" Rohan began.

She interrupted him. "Andrade was of the opinion that it was neither poison nor fatigue, but a kind of lightning flash across the brain. She'd seen it before in another Sunrunner—the *right* side was useless, but she could still function as a Sunrunner. Eventually she recovered completely. So you mustn't worry, Chay. Tobin's going to be all right."

"What about the man you knew?" Maarken asked.

She answered reluctantly, "He died. But it wasn't the seizure that killed him. He got back the use of his hand and arm, and was learning to speak more clearly and even walk a little. But the gifts were gone. One day he simply turned his face to the wall."

Chay raked his fingers back through thick hair. "So you're saying that as long as Tobin can still use sunlight, there's a chance she might—"

" 'Might'? 'Chance'?" Rohan snorted and grinned. Sioned hoped only she could tell how hard he was trying to hide his own fear. "Have you lost what pitiful wits you ever had? Chay, that she-dragon you were fool enough to marry is much too ornery to die so tamely. Do you think anything could get the best of her? I never heard such nonsense in my life. Now, go get some rest. Hollis, find him a nice, quiet bed somewhere. If you have to, weave him to sleep." Chay opened his mouth to protest and Rohan lifted a warning finger. "Don't force me to make it an order—because I will and you know it."

A tiny smile touched the older man's face. "Tyrant."

"Damned right I am. Maarken, see to your father's comfort. Or do I have to order you, too?"

Between them, Hollis and Maarken coaxed Chay from the room. His audience gone, Rohan wilted back in his chair. "Our grandfather died of this, Sioned. Did you tell Chay the truth?"

"Yes. It won't be easy, and it may take her until winter's end just to be able to speak again. But if there are no more seizures, she'll recover. That's the truth as far as I understand this sickness, Rohan. Feylin is the better physician—perhaps we'd better call her to Radzyn—"

He shook his head. "If Tobin doesn't improve, perhaps then. But I know my sister." He drained his winecup and got to his feet. "I'll go sit with her for a while."

"Oh, no you won't," she told him. "Betheyn is there, and she'll send for us if we're needed. But we won't be. Tobin must rest—and so must you."

"That sounds like an order, High Princess," he said as she rose and prodded him down the hall to their own chambers. "Have I ever told you how much I loathe managing females?"

"Repeatedly, but you should have thought of that before *you* were fool enough to marry *me.* Sleep off the journey and that wine, and maybe by this evening you'll be fit to talk to again. Imagine, ordering Chay around like that! You should be ashamed of yourself."

"I am," he murmured as he slid onto the embroidered quilt. "But not for the reason you think." He caught her hand between his own. "I feel guilty because I'm so glad it's not you lying there helpless."

Sioned gazed down into blue eyes dimmed with weariness and emotion. Twenty years ago, even ten, he and she could have ridden from Stronghold, stayed up half the night drinking, making love, or both, and been fresh as ever the next day. *We are growing old, my love,* she thought. *Tobin's illness is a hard reminder of that, isn't it? But I would rather grow old with you than be young again with anyone else.*

Rohan pressed her palm to his cheek, his eyes closed.

"Don't let me forget to tell you how much I love you," he said. "Ten times a day, at least."

"Only ten?" She bent to kiss his brow. "Rest now, beloved. I won't be gone long."

"Where d'you think you're—" He fought in vain against the sleep she wove around him. "Not fair," he mumbled, eyelids drooping.

"No, but necessary," she murmured, and kissed him again, and he slept.

* * *

Had Andry's twin brother Sorin lived to rule Feruche for more than the few brief years the Goddess had allotted him, Betheyn would have been his lady. It had been their intention to wed at the *Rialla* of 728. Instead, he had been murdered that spring.

They had met while Faolain Riverport was abuilding in the mid-720s. He had been invited there to give the benefit of his advice, for in the reconstruction of Feruche much had been learned about the use of iron that the Riverport architect wanted to know. Together Sorin and Master Wentyn spent long, happy days drawing plans and constantly revising them to improve the strength and the aesthetics of the new town.

But Sorin was never so busy that he hadn't found time to appreciate Wentyn's pretty daughter. There had been no instant understanding between them, no *ricsina,* the knife that pierces the heart, as so many others in his family had found. Rather it was a slow, quiet, comfortable thing, made clear to him only on his return to Feruche, when he found himself missing her more than mere friendship could explain.

After Sorin's death by sorcery, Andry—his only confidant in the matter—told their mother about the girl. A special trip to Riverport had been arranged before the *Rialla* that year. Tobin and Chay understood on first meeting Betheyn what Sorin had valued so much. When her father died the next autumn, they invited her to come live with them at Radzyn. There she had continued for the next eight years, returning their love and regard, treated by them and the rest of the family as the daughter she would have been had Sorin lived.

When Sioned went back into Tobin's chamber, Betheyn

was seated beside the bed, reading. The young woman glanced up at hearing someone come in and rose, leaving her book on the chair.

"She sleeps easily now, my lady," Betheyn murmured. "It's not that blank unconsciousness anymore, thank the Goddess."

"You've been sitting with her a long time, my dear. Why don't you go get some rest? No, I didn't have myself in mind to stay with her—I think while she sleeps Tobren can watch."

"It's no hardship, my lady." Betheyn gestured to the book. "I'm occupied, and I'd rather be here."

Sioned smiled. Tobin had always wanted a daughter; Maarken had brought her Hollis, and now she had Betheyn as well. It occurred to her that, fond as she had become of Meiglan, she would never think of the girl in those terms. It was an unworthy thought, and Meiglan didn't deserve it, but there it was.

She went to a table near the windows and looked over the little collection of medicines brought up with Tobin's book of simples. Sioned leafed through a few pages, seeing marginal notes in Tobin's untidy scrawl, Milar's precise script, even the thick strokes of Andrade's pen. That last brought an unexpected stinging to her eyes. Ridiculous; anytime she chose she could call up memory of Andrade's vibrant colors, a signature more evocative than a few lines of ink on parchment. But she did not often choose. Her emotions were too complex for easy remembrance of the woman who had taught her, brought her to the Desert to marry a prince, disapproved of her, chided her, loved her, and finally died trying to keep Pol safe.

Sioned wondered suddenly who would one day read her own book of simples—not a tame and commonplace volume like this one, but the translated copy of the Star Scroll secreted in her office. There were copious notes in those margins in her own hand, Urival's, and Morwenna's. Perhaps Jihan or Rislyn would study them one day. They were *diarmadhi*, both of them, though Rislyn was a Sunrunner as well. But sometimes Sioned thought that she would be doing them both a favor by destroying the scroll before they even learned of its existence.

She gave a start at Betheyn's soft touch on her arm. "My lady, what troubles you? It isn't just Princess Tobin."

"Ah, I've been obvious. I should know better—but I suppose it's because I'm tired." She made herself smile to allay Betheyn's doubts, so obvious on her gentle face. "Don't worry, Beth. Too long a ride and too much worry to find sleep just yet."

The quiet eyes held steady. "I believe it's more."

The words were spoken before she knew what she would say. "It's . . . it's that we're growing older. Time sneaks up on us. And one day it will steal the people I love." Events had stolen so many: Andrade, Milar, Maarken's twin Jahni, Maeta, Camigwen, Sorin. Urival's had been a soft passing, as had those of her brother Davvi and old Prince Lleyn. But the rest—Plague, sorcery, murder had been their lot. She felt old with the years they had not lived, that they had been cheated of, that she had survived without them.

Goddess, how morbidly her thoughts turned today—and without cause. Tobin was going to get better.

Betheyn replied, "I don't think it's time that steals. It's life that takes what we're unwilling to give. But life is all we have, and time to live it in."

Half my age and twice as wise, Sioned thought. "You're right, of course. How bitter it would be to treat either life or time as an enemy." She smiled again and started for the door. "I'll be back later. Be sure you get some sleep, Beth."

"Yes, my lady. Gentle dreams."

But Sioned did not return to the room where Rohan slept. She climbed the stairs to the curtain wall between towers and watched the sunset. Fire on Water—the stuff of conjurings and visions. Perhaps Andry had something after all in his idea of looking into the future. Sioned had herself glimpsed things long before they happened. Was it possible for a *faradhi* so gifted—and not all were—to court visions of the future? With *dranath* to augment power, and some mental and emotional discipline, it might become a reliable talent.

Yet if Sunrunners could foretell the future, would their lives be safe? Who would not scheme to gain control of such a person? And who among the *faradh'im* was strong and honorable and wise enough to use a gift like that?

But there was a more important question against which her tired mind had no defenses. She thought back over the events of her life—glorious successes and terrible losses—

and wondered, *If I knew the future, would I have the courage to live it?*

Her sense of humor did not rescue her, but mockery did. She had lived a life about which bards made songs—some of them even partly true. What right had she to feel sorry for herself? *The only thing wrong with me is selfishness. I'm growing old and one day the future's going to happen without me.*

"I thought you might be up here," said a quiet voice behind her.

She did not turn, merely reached back one hand. It was grasped in hard, callused fingers. "Hollis isn't as good at sleep-weaving as she should be," she said.

"She is, though. But I pretended and she went away." Chay stood beside her, holding her hand. "Beth says you're upset and wouldn't talk to her about it."

"Just moody. And tired. There's nothing to worry about, Chay. Tobin's going to get well."

He nodded. They watched the sea for a long time in silence, until he said, "Looks like something a Sunrunner would conjure, doesn't it? The wind's stiff tonight—whitecaps from here to the Small Islands, like little flames."

"I was thinking the same thing."

"Flames, or ripples of blood," he mused, then shook himself. "Goddess, what an idea. Maybe I need sleep more than I thought."

"Come inside, then," she told him, tugging at his hand. "And don't think you'll be able to pretend with *me*."

A sudden smile took thirty years from his face. "I wouldn't dare."

* * *

Pol arrived two days later, greeted by his parents' astonishment and the joyous news that his aunt was able to speak a few words and move a little. He came laden with wildflowers gathered along the road and once he saw Tobin awake, aware, and recovering, happily dumped them all in her lap.

You impossible boy! came her laughing voice on sunlight, and he nearly lost his balance at the shock. *That damned seizure didn't kill me, but now I may sneeze myself to death!*

Pol gaped. Her colors danced playfully around him and her black eyes sparkled with mirth.

Oh, stop looking so grim, you foolish child, and give me a kiss. She fumbled for a moss rose with her good hand and admired its sheen in the sunlight spilling across the bed. *Beautiful. Thank you, Pol. I hope you brought some for your mother—she's the one who thought of this, so I can speak to you. I can't tell you what it was like, being trapped inside my own skull.* Her gaze sobered and he knelt beside the bed, weak-kneed. *But I'm better. See? I can move my other hand and even bend my leg a little.*

The sheets shifted at her knees and her right hand crawled across the lace. He caught her fingers and smiled. *You're amazing.*

I always have been.

Her smile broke his heart. One side of her face was still perfect, the corner of her mouth curving and her brow lifting just as always, but the other dragged down, unresponsive.

"Would you care to explain why you're here?" Rohan asked suddenly.

He was grateful for the distraction, not wishing Tobin to see his anguish, and rose to face his father. "I had a look in at Stronghold a few days ago and found Morwenna, who naturally had to tell me where you were going and why. So here I am."

"She didn't say anything before we left."

"Stop treating him as if he was still fifteen," Chay said. "He's here, and welcome."

"Well, of course," Sioned agreed. "But I think yours is too volatile a presence at the moment, Pol—not to mention a filthy one! Go wash and change clothes. You stink of horse and sweat."

Ah, so that's why the flowers—to hide the stench! came Tobin's shimmering thought, and Pol grinned down at her.

Not fifteen, he remarked. *Five.* He gave her an elaborate bow, kissed his mother, and left the room.

Immediately outside in the hallway he encountered Daniv, Dannar, and a blonde, blue-eyed girl he didn't know. The first two were comparing stories of the journey to Radzyn. The latter tagged along listening with downcast gaze. They stopped on seeing him and performed the usual respects. He replied with a grimace, having as little use for ceremony as the rest of his family—except when it suited him.

"Goddess, such elegance!" he teased. "And I assume

you're beggaring my parents, Daniv, by eating everything in sight at Stronghold."

"I do my best, my lord," the young man said, grinning.

"I don't doubt it. Dannar—this could get confusing, two similar names—go save my dignity and run a bath for me before my mother throws me in a trough."

"I'll go with you," Daniv offered. "You can tell me all about that beauty you rode in on. I've been hinting to my father for years to buy me a Dragon's Rest gold for my knighting."

The two boys went off talking horses, leaving Pol with the little girl. She glanced up at him with frank curiosity and he suddenly realized who she must be. The eyes were unmistakable. "It seems I'm not the only one with pretty blonde daughters," he told her. "We haven't met, Tobren. I'm your cousin, Pol."

"I know, your grace," she said in a soft, low voice.

"Oh, you don't have to call him that, Tobren," Betheyn said behind him. He turned and smiled a greeting. "It's nice to see you again," she went on. "How was the journey?"

"My mother's ordered me into the nearest bathtub immediately. Beth, you've gotten uglier again."

"Many thanks, your grace," she replied, then winked at Tobren. "You only have to call him that if he's being horrid or you want to make fun of him." Tobren looked slightly shocked. Beth said to Pol, "She *is* pretty, isn't she? And so tall! Just twelve, three whole years younger than her cousin Chayla, but the same height." She ruffled the child's hair fondly.

"How do you like Radzyn and Whitecliff so far, Tobren?"

"Very much, my lord." She hesitated. "Is that what I'm to call you?"

"I'd be pleased if you'd call me by my name."

"I don't think that would be right, my lord," she said seriously.

"As you like," he said with a smile, but wondered what Andry had told her about him that she was so wary.

Betheyn caught his gaze. "Jeni must have been disappointed that she couldn't come along with your parents and hear about Goddess Keep from Tobren. I hear she's trying to convince her parents to send her there."

It was news to Pol that his mother's current fosterling,

Camigwen of Castle Crag, wanted to be a Sunrunner. "She has the gifts?"

"Their court Sunrunner thinks so. But Jeni's mother wants her to spend some time at Stronghold first."

Pol could well imagine. Alasen and Ostvel would be reluctant to send their daughter to Andry for training; the complexity of reasons was not something they could detail to the girl. How did one go about explaining that the Lord of Goddess Keep had been in love with her mother, and had once threatened her father's life because of it?

Tobren proved herself the child of her father by saying, "If she's gifted, it's her duty to be trained as a Sunrunner. Not to use the powers to the fullest is an offense against the Goddess."

"I agree," Pol said. "And I'm sure my mother will begin Jeni's education this winter."

Tobren caught her breath. "But that's wrong!" she cried. "My father teaches *faradh'im*! If you're not trained by him at Goddess Keep, you're not a real Sunrunner at all!"

Betheyn met Pol's eyes with a meaningful look. So this was what she'd wanted him to know about Tobren, he thought, and gave the girl an easy smile and a conspiratorial wink. "So I've always suspected. When my mother was teaching me how to conjure with Fire, she often told me I was hopeless!"

Tobren was still frowning. Pol wondered again what sort of tales Andry had told her about him; seldom did the family charm and his father's smile fail.

"My lord!" Dannar called from up the next flight of stairs. "Your bath's going cold!"

Radzyn boasted only a few real bathrooms, and these were for its regular noble residents and the suite kept for the High Prince. Most of the castlefolk—including Pol that night—bathed in portable tubs and had to be careful not to slosh too much water on the floor. He had been scolded more than once in boyhood for his playfulness in the bath. Being Desert-born, he delighted in water—as long as it wasn't something he had to cross. Rohan had never gotten over his wary nervousness of rain, but years at Dragon's Rest had accustomed Pol to downpours and even thunderstorms.

By the time he had washed and rinsed and stood draped in a thick robe, the priceless Cunaxan carpet was sopped.

He helped Dannar hang it over the window ledge to dry, then suffered himself to be prettied up to the squire's exacting standards. The dark violet tunic sewn with silver thread was paired with a snowy silk shirt above white trousers and short black boots. On his fingers were the moonstone that had been Lady Andrade's—his only Sunrunner ring—and the amethyst-and-topaz of Princemarch. The latter combination was repeated in the silver earring that swung close to his jaw.

"My, my," Rohan drawled when Pol entered the small family dining room. "What a gorgeous vision has graced us this evening. Tell me, my son, how long does it take to polish you up? You arrived a mere mortal like the rest of us."

Hollis arched a brow. "You don't give him much in that quarter, my lord High Prince."

Maarken grinned over his wine cup. "It always irks her that she can never make me jealous. But how can I be, when she only flirts with men who are disgustingly in love with their wives?"

Pol took his cue—behave as if this were any dinner—and laughed. "We're *all* gorgeous this evening. Especially you, Mother."

"Borrowed from Hollis," she confessed, smoothing pale green skirts decorated with black lace. "It's nice to know I still have a waistline."

"Which my cooks are attempting to ruin, by the look of the table," Chay said. "Let's sit down. I'm starving. You boys take your places, too—my people will serve tonight."

It was a rare treat for squires to be included with the grown-ups at table; they usually carved and carried all through a meal, and ate afterward. Daniv handed Tobren gallantly into her chair, doubtless dreaming of a time when he would preside over his own table as Prince of Syr at the splendid castle of High Kirat. The rest took their places at the square table, an arrangement more intimate than sitting all in a row at the high table downstairs. Instead of leaning across one's neighbor to conduct a conversation, all one had to do was talk across the napery, plates, and flowers. Still, there were advantages to a formal meal at a long table; one could sit at a distance from people one disliked or wished to avoid.

Chay put Betheyn beside him, then looked at the empty place to his right. Pol saw his throat work convulsively.

Then he said, "Tobren, you come sit over here by me, sweetheart."

It was Tobin's place and her namesake knew it. She blushed, hesitating, and Dannar quickly rose and escorted her to the indicated seat. Chay leaned back in his chair, beamed at them all, and announced, "How I do love being surrounded by pretty girls!"

With Tobren present, there could be no talk of politics regarding Goddess Keep. Rohan held forth with great enthusiasm on the subject of water clocks and the fascinating glass lenses his crafters were making until Sioned stuffed a wedge of bread in his mouth to shut him up. Maarken steered the conversation to the ever-popular subject of horses. It wasn't until taze and sweets were handed around and the servants were gone that Hollis brought up dragons.

"Abisel seemed rather fretful when she flew by a few days ago," she reported. "Friendly, but preoccupied. Is Azhdeen well? Did you get any odd feelings from him, Pol?"

"I offended him. He showed me something he wanted me to see, and I didn't believe him." Pol started to reach for a pastry, remembered his self-imposed prohibition against desserts, and refilled his cup from the pitcher of taze instead. "He conjured up something that looked like a dream, though it was very real to him. Father, do you think dragons dream?"

"Why don't you ask Azhdeen the next time you talk to him? What about it, Sioned?"

"How should I know? It's not something that's ever been an issue. They can *imagine* things—we'd never have received permission to build Dragon's Rest if Elisel wasn't able to imagine sheep penned up for her supper. But—dreams?" She shrugged. "I'll ask her the next time I talk to her."

Tobren heard all this with her blue eyes starting from her head. Chay noticed first, and smiled. "I know—sounds perfectly insane, doesn't it? Talking to dragons! But they can."

"Grandsir—*how*?"

"If I knew, I'd do it myself. Maarken? You want to explain it?"

"It's a little like Sunrunning, Tobren."

"My father taught me before I left Goddess Keep," she said with shy pride. "Does that mean I can talk to dragons, too?"

"Did he, now?" Pol asked, in a tone betraying nothing more than interest, but she suddenly stiffened in her chair.

Rohan smiled at the girl. "I've always wanted to be able to. When I was little I used to imagine flying over the hills and valleys just like a dragon, only *my* wings were made of sun- or moonlight."

"It's just like that," Hollis said with a warning glance at Pol. None of them had been aware of Tobren's ability; he wondered if any of them suspected Andry as strongly as he did of setting the least obvious spy imaginable in their midst. But what other motive could Andry have for teaching her? She was only twelve, absurdly young to know such things.

"I like Sunrunning," Tobren said, encouraged by her elders' interest, but still with a wary eye on Pol. "I can talk with Andrev and Valeda and Nialdan, and when I get homesick I can look at Goddess Keep—" She stopped abruptly.

"It's all right, heartling," Maarken said. "When I was a squire at Graypearl I used to get homesick, too. Didn't you, Pol?"

"All the time. And I didn't know how to go Sunrunning. But you know, Tobren, nowdays I sometimes go take a look at Graypearl, because I miss it. I expect you'll miss Whitecliff and Radzyn one day, too." His suspicions shamed him. What better way to soothe a little girl away from home for the first time than to teach her how to use light to talk with her friends whenever she needed to? Andry had plenty of faults, but he adored his children.

"Anyway," Maarken went on, "communicating with a dragon is done the same way as with other *faradh'im,* only you don't use words. You use pictures and feelings. The thing about dragons is that they always know the truth about you. It's impossible to hide your feelings from them."

"And they're fascinated by what we feel," Hollis added. "Almost the way we're fascinated by tiny babies—what must they be thinking and seeing and feeling? It's rather humbling," she finished with a chuckle.

"I can tell you one thing about dragons—don't ever get one mad at you." Pol winced. "Azhdeen nearly ripped my brains to shreds, he was that angry with me for not believing him."

"What had he seen?" Rohan asked.

"Dragons on water. I tried to point out to him that ships

look very much like dragons—sails for wings, the prow for the head, and so on. He took exception to being corrected. Dragons sailing the sea were what he saw, and that was that."

"I trust you were properly contrite in asking forgiveness." Sioned winked.

He laughed. "Mother, I positively groveled. We're friends again. But I'll think twice before I ever disagree with him."

"I should hope so," Chay said, entering the conversation for the first time. "If I was a Sunrunner, I'd *never* contradict my dragon." His voice was light and teasing, and he smiled, but there was a darkness in his eyes that Pol found perplexing.

"But that's another thing about them," Sioned mused. "Elisel isn't my dragon. I'm *her* human. I belong to her, not the other way around."

Rohan pulled a mournful face. "And here I thought you'd promised to be only mine forever. I'm wounded. My heart is breaking." He snatched a pastry off her plate and added, "And the seams of Hollis' lovely dress are going to break as well if you don't stop stuffing yourself."

The servants came in to clear the table and the party dispersed—for bed, for a walk in the moonlight, for games of chess. Pol claimed fatigue after the journey and went upstairs, but was unable to sleep for quite some time.

When would he not distrust Andry's every word and action? He resented what the mere thought of his cousin made him think and feel. He wasn't a suspicious man, or a jealous or vindictive one. He had offered Andry trust and friendship many times.

A certain fundamental honesty compelled him to admit that "offering" was not the same as "giving." Andry was as proud as he—and had been hurt more. Oh, he understood the man, even felt compassion for him. He had never forgotten what Sorin had whispered just before he died—to go gently with Andry. For Sorin's sake, he had tried. But Andry made it damned difficult.

Was his dislike based only on personalities? Somewhere along the years the easy cousinly friendship had been lost. He regetted it, but would not accept the whole responsibility himself. He and Andry were simply too different to like each other.

Or perhaps too much the same. Born of the same princely family, raised in the Desert, Sunrunners, powerful in those

arts and in politics—it might be that they understood each other too well.

Yet Andry's power could never seriously threaten Pol's. Lord of Goddess Keep he might be, but Rohan had seen to it that he knew his place. And Pol knew that his father's power as High Prince wasn't half what his own would be as Sunrunner and High Prince both.

And sorcerer, he reminded himself. There were things in the Star Scroll that Andry would never be able to do. He lacked the *diarmadhi* gift, similar to and subtly different from that of Sunrunners.

So we'll go on playing the game until one of us makes a mistake and the other pounces. I suppose it ought to comfort me that I'm the Dragon's son. Everybody knows what happens to anything a dragon considers prey.

But it saddened him that life had to be like that.

Chapter Seven

On the thirtieth day of Autumn, Faolain Riverport prepared to celebrate two events. The first was the annual harvest festival presided over by the sons of old Lord Baisal of Faolain Lowland. Baisath, *athri* of the thriving port, was the younger son; his brother, Miral, had inherited the family's main holding at Lowland. Good, tradition-bound farmers both, for all that one now lived in a town, they traded the festival back and forth between them. This year it was Baisath's turn, and the whole clan gathered in his large, comfortable residence for the occasion.

The second celebration was more personal. Miral's daughter Karanaya had finally Chosen a husband, and they would wed at the New Year. Naturally such an occasion warranted presents, and this touchy subject had brought together two ladies with very different aims. Michinida, Baisath's wife, was determined to spend the least amount of money possible; Kemeny, mother of the bride, was just as determined to see her daughter splendidly gifted at Michinida's expense.

They had been receiving merchants all morning.

"Too small, too flashy, too paltry," Michinida enumerated as a silversmith proffered various pieces of jewelry. "I want something simple and elegant, you wretch. Have you nothing worthy of anyone but a peasant's daughter?"

The man combed his beard and cast his dark eyes from side to side as if seeking spies. "Noble lady, if I show you my most precious things, I must respectfully beg that if you do not purchase them, you will not speak of them. Not their existence, and certainly not their price—"

"What insolence!" Kemeny exclaimed. "Are you insinuating that my dear sister-by-marriage would skimp money on my daughter's betrothal gift?"

Michinida frowned her annoyance. The woman was so vulgar—and so perceptive.

"Show us these marvels," Kemeny ordered, with a sidelong glance at Michinida.

The merchant sighed, fingering his beard, and placed a plain wooden box on the table before the women. He did not open it.

"Before viewing robs you of speech, gentle ladies, allow me to compliment you on the marvels of this place. Where I come from, we rarely see such magnificence. Why, there must be fifty rooms here!"

"Only forty," Kemeny said with a sliver of malice that instantly found its way into Michinida's breast and festered there. Lowland had forty-six rooms. "Open the box, be quick! I want to see my dear friend's gift to my daughter."

"Instantly, my lady. Only—" His fingers toyed with the hasp. "I cannot imagine why this fair abode is not guarded better. I saw only five soldiers on my way in. I tremble for my person if anyone gets word of what I carry in this box, should you not be pleased with it."

Michinida scowled. "The residence boasts a sufficient number of armed troops—almost seventy, I believe. But this is my husband's business, not yours. *Will* you open that box!"

He worked at the catch. "It hasn't been opened in so long, it's grown stiff. I beg patience." His fingers fumbled and poked. "Seventy seems a small number to guard so rich a prize."

"Who would dare attack?" Michinida laughed. "You are absurd, merchant."

"Yet there are stone ramparts on the river side, my lady. Ah, there, I think it's coming."

"So," Kemeny observed, "is winter."

"We have never considered it necessary to surround Riverport with walls," Michinida said loftily. "Oh, that fool architect wanted to, but as we rightly pointed out to him, to our east lies our own princedom. Rohan would have to go mad and Chaynal and their armies with him before they would fall on us. We are the most important trading center on the whole coast."

"Except for Radzyn, with its exclusive right to silk," Kemeny reminded her.

"Does Radzyn see the variety of goods that pass through

our warehouses bound for everywhere? It supplies the Desert. *We* supply three princedoms!"

"Lowland has the honor of supplying Stronghold itself," Kemeny purred. "For which service Sioned granted of her own purse the stone to build the keep."

"Oh, look, it's open," Michinida said, quelling the usual argument about whose was the more prestigious holding.

"Gracious ladies," the merchant said, "I show you now the most beauteous objects ever beheld." And he stood back from the table with a low bow, his eyes never leaving their awestruck faces.

Nestled on puckered white silk were six smooth, flawless black pearls. Not charcoal gray or purplish, as were sometimes found off Dorval, but black as night, overlaid with a hint of shining iridescence.

"Noble ladies," the merchant whispered, "the Tears of the Dragon."

Michinida was the first to recover her powers of speech, but even so her voice was hushed. "Where did you—were these lawfully obtained?"

The merchant stroked his beard and said nothing. When she dragged her eyes from the gems, he shrugged and very nearly winked.

"Not even the High Princess has such pearls," Kemeny whispered. Her hand went out, one finger extended as if to touch them, then drew back as if she didn't dare.

"The Tears of the Dragon," he repeated solemnly. "Nothing so magnificent exists anywhere. It is said they number twelve in all, and when together possess such power over any who see them that—" He shrugged to indicate his inability to express the colossal import of a complete set. "It is further said that they were wept by the mother of All Dragons for some mysterious sorrow, and worn by the Goddess herself."

"A pretty conceit," Michinida remarked as casually as she could. "But I'm not interested in stories, merchant. I'm interested in the price. I assume it is equally outrageous?" She felt queasy at the thought of the cost. She had intended to make Karanaya a nice present, but these must be worth a year's revenues. *Two* years'.

It was as bad as she'd feared. But with Kemeny there, she had no choice. As the bargaining commenced, the merchant wrung his hands, clawed his beard, clutched at his heart as if

the sums she offered were physically painful. But at last she wore him down to a payable, if expensive, price. Thrice what she'd intended to spend, of course, but halfway through the negotiations she had an idea. When she called in her chamberlain to arrange payment, she explained it, beaming.

"I have the most cunning notion! These pearls will start a family legend! The first of the—what did you call them? The Tears of the Dragon?—I'll give the first to Karanaya, and the second to your son's wife, Pelida—belatedly, true, but the thought is what matters. When my sons marry, they shall have the next."

Kemeny frowned and opened her mouth to protest breaking up the set—which naturally should go to Karanaya whole.

Michinida smiled sweetly at her. "Do you think it would be terribly selfish of us, my dear, to keep one each for ourselves?"

She looked at the pearls, thought of her daughter, and replied slowly, "We might keep one each . . . ah, in trust, as it were."

"I'm so glad you agree with me!" She didn't like giving up even one, but this was better than handing all six over to Karanaya. They fell to discussing how best to set their pearls—ring, necklet, earring? They did not notice when the merchant departed, his pockets bulging with gold, his beard split by a contemptuous grin.

* * *

A placid family evening at Gilad Seahold was shattered by a single scream. Lady Paveol pulled the face of her young son against her breast and cried out, "Oh, Goddess, how horrible!"

Lord Segelin surged to his feet, livid. "Get out! How dare you bring such foulness into the presence of my wife and child?"

The young juggler lost his balance. Six cups nimbly aloft an instant before smashed to the stones. "My lord—please, I meant no offense!" On his knees now, he tried to scrape together the shattered fragments, babbling all the while. "It's tradition in my family, we've always used cups made of—and now mine are broken! Where will I find more? These were given to me by my great-grandsire, who displayed his art in front of High Prince Roelstra himself,

earning a gold coin and six silver buttons! I hoped to make my way with them, but now—" He looked up hopefully. "Shall I sing for you, my lord? I have a fine and pleasing voice, and know all manner of songs—"

"*Get out!*" Segelin roared, and his son began to cry.

"A cradle song!" the juggler said desperately. "A soft song to soothe the young lord from his fright—"

"You and those horrible—*things*—frightened him!" He advanced from the sofa where his wife sat trying to calm the little boy, her face as bleached of color as the shards still littering the floor. The juggler scrambled to his feet and backed away, fingers tangling distractedly in his thin beard.

"My lord—please—don't kill me—!"

"Get out, or I'll do worse than kill you!"

He gave a high-pitched shriek and fled—not through the garden doors by which he had entered to amuse the family with his clever tricks, but out the main door and up the stairs.

"Goddess damn him!" Segelin yelled for his guards. The juggler led them a swift chase up to the top floor and across the wall, then disappeared into the stone tower that was the most ancient part of the manor.

"Wait, let me light a torch, my lord," one of the guards panted. "Those steps are uncertain enough by daylight, and it's gone dusk."

"Hurry up about it. When I catch the whoreson—do you know what he was juggling with? Do you know what those cups were made from?"

He spat onto the ragged stones, as if to rid himself of an evil taste in his mouth. The guard lit the torch and gulped at the expression on Segelin's face. No wonder the juggler had run headlong.

"I'm sorry, my lord, I didn't see what he—"

"*Skulls!* Hollow skulls with the jaws wired shut and the eye sockets filled with clay!" Segelin grabbed the torch and made for the entrance to the tower.

Guards followed with more light. Some went down the narrow, crumbling stairs, but Segelin climbed to the top of the tower. He'd guessed correctly; his quarry was no field prey with the cleverness to run to ground, but rather a terrified bird trying to take flight. The juggler stood shivering on the roof, arms wrapped as far as they would go around a huge triangular crenellation.

"I ought to push you over the edge," Segelin snarled.

"Oh, great lord, please! I don't know what came over me, I've never had so powerful a man angry with me before and I panicked—*please* don't kill me!"

Some of the shock had worn off by now, and Segelin's primary emotion was one of scorn for this trembling craven. He held the torch higher and saw that the stupid fool had actually wet his trousers in his fear.

"Bah!" he said, disgusted. "It would insult my blade to stain it with blood like yours."

"Oh, Goddess bless you, my lord, Goddess give you a hundred sons—"

"Pick yourself up, swine, and get out. And if I ever even *hear* of you within a hundred measures of my lands, I'll hunt you down and have your hands cut off. *Move!*"

He lurched to his feet and stood there swaying. "It—it's growing dark, my lord—I need a torch—"

Segelin took one from its bracket near the door and lit it from his own. It quivered and shook in the juggler's hand. A few steps, and he tripped over an unevenness in the old stones. The torch went sailing over the wall and down to the beach.

"By the Goddess' fiery eyes!" Segelin bellowed. "I never saw anyone so clumsy! Can't you juggle your own bones, or only the empty ones of others? Find your way down in the dark for all I care! I want you out of my keep *now!*"

The youth flung himself down the stairs. Segelin shouted to the guards, telling them to throw him out the main gate. Then he went to soothe his wife and son.

Nobody saw the juggler tidy his clothes, make a face at the dampness of his trousers, drink off the rest of the water from a small pocket flask, and start off at an easy, graceful lope into the deepening night, chuckling as he ran.

* * *

The moons rose early, bright enough to light her way. Not that Brenlis needed to see where she was going; the paths were familiar to her from childhood. She stepped softly through the pale grass, wilted but making a lovely sibilant sound against her skirts, until she reached the rocky cliffs. The smell of the sea filled her and she crouched down, picking up small rocks to throw down at the waves.

Her parents understood nothing. Nothing. She was the mother of a child by the Lord of Goddess Keep, and they asserted that as the baby's grandparents they ought to enjoy honors, land, wealth. Her influence with Andry should gain them favors from Prince Kostas—instead of being only lowly farmers, they could be important vassals, rich, powerful, intimates of their prince. They had been after her about it since her arrival, through the days it had taken to assure herself that her brother would recover from his illness.

Brenlis was nauseated by their greed, and had not scrupled to say so. But tonight they had used her brother against her.

We don't ask for ourselves. We ask for him, for his future. Why shouldn't he have the best? Why shouldn't he become a great lord with a fine castle and the chance for a rich wife? The Lord of Goddess Keep loves you. He'd do anything for you. You've given him one child—give him another, and this time make him marry you!

She hadn't cried until she had run through half a measure of drooping grass in the new moonlight. After wiping her eyes, she continued on to the cliffs, where she sat back on her heels to watch the glow of bonfires across the water at Faolain Riverport.

It was the harvest celebration tonight, she reminded herself. She was tempted to go, to lose herself in the crowds of laughing townfolk. She could pretend to be someone else, as she had done when she was little—as she had not had to do since going to live at Goddess Keep.

High Princess Sioned had understood. Brenlis had been brought to her attention by Lord Baisath, who had heard strange tales of a girl who sometimes saw the future. She had been invited to Stronghold and for the first time in her life Brenlis found someone who understood her. Sioned, too, had been looked on askance as a child, called fey and strange, something of an embarrassment to her family. Brenlis had warm memories of her sympathetic kindness. To hear some at Goddess Keep tell it, the High Princess drank dragon blood instead of wine and had taught her son the blackest sorcery. Brenlis felt guilty sometimes that she did not defend them, but who was she to contradict anyone there? Her two pitiful rings had been earned at great effort. She would never have any more, never achieve a rank that would enable her to speak of the gentle treatment she'd

known at Stronghold, the understanding woman who had sent her to Goddess Keep where she need no longer be afraid. Brenlis knew why people told stories about Sioned. They were afraid of her power.

But Andry was afraid of nothing. She wished she could talk with him now, bathe her wounded spirit in his love. But she didn't know how to reach out to him. The sun was difficult enough for her to use. Moonlight was completely beyond her. A part of her said that even were he with her now, within reach, she still would not know how to touch him.

He had worries of his own. She could not trouble him with her petty problems, not when he was frantic with concern for his mother. Brenlis had met Princess Tobin once during her brief time at Stronghold, and still could not quite believe that her own daughter was Tobin's grandchild.

Bitterness curled her mouth at the thought of the other grandmother. Merisel, Named for the long-dead *faradhi* Andry revered, had one grandmother who was a princess and one who was a grasping peasant. Brenlis would not ask Andry for anything, not even for her brother. She couldn't. He would do everything in his power—and she would have to give something in return.

Marriage. Though he had never asked outright, she knew he wished it. Lords or Ladies of Goddess Keep did not marry. But he would break that tradition as he had broken so many others. The power this gave her was frightening. She stared hard at the red-orange glow of the Riverport festival fires, and determinedly put him and her parents and everything else from her mind.

* * *

The last moonlight dappled patterns onto the intricate tiles of the oratory at Graypearl. Meath had never lost his amazement at this masterwork of the *faradh'im* who had lived on Dorval long ago. The floor and domed roof were a calendar, pure in function but not at all simple; it had taken Princess Audrite years of complicated calculations to replace missing or broken tiles accurately. The bulk of the oratory had been excavated from the ruins of an ancient keep on the other side of the island and transported here. It

was during an idle dig through nearby remains that Meath had found the Star Scroll.

"First of Summer, First of Winter, moons don't rise at all," sang a little boy as he leaped from one tile to the next, his brown curls bouncing. His voice was sure and surprisingly rich for his nine winters as he recited the lesson Meath had brought him here tonight to learn. "Fortieth Spring, Fortieth Autumn, it's early the moons fall!" He stopped on the Autumn tiles. "Meath?"

"Yes, O torment of my declining years?"

"The moons don't really fall down, do they? Wouldn't they break?"

"Audran, my pest, if they fell out of the sky we'd none of us be here to ask foolish questions."

"Then the song is foolish, too," Audran replied. "It says the moons fall, and they don't. Where do they go?"

"The other side of the world. There's more to the song—keep going. And don't land too hard on the midwinter tiles—they're very old."

"Older than Granna and Grandsir? Older than you?

"Even older than I, and I am exceedingly old." He grinned and gestured for the child to continue.

"Moons are full and white and clear," Audran sang, doing a complicated cross-step over to another set of tiles.

"Wait a moment. Where did you learn that? Not the song, the maneuver."

"From the squires. They've been teaching me how to fight with a knife." Suddenly Audran crouched and, wielding an imaginary blade, stalked Meath with exaggerated care. "I come in low and slow, and distract you with a feint—like this—then jump in and slash and slash until you're ribbons!"

"Gaahh!" Meath staggered back and clutched his belly. "I'm wounded! Great prince, don't finish me off!"

"Of course not," Audran scoffed, pretending to wipe a blade on his shirt. "You haven't taught me the rest of the song."

All at once Meath toppled to the tiles—careful of his sixty-four-year-old bones—and gave a whimper. Audran darted to him. In an instant the boy was prone and captive and Meath held a thin knife in front of his startled eyes.

"My prince," he said softly, "never leave an enemy merely bleeding. He may not be as badly hurt as he seems. And he may have other knives." Meath replaced the blade in his

boot. "And if the matter is serious enough to use your knife, it's serious enough either to kill him or scar him forever."

Audran barely breathed as the Sunrunner helped him up. "You scared me," he whispered.

"I intended to. If you're old enough to learn how to fight, you're old enough to learn the rules—the *real* rules, not the ones that apply when you're practicing with the other squires." Meath smiled and ruffled the boy's hair. "Forgiven?"

"Yes, I suppose so." Audran hesitated, then said, "Meath? You never called me that before."

"Called you what?"

" 'My prince.' You call Papa and Grandsir that, but not me."

Meath thought of the other little boys he'd had a hand in turning into men: Audran's father Ludhil and uncle Laric; Maarken, Pol. "You're growing up."

"I wish somebody'd tell that to my mother!" Audran grumped.

"Princess Iliena is a sweet and loving lady, and you're lucky to have her for a mother. But I understand." He glanced at the domed ceiling. "Now look what's happened. The moons have set and it's too late to go on with the lesson. Is that what you had in mind?"

"Meath! I did not!"

Laughing, they left the oratory and paused on the little footbridge over the stream that circled it like a miniature moat. This part of the garden was dark, for it was impossible to use the calendar accurately if torchlight interfered with the moons. Meath gestured, and a row of flames blossomed from wrought iron sconces set at intervals along the path back to the palace.

"Meath? Do the ones around the water, too, please?"

Obliging and indulgent, the Sunrunner concentrated. Audran clapped his hands as light flickered from the hundred small lamps that followed the course of the stream. Meath lit them in sequence, as if Fire sped from treetop to treetop in a miniscule forest. Audran leaned over the railing of the bridge and laughed to see the water ripple gold and red and orange.

"I want to be able to do that someday! Can I be a Sunrunner, Meath?"

"I'm afraid not, my prince," he replied gently. "There's no trace of it in your family. I'm sorry."

"Oh." Crestfallen, Audran turned from the display and sighed. Then, with the unquenchable spirits of the very young, he danced down the pathway singing the song about the moons again.

Meath chuckled and shook his head. He followed the boy, hoping Audran would not choose to make him play seek-and-find in the gardens tonight; his bones were aching from a long ride this afternoon, and he didn't relish the thought of trying to match pace with a nine-year-old.

He kept Audran in sight and as they neared the palace was astonished to see a guard hurry out, scoop the young prince unceremoniously up under one arm, and rush back inside. Other guards emerged, calling for Princess Alleyn.

"What is it? What's wrong?" he demanded.

"His grace said to find the children and get everyone inside at once."

A maidservant caught sight of Meath and cried out, "Do you know where she is? What's happened to Alleyn?"

"Try the lily pond, or the shed where she keeps her animals," he suggested. "Where is his grace?"

"Up top the walls, my lord."

He took the stairs three at a time, then two, and finally had to heed the screaming muscles of his thighs and the pounding of his heart. At last he reached the palace roof and stopped to catch breath enough to call out.

"Meath! Over here!" Chadric shouted.

Ludhil and Audrite were with him, as well as several guards and their commander. Judging by the way they breathed, all had only just arrived. They stared north out to sea, where the channel between Dorval and the continent widened into the Sunrise Water.

"Ships by the last moonlight," Ludhil said tensely, scraping the lank brown hair from his forehead. "The watch saw them clearly for only a moment."

"They're not ours?" Meath asked.

"We've none coming down from Tiglath, and none unaccounted for," Chadric said. "I received the yearly tally from the portmaster only yesterday morning."

"Port Adni?" Audrite guessed. "Einar? Waes?"

Her husband shook his head. "All in port for the winter. There won't be any early storms coming down from the

Veresch, or so Donato tells us from Castle Crag, and things are calm to the south as well over the sea. But by this time of year everyone with any sense has furled his sails."

Ludhil cleared his throat. "Father—the watch says he's never seen sails like these on any ship. Great squares, three of them, looking as if they're fixed in place. We use triangular, movable sails, and never more than two."

"New design?" Meath guessed.

"Not that I've heard of. And no one builds so much as a flatboat that I don't hear about." Chadric tapped an arrhythmic beat on the top of the low balustrade with fingers almost as weathered as the stone. "We must assume these ships are something less than friendly," he said with grim understatement.

"But who could they belong to?" Audrite exclaimed.

"I don't think that matters, Mother." Ludhil exchanged a glance with his father. "I think we'd better prepare ourselves."

"For what?" Then she gasped. "Oh, Goddess!"

Chadric turned to the commander of the guard. "Give the alarm at once."

Meath looked up at the sky and swore bitterly. "The moons are gone—and I can't use starlight!"

"On purpose," Audrite whispered. "This has been planned—timed."

Chadric frowned in the dimness. "I hadn't thought of that, but you're right. Ludhil, see to the defenses of the palace. Audrite, we'll need people to ride down to the port and reinforce the alarm. See to it, please. And Meath—"

"The useless Sunrunner," he muttered.

"Stop that!" Audrite exclaimed. "We need your wits and your experience!"

"And your Fire," Chadric said.

Meath had never kept count of how many times he'd told someone to sound the storm drum at Graypearl, warning of an approaching tempest. Now the drum began to thunder a different warning to the palace and the town below, and the beacon was lit atop Graypearl's soaring slender watchtower. Meath searched Chadric's eyes, the blue washed away in the dimness, and understood that he was about to break a Sunrunner's most solemn oath. He was about to use his gifts to kill.

* * *

A faint pungent scent of smoke awakened Brenlis. Stiff and chilly, she shifted in the little hollow—much smaller now than when she hid here as a child—and raised her head. It was not yet dawn; the east was soft and milky-skied, but stars still pocked the night that lingered in the west. She sat up and grimaced at the unpleasant dampness of her clothes. Residual anger nipped at her, resentment at being forced to spend the night this way. But for her brother, she felt unwelcome in her own home. The smell tickling her nostrils annoyed her further. Only the leftover fumes from the celebrations at Riverport, she decided; a little strong, but perhaps someone had grown careless and a house had caught. Standing, stretching, grateful for the clean salt spray as she faced the sea, she scrubbed her hands over her face and yawned.

It was then that she saw the dragons.

At least twenty of them, huge and gleaming dark and gold and silver, heads rearing proud and fierce from long necks half-submerged in the waves, white wings unfurled.

Brenlis cried out, thinking this another vision. But there was no queasiness, no lightness of spirit, no sense of being in two places and two times at once. This was real.

They were not dragons, those immense creatures floating toward the river's mouth. They were ships, lavished with bright paint that captured even this dim light. They picked up speed as the morning wind blew strong in the shoulders of their sails, these ships with the heads of snarling dragons.

She whirled around. Smoke billowed from the palely glowing Riverport, staining the eastern sky. Treachery there, faceless enemies mixed in with unwary townfolk, using the cover of festival bonfires to set the whole port ablaze. She sobbed with the horror of it, the deaths, the destruction. And she finally knew that she was living one of her own visions. She was standing on the cliffs near her home, just as she had done in the seeing—but the Goddess had not shown her enough.

"Andry!" she screamed, and fell to her knees on the stony ground. "Oh, Goddess, help me! Andry!"

But there was no light to use, no sun visible over the horizon. She covered her face with her hands and trembled, the cool wind fingering her dress as if to judge its worth as spoils of war. She begged the sun to rise, the Goddess to speed its passage into the morning.

Her need went unanswered. She looked up, tears streaking her face, and saw the last few stars winking mockery at her lack of skill. "I'll do it!" she shouted at them. "You're Fire, and I'm a Sunrunner! I can use your light, too!"

Now that she dared, now that she must, it seemed easy. Pale and silvery in a dark blue sky, the stars were made of cooler fire even than the moons. She felt chilled to the bone as she wove the delicate strands and cast them toward Goddess Keep.

Strangely, she forgot her terror and no longer smelled the thickening smoke. She flew along the starlight, enchanted. How beautiful the land was, mysteriously shadowed in the half-night. Here was the rich farmland she had passed through days ago, and there the dark ribbons of the Catha and Pyrme rivers, the gentle hills of Ossetia, the smooth expanse of Lake Kadar and its pretty manor and keep and pastures filled with horses. And then, finally, blessedly, the gray bulk of Goddess Keep.

But how would she find him? Surely he slept. Did the stars shine on him? They must. Otherwise she was lost. She searched frantically for his windows, looked within. The bed she had so often shared with him, richly hung with tapestries and covered in a white velvet quilt—his bed was empty, unslept-in.

She sobbed again and the sound jerked her painfully back to the coast of Syr. Where was he, how could she possibly find him? There was no hope for it—and the stars were almost gone. Her heart thudded sickly as she realized how close she had come to being shadow-lost. Shrinking into herself, she cursed her failure and her weakness, and whimpered Andry's name.

There was other noise now besides the whisper of windswept grasses and the pounding of the sea. She heard horses and the crash of windows, shouts and shrieks and the terrible clamor of swords. Fists pushed against her eyes so she could not see, breath held so the scent of burning and blood could not reach her, she rocked back and forth in mute agony, trying to deny what the Goddess pressed upon her. But with the sound came the scene, and the stench. This was no seeing of the future, removed from her, having no connection to her life and mind but the Goddess' power. This was real. She was seeing Faolain Riverport die. Worse,

she was *there*, drifting along the blazing streets as if she, too, were only smoke.

The enemy held the port. Their ships sailed in to safe harbor. Much of the town was ablaze, but they had been careful to spare the docks. From here they disembarked in their hundreds, tall bearded men with fierce faces. She saw them meet up with those who had gone around behind Riverport where there were no protecting walls, and with those who had joined the festival the night before to set fires that still burned. She heard them laugh, listened to their strange language that sounded a little like rituals sung at Goddess Keep. The words were slurred and rough, lacking the beauty of Jolan's poetry. She heard screaming too, louder and louder until she knew she must echo it or go mad.

Her own voice terrified her. But the sound helped. Her ears responded—her own ears, not the Goddess'—and the giddiness of vision left her. She raised her head, sucking in shallow breaths. Long shafts of sunlight poked through clouds of smoke. Dazed, she stared as if written in the sky was something she ought to remember. Sunlight. Something about sunlight—

Andry. She must find him. He must be told so he could warn everyone, tell them to make ready for war, tell them to flee—

Oh, Goddess—her family—her brother. She lunged to her feet as a faint cry came from the direction of the manor house. Running, stumbling as much as she ran, she topped the small rise and looked down into the sheltered hollow just as the torches were flung onto the roof. The dry thatch caught instantly. The door had been barricaded with boards torn from a fence. And there were more screams from inside, screams that gradually stopped.

Tall, bearded men paused to admire their handiwork. She counted twelve—too many for so insignificant a place. But then one of them called an order, pointed in the direction of the next small manor, and she knew they intended the same work at all the holds along the coast.

If it was Fire they wanted, then Fire she would give them.

A man bellowed in surprise and pain as flames sprouted from his chest. The one next to him was soon running like a wolf in a brushfire, trying to escape the blaze searing his back. She drew a circle of contracting Fire around one man

and sent it writhing up the crimsoned sword of still another. She ignited this one's hair, that one's eyes. Power flushed through her as if the Fire she called spread through her blood, lit her very bones. She began to laugh as she turned to kill the rest who had murdered her family, her brother.

She was looking straight at an archer's long, steel-tipped arrow. She set his drawn bow on fire in the same instant he released the string. And from a great distance she felt steel pierce her breast.

She knew there must be physical pain. But it was strange not to feel it as part of herself. What she felt instead was the fracturing of the pattern of colors that was hers alone, her unique identity. Her Self shattering, stained glass shards on the ground; her mind unraveling, threads picked from a tattered tapestry. By the time she felt the excruciating agony brought by iron in a working Sunrunner's blood, there was not enough of her left intact to scream, even with her mind.

The archer cursed and dropped his bow. The sorceress lay still, her eyes wide open to the smoke-filled sky. Her chest rose once or twice, rose no more. He knelt beside her, wiping sweat from his face, and tugged the rings off her fingers. Returning to his fellows—half of them dripping with hastily applied water, one of them curled in agony on the ground—he showed them the dainty circles and grinned. He'd wear them twined into the hairs of his beard, and gain high honor as being among the first to kill a sorceress.

PART TWO

Chapter Eight

There was a monotonous rhythm about the day, like the dripping of a water clock. Booted feet marched in precise meter from one dwelling to the next; boards were secured across doors and windows with steady beats of hammers on nails; even the shrieks of the dying had a certain cadence.

Along the strip of coast between the Pyrme and Faolain rivers, few survived to wonder who commanded the dragon ships. Gilad Seahold, signaled an easy prize by the torch flung over its walls, was gutted by fire, and all its people perished. Manors and cottages burned with their living occupants inside. The destruction was absolute. All that was taken were the horses. Plow-elk had their throats slit; food animals—swine, geese, goats, cattle—were burned in their pens or killed with a sword thrust and left to rot. The bounty of autumn harvest, stored in barns and sheds crammed with fruit, grapes, grain, and vegetables, was fired as well. The invaders brought no carts and took none to transport food for future use. They had no interest in salvaging what might feed their army; they were interested in horses and fire, and that was all.

There were no battles. The people in the holdings might not have existed, except for the slight trouble it took to kill them. There were no rapes, no maimings, no tortures. Simply death. Men, women, and children were of as little account as farm animals and food stores. Horses and fire; that was all.

The first village to burn was twelve measures in from the coast, a pretty place overlooking the river, where white flowers carpeted the hill in spring. By noon of that first day the hill and its village were black, but for the stark white bones of its ninety-six inhabitants.

The first substantial manor to burn was twenty measures up the Pyrme, a rich place with ten horses in a small paddock. An altercation broke out when two men claimed the same gelding. This provided the youngest son of the house a chance to run. The man who slew him was mounted on his father's favorite mare.

The first castle to burn after Gilad Seahold was thirty-eight measures from the sea, a minor holding of little importance to anyone other than those who lived there. Rising smoke had warned the *athri*, and he ordered his two grown sons, his daughter, her husband, and the castlefolk to prepare for war. His had once been a strategic keep, but a hundred years and more had passed since the last siege. There were weak places in the walls, and the moat had not been dredged in anyone's memory, and the great iron bars binding the wooden gate had grown rusty. The castle was ablaze before noon.

Again the yield was horses—only six this time, but of prime quality, the stocky Kadar Water breed characterized by white feathery tufts at ears and hooves. Neither as swift nor as elegant as Radzyn horses, still they were well-suited to carrying riders over long distances. Of the hundred men who had marched up the Pyrme River that dawn, over half were now mounted.

* * *

The sun rose with majestic unconcern, lavish with the light that was a Sunrunner's life, but Meath was in no state to use it. He knew he had crossed water; there was no mistaking the searing ache in his skull, the flashes of pain behind his eyes, the sore muscles of his stomach. He knew he had spent much of the night and half the morning lying rigid with misery in the bottom of a sailboat. He remembered the stars overhead quite clearly, mocking pinpricks of light that hurt his eyes. But the rest of his memory was confused by odd impressions of a long ride, ships, fire, arguing with Chadric—and seeing Audrite's birthplace, Sandeia, in flames. He understood none of it. A *faradhi*'s ultimate irony: his only certain memory was of that insane sail in the middle of the night, the sea crossing that had addled the rest of his brain. He could relive it in helpless detail from his first step into the boat to the time he was

carried onto dry land. He must have fainted then, and wondered with dull resentment why the Goddess had not allowed him oblivion long before.

Currently he lay prone in a thicket of berry bushes. He dared not raise his head—not yet, anyway, not until he was sure he could do so without losing consciousness again. So he concentrated on rearranging his memories into coherent order.

Graypearl was the start—and with that single word everything rushed in on him and he nearly groaned aloud. He had called down Fire on the strange, square sails while the ships were still in the channel, the effort and the distance so great that he sagged with exhaustion. No energy left even to rage that his work was so feeble, that not one ship had burned. But the town did, and he had joined Ludhil in persuading Chadric that there was no hope. The palace was indefensible. It had been lost the instant the invaders swarmed up from the beaches to the port.

"If this was a castle, we could bring everyone inside and wait for help from Radzyn or Riverport. But the hill and these walls are no fit protection."

Hurtful enough to remember the heartbreak in Chadric's eyes as he gave the bitter command to flee. Worse to think of topping the last hill after a frantic ride and finding Sandeia in flames. Sudden hope when Ludhil remembered the family's sailboats in the nearby cove; nightmare descent down the cliffs, already sick with what he knew would happen once he was on the water. And Chadric's anger when Ludhil thwarted his intention to stay and fight.

"Going into the hills, are you, and lead the resistance? You've got two choices, Father. One, you climb in that boat without a fuss. Second, I put you in myself. Which will it be?"

"You wouldn't dare!"

The younger man gave his father stare for stare.

Ludhil tricked them into thinking he would jump into the last boat as it breasted incoming waves. Instead he waded back onshore to join those for whom there had been no place on the tiny craft. They would meet up with shepherds and silk-farmers and pearl-fishers and fight the invading enemy. The scholar's slump gone from his shoulders, Ludhil had raised his hand in silent farewell to wife, children,

parents, friends, before turning to command his pitiable beginnings of an army.

But Iliena did something then that nothing in anyone's experience of her prepared them for. She stripped off her heavy cloak, broke the laces of the woolen skirt around her waist, and with a flash of long bare legs dove into the water. Shouts alerted Ludhil; he met his wife in chest-deep surf and carried her onshore.

Their sails were seen from Sandeia, but the wind cooperated and took them swiftly out to sea. Not that anyone attempted to follow—four small pleasure boats against the night sea? They would founder before reaching safety. One of them did, overloaded with panic-stricken servants. Meath had vague memory of sopping-wet forms crowding in beside him, weeping at the loss of others who were not strong swimmers. Someone sobbed hysterically that they would all be drowned; there was a sharp crack of palm against cheek, and silence but for a few whimpers.

That the other three boats came through safely was due to the skills of Chadric, Audrite, and the young woman who had taken command of the boat that would have been Ludhil's. But it had been a near thing just the same. Now they were on one of the Small Islands, it was full daylight, and they were only waiting for Meath to weave sun in the direction of Radzyn Keep and help.

He wished he could oblige. The only ships he'd ever been on were the sleek cargo vessels that took silk and pearls to the continent. He had never been sick like this in his life. His head felt ready to burst and every muscle in his body had twisted. He squinted into the warm sun dappling his face and beseeched the Goddess for strength. No Sunrunners ever died crossing water—they only wished they could.

Every breath hurt. He managed to get one elbow beneath him and lift his head. There was a girl nearby sitting watch over him. The sun shining on her hair turned it almost red-gold.

"Sioned?" he tried to say. But the sun exploded and he knew nothing more.

* * *

Evarin studied Andry's face carefully. "No, not yet, my Lord," he said with regret. "The eyes are still yours, and the chin is all wrong."

"Do you spend that much time staring in the mirror?" Andry grinned at him. "I never thought you so vain."

"Or pretty enough to gaze at myself in awestruck wonder," the young physician retorted lightly. "But it's the face I shave every morning, and, though ill-favored, my own. Now, narrower through the jaw, and concentrate harder on the eyes."

Riding was so instinctive that Andry didn't even have to think about controlling his horse, especially through the soft hills of Ossetia that rose in green-gold radiance beneath his mount's hooves. If only he could find the same effortless control over the spell he was attempting, he would count the day almost perfect. It was a fine, breezy autumn morning and they had made good time from Goddess Keep, using shortcuts that often bypassed the main road. A brief foray on the early sun had shown Andry that his mother was awake, sitting up, and glaring at Rohan, who had evidently taken it into his head to feed her her breakfast. The stubborn determination on both faces and the knowledge that she was recovering had made Andry laugh aloud. It was with a lighter heart and a smile on his face that he had set out today, and the ease of mind had prompted him to have Evarin teach him the shape-changing trick.

He was not a success. His features stayed his own. The Master Physician corrected and encouraged, but the likeness was not a good one. At last Evarin sighed and shook his head. "It's as if I'm looking into a mirror cast with a spell that will show only you—trying to match up the faces."

Andry relaxed his efforts and rubbed his forehead. The strain had begun to give him a headache. "I wonder if this trick would fool that mirror of mine. We'll have to try it one of these days."

"I don't think it would be confused. It identifies a person's colors, after all, not faces. And if you'll forgive my saying so, my Lord, this isn't a 'trick.' It has vast potential."

"True. But I don't know any woman I'd like to fool into thinking I'm her husband in order to charm my way into her bed."

Evarin laughed. "To which I'm supposed to reply, 'You'd never need to!' "

"Always tender of my conceit!" Andry grinned. "But admit it, this is just a trick for now, like my mirror. I've yet to figure out a use for the thing."

Evarin ducked a branch as they turned into a small wood. "It's a pity no more were found."

"I could still throttle Chiana for shattering the one Mireva used on her. But I suppose it wasn't her fault."

"There's nothing in any of the scrolls that mentions mirrors?"

"Not a single word. It's as if Lady Merisel didn't know they existed. I'd give a lot to find out how they work—but most of all how to make them."

"It makes me nervous even to think about it," Evarin admitted frankly. "But I know what kind of mirror I'd make—one to show exactly what was wrong with someone before the first hint of a complaint." He paused to let Andry precede him through a narrow passage between trees. "Imagine it, my Lord—knowing in advance about a canker or a rotting tooth before it began to hurt, when I could *do* something about it. I wouldn't have to rely on a faraway Sunrunner's observations and then make my judgment. I'd just say the name of the patient and see for myself."

Andry smiled at him. "Your idea of power is very simple, isn't it? A mirror of benefit to all. It wouldn't be that way with others. Which leads me to think that perhaps Merisel *did* know about mirrors, and deliberately suppressed the knowledge. She seems to have done that quite a lot."

"What sort of mirror would *you* make, my Lord?"

He considered. "I don't know. Perhaps—"

He never finished the thought, reining in so abruptly that his startled horse went back on its haunches. Down below, in a fold of the hills where the Pyrme River marked the border with Syr, a farmhouse roof was burning.

"Gentle Goddess! Quickly, my Lord, there may be someone who needs help—"

"No," Andry breathed. "Look at the doors and windows."

Rails torn from a nearby fence had been nailed across the entrance; the shutters were similarly barred. Smoke slithered from the sills, and as fire ate wood from the inside the gray-black tendrils grew to billowing clouds. Andry had been present at enough funeral rites to know the smell of scorching flesh. And this had no herbs or oils to disguise it.

"There's no one alive down there," he whispered, caught by horrified fascination. "They were deliberately trapped within and the house torched."

"But by whom? To what purpose? Prince Kostas can have

no quarrel with Prince Tilal! They're brothers!" Then Evarin gasped. "My Lord! Look!"

Moving north along the river was a group of armed men, their swords and shields and spears dancing with sunlight. Andry counted a hundred, over half on horseback. The colors carried on a pole before them were unknown to Andry—deep greenish blue like the sea, crossed with two vertical stripes of blood red. But the faces were familiar enough to stop the breath in his throat: dark faces wearing beards decorated with small golden beads. *One for each kill,* he thought dully. *One for each enemy slain.*

And how great a prize would be the Lord of Goddess Keep.

Outrun them? Tibaza was one of his father's stallions, quick and canny, and they had only Kadar breed. But their mounts were fresh; Tibaza had several days of hard travel behind him. And the carnage down below told him something extremely important: no one was being left alive. If they caught sight of him and gave chase, he trusted his horse's great heart and speed—but they would not rest until they found him. Better to escape notice, hide, and give warning. His eyes ached with the memory of Radzyn in flames.

Reining his horse around, he plunged back into the shadowy depths of the wood. Evarin followed. Andry hoped the enemy was far enough away not to hear—every twig that cracked beneath the horses' hooves seemed horribly loud to him. The words of Jolan's evening song came to him, an urgent plea to the Goddess now, not a pretty ceremony: *Lady, protect us from the dark time of night.*

* * *

What would my father have done?

The question haunted Chadric. Fortunately for his ability to function—not his peace of mind, he would never have that again and he knew it—his father's spirit did not haunt him. There was no gruff voice on the morning wind, no glimpse of aged eyes, faded but sharp, to pass scathing judgment. If there had been, he was certain he would have put his head in his hands and wept.

Meath had spoken of the old prince back at Graypearl. "Your father was never one to belabor the obvious, my

prince. Stop castigating yourself. Lleyn would have agreed that this is the only course open to us."

Chadric had hoped his self-loathing was more or less concealed. But Meath had been a student of Lady Andrade, she who had taught her *faradh'im* to read faces as easily as the pages of a manuscript.

Chadric sat apart from the others on the narrow beach, waiting for the sun to dry his salt-stiff garments, hoping that no one, not even his wife, would approach him. There was a certain solace in solitude right now. But it also left him alone with his thoughts.

The huge ships had birthed scores of smaller boats. From these the invaders swarmed up to the port and Graypearl itself. His lovely jewel box of a palace was not made for defense; it had never had need of defending. Knowing that if the port fell, the palace would be next, he sent his guards down to join the townfolk in fighting for their homes. Had he been even ten years younger, he would have joined them. He would have stayed, would have fought beside his people. But there was no place from which to fight. He had been a squire under Prince Zehava, a warlord who had forgotten more about armed conflict than anyone else had ever learned. Zehava had taught him how to take and how to defend, but not even he could have held this palace that was not built for war. Chadric had gallant people and brave guards and not enough of either to make a victory. Besides, he was too old. It had been fifty years since he'd raised a sword beside Zehava in battle against the Merida. Only a fool would stay.

It was Audrite who proposed Sandeia, snuggled in a cove on the southwestern coast of the island. There they could be safe, she said. They could take as many with them as there were horses in the stables. They could wait there for help to come, make a place for their people to rally.

So they mounted horses half-crazed with the smell of smoke drifting up from the port, and fled. The road to Sandeia was a familiar one to Chadric, even at night; it took him back to the rainy spring he'd spent convincing Audrite to marry him. Each morning he'd ridden to Sandeia, painfully aware of her father's decision that at the *Rialla* she would Choose her husband. Every bend in the road, every view of the sea between hills held memory of some persuasive speech formed during the day, some curse hurled against

himself that evening for not saying it right. But one afternoon she accepted him, and the next morning they rode back to Graypearl together.

They would never ride this way again, he thought as the measures lengthened behind him. He looked back only once. Graypearl was hidden, but the glow of fire was not.

"Don't, love," she had murmured beside him. "It will only hurt worse."

"It can't hurt any worse," he answered, and they rode on.

He had spoken too quickly. Sandeia offered no refuge. It was ablaze from granary to manor house. The anguish in his wife's eyes as her childhood home went up in flames hurt Chadric even more than the loss of Graypearl.

But the nearby cove and its sailboats had not been discovered. On the steep climb down the cliff Chadric fought a private battle with himself. It was the duty of a prince to protect and lead his people. He had failed miserably at the former—through no fault of his own, others would say. But he could still lead them to safety or against the enemy. He knew his people; never would they submit. Since the long-ago days when *faradh'im* had dwelled exclusively on the island, giving it a protection even more potent than that of the princes who ruled later, the proud and independent Dorvali had considered themselves above the petty conflicts regularly suffered elsewhere. None would meekly bend the knee to a conqueror. They would fight—not in the kind of battle Chadric had learned in his youth, but with stealth and cunning. He was too old to fight beside them, but he could be their symbol, their rallying point.

The foolish delusions of an old man, he realized now, narrowing his eyes to stare out across the channel. By daylight he could not see the flames he knew must still be burning. There was smoke, though, a grayish haze carried by the wind. He could do nothing but wait for Meath to recover and spin sunlight. Wait for Chay to send a ship from Radzyn. Wait for the blow to fall there—if it hadn't already.

I'm too old, he thought. *It galls me to admit it, but it's true. What's worse, I'm not the only one who'll realize that in the next days. Chay, Rohan, Volog—we're all of us too old. It's our sons who'll do the fighting.*

He watched the island until his eyes burned, as if to catch sight of his own son. Ludhil was a student of the world around him, not of war. He knew the meaning of the wind

and the currents in the sea and the ring-patterns in a felled pine; his careful, scholarly books were in the scriptorium on Kierst and in Rohan's own library. Chadric and Audrite had not raised him to be a warrior. But that was what events would make of him. He had only his long-ago squire's training to guide him, and he would have to use it well—or die. *I knew he'd stay, and his Iliena with him. From the moment he forbade it to me, I knew he'd do it himself. As a prince should. Fight well, my son. And forgive me for being too old to fight alongside you.*

* * *

Every instinct screamed for movement, action, flight. Andry forced himself to sit motionless, willing the enemy to look anyplace but where he huddled in the sparse cover of a glade. The soldiers along the Pyrme River had been only the first of the patrols he and Evarin saw that morning.

They had managed to avoid detection thus far. But they had not gained open sun long enough to weave light. The one time Andry had risked it, Evarin shook his arm to bring him back before he was halfway to Radzyn. Troops had come over a rise, and they were forced to melt back among the trees.

Andry had decided to head south, where the enemy had already been—a tactic that appalled his companion.

"I beg your pardon, my Lord, truly I do, but is this wise?"

"How long have you known me, Evarin?" Andry had asked.

"Three years, my Lord. But what has that to do—"

"One thing you must learn about me is that I loathe doing the expected thing. I get it from both sides: Andrade and my grandsire Zehava were exactly alike in that, if in nothing else. Anyone fleeing would logically go north, trying to outrun these vermin. Therefore we will head south." Evarin gaped. Andry gave him a tight smile. "It's not as insane as it sounds. They seem intent on obliteration, so I'm assuming they've left absolutely nothing behind them."

Suddenly the young physician's face showed both comprehension and horror. "Why should they stay to guard what's not there anymore—"

"It'll make grim viewing."

He was right about that—but wrong about the rest of it. In retrospect, he cursed himself for not slipping past the first group and riding east for all he was worth; the countryside was thick with patrols. They rode horses blanketed in the colors of Gilad Seahold—horses he could not outrun. Lord Segelin's liking for the Radzyn breed had provided the enemy with splendid mounts. Andry evaded them by riding through long measures of safe, deep forest. The sun taunted him, speckling the foliage with dancing gold he dared not use. He needed full sunlight.

Almost as great as his need was his fear of what he would see when his weavings took him to his childhood home. A ruined castle already in flames? A battle in progress, that he was too late to warn about? And what of the coast between Radzyn and Gilad Seahold, obviously fallen? Brenlis' family lived at the mouth of the Faolain. Was that farmhouse a smoldering husk, too?

At last, only a little while ago, he had gained a few free moments. The woods thinned as they descended a little hill, and below was a scene exactly like a dozen glimpsed along their way. Flames rose from the burnt-out shells of a home and outbuildings nestled in a fold of the hills. A plow-elk had escaped the barn. It was elderly, thin-shouldered, undoubtedly a family pet that fondness had kept from the slaughter now that it was too old to work. The silvered hide was singed and oozing, but the elk limped across a stubbled field as if in harness. For some reason this moved Andry as nothing else that day. He bit his lip until he could convince himself that the tears in his eyes were due only to the blood salting his tongue.

"My Lord!" Evarin hissed suddenly.

They had come within heartbeats of riding straight into an enemy patrol as it descended the opposite hill.

So now they sat their weary horses, helpless for the foreseeable future, and watched as the elk was carved up in laughing sword practice. They dared not slink back into the wood; any movement might alert those below. Andry wanted nothing more than to use the sunlight and slaughter them, toy with them as cruelly as they sliced into that pathetic animal.

"I can't kill them," he murmured. "Goddess knows I want to. But if I missed even one, the others would ride after us and we'd die. And of all people, I'm the one who

cannot be lost." He spoke without arrogance, without anything but knowledge of the simple fact of it.

Evarin kept his voice low. "We may be able to get some clear sunlight soon, my Lord."

"I just hope there's someone left at Radzyn to answer." He shivered. "Even now it may be too late."

"You! Tree-hidden!" The harsh voice shouted from behind him, deeper in the forest. Andry nearly fell out of his saddle. "Stay!"

The man spoke the old tongue—strangely accented, slurred where Andry would have given crisp pronunciation, but understandable and even familiar. He was fascinated by the changes wrought by centuries, but scholarly curiosity would cost him his life right now. He kept himself from turning to face the men who spoke a language outlawed on the continent for more than three hundred years.

The language of sorcerers.

Evarin tore off his riding gloves and began wrenching the eight rings from his fingers. "Quickly, my Lord!' he whispered. "All of them—the armbands too! You know enough to work the spell—hurry!"

Dark hair, dark eyes, and a beard with a dozen small golden beads worked in—Evarin's face was already changing. Andry slid rings and cuffs in a pocket and replaced his leather gauntlets. "Put your gloves back on—they'll see the paler circles on your fingers otherwise."

Evarin caught his breath, and jammed his trembling fingers into the gloves. "I'll talk you through it," he whispered. "Just as we practiced earlier. Black hair, dark brown eyes—see it in your mind, make the illusion real—"

Branches snapped like brittle bones under approaching hoofbeats. Maddening distraction. If he failed, perhaps Evarin could claim him as a prisoner. The younger man's illusion was perfect, almost effortless. Andry struggled, his heart pounding. As Rusina had said, it was much like weaving the guise of the Goddess around himself for a maiden's first-night. But this was no vague, concealing haze. This had to be precise. He had no mirror, only Evarin—but when the physician nodded quickly, Andry knew he had done it.

Together they turned to confront the ten mounted soldiers. One of them saluted by slapping his open left palm to the center of his chest. His beard was blue-black in the dappled sunlight. Andry counted ten gold beads. The others

wore no more than five, and two of them were beardless—not from youth but from application of a razor. Andry suddenly guessed that only with a kill could a man grow his beard and weave into it tokens of prowess. The relatively low rank displayed by these men at once eased his mind and worried him; his own habit of command might impress them so that he might get away with this, but they would also be eager to earn those gold beads. He wondered suddenly how many illusory tokens he had woven into his own illusory beard, and for a frantic instant could not remember. A slightly hysterical thought crossed his mind that his conceit had better be operating at full tilt. He had to outrank the leader or all was lost.

"My lord, we report." The man's right hand stayed on his sword.

Goddess in glory, Andry thought, *I really do understand him!* The man had said *tir'ri*: the personal possessive combined with the word for "lord" that survived in *athri*. He hastily returned the salute, noting that use of the left hand created freedom to strike a blow with the sword gripped in the right even while gesturing respect and friendship. And, oh, Goddess—what about his own sword? As if hearing his thought, the warrior glanced at the fine blade sheathed at Andry's side. As a highborn, he wore it as a token of his rank, and it had too many jewels. It was a ceremonial piece only, for who would dare assault a Sunrunner—whose rings were protection enough—let alone the Lord of Goddess Keep? Andry barely knew how to use the thing and for the first time in his life cursed himself for not completing the training for knighthood.

He shoved that thought aside, too, and concentrated on translating the man's fractured speech. There were little tricks of the tongue to it that grated on his nerves even more than on his ears—but he caught the gist of it.

"A beauty, my lord," the soldier said, nodding at the sword. "Spoil of Seahold? Wish we there!"

Andry replied with a nod, trying not to look relieved at the ease of his escape from what could have been a tricky explanation. And he had been recognized as someone of high rank, even a lord; that was excellent. He thanked the Goddess for his luck and beseeched her for inspiration.

It came in the form of a respectful question. "War sights good, my lord?"

"Very. Your report." Andry adjusted his accent to match what he had thus far heard. From the lack of reaction, he was a success.

"Thirty-seven kills, my lord, witnessed." He hooked a thumb over his shoulder at the beardless men. "Warriors at last."

Numbers were easy; *deg'im* gave him pause and he purposely relaxed so the word would come as automatically as when he listened to the sung rituals. Of course: plural of "kill." Simple, too, were the words for "witness" and "warriors"—*vaman* and *ros'im.* Absurd to congratulate himself on his linguistic skills. He had to get himself and Evarin out of here. Choosing his words from ones read in the scrolls, and with care to the slurring required, he said, *"Fey tiel, paliros'im."* Bold victory, clever warriors.

The man looked pleased. "Gracious my lord. Our duty. Woods watch until night. My honor is yours, my lord, if escapes."

So these butchers valued their honor, did they? Andry's guts churned as he remembered farms in ashes. What honor was there in such slaughter? *Why are these people here?* But he knew. Their speech, their dark Merida-like faces—they had come to destroy the continent they had lost so long ago.

But warriors respected strength and a commanding presence. It was time he displayed a little of both. "Excuse for challenging me?" Andry snapped.

The man blanched satisfyingly and his troops looked nervous. "Bad woods light, my lord."

"Truth, my lord," Evarin pointed out in a bad imitation of Andry's accent. "Be anyone, this light."

"Warrior speaks truth, my lord."

Andry shrugged, pretending to be mollified, hoping he was hiding near heart failure at hearing Evarin speak in the old language. "Caution good. Maybe spies—even *faradh'im.*"

To a man they spat on the ground. To a man their eyes grew narrow and fierce with hate. Andry nodded slowly. *So. I'm right. The vision was true.*

"Know to kill them, my lord! Any seen? Reason secret watch?"

"Why I watch, my business. Continue work." He gathered the reins, suddenly needing to be far away from here. Disguised or not, he was a Sunrunner and not insensible to the death of his kind promised in these men's eyes.

"My lord," the man said, bowing. "Honor to ride with us?"

Horrible question. To refuse without good answer would give them away. To go along would be an impossible strain. Andry didn't know how long he could support this spell; already he felt his muscles drawing tighter and tighter with tension. *Think!* he ordered himself. These warriors probably wanted a witness of high rank to attest to their kills. The idea of watching while they immolated another family—or, worse, being forced to participate in it—nearly made him vomit. *How I'd love to kill you,* he thought with longing as he pretended to consider the request. *But I can't. Not yet. Someone sent you out, and while you wouldn't be missed until nightfall, I can't take the chance.*

And he was taking too long to reply.

"We ride on," Evarin said.

The warrior's brow furrowed, but just as quickly he smiled. "Outer Isles speech! Talkmusic no more yours, my lord," he added generously to Andry.

Talkmusic—? Accent, the man was complimenting him on losing his Outer Isles accent. Andry's head was beginning to spin.

"Deep respect *aprus* when my lord returns *Azhchay.*"

For an instant Andry thought he'd used Rohan's other title—*azhrei.* But then he heard the difference, the final syllable that was his father's name. "Dragonhawk"—had they renamed their conquests already?

Then he recognized the other word: leader of a ship. Lady Merisel had used it in her histories. The visions swirled in his mind. Bearded men with bloodied swords, captives chained together on the beach below Radzyn—and dragon-headed ships. *Azhchay* was one of those ships. He could see them, smell salt and death, hear the screams—

Evarin's horse suddenly shied to the left, drawing all eyes, startling Andry from his trance. He got hold of himself and said, "Beautiful horse, but trouble! Home different, eh?"

"Father-thanks for spirit! Swift, strong—wind-mated! Victory horses, no matter bone-breaks!" He grinned and slapped the sleek neck of his Radzyn-bred mare. If his sword had been in his hand, Andry would have run him through.

He made himself ask, "Radzyn word today?"

The soldier acquired the look worn by people who have just heard a superior make an uncharacteristic mistake—too

respectful to show surprise openly, yet surprised just the same. "No, my lord," he said carefully, gaze flickering from Andry to Evarin. "Tomorrow."

Had he been standing instead of in the saddle, his weakened knees would have given him away. Radzyn was safe—for now. But the man's suspicion had been roused.

"Oh, my lord, Rathvin meant," Evarin said. "Names confused."

Andry grabbed the desperate cue and growled, "I know no difference?"

The physician made just the right face of frightened apology, which seemed to satisfy the enemy. Andry could not afford to linger and make another mistake. He grunted and gathered the reins. "All soon know success here." He saluted and guided Tibaza from the clearing. Evarin followed. It was too quick; they both knew it was too quick. They should have stayed longer. The similarity of names was a flimsy story—no warrior who had planned this invasion for years would confuse Radzyn, gem of the Desert, with any other holding. He felt eyes on his back like the pricking of knives as they rode from the forest into the open.

"I thought we were dead," Evarin muttered.

"So did I. I think we still might be." He flexed his hands; the palms of his gauntlets were soaked with sweat. "That was fast, Evarin. Where's Rathwin?"

"Rath*vin*. About thirty measures up the Catha, my Lord. I'm from these parts, remember."

"Thank the Goddess for whoever named it Rathvin!" Andry resisted the impulse to glance over his shoulder. "I started to lose it, didn't I?" He gestured to his face.

"Yes. That's why I had to dig a heel into my friend here." He stroked the gelding's flank. "Sorry, old son."

"Is it holding? Yours hasn't slipped at all."

"You're fine. But neither of us can keep at it much longer. Not without *dranath*."

"We become safer with every pace down this hill. I wish I dared a gallop."

"After all this picking through the trees, the horses would welcome it."

"Isulk, andraa—gev'im iseni." Andry softly quoted the warrior's praise of his father's beloved horses, captive between the thighs of these twice-damned enemies—Merida and sorcerer-sent. "Horses are why they'll attack Radzyn.

I've got to be able to work, Evarin. I've got to warn them." His hands ached for his rings.

The physician turned and waved. "The others are still in sight, my Lord. Damn! One of them's riding down to us!"

Four beads decorated the soldier's straggly young beard. He saluted smartly and said, "My lord, escort accept, I beg. Enemy hides."

Andry was sure then that he was suspect. But it hardly mattered. He forced himself to laugh. "Enemy? Peasants in hovels?"

"Lord's safety, my honor. Father-forbid any *faradh'im*—" He spat on the ground; a real ritual with these folk, Andry noted sourly. He knew that he should copy it. He could not.

Instead he demanded angrily, "Am I child, needing your sword? Return!"

"My lord, cannot. Orders—"

Evarin gave him a glance that said, *We're stuck with him.* Andry was compelled to agree.

"Ride ahead." *So that if I slip again, you won't see it. But I suffer your presence only until the first convenient place to kill you. They won't miss one in the hundreds, perhaps thousands, they've landed here.*

Have they already landed at Radzyn?

Gentle Lady, protect us from this dark time of night.

* * *

Tobin kept her eyes closed, drifting with Betheyn's soft, soothing voice as the young woman read to her. The autumn sun was soft on her cheeks and brow, reassurance of life. Until Sioned had come and she was taken into the sunlight, she had been afraid she would spend the rest of her life trapped and helpless within her own skull, a million things left undone—and, worse, unsaid.

She quelled panic and concentrated on the warmth suffusing her face and body. Chay had ordered the bed moved near the windows so that she might use light whenever she wished. Last night he'd caught her staying awake too late, and she'd been unable to tell him she'd been waiting for him to come to her so she could listen to his voice and watch the moons' silvery radiance on his face. Listening and watching were two of the three activities permitted her in convalescence. The third was sleeping—and she was still afraid of

that. Afraid she might not wake up again. But she would never have told him that, not even if she had been able.

Tobin had never been sick a day in her life. The Plague had spared her; childbirth had been absurdly easy considering her delicate frame; not even the wound in her thigh, that had left her with a limp as souvenir of the long-ago siege of Stronghold, had confined her to bed for more than a day. Sioned had warned her that speech and strength would be slow in returning, and she ought not push herself. But enforced inactivity was shredding her nerves.

Yesterday afternoon Rohan had read to her from a stultifying text on botany. Unlike their mother, who had created the gardens at Stronghold, Tobin cared nothing about plants. Neither did Rohan. His design had been to bore her to sleep; he succeeded only in irritating her. Glancing up at last from an interminable passage on rose roots to find her glaring silently at him, he had looked so naughty and guilty and silly that laughter had happened to her for the first time since her illness. More of a croak than a giggle, still her brother had greeted it with a delighted grin.

Today Betheyn was reading something infinitely more interesting: one of five gorgeous illuminated copies of Feylin's masterwork *On Dragons*, a present from Prince Volog. The author had one, and Rohan, and Pol, and one had been kept for the scriptorium. Ten more existed, but with simple line drawings instead of colored pictures. Tobin was proud that Maarken's sketches of dragon anatomy had been used extensively for the book. Tilal's daughter Sioneva had contributed drawings, too, showing a talent completely new in the Kierstian royal family. Sioned, wide-eyed at her namesake's skill, had remarked that nobody else of her blood had ever been able to draw a straight line with a ruler.

Tobin had looked through the book to admire the paintings, but had not had time since the *Rialla* to study the text. Betheyn would much rather have been reading an architectural treatise—an interest they shared—but knew how eager Tobin was to hear the contents of this extraordinary book. Feylin's lifelong fascination with dragons, even though she was cordially terrified of them, had produced the first scientific discussion of everything known about the creatures, with particular attention given to scoffing at foolish legends.

The first fallacy about dragons is that they are fond

of human flesh. Put a human in with a cow, a deer, an elk, a sheep, and a goat, and the dragon will invariably choose the sheep for dinner. Second choice appears to be deer or cattle. Elk and goats are favored only by very hungry dragons. There are tales of capture and feasting off humans, but all these can be explained (see chapters on Mating; Hatching Hunt; Famine).

Betheyn looked up. "I wonder who she volunteered for *that* experiment! Do you want me to continue with this, instead of looking up those chapters?"

They had devised a system of *yes* and *no*: Tobin's closed left hand indicated the latter, and an open palm meant the former. Today she managed a nod as well. Betheyn smiled.

"Good—this is the most interesting part. I can't wait until she tells why dragon's teeth are supposed to be magic. One story says if they're planted, trees will spring up. Another substitutes warriors for trees, and a third says the ground will be poisoned by them. My father once told me never to trust any superstition that isn't consistent."

Tobin felt a grin lift half her face. It still frightened her to sense it, and she knew there was good reason she had not been allowed a mirror. But it seemed that every time she used the muscles to smile or frown or try to form a word, she had a little more control over them. It was the same with wiggling her fingers and toes, moving her knee, raising her arm. She was still numb in many places, and recovery would be slow, but, by the Goddess, she *would* recover.

Betheyn resumed reading, the smile hovering around her lips.

As for the notion that princesses and/or virgins are a dragon's preferred meal, I suspect this to be a "warning" that takes on added significance when a dragon is said to be involved. Probably the disappearance of some young girl—virgin, princess, or both—was attributed to dragons. Popular lore is fraught with examples of ordinary, if tragic, occurrences blamed without reason on dragons. I have known several princesses and many virgins, most of them having had much to do with dragons in everyday life, and none have ever been accosted, let alone devoured.

"Am I to understand that no hungry dragons hovered outside your windows before you married?" Beth gave a sigh of comical disappointment.

A princess Tobin had been all her life; she had disqualified herself for the virgin part of it not long after she'd first set eyes on Chay. The memory brought another smile to her face.

It is further said that an angry dragon may be soothed by the sacrifice of a virgin, or a princess, or a princess who is a virgin. Happily, this legend has not been acted upon in many hundreds of years, probably due to this uncertainty about the nature of the offering. Dragons grow angry for two reasons: when their caves are fouled and when their hatchlings are killed. We would not much like it, either, if our dwellings were ransacked or our children butchered. Princesses, virgins, and/or virgin princesses would seem to be safe as long as we accord dragons the courtesy of leaving their homes and their offspring alone.

Betheyn chuckled. "I can just hear Feylin now, with that dry voice of hers! She must have had a fabulous time writing this—she sounds like a schoolmaster rapping knuckles for believing such nonsense."

Tobin wished that Betheyn was gifted in the Sunrunner way; they could have had a lively discussion of Feylin's sense of humor. It was infuriating not to be able to indulge in the pleasures of conversation, but she had to be patient. Speech would come back.

Another wickedness attributed to dragons is that their blood is poisonous. Experiments conducted on several animals have proved this to be entirely false.

"The difficulty being, of course, trying to get a goat to drink the stuff," Betheyn commented. "Remember when she told us about it? I laughed so hard I thought I'd suffocate!"

Recalling the hilarious account of Walvis' flat refusal to quaff a little dragon blood in the name of science, Tobin laughed. She winced at the sound. Beth looked startled for a moment, then hastily smoothed her expression. Tobin

closed her eyes once again as Feylin's tart refutations of dragon legends were read to her, slowly losing track of them as Beth's soft voice and the warm sunlight lulled her nearly to sleep.

Goddess greeting, my lady.

She thought for a moment that it was a dream. Recognizing Meath, she wove golden skeins and replied courteously to his salute. With her eyes closed she could almost see his face, formed of the glowing colors of his mind. But there was darkness shading them, and for all the habitual gentleness of his approach, she sensed urgency.

Then there was another voice, more powerful, the shades of amber and amethyst and ruby burning like flames. *Mother!*

She certainly was popular today with Sunrunners, she thought. First Meath, now Andry. . . .

Mother, listen to me!

There seemed to be some sort of argument going on between them. It was very confusing. They both seemed to need her with a bleak desperation that she must be imagining. In her present state, how could she possibly help them? She hovered away from the pair, trying to analyze the tenor of their colors as they grew more intense, both patterns now ablaze, painful even though she was removed from them.

"Tobin?"

Betheyn was touching her arm and the contact broke her concentration. She opened her eyes and tried to speak, but all that emerged from her lips was a meaningless grunt. But even as she looked up into the young woman's face, Andry took hold of her so forcefully that she cried out.

Mother—forgive me. You must listen. Riverport and Seahold and Graypearl are destroyed.

This made no sense. Invasion, fire, blood, destruction on a scale unimaginable—and death everywhere. Scenes of rich farms in flames were hazed about with Andry's fierce colors; Graypearl and Sandeia in ruins were tinged by the green-blue-gold that was Meath. She saw what they had seen, filtered through their identities. Her mind simply could not accept it.

It's all true, it's real—and Radzyn is next! You must get Sioned or Maarken or Hollis—they're none of them in the sunlight. Mother, hurry!

"Tobin!"

Beth's voice and touch again pulled her away. She heard

her own gasping breaths. A wine cup was held to her lips; she smelled herbs in it that would bring sleep and turned her head away.

"Sioned," she tried to say. She ordered her mouth to form the name. Could not. Furious at her body's weakness, she gripped Betheyn's hand with her left hand and glared up into worried eyes. "Pol," she said, and the single syllable was recognizable at last.

"I'll find him," Betheyn said, and hurried away, calling for Tobren to keep watch while she was gone.

Andry—Meath—what is this, who are they, why is this happening? The questions tumbled over and over in her mind, but there was no answer. *Andry! Tell me what this means!*

Her granddaughter Tobren appeared beside the bed, white-faced and frightened. She tried to offer the drugged wine; in a sudden access of strength she could not control, Tobin flung out her hand and slapped it away, staining the coverlet blood-red.

"Grandmother?" Tobren whispered. "Oh, Grandmother, please—"

She saw her namesake through a haze of angry, frustrated tears. Damn her traitorous body, damn damn *damn*—

Pol ran into the room, Rohan and Chay just behind him. Tobin groped for her nephew's hand, tried to pull him farther into the sunlight. When it was shining on his fair head, she saw his face go blank and blind.

Sobbing with relief, she sank back into the pillows, scarcely noticing as husband and brother fussed helplessly over her. Pol's colors shimmered about his head, eclipsing even Andry's until she marveled that neither Chay nor Rohan could see them.

The sightless blue-green eyes suddenly widened. "No," he whispered, and his fingers tightened around hers until she nearly cried out.

He told the others, swift words that cut deep and left behind stunned horror. Chay was on the move at once, racing from the bedchamber, shouting orders. Rohan stood still, staring at his son. Tobin's gaze flickered from face to face, seeing their hearts in their eyes. Pol was angry with a killing rage. But Rohan—Rohan was in pain. The wounds done to his people and to the land were wounds to his own flesh. She had seen this in him before, years ago, seen him

lead an army while he bled inside. Sioned had told her once that Rohan swallowed Fire, his own mind and heart a battleground, and it was only his terrible strength that prevented his being consumed. But Pol was different. He met Fire with a blaze of his own, the fury that now ignited his eyes and set his colors burning all around him. Pol *became* Fire.

Chapter Nine

Meath kept his eyes closed for some time after returning from Radzyn—not so much because he was exhausted, although he was, but because he was angry.

"Meath? Are you all right?"

It was a very young voice, very soft. He squinted up at a face framed in a cloud of red-gold hair. The girl touched his cheek gently and again he thought, *Sioned*. But it was not she. Alleyn, Ludhil and Iliena's daughter, wiped his brow with a damp cloth. Audran knelt beside his sister, both children watching with held breath. Meath smiled in reassurance.

"Lord Chaynal is sending a ship for us—a *real* ship, one to be comfortable in. Or, rather, one *you* can be comfortable in." He gave a comical grimace meant to bring answering smiles.

Alleyn regarded him gravely. "It hurt you, didn't it, Meath? Sunrunning."

"Not the work itself," he replied, more or less honestly. "It's a strain when I'm tired like this, but it doesn't hurt."

She pushed tangled hair from her face. It had long since come loose from its tidy braids, and in the sun shone with coppery and golden lights. Suddenly he *did* hurt, for the sight of this dainty little princess with her hair all awry and her clothes stained with salt water and mud. Petted and protected for all her thirteen winters, the world had abruptly shown Alleyn its worst face. Her home was ashes, her father and mother gone to war, her whole life disrupted.

But she was alive. Hundreds of other children were not. He concealed the anguish that would only weaken him, and glanced at Audran. The boy was round-eyed and silent, and when Meath looked at him he lowered his gaze to the sand in front of him.

"Audran? What is it, my prince?" Meath asked gently.

"Nothing."

"If you tell me, perhaps it can be mended." He nearly bit his lip at the futility of that statement. The only way to mend these children's world was to deal out more death. Remembering scenes glimpsed in Andry's memories, he began to think he would enjoy breaking his *faradhi* vow not to kill with his gifts.

Audran cast a quick look at his sister. She frowned and shook her head. To Meath, the boy said, "I'm just hungry. Is Lord Chaynal's ship coming soon?"

"Very soon. And I'd better go report the same to your grandsir." He knew the child had lied to him. He also knew he should not press for the truth. Rising stiff-kneed to his feet, he went to where Chadric sat gazing out at the sea with empty eyes. Meath crouched beside him.

"My lord," he said in a soft voice, "help is coming soon from Radzyn."

The prince nodded. "And?"

"My lord?"

"There is more, my old friend." Chadric had not even looked at him.

Meath knew there was nothing for it but to tell it all. "We are not alone in our losses—but we have our lives. Many do not. Syr and Gilad and the Desert have been invaded. Seahold and Riverport are rubble. Soldiers march up the river valleys laying waste to everything they see."

Chadric took up a driftwood stick and began drawing on the sand—idly, Meath thought for a moment, until he recognized the outlines of the continent's southern coast. When the rough map was finished, Chadric spoke again.

"Radzyn is next."

"Lord Andry fears so. They are preparing for war even now."

"And yet Chay sends rescue for us." Finally the prince looked at him. "Are you strong enough to go to Graypearl and see their preparations? They have had most of a day, after all."

Meath nodded, cursed himself for not having done it before, and sent a light-weave across the narrow sea.

Smoke billowed from the palace and the town below it. Bearded dark men were working very hard to keep the flames from spreading to the docks, which they would need

for their own ships. At Graypearl itself, soldiers swarmed with cold systematic method through the gardens, slashing every bush to the root and hacking tree trunks clean through. There was no looting of the palace's treasures, not even the taking of foodstuffs. Meath hovered closer to make sure, seeing through the collapsed kitchen wall that stores had been left to burn. As he understood war, it was waged for conquest, for revenge, but most of all for possession. Why capture a place if not to profit by what it contained?

He returned his attention to the gardens, and saw what he had most feared. The oratory was blackened, burnt out, its glass in shards after exploding from the heat of the fire. The men approached it slowly, with something of dread in their eyes until one of them picked up a stone and threw it. Fragments of glass shattered. In an instant the rest rushed over the little bridge and began digging their swords into tiles already damaged by fire.

Meath could not bear to watch any more. He set himself to an inspection of the little port, and found a thread of comfort when he saw that whenever one fire threatening the docks was put out, another sprang up almost immediately somewhere else. Someone understood that the place could not be left whole for enemy use. Someone worked with incredible stealth to set those new fires; Meath saw no one, as hard as he searched. He saluted them silently, and even tried to help a little, but the distance was great and he had never been much good at faraway workings. The unseen defenders must do it all on their own.

Then something else occurred to him. There were no corpses. None of the Graypearl dead were visible. He sought through palace and port, seeing only the tall, fierce men with golden beads braided into their beards. No survivors. He wanted to believe all had escaped yet knew this was impossible. Where were they?

Movement on the beach outside town caught his attention. A dark heap he had at first glance taken for piled driftwood suddenly took on other shapes, other colors: the black and gray and brown and blue of concealing cloaks. But there were also bare, blistered arms and legs; charred faces; dead staring eyes. A clean-shaven man wearing elaborate robes and a towering headpiece that was half-helmet, half-crown strode across the beach to the stacked bodies, his lips moving in rapid speech. He threw fistfuls of sand onto

the corpses and flung his head back with his mouth open in a triumphant howl. As last he lit a torch and set fire to the dead.

Flames caught on silk and thin wool and something —someone—moved.

Meath fled the island, sick with pain. He turned west down woven sunlight to Gilad. Lord Segelin's castle was a gutted ruin. There were no dead piled here, no remnants of a ritual pyre. It was as if Seahold had been empty for generations. It was the same for many measures inland, and the same at Faolain Riverport—and it was elementary strategy that it would soon be the same at Lowland as well. He fled over the farmlands between the river and Radzyn, pastures whose traditional enemy was the encroaching silent sand. The great towered keep was a hive of activity as it was readied for war; the port town was emptying of its citizens, all of them hurrying for the castle with nothing more than what they could carry on their backs.

But some had stayed behind. Masts were hacked from the ships at anchor, a forest of them toppling into the water and their heavy sails, rolled up for the winter, thrown in with them from the decks. The harbormaster, identifiable by the Radzyn badge on his breast, directed these operations, saving the ships from total destruction but rendering them useless to the invaders, and Meath grieved with him as he suddenly covered his face with his hands.

Only one ship stayed whole. It was already moving away from the port, a small vessel with a single huge triangular sail, heading due south for the Small Islands. Of all the ships at Radzyn port, this one alone would survive intact. Meath hoped Chay was right in not burning the rest—and then realized why he had not ordered that done. As fiery hulks they would be symbols of defeat and would take the heart from Chay's people before the battle had even begun. But this way there was a promise for the future—that there would *be* a future in which masts and sails would rise again on Radzyn's proud fleet.

Meath felt his own heart easing as he returned to the island. He reported to Chadric what he had seen, adding that he did not believe the enemy would be able to leave Graypearl before tomorrow at the earliest. The prince demanded particulars and, agreeing with Meath, almost smiled.

But when he tried to gloss over the damage to the palace, Chadric leveled a grim gaze on him and waited.

Audrite, who had joined them, cried out softly when she heard about the oratory. It had been her life's work, the expression in stone and tile and glass of her elegant, precise mind. She sat down in the sand and wept.

"Peace, my love." Chadric stroked her graying hair. "We're alive and soon we'll be safe. That is enough."

Meath made what he knew had to be his final effort of that day and found Sioned in the courtyard at Radzyn. The cool, quiet depth of her colors soothed him, even though darkness shaded their edges like soot.

Tomorrow perhaps, but certainly the next day, Sioned. Will you be ready?

We'll have to be, won't we? I haven't had time to see things for myself. What is it like, Meath?

They aren't interested in taking. Only in destroying.

Andry seems to think they're diarmadh'im. *But if so, why not use the gifts? Why rely on flint and steel for their fire?*

Capture one and when I get to Radzyn, we'll question him together.

He felt a ripple of bleak laughter. *You'll have to stand in line behind Rohan and Chay and Maarken—not to mention Pol.*

Sioned—if they really are sorcerers—

We'll deal with that when the time comes. By the way, my dear old friend, have I ever thanked you enough for finding the Star Scroll?

He returned at last to where Chadric and Audrite and the others waited for him. He was so tired that after telling them Sioned had been informed of the situation at Graypearl, he simply wilted onto a blanket spread for him in the sand. But he could not sleep, though he closed his eyes and pretended for the others' benefit. He could not rid his mind of an image of Sunrunners gathering to construct around Radzyn a dome of pallid, nearly invisible Fire, against which the invading enemy would smash its strength like waves on stubborn stone. It was too late to wish he'd learned the same—that he was more powerful and clever—that he could have done something, anything, to save Graypearl.

* * *

Andry could not allow himself the luxury of exhaustion. There was too much to do.

He had allies now besides Evarin—but they were not those he would have chosen. He had encountered Rohan's *Medr'im*, five youths of good birth and sufficiently accomplished at warfare to have dispatched the dozen enemy soldiers guarding the Pyrme River crossing. The astonishment of Andry's unwanted escort when he and Evarin quickly resumed their true faces was equal to the amazement of young Lord Gerwen at recognizing the Lord of Goddess Keep. The first did not survive long enough to express himself.

Gerwen pulled his sword from the corpse, introduced himself and his men briefly, then glanced back down with distaste. "Throw him in the river. He'll float down to where they can see him, and know that they're not unopposed in their slaughters." As the others did his bidding, he turned to Andry. "My Lord, I'm glad to find you safe and well—but you're the very last person I expected to see. The Goddess was thinking ahead when she put me by way of helping set up your tent at the *Rialla* this year."

"Otherwise you'd be launching me, too. Is the way clear across the river?"

"You would know that better than I, my Lord."

Andry arched his brows at the pointed hint. But he was grateful for the reminder that he was now free to work. "Keep watch," was all he said as he let his body take care of staying in the saddle while his mind wove the clean, fierce sunlight.

There were no interruptions. He came back to himself at last, bone-weary and refusing to acknowledge it, and saw that the shadows had lengthened substantially.

He told in spare sentences about the disasters at Faolain Riverport and Graypearl and Gilad Seahold. But there was worse news.

"A fleet of those dragon-headed ships hovers off Kierst-Isel. I think what they might be after is to capture that island as they did Dorval, then use it as a base to attack Einar, Waes, and Goddess Keep."

Response to this speculation surprised him. He knew Gerwen to have a sister married to a Waesian merchant so prosperous he could have bought and sold most *athr'im*; of the others, one had been introduced as the younger brother of an important landholder in the region of Einar. But though all five were deeply disturbed by Andry's words, and

the pair most directly involved paled visibly, not one suggested that they ride at once to assist in defending lands in which they had a personal stake.

Andry had never approved of the *Medr'im*, though they had been his own father's idea. He saw in them a direct challenge to a traditionally Sunrunner function—neutral observers who reported to the Lord or Lady any infractions of the greater law. He was skeptical about their uses as roving enforcers of the High Prince's Writ; he suspected that their devotion to the law was in fact devotion to their own importance, their pretty blue uniforms, and perhaps to Rohan for giving them something to do with themselves.

Their reactions now proved him wrong, at least about this group. Gerwen gave Andry a level look and said, "Your safety is more important, my Lord. We won't leave you. And I know you'll give warning in time."

Andry had not expected this degree of respect and faith from persons committed to Rohan. Perhaps things between them weren't as bad as he'd thought.

Evarin was eyeing the river nervously. "Forgive me for saying so, but you'd better do the rest of your Sunrunning before we cross *that,* my Lord."

It wasn't meant to be funny, but Andry laughed anyway. The *Medr'im* joined in, especially when the Master Physician pulled an affronted face. And for once Andry had no quarrel with a joke at the expense of Sunrunner dignity.

"The raft's only big enough for two, with horses," Andry said. "I won't be good for much after I'm on the other side, as Evarin so tactfully pointed out. He can go first, while I work."

"Very good, my Lord. Donaseld, help him."

The physician, already a little green around the edges, led his horse onto the raft and squatted down, one hand gripping his reins and the other tight around the low railing. Donaseld steered the raft with a large rudder to spare straining the guide ropes. Andry saw Evarin struggle for a moment, then give up and lean over to part company with his last meal.

Andry informed Prince Volog through his court Sunrunner of the disasters on the continent and the threat to his own shores. It came as no surprise. Pol had already surveyed the area and given warning. Andry was glad enough that his cousin had been busy. The *faradh'im* at Waes and Einar had

been similarly advised by Pol. But, being Andry's people, they wanted word from him alone about what to do. *Am I a warrior, to tell you how to make ready for battle? Ask the High Prince or my cousin Pol!* It annoyed him that he must defer to them, but he had little choice. His *devr'im* could not work at such distances, even had he been at Goddess Keep to lead them. It was galling to know that for all his preparations, he was still helpless.

But at least he could save Radzyn. He spoke with Torien at Goddess Keep, explaining his surmises and his intention to continue on to his parents' home.

There are Sunrunners enough there to use in its defense, Torien admitted, *but will they submit to your direction?*

If they don't, the castle will be lost. Whatever else he may be, Pol is no fool. Sioned will keep him in line—and so will Maarken if it comes to it. I won't need him that badly. There's strength enough among the others. You'll have to lead the defenses there, Torien. Don't begin too early, and don't wear yourselves out. They must be taught that Goddess Keep cannot be taken, but I'm afraid it's going to be a very long war for the rest of the continent.

We'll do all right. Have a care to yourself, Andry. If we lose you, everything is lost.

I have five zealous guardians dedicated to my safety. Give the children a kiss for me. And have you heard anything of Brenlis? I—

An urgent hand on his arm brought him back to the Pyrme. "Hurry, my Lord! Another patrol is coming!"

There was no hiding place. For a full measure north and south of the crossing the trees were sparse. The soldiers cresting the western hills into the river valley were mostly on foot, but armed with heavy bows and swords that glinted in the sunlight.

"Donaseld!" Andry shouted across the river. "Hurry! Don't wait for us—ride for Radzyn!"

The raft was just sliding into the sandy shallows. The *Medri* glanced around and waved. He grinned and pointed to Evarin, who sagged over the rail.

"Donaseld!" Andry called again. "Damn it, he doesn't hear me—"

Gerwen possessed a voice that could crumble stone at half a measure. "Make for Radzyn!" And he flung an arm toward the hills where the enemy was advancing at speed.

Donaseld saw the danger, lost his smile, and leaped from the raft into the water. He hauled his horse after him, then Evarin's, and finally picked up the Sunrunner bodily and threw him across a saddle. Donaseld mounted, grabbed Evarin's reins, and they were off as fast as he dared, with the half-conscious *faradhi* slung over the horse's back.

Andry turned to Gerwen. "You ride with me for Goddess Keep. The others can draw them off and meet up with us later. Quickly!"

There was an instant of hesitation, but Andry had been right to count on the authority of his rings. That perhaps there was some influence attached to him through his kinship to Rohan and Pol received grudging acknowledgment, but at this point he didn't much care. He needed their obedience and how he got it was unimportant. Perhaps the fact that he called Fire to the raft and it went up in unnaturally fierce flames had something to do with it, as well.

"Right," said Gerwen. "Donaseld will take good care of your physician, my Lord. Fendal, Kersion, Zadeen, take the north road to that ford at the Kadar."

Andry didn't wait to watch. He galloped off, with Gerwen right behind him on a Radzyn gelding as swift as his own Tibaza. He never once looked back over his shoulder to see how many were following him—a confidence instilled by absolute faith in his father's horses. It was only when Gerwen called to him that he drew rein.

"They've given up on us, my Lord."

He stroked his stallion's lathered neck. "I'll have a look," he said, and once again wove strands of sunlight. Evarin and Donaseld were well away from the river; the physician was now properly seated in his saddle, but had wrapped both arms around his horse's neck, hanging on with grim determination. There was no pursuit. Ten or twelve bearded men stood trapped on the river's west bank, cursing and furious. But then a body floated past the burning raft, wearing Desert blue. The face turned empty-eyed to the sky was that of Zadeen.

Andry followed the course of the river upstream to where it met the Kadar, then traced the greater river to possible fordings. He was just in time to witness the charge of six mounted soldiers. Fendal and Kersion could not risk swimming their horses across now—arrows would bring them down all too easily. Andry hesitated only an instant, then

called on the disciplines he himself had worked into a code of spells culled from the Star Scroll.

It was hard work, doing it alone. He had to be careful to leave no chinks in places he was accustomed to having others build for him while he supervised the whole. But he did it, as Sioned had done something like it long ago, and at a distance much greater than this. He wove the *ros'salath* in the space between the oncoming charge and the two men who had turned to defend themselves.

Had the situation been any less desperate, the sight might have been hilarious. The enemy slammed up against the weaving as if it were an invisible stone wall. Their beards parted in screams Andry could not hear, but could well imagine. They fell from their stolen mounts and huddled on the ground with their arms over their heads, still shrieking in horror at what they had seen and felt on contact with that wall.

Fendal and Kersion, prepared to wield their swords in a fight for their lives, instead saw their adversaries topple to the dirt screaming like terrified children. Fendal was the first to recover, slapping his companion on the arm and digging his heels into his horse's ribs. Andry hissed in frustration as the pair started forward to finish off the helpless soldiers rather than doing the smart thing and fording the river.

He had two choices: let the *ros'salath* fade, or let the two bump against it from the inside. Some deep unexpected part of him cried out against being the indirect cause of deaths—for through his skills he had rendered the enemy easy prey. It was a thing forbidden ever since Lady Merisel's time, the most solemn vow a Sunrunner swore. Andrade's face rose up in his memory, stern and implacable and ready to condemn him if he shattered his promise.

But she was long dead. He was Lord of Goddess Keep now, and his was the right to judge. Using his gifts he had killed before, destroying the man who had murdered his twin brother Sorin. Surely this was even more justified. Andrade would never even have guessed at the horrors Andry had seen that day.

And the choice the *Medr'im* made to fall upon and kill unhorsed men was none of his doing. He was not responsible.

He allowed the woven spell to crumble, and did not stay to watch as the soldiers were slaughtered. Instead he in-

formed Gerwen in terse syllables that Fendal and Kersion would shortly be joining them.

* * *

The sunlight was thick with Sunrunners all that afternoon. While the light held, news went forth from Goddess Keep and Radzyn to all courts and holdings with *faradh'im* in residence, and to the itinerants who traveled the farther reaches where settlements were few and far between. The concept of invasion was so unthinkable that many simply failed to react, and then refused to believe. But the authority of High Princess Sioned, Prince Pol, and the Chief Steward of Goddess Keep must ultimately be trusted. The incredible was accepted as true.

By sunset Sioned was so weary she could barely stand. The usual Sunrunner's headache—a sensation that one's scalp had become too tight—had burgeoned into a throbbing agony in her brain from the inside out. She trudged into the main hall of Radzyn Keep and winced as torchlight knifed into her eyes.

"Aunt Sioned!"

She barely recognized Daniv's voice, and certainly could not see him in the painful blaze of the hall. He put his arm around her waist and helped her to a chair. Sinking into it, she shut her eyes.

"Can I get you something? Wine? Food?"

"A new skull would be nice," she whispered.

"Will I do instead?" asked Rohan from nearby.

She opened her eyes—a vast mistake. They watered uncontrollably, as if she wept but was too exhausted to sob.

"Daniv, go make her grace's chamber ready. You, my love, are going to bed."

"Can't—too much to do—"

"And plenty of people to do it. Don't even dream of arguing with me. Can you climb the stairs, my feeble *faradhi*, or must I pretend I'm twenty-two again and carry you?"

"You'd give yourself a spasm." The whole world was falling in around them, and tomorrow or the next day they'd be in the middle of a battle, and still Rohan could make her laugh. She squinted up at him, knuckling tears. His face was gray with pallor, there were dark bruises beneath his eyes, and his shoulders slumped with a weariness as profound as

her own. And yet—and yet there was about him that quality he had bequeathed to his son: always shining, never tarnished, that mysterious brightness she loved so much.

"Did Chay order every damned torch and candle in the place lit?" she complained, wiping her eyes again. He helped her to her feet and they started climbing the stairs.

"The halt leading the blind," said Pol from the landing. "I don't know which of you I should offer to carry."

"Mind your manners, boy," Rohan said, "or I'll mend them at the point of my dagger. You don't look all that blithe yourself."

Sioned peered through tear-tangled lashes. The stairs were darker than the hallway below; she could see her son's face without fresh tears springing to her eyes. Pol looked almost as bad as she felt. Still, as with the father, the shining of him was undiminished. She wondered with a twinge of annoyance how in all Hells they did it.

"I'd sleep for three days if I had any sense," Pol replied cheerfully. "But I didn't inherit any and certainly never learned from *your* example." He came down to lend an arm to each, walking between them, and Sioned found herself having to make no effort at all in the climb.

Pol went on, "Radzyn port's empty, the masts and sails have been tossed, and everyone with the least claim to knowledge of one has been given a sword or bow." He hugged her tighter around the waist. "We're ready for them, Mother."

"And Meath? Have they all been rescued yet?"

"Soon. I don't envy them the sail—the wind's come up and it's getting blustery in the channel. Here's your room. Beth sent food up a while ago."

Sioned sank onto the bed and kicked off her boots. "Oh, Daniv, snuff those candles, please! My head is about to split wide open." Lying back, she stared up at the carved and painted ceiling that darkened into strange shadows as the light dimmed. "Is Tobin asleep?"

Daniv answered, "Lady Betheyn says she's fretful now that the sun's gone down. She's been out Sunrunning like the rest of you."

"And now she's going to *rest,* like the rest of us," Pol said. "Cousin, come share a cup with me before bed, if you would. I spoke to your father's Sunrunner earlier and she gave me messages for you. Sleep well, Mother."

Sioned gave a sarcastic snort. "Oh, of course."

Rohan sat down on the bed, a cup of wine in one hand and a slice of bread smeared with meat paste and cheese in the other. "Eat, drink, and don't argue."

"I will if you will," she challenged.

They shared the meal slowly, silently. At last Rohan stood and pulled the light quilt up from the foot of the bed. "Believe me, my lady, when I tell you that you *are* going to rest. Chay says everything's coming along nicely, Pol's right when he says we're ready, and Hollis is taking the moonlight watch, so you're unnecessary until morning. You're much too intelligent to refuse to rest when things are so well in hand."

"Don't patronize me," she said quietly, gazing up at him in the shadows. "I have enough wit to know when things are desperate."

"They may become so," he admitted reluctantly. "But they aren't yet. All we can do now is wait, Sioned. And remember, Radzyn is like Stronghold—neither has ever fallen to any invader."

"But who *are* these people, Rohan? What do they want with us? I went to look for myself and it makes no sense. They're not after spoils or riches or captives for ransom. They're just destroying. If you'd seen what I have along the Faolain and the Pyrme—"

"I thank the Goddess I have not." He drained the last of the wine down his throat and sat beside her, holding her hand. "Sioned . . . there's nothing more we can do tonight. And there aren't any answers. Not yet." He paused a moment, then asked in a colorless voice, "Have you talked with the other *faradh'im* about defending Radzyn?"

"If you mean about using spells from the Star Scroll —yes."

Rohan tightened his grip on her fingers. "If we stop the enemy here, we can march east to reclaim what they've taken. Kostas will attack from the north, Tilal from the west once he calls up his Ossetian army. If Volog's ships stay safe, we can use them to retake Dorval."

"Tidy," she remarked. "I doubt they'll cooperate."

"One's enemy so rarely does. But what else can I do but make plans based on the very little I know?"

"It gives you something to do," she murmured. "But we have a chance here, Rohan. Tomorrow. I'm not talking

about military things. I mean that we can terrify them. With sorcery."

A breeze sneaked through the castle and ruffled the tapestries gathered at the bedposts. Rohan pulled the velvet quilt closer around her shoulders. "What did you have in mind?" he asked finally.

With a thought, she lit a few candles near the bed. "It needs three of us, according to the Scroll. But that's only a ritual number."

"The *diarmadh'im* are very fond of three and its multiples," he mused. "They have a third deity, don't they? The Nameless One, or something of the sort."

"Three is only ceremonial as far as I can tell. I could probably do it all by myself, as I did when you fought Roelstra. But I'll have Hollis with me."

"Pol, too. I don't want him in the battle, Sioned."

"Neither do I. But it would be better to have him there than with me." She hesitated. "We must be protected, you see. If iron pierced us while we worked . . . an arrow, a sword—"

"Ah. I'd forgotten. But surely it would be safer for him to be with you and Hollis, surrounded by a wall of soldiers, than to ride into battle."

"*Not* with you," she murmured.

He was silent.

"Rohan—"

He shrugged. "I swore not to use my sword again . . . and I'm too old for this sort of thing. I felt that today, believe me. All the preparations—it was just like the campaigns against the Merida and Roelstra. It should have made me feel young again, shouldn't it? An old man reliving his youth. . . . But I felt a hundred years old. Maybe a thousand."

"Promise me. Please."

"Don't worry. Chay and I will direct things from the battlements. Or, rather, Chay will direct and I'll stand there looking princely and confident. Which reminds me, wherever you decide to work, everyone's got to be able to see you. My Sunrunner Witch weaving her protective spells. It's an argument for having Pol with you—so they're reminded of his power."

"But how do we keep a natural-born idiot from charging out to do battle?"

"It seems to me it's an even bet as to where he'd be safest. And whichever he perceives as being more dangerous, that's where he's sure to be." Rohan sighed irritably. "He's never been to war. I'm wagering he'll behave as stupidly as I did when I was eighteen and disguised myself as a common soldier to go fight the Merida."

She sat up and regretted it as her head spun—regretted, too, the bitterness that made her say, "Maybe we should have arranged a little war or two for him when he was young, so he'd know what it's like."

"No. Neither he nor I needed those skills. I had Chay. He's got Maarken." Rohan tucked one foot under him, careless of his dirty boots on the velvet. "Chay and I will supervise from here while Maarken takes the field. All you need do is gain us some time and confusion."

"And fear."

"You can't protect us long, I know that. If it was something like Fire that you could set and then not have to think about, that would be one thing. They aren't going to give up and go home, Sioned. Not until we kill so many of them that further battle is unprofitable. Give Maarken time to get the soldiers out and the gates locked up tight again. Cause as much havoc as you can."

"It's a pity we can't set those damned ships on fire."

He frowned. "What do you mean, *'can't'?*"

"Meath told me he tried and failed at Graypearl. The sails just wouldn't light—not with cold Fire *or* the kind that burns candles and torches."

"Another spell?" he guessed. "One against Sunrunner's Fire?"

"I don't even want to think about it. Andry believes they're Merida, doing *diarmadhi* work. But if that's true, why have there been no spells?"

"Maybe it wasn't necessary until now. And maybe you're going to be in the kind of battle Pol fought with Ruval."

Sioned watched his haunted eyes for a moment, then went into his arms and held on tight. "I hate this," she whispered. "I want our life back the way it was. Today when I saw Riverport—I wanted to run to you and tell you to make it right again, to put the world back the way it should be—" But in the next instant she said, "Listen to me—I sound like a spoiled child."

"I *wanted* to spoil you," he murmured, smoothing her

hair. "I wanted to make a life of beauty and grace, where we could love each other in peace, and grow old and smug at what we'd accomplished. Up until now I thought I hadn't done too bad a job of it."

"Oh, love. . . ."

"If I wasn't so damned tired, I'd make love to you so we could forget the last few days and not have to think about what happens tomorrow."

"If I wasn't so damned tired, I'd take you up on it." She made an effort and produced a reasonably honest chuckle. "I know you, *azhrei*. You don't care about peace for anything but uninterrupted leisure for your lusts."

"I beg to differ," he responded, blue eyes shining again. "I have only one lust, not several. Well," he amended, "it finds several modes of expression, but has only one form—red-haired and green-eyed."

" 'Modes of expression'? Rohan," she protested as his fingers framed her face and his lips brushed her cheeks and brow, "I thought we were exhausted!"

"Haven't you learned by now that you and I never do things the right way around? We celebrated our marriage somewhat in advance of the event—why not celebrate victory the day before we win it?"

"Do remind me sometime to lecture you on your improprieties," she murmured, twining her arms around him.

But they neither celebrated nor slept that night, for only a short while later Daniv shouted from the antechamber that contrary to expectations and their best information, dragon-headed ships rode brisk night winds from Graypearl to Radzyn.

Chapter Ten

In the spring of 705, Saumer of Isel informed his offspring that there would be marriages with Volog of Kierst's children; who wed whom was up to them. The two families were dutiful inheritors of a generations-old animosity; when his vassals raided Kierstian lands, Saumer laughed and rewarded them handsomely; Volog was equally gleeful and generous when his *athr'im* returned the favor. But it had been strongly hinted by the new High Prince Rohan that they cease picking away at one another's property. Because of his power, and because his princess was not only a Sunrunner but Volog's cousin, Saumer accepted the inevitable —though with very poor grace.

Obram, his heir, was obviously expected to marry the elder of Volog's daughters. Being an amiable young man, he presented himself to Birani, said and did everything pleasant and agreeable, and in 706 married her. The younger sister was her father's favorite and the real prize, but she was too young for Obram. Irony would have it that Alasen eventually wed Ostvel of Castle Crag, a man twenty years her senior.

No one, not even Rohan, had realized that for all the bickering that went on, the vast majority of people living along the border between the two princedoms got along nicely and conducted trade honestly. Rohan had thought that peace had to be built from the top down: that princes and lords must settle their differences and impose their will on the common folk. Kierst-Isel taught him how wrong he was. The islanders had been ready for peace long ago. It was their rulers who balked.

The marriage of Obram and Birani was the first step toward reconciling the families. They turned out to like each

other, and were happy. He died tragically a mere five years later, without a son to inherit Isel. Obram was mourned by both princedoms—Isel, which would have been his, and Kierst, which had grown to value him for his goodness to their gentle princess. And the two families' common grief was more unifying than any decree of the High Prince. It was cruel that this should be true, but it was.

Hevatia of Isel had not had to think very long before deciding which princess Volog's heir would marry. While Obram wooed Birani, she fixed Latham's regard on herself. Her two sisters were prettier than she, but she had one quality that Latham, possessing it himself, appreciated. She was ambitious.

At the *Rialla* of 698 she had looked over the men from whom she would Choose her husband, and found none to her liking. Not even Rohan, who seemed weak and foolish. In later years her mistake in judgment afforded her grim amusement. Hevatia understood and admired the High Prince's tidiness of mind even while resenting his use of her family to his own ends. It would have shocked her out of five winters of her life had she known how ashamed he was of it; she never noticed that no one had been similarly suborned since.

Being a young woman of ambition, she decided that Latham, and all that went with him, would be hers. Love, or even compatibility, had nothing to do with it. It helped that he was reasonably good-looking, possessed a tolerable degree of charm, and was ambitious enough himself to value that in a wife. They struck a bargain in the summer of 706, and at the *Rialla* of 707 were married, with all princes witnessing as new bonds were forged between the formerly opposing lands.

She did not love him, nor did he love her. She bore their first child, a son they named Arlis, three years after their union. The next year, Obram died and Arlis was heir to both princedoms. It was bitter fulfillment of an ambition neither Latham nor Hevatia had ever dreamed of, but once it was fact it became necessary to raise the boy with his future importance in mind.

Not only would Arlis rule the united island one day, but he was cousin to Sioned and therefore to Pol. Other kinsmen were the princes of Syr and Ossetia. If only through his relations, Arlis would one day be a very important man.

The parents agreed that their son's consequence must not depend on blood ties alone. Latham trusted Rohan more than Hevatia did, but neither of them wished to see Kierst-Isel become little more than the High Prince's vassal state. So Arlis was trained to understand and enjoy princely power. There was no better way to learn it than as Rohan's squire.

Until he was old enough to be fostered at Stronghold, Arlis spent every autumn at Zaldivar. Hevatia's two unmarried sisters doted on him; his grandfather Saumer spoiled him disgracefully. Hevatia never had the heart to chide them. True, she had to spend part of every year mending his ways, but he was a good-natured child and soon understood that what was permissible at Grandsir's was not a good idea around his parents.

If Obram's death united the families in sorrow, Arlis united them in love. Volog was only a trifle annoyed when Hevatia Named her second son after her father. At young Saumer's birth in 720, she was thirty-eight and could reasonably expect that she was done with childbearing—and creditably so, having produced an heir and a spare, as the saying went. But three years later she had the shock of her life. Not at the birth of her daughter Alathiel, but at the circumstances that produced it.

After sixteen years of marriage, her husband had fallen in love with her.

This confused Hevatia and embarrassed her profoundly. She could not imagine what had caused this aberration in a man she thought she knew inside out. She had grown no prettier; she showed him no special favor; she encouraged his new attentions not at all. They had evolved a comfortable relationship based on their children, their duties, their expectations for the future, and respect for each other's privacy. Each enjoyed a few brief, discreet dalliances through the years, with the usual understanding between civilized persons of high rank that any children Hevatia bore would be Latham's, and any sired by him on other women would be raised away from court. It was eminently practical, agreeable to both, and paid tribute to two rational minds.

But suddenly he shared her bed more nights than not, and, after the necessary number of gestational days, Alathiel was born.

And then something *truly* shocking took place. She found herself in love with her husband.

At eighteen, falling violently in love was as natural as breathing. At her age, it was ludicrous. At least, this was how she viewed her feelings at first. After a time, though, she didn't care if she made a fool of herself in front of the whole court and the island's entire population lined up to watch.

That autumn of 737, Hevatia and Latham celebrated the thirtieth year of their union, with ample cause for rejoicing. Arlis had succeeded his grandsire Saumer as Prince of Isel, was married to a charming girl, and had children of his own. Young Saumer was squire to Prince Kostas and would one day rule the important holding of Port Adni, which on Lord Narat's recent death had reverted to Kierst. Alathiel at fourteen was smart, pretty, and the light of all eyes—especially those of her aged grandfather Volog. She was with her aunt Alasen at Castle Crag, learning about the management of vast estates in anticipation of the holding or princedom she would help rule someday, for none doubted that she would make a splendid marriage.

At the celebration banquet, an old joke was dredged up by a minstrel: "Their graces are celebrating fifteen years of happy marriage—and fifteen out of thirty isn't bad!" They laughed heartily over that; for them, it was true.

While Graypearl and Riverport and Seahold burned that autumn night, Latham took Hevatia to a little cove some ten measures up the coast, where a cottage had been readied with every luxury. They had just fallen asleep after making love when stout boards were nailed across the door and windows. They never saw the men who swarmed ashore from longboats, or the dragon-headed ships anchored in New Raetia's harbor. They never knew of the battle, never rejoiced when the enemy was driven back onto the beaches and took flight for their ships. Latham and Hevatia burned to death in their huge, soft feather bed.

* * *

It had been Baisal of Faolain Lowland's lifelong dream to build a stone keep. For services to Rohan and Sioned in the war with Roelstra, he had been granted his wish. He had lived to see the completion of the outer walls and inner towers, and on his deathbed made his elder son and heir, Baisath, promise to finish the castle exactly as he had envi-

sioned it. This Baisath had done, but he added an embellishment of his own. A great admirer of moats, the new *athri* had made it his business to dig one around the magnificent new keep, wide enough to make a perfect mirror for golden-brown stone formed into airy spires.

The broad wreath of water was practical as well as pretty. At harvest time, river and moat were undammed so that fresh, swift water could do its cleansing work; the moat was naturally the destination of all the keep's refuse, and into it the middens emptied all year long. During the torrential rains of 727, Baisath and his family watched with held breath as the moat overflowed the dam and the fringe of grassy ground around the walls disappeared underwater. Even the narrow cobbled road leading halfway across the moat to the drawbridge vanished. Scraping up the mud left behind took all spring.

The annual cleansing rush of the river was never allowed to rise so high. When Mirsath led the refugees from Riverport to the castle the day after the invasion began, the water to either side of the causeway was a tidy three handspans from the edge—deep enough to deter a mediocre swimmer, but simplicity itself for a man on horseback.

Mirsath noted this with dull eyes. He must do something about it, he told himself. He was the new Lord of Faolain Lowland. His father was dead at Riverport with all his family, but for his cousin Karanaya, who rode with him, and his brother Idalian, safe at Balarat in Firon. Rage and grief and fear had sustained him through the wild night's ride from the burning town, but now that he was home his strength had run out. The resident Sunrunner, Johlarian, caught him as he toppled from his saddle.

"We heard," the *faradhi* said simply. "I've ordered everyone inside the walls, and everything that can be done is being done, my lord. No one will grudge you some sleep. I'll wake you at sunset."

Mirsath hobbled up the steps of the manor house, leaning on Johlarian's bulky shoulder. The glancing blow on his left leg had long since stopped bleeding, but the wound and the muscles around it had stiffened.

"I could sleep for days," the young man admitted. "Goddess, you've no idea what it was like—" Gulping back the memory, he glanced around distractedly as they entered the hall. "Karanaya?"

"Attended by your mother's women." Instantly the Sunrunner regretted mentioning Lady Michinida. "Lie down, my lord, and rest," he said even more gently, and steered the stumbling *athri* into a guest chamber off the main hall. Suddenly horizontal, Mirsath gave in to exhaustion and shock, and slept.

Johlarian watched his slumber for a few moments, grieving for his new lord and his old one dead at Riverport. There would be more deaths soon. The handful of guards Mirsath had brought with him, combined with a second handful resident here, plus the two hundred or so castle retainers and farmers, would be no fit match for the army he had glimpsed on sunlight at the High Princess' bidding. Sighing, the *faradhi* left the tiny chamber and found a kitchen boy to stand guard over his new lord's sleep.

Karanaya stood before the empty hearth in the hall, draining a wine cup. She was still in her betrothal finery, but it was a sorry mess after the frantic ride. Her yellow silk gown was in shreds from the knees down, expensive lace in tatters. She'd lost one gold earring and the matching armband in the crush of fear-crazed people left far behind. But she was wide awake, feverishly angry, and when she caught sight of the Sunrunner threw the empty cup to the floor.

"What's been done in our defense?" she demanded. "Don't tell me to go collapse like my cousin, either. He earned it by fighting our way free last night. I did nothing but sit a horse. Tell me what's going on here, *faradhi*."

Johlarian had never been an intimate of the family. Having been trained by Lady Andrade in aloof impartiality, isolation had never bothered him. He reported what he knew and what he saw, but never what he thought.

The lady heard him out, and swore under her breath. "All the farmers within the walls. . . . Goddess, we're going to be cramped." Then, sharply: "What did they bring with them?"

Johlarian blinked. "Why—I couldn't really say, my lady. Their household goods, I suppose. Anything they don't want to lose."

"In other words, their best cook pots but nothing to put in them! Does no one understand we'll have to survive a siege?"

The Sunrunner cleared his throat. "My lady . . . I think it unlikely."

"Survival, or a siege? Or both?" Not waiting for his answer, she beckoned to a guard wearing Riverport's colors. "Come with me," she said, and Johlarian could do nothing but follow in perplexed worry as she marched out into the courtyard, collecting men and women to her with imperious gestures.

"Strip every bit of food from your cottages and every blanket from your beds. And hurry up about it!" Johlarian stared at her. She turned to him and added, "And once we're done, *faradhi*, you're going to Fire the stubble in the fields. The enemy will find no living off this land."

"My lady—I cannot do that without an order from Lord Mirsath!"

Her pale blue-gray eyes were the color of flint. "Did I tell you what they did to our *faradhi*? They cut off his fingers and threaded his rings through their beards as decorations. *While he watched and bled to death.*"

No one had ever threatened Johlarian, obliquely or otherwise, in his life. Sunrunners were always treated with the most scrupulous dignity and respect. He gulped back nausea and nodded obedience.

"I'm glad we understand each other. But understand something else, *faradhi*. Whatever is required of you, you will do. If my cousin or I tell you to call Fire, you will do so at once. Whatever we order, you will perform. I don't care a damn for your oaths or your vows and I especially don't care what Lord Andry would say. You will obey, or you will be given to the enemy and *your* rings will shine from their ugly faces."

She strode away, calling for the drawbridge to be lowered. Johlarian stood in shock for some moments, trying to tell himself she was overwrought and didn't mean it. She meant it. Every word.

He trudged up to the top of the curtain wall, waiting in dull misery for her signal. If invasion was inconceivable, a Sunrunner coming to harm was unthinkable. Both had occurred yesterday. He had thought that when the keep fell, as it inevitably must, he would be spared and could bargain for as many lives as possible. That was part of the rules of war. Haunted by the vision of a *faradhi* slaughtered and defiled, he stared blankly out at the shorn fields, beginning to understand that in this war, there were no rules.

Karanaya's frightened little army marched back to the

castle leading sheep and goats and pigs, and laden with blankets crammed with food. She raised her arm to signal Fire. He summoned his energies and set a blaze in the stubble for a square measure all around.

"Spare our homes!" someone cried piteously from the courtyard below. And when Karanaya joined him on the walls, she confirmed the plan—but not for the reasons the peasants wished.

"When they come, and look into the cottages, you will call Fire to them and burn them inside." When he took an involuntary step back in horror, she gave him a grim smile. "Your rings are at present secure on your fingers, *faradhi*—and your fingers are securely attached to your hands."

"Yes, my lady," he whispered.

* * *

A south wind blew at moonrise, and the enemy positioned their great square sails to take advantage of it, skimming straight across the channel toward Radzyn port. Chadric and Audrite stood at the prow of the ship Chay had sent to rescue them, watching white enemy sails fill.

"As if the Father of Storms exhaled on purpose to take them there," fumed the captain. "We can't risk it, your grace. My *Sea Spinner* is fast, but she can't outrun them."

"Whitecliff?" Audrite suggested, but the man shook his head.

"Lord Maarken's holding has no harbor. We can't put in at the Faolain, nor anywhere along the southern coast." He eyed Meath, who was prone on the deck with his head in Alleyn's lap. "Pity your *faradhi* isn't up to taking a look—or to warning Radzyn. I've never seen any of them caught so bad with it, not even Lord Maarken. We'll have to go back around your island and north to Tiglath. It's not much of a port, but at least there's no word of enemy landings."

"They came upon Graypearl from the north," Audrite said, frowning. "Surely they'll have patrols along the coast."

"I doubt it, your grace. It's my thought that they came in three fleets—one at the Faolain, one for Kierst-Isel, and a third for Graypearl and Radzyn."

Chadric nodded. "There's little to be had by seizing Tiglath. The way is shorter and easier to Dragon's Rest and Stronghold from the Faolain."

"Exactly. No sand to hinder them." He snapped his fingers and a boy came running out of the moonlit darkness. "A warm cloak for her grace, at once. Her own is soaked through."

"Is it?" Audrite looked down at her bedraggled wrap. "From last night, I suppose." Shrugging, she looked once again at the huge ships crossing the ink-and-silver sea. If only Meath had recovered and gotten word to Radzyn earlier. If only the wind had allowed the *Sea Spinner* to arrive yesterday evening instead of well after dark. If only their second boat had not been pierced by wave-hidden rocks on landing at the Small Islands, forcing them to make two trips out to Chay's ship instead of one. Then at least they would have been at Radzyn by now. As it was, they could not even signal the keep that the enemy would arrive sooner than expected. Shivering, she thanked the boy for the thick wool cloak, and as she exchanged it for her sodden one she met her husband's gaze.

"Chay knows what's what when it comes to fighting," Chadric said. "Radzyn has never fallen."

She managed to smile, tried to match his confidence—forced though she knew it to be. "I don't give a damn if that idiot son of yours *is* past forty and taller than I am. When I catch up with him, I'll blister his behind for that trick he played."

"*My* son, eh?"

She nodded and turned her head from him to hide sudden tears, knowing that if she said another word, it would come out as a sob.

Chadric pulled her tight against him as the ship came around and headed out to sea. It would be a long voyage to Tiglath, and a tense one—for there might still be enemy ships waiting and there could be no news of family and friends with Meath incapacitated by seasickness. Fear and isolation and aloneness lay ahead, and awful uncertainty.

"About my son," Chadric said.

"Yes?" She was relieved that her voice held reasonably steady.

"If you're intent on taking him across your knee—I'll hold your cloak."

* * *

"But—they're beautiful," Pol whispered.

"Instruments of destruction usually are," Rohan mused. "Swords, knives . . . the elegant balance of a well-made ax, the perfect curve of a scythe. . . ."

They watched the dragon-headed ships make stately progress toward shore, and in Radzyn Keep there was a sudden, breathless silence. Beautiful the ships certainly were, gilded with the first pale glow of a cloudy dawn. Gorgeously painted heads rose from long, curving necks, winged sails arching in the wind.

"Azhdeen saw them," Pol said, still marveling at the magnificence of the enemy ships. "I didn't believe him. Are you sure we can't burn their ships with Sunrunner's Fire, Mother?"

Sioned didn't look up from lacing her quilted velvet tunic. "Meath says not."

"Even if we could," Rohan told him, "I would forbid it."

Pol stared at his father just as everyone else was doing—everyone but Chay, who nodded in quiet agreement. *"Why?"* Pol exclaimed.

"Do you want them here forever?" Rohan's eyes were bleak.

Chay said, "Without ships, they can't go home. We'd have to hunt down and kill every single one of them. Without ships, they must stay and fight to their last soldier—and possibly ours, too."

Rohan sighed. "Goddess alone knows what they covet here, or why. But if we spare some of the ships, the common soldiers will see there's a way to go back, and once enough of them start dying. . . ." He shrugged. "I will allow you your Fire, Pol. But not against the ships."

"Then let's try the landing boats. Hollis, you take the ones in the rear. Maarken—" Their stricken faces stopped him. "What is it? What's wrong?"

"I can't," Hollis whispered. "People would die."

"Your Sunrunner oath? Is that it? You were eager enough to learn the Star Scroll spell—a thing outlawed years ago!"

Hollis stood her ground. "Rohan and Sioned gave permission—or you never would have been allowed to teach it."

"You can't be serious! How can you scruple to use everything we've got against these people? You saw what they did at Seahold and Riverport—"

Maarken circled his wife with one protective arm. "We

made a vow, Pol. So did Sioned. The *ros'salath*, that we will help you do. But not this."

Incredulous, Pol began another protest. But his father interrupted. "Leave be. They swore an oath."

"Honor makes a wonderful shield against swords and arrows!" Pol snapped. "You may have sworn, but I didn't." He extended both hands, cloak billowing and rings glinting dully in the thin light. Sunrunner's Fire sprouted from the lead boat, then the ones behind it, flames that ran eagerly over wood. A cheer went up from the walls of Radzyn as the Sunrunner Prince worked.

But the dragon ships continued on their graceful course, while their hatchlings trailed tails of Fire like the homeless stars that sometimes fled through the night sky.

"*Those* burn," Pol muttered. "Perhaps Meath didn't try hard enough." And he directed Fire against the sails.

One sail became a sheet of Fire—but did not burn. All he accomplished was to make the ship even more terrifying: a dragon ablaze, like the one his mother was said to have conjured long ago.

Shock rippled through the group assembled on the battlements. Sioned stepped forward as Pol's hands fell to his sides. "Let me," she said, and fixed her fierce green gaze on the sails.

"So much for oaths," Pol muttered.

A greater Fire raged, angry red instead of Pol's deep golden blaze, but with the same result. Murmurings threaded through the sudden silence, dark whispers countered by a single bright hiss as Chay drew from its tooled scabbard the sword that had not tasted blood for the length of Pol's life.

"I swore an oath, too," he said. "I ask my prince to release me from it."

Rohan's answer was slow in coming. But after a time, after he searched his friend's quicksilver gray eyes, he unsheathed the blade he carried, borrowed from Chay's armory—shining, lethal, beautiful. "I release us both."

Pol forgot anger and humiliating failure. Standing before him were the architects of his peaceful, pretty life at Dragon's Rest—men he worshiped, men he wanted to emulate—men who now held swords with the easy assurance of trained warriors and the sorrow of awakened dreamers.

They were too old for war. Lean and fit as they still were, with the swords comfortable—too comfortable—in their

hands, yet Rohan was sixty and Chay nearly seventy. Where once their coloring had contrasted, golden and dark, now they were both silver. For the first time Pol's throat was gripped by fear. They were too old for this. It should not be happening, not to them. *We've lost before it has begun,* Pol thought. *Whatever happens, we've lost something they spent their lives building—Father, I'll get it back for you, I promise!*

The old friends gazed into each other's eyes for a few more moments, acknowledging between themselves everything Pol had been thinking. Then each turned to his son.

Nothing was said. But Maarken straightened as if his father had given an order, and, beckoning to the commander of the guard, vanished down the stairs. Pol followed his mother and Hollis to a vantage point at the side of the tower.

Hollis surveyed the beaches, her voice as calm as ever. "We'll wait for full sunrise. The clouds should blow away soon on this wind."

Pol watched his father and uncle, who stood side by side, together as they had always been. Grief had not left their faces, but Pol was startled to see something fierce and feral in their eyes. Old they might be, but beneath the serenity of age were two young men who had bathed their hands in enemy blood. This was what won wars, this elemental anger. Pol did not know whether to feel ashamed or relieved that he could find none of it within himself. He knew only sadness and pain, and a terrible weariness.

* * *

Far from Radzyn, on a lonely stretch of Ossetian road between the Pyrme and Kadar rivers, Andry and his escort of *Medr'im* were awake and in the saddle at dawn. It was cold, gray, the kind of morning Sunrunners hated, for it rendered their skills useless. Which was undoubtedly why the enemy had chosen autumn as their season for invasion, Andry told himself. Still, with rain there could be no battles or advances through downpour and mud. Which was undoubtedly why the strike up from the coast had been so sudden and so deadly. And why they sought to take the Faolain River to cut off help to the Desert—where it rained perhaps once in a hundred years. Autumn and winter could be brutally cold on the Long Sand, but ground could be

covered and castles taken. If Radzyn fell, and Faolain Lowland with it, a token force could be left in the south to hold it secure and the bulk of the army could be moved to the Desert before the heaviest rains.

Andry had glimpsed Lowland before moonset the night before. The enemy had spent a day making sure Riverport was utterly destroyed, every home and shop and warehouse and inn up in smoke. *And where is Brenlis, in all this horror?* he asked himself again, shaking inside. *Hidden away somewhere, little love? Find me, and soon, for I cannot find you—*

Soon the enemy would be at Lowland. It was already shut up tight, fields blackened by Sunrunner's Fire. The drawbridge was up, the moat overflowing. That puzzled Andry until he saw that the sluice gates to the river had been demolished to let the water rise. All well and good—but if the enemy could not get in, neither could the defenders get out to harass troops Andry knew must soon invade the Desert. A small force left behind could ensure Lowland's isolation while the main army marched past. Even so, at least Lowland would be denied them as a staging area.

Though they rode west, Andry's thoughts continually turned eastward to Radzyn. He would not be able to see things for himself until the sun finally made its appearance. If he was lucky and the Goddess was good to him today, the clouds might blow off in a strengthening wind by midmorning.

I should be there. I should be at my father's castle, giving the only help I can offer. Sioned had worked at a colossal distance to shield Rohan during his battle with Roelstra—almost the same number of measures as to Radzyn from here—but she had had help. She had seized the strength of every Sunrunner she could find, from Tobin at her side at Skybowl to Andrade and Urival and even Pandsala at the combat scene. Andry had no one but himself. It galled him to admit it, but there was nothing he could do—not at this distance, not alone.

So he rode west while his heart and mind yearned east, and cursed the clouds that kept him helpless.

* * *

Alleyn stroked Meath's thick hair and tried to screen the hot sun from his face. Her grandmother had told her to try

and get the *faradhi* to drink a little, but it was a losing battle against water-sickness. Alleyn didn't see why the element that had felled him should revive him, in any case. There wasn't any logic to it.

Audran came with a dipper filled from the fresh water barrels. "Is he any better?"

"No, and not likely to be until he's on land again." Angling Meath's heavy head, she helped her brother pour water down his throat. He moaned and coughed, but kept it down.

"Why didn't you let me tell him?" Audran whispered.

"He's got more to worry about than us," Alleyn snapped. She settled Meath in her lap again and glared at Audran. "Besides, maybe we just imagined it. We're not Sunrunners. Nobody in our family is a Sunrunner."

"I didn't imagine anything!" he retorted. "I felt it and so did you!"

"Hush up!" she hissed. "Who cares, anyway? If we can't make it to Tiglath, it's not going to matter if we're Sunrunners or sorcerers or both—or neither! And anyway, I don't see you getting sick."

"Not everybody does. Maybe we're special." Audran scowled and looked as if he'd pursue the subject, but his sister's fierce blue eyes stopped him. He gulped, lowered his gaze and mumbled, "I wonder where Papa and Mama are."

"I don't know," Alleyn said, her voice quivering a little. "But whatever you do, don't say anything to Grandsir. Or about what happened with us, either."

"He'd only worry," Audran sighed. But he squinted up at the sun with a speculative expression on his face anyway.

* * *

Pol forced himself to relax, allowing his mother to guide his strength into the weaving of the *ros'salath*. As he submitted, all information from his outer senses faded away. He knew there were shouts and battle cries, wind whipping his face and hair, salt spray stinging his nose, enemy troops wading ashore from the small boats, the lingering taste of blood in his mouth where he'd bitten his lip at his mother's first commanding touch. But all he really knew was the feel of her colors, strong and sharp. And for the second time in his life he recognized the difference between the *faradhi* gift

and that of the *diarmadh'im*. That it indeed was the second time confused him.

Sioned had told him once that it was like pressing one's hand to its exact match on the other side of a thin mesh screen: alike yet never touching. He hadn't felt that when fighting Ruval nine years ago, but now he knew what she meant. As she drew what she needed from him, he imagined one of the hands turning to clasp hers, while Hollis held onto Sioned's other hand with both of her own. But try as he might, Pol could not make the image of that second, different hand reach and grip and give of that other strength.

Stop that. You're distracting me.

He let the mental picture dissolve and concentrated on the colors whirling around him, in him. Sioned, Hollis, himself—a whole bright rainbow of jewel tints that threaded around and through each other to form a complex pattern. Usually Sunrunners likened their colors to a stained glass window, unique to each person. It was the easiest way to explain the inexplicable to a non-*faradhi* mind. But it wasn't that simple (he could hear his father's dry voice telling him that nothing was ever that simple). Patterns in colored glass, woven tapestry threads, sun and shadow on water—shifting subtly throughout life, changing with mood or stress, but always the same.

Pol gave himself over to Sioned's skill, curious at his lack of amazement. He was sure he had never felt anything like this before—as if he no longer had a body, as if everything he was had concentrated in the strange and beautiful thing she had made of herself and him and Hollis.

But to some deeper part of him, it was oddly familiar. And that other hand, the one that belonged to the sorcerer, turned its palm to show him a single gold coin. On it was his grandfather's profile: High Prince Roelstra. There was no similarity between them, no cant or contour that linked him to his blood-mother's sire. But all at once the face of gold turned, took on the colors and shadows of living flesh—and the leaf-green eyes laughed at him, eyes the color of his own in certain lights, or when he wore certain clothes.

He felt no fear of this man. But it was an eerily familiar face that grinned at him now, a face from his own memories. And that was impossible.

The hand closed over the gold coin with its living face, clenched into a fist raised as if to strike him for rejecting the

vision. He couldn't help it—he claimed his other hand, the *faradhi* part of him, and tried to break through the finely woven screen, smash that fist into oblivion.

Or lace his fingers with it, and become whole.

The idea flashed and was gone so fast that he barely knew it had formed. In his shock he felt sick, rent in pieces, as if the very thought of wholeness shattered him. The colors surrounding him fragmented, paled to shards of acid rime, needles of white slicing into his brain. The blankness of his physical being was now an agony of sensation having nothing to do with the logic of reality. He could *hear* whiteness, *smell* cold, *taste* lightning.

"Pol!"

Opening his eyes, he winced at shreds of sunlight. Hollis knelt beside him.

"Talk to me," she ordered.

He coughed, sat up, and wondered when he had fallen to the stones. "Everything still works—I think." He reclaimed one hand and rubbed his forehead. "Goddess in glory—my head's about to split open." Then he looked around. "Mother!" She lay senseless nearby, pale and spent.

Hollis soothed him with a touch and a tired smile. "She'll be all right—I have her word on it. She told me so after she finished stitching us both back together." She flung her thick, tawny-gold braid back over one shoulder. "I'll take care of her. Your father wants you downstairs. Hurry."

"But what happened?"

"I think we lost you, or most of you, and then I had the impression of . . . of swords." She paused to compose herself. "I've felt it before—only that time, it was a knife. I think they used iron against the *ros'salath*, Pol. Cut into it with swords." She attempted to help him up; they ended by helping each other, neither steady enough to stand alone just yet. "When you can, go to your father and Chay. Don't worry about Sioned. I'll make sure she's safe."

"Iron—" He swallowed hard. "You felt this before? When?"

"When Pandsala died."

He remembered the agony of it, and his mother's frantic work patterning the colors of a score of stricken faradh'im. But he also remembered that while iron was fatal poison to Sunrunners, it had a lesser effect on sorcerers. Like him. *Diarmadh'im* could work around it—painfully, but they could

function. He had not. He had simply fallen apart. "I failed again, then," he said bitterly.

"You couldn't know. None of us knew. It's not in the Star Scroll."

He'd forgotten Hollis was there—Hollis, who knew nothing about the true source of his power. "Damn Lady Merisel to all Hells! She must have known—yet she wrote nothing!"

"As with other things, perhaps she thought it too dangerous."

"She was fond of making other people's decisions for them." He tried out his legs, found them reasonably useful, and glanced over the walls. It seemed he'd be feeding his sword fresh blood today after all. With a last worried look at his mother, he ran headlong for the stairs, and forgot to wonder why submission to her weaving felt so familiar.

* * *

"Listen to them," Chay muttered. "Listen to their battle cry. Andry was right—Goddess help us, he was right."

The shout went up again from the enemy ranks: "*Diarmadh'im!*" It echoed off the eight towers of Radzyn Keep, all the way up to where Chay and Rohan stood watching the battle. Rohan wanted to put his hands over his ears to shut it out. They bellowed as if they had but one voice—and the discipline this implied was confirmed by the efficiency of the assault.

"As if it was the name of their lord, or their keep," Chay went on. "The way our people are shouting 'Radzyn' and '*Azhrei*' and our names."

"Maarken's breaking through," Rohan said, pointing to the wedge of mounted warriors slamming into enemy foot soldiers.

"That horse's ass—if he's not careful, they'll circle around and—" Chay ground his teeth, then beckoned to Daniv. "Run down and have my horse saddled, quick! And get me thirty riders—"

"Don't bother," Rohan interrupted. "Maarken's following the plan, Chay. Reinforcements are right behind. He won't be cut off."

Chay squinted and gave a snort of laughter. "In other words, he doesn't need the old man galloping up to his rescue! I don't know whether to be proud or disappointed."

Rohan divided his attention between glancing over his

shoulder at the stairwell door and peering anxiously down at the fray. With the collapse of the *ros'salath*, he had been expecting Pol to show up in one place or the other—and went a little weak-kneed when the young man finally arrived at his side.

"I'm sorry, Father—we failed," he panted. "They used iron—slashed right through it. It's a wonder we aren't all dead."

"It's no wonder magic is forbidden to Sunrunners in combat," Chay said. "Damn—there's that word again. Magic. I'm beginning to sound like my son."

Rohan suddenly remembered what Chay had said earlier. "What did you mean, 'Andry was right'?"

"He knew," Chay muttered, looking anywhere but at Rohan and Pol. "Saw this in some sort of vision. You know how I feel about *faradhi* seeings—"

"He knew. And said nothing, except to you." Pol's voice was lethally quiet.

"I should have believed him. It was my fault you weren't told. Don't blame him, Pol." Chay glanced at him then, with an expression as close to pleading as would ever appear on his face.

Pol was silent. Rohan pulled in a deep breath and, against all his protective instincts, said, "Arm yourself, Pol. Maarken needs you."

"I might as well go someplace I can do some good—or harm, as the case may be!" The deadly glitter in his eyes found an object that was not Andry, which had been Rohan's purpose. "I'll order Dannar up here—keep him with you. He's too young for this."

"And we are too old," Chay murmured when Pol had left them. "But if they can't push these bastards back onto the beach soon, our swords may drink today after all, Rohan."

* * *

Maarken had taken no wounds of any note—a slice here, a shallow puncture there—and he was only a little tired. But he knew the battle would have to be won soon. His right wrist, crushed in combat eighteen years ago, throbbed with pain. He had exercised it assiduously, making sure it was as strong as it ever would be again, but despite skilled physicians the broken bones had never mended properly. He

could move his wrist certain ways but not others—and swordplay demanded supple joints, especially in the wrist. He had accounted for more than his share of enemy dead, but muscles and tendons shrieked at the ill-usage. He could feel the wrist swelling inside his gauntlet. He figured he was good for a little while yet, but not much longer.

So it was all very simple. He had to win in order to get the wrist iced before it was damaged beyond help and crippled him forever. He could not swing his sword two-handed when on horseback, so he jumped off and, with a battle roar of "Rad*zynnn*!", led his troops forward.

Within moments his leather battle-harness was slick with blood. A dark-eyed warrior with a score of gold beads threaded through his beard managed to cut into Maarken's forearm, and the damaged wrist soon went numb. He still had the strength of his upper arm and shoulder. So he wrapped his left hand around his right to keep it steady, and hacked his way through five more bearded soldiers.

Screams, battle cries, calls for help, and the almighty crash of steel on steel deafened Maarken now that he was down here in the thick of things, rather than above it on his horse. He fought better on foot; proficient as a mounted knight, his real talent was face-to-face combat with a sword.

But this couldn't go on much longer. The first attack had come at dawn. It was now noon. The battle had gone pretty much as Chay had expected, the sheer numbers of the enemy more or less matched by the Radzyn defenders' knowledge of the terrain—and the fact that it was their land they were fighting for. But casualties were mounting on both sides. Maarken groaned when he saw the corpse of the young woman who had taught his children how to ride. There were others he recognized—too many. This couldn't go on much longer.

"Maarken!"

He took care of his current opponent and swung around at the sound of Pol's voice. His cousin was on horseback, cutting a swath through the enemy line to Maarken's left—doing a damned good job of it, too. He reined his big golden stallion around toward Maarken.

"Get up here behind me—we can get clear and call Fire!"

"No!" A hiss over his shoulder warned him just in time; he whirled, gutted the swordsman, and shouted to Pol, "I kill with my sword, not with my rings!"

"You idiot!"

And nearby three enemy soldiers became living torches.

"Stop it, *now!*" Maarken bellowed. "You'll get yourself killed!"

Suddenly the bearded warriors gave another roar of *"Diarmadh'im!"* Maarken had no time to think. He fought for his life as wave after wave swept down on him inexorably as a storm-tide.

He collided with a horse and someone grabbed his arm to steady him. He looked up into Pol's face, half-hidden by his helm.

"You don't have a choice this time—climb on!"

His cousin's strong arm hauled him up. It wasn't until he was perched behind the saddle, his legs at an awkward angle, that he realized his thigh hurt like all Hells. Pol pivoted the stallion and rode for the rear of their lines. Maarken hacked at a few enemy heads along the way with his left hand—and pushed his numb right fist into the bleeding wound just above his knee.

Some of the enemy had advanced nearly to Radzyn's walls, a knot of them assaulting the main gate, repulsed by arrows and kettles of boiling water from above. Pol galloped for a postern gate. It opened, Pol reined in, and Maarken slipped from the horse into his father's arms.

"Pol! Come back here!" Chay yelled.

But Pol was gone in a thunder of hooves back to the battle.

"Where are you hurt? Maarken, talk to me!"

With Chay's help, he limped inside the gate, heard it slam shut behind them and the iron bolts slide home. The passage through the thick walls was black as pitch; Maarken conjured a finger-flame to light their way.

"A couple of scratches, and this damned gouge in my leg. Nothing serious, Father—just enough to take me out for a while," he added angrily.

"For the duration—on my order," Chay growled. "I was watching. When you loosed your horse, I thought you'd gone down."

Maarken laughed in genuine amusement as they climbed the inner stairs. "*Your* son? You not only insult me, you insult yourself!"

They gained an inner chamber and Chay left him in Sioned's care. She looked ghastly pale, but her fingers were

sure and steady as she tended Maarken's wounds. "You didn't happen to see that imbecile I'm married to, did you?" she asked as she worked.

"*Rohan's* out there?"

"He and your father were protecting each other's backs. Then Chay saw your horse running free—and making free with his hooves along the way, I might add. How do you train those brutes, Maarken? Set them to knocking down inconvenient trees?"

A well-trained horse could take a man's head off with its hooves as surely as a whetted blade in a strong warrior's hand. Radzyn horses were *very* well-trained. Sioned knew that as well as anyone. She was talking to hide her fear.

"Father must be back with him by now." He flexed his wrist, which had been wrapped in cold cloths, and hid a wince behind a grin. "He's pretty quick for an old man."

"Say that to his face, you impudent child." She tightened the bandage on his thigh until he yelped. "There. It'll heal up just fine. But you're through for the day. Let's go see what's brewing outside."

She gave him a slim wooden stick to lean on and accompanied him across the courtyard. Horses crowded there thick as ripening grain, for every animal not needed to carry a soldier had been herded within the walls. The courtyard, big enough to encircle Maarken's whole house at Whitecliff, seemed shrunken. Once atop the walls, they looked down on the battle in silence for some time. At last Maarken swallowed hard around the lump in his throat.

"We've killed a lot of them, Sioned. But—"

She nodded slowly. "But they have killed many of us. If it stops at dusk, it will only begin again tomorrow at dawn. And it will continue until—"

"We're going to lose this, aren't we?" he whispered.

"You're the warrior. You tell me."

He turned blind eyes to the carnage below.

"We have two choices. Three. We can stay and fight—and die. We can stay and lock ourselves in and wait for help—and starve. Or we can leave."

"No," he said. "This is my home. My inheritance."

"To inherit a place, it is necessary to be alive."

"If we leave, there won't be anything left *to* inherit!"

"There will be no help," she said quietly. "The Faolain is theirs. Tilal and Kostas can't raise their armies in a day.

Ships can't get past the enemy along the southern coast. Graypearl is ashes."

"Remagev—"

"—is three days' march across the Long Sand. Walvis' little army is there, but. . . ."

When she said no more, he faced her again. Her green eyes lit with an unholy glow.

"The Long Sand," she repeated.

"What are you thinking?" he demanded.

"The Goddess is good to us, Maarken. Never doubt that she is very good to us." Before he could question further, she ran to the stairwell and vanished.

Chapter Eleven

Sioned watched as Rohan paced the tapestry-hung foyer, where they were miraculously alone for a few moments. Time enough to gulp down bracing wine, to talk without having to shout to be heard—or having to be careful that no one overheard.

"They're nearly at the walls," she said. "Choose soon, before the choices are gone."

Rohan wiped sweat from his forehead with one gauntleted hand, leaving behind a smear of dirt and blood. He had acquitted himself well, fighting beside Chay. But when battle fever overtook him, he had despaired to recognize how easily he became the accomplished barbarian again. He flexed the shoulder injured over half his lifetime ago and schooled his features against a flinch of pain. Much too old for this sort of thing. . . .

"Rohan—"

He faced her and frowned. "I don't much like the choices you present."

"Whatever we do, it must be done quickly, before we lose the chance."

"I can't give orders without consulting Chay."

"At least let us make ready. It must be decided soon."

"No. It must be *now*." He drained off what was left of the wine in his goblet. His gaze swept the length of the hall. "The first time I ever set foot here was—good Goddess, forty-four years ago. Maarken and Jahni had just been born, and old cousin Hadaan gave me permission to leave Remagev. My parents were here, too. . . ." He cleared his throat. "I thought this the finest castle and Chay the finest man in the world. I've never changed my opinion of either."

Softly, Sioned replied, "You first brought me here when

Andry and Sorin were born. I'd just lost our first baby. Chay took me for long walks on the beach, sometimes talking, sometimes not." She smiled fleetingly. "I adored him only fractionally less than I adored you. And I've never changed in that, either."

"This is going to kill him, Sioned," he murmured. "It's killing me right now."

"Here, within these walls, you're trapped. You need the Desert, *azhrei*. And the Desert will provide."

Rohan turned in a slow circle, memorizing a place he knew as well as his own Stronghold. It hurt to breathe; his heart suddenly seemed too large for his chest, throbbing painfully against the cage of bones like a frantic hawk. His left arm went numb, then tingled.

"Beloved? What is it?"

"I'm a coward," he said softly, trying to steady himself. "I'm going to leave it to you to tell Tobin. I couldn't bear it."

"As if telling Chay will be any easier," she murmured.

But neither the Lord nor the Lady of Radzyn Keep needed telling. Tobin, seated by her bedchamber window with Betheyn and Tobren beside her, had followed the battle by sunlight. When Sioned stepped into the pool of rose-gold afternoon glow, her voice was borne on colors darkened by grief and rage.

We can't hold Radzyn. We must leave, Sioned.

Kneeling before her, she rested her cheek on Tobin's useless left hand. "I'm sorry. I'm so sorry," she whispered.

It's not your fault sorcery failed. But I suppose Rohan thinks it's his fault that after thirty years of peace, we don't keep enough troops anymore to battle an army.

I think you're right, and Rohan does *believe he's failed—as a prince and as a man.*

My noble fool of a brother! Who could have foreseen this? We'll have to talk some sense into him once we're safe at Stronghold.

Not Stronghold, Tobin. Remagev. We'll lead them deep into the Long Sand.

Sioned looked up and saw the warrior princess in Tobin's black eyes. *Ah!* she said. *Excellent! We won't have to kill them—the Desert will do it for us!*

Sioned felt energy race through Tobin's slight frame. For a moment it seemed she would throw off her disability like

an ill-fitting cloak, spring to her feet, and start shouting orders. Only her hands moved. The reality of her physical infirmity sagged her back into her chair. But in another instant she squared her shoulders. *Damn it to all Hells—I'm as useful as a newborn foal. Worse—I can't even walk. What a time to start getting old.*

You? Never. Sioned smiled, then got to her feet and told Betheyn to pack saddlebags for herself, Tobren, Maarken, and Hollis. "Clothes, jewels, anything you especially treasure. I'll take care of Tobin's things. The squires can do for me and Rohan and Pol."

Tobren's blue eyes almost started from her head. "Are we leaving? But we can't! What about the horses? We have to save them."

Clever girl! Tobin's colors shimmered on sunlight again. *We can't let them have the horses, Sioned. That's probably why they attacked to begin with.*

"Your grandmother commends your quick thinking, Tobren," she told the child. "We should have thought of that ourselves. Beth, Dannar can do the packing. Send Daniv to tell Chay about the horses."

When they had gone, Sioned asked Tobin, "What besides your wedding necklets do you want to take?"

How frivolously romantic—and how like you, Tobin chided. *A change of clothes and a warm cloak. That's all. I take the most important things with me in my heart.*

And you call me *romantic!* Sioned went to the huge wardrobe, sorting through Tobin's dainty silk gowns and Chay's jewel-toned tunics and shirts; rich fabrics, elegantly cut and finely embroidered, so many recalling times both joyous and grim. The wealth of colors and textures crumpled suddenly in her clenched fists and tears sprang to her eyes. Stupid—why was she crying over shirts and dresses?

"Sion-ned?"

Tobin's halting voice alerted her. She wiped her cheeks on a blue lace veil and said over her shoulder, "You and Chay must account for half the silk trade all by yourselves."

There was no reply, and she didn't dare look at Tobin. She dragged out a few changes of clothes—not silk or velvet but sturdy leather and wool, durable garments that would hold up under hard riding and keep the wearer warm during brutal Desert winter nights.

She went to Tobin's dressing table and picked through the

jewel coffers, aware of that sharp gaze following her every movement. The wedding necklets, a few rings with particularly large stones, a carved sand-jade bracelet left by the Isulk'im in teasing apology for stealing a prize stud, a ruby pendant with diamonds that had been Chay's present on the births of Maarken and Jahni—once again her eyes clouded.

"Not to mention you seem to have most of the gold and gems mined in all thirteen princedoms," she said, cursing her unsteady voice. She stuffed the jewels into a velvet pouch and tied the laces. "Anything else? Letters you want to save, souvenirs—"

"Stop," Tobin whispered. "Sunlight . . . must t-talk . . . ."

She dreaded it, but did as so laboriously asked. *I'm here.*

I know what you're thinking. How can I leave this place where my sons were born, where my whole life is? If I think about it, I'll start screaming and never stop. So I won't think. Neither will you. Just do what has to be done. There's always time for grieving, Sioned.

I'm so afraid, Tobin—

I know. So am I.

* * *

Chay needed no one to tell him, either. He had been wise in the ways of war before Rohan knew how to wield a sword; battles against the Merida at Zehava's side had taught him reality early. He knew an untenable position when he saw it.

All he said was, "We'll wait for dark, then ride out in small groups. The *faradh'im* can discourage pursuit with a few bonfires—it might bend their oaths a little, but no serious breakage, I trust."

But when it came time to leave, and the first riders shot through the postern gate like arrows from a bow, and the Sunrunners had dappled the darkening battlefield with Fire, he gazed up at the eight towers of his keep with moisture gathering in his eyes. He caught Rohan's anguished look a moment later, cleared his throat, scrubbed a hand over his face, and said, "I'll go hurry the others."

Horses within the courtyard were tied securely together and led out in bunches of ten to twenty, accompanied by the grooms and trainers they knew best. But even though the enemy would be denied these animals, they could pick and

choose among those it had been impossible to bring inside, horses in far pastures and at Whitecliff. Chay couldn't decide whether the loss of Radzyn or his blooded darlings hurt worse. But when he reached his wife's chamber, he knew he'd gladly hand over everything he possessed if only Tobin could be safe.

Hollis had dressed Tobin in leather trousers and vest, a warm shirt, and a cloak. Her hair was braided tightly around her head. She sat straight-backed and calmly waiting for him. He paused in the doorway, knowing he should not glance around the room. All the nights, all the mornings. . . . The gleam of candlelight on silver at her dressing table caught his eye: her brushes and combs. The thought of enemy fingers touching them—he knew it was ridiculous, but he crammed them in his pockets anyway. When he faced her again, she was smiling, and the angle of the light spared him the ruined side of her face.

"I'll take your things downstairs," Hollis said, and tactfully vanished.

Chay knelt beside his wife. "Beloved, I know you're strong enough."

"When . . . was I . . . not?"

He gathered her in his arms. She weighed even less than the girl he had first carried into this room long ago—both of them laughing at the scandal they caused by leaving their own wedding feast. All the nights, all the mornings. . . . He kissed her hair and hurried down to the courtyard.

The chaos of frightened people infuriated him—not because his people were afraid, but because he could do nothing to ease their fear. Rohan waited at the bottom of the steps with Chay's favorite stallion. He held his sister while Chay mounted, then lifted her up to the saddle.

"Can you put your arms around me?"

She tried and failed, black eyes fiery with rage at her helplessness. Then her gaze shifted to the courtyard and fury became grief. This castle had been their life and their pride. By dawn it would be empty of them and all they had accomplished, befouled by the presence of enemies.

"Damn them all," he heard Tobin whisper.

Holding her tighter in his right arm, he kicked his horse through the low, narrow postern gate and into a headlong gallop across the fields. Rohan, Sioned, and Daniv rode with him, and three grooms leading a score of horses. There

was no pursuit; the Sunrunners had done their work well, and the enemy was too busy avoiding Fire to send more than a token force after them. Besides, soon they would have what they wanted: Radzyn Keep.

Chay never looked back. After a dozen measures he slowed the stallion to let the others catch up. Tobin's slight weight made no difference to the horse at all.

"Maarken?" she asked. "Pol?"

"Waiting farther on." She shifted in his arms, trying to turn, and he pulled her head gently to his chest. "No. We'll see it again soon enough." Pressing his lips to her hair, he added, "I'll get it back for you, beloved. I swear I'll win it back."

* * *

Chayla's fist closed around her pen as if it was the hilt of the knife, and candles lit earlier with Sunrunner's Fire flared in response to her emotion. The home of her ancestors had been in enemy hands a full day now, her family was fleeing across the Desert, yet here she sat with a medical text before her and orders to make detailed notes by morning. Remagev's *faradhi*, Relnaya, had decreed that no matter what, her education must continue.

It was an old trick and not a very subtle one. Chayla knew she was being kept busy so she wouldn't think too much. Absurd, of course—and the assignment itself was the wrong one to give, rife with descriptions of complications that might ensue after a serious wound. The treatments she was supposed to be memorizing were even now being used in earnest. Physicians sliced away fevered flesh with thin curving knives, applied steaming poultices, kept careful watch on dangerously deep gouges in case they festered. It was all too easy to imagine faces she knew and loved tightening with pain.

Perhaps Relnaya was more clever than she gave him credit for. Goddess knew this book was appropriate to the circumstances. She might have to use these techniques herself very soon.

Always supposing the wounded survived long enough to let her work on them.

Rage sparked the candles again, and the pen broke in her fist. She flung the pieces across the room, tempted to send

the inkpot after them just to hear the crash. Her even-tempered parents deplored her explosive anger, even while ruefully admitting she came by it honestly. Her grandmother's furies were legendary.

Thought of Tobin brought a surge of fear even stronger than anger. No one in her condition should be moved—and certainly not in a flight for life across the Desert. Not that Chayla could bring herself to believe that her indomitable grandmother was ill, let alone that Radzyn had been abandoned. Relnaya had forbidden her to share the sun with him today, and she hadn't enough knowledge to attempt it on her own. Distraction had been easy enough to come by during the light—readying a keep for war took every pair of hands. By rights she ought to be too exhausted to think. No use telling that to her frantic brain. It was night and she could do nothing but wait for two more days—and then her parents and family would be here. At least tomorrow Relnaya would ride the light to New Raetia, where Chayla's twin brother Rohannon was, so she could know him safe. Perhaps she could go along and learn enough to go Sunrunning on her own, and not be dependent on him. But she knew Relnaya; not a chance.

"Damn!"

Her own voice startled her. The candle flames jumped and quivered perilously near the curtains. Chayla doused Fire with a single thought and got up so fast her chair overturned. She couldn't stay in this room another instant.

But at the staircase she paused, irresolute. Had this been almost any other place, she could have lost her troubles in the scent of flowers and the sound of water. Remagev had no pleasure garden. Whatever miracles Walvis and Feylin had wrought here, roses were not among them. There were plots of kitchen herbs and medicinal herbs, and an arrangement of occasionally flowering cacti planted years ago by Sionell. But Remagev was an enclosed desert; its spring allowed it to live, but it was a desert just the same. There was no place where water ran free, and green growing things could shelter an angry, frightened, frustrated fifteen-year-old girl.

Well, if sand she was compelled to look at, then she might as well do it right. Reversing direction, she took the upper stairs two at a time. Perhaps sight of the moons bathing the Desert in silver would soothe her. Perhaps she could imag-

ine she gazed out on the sea from the heights of Whitecliff—the sea that was alive with dragon-headed ships.

Emerging into the night, she swung the heavy door shut behind her and nodded to the sentry on duty. He bowed his respects in silence and continued pacing the broad stones. Chayla looked out over the battlements to the stark landscape. The Long Sand was awash in moonglow, but not even her active imagination could portray the rolling dunes as the sea. To wander in a garden was to breathe in rhythm with life itself. To forget everything in the sound of the pounding sea was to hear the world's heartbeat. But if she lost herself in the bleak and barren plain before her, she might never find her way back.

She walked down the long expanse of hewn rock lit by torches, across to the tower, turned in a dark corner where flames did not reach, retraced her steps—as single-mindedly as the guard who trod the walls and watched the Desert.

By her fourth circuit one moon had fallen below the horizon, her sisters not far behind. Chayla glared at them. All that light begging to be used, and she knew nothing of how it was done. She was helpless to know what might be happening at New Raetia, or where her family rode through the night—

All at once Chayla swung around, scowling. Someone was singing to the music of a lute, a sprightly tune that offended her. The strings were plucked with effortless skill and a pure strong voice rose in a language she did not understand.

She followed the music to where a man sat in the darkness between torches, long legs crossed at the knees, a beribboned lute cradled in his lap.

"You're *singing*," she accused.

His fingers continued their supple dance across the strings, but he broke off the song. "Better than weeping," Kazander said matter-of-factly.

"How can you do such a thing—"

"—at such a time?" he finished for her, and in the dim light she saw the white flash of his teeth below his mustache. "Sweet lady, I am forbidden by my prince to go to his aid. I am forbidden to leave these walls to escort him and his to safety. I am forbidden to slice these enemies of my prince into dragon fodder. I am forbidden all that could be of any use. But I am not forbidden to sing." He shrugged. "So, I sing. It makes sense, if you consider it."

"It makes no sense at all!"

The lute fell silent. "And what would you have me do, my lady? Remagev is ready for war. My men are abed, cherishing the sleep they need and deserve. Those still awake listen for my lute and my voice. If you have no objections, I will continue."

"Continue what? Singing them to sleep? Do the Isulk'im need cradle songs?"

"You scorn what you don't understand." He strummed a light melody.

"Explain it to me," Chayla demanded.

"If there is time for music, then all is well," he said simply, and began to sing.

It *did* make a crazy kind of sense—the kind she was growing to expect from this odd man. She flushed, glad of the darkness that would conceal her reddened cheeks, and started to walk away from him. But he was a talented and sensitive musician, worth hearing; she gave a little shrug and sat down near him with her back against the wall. From this angle torchlight afforded her a clear view of his profile: proud, hawk-nosed, eyebrow and mustache black slashes against sun-darkened skin. The song went on for a long time, and she began humming a harmony to the chorus, wishing she understood the words.

"I liked that," she said by way of apology when he had finished. "What are the words?"

He cast her a sidelong glance as he retuned the strings. "If I said they were a poem inspired by the impossible beauty of your eyes, your formidable father and awesome grandsire might let me live just long enough to say my last devotions to the Goddess."

Chayla grinned. "Oh, no, my lord, you're wrong. They'd keep you alive for a *long* time. But I don't think you'd enjoy it."

Kazander laughed. "You've forgiven me!"

"What for? Oh—" She recalled being snatched up and carried half a measure across the Desert on his knee. "I suppose I have. Now, tell me what your song was really about."

He did not answer, instead starting another song. This one was quieter, and in her own language. The lyric was about the search for a white crown. It guaranteed its wearer everything from victory in war to gaining the love of a

reluctant maiden. A lot for one crown to do, even an enchanted one—which was the argument of the skeptical prince who had been told to seek it out.

"Did he ever find it?" Chayla asked when the song was over.

"Not in this version. In another he takes a different view, and succeeds. I like this one better."

"Really? Why?"

"Because its lesson is that we cannot hope to gain that in which we do not believe."

"That's not very optimistic."

Kazander chuckled. "Reverse it, then."

She thought for a moment. "If we believe in something, we can gain it?"

"We may seek it, which is not the same thing at all. But with courage, strength, and cleverness, we may yet succeed."

"But you like the version where the prince *doesn't* believe in the white crown."

He nodded. "The one in which he doesn't even try."

"I don't understand."

"I prefer it because by being a fool, he loses all. A more useful warning than when someone believes, tries, and succeeds. There are a hundred songs of similar theme. This one is unique."

"Do songs always have to teach lessons?"

"It helps the peculiarly stubborn." Shifting to get more comfortable, he said, "You may know this one, my lady. Will you take the woman's part?"

As she sang, she smiled to think what Kazander's listening men must think—let alone Walvis and Feylin and anyone else who heard. But as she concentrated, weaving her voice around and through his in the difficult melody, she forgot all but the song. Even Kazander's voice and lute were only the loom to the fabric of her own music. Did Pol's wife Meiglan feel this when she stood before her *fenath*? Did Sunrunners, when they stitched their colors with threads of sun- or moonlight?

Suddenly the framework of sound was gone. Chayla choked off the last verse and stared in embarrassed confusion at Kazander. He was on his feet, the lute abandoned on the stones.

"What is it?" She stood beside him looking out at the Desert.

"Listen."

She heard nothing, and said so.

"You've lived too long near the sea," he said, more sharply than he had ever addressed her. "Your ancestors were mine, at least in part. Listen to the oldest blood in you."

She thought he meant the ability to sense dragons before they appeared in the sky; her great-grandsire Zehava had passed that eccentricity on to his progeny. Chayla could not do it—yet. Pol had come into it late, too. But when she finally heard something at the very edges of her perception, it bore no resemblance to the sound of wings.

"If I didn't know better, I'd say that *was* the sea," she whispered. "Breakers in a storm."

"Yes," he answered grimly. "A storm. But not of the sea."

* * *

Back at least a couple of hundred years, the Long Sand had been a kind of white-gold river slicing the Desert in twain. Water holes along its edge had given rise to a string of temporary settlements, then permanent fortresses, and finally communities clustered around castles. But then the sand began to flow like a slowly swelling river, claiming one keep after another. Remagev was the only one still inhabited. Some of the rest had vanished completely under encroaching sand. The others served as way stations for travelers, empty rooms and crumbling walls offering protection from the searing heat—and shelter during sandstorms.

Before the survivors of Radzyn reached the abandoned keep that was their first goal, a dozen frantic horses stampeded into the stinging, wind-driven grit. Another ten injured themselves severely in panicky straining to escape the storm. Once within the walls, Sioned, Pol, and Hollis, who knew how to weave sleep, ran frantically from group to group of hobbled animals before sand blocked all light. Their hasty work in some cases was so sloppy that rather than peacefully dozing on their feet, the horses toppled to the ground.

People huddled beneath tentlike cloaks, backs to the wind. Rohan took Sioned under his own cloak for added protection. Made of thick red wool, borrowed from Chay's collec-

tion, it afforded better insulation than the light silk he had worn on the way to Radzyn. He could even hear himself think above the whining wind. He could also hear Sioned's painful breathing. He soaked a piece of his shirt with his water-skin and pressed it to her nose and mouth.

"Better?"

She inhaled and nodded. "Some. Our Desert usually speaks in whispers, Rohan. But now it sounds furious."

An ancient lyric about sand and the Wind Father beat through his mind in sibilant rhythm with the tempest. He murmured portions of it to himself.

The sands sing
a yearning song of beginnings
when rain sank into embracing land
when water-rich flesh fashioned proud fortresses
when water-blood flowed sweet-singing. . . .
the song changes
the Desert's arid soul mourns itself
its dead dry castles, its thirsting skin. . . .

Sioned moved closer in the blackness and spoke the poet's words of storm.

The sands shriek
the Desert wars against itself
raging anguish in the wind
no one answers for its lost life
yet there is strange vengeance in self-destruction
though flesh and blood are dry
the Desert's soul lives and grieves
given voice by the Father of All Winds. . . .

"The Storm God seems to be on their side, not ours," she finished.

"If we're trapped, so is the enemy."

"I hope the wind lashes their bones clean," she muttered.

"Goddess, but you can be vicious. Some might be appalled, but I've always found it rather exciting."

"I'm not in the mood for jokes, Rohan."

"Well," he said cheerfully, "we could discuss Denirov's rules of grammar, or Drukker's *Precepts*, or dragon statistics."

Sioned glared at him; not that he could see her expression

in the reddish darkness of Chay's cloak. Her voice was enough. "Why not be really creative and decide the meaning of life once and for all?"

"Heart's treasure, I thought you already understood that." He meant to kiss her lips and got a mouthful of dry, dusty hair instead.

"Nice try," was her comment on the kiss and the chiding. "But there's more to it than making love."

"An unfortunate truth." He kissed her anyway, with better aim this time, and caught the side of her mouth. "But I won't tell if you won't."

"Will you stop!" she shouted, totally out of patience.

Other low conversations around them ceased; then Maarken, in a deliberately provocative voice, called out, "Our High Prince chooses the damnedest times and the most inconvenient places, doesn't he?"

"With a wife that beautiful, who can blame him?"

"Who said that?" Rohan bellowed.

Sudden laughter defeated the storm, and Rohan would have been the last person to credit his own very personal magic for the miracle.

* * *

Visions came to Andry again in his sleep that night. Radzyn in ruins; dragon ships in the harbor; a boat drifting out to sea in flames, living sacrifices burning along with enemy dead; a hatchling dragon shot from the sky.

He woke before dawn, shivering and drenched in sweat. Cloud cover and unfriendly patrols had kept him bound all the previous day and evening. But the sky was clear now, and he waited in a fever of impatience for enough light to work with. His escort of *Medr'im* slept on in enviable peace. He did his pacing a considerate distance from them.

Ossetia was a sweet land—low forested hills alternating with pastures and farms, wearing autumn colors of leaf and flower that were a feast to Sunrunner senses. Andry saw none of it. He watched the eastern sky, counting his own heartbeats until thin golden rays slid through the trees on the near hills. Only a little while longer; only a few more breaths, readying himself for the first touch of sunlight on his face. . . .

The landscape spread out below him, shallow valleys, rich

meadows, harvested fields between the broad silver-blue ribbons that were the Catha and Pyrme and Faolain—tattered at irregular intervals by blackened farmhouses and enemy camps. He had no time for any of it. He sped along woven sunlight—and nearly unstrung the careful loom in his shock.

Radzyn was still standing. All eight towers. Every wall. Smoke did not billow from the stones, nor were there fiery fingers tearing at the last of the gutted ruin. Radzyn was whole, and he nearly wept.

But the burning ships bearing casualties—and captives—floated to sea on the tide. Dead faces shorn of beards, ritual chin-scars revealed, gazed empty-eyed at the lucent dawn sky.

And the dragon of his vision? Unable to watch the living burn with the dead, he cast about for the hatchling and did not find him.

Warriors gathered onshore to praise the dead turned as one, faces to the sky. Not hatchling, but dragonsire. Andry drew back; he had heard how Sioned and Maarken had once collided colors with a dragon. This one was blue-gray with silver underwings. The great jaws parted in a roar. He swept down with claws extended, circled the keep, soared out over the breakers to the dragon ships.

Andry tore his attention from the sire to the warriors. To a man, they were prostrate on their faces on the beach. Again he was so stunned that only instinct and training kept his weaving coherent. He had not seen this in any vision; the implications staggered him.

With a mighty wrench the dragon tore the carved prow from one of the ships and flew over the beach with his prize. Sunlight gilded the silver and blue-gray of him, sparked off the spines along his neck, turned his eyes to flame.

Small wonder the enemy groveled.

Andry followed the dragon back across the Faolain, careful to keep a respectful distance. The sire rode the wind with wings unfurled, twisting his head to rip the wooden dragon head to splinters with his teeth. The bits scattered along the regular route to the Catha Hills, where many dragons wintered. As Andry made his own way back to Ossetia, he remembered where he had seen this particular beast before.

Opening his eyes to the Ossetian dawn, he began to laugh. So Azhdeen didn't approve of dragon-headed ships,

did he? And those stupid, superstitious barbarians cringing in the sand—perfection. And quite possibly very useful. Pol would enjoy hearing about his dragon's exploit.

Pol, who knew how to construct the *ros'salath* from the Star Scroll copy in his possession, but was too inept to defend Radzyn with it.

Anger stilled his laughter. He turned on his heel and went back to the small camp, determined to say nothing about what he had seen.

Chapter Twelve

The day of the Battle of Radzyn, Tilal of Ossetia, Laric of Firon, and Edrel of River Ussh met in Pol's library at Dragon's Rest to make some hard decisions. But it was nearly impossible to believe in battle plans when a glance out the window yielded only peaceful orchards and quiet gardens.

Tilal rolled up a map of the southern princedoms and slid it back into place on the shelf. The long room was lined with Rohan's gifts to the palace: copies of all the volumes in his own extensive collection. Bound books and scrolls offered every conceivable subject—from medicine to metallurgy, history to animal husbandry, poetry to politics. For Tilal, who had been his squire for ten years, it was rather like walking into Rohan's mind.

But not Pol's, now that he thought of it. Rohan's heir had dutifully read what his teachers thought was important, but he was no scholar. Tilal smiled in rueful sympathy, remembering how he'd hated days spent in the library at Stronghold. But on taking possession of River Run, he'd missed the physical presence of books—their scent, the feel of parchment pages and leather bindings, the stark black elegance of script, the delicately inked drawings. He'd found himself ordering more books from Volog's scriptorium each year—and reading them. It would take him many years of collecting to bring Athmyr's library up to the standards he envisioned. But he was keenly aware that war threatened not just crops and castles. The books were in danger, too.

Edrel finished making copies of strategy notes and put down his pen. "I think we've covered everything, my lords. But I have a confession to make. My instincts are screaming

at me to gather what troops I can and start fighting. Trouble is, I don't know which way to march."

"West to your brother at River Ussh, or east to the Desert," Laric supplied, nodding. "I'm torn in two directions also—protect the princedom I was given, or fight alongside my brother to win Graypearl back."

Tilal fixed his gaze on the map of Ossetia still spread on the table. "I know. Gemma says she can feel enemy footsteps on our lands. My brother's princedom lies between two rivers held by the enemy." He glanced around at the library shelves again. "My mind tells me to take care of my own. But my guts demand that I defend my prince."

"Personal loyalty is one thing," Laric commented. "Duty is another. Perhaps it comes down to a choice of which course is most easily lived with. None of us can go in two directions at once. But who is more important—our own people, or the High Prince?"

"You know what Rohan would say to that, of course," Tilal smiled.

The other prince shrugged. "And he might be wrong. For there's a third presence, and a powerful one. Especially in the minds of the people. What do you think would happen if Goddess Keep fell?" A knock on the door turned their heads before any reply could be formed. Laric said, "Come," and Pol's court *faradhi*, Hildreth, entered hesitantly.

"Forgive me for interrupting, my lords," she said. "I thought you might need me."

Hildreth had left Goddess Keep ten years earlier with her husband and two sons, unable to countenance any more of Andry's changes in tradition. He had made no protest; neither Ullan nor the boys were gifted, and thus no loss to him. After three years as an itinerant *faradhi* in the south, Hildreth had severely injured her leg in an accident. Sioned, hearing of it, had asked Pol to invite the family to Dragon's Rest. Hildreth was an old friend, one of the group that escorted Sioned to the Desert in 698 to become Rohan's wife; Pol was glad to welcome her, the more so because she had been trained by Lady Andrade and was no champion of Andry's growing power.

Pol acted as his own Sunrunner, so there was little for Hildreth to do professionally. Her main duty was teaching —a task she enjoyed but which left the bulk of her gifts unused. In her eyes now was eagerness to function again as

a Sunrunner was meant to. Tilal, recognizing this with some surprise, reflected that for all her sixty-four winters she was like a strong young hawk kept hooded in the mews. She needed to be flown at prey.

"Thank you, Hildreth—and forgive me for not asking you here sooner. It's habit. I rarely conduct business with my Sunrunner in attendance."

"I wouldn't trust Fesariv, either," she replied forthrightly. "He thinks the moons rise when Andry gives them permission."

Edrel made an annoyed sound. "I'm a fool—I'd forgotten you rode Grib and Meadowlord, Hildreth. You'll know exactly the best route for his grace to take back to Athmyr to avoid the enemy."

"Avoid them?" Tilal forgot that his wife and daughter would be with him, and that he would command no more troops than his small personal guard and those that could be borrowed from Dragon's Rest. "I don't plan to *avoid* them. I plan to slaughter them."

* * *

Hildreth's foray on sunlight yielded horror. Radzyn attacked, a battle being fought, no telling who would win and who would be slaughtered. The question of defending their own lands or going to their princes' aid was thus solved for Tilal and Edrel: it was too late to help Radzyn.

Tilal had planned to speed his journey by swapping his own horses for ones kept at way stations along the road; Meiglan lent him enough spare mounts to make that unnecessary. He requested an escort of fifteen soldiers; she gave him thirty. When he thanked her, she expressed regret that she couldn't send more—while wishing she could keep all of them here, especially Tilal. He had fought in the war against Roelstra. That was many years ago, and he had only been a squire, but at least he had experience. She wanted him to stay and take care of everything while she hid in a safe dark place until Pol came home.

"I'll send your people and horses back when I meet up with my own," Tilal said. "Probably somewhere in Grib. I've sent word for my northern levies to join me while the southern protect the Pyrme River."

Jihan—irrepressible, willful—rode up on her new pony,

demanding to be taken along. Meiglan saw the others smile. She felt like hauling the child down and slapping her.

Kierun deflated Jihan's dreams. "You can't go, my lady," he said with the firmness of four winters' seniority.

Very few people had ever forbidden Jihan anything—and none of them had been twelve-year-old squires. She sucked in an outraged breath, but never got the chance to tell him what to do with his orders.

"My lord charged me to protect you and Princess Rislyn and her grace. And I can't do that unless you're all in the same place."

Meiglan nearly laughed. Protection from a child. The world had gone mad.

Tilal intervened hastily. "Lord Kierun is right. Your safety is his responsibility. You wouldn't want him punished if anything happened to you."

Her jaw jutted out, plain indication that she didn't care if Kierun swung by his thumbs for it. But she climbed off her pony and waved a sulky farewell.

"Don't worry too much," Tilal said kindly to Meiglan, but his green eyes were shadowed. "Radzyn's never been taken. Everyone there will be all right."

Everyone at Radzyn could die for all she cared, as long as Pol came home where he belonged. She bid Tilal and Gemma and Sioneva farewell and sought her chambers. She knew she ought to sit with Lisiel, who had been confined to bed by the physicians. But Meiglan did not want to be with a woman who had given her lord one son and might produce another very soon now. It was a reminder of what she had not yet given Pol.

At the *Rialla* this year she had summoned the courage to beg Sioned to tell her if a Sunrunner physician could help her bear a son. The reply had been completely unexpected: "You're worth much more to him than your ability to have children, my dear. You're not a brood mare! You are a princess." Simple enough for Sioned to say; she had given her prince an heir.

But though Meiglan could not bring herself to sit with Lisiel, neither could she think of a place dark enough and secret enough to hide in.

Thanys entered the bedchamber with hot taze and cakes. She served Meiglan and then set about sorting a basket of

clean laundry, talking on and on about the uproar in the kitchens as the servants prepared for a siege. Not that one was likely, but the chief cook had decreed that provisions were one battle Dragon's Rest would never lose. His underlings were commanded like soldiers on a regular basis; since word had come of war, he was even worse—

"Be quiet!" Meiglan shouted. Thanys was so surprised she nearly dropped an armful of lace bedgowns. "Do what you came for, but do it in silence!"

Sioned would never have had to raise her voice. Meiglan huddled in on herself in despair. She had learned it all so well, all the things to say and do. And she knew how hollow the words were in her mouth, how meaningless the actions. Other women of her rank—Sioned, Sionell, Tobin, Gemma, even hateful Chiana—would be doing something right now, secure in their authority, preparing for war as efficiently as they governed their daily lives. Meiglan had no example for war. She didn't know what needed ordering, organizing, overseeing. Her authority was empty without Pol.

When Thanys murmured that it was nearly time for the children's lesson, Meiglan stared in amazement. Pol was fighting for his life, and Thanys could prattle of the children's lessons? But as she glanced automatically at the water clock, her mind turning just as instinctively to the day's plan, she realized the older woman's wisdom. There was soothing comfort in routine that fooled the mind and heart into believing that nothing had changed. For the children's sake, life here must continue as regularly as possible.

For the children's sake? For her own. If she clung to the usual order of things, said what she always said and did what she always did, then perhaps she could convince herself that Pol was only out for an afternoon ride, that she could tiptoe into his chambers tonight and lie in his arms.

But there was a greater reason than her own need to behave as if all was well. People would see and approve, and say of her, *How calm our princess is, going about her everyday business as if the enemy didn't even exist!*

She prepared for the deception, knowing it depended on her ability to deceive herself. Stitchery, she repeated dully, she would be teaching the girls stitchery today. Monotonously, mindlessly plying her needle would present the very picture of serenity. She could even smile faintly at the irony

of it, for the woman who had unknowingly taught her this placid skill was the least peaceful person in Pol's whole family.

Tobin alone of the highborn ladies Meiglan knew was a notable needlewoman. She had faithfully studied every stitch of the embroidered blanket Tobin sent when Jihan and Rislyn were born, and by now was adept. Fingers that plucked the *fenath* with effortless ease had no trouble with the needle. She intended her daughters to master the elegant craft from childhood—it was the only one she could teach them of all the things they must learn, things that would make them powerful, self-assured women like Tobin and Sioned. Jihan and Rislyn would always be certain of their accomplishments and worth.

Meiglan left her own chambers with steps that sounded cheeringly confident to her own ears—and faltered before Pol's door. She glanced up and down the hall to see if anyone was watching, loathing her instinctive hesitation. This was her home, these were her husband's rooms; she could go in if she liked.

Once inside, she cursed her foolishness. Had she hoped to feel closer to him for standing by his bed, fingering his pillow? Or was this the hiding place she sought? She turned to leave, only to bump into Kierun on his way in.

"I'm sorry, your grace. May I help you find something?" the boy asked considerately.

Insane to be blushing and stammering in her own home. "No. Nothing, thank you, Kierun. I—I'm late for the children's lessons."

He bit his lip, then said in a rush, "Your grace, I hope I didn't presume too much with Princess Jihan this morning. It's just that—my lord said—"

"No, you were quite right, Kierun. It was just the right thing to tell her. She's so stubborn."

"I'll say," Kierun muttered, then turned fiery red. "Forgive me, your grace—"

"It's all right, Kierun. Go about your duties now." As she escaped down the corridor, she realized how fortunate she was that the only person who had seen her was also the only person at Dragon's Rest even shyer than herself. But Kierun had been assertive enough with Jihan. It was galling to find example in a twelve-year-old child.

* * *

"I told you it was a stupid time of year to cross the Long Sand!" Chay yelled, barely able to see Rohan in the stinging haze of sand.

"Cheer up—the road to Stronghold's probably even worse than this one!"

"*What* road?"

They hauled at their horses' reins, slogging through shifting sand that sucked at their boots like mud. The first storm had spent its fury in a single night. They'd had a day of clear riding before another blew in. Not nearly as fierce, still it caught them between shelters and showed every sign of lasting until evening. They were all old enough hands at living in the Desert to wade through, but it was hard going, and the journey to Remagev that should have taken three days looked as if it would last five, perhaps six.

Chay's main worry was Tobin. Incapable of walking, she was huddled against his stallion's neck, wrapped so tightly in a voluminous cloak that he wondered sometimes how she breathed. Every so often he reached for her hand, felt a reassuring squeeze, and swore that one enemy soldier would die by his sword for every instant of this nightmare. Strength and courage she should have been using to get well were instead expended in simply staying alive.

And then there was poor little Tobren. Desert forebears she might have, back a score of generations, but she had been born and raised at Goddess Keep on the Ossetian coast—a land wild enough in its way, with deadly winter storms, but wholly unlike this wasteland gone mad in the wind. It had taken Hollis and Betheyn together to coax her out of the shelter that morning. She hadn't spoken a word since. When the storm blew up today, she had begun to weep silently, too proud to draw attention to herself until Maarken lifted her from her saddle into his arms. A charming introduction to the land of her ancestors, Chay thought bitterly, wanting to rock her to sleep and ease the terror from her blue eyes. That was something else those whoresons would pay for in blood. They had made his granddaughter cry.

"I think it's letting up!" Rohan shouted.

"You always were a dreamer!" He adjusted the cloth

covering his face. "This damned stuff doesn't enhance my warrior's image any, you know!"

"Be grateful for wives with expensive tastes!"

Usually everyone traveling the Desert at any time of year—but especially in autumn—carried a length of fine-woven silk mesh for just this reason. But there hadn't been enough to screen all the people and all the horses. So the delicate undertunics worn by the highborn ladies had been ripped to shreds, and they and their husbands were swathed in softly perfumed lace. Chay had to admit it worked nearly as well as the silk—but he felt ridiculous.

He fumbled for Tobin's hand again, his heart catching when he felt her grip a little weaker than it had been. "Are you all right?" he yelled. The cloak nodded. "We can stop and rest if—"

"Chay!" Rohan yelled. "Somebody's coming!"

His hand went for his sword. How Rohan could tell there was anyone out there was a mystery; he couldn't see an arm's length past his own horse. He squinted and eventually the swirling sand assumed a shape, then another, then a whole group of shapes nearly the same color as the storm. "Maarken!" he bellowed. "Pol!"

But Rohan was gesturing peace. The shapes drew nearer, leading horses whose faces were wrapped in silk. Chay realized belatedly that these people were coming from the north, the direction of Remagev. The enemy could not have outrun and outflanked them so soon. Where were his wits? he asked himself. He wasn't just too old for this kind of thing, he was senile.

He drew even with Rohan and watched in surprise that quickly became amusement as one of the sand-colored shapes dropped to one knee.

"Great and noble High Prince!" a voice cried, and the other shapes descended likewise onto the sand. "The Mother of All Dragons has blessed your pathetic kinsman! He has finally found you in this likeness of the Sixth Hell! Have you or your beloved lady wife come to any hurt?"

"None!" Rohan shouted back. "I'm glad to see you—but, damn it, Kazander, I thought I told you to stay at Remagev!"

"Most honored prince, I could not!"

"Why?" Rohan demanded.

Kazander looked up. "Because, my prince, you are going the wrong way."

* * *

Tilal fulfilled his promise of slaughter sooner than he intended. Lacking a Sunrunner to spy out the land ahead, he had to rely on teams of mounted scouts. When, on the morning he crossed the Faolain River at a little-used bridge, one pair failed to return, he knew he was in for trouble.

"It's hellish, being out of touch this way," he told Gemma. "I don't know what happened at Radzyn, the news is days old—Goddess, I need a Sunrunner!" He fretted over this truth for a moment. "The last report that came to Dragon's Rest put the enemy at least a hundred measures south of here. I'd planned to look in on Velden at Summer River, use his *faradhi* to take a look. But now it seems we'll have to go around."

"Not around whoever got our scouts!" she exclaimed.

"I never suspected such a lovely face hid a warrior's heart."

Gemma shrugged. "If a warrior is what's needed, that's what I'll be. I'm no Meiglan, cowering in a corner, waiting for Pol to come home and make everything all right."

"Did she seem that way to you? I thought her very cool and capable about it all." He gestured to his squire and said, "Find Chaltyn for me, Malyander. We need to confer." When the boy was off on his errand, he continued, "Now that you mention it, I'm glad Edrel and Laric are there to make decisions for her."

"When we get to Athmyr, you needn't worry about *my* finding a convenient corner to hide in," she stated. "I'll hold the castle. But I swear, Tilal, if I have to bind and gag Sorin to keep him from following you off to war, I will."

"Just make sure nobody tells him about Jihan. Goddess, I really thought she was going to gallop after us. She had a look in her eyes like Pol used to get when he was her age. Impossible brat."

"Talking about little brother again?" Sioneva guided her horse nearer her parents, smiling.

"Obliquely," Tilal replied. "Don't say anything to him about Jihan's little performance—we're hoping he won't get any ideas."

"Not a word. Why have we stopped?"

"Take a guess," Gemma invited. "The scouts haven't reported back."

The girl's eyes rounded. "You're not going to lead a skirmish yourself, Father!"

"I'm forty-five, not ninety," he said a bit testily, and reined around as Chaltyn, the commander of his guard, rode up. A brief conversation divided the soldiers into two groups: one to hunt the enemy, the other, from Dragon's Rest, to remain behind. With a jaunty salute to his wife and daughter he rode off to the skirmish.

But, as he had unwittingly prophesied, it was no skirmish. It was a slaughter. They found the enemy in a copse where autumn foliage stained the forest yellow, rust, and brown. The two scouts were being systematically, almost ritually tortured. They did not scream because they could not; their own shirts had been stuffed so far down their throats that no sound could emerge. Tilal peered from cover at the sword cuts like bleeding ribbons across the man's back and the woman's breasts. He gave a signal, and his twenty fell on the twelve enemy—swiftly, brutally, and to the point.

The woman, one of his own guard, sobbed unashamedly when the gag was pulled from her mouth and cool water was poured over her wounds. "My lord—it was so quick, we had no warning—"

"You did all you could. I'm just glad you're both alive." Tilal hid sickness at the sight of her flayed skin. The war with Roelstra had been terrible—but prisoners had never been tortured. There were rules, and honor. What had been done to his scouts warned him that if, as Rohan sometimes said, war was the craft of barbarians, this enemy had made of it an art form.

"They spoke—we couldn't understand them," she went on, gasping as bandages were applied. "Panadi, he's one of Prince Pol's men, from near Rezeld, he thought he recognized a few words, like the old language, but—oh, Goddess—"

"That's enough for now. Rest." Turning to his guards commander, he said, "Search the corpses down to the toenails. We must learn all we can about these animals. I especially want those gold beads from their beards. And send someone back to her grace to tell her we're all right."

"At once, my lord."

He watched as the bodies were unceremoniously stripped. Not animals; just men, uniformly dark-haired and dark-eyed, built like bull elk. Clothing was laid aside for his inspection. Tunics of some rough-woven, undyed cloth that

was neither wool nor silk nor linen. Trousers the same, only dark. Shirts were of a thinner, softer version of the material, bleached white. Short boots of cowhide with surprisingly thin soles that, despite the long measures marched so far, showed little sign of wear. No rings, necklets, armbands, earrings, or other jewelry, except the gold beads. No underclothes, either. Just shirts, trousers, and plain tunics with a jagged design stitched in red on a black badge over the heart. Tilal cut one off with his knife, studied it, and decided at last that it was a stylized bolt of lightning.

Tilal got back on his horse and returned to his wife and daughter, thinking along the way about what those clothes might mean. All he came up with that he trusted was that the lightning might have some connection to the Storm God. Perhaps he and not the Goddess was the primary force in their lives.

But there was one other thing. Verbal exchanges had demonstrated to each side that the other's language was incomprehensible. Without words in common, there could be no communication. Yet the scouts had been tortured. If it had not been for information, it must have been for pleasure.

Tilal gulped down the bitter taste in his throat. Barbarians, indeed.

* * *

Mirsath paced the under walls of his keep, swearing under his breath. How in the name of the Goddess was he supposed to deter enemy advances while he was trapped inside Faolain Lowland? Yet the High Prince had been very specific and it was Mirsath's duty to obey as best he could.

The enemy had arrived three days ago. Since then Johlarian had spoken with Hollis several times. That Rohan and his family were safe at Remagev was welcome news; that he expected Mirsath to do something about the enemy was not.

They had set up a camp as riotous with color as the enclave of princely tents at a *Rialla*. Battle banners fluttered in the breeze; he supposed they signaled allegiances. They certainly were gaudy—bright orange striped with purple, livid green on pink, sapphire blue dappled in scarlet. Johlarian, sensitive to color like all Sunrunners, winced whenever he looked at them.

Mirsath winced, too, but not because he cared about the garish hues. He was more interested in the number of different flags and the total count of men fighting under them. Rohan had asked particularly about both. Bewildered and impatient—this had no bearing on how he was going to get out of this mess—he had nevertheless made his observations and reported back through Johlarian. Sixteen distinct banners and over seven hundred warriors. Sixteen opportunities for conflict between commanders, Rohan had replied with satisfaction; seven hundred chances for petty quarrels.

Mirsath had watched the camp, and, as usual, Rohan was correct. There were rivalries here as spiteful as any on the continent, expressed in taunts and jeers when the commanders weren't looking. On several occasions, soldiers camped under red-and-emerald banners had to be physically restrained from fights with those of the orange-and-purple. It was Rohan's opinion that despite the discipline they'd shown thus far, the enemy was too uncivilized to work together in a sustained effort for very long. Volatile and savage, evidently viewing war as glorious sport, their successes might make them sloppy or overconfident—preferably both—with a large dose of regional or tribal claims to superiority thrown in. Jealousy among the lower ranks often extended to those in command.

"His grace further says," Johlarian reported, "that an insult or two called down from the walls might be helpful. Their language is not ours, but he's sure we can think of ways to get the point across."

"The *point* is, what does it gain us?" Mirsath fumed. "So they don't like each other. So what?" When the Sunrunner's eyes began to lose focus, he added hastily, "Express that to his grace in different terms."

"Of course, my lord." A few moments later Johlarian frowned and shook his head. "The mind of the High Prince is a subtle one, my lord."

"I don't need subtlety—I need an army!"

An army was precisely what he was not likely to get anytime in the foreseeable future. His keep was stuffed and garnished for a siege and surrounded by a moat that, after judicious flooding, was obviously making the enemy think twice about an attack. But what kept them out also kept him in.

And Rohan wanted him to hold the invading forces here, prevent them from further advance. How could he do that when he was locked up tighter than a silk merchant's coffers?

"What does he think—that if we get them to fighting among themselves, they'll kill each other off and we'll be spared the trouble of a battle?"

"I don't know, my lord. Lady Hollis said that there are other matters to deal with now, and bade me farewell. Oh—" He brightened. "She also said that your brother, Lord Idalian, is safe and well at Balarat."

"At least *somebody* is." But he was relieved that the little brother he hadn't seen in seven years was far from the fighting. If anything happened to him and Karanaya, there would be one last member of the family—to rule over what? Riverport was a charred wreck, and if he didn't think of some way out of this, Lowland would follow it into oblivion.

He glared down at the camp that stretched all the way to the main course of the Faolain River. Sixteen different banners, seven hundred men. What was he supposed to do, have his archers pick them off one at a time from the walls? What was even more infuriating was that they seemed to be taking their ease, in no hurry to demolish his castle as they had done to Gilad Seahold. If they were smart, they'd march around him into the Desert before the rains began. The river already swelled with runoff from the north, where autumn storms had struck Princemarch and blanketed the upper Veresch in snow. The moat rose higher daily. Soon the Faolain would be impassable and they would have to attack in the Desert with what soldiers were already there. Still, he supposed the force that had taken Radzyn was large enough to take Remagev, too, possibly even Stronghold itself. That last didn't bear thinking about.

"My lord? I beg my lord's pardon—" One of the kitchen boys, promoted to page and very much on his new dignity, bowed with every other word.

"Yes, what is it now?" Mirsath asked wearily.

"My lord, five of the enemy are riding to the north wall, my lord."

He gave a short laugh. "Perhaps they plan to surrender."

The boy answered seriously, "I don't think so, my lord," and Mirsath gritted his teeth.

"Fetch Lady Karanaya at once." He beckoned to the Sunrunner and three archers and strode to the wall.

"*Athri* of Faolain Lowland!"

Mirsath gave a violent start. The shout was in his own language, not that barbarian gabble the enemy shouted up every so often. Five men on horseback—Radzyn breed, he noted angrily—had reined in at the moat. One of them held a banner. He recognized the colors with a shock.

"*Athri* of Faolain Lowland!" the voice called again, and the speaker stood in his stirrups. "Are you ready to talk sense?"

"I'm listening!" He gestured, and arrows were nocked to bowstrings.

"Have you a name?"

One of the archers yelled down, "You have the privilege of addressing the Lord Mirsath, *athri* of Faolain Lowland, honored with the friendship and confidence of his grace the High Prince Rohan!"

Mirsath raised a brow at the young man, who grinned and whispered, "It can't do any harm to remind them exactly who you are, my lord."

"I'm surprised you didn't give him my complete lineage. Nicely done. My thanks."

"My pleasure."

"Mirsath! So you survived Riverport! And is Lady Karanaya with you?"

"By Lord Andry's ten rings," Johlarian whispered at Mirsath's side. "Is that who I think it is?"

"Mirsath, what's going on?" Karanaya demanded, hurrying up to them. "Who is that, and why does he know our names?"

"It's Patwin of Catha Heights," he told her. "As for why he's here. . . ."

"Captive?" Johlarian guessed. "Under duress, with his daughters as hostages?"

"Let's find out. Lord Patwin! You may approach my walls along the causeway! Alone!"

After a brief conference down below, Patwin rode forward on his Radzyn bay. Mirsath, Karanaya, Johlarian, and the archers moved to the narrow balcony above the gatehouse. A solid wall behind and waist-high crenellations in front, the balcony had been built for the family's appearances during festivals and the New Year Holiday. The last time Mirsath had stood here, it had been hung with banners

and garlanded with flowers in honor of this spring's visit by the High Prince and High Princess. The people of Faolain Lowland had gathered outside to cheer them, then entered the gates for the solemnity of a law court followed by the happy chaos of a feast. A good day, a satisfying day. The kind of day Mirsath vowed Lowland would see again.

"My lord," he began as Patwin came within easy hearing distance, "I hope Catha Heights still stands."

"What? Oh, of course! Not a scratch on it. I'm pleased to see you alive and healthy, Mirsath—and the lovely Karanaya, too."

Johlarian whispered, "He doesn't sound worried. Have a care, my lord."

"Hush." To Patwin he called, "Your daughters are well?"

"Very, and prettier than ever. My eldest girl, Izaea, wishes particularly to be remembered to you."

Mirsath began to feel a little dizzy. Surely this conversation was unreal, this polite chat that might have been exchanged at a *Rialla* but was instead taking place in the presence of an invading army. He muttered, "He sounds as if he's having the marriage contract written up. This is insane."

"I quite agree." Karanaya leaned over the battlements. "Why are you here?"

Patwin began to laugh. And suddenly Mirsath understood.

"Haven't you been listening?" he hissed at his cousin. "His castle is fine, his daughters are fine, everything's fine. Duress? He's here because he wants to be!"

Her cheeks crimsoned with rage. "Because they'll give him something he wants?" Without waiting for an answer she already knew, she shouted down, "What did they promise you, craven? What's the price of treachery?"

"The princedom of Syr, of course!"

Mirsath pushed her aside. "And they'll do as much or more for me, is that it? If I surrender my keep without a scratch—the way you did!"

"Naturally there are rewards for cooperation. Why should I see the work of my ancestors in the hands of these barbarians? Catha is the jewel of the south, Mirsath. Could you see it destroyed? Speaking of the south—what would you say to that portion of the Desert—with Radzyn all your own?"

Now he *really* understood. "With Izaea as my princess?"

"Through my late wife, she's Roelstra's granddaughter. I've always pictured her as a princess." He swept one arm out to the side. "Look around you. It may take most of the winter to starve you out—but starve you will, and die, and so unnecessary. Work with the Vellant'im instead of against them, and they will prove generous. Mirsath, don't you want to be a prince?"

The royal title was the last word he ever spoke. An arrow sank into his chest, the fletching in Lowland's colors sprouting from his heart. He toppled from the saddle, dead before he slid gently into the depths of the moat.

"Nice shot."

Mirsath handed the bow back to the archer. "Thank you," he said calmly. "I hope I didn't hurt your arm when I appropriated your weapon."

"Not at all, my lord. Once again, it was my pleasure."

* * *

Word of Patwin's death got to Remagev that night by the moons. Rohan shook his head and sighed.

"It was a stupid thing to do, when you think about it. Mirsath should have agreed."

Sioned blinked at him across the taze that had been brought to their room. "So we'd have a spy in the enemy camp? Do you honestly think Mirsath capable of that much concentrated deceit?"

"Well, not Mirsath," Chay put in. "Karanaya, maybe."

"That's not what I was talking about," Rohan replied. "I meant that anyone looking at it rationally would consider Mirsath an utter fool. Keeping faith with his prince when his castle is hopelessly besieged? When accepting the offer could mean a princedom? A sensible man would have jumped at the chance."

Chay sent Sioned a warning glance and drawled, "Rohan, Rohan—you've corrupted these youngsters. They put loyalty to you above their own gain. You should be ashamed of yourself."

She took up the cause. "You're right, Chay, it's nauseating. He's taught them all sorts of bad habits. It can't be for his blue eyes or his pretty face. Why do you imagine they do it?"

"Rampant mental disability?" he guessed.

"All right, you two, enough," Rohan said. "Point taken. Remind me that if—*when*—we're handing out rewards to those who secured the victory, Mirsath has earned something special."

"But *that's* the point, you fool," Chay told him, completely serious now. "Do you think he expects a reward?"

"Rohan, you're thinking like a barbarian," Sioned added. "You don't have to pay them for their loyalty, my love. The coin you bought them with has nothing to do with gold at all."

Chapter Thirteen

Prince Volog, watching the course of a second battle for New Raetia laughed until his sides hurt. "Those idiots! What do they think women are—too delicate to be a threat or too stupid to give them a decent fight?"

His squire grinned back at him. "Whichever, my lord—our 'delicate' ladies are scything through them like spring wheat. What do you say—shall we pad all the armor so they face a whole host of women?"

The old man laughed so hard he had to sit down. "Oh, I can just see your grandsire! Chaynal of Radzyn Keep, with breasts beneath his breastplate! Rohannon, you have a wicked mind!"

They paced the upper walls of the keep, Volog leaning heavily on Rohannon's strong arm, and observed the battle with growing glee. By midafternoon it was amply evident that though the enemy finally condescended to cross swords with women as well as men, they would not be combing their beards in New Raetia's mirrors this night. Volog laughed again as they were driven back onto the beaches and into their longboats. But when he turned to Rohannon, his eyes were cold and grim.

"Bring me an accounting of their dead as soon as it's available," he ordered. "I want to know that Latham and Hevatia are avenged."

"Yes, my lord." Rohannon lent his arm to his aged lord as they descended the winding stairs. He didn't like the flush in the old man's cheeks, or the tremor in his hands. But at least he had roused from the shock of his son's death, and no longer sat staring dully at the fire. "They've tried twice to take us and failed twice. Do you think they'll need another lesson?"

Volog eyed him. "What you're saying is, if they do, can you help teach it? Don't think I don't know how it chafes you, escorting an old man around while others your age do the fighting. You're more use to me at my side, Rohannon."

"As you wish, my lord." He suppressed a sigh, then smiled. "Besides, my father and grandfather would never let you hear the end of it if I so much as stubbed my toe!"

The old prince's eyes twinkled. "What a value we place on ourselves, young lordling! Had you considered what they'd say to *you* if it was *my* toe?"

"Not a word. They'd flay me alive and leave me for dragon food!"

Grateful that he had made Volog laugh, he hoped the number of enemy dead would be sufficient to ease the old man's grief. Somehow he doubted it. How horrible it must be to outlive one's children. Only Alasen of Volog's two sons and two daughters was still living. Birani had died of a wasting sickness years ago, Volnaya in a shipwreck a few years after that, and now Latham was gone. Surely no pile of enemy casualties, no matter how high, could make up for losing his last surviving son.

Volog's page would keep watch over sleep the prince desperately needed, so Rohannon's time was his own. He climbed up to the curtain wall in time to see the end of the battle. As the surviving enemy rowed hard for the ships anchored off New Raetia, he couldn't help wishing that this had been a year for him to be Arlis' squire instead of Volog's. He was traded between New Raetia and Zaldivar the way Arlis himself had been, the way Riyan had divided his time between being Prince Chale's squire and training in Sunrunner arts under Lady Andrade. Not that Rohannon would be going to Goddess Keep. It wasn't that his father hated Andry; it was just that no one ever mentioned his name.

The theory behind Rohannon's back-and-forth education was that what he didn't learn at one place, he would learn at the other. The problem was that at Zaldivar he was the squire of a vigorous prince only twelve winters older than himself—but at New Raetia, of a man eight years his own grandfather's senior. He admired Volog, but life was infinitely more exciting with Arlis. If the young prince had been here, Rohannon would have been in the thick of the fight.

That would horrify his whole family, of course. But he

wasn't a child anymore. At fifteen he was an expert archer and not bad with a sword, either. He hoped to get his chance to prove it when Arlis arrived with the Iseli levies—any time now, Volog's court Sunrunner said. Pity they hadn't made it in time for this battle. Rohannon wanted his share of blood for the horrible way Latham and Hevatia had died. But there would be more fighting. Rohannon knew enough tactics to understand that the enemy must control Brochwell Bay to keep the northwestern princedoms and Kierst-Isel from sending help by sea. But if Arlis carried the fight to the water after rigging his merchant ships for war, Rohannon—son of two formidable Sunrunners—would never see battle at all.

That would please everyone at home, he told himself with a sigh. He believed in Rohan's ways of law and peace—but he also hungered to prove himself as brave and strong a warrior as his father, his grandfather, and his great-grandsire Zehava. Battle was in his blood. And at fifteen, compelled to watch instead of fight, that blood ran hot.

Rohannon descended to the main courtyard, where he could be of some use. He was unsaddling a feather-footed Kadar mare when Volog's page tugged frantically at his sleeve.

"My lord! We can't wake his grace!"

He outran the boy up the stairs. Servants crowded outside the prince's chambers; Rohannon pushed through and saw Tessalar, Rialt's fourteen-year-old daughter, kneeling beside the old man's bed. She looked up as he approached; tears streaked her pale little face.

"I brought taze, the way I always do this time of day, and he didn't wake. Rohannon—I think he's—"

"No!" But the coverlet did not move over Volog's chest, and there was no pulse in the bony wrist he lifted from the bed.

"I sent for the physician," Tessalar whispered. "But he and his helpers are tending the wounded."

Rohannon placed the prince's hand back on the quilt. "His grace won't be needing. . . ." He coughed around the lump in his throat and tried again. "You're right, Tessa—he's gone." He gazed down at Volog's smooth, peaceful face, untouched now by pain or grief or fierce laughter. All of life was simply and quietly gone.

"My lord?" It was the page, trembling in the presence of the dead.

"Not now," Rohannon said thickly.

"My lord, the guards commander sent me to ask for orders—"

With a thundering in his ears he realized that he was now the ranking highborn here. Until Arlis arrived—and how to tell him that father, mother, *and* grandsire were all dead? —Rohannon was master of New Raetia.

Battle was in his blood through a score of generations. But so was rule. He had been born of a line of princes; he was heir after his father to Radzyn Keep. He repeated that to himself, remembering that he had traditions other than that of the warrior to uphold. Absolute authority tempered by wisdom; leadership; the ability to oversee everything without forgetting individual needs or losing himself in details.

Rohannon straightened and drew a long breath. Responsibility settled silently on him, and it was not the warrior who shouldered it. Like knowing how to call Fire—capably, without having to think much about it—he began giving orders.

* * *

Maarken settled in the shade of Remagev's walls, wondering how a place that broiled by day could be so bone-chillingly cold by night. Autumn brought only small swings in temperature along the coast, blessed relief after the heat of summer, but here in the middle of the Long Sand there was no moisture in the air to hold the day's warmth. Hollis had blinked in surprise at the fire in their bedchamber hearth the night they'd arrived; Feylin, smiling, had told them they'd be grateful for it by midnight. Even with the fire, it took two thick Cunaxan wool blankets and a feather-stuffed quilt to keep them warm.

Now he was sweating. The morning's tour of barracks and stables had worn him out. Feylin hadn't allowed him up yesterday, not bothering to argue that after the exertions of battle, sandstorms, and the trek across the Desert, he had to have rest. She had merely observed that to see one's battle commander collapse on his face did not instill confidence in the troops.

Hollis' comment had been pithier. "Stay in bed, you

idiot. Do you think you're Pol's age?" It was some comfort to know that Pol, eleven winters his junior, was just as wrung out. But they'd spent one day resting. Now it was time to get back to work.

His task had been to inspect soldiers and horses to determine their readiness for another battle. Betheyn, daughter of an architect, was assigned to evaluate Remagev's defenses. Hollis took inventory of food, Sioned of military supplies, Feylin of medical stores. Pol was Sunrunning to every court not hidden behind cloud cover, gathering information, spreading reassurance that the High Prince was safe. Rohan himself was holed up with Chay and Walvis in the latter's office, poring over maps and planning strategy. And that madman Kazander had taken his men out to survey the terrain.

Everyone would meet at dusk, when it cooled off. Maarken told himself to be patient and take heart from the positive report he could give. The five hundred and six who had escaped Radzyn were in cramped quarters, but alive and grateful to be so. The wounded were made comfortable and tended as their injuries demanded. And out of three hundred and seventy-four horses, they had lost only twenty.

Maarken forbade himself to think about the hundreds more now in enemy hands. A clever foe, no doubt of it. In only ten days they had gained control of the major waterways, including Brochwell Bay; destroyed the Dorvali fleet that might have been used to transport soldiers; and gained enough mounts to speed their progress. Their hold in the south was sufficient to last through the winter, when rains would make fighting impossible. He remembered the winter of 704 as one long, gray, soggy misery. No one with any sense would attempt battle in such conditions.

Except in the Desert, where it rained once in a hundred years.

Well, those sandstorms ought to make them think twice, anyway. With time, Tallain and Jahnavi would come from the north. *This is our land, not theirs. We know and understand the Desert. And eventually, that will be our victory.* But he worried how many lives would be lost before "eventually" became "now."

He tried hard not to think about his people at Whitecliff. He had failed in his duty; he had not been there to protect them. He took scant comfort from the fact that his steward

was a canny old man who would know how to take everyone to safety—perhaps to Stronghold, which had never fallen. But then, neither had Radzyn.

Radzyn still had not fallen. It had been abandoned. That rankled, though he knew it had been the only choice. Had there been more warning—more time to gather troops and prepare—then Radzyn would still be theirs. But there had been no time, and now his patrimony was in enemy clutches—no sense regretting. He'd win it back. If it was damaged or even destroyed, he'd rebuild it. And Whitecliff, too, for when Rohannon Chose a wife. He owed his son what his father had given him. What fathers always owed their sons.

A few years ago, when the family had gathered at Stronghold for a New Year, he'd sat up very late with his father and Rohan over a cherished bottle of Syrene wine. Sioned's brother Davvi had yearly sent the finest vintages with a deliberately flowery letter of thanks in payment for a princedom—a joke among them, for he had been the rightful male heir to Syr. But Goddess help him if he didn't send his cellars' best; his sister took her wines very seriously. Kostas continued the tradition, though without the teasingly overdone missive. But that night had seen the last of Davvi's bottles, and by the time the final drops splashed into Fironese goblets, the three men were slightly drunk and very sentimental.

"Here's to him," Rohan had said, raising his glass. "Davvi started a minor lord and ended a prince, with sons ruling two lands."

"And not just by accident of birth," Chay put in. "I remember how he fought with us against Roelstra."

"So do I," Maarken said quietly. "And I remember how he gave me his new sword, given him by his son, to use against the pretender."

They sipped, savoring the wine. "A good man, a good prince, a good friend," Rohan murmured. "The kind we need more of. The kind who nurtured his princedom and gave it richer to his son. Not a bad life's work."

"The only life's work worth doing," Chay affirmed.

"Goddess knows both of you succeeded," Maarken commented fondly. "I hope I do half as well."

Memory faded into mists of wine, and Maarken shook his head. What he would give Rohannon and Chayla would have to be rebuilt. But he would do it. He must.

He had failed his people at Whitecliff; he would not fail his children. They were worthy of everything he could give them, and more.

His pride in his daughter was an almost unbearable ache. Chayla had worked with practically no sleep since their arrival, soothing fevers and cleaning wounds and sewing torn flesh so skillfully that there would be only faint scars. Soldiers he had worried about were sleeping peacefully, their injuries tended, their lives in no danger. She worked with calm efficiency, a physician born—and one day her art would outstrip that of Andry's much-touted Master Evarin. Of course, he had to admit with a different kind of pride that just looking at Chayla was enough to make a sick man well.

As for Rohannon—when they all met that evening, Pol spoke with special pride of his own about what his young cousin had accomplished at New Raetia.

"He's already organized scouting parties to clean up any lingering enemy patrols—like the one that killed Latham and Hevatia. The court Sunrunner says he's running the castle as if he'd done it since birth. And not a single person has so much as lifted an eyebrow at taking orders from a fifteen-year-old squire."

Chay cleared his throat. "The boy's had good schooling on Kierst-Isel."

"Nice try at humility," Walvis remarked, smiling. "Are you going to evade the truth, too, Maarken, or admit where Rohannon gets his abilities?"

Sioned's smile was tinged with sadness for the death of her kinsman. "Volog couldn't have left his castle or his princedom in better hands. Rohannon has done us proud. We needn't worry about Kierst-Isel—for now."

Rohan nodded. "Between him and Arlis, the island and its surrounding waters are as safe as they can get—for now."

"So are we," Feylin put in. "Medical and military supplies are quite adequate. But I don't relish the idea of having to feed all you lot for the whole winter."

"Gracious and noble lady," Kazander said with a bow in her direction, "do not trouble your mind. The Isulk'im can feed armies."

Walvis grinned at him. "Yes, but on what? Cactus spines? I've dined in your tents, Kazander. Mares are for riding, not milking."

"I don't know," Rohan said casually. "I rather liked that round of cheese you sent a few years ago, my lord *korrus*."

"The High Prince's grace is a man of rare discernment."

"I'm glad somebody here recognizes that. Leaving aside the problem of food for a moment," Rohan continued, "I'd like Pol to give us a summary of what he learned today. Feylin, will you make notes? Thank you."

"Going west to east—" Pol put a finger onto the map spread before his father. New Raetia was secure for the time being. Arlis was outfitting ships to attack the enemy by sea. Einar and Waes were untouched, the northwestern princedoms likewise. Ostvel was waiting for the last of the Veresch levies to arrive through early snow. Swalekeep was safe; Summer River was not yet directly threatened. Tilal had just reached Kadar Water, and the Sunrunner there had kept Pol busy for a long time with her report. He'd detail it later; for now, he passed on Tilal's opinion that Goddess Keep would be the next on the list of enemy objectives.

"Especially considering the concentration of Sunrunners there," he added. "The Pyrme is so far untaken, except for Allun's place—"

"What?"

"Sorry, Father, I forgot about that in my first report." Pol stared down at his hands. "Allun and his family have left Lower Pyrme with all their people. Abandoned it in advance of an attack—Cabar's orders. I found them on the road to Athmyr. His court Sunrunner told me that they left some rather interesting surprises behind, though."

"Such as?"

Pol wore his most innocent face. "Allun's complained to Cabar for years now that he needs new flooring above the great hall. Cabar never negotiated enough new Fessenden oak to replace the old—so Allun sawed through a couple of the support beams before he left."

Walvis choked with laughter. "And they'll all come tumbling down!"

"When Allun gets his keep back, Cabar will be forced to buy him a gorgeous new floor. Goddess defend me from such clever *athr'im*," Rohan drawled.

Pol grinned back. "Always assuming they get into the castle to encounter the deadfalls. The moat was drained. It's now thigh-deep mud—with a layer of pitch over it that the

Sunrunner will Fire once enough of the enemy are trying to cross."

"One *faradhi* can't call Fire from that kind of distance," Sioned objected.

"You did it to save Meath that time, all the way from Stronghold to Syr," Pol reminded her. "With help, true. Allun's and Tilal's Sunrunners were trained by Andry. They'll work together. Allun's man is confident they can do it."

"I see," she said quietly. "Go on."

"The rest of the news isn't too comforting. The Catha River is lost to us up to the Faolain. The Faolain itself—that's our major problem, but Kostas plans to take the Catha, follow it north, then come back down to Riverport—or where Riverport used to be," he added grimly.

"That doesn't do poor Mirsath any good at Lowland," Chay said.

"No. But Mirsath isn't Kostas' vassal. Kostas reasons that once he's got control of the Catha, Tilal can swing back around from Goddess Keep, meet him, then join Ostvel at the north divison of rivers. Then they march down the Faolain to the sea with a force that can't help but win."

Maarken frowned. "Superior numbers don't always equal victory. Not against an enemy as tactically smart as this."

"There's more," Pol said. "Rohannon told me that during both attacks on New Raetia, the enemy wouldn't fight female warriors. But the group at Radzyn did. Father, what you said about Mirsath observing petty rivalries—that plus this strange refusal to fight women means they're not one cohesive whole. My guess is they've banded together to fight, but it's not their natural state. The ones at New Raetia won't fight women. Sixteen different groups are at Lowland, some of whom don't like each other. It maks me feel much better. I was afraid we were facing one huge single-minded enemy, solid as the spire at Rivenrock. But evidence says otherwise."

"And yet they were efficient enough at Radzyn," Chay mused. "Graypearl was brilliantly done." He arched a brow at Rohan. "You always did attract the most amazing enemies."

Rohan's head tilted curiously. "Do you really think it's me they're after? I don't think they have much notion that I exist. We've ample proof that they're here to destroy, not conquer and hold—and they're especially interested in

Sunrunners. Mirsath told Hollis what happened to the Riverport *faradhi*." He turned to Pol. "If they know anything about us—or care to know it—you'll be their primary target, not I."

"Bring 'em on," Pol said, his smile turning wolfish.

Kazander cleared his throat. "The dread Lord of Radzyn and the most excellent High Prince and his worthy Heir know this, but I will bore them with it all the same. A man's status is measured by the quality of his enemies. Is it not obvious that the best warriors, the finest commanders, the most efficient strategies have all been used against the Desert? Why waste the strongest shafts and sharpest arrowheads against easy targets?"

Sioned cast him a sidelong glance, amused and yet mildly irked. "I'd prefer it if they didn't consider us so formidable. Maybe then we'd get the ones who scorn women fighters, or are too busy arguing with each other to be much nuisance to us."

Kazander shrugged. "The High Princess' wisdom is as vast as her beauty and her gifts—but it is desirable to understand the enemy one faces. They sent their best against the Desert. Therefore the Desert—and its High Prince—are their primary targets."

"Not to disparage Rohan's importance," Chay said "but they took Radzyn for my horses. Horses were all they took from other places. Granted that the enemy we face is different, but—"

"Radzyn's horses, Radzyn's lord—they had to get through you to get to Rohan," Walvis interrupted. "But what grudge could they have against the Desert that it's so essential to put their best troops here?"

"They didn't demolish Radzyn or Whitecliff the way they've done elsewhere," Pol pointed out, contrite as Maarken exhaled in sudden relief. "I'm sorry I didn't tell you that before—I'm going to have to organize my reports better from now on. Whitecliff is still standing. Untouched, in fact."

Maarken said quietly, "But not empty."

"No," Pol replied, hesitated, then added, "I think it's become the command headquarters."

"Not Radzyn?" Chay frowned.

"The castle's being used as a barracks," Pol said even more reluctantly.

Maarken made a strangled sound. "Those . . . *those*—in my mother's rooms?"

"Don't let her know," his father said. "Ever."

Kazander's eyes narrowed. "I respectfully suggest that the mighty Lord of Radzyn consider that before he reoccupies his keep, he orders it purified."

Chay snorted. "What *I* want to know is why Radzyn and Whitecliff aren't rubble."

Pol said, "They must want the Desert intact. This is the one place they haven't destroyed everything they could get their hands on. But why?"

Feylin reached for another clean parchment page. "Some ancient blood-debt?"

Maarken shrugged. "More logically, they're laying waste to the lands of their primary enemies. Radzyn and Whitecliff may still be standing for simple military convenience."

"But the Desert is no prize," Walvis reminded him. "We don't have rich farmlands or rivers or anything else that makes for an easy life. There are two reasons for war: revenge and increased wealth. If Feylin's wrong, and it's not the former, then these people are insane. The Desert has nothing to offer. All we've got are dragons and sand. Yet they sent their best against us. What's so special to them about the Desert?"

"I'm inclined toward the vengeance idea," Pol commented. "Although they could be doing as Maarken says—going after their main enemies, leaving nothing behind, and using the Desert as their base of power. After all, the High Prince does it. If the traditional centers in Syr and Gilad and so forth are gone, then other authority might be easier to set up. They could control everything from here."

Sioned rapped her knuckles on the table. "Let's deal with facts before speculations, if you please. We don't know who these people are, but we do know they're not one tribe or clan or princedom—however they're organized. Some of them refuse to fight women. Others have rivalries among themselves."

"Useful," Rohan mused. "Not much help to us here, but certainly something Kostas and Tilal should be aware of. Inform them tomorrow. And make sure Arlis knows about the other, Pol."

"He already does. Rohannon suggested all the battle harness be padded so every soldier the enemy faces has curves."

Chay snorted with laughter. "That's your mother in him," he told Maarken. "No sense of anyone's dignity but her own!"

"Clothes—" Pol said suddenly. "That's another thing Tilal mentioned. Two things," he amended. "First, their clothes are different from ours—not so much in cut as in material. He's never seen anything like that fabric. It's not silk or linen, although some of the garments are almost as soft and thin. It's not wool, either—although it can be rough-woven and thick. But he's sure it's all the same type, just like silk and wool have different weights. They have several kinds of leathers as well, some of it obviously cowhide, some of it unknown. And their boot soles are thin, but seem tough."

"No dragonhide?" Rohan asked. Killing dragons had been forbidden for over thirty years, but when a corpse was found—usually in the Desert or the Catha Hills—the hide was stripped and fashioned into gloves, boots, and riding leathers. The scarcity of the material made for soaring prices.

"None. But perhaps it's even more costly for them than it is for us, and these were only common soldiers, not even mounted. They also wear a kind of badge on their tunics—a jagged red slash embroidered on black. Tilal said it reminded him of a lightning bolt. He thinks it may have to do with the Storm God." Pol shrugged. "I think that's reaching a little."

"So do I," Sioned agreed. "If they're allied with the *diarmadh'im*, their deity is this mysterious, so-called Nameless One."

Chay asked, "What about weapons? Good manufacture on the steel?"

"Tilal didn't mention it, so I assume he found nothing out of the ordinary by our standards."

"He would've noticed. Tilal's a smart boy."

With a sly glance at his father, Pol quoted him: " 'Observe everything; it saves you the embarrassment of having someone else point it out to you later.' "

Rohan smiled. "Yes, he learned that lesson well, didn't he? What was the second thing?"

The spark of amusement in Pol's eyes turned to cold anger. "The two scouts had been tortured. We have no language in common. Whatever they said wouldn't have been understood. Yet they were tortured. For *pleasure*."

"Barbaric," Maarken said, his lips curling with revulsion.

"Tilal's exact word," Pol agreed.

"We learn more and more about the enemy," Rohan said after a moment. "I wonder what they've learned about us?'

"Not as much as they will learn in the near future," Kazander remarked with a casually ruthless smile.

Until that instant, Pol had seen this strange young man with his flamboyant speech as a kind of Desert curiosity, like the living walls of *athsina* cactus, big as a dragon and just as deadly, that one encountered sometimes in the north. But now he recognized in Kazander an eagerness to fight that matched his own. He hadn't felt this way at Radzyn; he had had no time to contemplate any reasons for the change. If he thought about it at all, he ascribed his feelings to anger and outrage and determination that not one more grain of Desert sand would be trod on by enemy feet.

But Rohan's lifelong habit was to wait patiently for events to develop. Thus Pol didn't even bother proposing the organization of a force that would take the battle to the enemy. Were this Princemarch, he could have ordered what he pleased. But the Desert belonged to the High Prince. He could contribute his ideas and skills—indeed, Rohan would be both disappointed and insulted if he did not—but he had no authority. Besides, what did he know of war? The other men here had all been in major wars. It was one of the Goddess' better ironies that Pol could not argue in favor of a battle he knew was necessary because he had scant experience of war. He had acquitted himself well at Radzyn, but one blooding scarcely qualified him to lead an army.

So he kept his own counsel, with a mental note to have a good long talk with Kazander—after making it clear that the *korrus'* comments must be couched in less grandiloquent phrasing.

Feylin had drawn them back to the summary of positions, and was saying, "Graypearl is in ruins, and the port town with it. Did the populace get away?"

"I didn't go looking for them," Pol said. "But Chadric would never have left if he wasn't sure that a goodly number of his people had made it to comparative safety."

"Dorval is a rotten place to fight a war—mostly steep hills meant for sheep and goats, not soldiers." Walvis pointed to the map. "The enemy has taken the only places they *can* take, Graypearl and Sandeia, along the coast where it's relatively easy terrain."

Sioned asked, "What about Chadric and Audrite? Where are they? Have they landed yet?"

Pol shook his head. "They couldn't go south, so I warned the Sunrunner at Tiglath to be looking for them. I didn't spot them today, but then I didn't have much time for a search."

"They're probably hugging the coast," Walvis said. "There are plenty of little coves to hide in. With Meath incapacitated, they can't know that the enemy came from the south."

"But from the northeast to Graypearl," Maarken reminded him. "A nice piece of confusion, that. And another excellent strategem by this group's leader." His blue eyes narrowed and his voice softened dangerously. "I appreciate Lord Kazander's idea that we are honored by the quality of our enemies, but I intend to impress some manners on this man—right into his brain on my swordpoint. He entered my house uninvited."

"Be glad he didn't burn it to the ground," Sioned told him. "Now that we've accounted for where these people are at the moment, I have a question almost as important—perhaps more so."

"Where they came from," Rohan supplied. "Any thoughts?"

"Their clothing is made of material unknown to us," Walvis began. "And they make a leather out of hide we can't identify."

"The beards seem to indicate full warrior status—particularly when the decoration is a Sunrunner's ring instead of gold beads." Feylin wrote as she talked, then glanced up. "Did you get accurate descriptions of those sixteen different banners, Pol?" When he shook his head, she told him, "Get them for me tomorrow, please. I'll leave a space in my notes."

"What else about them physically?" Rohan prompted. "They're dark—hair, eyes, skin—but not the taze-brown of a full-blooded Fironese like Morwenna, for instance. There's a reddish cast to their skin."

"They're big," Maarken said succinctly.

"You should know," Walvis commented. "You studied them at sword-length from dawn until well after noon."

"Closer study than was comfortable," Maarken answered, flexing his still bandaged wrist. "They shout '*diarmadh'im*' as a battle cry, the way we use the name of our holding or our prince. Their forging skills are equal to ours."

"They torture for amusement," Pol added.

Maarken nodded, continuing, "They're ruthless, merciless, barbaric—"

"And will probably receive help soon from their Merida brethren."

Chay's words stopped everyone's breath for a moment. Rohan recovered first. "Say that again," he ordered quietly.

"It was part of Andry's vision." He met Rohan's gaze and no one else's. "He didn't elaborate on what exactly he saw. But he was positive these people are Merida, or their close kin. I judge them to be the latter, since they don't fit the standard Merida physical type—they're bigger, and there's that reddish tint to their skins that you mentioned. Besides, who else is known to have been allied to sorcerers? The Merida were their assassins."

"That's why they use that battle cry," Pol murmured.

"Ruthless, merciless, barbaric. . . ." Rohan stroked the edge of the parchment map. It happened to be the section labeled *Cunaxa*. "Yes, that sounds familiar, doesn't it?"

Kazander rose abruptly to his feet. "My prince, I beg you will allow me to slaughter them for you! Their heads, their hands, or their eyes, whichever your grace desires me to bring back as proof—"

"Sit down, Kazander," Feylin snapped.

"The Merida are enemies of the Isulk'im even more than they are the enemies of the High Prince," the *korrus* said through his teeth.

"I'm from the north," she shot back. "I know what they are."

"Then you of all people—"

"Lord Kazander."

Pol watched his father capture and hold Kazander's fiery gaze. The struggle of wills was brief—and ended in Rohan's favor, as always. Pol had lost count of how many times he'd seen this done; it never failed to amaze him that this man could master anyone using only his eyes.

Kazander bowed low and resumed his chair. "It shall be as his grace commands," he breathed. "I crave pardon."

Sioned tactfully resumed the main discussion. "Even if these people are kin to the Merida, we still have no idea where they come from. We don't even know what they call themselves."

"Ah, but we do," Pol said, leaning forward. "Mirsath heard Patwin give them a name. 'Vellant'im.'"

"It *sounds* like our old language," Rohan said, frowning. "But is it? What are the possible meanings?"

Pol had seen ths countless times, too—his father presenting a problem, then sitting back to listen while others tried to solve it for him. *"Never do yourself what you can get other people who know more about it to do for you."* The speculations and suggestions came from other people—but the decisions were always Rohan's.

"Vellant'im," Sioned echoed thoughtfully, drawing the word out into its probable components. "*Vel* is sword. The *'im* signals a plural."

"They've got a lot of swords, all right," Walvis sighed. "Kazander, you speak the old tongue rather well. What do you think?"

"I use it in songs to delight ladies—and in phrases designed to insult Merida. Vellant'im," He repeated thoughtfully. "If the *t* is a corruption, then I make the name 'sword-born.' "

"But *lante* means mountain," Pol put in. " 'Sword mountains'?"

"Perhaps a clue to their lands," Rohan said. "Lord Kazander's idea makes their name a self-description—and, as Walvis pointed out, it's certainly apt. Pol's translation could identify their home. Mountains that resemble a rack of swords—or mountains with deposits of iron from which to *make* swords?"

Chay cleared his throat. "I know of nothing in any tales or legends that corresponds to either. Any of you?" Heads were shaken. Chay went on, "My verdict is to accept both translations—and I have no doubt that one of them is correct. After all, they use the name of sorcerers readily enough."

"Yes," Rohan murmured. "They use the name of sorcerers."

No one said anything for several moments. Pol shifted uneasily, as unwilling as the others to break the silence. Feylin did it for him.

"As a battle cry, you said. Then why have there been no spells? Why no word of sorcerers here rising in their support? And why haven't the Merida vermin come down from Cunaxa to join them?"

"You ask the most awkward questions," Walvis complained. "Someone's got to, I suppose. I don't know any-

thing about magic, but it's possible the *diarmadh'im* are massing in secret. The Sunrunners can't keep an eye on every mountain and hollow in the Veresch. Besides, when they came to support Chiana years ago, they hid well enough. It was only by accident that Donato discovered them."

"Perhaps they just don't *know* yet," Pol said, then felt foolish when his mother stared at him. "It's possible," he defended. "If they live isolated, then it could take some time to get word to them—even on starshine. And we've seen nothing to indicate that there are any sorcerers *with* the Vellant'im. Maybe there aren't. Maybe they're like the Merida in that, too—doing *diarmadhi* bidding but powerless themselves."

Rohan nodded slowly. "I see what you mean. It fits . . . but there's an itch in the back of my mind that says we're missing something."

"Sleep," Chay stated firmly. "We'll start this again tomorrow."

Nothing had been solved, as Rohan pointed out to Sioned in their chambers, but at least matters had been clarified.

"But—that Kazander!" He stirred up the fire in the hearth and added another log. Not of fragrant pine or oak; there was none to be had here. Remagev burned the woody husks of the gigantic *pemida* cactus for warmth on cold nights. "His spirit pleases me, but I'd feel better if he didn't remind me so much of a stallion who's never known a bridle."

Sioned climbed into bed and pulled up the quilt. "You've got the feel of it right, but the image wrong. He's like a hatchling dragon all grown up, but nobody ever told him he shouldn't still be able to breathe fire."

"Hmm. I wonder what the dragons will make of all this. Pol's Azhdeen was right about the ships, it seems. Did he see them coming, or do dragons have dreams of the future, too?"

"Andry knew, and told us nothing," she said slowly. "How could he betray—"

"He told his father. Who didn't believe him. That's not betrayal, Sioned."

"And does he now sit at Goddess Keep with a nasty smile on his face because he was right?"

"If you hold onto that attitude, you'll never be able to speak with him tomorrow."

She propped herself on her elbows, long hair streaming around her. "No! I won't do it! Tell Maarken or Hollis—"

"Maarken and Hollis aren't the High Princess. I'd do it myself if I knew how. You're the one who'll have to do the Sunrunning."

"On bent knee, with head bowed, begging to kiss his rings?" she snarled.

"Think it over," he advised. "I'm just going to look in on Tobin."

"Rohan, I *won't!*"

He gave her a small, knowing smile, despite the certainty that it would infuriate her, and left the room. Down the hall, Chay was about to get into bed beside Tobin, who was asleep.

"Shh—don't wake her," he whispered. "We can talk in the hall."

Rohan retraced his steps and they stood in the chill corridor. Guards walked the watch nearby, constantly pacing to keep their blood warm.

"What is it?" Chay asked impatiently. "Did Sioned kick you out? I know a bath every day isn't possible here, but surely you don't stink that bad."

"It's my plans she doesn't like, not my person." He explained his recent conversation with her, and Chay gave a low whistle.

"She may come around by morning—and then again, she may not. You should've been more subtle, Rohan."

"I'm afraid it's past time for that with Andry. But it's really your other son I wanted to talk about."

"I know."

"Know what?"

A stamping of cold bare feet, an irritated sigh. "That Maarken's got to have the title as well as the duties. I knew it while we were watching from the tower at Radzyn. Give me another title or none at all, it doesn't matter to me. But you have to name Maarken Battle Commander in his own right."

Rohan repressed his own sigh, one of relief. "For three reasons. First, the one you mentioned. Everyone must look to him first, not you or me or even Pol. Second, because he merits it. Third, because a public ceremony is the best sort of gathering right now—and honoring Maarken will be a

popular move as well as a smart one. We need something to draw us all together."

"Two more reasons," Chay said, a faint grin curving his mouth. "I'm too damned old to play these games anymore, and we all know it. And last but vitally important—Maarken needs the advantage with Andry that the rank will give him."

"I should have known I couldn't sneak that past you."

"You've taught *me* some disgusting habits over the years, too, you know. I never used to *think* so much."

"You always saw things for what they were. It was you who taught me to see reality instead of just my dreams."

"Your dreams changed things. My reality never could have." The grin widened. "Are we going to stand here complimenting each other all night while we freeze to death?"

Rohan laughed. "Situation desperate, feet turning to ice—why are these two idiots smiling?" he teased, and gave Chay a shove back toward his door. In his own chamber again, he saw that Sioned was pretending to be asleep. Just as well. He slid into bed beside her and lay on his back, watching the fire-thrown shadows on the ceiling.

Chapter Fourteen

A forced march had brought Tilal and his family to Kadar Water in excellent time. Lord Kolya, knowing his immediate need must be for a Sunrunner, sent his out to meet Tilal with the news that the entire holding was at his disposal. There was other news, too, after the *faradhi* spoke with Pol at Remagev and reported all that Tilal had heard and observed and done.

"Radzyn taken—I can't believe it," he murmured to Gemma as they rode into Kadar Water.

"Not for long, if I know Lord Chaynal," she replied, and he didn't have the heart to contradict her. There would be no quickness about any of this, no speedy resolution or retaking or routing of the enemy—and he wondered if he'd see his beloved Athmyr before spring.

He stayed one night at the holding and didn't sleep much. The gentle lap of the lake three floors below his bedchamber windows had a maddeningly irregular rhythm. When a drizzling rain began before dawn, he vowed that in no home he ever owned would he endure a tin roof. It would have been rude to rise before his host and thereby hint that the accommodations were not to his pleasure. So he left Gemma to sleep on and spread out a map before the hearth, huddling into a heavy, loose-woven wool blanket and making notes.

"What are you doing?"

He turned and smiled at the sight of his usually immaculate wife, rumpled and blinking in the rainy dawn. She was all sleepy velvet-brown eyes and vivid dark-auburn hair. The streak of white that had grown in before she turned thirty nearly vanished in this light.

"And don't tell me to go back to sleep, either," she

added before he could say anything. Rising, she dragged the quilt off the bed and came toward him. "Maps again? Where do you plan to do battle?"

"That's just what I was trying to figure out. Torhald, south of Athmyr, would be all right, but I don't want to lure them that far from the Pyrme. They don't seem interested in Ossetia for now—thank the Goddess."

"What about where the Catha and Pyrme meet?"

"We might get trapped between rivers. Besides, that's marshy ground this time of year and will get worse. If this were summer, it would be perfect."

"By summer, these whoresons will be dead to the last man."

He hid a smile. Gemma was a stubbornly single-minded woman who seldom changed her opinions. Though he loved her devotedly, he'd had occasion to regret her obstinacy. Now it amused him. "When you talk like that, I don't dare fail," he replied lightly.

"How I talk doesn't matter. How you fight does. You won't fail. What about near Rosmer's Ford? The drainage there is good—not much mud until midwinter."

"Hmm." He inspected the routes both armies could take to the site, calling to mind terrain the map did not indicate. "We'd have to draw them across the river to do it—but the river would be at their backs."

"Take a Sunrunner along to Fire the bridge," she suggested.

"Sunrunners are what I'm really worried about," he admitted. "The enemy has failed twice to take New Raetia. They're going to give up soon and take their war elsewhere. They don't need Einar—all they have to do is leave a few ships patrolling the strait. But Waes is the entry to Meadowlord. If they march across and link up with their people on the Faolain. . . ." He pointed out the probable strategy on the map. "If they decide against Waes, Goddess Keep is their next choice."

"I thought you'd told Pol that's where you definitely think they're going."

"I've reconsidered. I think I'm too influenced by the fact that Goddess Keep is in Ossetia. Waes is the more logical choice."

"And yet they shout *diarmadh'im* in battle." Gemma reached to stir up the fire, wielding an iron poker with savage intent. Tilal pulled the maps away from the sparks.

"Any member of our house worth his wine appreciates a gamble. Do you share the family instinct, Tilal?"

"Wife and cousin, I take Sioned's view—she never wagers except on a sure thing. And there's nothing certain about this. Waes or Goddess Keep? Which do they want more?"

"If you go to Waes, you'll be backtracking."

"If I go to Goddess Keep, it'll be just that much longer before I can join Kostas."

Gemma settled down beside him and sighed. "I admire Andry's taste in poetry, if not his politics. Other than that, we owe him nothing—except that he's on our land."

"His land, our princedom," he pointed out. She tended to see Goddess Keep as another Ossetian holding, and Andry knew it. "Besides, we owe him our protection. All the princes do."

"Then let them come to help! Where's Velden of Grib? Cabar can't send anyone from Gilad, he's too hard-pressed himself, but what about Chiana? If we made it here from Dragon's Rest in so few days, she can march down from Swalekeep in even less."

"Chiana? Defend the place where she spent six miserable winters as a child? Not likely, love. She'll have to come to the aid of Waes, since that's the gateway to her princedom." He paused a moment. "And isn't it amusing that we all automatically assume it's Chiana who'll be giving the orders, not Halian."

"He's not capable of ordering a new shirt."

"We judge our princes harshly, my lady."

"We judge our princes by the one we know best, my lord," she retorted.

There was a soft scraping at the door, and when Tilal called permission to enter, Malyander brought in a pitcher of steaming taze. Tilal's squire was heir to this keep, but being unexpectedly home did not excuse him from the usual duties. Tilal asked him to put the tray on the floor beside the fire, and then said, "Is your father awake yet?"

"Yes, my lord. He's anxious to speak with you at your convenience."

"I'll be downstairs shortly. No bath today—Goddess, dirt is what I hate most about war!—but I've got to have a shave. We leave as soon as everyone's ready."

Tilal met Kolya at the stables. Half the Dragon's Rest horses would be returned there by the troops Meiglan had

lent; the other half, plus those Kolya owed his prince in war, would suffice to mount Tilal's forces. The rest of the Ossetian levies were assembling at various points along the road. Gemma would take troops enough with her to Athmyr for its defense and, Tilal hoped, some effective raids to discourage an enemy attack on the castle.

"Are you sure you won't take more?" Kolya asked as Tilal chose a fine gray for his own use.

"No, but I appreciate the generosity. My other *athr'im* are well-mounted, thanks to your breeding program. When I look at the numbers from your father's time and compare them with yours, I can scarcely believe it."

Kolya's worried face cleared for a moment. "Getting the occasional jump on Radzyn is my chief pleasure in life."

"More than occasional. Your horses took plenty of prizes at the races this year." Tilal ran his hand over the stallion's muscular shoulder and down one leg to the white feathering around the hoof. A huge russet eye regarded him with suspicion, but Tilal knew how to manage these horses. The trick was to familiarize them with the rider's touch, scent, and voice—and then stare them down. "Rondeg here is a match for anything Chay has in his stables."

"Except they're not in his stables anymore." Kolya's smile was replaced by a grim frown. "And one reason I'd like you to take more of my beauties is that I don't want those barbarians on their backs."

"I understand. But don't worry. We'll get them before they're within reach of you. I'd like you to hold the rest of your horses in readiness if they're needed."

They left the stables after ordering two wary grooms to saddle the big stallion for their prince. The courtyard was controlled chaos. The group Gemma was taking with her to Athmyr was nearly one hundred strong. Tilal's force was twice that, waiting outside the walls.

Kolya took Tilal aside. "My lord, I've hesitated to mention it, but—"

"Go on, Kolya," he prompted, trying to be patient even though he itched to be on the road. Trouble was, he hadn't yet decided *which* road.

The *athri* met Tilal's gaze levelly. "My lord, your squire is my only son."

That brought Tilal up short. One of Rohan's most inconvenient rules of governance was that a prince must always

try to see all sides of an issue. At question here was Tilal's right to the services of his squire—and the right of a lord to the safety of his only heir.

As he looked into Kolya's tense face, there was no need for imagination to recast himself as a father with a precious child at stake. Goddess be thanked that Sorin was only nine; he would stay at Athmyr with Gemma and Sioneva, safe. But Rihani was seventeen, and with Kostas. True, he was of an age and at a point in his training that he could acquit himself very well in a battle—and Kostas would be careful. But Malyander was only twelve, and an only son.

"I'll miss him," Tilal said quietly. "The difficulty is how to present it to him so he's not shamed by being left behind. He's very proud, but more than that, he's got a powerful sense of honor and duty."

Kolya's face changed as he realized that his son would not be put at risk in war. He swallowed hard. "Thank you, my lord," he murmured.

"Perhaps if I say I want him here to use what he's learned thus far about defending a keep? You were never fostered, as I recall," he finished unwisely.

Kolya looked anywhere but at him. "I was only five when my father died in the Plague. It was decided that I should stay here rather than spend years at someone else's holding. I never learned the art of war."

"That's the way Rohan wanted us all to grow up," Tilal mused.

"You're gracious to overlook my inferiorities," the *athri* replied bitterly.

Tilal knew he didn't have time to restore Kolya's sense of self-worth; he made time anyway, because it was what Rohan would have done. He hoped he could do it in the same style. "Art? Sweet Goddess, what art is there in knowing twenty different ways to butcher an enemy army?" He gestured at the big gray and all the horses nearby. "*That,* my friend, is your art."

"At least I'm some use to you, then."

Tilal grinned as the stallion bared formidable white teeth. "If that beast doesn't chomp my head off first!"

Kolya snorted with laughter. "Only meat-eating horse I ever met. I'll protest about Malyander a bit, my lord, if you don't mind. His pride will need it. I remember being that age."

As Tilal gave the squire his orders and his reasons for them, he reflected that he seemed to be making a habit of convincing children to stay where they belonged. Malyander listened wide-eyed, brightened when Kolya objected that a squire's place was with his fostering lord, but reached the conclusion they wanted him to. His mother nearly ruined all by casting a glance of appalled betrayal at her husband when he made his protests. But the boy, after a gulp of regret that he wouldn't know the excitement of battle, shook his head.

"I want to help fight," he admitted. "But if Prince Tilal needs me to be here, then I have to stay."

Gemma's subtle but firm physical restraint prevented Lady Matiya from clasping her darling child to her breast, but not even a stern look could keep her from bursting into tears of joy. Malyander sighed impatiently at his mother's display and turned to his father.

"*You* understand, don't you, Father?"

"Yes. I'd rather we could fulfill our obligation to our prince," he said, and it was only partly a lie, "but if he orders it, we must in duty obey."

"*That* was chancy enough," Tilal murmured to his wife as they rode from the keep. "But Kolya was right—the boy's too young."

"You were no older."

"I was a second son."

"Did your father love you any less or worry about you any less because he had Kostas?"

"I know what you're really saying," he told her gently. "It's Rihani, isn't it? Why do you think I'm anxious to join Kostas? I trust him, but I have to be there, Gemma. I have to see Rihani safely out of each battle with my own eyes."

They rode on in a misting rain for which Rondeg had no liking. The stallion signaled his displeasure with flattened ears and teeth bared at any horse foolish enough to get within reach. Tilal did not discipline him; experience had taught him that the reaction meant he was willing to defend his rider. Tilal had already demonstrated his authority with a solid whack to the stallion's cheek when he reared as Tilal mounted. Radzyn horses were sweeter of temper, but a Kadar stallion was worth the trouble.

As they neared the main road, the clouds parted to give the sun a look at the land. Tilal squinted in the sudden

brightness. That wooded rise up ahead, that was the crossroads where he must part with his family. He told himself they'd be safe, that Athmyr was a stout castle that could hold out at least as long as it would take him to arrive. And thus far the enemy had shown little interest in pushing west to Brochwell Bay, being content to control the central rivers. But his solace lay in Gemma's adamant vow to hold the keep as long as there was breath in her body. One did not doubt a woman like that.

From down the column a voice Tilal recognized shouted his name. Not his title—his name. That surprised him less than the tone: frantic, almost terrified. He reined his horse around and rode to find the man, an aged retainer who always accompanied him to *Riall'im*.

"Chaltyn? What the—oh, Goddess," he breathed, and jumped from his saddle. Chaltyn knelt on the ground beside Sioneva, who had tumbled off her horse. Her eyes were wide open and glazed—but not because she had hurt herself and was stunned. Tilal had known that look since childhood: since becoming squire to a prince with a Sunrunner princess.

"Tilal—my lord, she fell and there was nothing I could do to—"

"You others, get back!" He cradled his daughter's head in his lap, stroking her dark hair that had come free of its pins. "Wine, quickly!"

Chaltyn gave him a full wineskin. But he didn't open it, not yet. Not until Sioneva's blue eyes blinked and focused. Tilting her head up, he poured a mouthful down her throat. She choked slightly, then grasped the skin herself and took a good long draught.

"Better?" Tilal asked.

She nodded. "Mother of All!" she breathed. "So *that's* what it's like!"

Gemma had joined them by now, on her knees in the mud. "What, heartling?" she asked gently.

"Sunrunning," Tilal said succinctly. "Who was it, Sioneva?"

"L–Lord Andry," she whispered, marveling at this strange, wonderful, astonishing thing that had happened to her. "It was like bathing in color—"

"Damn him!" Gemma hissed.

"No, you don't understand!" Sioneva propped herself on her elbows, her eyes shining. "It was *beautiful!* Like being

immersed in water that I could feel and taste and smell and even hear—only it wasn't water, it was color!"

So he had a Sunrunner child after all. He'd wondered as his sons and daughter grew if the gift brought by a *faradhi* who married a prince of Kierst would touch his children as it had touched Sioned. Tilal's father had not been a Sunrunner; neither were his two sons. Sioneva had never shown any signs of it; she was never ill while boating on the little lake at Athmyr, but then some Sunrunners were affected by nothing less than an ocean in a storm. But that she was indeed *faradhi* was in no doubt. He knew the gift was in his family; it was not unknown in Gemma's branch of the Syrene royal line. Now they knew for certain, courtesy of the Lord of Goddess Keep himself.

"I'm glad you enjoyed it," Tilal said, thinking of Alasen, who had been terrified by the revelation of her gift. "But now that you seem to have become my Sunrunner, what did Lord Andry have to say?"

The wonder left her face. "Father—this morning he spotted ships sailing down from New Raetia to Goddess Keep!"

Neatly solving the problem of where to go and what to defend, he thought. The Goddess must be looking after her own. He hadn't consciously waited, as Rohan would have done, for events to show him what action to take. But if he'd marched directly for Waes from Kadar Water instead of escorting his ladies to the main road, there would have been no Sunrunner for Andry to contact, no receipt of any message. He'd have to tell Rohan that a philosophy Tilal did not really believe in had worked.

But how had Andry known about Sioneva?

He smiled at her. "When I see Andry, I'll thank him for his skill and care of you. Can you ride? You and your mother had best start for Athmyr."

"But you can't send me there now! You'll need me!"

"I know what I need to know. Goddess Keep will soon be under attack. I can get there in time—but not if I'm worried about whether you'll stay on the road home. Promise me, Sioneva."

Her delicate brows slanted in a frown. Another princess with a will of her own—but this one had the maturity to recognize necessity. She sighed, pushed the hair from her face, and nodded. "Yes, Father."

He helped her to her feet. She and Gemma tried to brush

the mud off their clothes and succeeded only in getting their riding gauntlets filthy. Tilal nearly called for Malyander to fetch fresh trousers for all three of them before remembering he had no squire now.

Their horses were brought—Rondeg glaring, the others sidestepping out of his way. Tilal realized with a shock that this was farewell.

"Gemma—" He couldn't find the right words to tell her good-bye. "I'll get news to you at Athmyr as soon as I can." Suddenly he gathered wife and daughter to him. "I love you. Stay safe."

Gemma kissed him in public for the first time since their marriage ceremony, startling him so much that he lost all capacity for speech. Just as well; she was on her horse an instant later, directing Chaltyn to keep the prince healthy or else. Tilal watched them ride away for a few heartbeats, then swung up onto the gray stallion's back. This time Rondeg neither reared nor bucked. He bared his teeth at the nearest horses just to remind everyone of his status, then slid into an easy gallop as Tilal led his troops west and south to Goddess Keep.

* * *

"So Tilal's coming. Let's hope he makes it before the enemy." Torien paused in his nervous pacing of Andry's bedchamber. "How *did* you know about Sioneva?"

Andry sank more deeply into the cushions. He was not in the best of moods. He'd had a nasty little chat with Sioned on the morning sun that lingered in the knotted muscles of his neck. How dare she tell him she expected regular reports from every Sunrunner on the continent, as if she were Lady of Goddess Keep? Taking a long swallow of wine, he rubbed his aching forehead and winced at the splatter of rain beginning outside. He'd cut it fine this time. Another few instants and clouds would have blown over the sun.

"Endless genealogies—and the mirror," he said.

"Gentle Goddess," Torien breathed. "I'd forgotten."

"So do I, most of the time. It's more of an irritant than a help. I always suspected one of Tilal's children might be *faradhi*. It's in both families. Those genealogies that drove Andrade nearly insane practically guarantee it."

"This rain is going to guarantee *my* insanity," Torien

grumbled, casting a bitter glance out the windows. "They knew the season to attack, didn't they? How much sun do we average in autumn and winter—one day in ten? Twenty? At least they can't march through knee-deep mud."

"Rohan did. Oh, not far, and with my father taking care of strategy he only had to fight a couple of battles against Roelstra. But he did it. And how many more battles do you think necessary? They own the Faolain and the Catha. They'll add the Pyrme before winter hits. All they need is Waes and Goddess Keep before spring. That's when the war *really* starts."

"You mean our war, not theirs."

Andry considered. "I hadn't thought of it that way. Our war to take everything back will have to wait. It's been all theirs up until now—with the exception of New Raetia." He smiled. "Ah, Rohannon is a kinsman to be proud of! What a *faradhi* lord of Radzyn he'll make one day!"

"Have you spoken with him?"

"Not yet. Sioneva was essential; Rohannon can wait. He knows what he's doing and he's doing it very well. Goddess Keep is what's important right now."

"The home farms are emptying. We can hold our people plus a hundred or so from the villages. But that's all."

"Our gates are open to all, Torien. No one will be turned away from Goddess Keep. They're welcome as long as they don't interfere with the *devr'im*." His smile thinned. "Besides, I want as many witnesses as possible. But you wanted to know how I figured it out about Sioneva."

Andry took the bulky genealogy scrolls from their case on a shelf and unrolled them onto the carpet. Real parentage and lists of illegitimate children were included here, unlike the official records downstairs in the library and at Castle Crag. But the essential lie, the one about Pol, was missing. Andry kept that one to himself.

Andrade had in her time kept charts as complete as she could make them of various bloodlines. Of course, the princes and *athr'im* knew their forebears back hundreds of years, but the common folk rarely bothered. Yet it was from these commoners that the overwhelming majority of Sunrunners came—becase marriage between trained *faradh'im* and highborns had been, if not exactly forbidden, then strongly discouraged.

"It's fact," Andry told Torien as they settled onto the

rug, "that those with *diarmadhi* gifts pass them on to all offspring without exception. With *faradh'im,* the skills are guaranteed only if both parents are Sunrunners. Sometimes parents who are ungifted themselves produced *faradhi* children—"

"—which invariably shocks them speechless," Torien chuckled.

"It certainly did my father," Andry agreed, "when he found out about Maarken and then about me." For lack of a better term, Andry called people such as his father "halflings." Their gift in combination with a full Sunrunner could make for *faradhi* children.

The puzzle of Alasen made sense only if Andry accepted this halfling idea. Neither of her parents were gifted, and none of her siblings—but Alasen was. Ostvel, too, must be a halfling; their eldest daughter, Jeni, was *faradhi.*

So was Sionell's daughter Antalya. Sailing with her father off the Tiglathi coast one day five years ago, not a dragon-length from shore Antalya turned green and fainted. There had been a repeat scene on the lake at Skybowl later that summer. Speechless? Tallain, Sionell, and her grandparents had practically joined her in her faint.

"It's something like eye color," he mused. "Two blue-eyed people can't have a brown-eyed child—"

"Unless the father isn't really the father."

"Yes—which is a dead certainty if the baby turns up with dark eyes. That was Barig of Gilad's problem—his mother is definitely Cabar's aunt, but the only thing certain about his father is that it wasn't the man she married. But the analogy is fairly apt for Sunrunners. Two of us can't have ungifted children. But people with brown eyes *can* have a blue-eyed child."

"Halflings," Torien said, tracing Tilal's and Gemma's lines with one finger across the complicated parchment.

Andry nodded. "And the mirror can tell me who's what. It breaks down when we start talking about sorcery, of course."

"Can I have a look at it?" Torien asked. "I'd like to see it at work again."

Formerly the property of an old socerer woman who lived—and died—in the Veresch, the mirror reacted differently to the names of *faradhi,* halflings, sorcerers, and those with both gifts. The first appeared with their colors clearly

defined around them; the second with a faint aura called an *aleva*, or "fire circle." Full-blooded *diarmadh'im* were defined by blackness in the mirror—which Andry considered appropriate enough. Those such as Pol, both Sunrunner and sorcerer, appeared with their colors limned in eerie silver. Everyone thought that Riyan was both as well, but the mirror had told Andry long ago that the man was all *diarmadhi*. His queasiness when crossing water was not due to Sunrunner blood, but to a normal physical reaction.

He went to the closet where the mirror was kept, shrouded and seemingly unimportant, and carried it near the hearth. Whisking the blanket from the glass, Andry conjured a fingerflame.

"Sioneva," he said, and the girl's image appeared—with the glow of full Sunrunner gifts around her head. "You see?" he remarked to Torien. "Halfling parents, *faradhi* child."

"What about the others?"

"Rihani," Andry told the mirror. The boy's face was very like his sister's—they shared the same brown hair and blue eyes, the same resemblance to Tilal about the eyes and Gemma around the brow and jawline. But what was brilliant surrounding the girl was barely visible in the boy: halfling.

Andry identified the third sibling aloud, Named for his own dead twin. Goddess, how much it still hurt to think of his brother. The mirror showed him Tilal's son; it stayed blank on hearing the names of the dead.

Young Sorin looked like neither parent, and where he'd gotten those gray eyes was problematical, but by the usual odd trick of kinship he was unmistakably the brother of Sioneva and Rihani. He was half a Sunrunner, and therefore useless to Andry.

"Well," sighed Torien, "that's two fewer *faradhi* princes we have to worry about. No problems with Ossetia in the future."

"No? Your vision doesn't extend far. What if Sioneva marries a halfling lord, and their children are Sunrunners? What if Rihani Chooses Antalya of Tiglath, say, or my niece Chayla, and his children turn out the same? It's generations we're speaking of, Torien. The trouble is, I don't know whether to encourage it or stop it."

The steward was barely listening. As each name was

spoken, the face in the mirror changed. Torien blinked into his own eyes and Andry grinned at his discomfiture. It was a bizarre thing indeed to be standing at the wrong angle for a direct reflection, and yet to see one's own face in this mirror.

Torien felt his sidelong amusement and shrugged irritably. "Perhaps just this once you could ask Brenlis to look into the future and—"

"No—oh, Goddess, no!"

Andry put both hands to the mirror's cold surface. He called Brenlis' name, frantic with fear, clawing the glass.

Empty; blank nothingness; the mirror's response to the names of the dead.

Chapter Fifteen

As Tilal heaved his saddle onto Rondeg's back, Chaltyn gripped the bridle in one hand and rubbed his balding pate with the other. "I don't like it, my lord," he stated frankly. "That bunch of—mind your teeth or I'll hood you like a hawk, you misbegotten brute!—those song-singing Sunrunners can't fight. It will be just us against Goddess alone knows how many of those savages."

Tilal kneed Rondeg in the belly; air whooshed from the horse's lungs and tufted ears were laid back. He quickly tightened the girth. "Nice try, old son," he told the stallion. "But I know your tricks by now. I know Sunrunner tricks, too," he added to Chaltyn. "You don't believe in rumors, do you?"

"I believe in nothing I can't grab with my fists," the old man growled. "I know the rumors, my lord. That a magical wall goes up at their bidding, turning warriors and horses to stone." He snorted. "You'll never convince me I'll soon sit a granite gelding."

"Don't fancy yourself as an equestrian statue? No more do I. But it's fear woven into the wall that makes enemies *wish* they'd turned to stone." Sioned had told him the story of the battle at Dragon's Rest nine years ago—a battle that had ended before it even began. Just where the gorge widened into the valley, Andry had constructed a spell from the Star Scroll. Those contacting that invisible wall slammed into their own worst nightmares.

"Wall or not, they'll need us to do their fighting for them."

"Agreed." The *ros'salath* would keep the Vellant'im out of Goddess Keep, but it would not kill. That was Tilal's job.

He inspected Rondeg's leather battle harness, the equine

equivalent of his own, covering breast, upper limbs, and back. Kolya had insisted he take the armor along with the stallion; a commander unhorsed was a very bad idea. Tilal's gear was a gift from Kolya as well, the leather hastily redyed in Ossetian dark green. Matiya had fashioned a plume for his helm that resembled the wheat-sheaf symbol of his princedom. He also wore the belt of Desert blue and the gold buckle of his knighthood, given twenty-five years ago and brought out for the *Rialla* this year. It had been Pol's notion that older men should wear the symbol of their status to honor new-made knights. Tilal was glad he would be carrying Rohan's color into battle with him. He only wished he had the High Prince's banner as well to fly beside his own.

The symbols and the substance were ready. He mounted and made a brief tour of his troops. Those gathered from around Kadar Water had been augmented by levies from elsewhere in Ossetia, until he commanded a respectable army of cavalry, bows, swords, spears, and scythes. Something Rohan had said years ago came to mind—that people fight for their own land with a fervor not born of mere loyalty to a prince. Tilal had no illusions that his four hundred and sixty-three followed him for himself alone. He was a just and able prince, generous, faithful to the law. His work in the war against Roelstra at so young an age was a source of pride to his people; he had a handsome wife and a charming daughter and two strong sons. The Ossetians loved him well—but for all that, he was a foreigner, a Syrene-born second son of River Run's *athri*. It was just as well he had no territorial ambitions and did not make war to amuse himself; through duty his people would have followed him, but they would not have fought as they were about to do.

And, ultimately, fight for whom? Andry. Goddess Keep was on Ossetian land; it was only good tactics to stop the Vellant'im there. But that Andry would be the primary beneficiary of spilled Ossetian blood did not sit well with Tilal.

The Lord of Goddess Keep annoyed him on several counts. Tilal had philosophical differences with Andry over the direction *faradh'im* had taken in the last eighteen years. He looked askance on rituals and mysteries. His nature inclined him toward easygoing, friendly, unsuperstitious relations with the Goddess. But even if he had agreed with Andry, there was a deeper problem that was at once—paradoxically—

intensely personal and overwhelmingly political. Neither the man nor the prince in Tilal appreciated Andry's self-chosen position as rival to Pol's power. He was on Pol's side, simply and irrevocably. Family feeling was part of it. He also genuinely liked his cousin as a man. As a prince, he deplored the inevitable clash of two strong wills. And he had the uneasy feeling that this war would see a headlong collision between them.

But that was not his immediate problem. He nodded to Chaltyn his approval of the disposition of troops, beckoned to his banner-carrier—a place that would have been Malyander's, now held by a woman archer from the southern coast—and began the march. They would reach Goddess Keep by noon, set up camp, and wait for the Vellant'im to land on the beach below the wrinkled cliffs. Tilal had several ideas about using those cliffs to his advantage, and as he led his army across the autumn-rich meadows of their princedom, he was smiling.

* * *

The alarm was called just after dawn. The Sunrunner on watch had no need of sunlight to see the dragon-headed ships; they were less than twenty measures off the coast and sailing fast.

Torien was informed first. He nudged his wife awake, threw on some clothes, and sent warnings to the home farm and the villages. Then he went to have a look for himself.

Jolan was already up on the battlements, gazing out to sea. She didn't spare him a single glance as he stood beside her in the crisp morning air.

"By the Father of Storms—magnificent," she breathed. Daughter of pearl-fishers along the Dorvali coast, she appreciated a fine spread of sail. Torien, born near Snowcoves in Firon, could not help but agree with her. Admiration for the ships momentarily banished all other thoughts.

Oclel appeared at Torien's shoulder. "They'll hit Trenchwater soon," he said. "That gives us some extra time."

Wrenched back to practicalities, Torien nodded. The deep ocean floor gorge, hinted at by a swath of midnight-blue water, had a current as strong as the Faolain in spring flood. The captains of regular cargo ships knew how to negotiate

Trenchwater. It would slow the enemy's progress—or so he hoped.

"I'll wake Andry—if he's not already up. Oclel, you start the drill. Everyone knows what to do."

"They'd better," Oclel replied in a voice that boded ill for slackers or those of poor memory. "As for the farmers and their noise—they'd best behave and not get in anyone's way."

"Kind but firm," Jolan reminded him, smiling a little. "Don't bite their heads off. War is new to them."

"And the rest of us have been doing it all our lives?" Oclel asked. "I won't have their pigs squealing underfoot while we work. They'll do as they're told and stay where they're put or they can go take their chances outside." He squinted at the dragon ships. "No one's thought to find Tilal yet, I suppose?"

Jolan shrugged. "We can keep them busy until he arrives."

"I don't like being beholden to him," Oclel muttered. "He's Rohan's, down to his last breath."

"He's prince enough not to gloat to our faces—unlike his brother."

Torien elbowed his old friend in the ribs. "Be glad it's not Kostas marching to our defense. We'd never hear the end of it."

They went about their tasks, Jolan keeping pace with Torien to Andry's door. "Having seen those ships, I don't wonder Chadric fled," she murmured.

Torien stroked her cheek, his fingers brown as taze against the white-rose paleness of her skin. "But you haven't forgiven him."

"Would you? My parents, my sisters and cousins—Goddess only knows what's become of them. All I saw on sunlight was their village. Burned to cinders."

"We'll look for them again soon, love," he promised. "Perhaps they're with Prince Ludhil."

"And perhaps they're all dead." Jolan straightened and continued more briskly, "I'll go prepare the wine."

"Make it fairly strong. We may be at this a while."

This was Andry's opinion as well. He was awake and dressing when Torien entered his chambers. The steward barely had time to report what had been seen and thus far done before the outer door burst open and Andrev ran into the room. The boy skidded to a stop at his father's side.

"Valeda says I have to stay with the *children!* I'm thirteen, Father, old enough to be your squire! Please let me!"

Torien saw amusement war with consternation in Andry's blue eyes. The son was the image of the father in that feature as well as the lines of mouth and jaw and the sweep of thick hair back from the temples. But Andrev was blond like his mother Othanel, who had died ten years ago attempting a Star Scroll spell. Since spring, Andrev's height had started to go up and his voice had started to go down—but as he repeated his plea, the latter cracked back into a childish treble.

"I can hold the banner and I've been practicing with sword and knife and Oclel himself says I'm pretty good—please, Father!"

After a moment, Andry said softly, "No."

"But *why?*"

"Because—" Andry hesitated, and Torien saw the reasons in his eyes. Andrev was his eldest son, soon to begin the training that would make him Lord of Goddess Keep after Andry. Since his eleventh year he had been wild to be fostered at some court—preferably in the Desert, like his half-sister Tobren—and become a real squire like other boys of his age and high birth. His father had forbidden it.

Torien said, "Because the battle we'll fight won't be with swords or knives. Your skills will better serve to protect your brother and sisters." He had little inclination for and less experience with children, despite the dozens at Goddess Keep—and Andrev was no fool. But for a disgusted glance, the boy ignored him.

"I could stand guard. I won't get in your way, Father, if you're worried about that."

Andry shook his head. "I wasn't. But I'd have to worry about your safety, and that would distract me from what I must do."

The boy's cheeks flushed. "I'm not like Joscev, that you have to rescue me from the roof or keep me away from the unbroken horses!"

"I know. But I'd worry about you all the same."

"But, Father, I—"

"Enough, Andrev. I have things to do, and you're keeping me from them." Even Torien recognized that this was the wrong thing to say. Hastily—but too late—Andry added, "We'll talk about your fostering once this war is over.

Would you like to go to Kadar Water, or perhaps Kierst-Isel like your cousin Rohannon? Think about your choice."

"Once the war's over, I won't be any use to you," Andrev said, stiff pride trying to conceal angry disappointment. "I'll get out of your way now, Father."

"Andrev—" He extended a hand, but the boy was already out the door. Andry sighed. "He won't soon forgive me for this."

"Andry, he worships you."

"When he was little, yes. But he's growing up. At his age, all I wanted was to prove myself—but in Sunrunner arts, not those of war. I suppose it's my father and grandfather in him." Shrugging, he donned a white wool tunic and belted it around his waist. "Let's get started. I want an estimate of when Tilal will arrive. And Trenchwater won't slow these people down long, you know—they've come from Goddess knows where through Goddess knows what kind of seas. We're not dealing with casual sailors here."

That became obvious when Jolan checked on the ships' progress. "Faster than I thought," she admitted as the *devr'im* assembled in the gate tower. Indicating the wine cups on a low table, she said, "Drink up. We've got work to do."

Torien watched the others find their individual goblets. Commissioned from a Fironese crystaller, each of the nine had been designed by Andry in the primary colors of each *faradhi*'s gifts. Jolan's was a scene of underwater pearl-beds, amber and emerald seaweed bending delicately in the current; for Oclel, born in the Veresch, a black wolf paced among ruby flowers near a sapphire river. Rusina paused to admire her cup before drinking; the glass showed a gray-white cat stalking blue birds through a grassy field. Everyone knew who Andry cast as the cat.

Ulwis drank her wine slowly, sunlight glistening off topaz-gold hawks wheeling above the blue-and-purple mountains of Cunaxa where she had been born. Nialdan's had birds, too: red-feathered sea geese nesting in emerald grass on the beaches of his father's holding near Waes.

Valeda drained her cup and set it down directly in the light; the complex design, mostly green with pinpoints of red flowers, depicted the circle of trees near Goddess Keep with its pond and rock cairn. It was a reference to her main duty here, that of making boys into men under the guise of the Goddess.

Torien's was in shades of red and amber and blue, sunset over the sea. Deniker's goblet must have caused the crafter many false starts before he got that unusual jade green right. Into the opaque green sea a blue waterfall tumbled, foaming white at its base.

But Andry's was the most impressive, as was fitting. A ruby-bright dragon soared above his native Desert, amber beneath a sky streaked with amethyst clouds. The colors were augmented by bits of crushed jewels blown into the molten glass itself—a triumph of the crystaller's art. Empty now as he turned it by its stem in the sun, it spat color onto the walls.

"Feeling it yet?" Andry asked quietly.

A few nods; those who had not yet finished their wine quickly did so. By the time Torien joined the others on the sunlit balcony above the gate, the *dranath* had heated his blood and sharpened his perceptions. The faces of the others showed the same heightened awareness. Incredible, what a pinch of harmless-looking herb could do.

The configuration of strengths had been worked out years ago and tested many times—but never against a real attack. Yet Torien sensed no nervousness in the group, sure of themselves and especially of Andry. As core of the *ros'salath,* he was in the center. Flanking him were Nialdan and Rusina. Oclel stood at his wife's side, Jolan next to him, and Valeda last of all to anchor that portion of the weaving. To Nialdan's right were Ulwis and her husband Deniker. Torien took his place at the far end, and they were ready.

Oclel needn't have worried about distracting noise. The morning was quiet here, all the farmers and villagers inside the keep now, with thick stone walls between them and the *devr'im.* Neither was there any sign of the enemy. There was only the silent expanse of shorn fields bordered by red- or gold-leaved trees in thin autumn sunlight. But the quiet held warning: no birdsong, no grunting of plow-elk, not even the squeal of mice caught by hunting cats.

"No sunlight," Andry murmured. Torien shifted his plans to allow for this, agreeing with the judgment. Had it been a cloudless day or a clear night, they could have used sun, moons, or stars without fear. But the autumn sun was unreliable, and could catch any working Sunrunner in clouds. So they would conjure only: more difficult, but safer.

Slowly, for they had time yet, and carefully, for this must be done right, the three anchoring minds gathered in the strengths of their subordinates. Torien had heard Valeda liken herself to a master weaver and a loom, with Jolan and Oclel the bright threads. Torien preferred to think of it in the terms of his Fironese homeland: he both crafter and window, Ulwis and Deniker the shapes of colored glass. But neither image was entirely analogous. Threads snapped or unraveled; glass splintered or broke. What was fashioned by the *devr'im* that morning would do none of those things—unless one of them was pierced by iron. Torien had no real fear of that for himself. He was part *diarmadhi*. It was his shame but it might mean his life. Those of that blood experienced terrible pain if hit by iron; Sunrunners died.

He worked, and made of the gorgeous blues and greens and golds and reds and Ulwis' strange glowing purple a pattern of surpassing beauty. As crafter he fashioned the window; as window he was part of the pattern. But what was beautiful to see and be on his side was, in the way of all things, the opposite on the other. He had been on that other side several times. He knew the horrors waiting for those who came close enough to touch.

Jolan had made a poem of it, something about what was light becoming darkness, what was pleasure becoming pain. Fragments of her words skittered through his mind, distracting him. He chased them away with a promise to hear her sing the poem when victory was theirs.

Sensing that Andry waited, he presented his splendid window for use as if it were a shield. Valeda's image of strongly woven fabric cloaked Andry; the Lord of Goddess Keep's own concept, that of a sword with Nialdan as the solid hilt and Rusina as the glowing moonstone blade, completed his armament. Andry, who had never ridden to war, was ready for battle.

They left their dragon-headed ships for the beaches, scaled the cliffs, marched in good order across the fields. Torien felt but could not see them. His physical senses were useless, just as during a Sunrunning. He had no flesh, no blood, no body to feel the deep trembling excitement brought by *dranath*. He was the window now, pieces of brilliant glass melded together by power. He was his Lord's shield, as others were his cloak and sword. Those who encountered him would collide with nightmares; those who touched the

cloth would be shrouded in hideous visions; those who braved the sword would be pierced by terrors. Let them come.

He knew when they approached the keep. He waited for Andry to use him. But Andry waited, too. If Torien had once known why, he had forgotten. He wanted to feel those minds crash into the seething darkness of him that for him was light. He was as eager for it as a hungry dragon for the kill, as a boy for the smile of his first love, as a man for the bed of an adored wife. This was what *dranath* gave him.

If he had known anything but the most tenuous connection to his body, he would have parted his lips on a cry of joy and possession and triumph. A pitiful ungifted mind shattered on its own worst fears. Shattered on the shield he had given his Lord against their enemies.

The first of many—but not enough. They drew back, and he quivered with rage. *Come to me, come to me,* part of him sang. *Come to me and die.* For this was the secret Andry had told none but him. The practice was for practice. This was lethal. Minds shattered or shrouded or pierced would remain so, to the death of the flesh as surely as if they were Sunrunners shadow-lost.

Had he been wholly of his body, he would have bellowed challenge, jeered their cowardice. The eager hunger surged and he knew he must glow and vibrate in the air like a shimmer-vision on the Long Sand. *Come to me!*

When they came, it was not with unguarded minds. It was with iron.

His body screamed with the pain of it, colors rent asunder by the onslaught of fierce bright steel. But he held. Crippled. Not yielding. Repair the crumbling glass, rethread the shredding weave, reforge the sword. *I can. No one else.*

He did it, and the Sunrunners did not die. He found unexpected strength in Ulwis, she of the dark Merida face who denied possessing that blood, and used her. What he presented to Andry was not the adamantine shield and enveloping cloak and shining sword of before, but it served. It served.

* * *

Tilal was silent as he strode through the gates of Goddess Keep. Chaltyn hobbled along beside him, favoring his left thigh. The prince was unhurt but for the usual bruises. But

of his four hundred and sixty-three, eighty-one were dead, twice that many injured. The enemy had been driven back down the cliffs, back to their longboats and their dragon-headed ships. Goddess Keep was game bigger than they had teeth for. Tilal knew why they did not linger off the coast to try again, as at New Raetia, but instead set limping sail around the cape for Gilad or Syr or the Desert. Andry had defeated their minds. Neither Tilal nor his soldiers had been necessary at all.

A blond boy with Andry's blue eyes pushed through the crush of Sunrunners and castlefolk, villagers and farmers and Tilal's own people. "Your grace? May I escort you to the Lord's chambers?"

Tilal nodded curtly, not trusting himself even to open his mouth to be civil. A path was cleared through the noise to the keep. As they mounted the inner stairs, Tilal decided it was both a good thing and a bad thing that he must slow his steps for Chaltyn to keep pace: good because it prevented him from pelting up to Andry's rooms and wringing his neck, bad because he had even more time to seethe. He told himself to remember his love for Chay and Maarken and Pol and especially Rohan. They needed neither the personal anguish nor the political disaster Tilal's fury was quite capable of causing right now. But stronger than feeling or practical wisdom, the memory of his dead and wounded threatened to ignite him like a bin of oil-soaked wood.

The Lord of Goddess Keep was waiting for him in an audience chamber rich with color, hung with fine tapestries, furnished with fruitwood chairs and velvet cushions. Andry sat in what looked suspiciously like a throne, all carved and elaborate. Flanking him, standing, were persons Tilal recognized as the Chief Steward and the mother of one or another of his children—Tilal neither remembered nor cared which. Andry and the woman looked exhausted. The steward looked half-dead.

"His grace of Ossetia," the boy said, the form correct, the voice hushed.

"Thank you, Andrev. Bring a chair for his grace, and then leave us."

"Yes, my Lord."

So he made his own children address him by his title? How charming. How like Andry. The irritation of years

flared, and it was no surprise that this one small thing had brought him to despise Andry at last.

Tilal nodded thanks to the boy but did not sit down. He looked an order at Chaltyn to get off his feet; the old man balked for a moment, then sat down in the presence of his prince—and the Lord of Goddess Keep. Andry's brows did not stir, but the steward's did.

Tilal had tried to calm himself enough on the way here to come up with a really blistering first sentence. Now, seeing Andry composed and waiting to be addressed, as if *he* were the prince and Tilal nothing more than a moderately useful servant, he said the first thing that came to him.

"Who in all Hells do you think you are?"

"Not a question requiring an answer," Andry observed. "But to be pedantic, I am Lord of Goddess Keep, and not answerable to you. I am, barely and regrettably, answerable in some things to the High Prince."

"*Answerable* to him? He'll fry you! How dare you use your gifts this way?"

"What way is that, your grace?" the woman asked.

Tilal ignored her. "We saw the dying—so much for the *faradhi* vow not to kill! Goddess in glory, Andry—do you know what you did to them? Did you have any idea—"

"You care no more for enemy deaths than I do," Andry replied quietly. "You yourself killed enough of them today."

"Clean kills, my Lord!" Chaltyn burst out. "Not leaving a mindless, whimpering husk that flinches from wind whispering through a blade of grass!"

Andry held Tilal's gaze with his own—but on a man who in many years at Stronghold had been taught what tricks Sunrunners used on the ungifted, the tactic was useless. Tilal was no ignorant, awestruck youth; he was a prince, familiar with Sunrunners, and had no intention of being caught the way it was said dragons snared their prey with a glance.

Andry recognized it, and his expression changed fractionally. "It's not the deaths that bother you," he reiterated.

"You made sure I saw them, didn't you? I and all my army. You killed close on a hundred of them—but no more. Why is that, Andry? Did it take too much out of you? Would it have been too tiring to confront the whole army? Was a hundred enough to create the right impression?"

The woman sucked in an outraged breath. No one spoke

to the Lord of Goddess Keep this way. Andry placed a hand on her arm.

"You *waited!*" Tilal spat. "You wanted enough witnesses to spread a tale of invincibility. I *saw* it, Goddess damn you—my people were fighting and dying! Those bastards were almost at the gates and you *waited* until then to work your spells!"

"Valeda," Andry said to the woman, "you see before you a prince trained by my uncle Rohan, who sees clearly—and understands the meaning of what he sees. But he never learned to control his temper or his tongue." He rose from his chair, and Tilal was not so far gone in rage that he missed the stiff weariness Andry tried to hide. "Yes, Tilal, you're right. I waited. But you don't yet understand why. It wasn't to see your soldiers killed. Rohan's own law allows me to employ the *ros'salath* in defense of Goddess Keep."

"So that's what you're after," Tilal breathed. "Pol failed at Radzyn. You're putting Rohan on notice that you *won't* fail. That he needs you. That you should have free rein, you and your—"

"Devr'im," Andry supplied. "You'll recognize the root words. It's a term of my own devising."

He recognized them well enough: "lords of light." A pretty word with horrible implications.

"And once you've done all this," Tilal said slowly, "once you've destroyed the enemy . . . will we then call *you* High Prince?"

"You insult me with more ambition than I possess." Andry took a few steps toward him. "Listen to me, Tilal—cousin," he added with a sardonic smile, and the word used between princes grated on Tilal's ears. "We *are* cousins, you know, if only by marriage," Andry went on. "My only ambition is to cleanse all lands of these barbarians. The rest of you are failing—my blood-cousin Pol being a prime example. I and my *devr'im* can succeed, but only if we're allowed to work freely. That's the message I wish you to convey to Rohan. It's very simple. Let us work, and we'll drive these savages out. What other hope is there?"

Tilal's fingers twitched as he reconsidered his earlier notion about wringing Andry's neck. No, there was a better way to do it, to fell him and leave him alive and in pain.

"I knew and loved your brother Sorin," he said through his teeth. "For the first time, I'm glad he's dead."

He paused just long enough to watch the poisoned shaft strike home. With a sharp gesture to Chaltyn, he turned on his heel and stalked out of the chamber—before his hands really did find and break Andry's neck.

* * *

Chaltyn dissuaded him from leaving Goddess Keep that very evening. "It was a hard battle, for all that we won it," he said. "Our people need and deserve at least one night's sleep before they march again."

His prince snarled at him. "I don't care if it's only half a measure, I want out of here *now!*"

"That would be a great unwisdom," the old man scolded. "Stay the night. Use up Andry's substance instead of our own. We've a long enough walk ahead of us to the Faolain and your brother—and fighting enough along the way to get the taste of Andry out of your mouth."

By the time he was out in the courtyard again, he had cooled enough to recognize that Chaltyn was right. "Very well. But I'm not sleeping within these walls tonight."

"Yes you are." Tilal stared; Chaltyn leaned closer. "Have you forgotten that the High Princess your aunt still has friends here? You need a Sunrunner, my lord."

He gave in with poor grace. "And a bath. I stink of Andry's presence."

Emerging from a long soak that soothed his muscles if not his mind, he found an excellent meal waiting for him in his chamber. When he was finished, he rang the little bell beside the bed. The boy who came to take the tray was none other than Andry's blond son.

"More wine, your grace?"

"No, but thank you. I'll sleep well enough on what I've already had. Andrev, isn't it?"

"Yes, your grace."

'It's 'my lord,' actually." He recalled Andry's mocking words—and how the boy had used a title to his own father—and added, "We're cousins, of a sort. You can use my name if you like."

A quick smile reminded him suddenly of Sorin. Andry would never forgive him for what he'd said—but he would not have taken it back even if he could.

"We're kin by marriage, I know," the boy said, and

began unpacking fresh clothes from Tilal's saddlebags for the morning. "My sisters and brothers didn't believe me when I pointed you out to them during the battle. And now I see you have green eyes, like the High Princess."

"My father was her brother. So you watched today, did you?"

"Oh, yes! I counted how many you unhorsed. That's a real fire-breather you were riding. Don't let my father hear me say it, but some of Lord Kolya's horses are even better than my grandsir's."

"Some of them," Tilal grinned. "But don't let your grandsir hear *me* say it!" He stretched and pulled a face as a sore muscle twinged in his back. "Thank you for your service to me tonight, Andrev."

"I saw that you don't have a squire, my l– Cousin Tilal."

"Not at present. No, you needn't polish my sword, though I appreciate the thought. It's late."

"A fine blade," the boy said wistfully, running a cautious finger over the gold-chased hilt.

"Unsheathe it if you like—but be careful, it's got an edge like a dragon's claw. I gave it to my father many years ago, and he left it to me."

"Is it the same one my uncle Maarken used to kill the pretender?" Andrev breathed, eyes shining.

"The very same." Tilal hid a grin. So Andry had a would-be warrior for a son, did he? *That* must go over well.

"Thank you for letting me see it," Andrev said, sliding the blade carefully back into the scabbard. "Good night, Cousin Tilal."

"Good night." He settled back in bed to rest, but not to sleep. Chaltyn had promised to find and send before midnight a Sunrunner loyal to Sioned and Rohan. But despite his determination to stay awake, he was drifting off when his door opened and light spilled into the room.

"Who's there?"

Shadows returned as the door swung closed. "My name is the one piece of information you may not have, your grace," a voice whispered, so low-pitched that he couldn't tell if it was male or female. "I swore to the High Princess."

Tilal didn't trust Andry out of sword reach and he felt very odd around the edges of his perceptions. Like something tugged at part of him—not to draw him forward into the light, but to throw a blanket of mist over him. Struggling

through it, he asked casually, "You knew her, I suppose, when she came here at thirteen."

"Since the day she arrived—at age twelve."

"And had a room in the west tower."

"The fourth floor of the central hall. Satisfied?"

"Not yet."

A dry chuckle. "You're a suspicious man, my lord."

"In Andry's keep, do you blame me?"

"Not at all."

"What was Sioned wearing the day she arrived here?"

"Oh, dear. How can I remember that far—wait. It must have been the green wool gown with the black sash. She insisted on wearing it until it was nearly in tatters, long after she grew too tall for it."

Tilal relaxed. "My father sent her one almost like it when I went to Stronghold. Green and black are River Run's colors. She told me about that other gown when she unwrapped the box."

The shadows laughed softly, and their mist cleared a little. "I am believed on the strength of a length of wool! What shall I tell her on the moons?"

He gave a brief summary of his encounter with Andry. "You can also tell her I came within a hair's breadth of throttling him. Now, what can *you* tell *me?*"

"Something happened to disrupt the *ros'salath* but was corrected. The weave wasn't restored to its former strength. It no longer killed. But it was still strong enough to turn them from us to easier quarry. Your army."

"Easier?"

"Your pardon. I meant more traditional fighting, where a sword is a sword—and not a knife through the mind. Not a perversion of *faradhi* gifts."

Ashamed of his outburst and feeling deeply for the disgust and pain in that voice, he nodded. "Are there others who feel as you do?"

"Forgive me, but that's another question I can't answer."

"Doesn't matter, I suppose. It's not something I understand or can do anything about. I need a favor, though. Is there someone who can come with me on the march? All I need is communication. I don't want a warrior."

A short silence ensued. Then the voice whispered on a sigh, "No one. Andry would know if even one of us slipped out. If he offers you a Sunrunner, accept. The spy you know

is less dangerous than the one you don't—and, as you say, you need communication."

"He won't offer."

"Perhaps you're right. If that's all, your grace, the moons are rising and I should be quick about this. There may be cloud cover."

"Just one more thing. My love to them—and if Sioned contacts Athmyr—"

"It has already been done. Your lady knows you safe and unharmed."

"Thank you."

The wedge of light appeared and vanished once more. Tilal sank back down in bed, and was too tired to think for more than a few heartbeats before he was swallowed in sleep.

* * *

Andry did not offer a Sunrunner. Neither did he come down to see Tilal leave at dawn. Chaltyn reported that a delegation from the common folk had come pleading for troops to be left behind in their defense.

"And what did you reply?" Tilal asked, staring at the road from between his stallion's tufted ears.

"To trust in the Lord of Goddess Keep—and if that brought no comfort, try the Goddess herself."

"It pains me to leave them without swords. But I won't have my people die for Andry's sake. Not again. The cost is too high—and I'm not talking about what I owe their families." One of Tilal's duties after this was all over would be to travel to every farm, village, and holding that had suffered a loss and offer the life-token due the survivors of a soldier dead in a prince's service.

They rode on in silence. Clouds that had drizzled two days ago and parted yesterday were threatening rain in earnest. There would be no tales spread on sunlight of Andry's power today.

About forty measures from the keep, when it was getting on for noon, Chaltyn rode up from an inspection of the column with another rider at his side. Tilal knew he shouldn't have been surprised that it was Andrev.

"See who I found, my lord," the old man said, "stuck between the horse and the archers."

"You need a squire, Cousin Tilal," the boy said simply. "And a Sunrunner."

Chaltyn stared at him. "You know how? At your age?"

"I know how."

"Where does your father think you are?" Tilal asked.

Andrev blinked. "With the others, helping the villagers return to their homes. They won't miss me until sundown. If then," he added.

By the Goddess, Andry would be livid—and after yesterday's events Tilal couldn't resist a decision guaranteed to infuriate the Lord of Goddess Keep.

"Very well. I need a squire and a Sunrunner. We'll take care of the formal swearing later. Chaltyn, go find him a tunic of the right color."

Andrev's blue eyes shone. "Thank you, Cousin Tilal!"

"His father won't thank you," Chaltyn muttered.

"I know." Tilal barely restrained himself from adding, *Ask me if I care.* "Andrev, from now on it's 'my lord.' You're in my service now."

PART THREE

Chapter Sixteen

It was impossible to keep things from Tobin. Even crippled, she could command information so powerfully with just her eyes that not even her lord and husband could keep his mouth shut. Or perhaps he was the one with the least resistance. Whatever the case, Tobin knew most things only a short while after the others did.

Since their arrival at Remagev it had become her habit to spend the day in any available sunshine. Feylin gave her a corner chamber, with one window facing south and the other west. Sioned, knowing what was in Tobin's mind, extracted a promise from her not to go Sunrunning unless one of them went with her in case she faltered. It had been a long while coming, but, once given, Tobin kept her word. After all, nothing was said about passively receiving the messages of other *faradh'im*.

A glorious sunset was just beginning, and Rohan had come to enjoy it with her. Tobin knew why her crafty brother had come now instead of earlier: Tobren had come to sit with her, too, and in the child's presence there could be no imperious glance ordering him to talk.

The girl perched on a stool by Rohan's chair, sewing a sling to support her grandmother's arm once she was able to get about—which Tobin swore would be tomorrow. She had recovered from the flight across the Desert and was back to where she had been before Radzyn was attacked: ready to try walking with a cane to support her bad leg. She felt strong enough. And she knew if she spent one more day confined to this room, pleasant as it was, she would start screaming.

Rohan did not have much to choose from in Walvis' library, so he read aloud from Feylin's dragon book which

Tobin had insisted Sioned pack. Tobren's steady stitching paused every so often as she looked up in amazement. Though she was still skittish around Pol, Rohan had won her over. She wouldn't call him by name yet, but Tobin knew it was only be a matter of time.

In the deep western light, their pale hair was nearly the same color—Rohan's gone silver with his years, Tobren's paled by exposure to harsh Desert sun. Tobin wondered what the child's mother was like—a woman she had never met and about whom Tobren never spoke. That was unnatural, as far as her grandmother was concerned. But then, so little about Andry's begettings and what passed for his family life at Goddess Keep was usual.

Such thoughts irritated her. She concentrated on Rohan's voice as he read. It was the chapter Betheyn had enjoyed so much, ridiculing dragon legends.

"I didn't know the one about dragon spines being poisonous," Rohan said. "Teeth, talons, and blood, yes. But spines?"

Tobren frowned as she rethreaded her needle. "Maybe it's like the scorpion. Or a serpent's fangs."

"Probably where the idea originated. But, as Feylin writes, the spines would have to be hollow to hold poison. So would teeth and claws."

"With the teeth, it could be their spit," she reasoned.

"Hmm. Hadn't thought of that. But I'm living proof to the contrary." He rolled up a sleeve, revealing a scar on his upper arm. "Talon. If I'd been slower, I'd have teeth marks, too. I'm positive the old dragonsire spat on me."

Tobren caught her breath. "He did? When?"

"A *very* long time ago, when I was young and stupid enough to go chasing dragons." He smiled down at her. "I've kept a respectful distance since!"

She laughed. "I should think so, my lord! I like hearing about dragons."

"They're in your blood, Tobren. There's no escaping love of them if you're Desert-bred. It was said your great-grandsire could tell when dragons would come just by the shape of the clouds or the feel of the wind. It runs in the—"

He stopped abruptly. The little girl's face had taken on that strange, glazed look he and Tobin knew so well. They both held their breath until she was back with them, conscious of their presence again.

"Who was it, Tobren?" he asked gently.

"Andrev! Oh, he's done a terrible thing, my lord! He's going to be in awful trouble with Father!"

Rohan traded glances with Tobin. Neither of them was used to Sunrunning in a child, but Andry taught his sons and daughters young. "What has Andrev done?"

"There was a battle and we won—but Andrev ran away! He wanted to help during the battle but Father wouldn't let him. So he ran away when Prince Tilal left. He says he's Prince Tilal's squire now, sworn and accepted and everything. Can he do that, my lord?"

"He's thirteen?" When she nodded, he said, "Yes, Tobren, he can do that."

It was a very old law Tobin knew Andrev was unaware of—so was Andry, or he would have invoked it when he was that age and frantic to get to Goddess Keep. Such a thing hadn't been done in lifetimes. But it was legal for a boy in his thirteenth year to pledge himself as a squire where he pleased. If he did so against his parents' wishes, however, they were under no obligation to take him back. He risked his inheritance and might have to settle for whatever place and income his fostering lord would give him. It was no secret among their family that Andry intended Andrev's inheritance to be Goddess Keep itself.

She met her brother's gaze again. What was Andrev thinking of, to do such a thing? And Tilal, to accept him?

Rohan said, "We'll have to send to your father so he knows where Andrev is, and that he's all right."

"He'll be furious," Tobren murmured.

He'll blister that child's bottom for him, sure enough, Tobin thought. *And deservedly. Whatever possessed Andrev to run away from home?*

Then she remembered something Rohan had said once about Pol. *"I used to worry about him. He rarely got into scrapes—that I heard about, anyway—and he was altogether too mannerly as a child. But I stopped worrying the day he ran away from home in a fury when he was eleven. That showed spirit—took me a lot longer to get up the nerve to cross Father's will. Pol had the courage to go off on his own. But he came back, which showed he had the sense to realize that at his age, he was too young. Spirit, bravery, and brains, Tobin—just like your boys. That's how I knew he was all mine, and not Ianthe's."*

Andrev, too, had now run away from home. The problem was how to return him before Andry went raging after Tilal. But if the boy had already sworn, it was legal—and Andry couldn't reclaim his son unless Tilal consented. But why had he accepted Andrev in the first place?

That question exercised the minds of those who met after dinner in Rohan's chambers for the regular evening discussion. Nothing had been heard from Goddess Keep, so they had no account of the battle itself beyond Andrev's sparse information that there had indeed been one. Sioned, whose last encounter with Andry had left her shaking with fury she could not allow herself to express to its object, flatly refused to be the one to talk to him this time.

"He's *your* brother, Maarken," she said tersely. "*You* deal with him."

"If there's sun enough tomorrow, I will. I know what he'll say, though. He'll demand Tilal release Andrev and send him back."

"Of course," Pol said. "But I don't think that's a very good idea. Chay, Maarken, please forgive my bluntness—but his son's involvement in this war is our best guarantee that Andry will help where it's necessary."

Rohan arched a brow. "Still kicking yourself over what happened at Radzyn, I see."

Pol's color heightened a trifle. "I failed. I'll bet Azhdeen's hide that Andry didn't, and kept them out of Goddess Keep so Tilal could hack them to pieces in the field. Like it or not, we need Andry. And I *don't* like it."

"Consult your dragon before you wager his hide," Walvis murmured. "Which is to say, wait until we get a full report of what went on there yesterday. If Tilal was angry enough to accept the boy, which was guaranteed to make Andry cross-eyed furious, then much may have happened that we know nothing about."

"The great *athri* is wise." Kazander touched his fingertips to his heart. "No powerful, sane man deliberately insults another powerful man unless he has already received a mortal insult himself."

Sioned lifted her hands in a gesture of disgust, her ring spitting emerald fire. "So Andry's livid, Tilal's in a rage, and our only source of information about the whole mess is a half-trained thirteen-year-old boy who's run away from

home. Delightful. Simply delightful. What other happy news tonight?"

The rising of the moons brought a fuller account of the battle at Goddess Keep—from Sioned's friend there, not from Andry. Feylin scribbled everything in her records when they all met again at midnight.

Pol smiled tightly. "He wanted us to come begging. But to get his son back safe, he'll have to help us fight this war."

Chay drooped in his chair, his graying head bowed. Maarken rose to his feet and left the room. After a moment, Hollis gave Pol a single cold glance and followed her husband.

"Nice work," Rohan commented sourly. "We all understood, Pol. You didn't have to say it aloud."

"I'm not the one who put conditions on help that should be freely given! We princes have a duty to protect Goddess Keep—which Tilal has done. What's Andry's part of the bargain, in return for defending him and his?"

Sioned folded her hands. "There is no law, no tradition—he can demand what he likes in return for his help. And if it's Andrev back at Goddess Keep, we just might have to oblige him."

"He wouldn't dare," Pol said flatly. "He *owes* us. And he can't let people keep on dying in a war he could stop!"

"Oh, this will look fine, won't it?" she retorted. "The only reason the Lord of Goddess Keep supports us is because his son is at risk. That's not what Andrade had in mind when she named him her successor. She wanted you to work together. You wielding the power of a prince, he that of Goddess Keep, Sunrunners in common with a mutual goal."

"I won't crawl to him," Pol said stubbornly. "And I won't try to convince Tilal to release Andrev."

Chay glanced up, quicksilver gray eyes robbed of their light. "Pride has a bitter taste when you're drinking loser's dregs."

Pol shrugged. "I don't think we need Andry to win this war at all. We can learn the weaving ourselves. I know the basics. I've got powerful *faradh'im* of my own to work with. I—"

"Your own?" Sioned began angrily, but Rohan silenced her with a look.

"Pol," he said quietly, "by all accounts, the *ros'salath* at

Goddess Keep killed. Your mother and Maarken and Hollis took oath—"

"That didn't stop Mother, a long time ago."

Sioned's fists clenched around rings that were no longer on her fingers. "You know nothing about that. Nothing."

"But it's true, isn't it?"

Kazander was caught gaping at this revelation. He quickly smoothed his expression. "These are matters of more weight than I have shoulders to carry. If the High Prince and High Princess in their graciousness will excuse me—"

"Yes, of course," Rohan said, distracted. The *korrus* stood, bowed, and hurried from the room.

"You killed with the gifts, Mother," Pol said relentlessly.

"I've paid for it ever since! As you pointed out at Radzyn, you never made that vow. I don't want you to have to pay for *that* for the rest of your life."

"What kept *faradh'im* safe was that vow," Chay said. "It's my shame that my own son has broken it. That if we are to win this war, he'll have to break it again." He sighed quietly. "It's his choice, Pol. His oath forsworn, his decision to do what he knows is wrong. He just doesn't seem to understand how wrong it really is. How dangerous."

"If Andry wants to dishonor himself, that's his business. I never swore. There's no oath for me to break. Besides, if it saves just one of my people—"

Rohan stood abruptly and began to pace. "Honor! Haven't you been listening? Chay's talking about your life! Who do you think that vow is meant to protect? Princes trust Sunrunners not to choose one side or the other. If they ever thought Sunrunners would *kill,* do you think any of you would be left alive?"

"In the last forty years people have gotten used to at least *one* Sunrunner choosing a side." Pol looked pointedly at Sioned.

Rohan snapped, "And do you have any idea how hard it's been for her? She was the one who drew the line between respect for what she *could* do and certainty of what she *would not* do. The line you intend to cross."

Feylin and Walvis watched them square off across the broad table, barely aware of held breath. Sioned sat with head bowed over her laced fingers, Chay with his chin sunk on his breast.

Pol gestured impatiently. "Andry broke his oath years ago when he killed Marron. You punished him for it. If you hadn't, the other princes would have been at your throat. Then they would have gone after the Sunrunners—"

"After *you,* Pol."

"—except that you're the High Prince, and they knew there was nothing to fear from Andry—or from me. Your authority will work again. If we need to use him—something I'm still not convinced of—Andry can be kept in line."

"I disagree. Word will spread and demands will begin for him to use this *ros'salath* in the defense of the continent. I must allow it, they will say. Either that or set my Sunrunner prince of a son to do it." There was sudden anguish in his eyes. "How do I watch you do a thing I know to be wrong? That breaks all law and tradition? A thing that will make you hated and feared and put you in mortal danger for the rest of your life?"

Pol replied levelly, "If Andry won't do this without imposing conditions, then I must. Would you rather have everyone looking to *him* instead of the High Prince? Would you see him *become* High Prince and Lord of Goddess Keep both?"

As Chay made a soft sound, Feylin glared at Pol. "If I thought it was power and prestige alone you were concerned with, I'd take you over my knee—prince or no prince," she said.

"I'd be lying if I said I wasn't worried about those things," Pol returned forthrightly. "Andry and I have never trusted each other. But if he proves the salvation of the princedoms, think what we'll have to deal with! Father, you talked about my life being in danger. The same holds true for Andry—and *all* Sunrunners."

"You're wrong." Chay's voice was barely audible. "It's not the same. You'll be High Prince one day. Andry will not. If it was power and prestige he wanted, I'd march on Goddess Keep myself and break him. But all he's ever wanted is to be Lord there. I don't know how you became rivals, but it's crippling you both. That cripples *us* in fighting this enemy. I agree with you, Pol, that he and the *faradh'im* are in little danger once the war's done if there's a strong High Prince for balance. But if *you're* the one to kill with the gifts—do you see? You're more dangerous, and there-

fore in more danger, than Andry. You will become exactly what they all fear most."

There was a brief silence before Walvis cleared his throat. "Pol, you'd put your father in the impossible position of having to punish you as he did Andry—either that or set aside the law. If he did that for Andry, it would be accepted—barely. If he did it for you. . . ."

"By not punishing," Rohan said inexorably, "or by canceling my own law, I condone. The scrolls give me authority over Goddess Keep. It is held of the High Prince. Lady Merisel provided a final check on their power—just as even a prince who is not a soldier has final authority over his armies. By allowing Andry to kill, I show that it is acceptable to me. That it may be done again—"

"You don't care about the Sunrunners," Pol said. "Not when it comes down to them or me—which is the real issue here. You'd rather Andry did the dirty part of it so your precious son won't get sullied."

"I can live with his danger better than with yours," Rohan snapped.

"Andrade wanted a Sunrunner prince. Well, here I am, Father! You think she wanted both powers in one man. *I* think she meant me to protect *all* people—gifted or not, Sunrunner or not, highborn or not."

"Yes," Sioned burst out, "here you are! Prince and Sunrunner and with power enough for twelve. And unbound by the traditions of Goddess Keep. If Andrade had lived, you might have become a Sunrunner by earning your rings. But you didn't." She paused. 'You are as much a renegade as the man Roelstra corrupted using *dranath.*"

Pol stiffened. "Do you have so little faith in how you taught me that you think—"

"I *know* that power once used is easier to use a second time. And a third. Until you forget reasons and simply use it because it's convenient." She stared at her hands again.

"Thank you for your confidence, Mother," he said bitterly.

"Stop it!" Rohan exclaimed. "And get out, all of you. This is over."

"No, my lord." Sioned rose and stood beside him, facing Pol. "I want your promise. Swear in front of the High Prince and these highborns and a Sunrunner of seven rings that you will not use your gifts to kill."

Chay straightened as if hit by lightning, and made a little

warding-off gesture with one hand. Walvis and Feylin sat mute and stricken.

"Swear," Rohan echoed.

Surging to his feet with his fists clenched, Pol opened his mouth to refuse. But his father's eyes had caught him. He wrenched his gaze away, looked at his mother—no better, perhaps worse. Absolute authority, adamant command, power that practically sparked from their fingertips—here in two people was all that Andrade had hoped to combine in one. In him.

Could he swear with the qualification that he could break the oath if he must? No. There was no compromise. Was he Andry, to make an oath and break it?

He was seized by their eyes, Desert-sky blue and midsummer green. They were compelling the words, making them a condition of their trust. He felt his lips part and the phrase form on his tongue.

And then Sioned made a mistake. "Swear," she said, "or I promise you, if you do this thing—"

He didn't let her finish, unable to bear a condition set on her love.

"I swear to *nothing!*"

* * *

She kept silent until they were alone.

"Oh, Goddess—Rohan, what have I done? Why did I say that?"

"I would have said it myself an instant later."

"So many years I was terrified that he'd hate me for keeping the truth about Ianthe from him. Despise me for what I'd done." She paced nervously, her voice quick and clipped. "I wronged him when I doubted him. I wronged him again tonight. I should never have demanded it. He's too proud. I should have let him come to it himself. Learn for himself."

"Power doesn't frighten him. That's what he must learn, beloved. I thought after the battle at Rivenrock . . .but *he* didn't kill Ruval. The dragon did."

"Rohan, we need Andry on any terms we can get him. We can't let Pol—"

"No. I am High Prince for all people, Sunrunners like everyone else, just as Pol intends to be. Andry doesn't see the danger he'd put himself in."

"Not that he'd thank you for pointing it out, any more than Pol did."

"At least Pol sees it when it's shoved under his nose. Andry would smile as they acclaimed him their savior—and never understand when they began to fear him. He's not wise enough to tread that line, Sioned. He doesn't even understand why there must be such a line. Power doesn't frighten *him,* either."

* * *

Sionell stood with her husband on a wall of their city and squinted into the hazy distance. "Still no sight of them yet. Perhaps we should send out a ship to find them and guide them in."

Tallain shook his head. "They'd panic at any sail. I know I would, in their position."

"You've never panicked in your life—well, except when you held Talya for the first time."

"That wasn't panic. That was the absolute certainty I'd drop her and then you'd flay me alive for—look! Is that them? Those look like Chay's sails."

"At last! Goddess be thanked!"

"Poor Meath is probably half-dead of seasickness. And Chadric must be frantic. I'm glad we have good news about Ludhil."

Sionell caught her breath. "Tallain—I count two ships, not one!"

"Enemy?"

"Silk ship!"

Tallain took her hand and made for the steps. "We'll have to find room for them. They'll be exhausted."

"And hungry and filthy," she added. "We've been ready for days, but we can't take all of them in the castle."

"I'll send Lyela to the guildmaster with a request for housing. She gets along with him—Goddess knows how."

"Lyela gets along with everybody. I'll never believe Kiele was her mother."

They hurried down the wall stairs and across the city square to their residence. Sionell hiked her skirts to her knees, cursing herself for not having worn trousers today instead, and the populace got a view of long, shapely legs and neat ankles.

Horses were dispatched to the cove immediately. Tallain and Sionell followed a short time later to welcome the Dorvali, and were surprised that only a few had chosen to ride. Most were so grateful to feel firm land beneath their feet again that walking, though chancy for the first few steps, was a gift from the Goddess. Meath stumbled along with two burly Tiglathi guards holding him up. He smiled weakly as he caught sight of his hosts, looked vaguely bewildered for a moment, then crumpled to the ground.

"He *would* try to stand up," Audrite commented, shaking her head. "Just as he *would* have us continue on by ship when we could have landed anywhere and walked." She embraced Sionell. "I won't ask for news now. And neither will Chadric," she warned in her husband's direction. "It can all wait."

"There's one bit of news that won't," Tallain said. "My Sunrunner found Ludhil and Iliena only yesterday, camped in the mountains near the old *faradhi* keep, safe and sound."

Sionell was glad that Tallain had seen fit not to mention the rest of it—that most of the people with Ludhil were farmers and villagers, not warriors, and the prince had been about to lead a group on a raid of enemy positions. That news could definitely wait.

As they walked back to Tiglath, Chadric told the tale of their journey. "The wind kept shifting—I swear the Father of Storms is on their side, not ours—and we had a terrible time making headway. When we rounded the north side of the island, we saw four of their ships chasing Master Nemthe." He nodded to the silk merchant, who huddled on horseback muttering complaints. "We were the bigger prey. But Captain Ennov knows his ship. I'm buying his contract and the *Sea Spinner* from Chay once this is over, I don't care what it costs. The man uses the wind the way Sunrunners use light."

"We looked for you days ago," Tallain said. "*Everybody's* been looking for you. My Sunrunner's informing Remagev and Dragon's Rest that you've landed safe, but they'll want details."

"Has Aunt Lisiel had her baby yet?" This from Audran, dancing along at his grandfather's side with the limitless energy of the young.

"Not yet," Tallain said. "But they're all safe and well."

"Details," Chadric mused. "After we escaped, we met up with Nemthe's ship and continued on. The wind drove us

into some of the coves, and thirst into a few more. I could map your coast by now, Tallain. We would have had Meath send word so you could get horses to us, but we couldn't even get him out of the ship to recover. And he wouldn't let us wait long enough in any one spot—the ship was faster, he said, and easier on the children. So we found what food and water we could, waited for a breeze, and then sailed on."

"Water?" Sionell asked. "Where?"

"Three places I'll bet nobody knows about. I'll mark them for you. We were driven out of one by a sandstorm, so it's possible it's disappeared beneath half the Desert. But Rohan will want to investigate. If watches are set up, next time we'll have warning."

The castle at Tiglath, the oldest part of the town, was large enough to hold the highborns and their personal retainers. But the city's population had swollen in recent days with the influx of men and women called to arms. The housing kept for them was full. So the rest of the Dorvali were welcomed into private homes—servant, guard, or commoner, it made no difference to the Tiglathi, who had only to be informed by their guildmaster that help was needed before they opened their homes. Master Nemthe created a minor stir when he asked why he was not being housed in the castle, as a man of his importance and wealth deserved. Chadric gave him a single cold glance, and he subsided.

Vamanis, Tallain's court Sunrunner for the last six years, met them in the main hall with messages of relief and joy from Remagev and Dragon's Rest. Tallain sent the Dorvali up to their rooms, where baths and food had been readied for them, and himself gave Vamanis a summary of Chadric's tale.

"If the sky's clear, see what you can find out about Prince Ludhil's raiding party. I'd like to have some good news for his parents."

"At once, my lord."

After a moment's hesitation, Tallain added, "And see what's going on in the known Merida holdings in Cunaxa." Vamanis blinked, swallowed hard, and nodded. Tallain watched him go, then murmured to his wife, "I'd better have that section of wall shored up."

He could have said nothing to shock her more deeply. For the more than thirty years since the Merida's last incursion, a small part of Tiglath's walls had lain in rubble—symbol,

Lord Eltanin said at the time, of his belief that the walls Rohan would build would be stronger than stone could ever be. Tallain shared his father's faith in their prince—or so Sionell had always thought.

She said slowly, "Wouldn't that be just the same as inviting the Merida to come break them down?"

"It's going to be a long war," was all he said.

* * *

Andry approached his mother quietly, the restraint imposed on him by her illness serving his purpose well. He must not reveal the fury that gripped him every time he thought about Andrev. He must not reveal the hurt.

She sat in the morning sun, and she was smiling. It pierced his heart that one side of her face did not obey the laughter in her black eyes. She held a cane in each hand, a little unsteadily in the right but firmly in the left. Sliding to the edge of her chair, she levered herself up—and stood.

Her balance was precarious for a moment. Then she took a step. And another. Tobin the indomitable, he told himself gleefully. He should have known. Absolutely nothing defeated his mother.

She made her slow way to the window seat, scowling fiercely with half her face, the other side twitching along brow and mouth. At last she turned slightly on her good leg, fumbled with the canes, and plopped onto the seat. He could almost hear her triumphant laughter.

"Brilliant! And I promise I won't tell on you."

"Andry? Andry, where are you? Are you safe?"

"Perfectly. Does Father know you're walking?"

"It's to be a surprise. Goddess knows he needs something to smile about for a change."

She turned her face to the sun, eyes closed. *Oh, Andry—this war is bad enough, but to be unable to move, to help—and to have no word from you—are you sure you're well? And the children?*

But for Andrev, about whom I know nothing. He grappled with his emotions, somehow managed to retain calm. *I was hoping you might have some word for me about him.*

With Tilal. Andry, I know you want him back with you. So do I, when it comes to it. An army is no place for a child.

That's putting it mildly. Will Rohan order Tilal to give him up, or not?

I don't know.

Will he release me from that prohibition about using Star Scroll spells to defend places other than Goddess Keep?

I don't know! Andry—you killed *with it. Think what that means!*

He made no reply.

She tried again, desperation tingeing her words. *You're Lord of Goddess Keep. You can do as you like with your Sunrunners. Rohan can't stop you. Frankly, he'd be wrong to try. But you must understand—*

I understand that he's willing to lose this war for a point of pride!

No. Don't you see? The vow protects you.

And has Pol sworn it, Mother? he asked with poisonous sweetness.

Her eyes opened wide to the sun, tears welling in them. *It's said you knew what would happen at Radzyn years before it came to pass.*

He hesitated, then decided he owed her the truth. *What I saw and what really occurred were different. I saw the keep in ruins. I saw them kill a hatchling dragon. But Radzyn stands. A dragonsire flew over and ripped the figurehead from one of their ships. It was different from my visions, Mother.*

When did this happen? What else did you see?

I watched the day after the battle. When the dragon came, they fell to their knees in terror. They may know about dragons, Mother, but I don't think they encounter them often. I'd hoped what he did to the ship would be taken as a portent—but evidently not. They're building strange things at Radzyn now, using all the wood they can find. I don't understand what those things are. They'll march soon. Rohan has to do something, and quickly. He has to decide.

I . . . I don't know what to tell you, my son, she admitted sorrowfully.

Then tell this to Rohan: I will do everything in my power—and it's considerable, as you now know—to help him win this war. But I must be allowed to work freely, and I must have Andrev back. Those are my terms. They won't attack Goddess Keep again, Mother. They learned. Pol tried at Radzyn and failed. I and my devr'im *are Rohan's only choice. He can make no other.*

And when it's over, what will your terms be then?

He flinched at the bitterness. *Do you know what else I saw at Radzyn? They heaped their dead onto a ship and sent it out to sea in flames. Those they had captured were on board, too. They burned, too. Life-offerings to the dead.*

Her colors shivered in horror. But her words were firm. *And do you know what they do when they kill a Sunrunner? They weave the rings into their beards as tokens of triumph.*

Andry drew away, just as horrified, and fled, her despairing cry of his name echoing in his mind.

* * *

"So Ludhil's organizing an army," Rohan mused. "No insult intended, but I never saw him as the military type."

"He's doing what he must—as are we all," Chay pointed out.

Walvis gave a comical grimace. "Another of your uncomfortable reminders."

They were out walking on the plain where Walvis held his annual little war, a place which might see war in earnest before too many more days had passed. No skirmish to capture the opposing side's banner, but a battle that would kill hundreds. The Desert had not failed Rohan; Sunrunners reported scores of corpses half-buried by the sandstorm. But the mass pursuit he had envisioned, with half the Vellanti army perishing in the Long Sand without a single battle, had not come to pass. Either the enemy was smarter than he'd thought, or they had something else in mind for him and his than was happening in Gilad and Syr.

"This isn't a bad place for a pitched battle," Chay remarked. "We'd have the advantage of position, and the morning sun glaring right into their eyes."

"So I always teach," Walvis said. "And we've got a tidy force at our disposal. My group and those you brought from Radzyn, plus Kazander's wild men. We ought to do very well."

Rohan kicked at a loose stone.

"Those wooden things of theirs puzzle me, though," Chay went on. "Like long carts with movable pieces. Seems they brought the basics with them, wheels and so forth. Hollis says they're putting two horses each between the shafts."

Radzyn horses, pulling carts. That almost hurt worse than thinking of the enemy in their saddles.

"Do you suppose they simply mean to travel in comfort, and then jump off when they do battle with us?"

Rohan glanced at Walvis. "I'm no military man, either. But I don't like this. They wouldn't bother bringing wheels all this way and then spend time assembling those contraptions—whatever they are—unless they're important."

"And you don't want to come up against them?" Chay asked.

"Not if I can help it. Not without twice the number of troops we've got now. I can't call Tallain down from the north, not if the Merida are involved. I've got a nasty feeling—and he agrees with me—that they'll break out of Cunaxa soon."

"Prince Miyon—" Walvis began, then stopped.

Chay snorted. "Question and answer in a single name."

Rohan barely heard them. "I can't pull people from Stronghold or Skybowl. Help from the west is impossible, at least until Kostas retakes the Catha and turns north, then comes back down the Faolain. I can't blame him for wanting to clean up Syr first, but it does leave me in something of a bind."

"You could order him to it," Chay said.

"But you won't," Walvis added. "The enemy controls nearly all Syr and Gilad. We've only lost our coast."

"Exactly. So I have what I have and must make do." He watched a pair of hawks circle in the brassy sky. "I have the Desert," he murmured. "That's more than the rest of them have. Another sandstorm's coming—I can taste it. But by winter there'll be only the day's heat and the night's cold to slow them down. Everything tells me I have to make a stand here. I have to choose battle. Kill as many of them as possible. Save Remagev as I could not save Radzyn—"

"Don't start," Chay warned. "I won't have you blaming yourself for that, my prince."

Rohan smiled briefly. "You know I hate it when you call me that."

"Would you prefer Kazander's style?" He clasped his hands to his breast and intoned piously, "O Most Great and Noble and Wise High Prince, Lord of Dragons, Whom the Sun Bathes in Gold and Glory—"

Rohan knew he was being maneuvered into laughter, and was glad to oblige. "Please! I've just managed to get him

down to the occasional 'great' and 'wise'—don't you dare encourage him!"

* * *

"Remember what I told you back home, lamb. You must be very good and very quiet, and do just as you're told."

"But I've *been* good, Lady Cluthine. Where's my surprise?"

Rialt paused in his circuit of the campfires at hearing his son's voice, a slight smile easing the grimness of his expression. At barely four, Polev knew a bargain when he heard one. His silk merchant grandparents would have been proud of him.

Cluthine, granddaughter of Clutha of Meadowlord and niece of the current ruling prince, was laughing at the child's demand. But Rialt heard the strain in her voice. She had not been well this year, and the flight from Waes would do her no good.

"So you're holding me to the contract, are you?" she asked the child in playful tones. "Well, you may have your surprise tomorrow."

"Why not now?"

"Because it's late, and time to sleep."

"But Mama hasn't tucked me in. And I'm not tired."

Cluthine sighed. "Don't you remember about being very quiet? Don't you want to hear the stars talk to each other on the wind?" Her gentle voice fell to a soothing murmur. "Listen, Polev, and you can hear them. The moonlight all silver and mysterious, the stars whispering. . . ."

Knowing his son's sleep would be watched over by a loving friend, Rialt walked on to where his wife was readying a bed of blankets. Her thick black braid fell over a shoulder, and as she tossed it back she glanced up.

"It's not much," she apologized, gesturing to the bed.

Amused, he replied, "Did you think I expected silk sheets?"

"I promised when we married that I'd be the best wife in the world."

"You are, Mevita. But I haven't made it easy the past two days, have I?"

"That's not your fault." She sat down cross-legged. "Will we reach Swalekeep tomorrow?"

"Barring any unpleasant surprises."

"If only Cluthine and I hadn't sent our best jewels to be

cleaned," she fretted. "I could have bought you and Polev a decent place to sleep tonight. Why did you have to be so silly about not selling my wedding necklet?"

"I'll part with all my gold before I'll let you part with that." He crouched beside her and warmed her hands between his own.

"If it can gain us food and fresh horses, and you a good night's sleep, I'd consider it well lost. You'll have to save the gold for Chiana and Halian."

"Thina doesn't think so."

Mevita shrugged. "She's an innocent. She believes they'll be overjoyed to shelter us."

"Halian will, anyway. He's fond of his niece." He squinted into the starry sky knowing that by morning clouds would blow inland from Brochwell Bay. Storms this time of year held pretty much to a five-day cycle; tomorrow would see another downpour. He hoped it wouldn't come until late afternoon, when, with luck, they should be at Swalekeep.

He had no illusions about the welcome he himself would receive. Halian had never appreciated Rohan's making Waes a free city, subject only to the High Prince. Chiana had never appreciated Rialt's close ties to Pol—the usurper who ruled in what she considered her son Rinhoel's rightful place. But at least Halian liked Cluthine, for all that she had chosen to stay on at Waes when her mother, the former regent and Halian's sister, died. And their party had another asset in Princess Naydra. Chiana could scarcely refuse to receive her eldest surviving half-sister.

He said as much, and Mevita nodded. "She won't have any choice. It galls me, though. She always treats you like a peasant."

"Well, for all my courtesy title, I was born only a few steps above peasant on the social scale." Rialt kissed her fingers. "I don't care how she treats us, so long as she gives us a roof over our heads until we can start for Dragon's Rest. How's Naydra?"

"As well as you could expect. Narat's ashes are barely cold." Mevita gave him a sudden, quick embrace. Just as abruptly she drew away and jumped to her feet. "If I don't kiss Polev good night, he'll never go to sleep."

After six years of marriage, Rialt was accustomed to his wife's ways. The more deeply she was moved, the more hurried and brusque the expression of what she felt. Usually

she was as quiet and steady as a hearthfire. But her feelings were sometimes like the powders tossed on flames that caused surges of color.

Rialt spared a smile and a shake of the head for Mevita's idiosyncrasies, then rose to complete his inspection of the camp. It was cold, and he stuck his chilled fingers in his pockets. His right hand encountered the little silver dragon Pol had given Mevita on the birth of his namesake. The hinged neck had opened to reveal a delicate amethyst bracelet coiled within the dragon's body. It was the only thing besides clothes and his wedding necklet that he had taken from their private chamber in the residence in Waes.

Fully six hundred people were in his keeping on this journey to Swalekeep. Despite the speed of the city's evacuation, all had been done with tolerable efficiency. Determined on order, Rialt's commands had been backed up by sword-bearing guards. He was no fool; he knew what panic had been inspired by the disasters in the south. The only choice he gave his people was where they would go: east with him to Swalekeep, southeast to Prince Velden's Summer River, or due south to Kadar Water. Communication arranged through Goddess Keep would warn of the arrival of refugees from Waes. There was no way to inform Chiana—the victim of sorcery nine years ago and now half-frantic in the mere presence of *faradh'im*, she had thrown her court Sunrunner out. Her privilege, of course—Miyon of Cunaxa felt the same way—but damned inconvenient.

Then again, neither Chiana nor Miyon desired Sunrunners to observe and report to Andry, and thence to Pol. They did not understand that the pair did not speak to each other unless absolutely necessary.

War was surely making it necessary. Rialt paced off the perimeter of his camp, pleased that most people had fallen into exhausted sleep watched over by sentries. The last two days had left them in shock. Prince Tilal, marching north, had not been able to arrive before the swift dragon-headed ships. Rialt had recognized the inevitable at once, but fought against it until his *faradhi* conveyed Lord Chaynal's brutal judgment: Waes would not last a day. So carts were piled high and plow-elk requisitioned from the fields to pull them. The Waesians left the homes of their ancestors behind, but not intact. Docks, warehouses of food and wool and silk, shops, inns—anything the enemy could use was systemati-

cally destroyed. It was the misfortune of the poor that they lived in houses made of wood, not expensive stone. Their parts of Waes were still burning. But the luxurious residences of the merchants and other wealthy denizens of the city were safe—though utterly empty.

"The Lord of Radzyn says that—that they should be encouraged to land here," the Sunrunner had reported, sickly pale. "They must invest the armies here that could not take Goddess Keep or Kierst-Isel."

"But what made them turn from the south?" Rialt exclaimed. "They'd sailed around the cape from Goddess Keep—"

"Who can tell what motivates these savages, my lord? The Lord of Radzyn says that when Prince Arlis sails his fleet and Lord Ostvel marches from Castle Crag, the enemy will be crushed between."

Ambitious, daring—and sure to infuriate Chiana, for Swalekeep was within easy marching distance from Waes. But Chay had counted on that. The threat would encourage her to commit Meadowlord's troops to save her own skin. It would be Rialt's job to convince her to do so.

If she deigned to allow him into her presence.

Chiana was as welcoming to the widowed Naydra and as icily condescending to Rialt and Mevita as he'd anticipated. But her fury at their news was worse than he'd thought. He told her and Halian in private about Chay's plan—all except the part about kicking Chiana into calling up the troops—and was privileged to witness a rage that made even her husband blanch.

When she finally paused for breath, Rialt bowed and murmured, "Be that as it may, your grace, I respectfully but strongly urge that at the very least, you have your people see to the gaps in your walls."

With that, he retired to the small chamber he would share with his wife and son—not *quite* in the servant's wing of the keep. The windows overlooked a rainy street just beyond the low walls. A copper pot in the middle of the threadbare rug testified to a leaky roof. Naydra and Cluthine had naturally been given suites; Rialt's Sunrunner had been shown the door and told she must find lodging with the other Waesians somewhere in town.

"Your ears look bruised," Mevita remarked on seeing him.

"She has a powerful voice, does her grace of Meadowlord." He sat down in a rickety chair, winced as it squeaked, and took his son onto his knee. "Well, was your surprise worth the trip?"

"I have a new pony! Lady Cluthine and Princess Naydra showed him to me before the rain started. His nose is all white, like he dipped it in a bowl of moonlight, Naydra says. And there's a big garden here, Papa, much bigger than at home. But I miss the sea."

"So do I. We'll go back to Waes as soon as we can. I'm glad you like your pony." He reminded himself to thank Cluthine.

"Run have your dinner, button," Mevita said, plucking the boy off Rialt's lap and setting him on his feet. "Do you remember the way to the hall?"

"Of course I do," Polev affirmed, and scampered off.

"The hall?" Rialt asked.

"Chiana might *want* to feed him in the kitchens, but he's your son, not a servant. He'll eat in the hall—and at the high table, too."

He grinned. "I suspect, my dear, that you're a snob."

"If you promise not to laugh at me, I'll tell you a secret. On the way here, both Naydra and Cluthine told me to stand up to Chiana. If the High Prince intends her to listen to you, she has to be reminded who you are."

"We shall prepare to be arrogant and stubborn about our privileges, then—even though there's very little left of Waes for me to be Lord Regent of," he added, suddenly tired and depressed.

"Tell me what Chiana said." Mevita sat on a wooden footstool beside him. "We heard her all the way from Naydra's chambers—but not the exact words."

"She has a remarkable vocabulary," he admitted. "Even Halian looked impressed. But I won't repeat what she said in the presence of a lady."

"Thank you, my lord."

He smiled and shrugged. "I don't like to say it, but I can see her point. You know there've been rumors that she's going to wait it all out, let everyone else do the fighting, and then start her own war with her own armies fresh."

"There've been other rumors, too. Meadowlord has hardly been touched."

"That's strategy. Graypearl, Radzyn, Gilad, Syr—those

are the places to take first and hold fast. In twenty or thirty days, Meadowlord will be mostly mud, impossible to fight in."

"But not impossible to ship supplies from Swalekeep down the Faolain."

He stared down at her angry dark eyes. "Are you suggesting she's made an agreement with the enemy? Like Patwin?"

"She yelled for a very long time," Mevita said shrewdly. "Maybe longer than strictly necessary. And she *is* Roelstra's daughter."

"So is Naydra, and there's not a vicious bone in her body."

She gave him a patient sigh. "Rialt, what did they promise Patwin? What could they offer Chiana that she's wanted forever?"

"A princedom," he said slowly.

"A specific princedom," she corrected.

He scrubbed one hand over his face. "My wits are too thick to make any judgments tonight. Let's go down to dinner. And while I don't really care if I'm served in the kitchens or outside in the rain, I'll make the effort and stand on my rights."

"Oh, *you* needn't be obnoxious about it," she assured him quite seriously. "I'll do all that for you."

* * *

At sixteen, Prince Rinhoel of Meadowlord was the spit of his grandfather. The height, the black hair, the proud aristocratic features, the eyes pale green like new leaves —he looked so much like Roelstra, in fact, that people who remembered the late High Prince assigned his character to Rinhoel as well. This was a mistake and an injustice that irritated the youth profoundly. Roelstra, in his view, had been a fool. Rinhoel was anything but.

From his father, Prince Halian, he inherited only the angle of his chin and a taste for luxury—but not its idle enjoyment that made Halian so easy to manage. Outward shows of wealth were to impress and intimidate, though he also appreciated fine things for their beauty and comfort. But for Rinhoel, pleasure consisted of pursuit, conquest, and possession—of coveted toys when he was little, of girls as he grew older, of the knighthood he had not earned, and,

increasingly, of power. He prided himself on single-mindedness. Roelstra had directed that quality toward getting a son. Rinhoel shared with his mother a larger goal, one that did not depend on the whims of the Goddess but rather on their own cunning. They wanted Princemarch.

Chiana had come close nine years ago. She had come even closer to being executed. The assault on Dragon's Rest might have succeeded, but for sorcery. Still, sorcery had been her salvation as well—she had been its victim, and that was what had saved her from the consequences of her actions. She was reminded of it every time she looked at her hands, scarred by glass shards of a mirror she had been forced to destroy. Terror had made her meek for some years afterward. But with Rinhoel's approaching manhood, her old ambitions had surged up once more.

Mother and son knew and accepted that they could not gain Princemarch by military conquest, the way Rohan had seized it in the first place. They could not recover it by legal posturings about Rinhoel's blood claim, even though Chiana had been but six years old when forced to sign a parchment disinheriting herself and all her issue. There was only one way to gain triumphant entry into Castle Crag. Pol had to die.

Thus far he had not obliged.

Roelstra's daughters had produced other grandsons. Ianthe's three were dead. Danladi's son Daniv had been tamed by service as Rohan's squire, his future as Prince of Syr, and affectionate ties of kinship through Sioned, his father's aunt. Rohan had made sure that no dangerous dreams festered in Daniv.

And Syr did not border Princemarch. Meadowlord did. With Pol gone, the conveniences of geography would naturally lead the other princes to confirm Rinhoel's claim instead of Daniv's—so much tidier. Still, Rinhoel could not take possession until Pol died. Or if he married one of Pol's daughters.

Jihan and Rislyn were half his age. Years would pass before their marriages would even be considered. Chiana had looked the pair over at the *Rialla* this summer, deciding that gentle Rislyn was the better prospect. Jihan was too willful. Having settled the question in her own mind, she had informed Rinhoel of his future bride's identity and instructed him to make himself into everything Pol could

wish for his precious little girl. Once they were married, Pol could be discreetly removed and Rinhoel would at last be at Castle Crag in his grandfather's place.

On this course of action mother and son had not agreed. Rinhoel had no intention of playacting to impress Pol for the next ten or twelve years. And, he added shrewdly, did his mother really wish to spend even more of her life waiting? Far more attractive was the notion he held out to her that if the twins were disposed of, he would be the best heir to Princemarch. Pol could not ignore him then. Not him, or his mother. By the next *Rialla*, Rinhoel would be twenty. He could spend the next three years forging alliances with various princes, so that when the twins died and an heir must be found, he would be it.

But now had come this bloody onslaught from the south, and with it the opportunity of a lifetime.

Mirsath's fortuitous murder of Patwin had been the first opening. Aurar, Patwin's youngest daughter, whose birth had been her mother Rabia's death, was currently living at Swalekeep. At the news she became a fire-breathing she-dragon. Rabia had been Chiana's full sister, both of them daughters of Roelstra and Palila, and Chiana was pleased to see resemblances in temperament and ambition between herself and her niece. But Aurar's demand that an army be sent to level Faolain Lowland and avenge Patwin's death had needed redirection. The girl proved herself clever by heeding Chiana's advice.

"My darling Aurar, I share your grief. Mirsath will be dead soon enough, I promise. But we must be cautious. What your beloved father worked so hard to gain for you can still be had. I can't send an army, you must understand that. But I *can* send you and a large escort down to recover your dear father's body for proper burning. They will allow you through as the daughter of their valued ally. And while you're there, you will present certain propositions to them—in exchange for establishing you as Princess of Syr in your own right."

Aurar liked the idea of being a ruling princess. She was Roelstra's get for a fact, Chiana had told Rinhoel.

"Not that she's going to sit her pretty bottom down at High Kirat for an instant," she added. "Syr will go to you, of course."

"I never doubted it, Mother. But perhaps I should go with her."

"We can't risk you. I mean no slight to your bravery, my heart, but you must remember that these people are barbarians."

So Aurar had departed with a suitable escort, all attired in mourning gray. She returned with Patwin's corpse—and answers to Chiana's offers.

"Ostvel is gathering the levies of Princemarch. Kostas and Tilal are in the field. If Rohan wins in the Desert, his armies would land on us, too. I pointed that out as you asked. But they've taken most of the Faolain River, so ships can sail by night to supply them."

"With the winter cloud cover, the Sunrunners won't see a thing," Chiana concluded gleefully. "Aurar, my love, you've done brilliantly!"

But now there was a new threat, from a portion of the enemy army not yet privy to the arrangement. Rinhoel met with his mother after dinner the night of Rialt's arrival, and demanded to know how Chaynal could be so stupid.

"Stupidity is a thing unknown to the Lord of Radzyn, and you'd better remember it," she snapped. "Rialt says they hope to lure forces unsuccessful on Kierst-Isel to Waes, and trap them between Ostvel and Arlis. It's a good plan, but it puts us in danger until we get assurances of safety from these savages."

"Aurar can act as go-between. And if she fails, I'll wring her neck."

"I have no interest in how she dies, but restrain yourself until we hold Syr, if you please. For now, we have these filthy Waesians to house and feed. And that impudent bitch, complaining about her room and insisting they sit at table with us! The arrogance of the woman!"

"That miserable brat of hers kicked me when I told him to shut up tonight. But we have to endure them, Mother. It'll look suspicious if we don't."

"Rinhoel. . . ." Her hazel eyes brightened. "They make perfect hostages! Pol's fond of Rialt—Goddess knows why a prince consorts with a merchant's son who used to be his chamberlain. Desert folk have always had despicable manners. My stomach curdles every time I think of that *nothing* Ostvel as Lord of Castle Crag, married to a Princess of Kierst!"

"Hostages?" he prompted before she could reiterate her entire list of Rohan's offenses.

"What? Oh, yes—well, they're bound to find out we're helping the enemy eventually. When they do, we'll have Rialt and his odious little wife and brat. We must keep them here at all costs."

"And give them better chambers?" he asked sarcastically.

"In a few days. Perhaps." She shrugged her annoyance. "But we can't let them go to Dragon's Rest. They're too valuable here."

* * *

This was Rohan's view, as well—though for different reasons. Rialt met his Sunrunner at an inn the next afternoon, and once the woman had finished conversing with Hollis on the sunlight, it was all decided. He and Mevita and Polev would stay at Swalekeep and observe Chiana. News of Aurar's journey to recover her father's body had intrigued the High Prince greatly. Rialt suspected he was right, and some sort of bargain had been struck. He would wait, watch, foul Chiana's plans in small ways if possible, and report everything to Rohan and Pol through his Sunrunner.

When he returned to the castle Rialt apologized to his wife for not having credited what she had known instinctively: that Chiana saw a chance to gain Princemarch, and didn't mind bedding down with the barbarian enemy to do it.

Chapter Seventeen

On the fifty-eighth day of Autumn—twenty-six since Graypearl, Gilad Seahold, and Faolain Riverport had been attacked, twenty-three since the fall of Radzyn—they found out what the wooden contraptions were for.

A score of them snaked across the Long Sand on huge, spoked wooden wheels, drawn by Radzyn horses broken through Goddess only knew what cruelty to the unfamiliar work. Heavy bits dragged at their mouths, secured by wide straps across forehead and nose; thick leather harness bound them breast and rib; reins threaded through brass guide rings to the men driving the horses.

"Do they actually plan to *fight* that way?" Walvis marveled as the bizarre frameworks pulled into what they assumed was a planned formation on the flat plain where battle would be fought. "Are those barriers?"

"How should I know?" Maarken rubbed his sore right wrist absently, scowling into the distance. "I don't like this at all."

Chay leaned his elbows on the low wall between crenellations, hands clasped before him and shoulders hunkered down. "I suppose they might be obstructions of some sort, to stop our mounted soldiers. . . ."

"Or for their troops to hide behind during our charge," Pol contributed. A moment later he shook his head in frustration. "What in all Hells *are* those things? And why are so many of their men racing around gathering up the biggest rocks they can find?"

"I think we're meant to be frightened," Rohan mused. "Or at least extremely nervous."

"It's working." Walvis spoke dryly, but his eyes were

shadowed with worry. "How do we plan a battle against something we don't understand?"

As high, thin clouds burned away above them, they watched the unwieldy frames become something terribly logical. Wheels were blocked with large boulders while ropes were attached in various places. From the middle of each rose an armlike pole ending in a broad hollow like a cupped palm. Ropes leading from these bowls were wound laboriously into a section of the frame, much as chains were wound to lift a drawbridge.

A tall, massively muscled warrior whose beard seemed made entirely of gold beads stood a few paces in front of the array, one arm upraised. When he swept his hand down, there was a mighty rush of air and a simultaneous *thwanng* from all twenty machines as the ropes' tension was released and the empty hands flew upward.

Rohan gulped hard. "Now we know."

Pol had already thought beyond the effect to neutralizing it. "How many would it take to swarm one of those things and topple it?"

Chay nodded slowly and turned his head to look at Rohan. "My prince?"

In a colorless voice he replied, "We are their equals in conventional war. These tip the balance in their favor. Therefore, we must find some way of canceling the threat. It would cost too many lives to use foot soldiers against them."

"In other words, you're open to suggestions," Walvis murmured.

"Always."

Before anyone else could speak, Pol said, "There's only one way. Fire."

It was the first time he had addressed his father since the night he'd refused to swear the Sunrunner's oath against killing. It was not lost on either that this was really the same discussion. Blue eyes met blue-green, each man knowing that it would come up again and again—until one of them relented. And neither of them would relent.

"Not from me," Maarken said quietly, but there was anguish in his voice.

"I wasn't going to ask. It'll be my responsibility." But Pol couldn't quite keep the tinge of scorn from his voice.

His cousin glared at him. "I've done it before—that's what you're thinking, isn't it? I called Fire to a wooden

bridge. But that was cold Fire, Pol. Not the kind you intend to use. It didn't kill."

"Only strongly discouraged people from crossing that bridge, or venturing onto it to put the Fire out," Pol snapped. "What's the damned difference? And how do you know I won't use the same kind of Fire?"

"Because I know *you*. Here's your chance to demonstrate you're just as powerful as Andry! How can you be a ruling prince, a husband, a father, nearly thirty-three winters old—and still such a child?" He stalked off, limping on his wounded leg and shouting for his wife and a squire.

Pol gritted his teeth. Maarken had been closer to the truth than he liked to admit, even to himself. What Andry had done still infurated him. But the insult from a man he worshiped stuck in his throat like a knife.

"I suppose you agree with him about me," he said to his father.

"Do you?"

Pol felt every muscle in his body tense. "Perhaps you think I should ride back to my princedom, my wife, my children, my next birthday, and my toys."

"Don't be a horse's ass," Chay said tiredly. "You don't understand Maarken. *I* can condemn what Andry did. I'm his father. But Maarken's his brother—and swore the same vow. What Andry did violated everything Sunrunners are, but by the Goddess, it *worked*. Don't you see how much Maarken's tempted to do the same?"

Rohan said softly, "The means of Andry's victory may be justified in its end—to Andry. But not to Maarken. And it's tearing him apart, not just for himself but for his brother."

"It seems to me," Pol said in equally low tones, "that those of you who are *not* Sunrunners do a great deal of philosophizing about those who *are*."

His father's brows knotted over narrowed eyes. "And what about those of you who are *diarmadhi*?"

A muted gasp from Walvis reminded them of his presence, and Pol froze. *He doesn't know about me—*

But he did now.

Pol looked down at his father. "*You* tell him how it happened," he said curtly. "It's not a story I have the stomach to repeat right now."

As he strode away, he heard Walvis mumble something about not wishing to know, that it was not his right to know,

that he had no need to know. Rohan said, "It is your right, and there is need." Pol hurtled down the stairs before he could hear any more.

* * *

The battle was brief and vicious. Pol, standing on Remagev's walls, called down Fire on the wooden arms that flung their huge handfuls of stone at the keep. Like the sails and the dragon ships, they did not burn.

Some of the machines spewed colossal boulders against the walls, while others used smaller stones to terrify Remagev's inhabitants. No one had even heard of a battle fought this way. It was as if the sky itself assaulted them.

Failure turned Pol into a madman. He armed himself in a frenzy and tore the reins of a war stallion from a Radzyn soldier's hands and pelted out the gates roaring *"Azhrei!"* at the top of his lungs. Rohan saw him go, and wanted to cover his face with his hands. But he watched his son's slaughters resolutely, telling himself it was not a prince or a Sunrunner their people needed, but a warrior. A barbarian. Pol was living up to a heritage older than Rohan's rule of law.

Fighting was a nightmare. The initial charge was too fast, horses and soldiers frantic to escape the heavy stones showering down from the sky. For a time Maarken lost control of the cavalry through no fault of his own. And there was no way to regroup, for the machines could be adjusted to direct stone at any target.

Kazander's horsemen dealt death enough; Chay's and Walvis' people did the same, mounted and afoot. Maarken had given the heartbreaking order that whatever horses could be killed should be. So not just enemy soldiers but Radzyn horses were butchered, a sword through the heart or the brain once their riders were unseated. Some were taken and hauled back to the keep, but the primary object was to deprive the Vellant'im of their stolen, essential mounts.

But it was the Desert force that was finally compelled to withdraw behind Remagev's massive gates as the machines—untouched in the battle—continued their fire against and into the keep. This seemed likely to last all night.

"The walls will hold," Walvis told Chay. "It'll take more than a few rocks to—" He ducked instinctively as a clatter

sounded in the empty courtyard outside. "—to break through."

"If they don't drive us mad first with their stony rain," Chay growled. "Go get your arm bound up. It's bleeding."

Despite the brevity of the battle, there were many casualties to be attended. Sioned, Feylin, Chayla, and the others who knew enough medicine worked until long after dusk, while the pounding at the walls continued.

"We killed many," Kazander said as Chayla bound up a cut on his arm. "So did they. But they have more people to lose."

She tied off the bandage, inspected it quickly, and said, "Are you hurt anywhere else?"

"No, my lady." He rallied briefly, giving her a tired smile through the dirt and sweat caking his face. "But if I were, the sweet healing touch of your hands would cure me instantly."

"Fool," she snorted. But as she moved on to the other wounded, her bloodied fingers brushed lightly over the back of his hand.

Chayla's beauty had made her the favorite among the young men who came to Remagev, though her scant sympathy for the scrapes and bruses taken in training kept most from falling headlong in love with her. But these wounds were real, and their fighting skills were the only reason her patients had survived to become her patients.

That evening she found in herself what the finest physicians must have and must hide: compassion. Its discovery turned her from efficient crafter to genuine master. She had studied medicine because she had a talent for it, because the workings of the human body fascinated her. But the girl who memorized texts for their intellectual challenge that night became a Healer. She felt each wound as if it was her own—and learned to conceal the pain. For if these people could bear their hurts in proud silence, who was she to weep?

Just the same, her father came upon her late that night in Sionell's little cactus garden, hunched over and gasping as she tried not to cry.

Maarken had not fought long that day—his wrist was still painful and his thigh had not healed sufficiently to permit it—and thus there was no physical exhaustion to take him to his bed where his wife insisted he belonged. So he limped

downstairs, not wishing to be up on the battlements where his father and Rohan stared at enemy campfires. He could feel the Vellanti presence all along his skin; he didn't need to look at them to know they were there.

The dim golden beacon of his daughter's hair snagged his attention long before he heard her muffled sobs. A father's first instinct rose up in him: *Who has hurt her? I'll kill him for it*— But no one was to blame. His heart ached and he wished she was still a little girl who could be sheltered, protected, spared all ugliness. He thought of that other bright blond head, twin to Chayla's, those other young shoulders bending under a weight too heavy. Rohannon didn't even have his family around him. He was alone. Maarken resolved that if there was enough sun tomorrow, he would find his son and give what comfort he could.

But Chayla he could help *now*.

He was sitting beside her with his arm around her before she fully realized he was there. "Hush, little one," he whispered, rocking her. "Ah, love, it breaks my heart to see you cry."

"I'm not c-crying," she managed, hiding her face against his shoulder.

"Of course you're not. Forgive me."

"It's just—I couldn't help!" she burst out. "Not enough. I worked and worked and I did it right and they'll heal and they're not in any more pain but it isn't *enough!*"

"You did all you could," he said, feeling helpless, wishing again she was still a child with simple hurts to soothe.

"I know," she said impatiently. "If not for me, some of them would lose an arm or a leg, or their wounds would fester, and more would die—but it was as if my skills were there to serve the *war*, Papa. Do you understand? I want more than anything to be a physician and help people—but I don't want it to be *this* kind of help!"

He stroked her silky hair, understanding better than she could ever know. He loved being a Sunrunner, loved the feel and taste and scent of colors on light. He took pride and pleasure in his skills. But he didn't want to be forced to use them in war any more than his daughter did.

Had Andry been forced into it, or had he grabbed at the chance? It didn't bear thinking about. If the reality of it tore at him the way the very idea of it tore at Maarken, then he was going through all Hells right now.

But Chayla could endure using her skills in the service of war, and Andry was doing the same. Could Maarken do any less? Was Pol right? Had the time passed for pretty notions of honor and oaths and Sunrunner ethics?

Had Andry *wanted* to kill?

"Listen to me, heartling," he said. "We all do what we must in the service of life. That's how you must think of it. We've been trapped by this war. You fight by being a healer, Chayla. What others try to take, you can give back through the skill of your hands and eyes and mind." He held her closer. "If war is darkness, then you are light. But there's a price for it—paid in the coin of your own heart."

"Papa, *they're* paying in blood."

"I know. I know." Blood was simple and pure, like new-minted gold. It was handed over in pain and suffering, but the accounts were balanced. He had been wounded in battle several times; he understood the reckoning of that debt. But those who healed, or commanded, or had power beyond that of swords and arrows—their payments were more complex, not so easily given, not so cleanly summed.

Chayla shivered, then sniffled and wiped her eyes. "I hate it. I understand what you said that I'm serving life by healing it—but it's work I shouldn't have to be doing. It's like—it's a corruption of physician's work. We didn't ask for this war. We didn't do anything to deserve it. It's not fair."

"No, it's not. But there's wealth enough among us, heartling, to settle accounts." A bitter wealth of blood and heart and spirit—Goddess keep them from spending it all.

"I shouldn't be sitting here feeling sorry for myself," Chayla said, tears fading from her voice. "I have to go look in on a couple of people."

"It's late. Let someone else do it."

He knew the words were a mistake as soon as they left his mouth. She drew away and looked up at him and with her wide, sad, beautiful eyes, a little smile on her face, and suddenly he knew she was no longer fifteen winters old.

Maarken shrugged. "I'm your father, I can't help it."

"I'll bet you'll say the same thing to Rohannon next time you talk to him." Rising, she leaned down to kiss his brow. "*You're* the one who needs to sleep."

He grunted. "My daughter, the physician. I just hope kissing your male patients isn't part of the prescribed treatment."

"I took an oath to kiss only the ones who're better-looking than my father and brother—and there aren't any."

He saw her square her slight shoulders as she walked away, the momentary lightness brought by her smile fading as *oath* lingered in his mind. He sat outside for a long while, and his wrist and leg stiffened even more with the growing cold. In fact, he expected Hollis to appear any instant with a cloak and a scold to come in before he froze. But it was Kazander who arrived with a heavy length of close-woven wool over his arm. The young man bowed low, presented the cloak, and as Maarken put it over his shoulders bowed again.

"My lord Battle Commander, there is word from Stronghold."

"Oh, Goddess—it hasn't been attacked, has it?" He started to his feet.

"No, my lord. Be easy. The Sunrunner Morwenna conjured in Fire and Water at Stronghold today, watching the battle here. The stars give few threads tonight, but enough to weave. And the revered Guard Commander Myrdal says there is a way out."

"A way to defeat their rain of stones? How? Tell me!"

Kazander bent his head again. "Forgive me, my lord. I should speak with more care. There is a way out of Remagev, by which all may escape to safety."

"Running—again." He couldn't stop the words, or the bitterness.

"I agree, my lord," Kazander murmured. "But. . . ."

"Yes. Go on."

The young man looked up, a feral smile lifting the ends of his mustache. "I have an idea or two that might meet with my lord's approval. The vermin may walk into Remagev—but few will walk out of it."

* * *

Pol listened to Rohan outline plans for an orderly retreat. It was all he could do to hold his tongue and his temper. *He is High Prince, not I,* he reminded himself again and again. *I can't speak in front of the others. I must say nothing. But, Father, you are so wrong!*

Remagev would be abandoned—prepared with deadfalls. Rohan had taken Kazander's advice about that, though

probably only because Myrdal had originally suggested it. Giving up another keep, no matter how lethal a trap it became, clotted in Pol's throat and would not be swallowed. He told himself his father knew what he was doing. But no matter how much trust showed on the faces around him, no matter how much faith he had in Chay's and Maarken's military acumen, to run away was cowardice.

"Understood?" Rohan said at last, and everyone nodded. "Very well. Sioned, Hollis, Maarken, make sure our people elsewhere are informed. Especially Riyan and Ostvel."

"He'll be marching across the border into Meadowlord soon," Sioned mused. "Dear old Clutha always did have fits at the very thought of his precious princedom becoming a battlefield again."

"Well, Ostvel won't get any help from Chiana." Maarken hesitated, then cast a sidelong glance at Pol. "What about Miyon?"

Pol replied, "I won't waste a single arrow defending him."

"I can't argue with your sentiments about his worth," Chay said, "but I do take exception to your grasp of tactics. Cunaxan steel is as vital to an army as Radzyn horses." A muscle in his jaw twitched as another hail of stones spattered the courtyard below, but he continued steadily, "The Vellant'im are now superlatively mounted. We must see to it that they're not similarly armed. Rohan, what if Tallain and Jahnavi divert some of their people to Cunaxa? If Miyon's armories are taken, the enemy could supply their people forever, using the dragon ships."

"Why do you think I ordered them both to stay in the north? Miyon will be defended whether we like it or not. The problem will be getting him to send his own people to help. We must convince him that we're his best hope of holding back an invasion."

Hollis nodded slowly. "Jahnavi is an able soldier—like his sire."

"Who learned from Chay," Walvis said.

"Who learned from Zehava," Chay added. "Rohan, what do you think *he'd* do?"

Rohan smiled tiredly. "The only thing I lack right now is my father's voice on the Desert wind telling me I'm losing the princedom it cost him so much to secure."

Pol was relieved when his mother turned the conversation. None of them could function if they started speculating

on what might be. There was too much at stake dealing with what *was*. "When I contact Tuath, I'm going to have Rabisa take the children to Feruche. A trip across the Desert is dangerous, but a siege would be worse."

"What about Sionell at Tiglath?" Hollis asked.

"Do you honestly think she'd leave?" Pol countered with a slight smile.

Sioned smiled, too. "Even if she would, Antalya wouldn't. Goddess, but that child is stubborn."

"Talya won't leave without her mother, Sionell won't leave without Tallain, and Tallain wouldn't leave if you put a sword to his throat." Rohan shook his head. "I envy them their simple choices."

Dangerous sands again, Pol thought, and again his mother provided the lifeline. "Now that we've settled Miyon's future without his permission, I suggest we see to our own—and especially the enemy's. We begin at dawn tomorrow, I think." She shook her head, smiling. "Myrdal never ceases to amaze. Ninety-two last summer, and sharp as Fironese crystal."

Walvis folded his arms and said, "Until I see for myself, I'm not going to believe there are ways out of here I don't know about. And secret rooms! I practically rebuilt Remagev from the ground up and I never had a clue!"

"There's nothing about Desert castles she doesn't know. I was twenty-eight before she finally showed me the secrets of my own keep. And even then she didn't show me all of them." Rohan paused, gazing at his friend and former squire. Before he could speak again, Walvis shook his head.

"They won't destroy Remagev any more than they did Radzyn," he said. The solid thunk of a huge boulder against the outer wall mocked him. "They *won't*," he repeated.

"When I gave you this castle, it was almost in ruins. I don't want you to come home to the same thing all over again."

Feylin laughed aloud. "Five steps into the main hall, and what Allun did to them at Lower Pyrme will seem a New Year Holiday by contrast. They won't get far enough in to break a single dish."

"And even if they do," Walvis added, smiling a little, "I need a project to occupy my old age."

Pol heard them with growing wonder, knowing he should not be surprised. Their words were a tribute to them—but

also to his father. People would follow this man, trusting him, loving him, into any Hell he cared to lead them. They knew he would lead them back out again in triumph.

Rohan rubbed his face briskly. "Get to your beds, then, so your wits are about you for this little welcome-to-Remagev party we're giving them. Pol, stay for a moment, please."

While the others took their leave, Pol braced himself. Once they were alone, and the erratic splatter of rocks sounded even louder, Rohan blew out a long breath and shrugged an apology.

"I know I've been speaking as if your people are mine. If you have objections—"

"None. You know that."

"Then tell me why you're looking so grim. Is it that I had to tell Walvis about you?"

"No. I'm sorry for the way I acted. Maarken was right—it was childish."

"The oath, then?"

"Not that, either. We both know where we stand on that."

"Yes, we do," Rohan murmured. "Am I going to have to pry it out of you, Pol? Whatever differences we may have, we're still father and son. And the work we're involved in means we have to tell each other the truth."

"Father. . . ." He groped for words to tell this man he was wrong.

Shrewd blue eyes narrowed slightly. "Ah," was all he said.

"We should stand and fight," Pol said, trying to sound calm and reasonable. "Stop them before they can kill any more of our people. Deal them a blow so crippling they'll run back to their dragon ships. Lure them into the Desert, away from their machines. It'll be an even battle, Father. We have to fight them *now*. They're setting up to conduct a long, long war. With the southern rivers as supply lines, they won't hunger or thirst—"

"They'll die of both when we raid and raid and keep on raiding."

Pol felt his lips curl. "Strike and run, when we could finish it all with a couple of real battles?"

Rohan looked thoughtful. "In other words, you want me to *do* something."

"Yes!" The passion of pride and anger broke through his

careful respect. He sprang to his feet, almost shaking. "How can you give up Remagev, when Walvis and Feylin struggled for years to rebuild it? Radzyn is lost, and Whitecliff and Riverport—what does it take to make you do something?"

"I cherish my freedom, Pol. It's something you haven't yet learned—never having been a prisoner."

"The freedom to run away?"

Rohan sighed. "Freedom lies in not taking action until there is nothing else to do. But you don't understand that."

"Enlighten me," Pol said through his teeth.

"If I order another battle, if I act to bring this war to an end, *we will be slaughtered.* There are too many of them and too few of us. I know what will happen. But I do *not* know what the consequences of waiting will be. Thus I'm not trapped. I have room to maneuver. I'm free."

"Free to do *nothing?*" Pol cried in frustration.

"Exactly. Free as a dragon in flight. Do they fly headlong into a storm? No. They wait it out. The storm is a trap, Pol. War is a trap. By acting to bring a battle, I deprive myself of freedom of action. I trap myself and all my people—and they die for it."

"You were quick enough to fight Roelstra!"

"And I did it very efficiently, too—because I had no other choice. It all became very simple, Pol. Him or me."

"Have you forgotten how to fight, then?"

His father's expression remained one of detached contemplation. "I regret having to say this about my own son, but for an intelligent man you can be a thundering great fool."

Pol's spine became a sword blade. "Then explain it and cure my idiocy," he said coldly.

"Use your eyes, boy!" Rohan snapped, all the deceptive mildness gone. His eyes flashed and he flung one hand out toward the window where the Desert waited. "Look at it! Could someone who's never lived in it live off it? That's your battlefield, Pol, hundreds upon hundreds of measures of it, without a drop of water or a blade of grass or a single handspan of shade! The Desert will win our war for us. I won't give up one life unnecessarily—not when the Long Sand will take more lives than swords and arrows ever could." He raked Pol with a contemptuous gaze. "You've lived soft and fat in Princemarch for too long, woken to green fields and trees and more water than you'll ever need. Enlighten you? Look at the Desert until you understand

again what it's like to live off it the way Walvis taught you in childhood—the way the enemy can't. Bleak and lifeless—and the most beautiful land in the world." He fell silent, rose to go, then turned long enough to say, "Don't speak to me again of battles, boy, until you've really led one. And remember that if I have my way, you never will."

Goaded beyond caution, Pol lashed out. "Oh, yes, the great scheme! Peace and plenty, no swords, no war—nothing but talk and maneuver and waiting for people to see things your way! Why don't you invite the enemy to dinner? Give them a banquet and reason with them! Or buy them off—now, there's a thought! There's gold enough at Skybowl. Surely you could pay them off the way you did the Merida, your first year in Zehava's chair!"

There was no perceptible stiffening of Rohan's muscles, but suddenly Pol wanted to back out of reach. He should have followed this instinct. Though he was half his father's age, a head taller, and heavier by two silkweights, Rohan suddenly had him pinned face down on the table like a side of beef with one arm crooked behind his back. His wrist was caught in viselike fingers and for a moment he thought the bones would snap.

"Now I know you for Ianthe's son," Rohan hissed in his ear. "No child of Sioned's could be so stupid! Listen to me, and listen well. If I could buy the enemy, I would do it. But I can't. If you had the sense the Goddess gave a plow-elk, you'd see that. Don't you understand? They don't want our substance, they want our lives! But you're so arrogant and eager for blood and battle—how can you scorn the lives in your care?"

Pol struggled and got his shoulder nearly wrenched from its socket for his trouble.

"Stay still, boy. I'm not finished with you yet. It's a fine palace and a soft civilized life you've made for yourself with the peace I gave you. But you're a barbarian. You're the kind I've spent my whole life fighting."

Pol's muscles spasmed involuntarily at that. Rohan tightened his grip and laughed bitterly.

"Tell me, my civilized son, how did it feel to kill? Fires the blood, doesn't it? That wonderful gush of omnipotence—did you like it, Pol? I did. But at least I knew what it was. Strip away the years and the deeds, and there's your real

face grinning at you, with a hundred generations of savages in its eyes."

"Damn you—let me go!" Pol spat.

"So you can indulge yourself in another battle? Risk your life for the pleasure of killing some more? Ah, no. You're too important. Doesn't it gall you to be protected? I don't give a damn for your hurt pride or your contempt for my methods—past or present or future."

"Then break my sword arm and have done with it!'

"You'd still be able to give orders. You'd send men and women to fight and die in a battle they can't win, just because you think you should put up a fight. I know savages. I know your kind." Abruptly Rohan released him and turned away.

Pol barely kept himself from collapsing onto his face across the table. He glared at his father's back, resisting the urge to rub his aching shoulder. "And you put me where I am, didn't you?"

"Perhaps you're the right man for the work after all," Rohan observed. "Perhaps only a barbarian can defeat barbarians." He paused at the door and glanced over his shoulder. "Take heart, Pol. If I die somewhere along the way, you'll be High Prince and get your chance to play the warrior. You ought to do very well—you seem to have all the right instincts."

"The same instincts you used when you killed my grandfather?"

If he had expected to draw blood with that, he was disappointed. Rohan gave him a small, vicious smile.

"Exactly the same, my son. Exactly the same."

Chapter Eighteen

Maarken stood at the north postern gate, a fingerflame conjured near his shoulder. "Yes, that's it—right through here and out to the Long Sand. Meet up with the others at the ruins of Sandfall, then continue on to Stronghold. Goddess watch over you."

The Vellant'im directed their bombardment of stones at the walls and courtyard only. Maarken would have considered this stupid, but for the fact that they could not have guessed that yet another keep would be abandoned. He hated what they were doing—they all did—but with Rohan he believed in the strength of the Desert. Their Desert.

He was learning not to flinch, but the irregular pounding of stones was maddening. With Kazander he prowled the barracks, selecting soldiers to ride out by night with the wounded who could sit a horse. Traveling with only the clothes on their backs and the swords at their belts, they would wait in the half-hidden shelters along the way. Six groups of twenty each departed between midnight and the black time before dawn—ten able-bodied to protect ten wounded. They rode dark horses with bridles wrapped to stifle sound. Maarken listened for alarms from the Vellanti camp that would mean discovery, but there was only the incessant, nerve-shredding rattle.

"They use the bones and teeth of the Desert against us," Kazander murmured as rocks danced their way down the barracks roof.

"But they don't understand her flesh," Maarken replied, surprising himself with the imagery. Kazander was contagious.

The young man grinned beneath his mustache. "May they sink into her soft golden arms like eager lovers—and die of her caress."

He couldn't help grinning back.

They passed Feylin and Chayla, dozing fitfully in the part of the barracks sectioned off for the wounded. Maarken paused to stroke his daughter's hair. She murmured in her sleep and awakened, blinking at the tiny flame that followed her father through the night.

"What—? Oh. Papa. Is it time yet?"

"No. Go back to sleep."

Shaking her head, she stood, stretched, and grimaced as a clatter hit the roof again. "The sooner we get out of here, the better!"

"Absolutely," he agreed, and smiled before walking away, the fingerflame tagging dutifully beside him.

Kazander accompanied Chayla to the well just outside, drawing water while she waited in the safety of the arcade. Neither of them said a word until he returned to her, blithely ignoring the rain of large stones ten paces away.

"I suppose it's too late for music." She gave him a rueful sidelong glance.

He did not pretend to misunderstand her meaning; she was not talking about the time of night. "Never, my lady. At Stronghold, I promise to make you forget all this."

"For the length of a song, anyway." She smiled, and his heart turned to water.

Rohan and Sioned actually lay down between blankets for a while at midnight. She mimed sleep better than he did. As he slid from under the covers and reached for his clothes, her soft question about where he thought he was going startled him into a muffled curse. He accused her of faking sleep to her own purposes; she replied that her purposes and his were pretty much the same. He admitted it ruefully, they smiled a little, and got dressed to go downstairs again—he to the stables for a conversation with the grooms, she to help Hollis with the packing before preparing a trick of her own.

Chay, Betheyn, and Walvis sat in the latter's study, poring over drawings of the keep. Sioned had earlier made a list relayed from Myrdal through Morwenna. Beth, daughter of an architect, carefully marked the little secrets and explained to the astounded men why each was not only plausible but logical, even elegant.

"I knew about the room off the main stairs, of course," Walvis said. "But there can't be a second room just behind it. Where would it fit?"

"Here." Betheyn chuckled as she pointed to the plans. "Oh, I wish I'd met whoever designed this castle! See how this room tucks in neat as you please? I like the passage under the gatehouse, too. All those tiles set at intervals in the ceiling, with matching ones on the floor above—but they're not *on* the floor, they *are* the floor, with empty air between them! All we need do is smash through and rain hot oil or water or whatever we like down on them."

"But we can't leave someone behind to work it," Walvis objected. "What use it is if—" Suddenly he gave a whoop of laughter. "When the inner gate opens, a bell rings up in the gatehouse! Connected by wires! Set hot oil in pots beside the holes, wire them through the bell-hole down to the gate—and when the gate opens, the wire pulls the pots instead of the bell, and they're drenched!"

"I like it," Chay announced. "What else have we got, Beth?"

"There's another series of ceiling holes in the long arcade between the postern gate and the barracks. Supposedly, they let in light." She chuckled.

Walvis looked more shocked than ever. "Feylin and I have been trying to get rid of the noise for years! We almost tore it all down once to rebuild it!"

Beth nodded gleefully. "The stones shift. If we move enough of them out of position ourselves, when the postern opens, half the arcade ceiling falls in."

Chay grinned broadly. "You've got a flair for this kind of thing, my dear."

She looked startled for a moment, then shook her head. "It's just that I remember when Sorin was finalizing the plans for Feruche, Myrdal put in the same kind of deadfall—just in case. We laughed over it all night."

"*All* night?" Chay asked.

Betheyn turned a delightful shade of pink. He winked at her. She became even more flustered and took refuge in Sioned's notes. "Myrdal says there's an underground room here—"

"There can't possibly—" Walvis sighed. "Ignore me. Go on."

She smiled her sympathy. "I know—it's rather unsettling, isn't it? Anyway, the granary floor can be rigged to collapse. She's not sure how. But it'd be very useful because below it is solid knives."

"Stronghold's supposed to have one like it," Chay mused. "We'll make an inspection tomorrow morning and think it over. What else?"

"A passage and a stairwell that go nowhere. I'm not sure how to use them."

Rohan came in then and was apprised of Remagev's hitherto unsuspected deadfalls. Having spent five years here as squire to his kinsman Hadaan, and having had a hand in the refurbishing, he was as startled as Walvis.

"You've got to admire these people," he said. "Sunrunners and sorcerers traded castles back and forth as their fortunes rose and fell—and left little surprises for each other. Must've made life interesting. I know how the knife chamber works at Stronghold, but it's all in stone. You say the granary floor is wood. That may be a problem."

"Well, there's enough else here to keep them busy," Walvis replied.

"Rohan, where have you been that you stink of horse?" Chay asked suddenly.

He grinned. "I've been playing physician."

The older man drew himself up. "What have you *done?*"

"We're splitting up into four groups when we leave. That doesn't do us much good unless they split up to follow. Sand doesn't hold hoofprints. So I'm giving them something to track."

Chay gave him an awful glare. "Sacrifice even one of my horses, and I'll leave a trail to follow—in your blood!"

Betheyn's eyes widened, although years at Radzyn had accustomed her to its lord's sense of humor. Rohan, who had known him roughly seven times as long as she, pretended outrage.

"Chay! Not horse blood, and certainly not horse bodies! Horse shit!"

Walvis shook with laughter. Beth frowned as she tried to puzzle it out. Chay let out an explosive breath and nearly took a swing at his prince.

"The ones we're riding to Stronghold will be cleaned out by morning," Rohan explained blithely.

Betheyn hesitated. "But won't they know the difference in the—the—"

"Texture?" Walvis supplied helpfully.

"I thought of that. The others won't be dosed. They'll be fed as usual—and enough fodder taken along to keep them nice and regular along the way."

"Rohan, only you would think of such a thing." Chay grimaced. "My poor sweethearts and their ruined digestion!"

"Better theirs with a dose of salts than yours with a sword in your guts."

* * *

Pol and the two squires, Dannar and Daniv, spent part of the night helping pack various instruments of war that must not fall into enemy hands. The armory was denuded of extra swords, shields, spears, knives, and battle harness. Some were parceled out to those leaving Remagev that night, after careful wrapping to ensure silence.

Occasionally Pol paused to stroke the hilt of a fine Cunaxan sword, wondering when his fury would find outlet in its use. He didn't know who was its primary object: his father, for prohibiting the battle that sense demanded; his father-by-marriage, from whose lands these swords came and whom he had to protect whether he liked it or not; or the Vellant'im responsible for all this.

After he sent the boys upstairs to see to the personal possessions of those they served, he sat on a bench near Sionell's cactus garden and finally admitted that the only person he could rightfully be furious with was himself.

Lived soft and fat at Dragon's Rest, had he? Literally as well as figuratively; he'd lost flesh these hectic days of autumn, but his belt was still a bit tight. In battle he'd not moved as swiftly as he'd expected, and was sore in places he shouldn't have been. But at least he'd *done* something. At least he'd fought. Rohan was too old to join in the actual battle, of course—but his was the power to order battles fought. A thing he refused to do.

What angered Pol more than anything was the anger itself. What was wrong with him? He felt all unbalanced, every nerve raw, every emotion magnified as if by one of those pretty, useless lenses his father enjoyed peering through. His mind snagged on the image, and he realized that part of his trouble was that he felt as if he were on the wrong end of that lens, being inspected for flaws. Rohan found plenty, Goddess knew; Pol had seen it in his eyes.

Well, perhaps it was time he did a little examining of his own. Perhaps the problem wasn't with him. Perhaps it was

Rohan. The tough question was whether he still trusted his father. He rubbed his aching shoulder and frowned.

He knew how Rohan's mind worked. But he wondered if his father understood why he did what he did—or, more to the point, *didn't* do. Forcing events put one in control of them. That was power. Rohan was wary of using his power. Pol even understood why. There had been times when it scared him, too. But to fear its necessary use . . . was he calling his father a coward?

He bent over, elbows on knees and face in his hands. *Do something,* he begged silently. *Win this war or give me leave to win it for you. Make me believe in you and trust you again.*

The moons had risen late, three pale glowing discs behind the haze. Pol gave a start as he felt light break over him, free of clouds. Straightening, he wondered if it would last long enough to weave. But where would he go? Radzyn, Whitecliff, Riverport, Graypearl—and torture himself with sight of the destruction. Syr or Ossetia, where armies fought battles he wasn't allowed to. Goddess Keep, where Andry slept—or Dragon's Rest, where Meggie probably could not sleep. Guilt stung him. She hadn't been in his thoughts more than an instant in the last days. She must be terrified, poor darling. But Dragon's Rest was remote and secure. Laric and Edrel were there. He had nothing to worry about regarding his family and his palace. He had more immediate concerns.

He plaited moonlight automatically, not knowing where he would fling the strands, not caring. It was blessed escape, exercise of well-loved skill. Clouds had blown northeast, and no new ones billowed up from Dorval, so he could take his time and enjoy his creation. The power he was allowed to use.

Faolain Lowland was surrounded by the enemy. He left it quickly behind and avoided Riverport, seeking High Kirat instead. The immense keep sat its hilltop like a prince his throne. Sentries walked the torchlit walls, and there was a light behind the fine glass windows of Princess Danladi's chambers. Light, too, shone from the court Sunrunner's windows, but thin pale curtains were drawn and Pol could not pass through them.

He moved on to Catha Heights, wanting to see how Patwin's splendid castle did now that its traitorous *athri* was

dead. The place crawled with Vellant'im—walls, courtyards, battlements, even the famous gardens Pol had despaired of bettering when planning his own at Dragon's Rest. He left, still sickened by Patwin's betrayal. Too bad Mirsath was such a good shot with a bow—the death should have been slower.

Through the Catha Hills, small lakes shone like silver coins sewn together by bright ribbons of rivers. Thick forest hollowed into meadows that always rippled with flowers. Pol felt his spirit ease as he hovered above the land. Half his heart belonged to the Desert's stark, sere beauty, but the rest of him breathed of green woods and broad meadows and water.

And dragons—ah, dragons. He saw them emerge for a night's hunt from hidden caves. These were their wintering grounds, where deer and elk stayed fat and storms were soft. He drew back, not wishing to collide with a dragon by accident as his mother had long ago. But then he recognized a blue-gray sire silvered by moonlight and smiled, following Azhdeen back over High Kirat to the mouth of the Faolain.

The dragon's purpose was instantly known to Pol. A certain kind of fish lived only in the deep, broad estuary where salt water met fresh. Pol had experimented with stocking a pond at Dragon's Rest, but all the fish had died. Evidently Azhdeen had a craving for it tonight. Pol grinned as five huge dragons soared high, plummeted down, and time and again came up gulping.

It took them quite a while to eat their fill. Pol had always wondered how they avoided swallowing half an ocean of water along with their meal, but surmised they used their teeth as a strainer. Azhdeen finally flew to a large boulder above the sand, belched his satiation, and shook his wings dry.

It frustrated Pol that he wasn't near enough to conjure the pictures by which they communicated. He needed to touch Azhdeen's riot of rainbow colors, feel the dragon's pride of possession as he conversed with his human, siphon off some of the dragon's supreme confidence to bolster his own. It was better than *dranath,* that feeling—he'd taken it once in wine just so he'd know what it did, and concluded that time with his dragon was infinitely more sustaining.

Azhdeen rose from his rock into the air. Pol skittered back from him too late. They were caught in each other, tangled like yarn in the wake of a playful kitten.

The dragon missed a wingbeat, recovered, and opened his jaws in a roar. The other dragons instantly fled into the night. Pol retreated from the clash of colors, sliding back along his woven moonlight.

Azhdeen followed.

The empty husk of Riverport lay below. Azhdeen circled it, jaws open in a long, keening howl. And Pol heard him. He saw the blackened ruin down below and he saw the dragon flying above it and as Azhdeen bellowed again he heard his own voice cry out softly at the same time.

Reeling, he tried to unthread himself from the dragon. But they were still chaotically entwined, perceptions and emotions spun together. Azhdeen was the stronger; Pol struggled to keep himself from being wrapped in the dragon's powerful colors—and feelings.

The tense skeins loosened a little. His own emotions welled up. He had failed at Radzyn, and at Remagev; he no longer fully trusted his father; he had no plan for certain victory over the enemy. At last he realized that the reason he was so furious was that he was ashamed.

Azhdeen shook his head in confusion. Humiliation was unknown to him. No other sire had ever bested him in combat; none of his chosen females had ever escaped him. His throat pulsed in a series of short, sharp cries and the whirl of colors intensified, skimmed nearer to Pol's own. He was more ashamed than ever that he had burdened the dragon with his uniquely human emotion.

Azhdeen took exception to what Pol was feeling. He spread his wings wide, baring his teeth in fury. Any attempt to soothe him was foredoomed to failure. Dragons had complex colors but very simple emotions, and were utterly single-minded. What they felt, they felt with every nerve.

Pol concentrated on unsnarling the delicate moonlight. With every link lost between them, Azhdeen grew more upset. Pol cursed himself and ripped away from the dragon, to the accompaniment of what felt like a dagger-thrust in his skull. He fled back to Remagev as fast as he could.

Azhdeen followed. Not with his wings, but with his colors.

Shock gushed from them both in waves of blinding light. Pol held his head between his hands as if to keep his skull together. He could hear-taste-smell-touch-see the dragon's voice, just like a Sunrunner's voice, but the dragon had no

words. Cries and shrieks and deep-throated growls filled his brain and drowned his senses.

Please! Don't! Azhdeen, it HURTS!

The abruptness of the dragon's leave-taking hurt even worse. Pol gasped in air, blood pounding acidly along every nerve. It took forever for his vision to clear, and longer still before he dared lift his head.

He'd toppled from the bench to the fine gravel path. The moons shone cold on Sionell's little garden, white-frosted the twisting shapes and the walls and towers of the keep. Pol shivered and rose carefully, aching to his bones. Once he regained the bench he could move no more, and sat hunched and shaking until the moons fell.

* * *

It was Dannar's very bad luck that morning that the outer door of Lord Chaynal's rooms was open. He took it as invitation to enter. Two paces into the antechamber he stopped in his tracks, the errand to fetch his lordship for the High Prince flying clean out of his head.

"Get back in bed, you stubborn bitch!"

The inner door was open, too. Princess Tobin was standing—surprise enough. But the sight of her fiery black eyes reminded him of a conversation between his brother Riyan and their father about the princess' marriage contract. Dannar reflected that she didn't need a knife; she looked perfectly capable of running Lord Chaynal through with one of her canes.

"Senile—old—fool!" she hissed. "Get . . . Sioned!"

"No!"

She was facing the door and saw Dannar. Pointing the cane at him, she grated, "Sioned. *Now.*"

The boy scurried from the room. By the time he returned with the High Princess, Tobin was seated by the windows, weak morning sun on her face. Chay was hauling on his boots. Rising, he stomped each foot to fit the boots more securely and flung a fulminating look at his wife.

"Shriek yourself into another seizure, then!" he snarled on his way out. "Shatter the sunlight for all I care!"

Sioned gave a low whistle. "What did he do that you deserved *that?*"

Dannar blinked. What *Lord Chaynal* had done that made

Princess Tobin deserve a tongue-lashing? In all his eleven years, he had heard his own parents shout at each other exactly once. When Alasen and Ostvel fought, they did so in a silence colder than icicles dripping off Castle Crag in winter.

"Idiot," Tobin snorted. "Sunlight. Please."

"Wait outside, Dannar. I need you to help me later."

He stood in the corridor and listened to the sudden silence, not understanding why a man like his lordship put up with such rages. When *he* married, his wife would be quiet and respectful and never raise her voice or glare at him or—

"Dannar? Ah, there you are. Will you carry this for me, please?"

He accepted a large, heavy bound book from the High Princess' hands and read the title. "Lady Feylin's book on dragons?"

"Yes. And we're going to have to find her notes as well. Sweet Goddess," she sighed, "as if I didn't have enough to do today! But this is important—and we're more capable of doing it than Princess Tobin."

"She seemed very angry, my lady," he offered as they walked down the hall.

"Lord Chaynal is a little overprotective." She chuckled. "What he doesn't know is that she's been up and walking very nicely for some days now. But today he caught her at it."

"What's so important about the book?"

"The princess has quite rightly reminded me that the Vellant'im are very much in awe of dragons. Lady Feylin manages to demolish all misconceptions about them in her book."

Dannar mulled that over. "Oh—I see! If they knew the truth about dragons, they wouldn't be scared anymore."

"Precisely." She paused suddenly and smiled. "Listen to it, Dannar—the *quiet*."

"Maybe they ran out of rocks."

She laughed and went to open the library door.

To Dannar, there weren't enough books in the room to merit its being called a library, not compared to Dragon's Rest and Stronghold and his parents' collection at Castle Crag. It was more like a workroom, the large table strewn with parchments and books and scrolls.

"We're not going to *burn* all these books, are we, my lady?"

"Good Goddess, no! We're going to hide them. But we must burn some," she added grimly. "Just enough to make it seem we burned them all." She went to the narrow bookshelf on the east wall, reached behind it, and muttered something before turning to him again. "Dannar, help me shift this aside."

Mystified, he did so. She felt the stones with slim, clever fingers, and a few moments later tossed a smile over her shoulder.

"Your father says there are all sorts of secrets like this at Castle Crag. Did he ever show them to you?"

"I know about the one in his office. He showed me how before I left."

"This one works along the same principles. You wiggle your finger into this space—so—and push in while pulling the little catch to the left, and—"

The wall moved back and to the side. Not just a section of stone, as at Castle Crag, but half the wall. Dannar gaped.

"Come on, let's start stacking the books in here."

They made quick work of it, as there were little more than a hundred volumes to be moved, but it was dusty work just the same. They were both coughing and sneezing before they were done.

"We'll keep these for burning." Sioned pointed to the scrolls and parchments left on the table. "And the dragon book as well."

"There are other copies, aren't there?"

"Quite enough. Although it grieves me to lose this one. . . ." She ran dust-grayed fingers over the leather binding.

"Isn't there some way we can save it, my lady?"

Her head tilted to one side as she regarded him. "Do I detect the makings of a scholar?"

He shrugged, uncomfortable with the question. "It's a beautiful book. It's not right to destroy beautiful things."

"I agree. But Tobin insisted. She says the one we partially burn has to look impressive."

"Partially?"

She only smiled.

A little while later they had closed up the wall and moved the shelf back into place. They also made a sufficient mess

of the room to suggest hasty sorting of vital scrolls and parchments. Walvis possessed no rare or unique volumes, but still Sioned chose ones she knew to be outdated or so common as to make scant difference if they died. That was how she thought of it: she was about to kill books.

With little to do besides practice walking, Tobin had had much time for thought. What puzzled her most, she had told Sioned on sunlight, was the reaction of the enemy to dragons. *Andry says they fell on their faces—as if they were not just terrified, but worshiped the beasts.* Goddess alone knew how many dragon legends were believed by the Vellant'im, but it was Tobin's opinion that with Sunrunners able to speak to dragons, it might be possible to use them in some way. *Any advantage we can get,* had been her reasoning, and Sioned agreed.

But it reminded her of a conversation with Rohan after her first contact with Elisel. *"Dragons in battle—if there's a way to do it, someone will."* She swore it would not come to that. Still, if the Vellanti fear of dragons could be used against them. . . .

Which meant that they must not find this book, or Feylin's notes. The latter she tidied as best she could and rolled into a scroll case for packing. But the book, Tobin's copy with Maarken's drawings faithfully copied and painstakingly colored . . . this book had to die.

She had Dannar drag over the large iron brazier that warmed Feylin's feet on cold nights when she worked, and called Fire to it. They fed the flames with page after page of books and scrolls. Sioned hoped there would be enough ash and half-blackened parchment to suggest the burning of many, many books. She glanced around the library. Ransacked shelves with harmless volumes scattered on them and the floor; tallies of glass ingots and goats and other produce left lying there as if too unimportant to burn—yes, it just might give the right impression.

But the most important illusion was still to be conjured.

"You take half," Sioned told the squire, and cut pages from the heavy binding with her belt-knife. It was hard going, but eventually the book lay in shreds on the table. "Look for things you'd want the enemy to know, things that would frighten them. We'll save those pages and burn the rest."

Dannar coughed smoke from his throat and said, "I've

seen my lord speaking to his dragon, my lady. Is that something we'd like them to know?"

"Hmm. If you run across anything like that, let me look at it."

She had the last-half of the book, including a section wherein Feylin listed all the superstitions about dragons without comment. If the author had been present, Sioned would have kissed her; nothing could be more perfect for her purposes than stories of princesses and virgins sacrificed to angry dragons, warnings about poisoned blood and teeth and talons, cautionary tales about not looking into their eyes and never entering their caves. That last was fine advice, actually—dragons would never use the Threadsilver Canyon caves again, for people had been gathering up gold there too long.

Sioned ripped those pages out and set them aside. The rest was the last bit of a comprehensive dragon anatomy. Feylin had worked from the skin in; Sioned scanned sections on heart, lungs, and digestion, recalling days at Skybowl when Feylin had systematically carved up a dead dragonsire to find out how he worked.

"I think all this has to go, my lady," Dannar reported. "The first part makes fun of the legends."

"Absolutely, it must go. But we'll leave them some of the bones and wings to chew on," she added, grinning. "And a bit of the guts as well."

He grinned back. But they both sobered as the beautiful script and painted pictures were eaten by flames.

"Now for the hard part," she muttered. "Hand me these pages one at a time, Dannar. I have to burn enough to make it look good, but not too much."

Myths, warnings, superstitions, charms for appeasing or avoiding, a little anatomy—all of it was artfully scorched. Sioned held each page by the upper corner and directed a tiny fingerflame to burn most, some, or a little of the parchment. When a page was burned to her satisfaction, she let it drop to the floor where Dannar stamped on it a few times to put out the flame and then kicked it to whatever corner of the room he happened to be facing.

"Princess Tobin planned to do this herself, didn't she, my lady?"

"Yes. Page by page, hating every moment of it—just like us. But she's a clever woman. This book is more use to us

half-burned than whole." She coughed at the smoke. "What do you think? Will they buy this little scene?"

Dannar stood at the door and surveyed their creation. At last he smiled. "I think they'll pay more for it than they know, my lady. But the brazier should be kicked over. And a chair, too. We're supposed to have done this in a hurry."

"How did you learn to be so devious?"

"Not me—my sister Jeni." He chuckled. "She was always the one who made it look like somebody else besides us did the damage."

When all was arranged to their satisfaction, Sioned called Fire to the book's cover—careful to leave the title intact. The back cover she singed and kicked into the pile of ash near the overturned brazier.

"That's that," she said, taking the scroll case of Feylin's notes and locking the library door. "There's something else I'd like you to help me with. In the kitchens, this time." She smiled grimly. "That I can't boil water is the joke of my whole princedom. But this recipe calls for sorcery, not seasoning."

Pol's headache succumbed at dawn to a noxious medicine. He went to Chayla for it because Feylin would have asked questions he wasn't particularly eager to answer. Not that Chayla missed his bleary eyes and the wince brought by sunlight, but she only arched a brow and mixed herbs into half a cup of wine.

"I should warn you it tastes like a middens."

He bolted it down. "I never met a medicine that didn't."

"That's why I thought up this." She handed him a small wafer. "Slide it under your tongue. It'll cure the taste."

"Thanks." After a moment he nodded. "You're right. Skillful *and* merciful as well as beautiful—you'll have to beat them away with a stick, Cousin." When she sighed, he shrugged an apology. "Been hearing that a long time, hmm?"

"It was old before I learned how to walk." There was no smug pride in her voice, nothing but rueful resignation that people would always remark upon her beauty.

"Well, then, you ought to be used to it by now."

"Are you?" she asked pointedly.

It had been a very long time since anyone had embarrassed him about his looks—though, unlike Chayla, he had long ago learned how to use them. He winked and left her to attend to her patients, himself seeking out Betheyn.

He had noticed something about the arrangement of deadfalls at Remagev that had escaped the others—perhaps because of them all, only he had built his palace stone by stone and watched Myrdal's suggested "improvements" being constructed or installed. Remagev's design herded invaders to the west door.

"What about the granary?" Bending over the architectural plans, Beth answered her own question. "No, I see—that discourages them from getting in through the kitchen side."

"Right. I thought there might be some clue in the glassworks, but they were completely rebuilt in 710. Anything useful there is gone."

"But why the west door?" She frowned, tracing the path with one finger. "It looks an ordinary hallway, my lord, inconvenient for the rest of the keep."

"Locked and ignored for Goddess alone knows how long," he agreed, assuming his most innocent face.

A delicate snort greeted his portrayal of virtue. "Let's ask Lord Walvis."

They found him up in the gatehouse, helping smash floor tiles. Spearheads, ruined in a good cause, were breaking through brightly colored Kierstian ceramic to reveal arm-length shafts beneath. The lower tiles shattered with more difficulty, being unworn by years of bootheels.

"The west entry?" Walvis asked when they posed the question to him. "No, we've never used it. Why?"

"How long has it been locked?"

"Lord Hadaan and I opened it one summer to see if it'd help ventilation. But it sucked up the afternoon wind like a blast furnace, so we locked it again. That was—oh, twenty or thirty years ago, now."

Pol led Betheyn back down the stairs to the sound of more cracking tiles. "You see? It's inconvenient, it's useless for cooling, it's got no purpose at all. So why build it?"

"Is there something like it at Dragon's Rest?"

"There are ways of herding people where you want them to go—in our case, to the upper corridor of the servant's quarters." He did not elaborate on exactly what waited up there after proper preparation. "I'd make a pretty substantial wager there's something about that west entry we can use."

Feylin jingled with the key to every lock at Remagev on a

chain attached to her belt. Unable to remember which applied to the west door, she gave them the whole collection.

"This could take all day," Pol sighed, surveying the stiff locks set at shoulder level in the twin doors.

"Not at all." Betheyn selected a key. Pol bowed an apology as the lock yielded. He shoved the doors open, hinges creaking a protest. "Needs oil," Beth commented critically, and led the way inside. Sunlight didn't reach very far in and there were no windows. He conjured a fingerflame, startling her slightly as she paced slowly forward.

"How would it work?" she mused as she walked. "They come in slowly, suspecting more traps. Double doors, no other exit. Hmm. Low wooden ceiling—*not* the floor of the room above, which is stone. They reach the door, open it—" She tugged at the heavy iron bar crossing the wood.

Pol heaved at the bolt and it slid into the stone wall. Halfway in it stuck, one door freed. He pushed harder. The iron moved, caught again, and sound snaked across the ceiling toward the entrance.

Betheyn gave a delighted cry. "The catch springs the outer doors by a connection through the ceiling! I *thought* they were a touch too stiff. Trap the enemy in here and herd them through—"

"To freedom," Pol pointed out. "And access to the keep."

"Not necessarily."

He slanted a frown at her smug smile. "What do you know that I don't?"

"It's noon and the only light is from your little Fire. If they come in at night, and if we fix the catch, then the only way out is through this door, leading into the corridor. But *that's* locked from the other side."

"I'm beginning to like this," Pol said with a grin. "But we can't just trap them, Beth. We ought to entertain them while they're trying to get out. And I think I know a way to do it."

Chapter Nineteen

It took a while to hunt down ingredients for the recipe Sioned had in mind. Feylin gave over some of her medicines without comment, though her brows crept almost to her hairline at a few of the requests. Concoction took the better part of the morning, even with Remagev's Sunrunner, Relnaya, helping. When Dannar came with news that everything was ready for departure, she had finished.

The squire peered into the vat of thick paste on the butcher block. "What's that, my lady? It smells awful."

"That's the one drawback. Can you go find me a large amount of some very strong herb? Try the storerooms."

"What about *pemric*?" Relnaya suggested. "That ought to do it."

It did. Crushed seeds were added, and the resulting pungency masked the stench. Sioned spooned half the paste into a copper pot and thinned it with water until it was runny. "Dannar, please take this to Lord Walvis. He'll know what to do with it."

"But what *is* it?" the squire asked again.

"Don't touch it!" she exclaimed as the boy extended a finger to a drop on the table. "That's been diluted, but it'll still burn like fire and cramp your hand. It's something Lord Urival taught me how to brew from the Star Scroll."

"Sorcery?"

"Yes indeed. There's not exactly an oversupply of water here, and that or boiling oil won't stay hot long enough to do any damage. So I made this."

Dannar looked warily into the cauldron. "I think I know what you're going to do with the paste—smear it on anything they're likely to touch, right?"

"Door handles, chair arms—and the well-ropes, for when

they try to wash it off. I want Remagev to burn like fire up one side and down the other."

"I'll take the upper floors," Relnaya said.

"Thanks. That frees Hollis and Beth for elsewhere. I'll do the downstairs. We'll wait until everyone's out of the keep before we start. And take a pail of water along in case you get any on you."

The squire departed, and the two Sunrunners were scooping paste into three large bowls when a muffled crash sounded. It came again, and again, and yet again. Suddenly there was accompaniment: a scandalous ballad howled at the top of two sets of healthy male lungs.

Sioned glanced up, curious but not alarmed. "Ingots, I should think. And I recognize my son's charming voice. I believe the other is Lord Kazander."

* * *

One crate of half-silkweight glass ingots, each about as heavy as a healthy newborn baby, was half empty by the time they finished all twenty-four verses of "The Lord and the Swordmaker's Daughter." It was easier to keep rhythm to the song Pol began next—"Swalekeep's Secret Stair"—but Kazander didn't know that one, so he switched to "How Many Times Tonight, My Lady?" By the fourth verse they were laughing so hard they could barely lift the ingots from the second crate, let alone smash them with sledgehammers.

The first glass had been demolished in grim silence. Then Kazander started humming. Soon they were bawling out lyrics emphasized by crashing glass. Pol had never had so much good, destructive fun in his life.

The "entertainment" for the Vellant'im trapped in the hallway had met with Kazander's gleeful approval. The *korrus* had pointed out that the enemy wore soft boots, not stiffened leather; glass shards would slice right through to the soles of their feet.

"This is the only exit," Pol had explained, showing Kazander how Betheyn had fixed and oiled the springs and hinges. "It's made so that the outer doors close only if the bolt slides all the way into the wall, past the catch. And there's no way to open it again without resetting the spring. They could burn the outer door down, true—but the *really* interesting part is that the ceiling comes apart on the catch.

The wires were broken, but Beth fixed them. So we can fill the false roof with glass, too, and get them no matter what."

"Lady Betheyn," Kazander said thoughtfully. "Has she a husband? Would she like one?"

Pol swung the huge hammer down on another ingot, laughing even harder as Kazander pitched his voice high through his nose for "Lament of the Old Man's Bride." They were both half-hysterical and Pol knew that when they finished he would be utterly wrung out—but he didn't care. Anger and tension melted from him like a spring frost. He took the man's verses, changing his voice for every suitor who offered to comfort the neglected lady, played by Kazander. Soon the *korrus* was laughing so much he couldn't finish the song. When he got his breath back, he demanded to know where a gently reared and tenderly sheltered prince had learned such disgraceful songs.

"You'd be surprised," was all the reply Pol would give. Kazander laughed again, raising his hammer as if to beat a proper answer out of him.

"Don't aim for his head," a dry voice advised from behind them. "He's got a skull like rock and you'd make no impression."

Both young men whirled. Rohan stood limned by sunlight, arms folded, leaning casually against the wall. The hammer dropped from Kazander's suddenly strengthless hands. Pol felt the back of his neck twist with renewed tension.

Rohan shook his head. "The very least you could have done was invite me to the party." He picked his way through the shards on the floor and hefted the abandoned sledgehammer. "May I play, too?"

Kazander bowed nearly in half. Rohan selected an ingot, tossed it onto the floor, then swung the hammer in a vicious arc. The glass shattered in all directions and he laughed aloud. Pol realized how long it had been since he'd heard his father laugh.

"Try it set sideways," he suggested, placing another ingot on the floor.

They finished off the rest of the second crate, Kazander relaxing enough to take a smaller hammer and hack the larger pieces into splinters. The trio swung and shattered and laughed like madmen, and were exhausted when the ingots were gone, but it was a good weariness. When Rohan

left them, after thanks for the fun, Pol could almost fool himself that there was peace again between them.

"Forgive me if I speak too freely, my prince," Kazander said as they donned thick leather gloves to gather up shards for the trick ceiling, "but he's not as old as I thought."

Pol smiled. "I suspect he's not as old as *he* thought either."

* * *

The back of Rohan's neck itched as if arrows—or those infuriating stones—were aimed straight at his back. He stretched cramps from his muscles, trying to regain the lightheartedness brought by the mad glass-smashing, but it was no use. It occurred to him how nice it would be to find Chay and Maarken and Walvis and get roaring drunk. But he'd learned long ago, in another war, that at such times vast amounts of wine only made him more and more sober.

A depressing thought. He rotated his left shoulder against the nagging ache in that arm and tried to look confident as he inspected the progress of arrangements for the enemy's welcome.

There was nothing unusual for the Vellant'im outside Remagev to hear that day and evening, only the sounds of a keep making ready for siege. They camped under one flag and there were no petty arguments witnessed from Remagev's walls, which suggested that there were no jealous factions here. Discipline and prowess had been amply demonstrated; these troops were the best the Vellant'im had. Kazander's notion that it complimented Rohan's reputation flattered him not at all and comforted him even less. They could have no interest in him personally. They wanted the Desert.

Tobin thought it might be because of the dragons. But the Desert wasn't the only place dragons were found. They wintered in the Catha Hills and summered in the Veresch. They only mated here. There must be something else about his princedom that the enemy wanted. He didn't flatter himself that it was him.

The Desert was known for three things: sand, dragons, and gold. Coveting the first was preposterous. He tended to doubt that anyone would risk so many lives and go to so much trouble for a sight of dragons. Gold was the only thing that made sense. But *which* gold? The legitimate mines

everyone knew about—or the secret gold gleaned from dragon caves?

Had his objective been that wealth, he would have done precisely what the Vellant'im were doing. He would neutralize help from elsewhere while surging up from the south into the Desert. Radzyn had been left whole so it could be searched and used as a base. The same would probably happen at Remagev. Those mechanical arms could just as easily have thrown fire into the keep, but had not. Remagev would remain whole.

The false trails from the keep would not fool the enemy long. On realizing the tricks, they would head for Stronghold—where any idiot could walk in to Rivenrock and gather as much gold as he liked.

Only for the past three mating cycles had the dragons used Rivenrock again, after shying away from the place since 701. Their numbers had increased to levels that finally convinced Feylin they could survive even another disaster like the Plague. In memory Rohan still saw the raging flames that had cleansed the canyon, Fire called by his son in fulfillment of the Treaty of Linse: "And the Desert shall be of the House of Prince Zehava for as long as the Long Sand spawns Fire." Ah, what it had cost Rohan's father to wrest that from Roelstra: years of fighting the Merida, years of living with a sword in his hand. It could have cost Rohan's life, too—at eighteen, during Zehava's last Merida war, he'd disguised himself and marched into battle. On hearing this news, his mother had treated all of Stronghold to one of her more spectacular furies, and his father nearly had a seizure—but he'd also knighted his son on the field.

Rohan now fought another war for his princedom, but this time there was gold to protect as well, and dragons. If people climbed through the Rivenrock caves with their scent and their leavings and their fingers seizing golden sand, dragons might not return there. Without caves, unmated females would die and the population would plunge. Rivenrock was but fifty measures from Stronghold. Rohan would be leading the enemy almost into the canyon mouth. They would find it, foul it, and when the next mating year came, dragons would die.

But he had nowhere else to go.

"My prince, it's time," said a quiet voice at his side.

Rohan concealed a start as Walvis interrupted his thoughts.

He hadn't realized how quickly daylight had given way to evening. The courtyard was packed now, but so nearly silent that he could hear the flutter of the few torch flames in the slight breeze.

"Remagev is yours," he said slowly. He couldn't give the order himself. But he had to watch. He had to stand by his *athri*'s side, the picture of serene confidence and sly amusement at the tricks they were about to play on the Vellant'im. In all his sixty years he had never had to work so hard to hide his emotions—not even during that long summer of pretending he had not loved Sioned from the instant he saw her face in Fire.

Still, he was good at it. He'd learned hard and young. But it never got easier. He dreaded the day it did, for it should *not* be easy.

Horses were brought to the main steps, and he and Walvis mounted. He felt his back twinge and a genuine smile flickered over his face as sore muscles reminded him of his afternoon game. The crowd in the courtyard broke into four groups. He would lead one to Stronghold by the quickest route—both for safety's sake and that of the horses, which had not been fed since the previous night's purging. They'd been well watered, but there would be nothing for them to drink until Stronghold. The other three groups—whose well-fed mounts would keep the Vellant'im following after, or so Rohan hoped—would head north, northeast, and due east before turning for Stronghold. The latter group worried him most; their mounts would go without fodder longest, probably for at least three days. But he had faith in Chay's horses. Only the strongest had been chosen for this group.

Last night Daniv had volunteered to go with those riding north under Pol's leadership. Sioned informed her great-nephew that he would do no such thing. Rohan overruled her. Daniv was a mature sixteen, tall for his age and eager to prove himself.

"We won't be gone that long—two days out, one back to Stronghold. And I'll be careful, your grace."

"So I'm 'my grace' now instead of 'Aunt Sioned,' eh? Very proper, very dutiful—and it doesn't fool me at all."

"Peace," Rohan ordered softly. "I accept your offer. Besides, Rihani is fighting in Syr with your father's army, and we can't let your cousin collect all the glory, can we?"

When Daniv left them, glowing with excitement, Sioned

rounded on her husband. "How *could* you? There's nothing glorious about war and you know it."

"Leave him his illusions a little longer, Sioned. They'll shatter soon enough. Illusions always do."

So Daniv rode forward at Pol's side to salute the High Prince. Rohan searched his son's eyes. Yes, he'd been right to walk in on the glass-smashing scene. He and Pol were friends again. They still didn't agree, but at least resentment no longer smoldered in the blue-green eyes.

The pair turned smartly and joined the fifty soldiers who would take a two-day journey due north. Daniv was confident, with an easy authority that proclaimed him a prince. He did not remind Rohan of himself at the same age.

Prince Velden's nephew, Sethric, organized his hundred before making his bow to the High Prince. Four years older than Daniv, those years were the difference of a silkweight of muscle and half a handspan of height. Remagev had toughened him, given him poise. Rohan thought what a fine *athri* he would make when he returned home—if there was anything left of Grib to go home to.

He hid the pessimism with a smile. *Goddess, but I certainly am good at this,* he thought cynically; even with so many years between wars, he hadn't lost the knack. He could still hear his asinine little speech on the day he'd joined Chay and the southern levies to fight Roelstra. Then as now he showed them a prince certain of victory—and never let them know what he truly felt. They needed and trusted him. He owed them a calm face and straight shoulders and untroubled eyes. Sethric responded as people always did, with an answering smile and an even lower bow. Yes, he was very good at this. Always had been.

Maarken, however, knew what was behind the mask. He would be in charge of the most dangerous diversion, and his journey to Stronghold would cross the enemy line of march as they tracked Pol and Sethric. His horses would have nothing to eat and precious little water while crossing the Long Sand. Of them all, Maarken understood how perilous this whole plan was, and how necessary. As he made his bow, there was limitless compassion in his gray eyes.

Rohan guided his horse to Remagev's main gates, watching the Isulk'im ready their mounts for an insanity planned by Kazander. The *korrus* smiled happily at Rohan and gave the characteristic salute. Rohan returned it, privately

astounded at the delight this man took in risking his neck. His men were just like him. They had accounted for ten Vellanti dead each in the battle two days ago, and taken only minor wounds.

Glancing around to make sure everyone was ready, Rohan caught sight of Sioned, Hollis, and Tobren at the doors of the main hall. His princess lifted one hand to signal that her vicious little brew had been applied within the now empty keep. Then she vanished back inside.

"My lord *korrus*," he said to Kazander, "may the Mother of All Dragons keep you from harm within the shelter of her wings."

The Isulki looked a bit startled. It was an ancient blessing, and one that few outsiders knew. Kazander bowed again and replied with an even older one.

"Most High and Honored Prince, may She be in your eyes and in your looking, in your ears and in your listening, in your hands and in your doing, in your mind and in your knowing."

Chay would disagree with that, he told himself with a touch of whimsy. *He always did say I think too much.*

Walvis signaled the inner gates open. The wires had not yet been connected to the pots of Sioned's liquid fire; Walvis would do that himself just before he rode out. Another Fire had been quenched since dawn: Sioned had summoned Air to scatter the cooling ashes of the dead. Chay had lost thirty, Walvis twenty-six. Not a high count as battles went. He remembered sitting in his father's tent after that last terrible battle against the Merida as Chay gave the casualty report. Zehava had heard it in silence, then remarked that most people would consider five hundred dead a fair price for a princedom. Appalled at the time, it had been years before Rohan realized that his father had not included himself in "most people." But Zehava was long dead and the apologies spoken only to the silent sky by the time Rohan finally understood. He wondered what "most people" would consider a fair price for a whole continent.

The main gates parted wide enough to let Kazander and twenty of his men ride through at a gallop. It was the *korrus*' mad plan to charge around Remagev at top speed, shrieking war cries all the way. Not only would they startle and distract the enemy, but they would see whether sentries patrolled the shadows around the keep. Maarken had been

of the opinion that Sunrunners could conjure Fire for a look, but Kazander grinned and said it would be more fun his way.

It certainly sounded as if the Isulk'im were enjoying themselves. Rohan could imagine them tearing around the walls as if this was *Rialla* race day; he didn't have to imagine their roars of battle. Twenty-one of them, and they sounded like an army. They yelled his name and Pol's and Kazander's, punctuated with *"Azhrei!"* and bone-chilling screams. A reluctant smile came to his face as heads swiveled to follow the sounds. Yes, just like race day. Only they rode not for gold or jewels, but for lives.

One of Kazander's men stood ready at the gates, counting to himself. Rohan felt his nerves twinge as calls went up from the Vellanti camp, rousing warriors from after-dinner indolence into battle harness. The Isulki noise grew louder and the one on duty suddenly wrenched the gate open—a split second before Kazander hurtled through alone and reined to a halt, laughing.

"Not so much as an arrow did they loose, Noble High Prince!" he exulted. "And only twenty of them scattered around the outer walls—now running to mount up and follow my men! We could leave walking and they wouldn't catch us!"

"We'll gallop just the same, if you don't mind." The young man's cheerful enthusiasm was invigorating. Rohan began to think this might work after all.

Pol's fifty were the first to leave. Rohan saw him give a sweeping gesture with one arm, and then lost him in the crowd thundering through the gates. At the last instant Kazander took off after them, yelling over his shoulder, "He's lived in Princemarch too long!"

"That boy is insane," Chay observed.

"Completely. But he's right. It's years since Pol spent any amount of time in the Desert. Frankly, I'm glad Kazander's going with him—I've guards enough for my precious princely person, thank you very much."

Chay made a face at him. "More fun to be had with the young dragon than the old one, anyway." More briskly, he went on, "The quickest of the enemy will be mounted by now and following the Isulk'im to find out what the hell they think they're doing. The next group will go after Pol

when they can. Sethric, wait for her grace's signal and take your hundred out through the main gates."

"Yes, my lord." He saluted again. "Until Stronghold!"

Rohan could not see Sioned on the upper walls, but he and everyone else jumped when a torch suddenly blazed nearby. Her signal. Sethric led his riders out at top speed.

Chay frowned as he glanced at Rohan. "This is the tricky part. Will they follow our diversions or wait for *us*?"

"I think they're sufficiently confused, my lord," said Relnaya, a sly smile on his face. "Lord Kazander's men will join Lord Maarken once they've outrun their escort." He snorted. "They sit their horses like chairs."

"They sit my grandsir's horses," Tobren reminded him. "It may be a closer race than you think."

Rohan hid another smile and waited for Sioned's next signal. It seemed a long time coming. Perhaps the Vellant'im weren't going for it. Perhaps too many of them were staying behind. Rohan had offered temptation; what if too few succumbed? And it was such delicate timing—how long to wait for them to saddle up before signaling the next group to leave? Rohan had hoped that chaos would break down efficiency, that warriors who worked together so well would be separated by the frantic speed necessary to follow the Desert troops. Those who were ready first would set off first, with discipline in a shambles and their only thought to overtake these crazy people who thought they could escape.

And what if he'd been completely wrong, and only token forces went after Pol and Sethric and Maarken, and the bulk of the army stayed to occupy Remagev?

He'd gotten away once. To do so again would be a slap in the enemy's face. He reasoned that pride would send large numbers of Vellant'im into the Long Sand to foil this second escape. If this happened against their leaders' wishes, so much the better. But he couldn't be sure, despite his experience in dealing with barbarians.

Another torch flared to life, and Maarken dug his heels into his stallion's ribs. The gates were flung open and hauled closed behind the last of Maarken's group in an impossibly short time. Rohan let out a long breath and rubbed his arm absently.

Myrdal's secret exit from Radzyn was back where the keep abutted natural stone. It was just horse-high and wide enough for only a single cart to pass through. Chay would

lead, Rohan bring up the rear—over vehement protests—with Walvis leaving last of all after wiring the gatehouse and arcade. The first two torches were abruptly extinguished and the courtyard was plunged into near-total darkness. It was time.

Feylin ran up, breathless with exertion and excitement. "You should *see* them scrambling out there!" she cried. "Almost all the men who still have mounts and are capable of riding them are saddling up to follow! It worked!"

Not until we're all safe at Stronghold, Rohan thought. But he didn't say it aloud. He glanced at the line of people filing slowly through to the hidden passage—they moved in smooth order, without panic or delay, but it was going to take a long time. Those who could ride must mount; the wounded who were too unsteady to sit a horse alone must take a second rider up; carts carrying supplies and the seriously hurt had to be protected by the uninjured warriors Rohan was taking with him. When they met up with the groups who had spent the day in shelter, there would be more defenders—at about the same time as the Vellant'im caught up with them, or so Rohan was gambling. But he wasn't sure it was a bet his wife would take; she liked better odds.

The by now familiar twang of stressed wood and ropes warned them an instant before stones hurtled down. Rohan cursed and tightened his grip on his horse. The chaos he'd so carefully planned against began to invade the courtyard, borne on screams of fright. Many people went down; everyone else ran for cover.

"Damn! We'll have to move even faster than—" Rohan suddenly stood in his stirrups and yelled Chayla's name. She had run out into the courtyard to help the wounded. More rocks pelted from the night sky; Chayla and those trying to retrieve the injured huddled with arms over their heads until the rain stopped.

Relnaya darted out to where Chayla was staunching blood from a child's head wound. The Sunrunner picked up the little boy in one arm and hauled Chayla to safety with the other.

All at once an almighty crash hit the main gates. Rohan yelled a warning up at Walvis, wincing as iron-reinforced wood shuddered again.

"I heard!" came the shout from within the gatehouse. "Close the inner gates—I'm almost done!"

He called Dannar over and told him to speed things up at the passage. The squire jumped at the next shock and darted through the tense crowd. Rohan willed everyone to stay calm, to keep from shoving each other and turning this into an enemy victory.

He caught sight of Hollis taking the stairs two at a time, long tawny braids flying. She was supposed to have left with Chay and Tobin, but it was a little late to yell at her for it now. She disappeared into the gatehouse and a few moments later the battering at the gates stopped. Just visible over the walls was a yellow-white glow. Sunrunner's Fire.

He reined his horse around and rode up and down the line of nervous people, hoping his presence would be enough to settle them down again. Thus far they had not panicked—but he knew how quickly it could happen.

So he smiled and told them, "They're busy running after the others and running away from Lady Hollis' hospitality. I can't understand that, personally—don't they know how cold it gets here at night? She's only seeing to their comfort. Just move along and watch your heads, you tall ones, once you're mounted up—or make sure you get a very short horse!"

They laughed up at him and he grinned back. No, he hadn't lost his touch.

Sioned finally arrived, gasping for breath and with a wicked gleam in her eyes. "I would've been here sooner, but it took me a long time to get the knack of breaking the bowls right."

"Would you care to explain that?" he asked as Dannar led her horse up and she swung into the saddle.

She laughed, well aware of the people around them who listened. "When it became clear they weren't going to wait until morning to invite themselves in, I put the leftover paste to excellent use. Beth and I left pots of it over hot coals. By the time the pottery breaks from the heat, we'll be gone—and the Vellant'im will be breathing the most horrible stuff you could imagine. Beth is putting the last bowls in the glass furnaces now."

"You are the most cheerfully vicious woman I ever met!"

"I do try not to disappoint you," she said with a sweet smile.

Sioned had finished the spell that eased fear. Rohan leaned precariously over to kiss her in gratitude. Whistles and

applause made his cheeks burn, but panic laughed away would not threaten again. Not for a little while, not until they were beyond the walls and had to rely on other protection.

"Damn it, Hollis, come on!" Walvis' voice came from within the gatehouse.

Dannar grabbed two horses and led them to the wall. Walvis was down first, and jumped into the saddle from the steps. Hollis was close behind him. The glow of her Fire was gone outside. It wouldn't be long before the Vellant'im began battering the gates again. But Walvis' fierce grin told the story as he rode up. The Vellant'im would walk into a Remagev rife with deadfalls—*if* they had the courage to explore past the gatehouse ceiling's burning rain.

There were sounds of battle outside now, steel on steel. "They've found where we're getting out," Hollis said. "Let me go up and help."

"Not necessary," Rohan told her as another glow crept over the walls. "Look. And listen."

The ringing of metal stopped. Scant moments later the whispers came back from the front of the line: Princess Tobin and her granddaughter were at work with Fire.

"Tobren?" Sioned exclaimed. "When did she learn—and why am I complaining?" she interrupted herself in disgust.

"Is the arcade rigged?" Rohan asked, and Walvis nodded. "Then let's go."

The diversions had worked, for the most part. The enemy was divided and riding in four different directions; Fire would keep them at bay while Rohan's group escaped; Remagev itself would take plenty of casualties as it collapsed and smoked and rained glass shards. He was protecting his people while giving the enemy ample opportunity to destroy itself, both here and out in the Desert.

But in spite of knowing he had done all he could, in spite of a lifetime of keeping peace with laws instead of a sword in his hand, a part of him still had fierce, proud memories of battle. It had ignited his blood at Radzyn and now stung him again. To kill those who were killing his people, the world he had created, his life's work—Goddess, how he wanted to be Pol's age with a sword in his hand.

Sioned wrapped her dark cloak more closely around her and rode outside the walls to take over the Fire conjuring. She would lecture them later on the folly of what they'd

done. Or perhaps not—for arrows were flying through her wall of flames, shot blind, and if one of them struck her. . . .

She spared a puzzled frown for the fact that the iron did not stab as it had with the *ros'salath*. But this was no weaving. It held none of her essence. She was not bound into it as she had been into the complex working. But it was hard work just the same, and she was grateful when hands took her reins and led her horse along for her.

The hands were Tobren's. She shared a saddle with her grandmother, who had not yet regained enough strength in her hands to guide a horse. The admiration in the child's eyes for Sioned's easy skill was born of intimate knowledge of *faradhi* ways. Still, Tobren was wary of her. Goddess only knew what Andry told his children about the Sunrunner High Princess. When Hollis joined them and said, "I'll take the Fire. You're the only one who can weave starlight," Tobren's face clenched like a fist.

Sioned spun cool white light and surveyed the turmoil in the Vellanti camp. Their numbers had been substantially reduced by chasing after the other groups. She ranged a little farther, counted pursuers, and by the time her lord rode up had a heartening report for him.

"About forty are after Pol, fifty after Sethric, and Maarken takes the prize with nearly seventy."

Rohan's eyes reflected Hollis' Fire. "Then Pol's about evenly matched, Sethric outnumbers them—and I pity anyone who crosses Maarken's path."

"I don't feel sorry for them at all," Tobren stated as she yielded Sioned's reins. "I wish I was a real Sunrunner —I'd do like Papa and kill them!"

Tobin's eyes closed briefly; Sioned glanced away. It was Rohan who answered the girl.

"Your father is a very brave and clever man, Tobren. But it must grieve him to use his gifts in so terrible a thing as war."

"The Goddess chose Papa and made him Lord of her Keep. If she didn't want him to use his gifts, she wouldn't have given them."

The logic was inarguable—but that didn't make it any less wrong. Rohan knew there was no way to convey that to this proud child, even though his sister's eyes pleaded with him to say something—anything. He drew breath to make a try, but all at once was incapable of saying anything at all. The

rush of wings was in his head, the tingle along his bones, the strange instinctive sureness that a dragon was near.

The roar of an enraged sire was unmistakable. Hollis was so stunned that her Fire sputtered down to a mere trickle of hip-high flames. But there was light enough to see the dragon by—and the Vellant'im. To a man they leaped from their horses and prostrated themselves on the sand.

"I don't believe it," Sioned breathed.

"It's Azhdeen—he must be looking for Pol." Rohan shook himself. "Take the Fire from Hollis and get these people moving! We may not have long." He kicked his horse to the line of Sunrunner's Fire. Standing in his stirrups, he lifted his arms high and in a terrible voice bellowed, *"Azhrei!"*

Sioned had a dangerous urge to laugh. It grew stronger as Chay started singing as loud as he could. The song was taken up by hundreds of voices—a ballad over thirty years old, fulsome in its praise of Rohan's virtue, strength, and cunning. She knew at once why Chay had chosen it: *azhrei* figured prominently in the chorus, the one word they could be certain the Vellant'im understood.

So, under cover of Sunrunner's Fire and a self-serving song and the angry howls of a dragon anxious about his human possession, they escaped Remagev.

Chapter Twenty

"So they got away," Rinhoel said. "Too bad."

His mother cast a quick, nervous glance at the door that had just closed behind Rialt. "Hush! We're on shaky enough ground without his overhearing remarks like that!"

"Oh, come now, Mother! It's all legal. The treaties say that whenever one princedom attacks another, the rest must go to the victim's defense. There's nothing anywhere about being attacked by outsiders." Rinhoel snorted. "Trust Pirro to think up something like that, anyway, to justify his cowardice."

"But it works just as well for Cunaxa and Firon as it does for Fessenden—and us. Only *we're* not cowards." Chiana paced the glass and velvet audience chamber, the mourning gray she wore for Patwin billowing in stiff silk folds around her. "If Rohan wins, we lose everything. He's always won before."

"It's time he lost for a change. Do you want Princemarch or not?"

The blunt question went to the heart of ambition and resentment and fury nurtured for a lifetime. All of it spurted forth like poison from a lanced wound. "Yes. By the Goddess—*yes!*"

"Then act like it. We have allies now. What they want for themselves coincides nicely with what we want for us. If we work together, we can have everything. Pirro gave us a legal excuse to withhold active support—as if we needed it, with our own borders threatened!" He laughed softly. "Not even dear Aunt Naydra dares scold us for not sending our armies to Syr or the Desert. And everyone understands why we've called up the levies. No one needs to know they're meant to seize, not defend."

Chiana subsided into a velvet chair. "You're right, my treasure. You're right. Forgive me. But the only times I ever tasted victory were when I married your father and when I gave birth to you. I can't help my nerves."

"Mother, this time it won't be just a taste. We'll both be drunk on it for the rest of our lives."

She smiled. "I count marriage as a victory only because it gave me you."

"I didn't think it was because you adored the Parchment Prince."

"Rinhoel!" She giggled at the nickname bestowed on Halian for his uselessness. Before she'd married him, he had chafed against his father Clutha's iron rule that kept him powerless. For a time after the old man finally died, she'd thought Halian would actually rule Meadowlord. But the habit of idleness was too ingrained by then. Chiana had spent about half a year regretting it while she nearly foundered in unaccustomed statecraft, until one day she realized she was more of a prince than he would ever be. Thus she encouraged his pursuit of pleasant diversions—and ruled Meadowlord as she liked. And she liked it very much. For fifteen years now Halian had signed what she gave him to sign and read aloud what she gave him to read during law courts. The Parchment Prince.

Rinhoel dismissed his father with a wave of his hand. "Discussing dear Papa is a waste of time. We have other things to talk about. Rohan's on his way back to Stronghold. Tilal and Kostas will soon be bogged down in winter mud. Storms have sent Arlis back to New Raetia after only one skirmish in Brochwell Bay. But there *is* a place where fighting is not impossible in winter. Do you remember that miserable summer I spent at Remagev two years ago?"

"Not as vividly as you do."

"Well, yes," he admitted with a grimace. "A killing climate, all of us dumped into a barracks without thought of rank or position or birth—but that wasn't as bad as the so-called training. Free labor for Lord Walvis, more likely, cleaning that ancient pile and mucking out stalls." He shrugged off the memory. "But I did make an interesting acquaintance there. And he showed up here a few days ago. I let him cool his heels and then met him in town last night. But today our friends from the south arrive, and I thought Birioc might make a useful addition to our conversation."

Chiana frowned. "I don't recall your mentioning him. Who is he?"

"Nobody, really," was the casual reply. "Just one of Miyon's bastard sons—by a Merida woman."

She choked. "A Cunaxan prince? *Merida?* How did he ever get into Remagev?"

"By lying, of course. Cunaxans are all liars, and the Merida are worse than Cunaxans. He got in claiming to be the heir of some minor holding on the Desert border. That played right into Walvis' pretty idea about making us all one big happy continent."

"The notion of a peasant," Chiana observed.

"Actually, it wasn't that big a lie about the holding—Miyon gives crown properties to his mistresses to provide his bastards with a name."

Chiana nodded. "Meiglan's mother held Gracine Manor until she died."

"Birioc's mother got a place called Catchwater. But she didn't live to see it. It's all rather pathetic. He says his mother was a princess of the Merida, but that's probably another lie. Her people sent her to Miyon to get themselves a royal heir. He didn't know what she was or he wouldn't have touched her—not even Miyon is that stupid, to give the Merida a claim on him. But the child was born, the mother died, and the servant who raised Birioc was Merida, too."

"Quite an indoctrination, I should think," Chiana remarked. "I trust he sacrificed honor to survival and did not receive the chin-scar."

"What do you think?" he snorted.

"I see where this leads. Miyon still doesn't know his son's real heritage, does he?"

"Not a whisper of it. He's younger than our dear future High Princess—about twenty-one now, I think. He stayed the whole year at Remagev because his father ordered him to. Miyon wanted to know exactly what goes on there. What the ass doesn't realize is that his half-Merida son got an education in warfare and leadership that *won't* be to his father's advantage."

Chiana thought all this over, then bit her lip. "Rinhoel . . . I agree this Birioc could be of use. But the Merida were the sorcerers' trained assassins."

"I know that," he replied impatiently. "But when the

Vellant'im finally march on Stronghold, Birioc's people can keep Tallain and Jahnavi too busy to come to Rohan's aid. The Desert is the only place you can fight a war in winter. A Merida attack on Tuath and then Tiglath would serve our purposes—and Miyon's. *And* the Merida's."

Admiration shone in her eyes, but still she wavered. "The reasoning is flawless, my love, but . . . sorcery?"

"If the Merida could work spells, do you think Rohan would be High Prince? Do you think he'd even be alive?"

"But the Vellanti battle cry—"

"They haven't done any sorcery either. I'm convinced that they can't. Why use up so many lives in war if you could weave a spell and kill the way Andry did at Goddess Keep? The Vellant'im aren't here to soften us up for death by sorcery, Mother. If *diarmadh'im* were going to do anything, they'd have done it. Personally, I think that wherever these people come from, the sorcerers are all dead. It's just something they shout to remind them of past victories and inspire them to new ones."

"You may be right. But it's puzzling just the same." She pushed it aside and spoke more briskly. "Very well. I'll see Birioc. What should I call him?"

"He's hungry. A 'my lord' here and there will feed him."

"No, make it 'Prince Birioc'—for his mother's sake, if not his father's."

Rinhoel went to her side and kissed her cheek. "You're the wisest woman in the world—as well as the most beautiful."

"You're not a bad liar, yourself." But she smiled fondly up at him, adding, "High Prince Rinhoel."

* * *

High Prince Rohan escaped Remagev but not pursuit. Pol's dragon abandoned the area soon after everyone was out, and shortly thereafter the Vellant'im dared lift their faces from the sand. It took them a while to recapture their horses—Radzyn animals familiar with dragons on the hunt ran like fire through a hayloft—and this gained Rohan a little more time. But pursue the enemy did, though not in great numbers. It was Sioned's opinion that his "mighty *azhrei*" performance had scared most of them witless.

"I'm surprised Azhdeen stayed as long as he did, after he was unable to find Pol," she mused.

Tobin's black eyes sparkled with laughter. "Liked the music."

"Do you think so?" Rohan asked, then shrugged. "It's as good an explanation as any, I suppose."

Tobin leaned over in her saddle behind Tobren and poked her brother with a cane. "Feylin's legends!"

They stared at her until Betheyn chuckled softly. "None of you has gotten that far, but we were reading it the other day. There's a very old story about a virgin princess who saved herself from becoming a dragon's dinner by singing him to sleep."

Rohan looked blank for a moment, then chuckled.

Beth went on, "There's another one about rallying dragons to the defense of a castle by a bard who stood on the battlements howling some song or other."

"I'm organizing a choir the instant we get home," Sioned stated. "It probably won't work on dragons, but it might scare the Vellant'im."

"I prefer to trust Stronghold's walls, thanks all the same," Rohan said.

A pack of about thirty Vellanti warriors was met and discouraged from further pursuit by the remains of the Radzyn guard. Rohan was beside himself when he found out Chay had actually led the assault.

"You senile, old—are you in your dotage? Do you think you're twenty-two again? What in all Hells possessed you to risk your damnfool neck like that?"

Chay was unimpressed. He flexed his sword arm and commented, "It's not what it once was, but it still works."

With an incoherent growl, Rohan rode away to the front of the column. He didn't know if he was angrier at Chay's imbecile action or the fact that he could not go and do likewise.

Sioned ventured out on starlight once more, and returned smiling. "Sethric is outdistancing the enemy, Maarken has a good lead—and as for Pol, Azhdeen is flying escort with predictable results!"

Had this been spring or summer, Desert skies would have been thick with dragons. Rohan cursed enemy timing and urged his people to hurry. The carts moved along, filled with wounded and supplies, but who could tell when the Vellant'im would recover from abject terror of dragons and follow at speed?

At dawn Hollis wove sunlight. "Perfect," she sighed at last, her tired eyes regaining focus. "They seem much more interested in Remagev than in us. But it's cost them." She smiled. "Smoke rises from the glassworks and the kitchen. Also from the west entry—but I counted close to a hundred limping back to camp on bloodied feet."

"So my ingots weren't destroyed in vain." Walvis stroked his beard and slanted a sly look at Rohan. "Let's see—at the price arranged at the *Rialla* this summer, multiplied by two crates, you owe me—"

Sioned gave a derisive snort. "This from the former squire I had to teach how to count above ten without using his toes?"

"Your glass can wait," Chay declared. "He'll pay for my horses first."

"Not at your prices," Sioned retorted.

"But what about my ingots?" Walvis asked plaintively.

"And my horses?" Chay demanded.

Dannar and Tobren stared slack-jawed, never having heard such exalted highborns squabble so. It took a few moments for them to notice that the people around them were following the exchange with expectant grins.

"Enough!" Rohan exclaimed. "Or I'll rewrite your charters, take my castles back, and you can go beg a tent from the Isulk'im!"

"If they'll have you, which I doubt," Sioned finished.

It was the signal for everyone to laugh and move on, spreading the tale along the column. Rohan blessed his people for making it so easy for him. Remagev and Radzyn lay abandoned behind them; ahead lay a hard forced march to Stronghold with the enemy in pursuit. Anyone in his right mind would have been terrified. But his people could still laugh. He watched them walk past him with tenderness and pride nearly overflowing his eyes. Sentimental—even foolish, perhaps—but how he loved their refusal to despair.

Their belief in him was harder to observe. *Clever, crafty, cunning High Prince. Live up to your reputation,* azhrei. *It means lives.*

* * *

At midmorning Birioc was at last admitted into Princess Chiana's presence. He came in frowning and prepared to be

insulted. Bastard get though she was, still she looked down on others of her kind from her secure position as true ruler of Meadowlord. But she called him "prince" and clasped his hand in both of hers, and sat him beside her on a spindly-legged velvet couch, and poured wine for him with her own hands. He was young enough to be flattered, but old enough to be suspicious. Her hazel eyes were entirely too eager.

Rinhoel, equally welcoming, left them after a few moments to escort in another visitor. While he was gone, Birioc took the opportunity to make his position clear.

"We are totally uninterested in defending other princedoms, your grace. We want back what is ours, and this is our chance."

"Your aims coincide perfectly with ours, Prince Birioc." She dimpled charmingly. "We want certain things as well—and the key to obtaining them is the defeat of High Prince Rohan."

"I'm glad we agree. What do you propose our part to be? Before you answer, I must warn you that even if we were inclined to fight for land not our own, we haven't enough troops to do so."

"I appreciate your candor. I will answer with equal honesty. All you must do is to keep Rohan's northern army occupied. The southern levies have assembled at Stronghold and the Vellant'im will keep them there. You see, what you desire and what we desire is the same thing."

"Not entirely. We want Tuath and Tiglath back. We want Skybowl and Stronghold."

"And Feruche?" Her smile grew a trifle fixed.

"And Feruche," he returned firmly.

"It is part of Princemarch."

He smiled thinly; his father had told him she would be intractable on the subject of any handspan of Princemarch soil. "It is not negotiable."

Chiana's brows quirked down and her lips tightened. Then she smoothed her expression and asked silkily, "I expect you want Radzyn as well? Do you truly expect to hold it?"

"Until it falls into the sea," he assured her.

"What of Riverport and Lowland?"

Birioc smiled. "You get to the point, don't you, your grace?"

"There's very little to be gained by dancing around it, my lord."

"Riverport and Lowland *are* negotiable." He didn't add that his father had told him to concede everything south of the Long Sand if necessary. Miyon wanted Stronghold as devoutly as Chiana wanted Castle Crag. When one engaged in reshaping princedoms, one could say what one liked. Possession when the dust cleared was what counted.

"We will discuss it further," Chiana said.

"Oh, yes, we certainly will," he agreed.

Another tiny frown, another hasty clearing of her expression into amiable lines. "There will be plenty of time once Rohan is gone, after all. We can settle all the little details once he's dead and Pol with him."

Birioc nodded.

"Ah," she said suddenly, rising. "Our other guest has arrived."

The bronze doors of the presence chamber opened to admit Rinhoel and a man who could have been one of Birioc's Merida uncles. He felt his jaw drop a little and hastily closed his mouth. The man was tall, with a warrior's heavy shoulders and lean belly. A lush black beard threaded with dozens of little golden beads covered most of his face, but the sharp nose, wide mouth, and long, dark eyes were Merida. Birioc knew he was staring and couldn't help it.

"Brother!" the man exclaimed, his accent harsh, the word thick on his tongue. He embraced the startled Birioc so forcefully that the young man was sure his bones would crack.

Chiana and Rinhoel were just as astounded. The big man laughed deep in his chest, his dark eyes gleaming.

"Lost to us generation on generation ago—and now found. Those of the Sacred Glass remember nothing of us. But we remember them."

"I'm fascinated," Rinhoel murmured. "Please go on, my lord."

"Later. Another time." He made a belated bow to Chiana, raking her appreciatively with his eyes. She blushed. "You barbarians breed fine women. My wives would kill to possess such eyes."

Flustered, Chiana turned helplessly to her son. "Rinhoel . . . ?"

"Your pardon, Mother. I present to your grace Lord Varek, second battle lord to the High Warlord of the

Vellant'im. My lord, you have the honor of being in the presence of the Princess Chiana of Meadowlord."

Lord Varek bowed again, than glanced at Birioc, who was having trouble swallowing. "You have heard my name, my brother," he said shrewdly.

"I—" He gulped. It had been his grandfather's name. He stammered out as much and Lord Varek nodded.

"And did he die bravely, with his sword in his hand?"

"Y-yes. Against Prince Zehava."

"Father of this Rohan High Prince. I see. He will die for it," Varek said with casual certainty. "We are indeed brothers. If my name was your grandfather's, then one of his sons must have been Beliaev, like my own eldest son." He frowned in concentration as Birioc gaped. "And *his* sons—"

"My uncle had no children. He died in battle at Tiglath."

"Who killed him?"

"Lord Walvis of Remagev."

Dark brown eyes turned black. "Remagev of the dragon! This Walvis will die, too."

"My lord," Rinhoel said, trying to gain control of this bizarre conversation, "this is Prince Birioc, son of Miyon of Cunaxa by a Merida princess."

"Birioc is the name I would have guessed." Varek embraced him again. "*Tir'deem,* our people will have revenge."

He recognized the word—old language for "my brother." But how were they brothers? What connected the Merida with these savages?

They all sat down at Chiana's invitation and she poured wine. The princess grew rapidly more annoyed as Varek ignored her and spoke directly with the men. Birioc found it amusing that Roelstra's arrogant bastard daughter could not get a word in edgewise.

"The High Warlord says to you, many thanks for food and wine," Varek began. "The High Warlord says to you, swords and horses would be better."

"We need them for our own aims," Rinhoel pointed out.

"Your aims are ours."

"Not necessarily," Chiana began, but Varek went on as if she had not spoken.

"Death to Prince Rohan. Death to *faradh'im*. We want the same."

Chiana tried again. "Of course, my lord, but—"

"The High Warlord says to you, we will kill Rohan

and *faradh'im* for you if you kill Rohan's armies in the north."

"That's exactly why Prince Birioc is here," Rinhoel put in. "His father, Prince Miyon, rules Cunaxa. He—"

"I speak for myself, my lord," Birioc said sharply. "We will take care of the north for certain considerations."

"And arms? Fine Cunaxan steel?"

Birioc was betrayed into blurting out, "How do you know about—"

Lord Varek gave him a serene smile. "It is a great fool who sails a strange sea without a map."

"You've been here before," Rinhoel breathed.

"Not I. Others."

Birioc exchanged an appalled glance with Rinhoel. Chiana cleared her throat and leaned forward.

"Then you know how difficult it will be for you to take Stronghold."

This time he deigned to hear her. "The High Warlord says to you, give us horses and steel and we will take Stronghold and kill Rohan and his *faradhi* son."

"If you want *faradh'im*, why not take Goddess Keep?" Rinhoel asked.

"They are unimportant." Varek dismissed them with a wave of a battle-scarred hand.

"I think I understand," Birioc said slowly. "All the other attacks—they're designed to keep everyone busy, just as we're supposed to do in the north. Your real goal is Rohan."

"*Tir'deem*, you are wise." Varek inclined his head and placed both hands to his brow.

"But why?" Chiana demanded. "There's nothing I'd like to see more, but why the High Prince? What's so important about him?"

Varek fixed her with a forbidding ice-and-fire gaze. "It is enough that the High Warlord wishes it. Do your servants question *you?*"

She sucked in a breath. "*I* am not one of his servants, and I insist upon knowing why you think Rohan is so valuable!"

He flat out ignored her again. Birioc had difficulty restraining laughter as Chiana made the mistake of losing her temper and swept from the room with what he supposed she considered an impressive show of infuriated insult.

Rinhoel seemed torn between outrage that his mother had been slighted and a natural desire to keep vital negotia-

tions going. Birioc was interested to note that the latter won. So, he thought, the whelp is practical, at least.

To Lord Varek he said, "If we come from the north and you from the south, the Desert is ours."

"There are many other things to consider," Rinhoel said quellingly. "The Lord of Castle Crag and the Princes of Ossetia and Syr are on the march. My grandsire, Prince Clutha, was right in that Meadowlord is forever the battleground. This time it won't be. I don't intend to inherit a ruined princedom."

"Is Meadowlord what you intend to inherit?" Varek asked, all innocence.

Birioc smiled. This unexpected kinsman was someone he understood, someone he could work with. They would use Chiana and Rinhoel the way Chiana and Rinhoel obviously planned to use them. Neither he nor Varek cared for anything but the deaths of Rohan and Pol. And when it was over, the Vellant'im could have the southern Desert, and welcome. It would be all one, anyway—with the Merida ruling at last. All that remained was for Birioc to force Miyon into naming him heir to Cunaxa. A few battles around Tuath and Tiglath would provide ample opportunity to eliminate his half-brothers. Easy as sliding down a sand dune. He met Varek's dark eyes, saw them glint above the luxuriant gold-studded beard. Perhaps, Birioc thought, he ought to grow one, too.

* * *

It began to snow in Firon long before the official beginning of winter, drifts piling high and white around Balarat. On the Cunaxan side of the Veresch there was bitter cold and dry frost but only occasional snow, but on the Fironese, horse-high and sometimes even dragon-high drifts numbed and paralyzed the land from late autumn to late spring. People sometimes observed that it was no wonder the Fironese created such marvels in glass. What else had they to do half the year, and what other warmth than their kiln fires?

Idalian of Faolain Riverport regarded this year's snow as his sworn enemy. The preceding six winters at Balarat as Prince Laric's squire had seen him at first astounded, then delighted, by the white mantling that offered chilly reminiscence of Desert sand dunes. But this year all of young

Prince Tirel's pleas to come outside and play fell on ears deafened by grief and anger. If not for the snow, he could be traveling south now, to help in the defense of Faolain Lowland and what remained of his family.

Idalian had no idea how long he stayed in his rooms, trying not to remember, trying not to weep, failing miserably at both. Parents, aunt, uncle, cousin, all of them but his brother Mirsath and their cousin Karanaya gone—it was more than he could comprehend. He'd last seen them all six years ago, at his farewell banquet. The hall had glowed with candles and resounded with laughter; minstrels had played, and if Idalian at thirteen had been too young to appreciate the opportunity to dance until midnight, there had been jugglers and mimes enough to occupy a boy's attention. His father had been near to bursting with pride that his younger son would be squire to a prince—and at the honor of having the High Princess herself present at their table. She had come to add her congratulations on her way home from a visit to Syr.

Sioned had not forgotten him. She had found time in between her heavy responsibilities to send him a message of sympathy and comfort through Balarat's court Sunrunner. Idalian was grateful, but he could not relate such words to himself. Surely, *surely* it was impossible that almost his whole family had been wiped out.

Prince Tirel was miserable at his friend's grief, but he was still just a seven-year-old boy. When his uncle Yarin arrived from Snowcoves, Tirel mostly forgot Idalian's sorrow in the excitement of showing his cousin Natham all his toys. But one day he came up to the squire's rooms, just down the hall from his own, and begged to be let in for a talk.

Idalian, who had been sitting by the windows hating the falling snow, was puzzled by a word the boy used. "Conference? What do you mean, my lord?"

"Isn't that what they call it when Papa and Mama talk to their ministers?"

"Yes, but I'm only a squire."

Tirel set his jaw. "When my father is away, I am Prince of Firon. And I can make you my minister if I like."

Idalian settled the boy into a chair near the fireplace. "This sounds serious. What need do you have of a minister?"

After a quick glance around the empty room, Tirel whispered, "I don't like my uncle Yarin."

"Because he makes you keep at your schooling, and won't let you play with Natham all the time?" He smiled.

The child leaped up, crimson-cheeked, gray eyes flashing. "I'm not joking, Idalian! When I told him that I'm prince when my father isn't here, he said to go play with the toys he brought me from Snowcoves!"

"You're very young, Tirel," Idalian began.

"I thought you were my friend! You sound just like Uncle!"

The boy's betrayed expression—and the unwelcome comparison to Lord Yarin, whom Idalian didn't much like either—startled him. "I'm sorry. I shouldn't have said that."

"No, you shouldn't," Tirel stated. "And anyway, I'm not too young to know that Arpali isn't really sick, like my uncle says!"

"What?"

"I haven't seen you for a long time," Tirel said in peevish tones. "You don't know what's going on here. I wanted Arpali to send a message to Dragon's Rest to let Mama know I'm all right. First Uncle said there were too many clouds for a Sunrunner to work. Well, there were, that day," he admitted. "But the next day the sky was blue, and I asked again—but Uncle said she was sick."

"How do you know she's not?"

"I went to her room. One of Uncle's men was outside, like a guard!"

Idalian tried to appear properly shocked. "Perhaps he was just there to keep people from bothering Arpali's rest."

"Or to keep her from getting out!"

"My lord, I can't think of any reason why your uncle would—"

"You *are* just like him! You don't believe me! You think I'm a stupid little boy who should go play!" Tirel ran headlong from the room before imminent tears of frustration could humiliate him.

Idalian gnawed the inside of his cheek, knowing he ought to go after the boy and soothe him somehow. But Tirel had always liked Lord Yarin before; the man had insulted the child's self-importance, but that was no reason to suspect him of anything sinister.

Still, the child's hurt weighed on his mind. In a way he was grateful to Tirel for giving him something else to think about besides his family. It reminded him that it was time he

resumed his duties, offer his services to Lord Yarin. He still wanted to go home—even if there was no home to go to. He might have helped at Lowland, but snow made travel impossible. It was fortunate for Yarin that he had come early from Snowcoves; this was no time of year to be on the road.

Idalian resolved to set his grief aside and resume his duties. First he would have to make himself presentable. He felt filthy and a mirror showed him a substantial growth of beard. Servants brought buckets of hot water and a tub up to his room, and when he had washed, shaved, and dressed he went down to the kitchen for something to eat.

"How's Arpali?" he asked the cook as he broke the crust of a new loaf to sop up the last of his soup.

She shrugged plump shoulders. "I don't know, I'm sure. The meals come back half-eaten."

"Our Sunrunner must really be sick, then, to turn down your cooking."

"Pretty words from a young man who hasn't eaten a thing!"

"Sorry. No insult intended, Nolly."

"I know, child." She patted his hand. "It's a hard thing. I lost my parents in a gale blown straight from the cold, cruel mouth of the Storm God himself in all his fury. You think of your duty to the High Prince, and to our own lord, and especially the youngling who depends on you while his parents are away. I know you want to go home, but you can't. Not while Prince Tirel is all alone."

Idalian pushed away the empty bowl and stood. "I don't have a home, Nolly. Riverport is *gone*."

"As long as two stones stand atop each other, your holding is your holding. Think of that, and what your family would want of you. You can't bring back their lives, but you can live your own to honor them."

He studied her face for a moment—dark as taze, round as a moon, plain as an old boot—and leaned over to kiss her cheek.

"Do that again, boy, and you won't get out of this kitchen clothed."

He laughed, backing away as if terrified. She snorted and ladled more soup into a bowl.

"Take this to Arpali with my compliments, and word that if it doesn't come back empty, I'll come pour it down her throat."

The man outside the Sunrunner's chamber was definitely there to guard her. No other interpretation could be put on someone who stood duty bearing a sheathed sword and a knife in his belt. Idalian asked to go inside. He was told Arpali was asleep. He tried to insist. He was strongly discouraged by a steady, cold gaze and the hand that shifted slightly but meaningfully toward the knife.

He didn't argue. Leaving the soup with the guard, he went to find Lord Yarin, intending to offer his assistance wherever and however required. The rebuff he received would have stung him to a fury matching Tirel's, had he been just a little younger. But at nineteen winters he was old enough to recognize that his help was scorned in deliberately insulting terms—an unnecessary thing, calculated to make him stalk off in a sulk. Part of him wanted to inform his lordship in no uncertain terms that he was the sworn man of the High Prince himself, and therefore not to be trifled with. He hushed the voice and bowed himself from Lord Yarin's presence. Then he sought the oratory, where he could find some privacy to think.

Over the next days he observed Yarin's people carefully. There were quite a few guards present, surely more than were needed for escorting their lord and his lady and heir to his sister's castle. Also in the party were Yarin's steward, chamberlain, and several other functionaries whose attendance was not strictly necessary. Idalian supposed they could be explained away with the excuse that everyone tried to wrangle a trip to Balarat whenever possible, even in winter; it was a beautiful and comfortable castle, commanding a hill overlooking a deep valley. But somehow Idalian had the feeling that all these people had not come to appreciate the icy splendor of a keep crystaled by snow. Yarin's stated purpose for coming to Balarat was to protect his sister's son from rampaging invaders. Idalian suspected he had fled Snowcoves in case of attack from the sea. But as the days passed he reconsidered. The barbarians had shown not the slightest interest in any land north of Princemarch. And who would be fool enough to try sailing through ice-crusted waters, anyway? Winter was a strong defense, and winter had walled up all Firon tighter than a dragon's hatching cave. So why was Yarin here?

There was no word of Arpali other than that she continued weak and ill. Idalian attempted again to see her, and

again was denied entry. By this time it was clear that the servants were taking their orders from Yarin's people, supervised by his wife, Vallaina. The more Idalian saw, the less he liked it.

A fine day came, bitterly cold but with an irresistible glisten to the snow. Idalian thought that Tirel—who hadn't spoken to him since their "conference"—would enjoy a romp outside. Vallaina gave permission, but sent along two guards and her son Natham. Thus Idalian's chance to make it up with Tirel was ruined.

But he had another idea, and acted on it once Natham was thoroughly soaked from a snowball skirmish. He suggested a warming visit to the glassworks. Natham cared nothing for the craft that was the wealth of Firon; he and the guards returned to the castle.

By the fierce glow of hearths where ingots from the Desert were fashioned into everything from wine bottles to windowpanes, Idalian apologized and told Tirel that he, too, was suspicious. It was all the opening the boy needed.

"My schoolroom is right above Arpali's chamber. I've been sneaking in at night and thumping on the floor—and last night she stopped thumping back. Do you think she's been hurt?"

"Nobody would dare harm a Sunrunner!"

"Uncle Yarin would," Tirel said, and the name was laced with loathing.

"Don't be silly. You just don't like him," Idalian said, but his heart was racing. "You're being treated all right, aren't you?"

He shrugged. "I have my lessons, and I play with Natham—he's such a pain, and he can't throw a snowball for spit!"

Idalian grinned. "I saw. But I thought you used to be friends."

"He's different. He says he gets to choose what to play because he's older than me. But I'm the prince, not him."

"He's your guest. You should be gracious, Tirel."

"That's not what I meant! He's acting like *he's* a prince. You know how, since Papa and Mama went away last spring, the steward comes to tell me things? It's boring, but I guess I have to learn to like it. Well, now she doesn't come talk to me anymore. Natham says it's because I'm too little. But I wasn't even seven last spring when she talked to me and

now she doesn't! *I* think it's because I'm not supposed to know what's going on."

Only a fool would fail to see the signs now. But how could Yarin think he could take Firon, when Laric was kin and friend and ally to Prince Pol?

Simple, he realized suddenly. Everyone had problems more urgent than making sure Firon stayed in the hands of its rightful prince. There were battles being fought in the south that no one here knew about. Not that they could *do* anything, with snow blocking all routes out of the princedom and the harbors frozen. But at least Arpali could have kept them informed.

And could have told others what was happening at Balarat.

She was not sick. She was being held captive so she couldn't use the sunlight. If no news could get out, then none could come in, either. Doubtless with the war so far away and nothing to do with him, Yarin considered the trade more than even.

And how a sweet, pretty lady like Princess Lisiel could have such a snake for a brother was beyond Idalian's understanding.

"I think you're right," he said abruptly. "But there's not much we can do about it for now. No, don't argue," he warned as Tirel's face clenched up. "You're smart and you're a prince, but you're still only seven years old. And I may be the brother of an important Desert lord, but I'm still just a squire."

"We need Arpali," Tirel asserted. "When Lord Andry finds out about this—"

"I'll work on it," he promised, but was thinking, *What can even he do from Goddess Keep?* The last he'd heard, it had been attacked. Unsuccessfully, to be sure, but it was still in danger. Everyone was occupied with the war. There would be no help from anyone.

Tirel hunkered in on himself, shivering despite the blazing heat of glass kilns. "Idalian—what're we going to do?" he asked in a small voice.

"I don't know." He put an arm around the child. "We're not alone, my lord. There are plenty of people loyal to your father, and Arpali—"

"But she's a prisoner. We're prisoners, too, aren't we?" he asked forlornly. But just when Idalian thought tears were imminent, Tirel straightened up and scowled. "Firon doesn't

belong to Uncle Yarin. High Prince Rohan gave it to *us* and nobody's going to take it away."

For the first time he envisioned Riverport in the present—not as it had been six years ago when he left it, not as it must have been when his family was butchered, but *now*. What his father had built was in enemy hands and under enemy bootheels. But it was *his*, just as Nolly had said it was. Just as Firon belonged to Tirel and his family. These unknown savages had taken it away, but they weren't going to keep it.

He gave the young prince a grim smile. "Your Uncle Yarin may make a try at it, but we'll stop him. See if we don't."

* * *

Ostvel shook rain off his cloak as if to rid himself of amazement as well. He stood in the silent gray streets of Waes, staring at empty windows. Tilal was beside him, their personal guard waited nearby, and all of them were as unbelieving as he.

"I know you said that Rialt managed to clear everybody out—but this is crazy!" Tilal said at last. "It hasn't been touched!"

"Just the places they themselves burned," Ostvel agreed. "Can it be that the Vellant'im landed and left?"

"I don't think so. There are foodstuffs in some of the houses. Even the Vellant'im have to eat. They can't have brought enough to last all winter. Waes as it stands is an open invitation to walk in and resupply. But there's no sign they even sent a scouting party."

"So they didn't take the bait." Ostvel resisted the need to rub some warmth back into hands that ached from the cold and damp. "It's unnatural, Tilal. It makes no sense."

"Do you think we dare camp where they did not?"

"Are they waiting for us in corners, do you mean?" He shook his head. "I doubt it. But have the whole city turned inside out just the same before we let the rest of our troops in. We might as well spend a night in real beds beside real hearths if we can." His sore joints felt better just at the thought of it. What was truly crazy was a man of his years traipsing around the countryside leading the armies of

Princemarch. He deserved a placid old age in his own keep with his beautiful wife to keep him warm.

Tilal gave the order to inspect every building, then glanced up at the lowering sky. "It'll rain for the next three days, looks like. No chance to tell Sioned about this."

"Damned gold-beards knew exactly what our weakness is, to start a war just as the rains came. It'll fret Sunrunners more than it does us, though. When I was at Goddess Keep, everyone walked on tiptoe around Andrade all winter long."

Tilal laughed briefly. "Everyone walked on tiptoe around her anyway. I hope the innkeepers didn't take all their wine with them. I could do with a nice mulled Syrene red about now."

"That's the first thing they'll have loaded into their carts. But maybe Rialt left something interesting at the residence. Come on."

Waes was confirmed to be exactly what it seemed: empty as a broken dragon egg. Tilal gave strict orders for watchfulness and sobriety, however safe the city seemed and however many casks of wine were found to warm the night chill. He did not intend to be trapped here as they had hoped to trap the Vellant'im.

Ostvel's army consisted of soldiers from Castle Crag, the levies he'd gathered to him on the way down the Faolain, and forces led by two young lords who had chosen to accompany their troops. Draza of Grand Veresch was twenty-eight, grandson of old Lord Dreslav by one of his many mistresses. That the youth was illegitimate had never mattered; his only competiton for the inheritance had been a fair-born uncle who wanted only to spend his life in the high mountains hunting wolves. Draza had a wife and two small children; it was the first time he had ever been separated from them and admitted bashfully how much he missed them. But the need for revenge was stronger; his half-sister Pelida had been married to Gevnaya of Faolain Lowland, and had died with him at Riverport. Usually the quietest and most gentle of men, Draza wanted blood.

Kerluthan of River Ussh, three winters Draza's senior, was the elder brother of Pol's former squire, Edrel. Their sister Paveol had died with her husband and son at Gilad Seahold. No matter how much Kerluthan might miss his own wife, he had vowed not to return to her until he had the deaths of half the Vellanti army to his credit.

The emptiness of Waes infuriated him. "Where are the whoresons?" he demanded as he stalked into the residence, violent gestures spraying the carpet with raindrops. The late Lady of Waes, Roelstra's daughter Kiele, had chosen the Cunaxan rug. Ostvel felt a sudden twinge at being in her house.

Tilal's shrewd green eyes noted the emotion flitting across Ostvel's face, but he addressed himself to Kerluthan. "We'll find them. Now that your troops and horses are decently quartered and fed, my lord, why don't you do yourself the same service?"

"I'd feed better and sleep happier after some worthwhile exercise," Kerluthan grumbled, but went away with Draza to see what the squires had found in the kitchens.

Tilal regarded Ostvel pensively. "What were you thinking just now?"

"You've got Sioned's eyes, all right." Ostvel shrugged. "I was thinking of Kiele, if you can believe it. She lived here, after all." Settling into a soft chair, he added, "I was remembering . . . how she died."

"Ah. Not a pleasant *Rialla*, that. Except that I won my Gemma there."

"And I, my Alasen." He would never understand how or why. Neither would he ever know what had made him throw a knife to Lyell so he could kill Kiele and himself before Sunrunner's Fire got them. Well, that was a lie. It hadn't been the first time he'd taken responsibility for a death so that it wouldn't burden someone else. As he had killed Ianthe to spare Sioned her blood, so he had provided Lyell with the knife to spare Andry. Not that the Lord of Goddess Keep had been any more grateful for it than Sioned. But at least *she* had come to understand why he had done it. Andry had never forgiven him—and not just for stealing Lyell and Kiele's deaths from him. Ostvel had won Alasen. That was what Andry would never forgive.

Andry's eldest son came in, carrying a tray loaded with cheese, soup, and wine. "The cheese is a bit smelly," he apologized. "We had to carve a lot of it off that had gone bad. And there's no bread to go with it, though Chaltyn has put some people to work baking for tomorrow morning. But the soup's good and hot, and the wine is from Catha Freehold."

Tilal exchanged an amused glance with Ostvel. In the

scant days since he had become a squire, he had thrown himself into his duties with a dedication bordering on fanaticism. There was no doubt in anyone's mind that Andrev was precisely where he wanted to be, doing precisely what he wanted to do. On first recognizing Tilal's new squire, Ostvel had been appalled. After a little thought and a brief conversation with Tilal, he had agreed with the prince's reasoning: Andry couldn't hold himself aloof from the war if he had so personal a stake in it. Though he had done just that so far, Ostvel knew it wouldn't last. Faults Andry had, but paternal indifference was not one of them.

As Andrev served them their meal, Ostvel glanced again around the room. The eccentricities of the residence did not extend to its individual chambers. Three houses had been made into one by knocking down a few walls, building others, adding staircases to connect different levels, and otherwise attempting to make coherent a structure that balked at every turn. But the separate rooms were graceful and well-appointed. The residence had not been so long empty that the polish had gone off silver and brass fixtures, although a thin layer of dust had accumulated on the table-tops. There was even wood enough for a night's fire left in a decorated bin beside the hearth. Andrev piled some onto the blaze he'd made earlier, called Fire to the new wood, and bowed his way out.

"He's very casual about his gifts," Ostvel remarked as he spooned up the thick soup.

"You would be, too, if you were Andry's son." Tilal bit into a slice of cheese. "Not bad—this type's always better for aging. I just hope Sioneva's introduction to her talents hasn't left her frightened or bewildered. Andry was careful, and for that I'll thank him—"

"If you ever decide to speak to him again," Ostvel interrupted with a knowing smile.

Tilal grunted inelegantly around a mouthful of soup, swallowed, and said, "I suppose I'll have to, one of these years. Next summer maybe, at Dragon's Rest, when Rohan calls everyone together to sort things out."

"The last time he did, I got Skybowl," the older man drawled. "Something of a surprise. I hope he doesn't decide to give me Meadowlord this time."

The prince choked on his wine. "What?"

"It'd be just like him, you know," Ostvel went on, enjoy-

ing the effect of his statement. There was little else to enjoy about this situation. "In trust for my son Dannar, of course, since he's the one with royal blood in him, not I. But I have a very uneasy feeling I'm going to be changing residences again. Ah, well. At least it'll be to a castle that doesn't turn to ice every year."

"Turn around and go back to the beginning," Tilal pleaded.

"Isn't it obvious? Why aren't the Vellant'im in Waes? It's wide open. Even if they suspected a trap, at least they should have foraged for supplies, as you mentioned earlier. But they've shunned it as if it oozed poison. Why?"

"They outthought Chay—which has to be a first."

Ostvel shook his head and poured himself more wine. "No. Not that Chay is infallible—and don't ever tell him I said so. The truth is that the Vellant'im were warned." He smiled mirthlessly as the green eyes rounded.

"But they couldn't have known we'd—"

"Couldn't they? There's nothing to stop them coming here and taking what they want—lolling here all winter in these very rooms, if they pleased. You and I couldn't have gotten here any faster than we did—which means they had ample time to strip the place. But it hasn't even been touched. They were told not to come here at all."

"Chiana." The name was a hiss.

"Chiana," Ostvel agreed. "Rialt suspected her—or rather his very perceptive lady did—almost the instant they got to Swalekeep. Chiana threw a fit when she learned that Waes was open to invasion, supposedly because nothing lay between her and attack from the west. But she also knew that you were coming from the south and I from the north. We are the millstones, Tilal—but the grain is missing."

The prince looked as if he would throw his wineglass into the fireplace. "She saw the trap and warned them. She's working with the enemy."

"She wants Princemarch. More to the point, she wants to enter Castle Crag as its owner. *My* castle, that my prince gave me and that my son will hold when I'm gone." He heard the fierceness and made his voice lighter. "So you see that Chiana and Rinhoel will die for high treason, and Meadowlord will be forfeit, and our cherished, sadistic Rohan will probably give the damned place to *me* next summer."

Tilal snorted. "Alasen would laugh herself into a seizure if she could hear you complaining!"

"I've been surrounded all my life by women who find me hilariously funny," he replied in an aggrieved tone. "Alasen, Sioned, Tobin, my daughters—you never met my first wife, did you?"

"No, but I'll bet she's laughing at you, too, on the night wind."

"I have every faith that she is."

They stayed silent until Andrev appeared with a pitcher of hot taze and cups. Tilal roused himself to ask if the boy had eaten and found himself a bed.

"Yes, my lord. Your chambers are ready for you upstairs. We aired them as best we could, but with all this rain. . . ."

"I'm sure they're fine. Go to bed, Andrev. It's been a long day."

"Yes, my lord. I'll just build up the fire a little." Again he stooped to put wood on the hearth, and urged the flames higher with *faradhi* arts.

When he bowed his way out, Tilal said, "No, not shy about it at all, is he? I'm told he knows his sister Tobren's colors and can speak with her on sunlight. If we ever see any again, I'll have him report to her and she can tell Rohan all this."

Ostvel nodded and sipped at his steaming mug. "When Sioned first came to Goddess Keep, she was wary of her gifts. I remember the night she and Cami had to call their first Fire for Andrade. We talked afterward, the three of us—and for Sioned it was in the way of a confession. 'I always thought I was odd, strange, not like other people,' she said. 'But until I came here, I didn't know it was because I was special.' "

"My father told me that one night, when she was sitting with him and my mother in the solar at River Run and the fire needed stirring, Sioned lifted a finger and it blazed up. Sunrunner's Fire, without even thinking about it." Tilal sighed. "My mother didn't much like that, or her. She was always 'your father's Sunrunner sister' that we didn't talk about. I was—oh, six, I suppose—when she married Rohan. Mother was more inclined to mention her after that! Then I went to Stronghold as a squire and saw for myself."

"The Sunrunner witch," Ostvel supplied, smiling.

"I'm surprised Mother never used that name."

"I'll bet Andry does."

"Reluctantly." Tilal reached for the pitcher of taze. "When do you think he'll emerge from Goddess Keep?"

"Sometime after the first battle Andrev is in, I should imagine."

"Stubborn son of a—" Tilal laughed suddenly. "Yes, he *is* a son of a she-dragon, isn't he?"

"Down to his toes. Tobin's the only one he still speaks to. I hope she can make him see sense."

"Well, it's still my opinion that we don't need him. We can beat these savages on our own. Andry can either sulk and lose all respect, or he can forgo his conditions and fight beside us and take what credit he can get for it. But either way, we're going to win."

Ostvel nodded, though he was thinking, *But how much and how many are we going to lose along the way?*

Chapter Twenty-one

The day after Birioc met his distant kinsman, Tirel and Idalian made their pact, and Ostvel and Tilal rested their armies in Waes, Rohan entered Stronghold. The next dawn brought Sethric of Grib, bearing tokens of a Vellanti defeat out in the Long Sand. Clothing, swords, knives—even gold beads painstakingly unthreaded from thick black beards—he presented it all to the High Prince on the main steps.

"I know your grace is interested in such things," he said with a low bow.

"Good work. Did your people take any hurts?"

"Minor scrapes. We didn't lose anyone and recovered several of the horses stolen from Radzyn," he added in Chay's direction. "Your trick with our own horses worked perfectly, your grace. Some of the enemy kept following but lost us when we turned for Stronghold. There wasn't anything to track us by."

"Excellent. Then perhaps it will work for my son and Lord Maarken as well. After you've washed and eaten, come back and give us the details of the fight."

"I can tell it all now."

Rohan smiled slightly. "But you'll tell it in more comfort later. There's time, my lord."

The young man hesitated. "Your grace—I just wanted you to know. . . ."

"Yes?"

"You're not at all what my uncle Prince Velden says you are."

Chay gave a complex snort. Rohan only nodded. When Sethric had been taken upstairs by a page, he slanted a look at his brother-by-marriage.

"Go ahead," he invited. "Say it."

"Say what, my prince?"

"Don't make innocent eyes at me. I know what you're thinking."

"Then there's no need for me to say it out loud, is there?"

"No, but you'll enjoy it."

Chay grinned. "So will you, for all your protests that you don't do it on purpose. Very well, here it is—that boy's ready to give over loyalty to his princedom, his own kin, and whatever inheritance Velden's promised him for the sake of swearing himself yours. He doesn't even want a holding—just the chance to follow you and be within sight of your princely face and dragon's eyes."

"Oh, I don't think it's gone that far yet," Rohan commented. "I'll bet he's still wondering why I didn't order a massive battle on the Remagev plain."

"At this point, do you think he cares? He's young, he's seen action and won, and he's alive to be smug about it."

"If that's all that's necessary, then Pol should come back singing my praises." Repressing a sigh, he added more lightly, "I've never seen a dragon with blue eyes."

"I have, *azhrei.*"

* * *

At first, after he knew Brenlis was dead, Andry had been unable even to look at their three-year-old daughter. Merisel had her mother's blonde hair and delicate little face, and her mouth curved in Brenlis' sad-sweet smile. It hurt to be near her. But as the days wore on, he found comfort in the resemblance and spent more time in the nursery playing with her, reading to her, or just watching her sleep. When Torien or another of the *devr'im* wanted to find him, that began to be the first place they looked.

His other children were old enough to mark the change in the frequency of their father's visits. At ten, Chayly was Valeda's to the quirk of her eyebrows; Joscev, not quite seven, had long been in his half-brother Andrev's shadow. Indeed, the boy seemed made of shadows: of all Andry's offspring, only he was black-haired and brown-eyed, like his mother, Ulwis. Had Andry looked, he would have seen his own jaw and cheekbones in Joscev's face, and his own smile

on Chayly's mouth. But he did not look at them. Only at Merisel.

She enchanted him as thoroughly as her mother had done. He lavished on her all the love Brenlis had never allowed him to give her. But there was a difference between mother and daughter: Merisel adored him in return and cried when he was called away to his duties.

"You're spoiling her," Rusina observed as Andry kissed his daughter's tear-streaked face and handed her over to the nurse.

"No, Merisel, you mustn't cry! Papa will be back to tuck you into bed. There's a good girl."

"And hurting Chayly and Joscev," Rusina added as they left the room.

He gave her a sidelong look. "When did you ever concern yourself with my children—even the one you bore me?"

She tossed unruly dark curls from her eyes. "Tobren turned out just fine without me. I don't think the others much care about who tends or teaches them. You're the one who's important in their lives."

"And they all know I love them."

"Even Andrev?"

"I can deplore his actions without ceasing to love him."

"As your father does with you."

Andry grunted and led the way down the staircase. "Are the horses saddled?"

"Yes. I still think this is unwise."

"If I spend one more day pent up in the keep, I'll go mad."

"Not even Merisel can distract you from boredom?"

"Stop it, Rusina," he warned.

"Yes, my Lord. Of course, my Lord. As you wish, my Lord."

He had never hit a woman in his life. The impulse to slap some respect—or at least a little fear—into Rusina disgusted him. He strode into the courtyard, hoping the chill autumn air would cool his anger. Oclel turned his head when Andry spoke his name, thick fingers testing the saddle girth he'd just tightened, moving to tighten it some more.

"I could do with a good gallop," the younger man said. "Do you mind if I come along?"

"I'll be glad of the company," Andry lied. He'd wanted to spend some time alone in the fresh air, riding beyond

fields still trampled down by two armies into unspoiled countryside. Especially did he want to escape the growing village of tents and lean-to shelters around the keep. What was he supposed to do with all these people? The Goddess had shown him nothing of this in either vision or dream.

Having given Oclel permission to accompany him, he could hardly send Rusina away. She climbed into a saddle as if she straddled a trestle bench. When Oclel rolled his eyes skyward at his wife's ungraceful performance, Andry felt a smile tug his mouth. He had never known so oddly mated a couple as this: the brawny, plainspoken soldier's son from the Veresch and the frail, acid-voiced *athri*'s daughter with a few drops of Fessenden's royal blood in her veins.

Not that anyone would wish to own to a relationship to Prince Pirro, Andry reflected as they rode through the gates. Pirro huddled up there in his chilly stone keep, far removed from battle and with every obvious intention of remaining so. Andry had to admit privately to a grim amusement that the prince had used the fine points of Rohan's own laws against him. "Defend only from attack by other princedoms," indeed. Good Goddess, what was wrong with these people? Didn't they understand that nothing less than retaking the entire continent would content these *diarmadhi*-inspired Vellant'im?

As for the refugees clustered around Goddess Keep—did they think Andry could wave a hand, say a few words, and remove the threat forever? His mouth quirked in a bitter smile. Hand-waving and speech aside, he could indeed have done something about the danger—if only Rohan and Pol would let him. Their foolish tactic of letting the Desert kill the enemy for them was hopeless. If only they would send for him and his *devr'im*.

"A glorious day, my Lord!" Oclel exclaimed happily. They had left behind the tents and the mangled fields, and were riding up the road that, within a few measures, would branch off to the coastline. Andry hesitated. His intended destination lay to the west, but it was indeed a beautiful day—perfect for a good run. Impulsively, he decided to give the stallion his head.

Rusina called out Andry's name, then laughed and challenged her husband to a race. The thunder of hooves was a good sound, bright as drums beating time to a dance—not

the heavy thuds that echoed the pounding of a fear-sick heart.

Andry finally halted atop a little rise. He stroked his horse's sweaty neck, catching his breath after the wild gallop. "Ah, we're both out of shape for this kind of thing, my lad! It's been too long." He walked the stallion in slow circles while the others, riding lesser animals and not raised in the saddle as he had been, caught up.

Oclel complained good-naturedly about Radzyn get—the two- and four-footed variety. Rusina had lost her cloak, and Andry offered her his own. "I never get cold, you know," he told her. "It's the Desert sun in my bones."

"If you say so," she said, clasping the white wool around her. "I'd like to go to the cliff forest, if that's all right with you. Valeda needs some fresh wildflowers for the children's lessons, and what with the battle and now all these tents, everything within two measures of the Keep has been trampled."

"Still doing her favors to apologize for borrowing her face, I see," Oclel teased. "Very well, my lady. Fringecup and autumn bower and blue-hoof it is. We may even find some wooly-buttons. It's about time for them to bloom."

They rode across the fields to the boundaries of the Goddess' forest. Tethering their horses—one did not enter these precincts except on foot—they separated, keeping track of each other by the sound of twigs snapping underfoot in the dense undergrowth. Andry returned with an armful of color to find Rusina glaring in disgust down the road back to Goddess Keep.

"What happened?" He looked around for the missing horses.

"What does it look like?" She shook a broken branch.

"Well, it *is* their dinnertime. And it's not too long a walk home." Approaching her, he peered at the jumble of flowers in a fold of his cloak. "What a mess."

"You may as well dump yours in, too. We can sort them later."

Adding his collection to the tangle, he said casually, "I think I'll look in at the tree circle."

"Are you sure the Goddess will be at home?"

"There are ways of coaxing her when she's feeling shy." He reached in his pocket and brought out a scrap of parchment folded around *dranath*.

When Rusina spoke again, her voice had lost its sardonic edge. "Andry, be careful with that. The added strength isn't worth the risk."

"I'm touched that you care," he replied in silken tones. But when she didn't snap back at him, he shrugged an apology. "I have to know."

"And if you see things even more terrible than what's already happened?"

He made the effort to smile. "You mean it can get worse?"

"You don't usually ask stupid questions." Rusina scowled at the flowers. "Valeda had better appreciate this. Let's go home, Andry. It's late. Oclel!" When there was no answer, she sighed her annoyance. "Hundreds of Sunrunner men at the Keep, and I have to Choose one who loses himself not on sunlight, but in flowers. Oclel!"

They listened for him and heard nothing. She drew breath to call out again. Andry gripped her arm.

"No," he whispered. "Hear the stillness?"

"As if there were wolves out hunting," she breathed.

He pulled Rusina up and flowers tumbled from the cloak, scattering onto the dirt. "Get moving," he ordered quietly.

"No!" she hissed.

"Shut up." He froze as bootheels crunched dry leaves. Anyone meaning them harm would have been quieter. Catching a glimpse of blue wool, he exhaled in relief and called out, "Oclel, you idiot, you gave your wife a terrible start!"

The tall Sunrunner emerged from the trees. His blue tunic was spotted mid-chest with darkness. As he staggered forward and fell, a matching stain on his back showed where the sword had entered his body and gone all the way through him.

Rusina shrieked his name. Andry started for him, but Oclel waved him back.

"No! Get away Andry—close behind me—"

"Oclel—"

"Run!" The few extra moments of life lent by urgency and fear faded from his blue eyes, and he was dead.

Men crashed through the forest now, having given up hope of a surprise attack on hearing Rusina's scream. Andry swung around, trying to detect their direction. His gaze flickered to the broken branches where reins had been tied. *Stupid!* he raged uselessly at himself; one horse might escape, but all three?

Escape—he grabbed Rusina's arm as she stumbled past him, trying to reach Oclel's body. The one thing he could not do was break into the open; they would be perfect targets. So he clapped a hand over her mouth to stifle her sobs and hauled her with him deep into the trees.

Plunging into the frail shelter of a glade, he clasped her against him and stared hard into her tear-filled eyes. "Be silent!" he breathed. "Oclel died to protect us—will you make his death meaningless?"

She stopped fighting him, limp for an instant. Then she straightened, and hate was in her eyes. When he touched her cheek in compassion, she jerked her head away.

Andry listened. The enemy was quiet now, more cautious, having lost track of them. Twenty paces away, a brown furry shape skittered up a tree; an arrow's whoosh and thud, and the animal was pinned to the bark. Then there was silence.

Rusina's heartbeats hammered against Andry's chest. "They'll find us," she whispered. "We have to move."

He shook his head. "When they do. Noise."

She nodded and glanced back to where Oclel lay. "Fire. Please, Andry."

He could see a fragment of blue tunic through the foliage. He called Sunrunner's Fire into a burning shroud for his friend's body. Rusina trembled beside him, as if battling new sobs.

Andry hadn't thought about the enemy reaction to the sudden flames. But he used the startled uproar to cover the noise he and Rusina made as they ran. He made instinctively for the tree circle, cursing the enemy for invading this most sacred of *faradhi* places.

I can weave something—Fire, a sorcerer's spell, anything—just get to the circle, the Goddess will help me, she must—

Rusina tripped and fell, moaning. "Come on!" he cried, crouching to pull her up. "Almost there—"

"Can't—my ankle—leave me here, Andry—"

"No, damn it! Get up!" He took her arms and she got both feet under her before collapsing facedown into the carpet of dead leaves.

"Faradh'im!"

Andry lifted his head. All around him were footsteps, invisible enemy plunging through the forest. They came from every direction—even that leading to the tree circle.

Rusina moved beside him, turned, propped herself on one elbow. "Andry."

He looked down at her face. At his own face.

* * *

Birioc came away from Swalekeep with more than his father had ever dreamed of getting. It was all settled—not just in private among himself, Varek, Rinhoel, and Chiana, but in secret between Birioc and his kinsman. Though he would not discuss the latter with anyone but his Merida uncles.

The Vellant'im would hold the south through the winter, taking Faolain Lowland as soon as it was convenient and beating back any attempts by Kostas to retake those portions of Syr now in Vellanti hands. Storms would close Brochwell Bay until spring, so they needn't worry about Firon, Fessenden, or Kierst-Isel. Gilad lay bleeding. Grib would have to be brought into the fold, but Chiana was confident of her influence with Prince Velden. It had been Rinhoel's suggestion that if Velden balked, Meadowlord's armies could go to his "defense" and make sure that he died in the process after a light battle with the Vellant'im for show. This plan was held in abeyance until Velden could be sounded out. But it revealed to Birioc that Rinhoel was growing weary of sitting in his nice, safe home. It was a change from the summer he'd spent at Remagev, when he'd sulked and complained about too much work and not enough leisure. Birioc had despised the young prince then and had not altered his opinion, but Rinhoel's usefulness outweighed personal feelings. Birioc had cultivated him two years ago, and would not risk the harvest for the paltry pleasure of telling Rinhoel what he thought of him.

Dorval was completely eliminated from the conflict, although reports spoke of a sizable group in the hills that conducted lightning raids. These were more irritant than danger, but valuable time was wasted chasing these people down—and the Vellant'im were frustrated when their foes melted away amid the crags and dales.

The armies of Princemarch and Ossetia were a major concern. The trap at Waes had been avoided, thanks to Chiana's timely warning. Miserable weather would slow down any advance. Tilal and Ostvel must be kept busy, however,

so that Meadowlord could seize Dragon's Rest at the appropriate time and then march for Castle Crag. But under no circumstances must Tilal and Ostvel be allowed to join Kostas.

As for the Desert—the Merida would take Tuath, then Tiglath, then Feruche while the Vellant'im lunged up from Radzyn to Stronghold. When Lord Varek was asked why they had allowed themselves to be sidetracked to Remagev, he replied that Stronghold was not the objective. Rohan was. He would not explain why.

But Birioc could make a fair guess. In his years as High Prince, Rohan had managed to forge divisive princedoms into a workable whole. Not a seamless one, but what he melded together through law and his own personality had held secure for the length of his rule. With him gone, the beleaguered princedoms would splinter. Pol hadn't his father's strength. Even had he possessed Rohan's combination of will and cunning and leadership, he was a Sunrunner, a breed no one with half a brain trusted. Miyon had always paced a pretty path between pursuit of his own aims and the appearance of loyalty to his daughter's husband. Birioc knew that Pol trusted Miyon not at all—but he had to behave in public as if he did, and that would work to Merida advantage. It remained only to convince Miyon to play his part in the proceedings. Birioc didn't think it would be difficult. Miyon had loathed Rohan all his life. The trouble was that no contempt went with it; his hate was prompted by fear.

This much of the plan was known to Chiana and Rinhoel. There was another part, the secret part, agreed to by Varek and Birioc alone. Once the princeling and his poisonous mother had completed their tasks, they would be dealt with as befitted traitors. Varek was willing to flatter them, work with them, and above all use them. But he despised them as deeply as Birioc did. They were betraying their own kind. They would die for it.

"But you and I, we are of the same blood," Varek had said. "The High Warlord will rejoice in this reunion with our brothers of the Sacred Glass."

As much as Birioc wanted to know the specifics of the relationship—which would tell him where his people had come from and why—he did not press the point. It was enough that there was an ally at last, a vast and ruthless army to crush Rohan and all his get. The Merida had been

promised the Desert in ages past. Finally, *finally*, they'd have it.

He rode back to Castle Pine as quickly as terrain and weather would permit, too filled with triumph even to curse the passage of days. The Merida had waited hundreds of years for this. They would not mind waiting a little while longer, especially when victory was certain.

* * *

Born to a prosperous family of silk merchants on Dorval, Rialt had been trained from boyhood to equate efficiency with profit. What worked for a business worked just as well during his four years as chief steward at Dragon's Rest, and even better when he ruled Waes as its regent. Though his efforts at Swalekeep were of much smaller scope, the same principle held true. Only this time the yield of his organizational skills was not coin but information.

If he was the commander of this endeavor, then his chief captains were his wife and Lady Cluthine. Mevita befriended a variety of servants within the castle, all of whom had some grievance or other against Chiana. She heard their grudges with sympathy, culled useful information, and reported back to Rialt. Cluthine, with access to the nobility, especially her uncle Prince Halian, did the same on a higher scale. By comparing the two versions of what went on at Swalekeep, Rialt got a fairly accurate view of things.

And was horrified.

He was compelled to admire Chiana's stealth in getting the Vellanti lord in and out with no highborns the wiser. Her attitude toward servants—that they were nothing more than hands and feet for her to command—was her mistake. The man was seen. Less care had been taken with Miyon's son; his identity was confirmed by Cluthine. But sure knowledge of what they were all up to came to Rialt from a unsuspected and astonishing source.

It happened while he was out riding in the parklands beyond the walls. Polev had begged to be allowed to exercise his new pony. The overcast sky yielded a fine intermittent mist but no real rain; properly bundled up against the chill, there was no danger to anyone's health. The greater danger, indeed, was to stay cooped up indoors. Cluthine

and Naydra, feeling the same restlessness, came along with the young Princess Palila.

Rialt did not share the automatic reaction of most older people to the girl's very name. Roelstra's treacherous mistress was a figure of legend to him, not a real memory as she was for Naydra. Still, being a fair-minded woman, she went out of her way to treat this second Palila with kindness. Rialt had seen several examples of this since coming to Swalekeep, and quickly realized that the attention paid her by her aunt and her cousin Cluthine was the first she had ever known. It was plain enough that her mother ignored her, her brother scorned her, and her father barely knew she was alive. Palila had been raised by Halian's three bastard daughters, all much older than herself, whom it had pleased Chiana to make little more than servants. Resentful, they took it out on the child. Palila was almost pathetically grateful to escape Swalekeep for a morning ride.

"She's a sweet little thing," Naydra commented to Rialt as they watched the children race their ponies. "Astonishing, with so poisonous a mother." She smiled. "But then, my father wasn't exactly beloved of all who knew him."

"You, however, are," he replied. "That's not flattery, my lady, it's the truth. I know how fond Pol is of you."

Naydra was sixty-four and looked it, but a sudden blush took thirty years from her face. "And I of him. Rohan and Sioned gave me a life I loved. I will miss it, and my dear lord. But I must say I'm glad he won't have the grief of seeing his merchant fleet fitted out for war."

"I had the honor of working with Lord Narat often. He will be missed. And I agree, I'm glad my parents didn't live to see Graypearl destroyed."

"Do you have relatives still on the island?"

"My sister and her family. I only hope they escaped with Prince Chadric." He shrugged, uncomfortable with a worry he could do nothing about, and changed the subject. "Not to be subtle about it, but speaking of Chiana—"

"You need proof of her betrayal," Naydra said calmly. "I have none. I wish I did. We all know it's true and we'd all like to see her die for it. But we have neither arms nor authority to act if proof is found. We need Lord Ostvel as the High Prince's representative. More importantly, we need his army."

"Succinctly put, my lady. All I can do is watch and wait. It's maddening to be so helpless."

"It's something I grew used to when I was young." She smiled again in bitter memory. "I believe Chiana shares with our father a joy in seeing others flail about like beached fish. She's certainly entertained by you, if you'll forgive my saying so. Only last night she worried very sweetly about giving you something to do to occupy your time here."

"Let me guess—Rinhoel suggested putting me in charge of the servants."

"Shipping, actually."

Rialt perked up. "Did he, now? That could be the best place for me."

"If your lady wife will allow it." Naydra chuckled softly. "I do like her. She can turn Chiana scarlet or white at will. It's marvelous."

Polev came thundering up on his pony, Palila right behind him, Cluthine following more sedately. "Did you see, Papa? I won! And I bet I could beat those horses down there, too, if Lady Thina would let me," he added with a sidelong glance at her.

Rialt peered down the hillside to the main road. A knot of riders was escorting heavy baggage wains south. He could guess where they were going. Chiana would say, of course, that supplies meant for Kostas had fallen to a convenient enemy "capture" or two, fulfilling her bargain with the Vellant'im while leaving her blameless.

Yes, a job overseeing the shipping down the Faolain would be excellent—and what fun it would be to salt the grain. He grinned to himself and started planning how to convince Chiana to give him the job. He was a lowly merchant at heart, bred to hard work and not the elegant ways of a highborn lord; he would willingly soil his hands to spare her own exalted person; he would be proud to contribute to Prince Kostas' efforts as his station in life allowed, for actual physical battle was the duty of great lords and princes—no, best forget that one, as it might be construed as a veiled insult to Rinhoel.

His attention snagged on a word in the conversation that continued around him. That word was "Cunaxa," and it was spoken by Princess Palila.

"—me to call him a prince, even though his mother wasn't

married to Prince Miyon and bastards are always called 'lord' or 'lady.' Are Merida royal, Aunt Naydra?"

"They would have it so," was the calm reply. "How did you meet him?"

Palila looked like a child caught in a misdeed. "I—I went to ask Rinhoel to take me riding with him. He was very angry when I came to his room."

"It wasn't your fault, dear," Cluthine told her. "Rinhoel's servants were to blame, not you. If he ordered privacy, they should not have let you in."

"But I'm the one he yelled at," she sighed. "Prince Birioc was very kind, though. He said I was pretty. But I think he was just being polite."

Rialt wanted desperately to ask her what she might have overheard, but Naydra and Cluthine had more of the girl's confidence than he. They would gently extract the information. So he smiled at Palila and said, "I don't think so at all. You have your father's blue eyes and your mother's auburn hair, and that's a very striking combination."

True enough, but the timid little face was a closed one, cautious and quiet. His compliment made her recoil with embarrassment that verged on fear. He wondered if fourteen years of Chiana could ever be overcome, or if it was too late. His own daughter Tessalar was just Palila's age, that lovely time in a girl's life when she begins to discover who she is. But though Palila was physically mature, her spirit had been stunted. He saw little hope for her until he remembered another painfully shy, insecure girl. Freed from her father, Meiglan had bloomed. Perhaps Palila would too, given the chance.

He purposely took Polev and Naydra ahead with him on the ride back, to give Cluthine time to speak privately with Palila. By the time they reached the stables, she nodded success and asked him to escort her to the shops for ribbon to match her new gown. Polev was taken indoors by Naydra on the bribe of two stories and a game of blocks.

Cluthine waited until they had left the stables before saying, "Palila overheard Rinhoel say 'your mother's Merida blood' in conversation with Birioc. Thus he's Miyon's son by a Merida woman."

Rialt kicked at a loose cobblestone. "The least important aspect of it is military supplies—swords and shields. But in order to get them they'll need Tiglath to ship from. And

since Tuath is on the way, they'll probably take that, too. Damn!" He glared up at the gray afternoon sky. "I've got to get word to Pol!"

"Your Sunrunner is helpless until this gloom lifts. Would it be better to send a rider?"

"I don't know," Rialt said slowly. "Apart from the time involved, Chiana's people may be watching for a messenger. You know this area better than I. Do you think we'll get some sun in the next few days?"

"If the Goddess is good to us. I'll say a special prayer in the oratory tonight. And let's hope that Lord Andry uses his influence."

Rialt nodded, unwilling to discuss Cluthine's acceptance of the new aspect credited to Andry in his role as Lord of Goddess Keep. Intercessor with the Goddess? Absurd. But people believed it.

He left her to decide among various ribbons and made a brief detour to a nearby wineshop. The serving girl was married to one of Chiana's footmen, a young man on Mevita's list of friendlies. The girl agreed to get a message to his Sunrunner after dark. Rejoining Cluthine, he chose ribbons for his wife—and, on impulse, Palila—and they returned to the palace.

But that night he waited in vain at a little park near a broken section of Swalekeep's outer wall. It was long past midnight and hard rain was falling by the time he gave up. The next day he went to the man's lodgings. The *faradhi* lay in bed, eyes closed. The innkeeper herself had cleansed the blood from the head wound that had killed him.

"Cutpurses, my lord," she said. "He was found in the gutter yesterday sunset. But, bless the Lord Andry's grace, they didn't dare take his rings."

"Cutpurses, nothing!" Rialt fumed in private to Mevita. "Chiana had him murdered—our one link with Pol! Andry's not going to have her punishment, by the Goddess. I'll set her afire myself—while she's still breathing!"

* * *

Rohan was also contemplating physical mayhem, though nothing quite so drastic, as he paced furiously up and down the priceless carpets in Stronghold's Summer Room.

"I'll take him over my knee, prince or no prince. What does that fool think he's doing?"

"Rohan," his wife said reasonably, "there are times when I, too, would grab him by the ears and shake him—if I could reach up that far."

"He had his orders. Three days at the most—and it's been four! How dare he go out looking for a fight with the Vellant'im?" He whirled and stabbed an accusing finger at her. "You never made him swear, not you or Urival or Morwenna while you were training him! I should've let him go to Andry after all! *He* would have kicked some sense into him!"

The unfair indictment and the idiotic statement that followed lit Sioned's own temper. She damped it and answered in an only slightly raised voice, "I don't see what that has to do with anything. He's going out of his way to find a fight, but it's to use a sword, not sorcery."

"He's being willfully disobedient. He's ignoring direct orders. He—" Breaking off, he scowled at his sister, who was shaking with silent laughter. "What's so damned funny?"

"You." Tobin glanced at the windows, but the sparse sunlight was at an inconvenient angle. So, laboriously, she spoke aloud. "Chay said years ago . . . nothing *wrong* with Pol . . . polite, obedient . . . knew he'd g-grow out of it!"

Rohan snorted. "Well, he *has*. And I do *not* find it amusing."

All three of them jumped as the dragon horn sounded from the gatehouse. Sioned exchanged a glance with Tobin, both of them hoping Pol would understand his father's anger as only a natural expression of worry.

Wrong.

Pol and Kazander rode in laughing, in perfect charity with each other and the world. Their tired horses were led away to be adequately fed and watered for the first time in days. The soldiers saluted their High Prince and at his nod were released to go take their own ease. But Pol and Kazander bounded up the steps, obviously expecting to be hailed and welcomed and made much of.

"Father, you should've been there! They fell flat on their faces when Azhdeen flew over—and before they could get off their knees, we had them! Sorry we're late, but we chased a few stragglers halfway to Skybowl—they were so scared they went north instead of south!"

"Mighty *azhrei*, your humble servant bows to you in thanks for such excellent sport and in apology for not coming sooner with news of the victory gained in your noble grace's name."

Rohan surveyed them coolly for several moments, just long enough for their happy grins to fade. Sioned held her breath and silently begged her husband, *Don't say it!*

He never got the chance. A deep, querulous voice rose from the crowded courtyard: "Where's that foolish hatchling? Pol!"

Sioned exhaled in relief. Myrdal, ninety-two winters old and more autocratic with it than ever, stumped forward to the steps, her cane prodding people aside. Pol bent and enveloped her frail old bones in a careful embrace. Rohan's shoulders shifted in an irritated shrug, but the moment for lecturing Pol was gone.

But Pol had not missed the look in his father's eyes. Later, after the tale had been told—in Kazander's inimitable style—and the young men had bathed and eaten, Pol sought out his mother. She was alone in the library-office she shared with Rohan.

"Mother, what in all Hells is the matter with him?"

"Here it comes," she muttered to herself. She pushed aside the lists made by Feylin of stores and supplies—not a comforting total, considering the mouths to feed—leaned back in her seat, and gestured Pol to the chair opposite hers. Rohan's chair. When he hesitated, she arched a brow at him. "Oh, sit down. It'll be yours one day. You might as well get the feel of it."

The sunburn acquired out on the Long Sand deepened, but he sat. "Why is he so angry?"

"You're a smart boy. You figure it out."

"Oh, Goddess! Not you, too!"

"No," she admitted. "But I can see his point."

"So I was late. Don't the enemy dead count?" Then he made a face and answered his own question. "I know, I know—not when it was me out there leading the battle. What was I supposed to do, Mother? Let them get away?"

"Of course not. But you must understand how vital your safety is. If anything happened to you, your heirs are little girls barely eight winters old. That's the political side of it. The other. . . ." She sighed quietly. "I kept an eye on you out there, but—"

"—but why didn't I keep you informed? Either I'm a prince or I'm not, Mother. Either I lead or I don't."

"Rohan let you go against his better judgment, against his deepest feelings—"

Pol frowned. "*Let* me go? Ah. I understand. Give the prize stud a good run every so often to make him think he's still free, but keep an iron hand on the reins just the same." He rose. "Thank you for making it clear, Mother. I'm in your debt."

"Pol—"

"If the stallion doesn't behave himself and ride where he's reined, will you geld him?"

"Stop it!" she ordered. "If you equate manhood with using a sword, then you've spent thirty-three years not listening to a word any of us have said! You don't need reining, you need a curb bit and spurs dug into your stubborn ribs!"

"Why is Maarken allowed to do what's forbidden to me?" he challenged.

"Because he's expendable," she answered brutally. "You're not."

"And when the Vellanti army comes here, as we all know it will? Will everyone be sacrificed to my safety? All of Stronghold? All these people, expendable?"

She met his gaze steadily. "Down to your father and me."

"I don't accept!" He leaned over, bracing his fists on the parchment-strewn desk. "That's not what being a prince is. I've been well-schooled, Mother. I've listened. There hasn't been a major war since Roelstra died because Father doesn't fight with swords—he uses himself as the battlefield. His mind, his feelings, his skills as a prince. He fights that way so his people don't have to take up arms. That's his sacrifice—don't think I don't know what it's cost him. Well, now it *has* come to swords. There's no way to avoid it. Are you saying that after all you've taught me, I must be less of a prince than he?"

Sioned knew she was too angry and frightened to find the correct reply. Pol was right. So was Rohan. And damn them both for it.

"I was never educated in the fine points of cowering in a corner," Pol said quietly. "Don't ask me to learn now."

She drew in a deep, almost painful breath. "I must ask

something of you. It won't be easy but it's the one chance to make peace with your father. If you—"

"I know what you want," he interrupted. "I can't give it to you. I won't swear your oath, Mother. I need all I am to defend my people and my princedom."

She bent her head. "Then there's nothing more I can say."

"I suppose not." He started for the door, his bootheels emphatic. She glanced up as he hesitated, saw him turn, his blue-green eyes shadowy. "Mother . . . you must have known what you did when you took me from Ianthe. You must have known what I'd become. You *made* me, you and Father and Urival and Chay and all the others—all I'm asking is that you have faith in what you created."

"Never think that I don't."

"Then let me be what I am."

She had never asked that for herself. In childhood she hadn't known what she was. After she found out at Goddess Keep, marriage had given her another identity, one that clashed with the *faradhi*, one that Andrade deplored even though she had been its cause. *Princess or Sunrunner?* was always the Lady's question. *Both*, Sioned always replied—but princess first, the princess Rohan had taught her to be. But Pol was prince, Sunrunner, and sorcerer, all three.

"Mother," he was saying, "do me and yourself the honor of believing I can use what I am with wisdom."

"It's not that. It's—" She stopped, helpless.

"What, then? Help me understand. Is Father angry because he thinks I was in danger—or because he perceives another disobedience? I never swore the oath and I never will. It's not childishness or spite. I *can't* give up anything that gives me a weapon to use against these people."

"You can't use it alone."

"There must be other gifted people somewhere who understand necessity."

She tried one last time. "Rohan knows how to make war. As you pointed out, he *hasn't* for the length of your life. There must be another way for you, too. There has to be a way that doesn't twist the *faradhi* part of you. Please, Pol—I won't ask a formal swearing, just a promise to me and your father in private. Please." Sioned was trembling with the effort at control. "I'm frightened for you, my dearest—I

don't want the joy of being a Sunrunner to turn bitter for you, with the memory of deaths—"

"Andry doesn't seem bothered."

"Andry is not my son!"

Pol gave her a thin smile. "So. Somebody finally admits that Andry is expendable, too."

"Pol!"

But he was out the door, heedless of her frantic cry. Sioned slammed both fists hard on the desktop, rattling inkwells and loose pens and the boxes containing their various seals.

"Damn," she said wearily, all the strength gone out of her. "Oh, damn."

* * *

Their speech was so thick Andry could barely understand them. None had more than a few gold tokens in his beard, though one of those beards was liberally streaked with gray. There had been eight of them originally; on the way through the forest, Andry saw the corpses of the three Oclel had killed.

The Sunrunners were herded along at swordpoint. None of their captors dared get closer than that—not after two Andrys faced them in the clearing.

Andry mimicked Rusina's limp as they walked. Her changing was perfect, down to the color of the eyes. They both wore riding gauntlets, which effectively hid their rings and his wristbands. There had been some argument among the Vellant'im, difficult for Andry to follow, that Rusina must be the true and he the false image, for she had on the white cloak by which they had identified Andry from the trees. But nothing had come of it. Their prize, the Lord of Goddess Keep—whichever one was really he—was too valuable to make guesses. They would wait and see which lost the shape during sleep.

They were taken to the north edge of the woods, where seven horses were tethered. Three of them belonged to Goddess Keep. Andry glanced at his own blue eyes and saw his own head nod bitterly. No riderless mounts would gallop back home to alert Torien to danger.

It was hard, watching the eldest of the men climb into his own Tibaza's saddle. As Rusina was prodded toward an-

other horse, she stumbled on her bad ankle and cried out—but her voice was low and deeper than her own, not quite a man's but not wholly a woman's, either. Andry marveled at the liquid ice that must run through her veins.

They descended the cliffs and rode along the beach. The Vellant'im were smug and excited, despite the shock of two Andrys. That they had not fled in terror told him they were familiar with *diarmadhi* tricks. Yet no sorcery had been used in battle—thus far—and the puzzle of it would not form a logical pattern in his mind.

What he *did* know was that the Goddess had in a bizarre manner put him by way of some answers. As the enemy talked among themselves, he learned that they had been left behind after the battle at Goddess Keep, and had been surviving ever since by stealing. They must move more silently than the sunlight, he thought. Then again, with all the people crowding around the area these days, who would notice a few thefts?

They came to a narrow cave and dismounted. Within, cold and sea-damp, Andry and Rusina were gestured to sit on flat rocks circling a dead fire pit. The horses were urged back into the darkness, and ropes slung around stones to keep them penned. There was the smell of fish and salt, and, from the back of the high-ceilinged cavern, human and equine waste. Rusina nearly gagged as a gust of wind from an unseen chimney blew the stench over them.

The Vellant'im then left them, one man remaining by the cave mouth as guard. Andry looked himself in the face.

"Quick thinking," he said with hardly any voice.

She shrugged beneath his white cloak.

"I'll get us out of this."

"Until you do, give me the *dranath*."

He passed over the little scrap of parchment. She choked down half the drug and within moments he felt the impact of a strengthened illusion. She was delicately made and not a tall woman, but now there was not the slightest difference in their forms. Except that she was shivering.

He conjured Fire and warmed his hands at it. After a little while the convulsive tremors left her. She bent her head, but not before he saw the gleam of tears.

"I'm sorry. He was dear to me, too."

She made no reply.

"Take off your gloves and rings." He stripped off his

own, and the wrist bands. She tore off a piece of her undertunic to tie them in along with her own. "We have to escape before either of us gets too tired."

"With this much *dranath* in me, do you think I could sleep?"

"But we have to learn as much as we can," he went on. "They're left-overs from the battle, cut off from the main army's retreat. They don't think I can understand their language. They might let something slip."

"By all means."

"You know why I have to stay as long as I can, don't you? I may learn something I can use, something about their plans, their origins—"

"You don't need to justify yourself to me."

He bit his lip. "Why did you do this?"

The eyes that stared at him were his, but the incredulity in them was her own.

"You didn't want the daughter I gave you. You don't have much use for me at all, in fact. Why save my skin?"

"Because you are what you are."

Simple answer, implying more loyalty than he'd ever expected from this prickly woman. But not to him personally, as was the case with Torien and Nialdan and the others of his *devr'im*. He was Lord of Goddess Keep. Had he been Rohan or Pol, the loyalty would have been for him alone, out of love. But this would do. It would have to.

* * *

The Vellant'im had found the little spring, just as Maarken hoped. They would have been blind not to—he had practically led them by the beard. His own people had watered there the previous day, and according to the plan ought to have been far away by now, back across the Long Sand headed toward Stronghold. But during the rare moment of ease and coolness in the midday heat, Maarken had first toyed with and then presented the idea of an ambush. His two senior warriors, one from Radzyn and the other from Remagev, considered, glanced at each other, and nodded.

Chay's man, Abigroy, said, "It'll spare us having to look over our shoulders so much, my lord, if we're rid of them now. I say we do it."

"Yes," drawled Catla, idly stroking the embroidered blue

and white badge of rank on her sleeve. "Never much fancied bearded men, myself—saving my Lord Walvis, that is."

As new Battle Commander of the Desert, Maarken could have ordered anything he pleased. But he knew the way his father had done things, and could not imagine any improvement on Chay's style of asking how his people felt about a tactic rather than informing them of the course they would follow. Besides, he didn't have an autocratic bone in his body; all Tobin's taste for absolute command seemed to have gone to Andry.

So Maarken's soldiers crouched behind the escarpment above the spring while the enemy drank so much water that they sloshed when they walked. Maarken had left his horses half a measure away, intending to collect them riding the recaptured Radzyn mounts of the enemy. His father would appreciate that. Sometimes he thought Chay was more upset by the loss of his treasured horses than of Radzyn itself.

Bellies full, the Vellant'im stretched out for a brief rest in what little shade was provided by overhanging rocks and exactly four dry, stunted trees. The spring barely merited the name—a feeble burble perhaps the size of a man's circled arms—but to a traveler through the Long Sand, it was as wide as Lake Kadar. Rohan had said the Desert would do their work for them, that they knew this land and the enemy did not. Maarken nodded to himself and ran his thumb lightly along his sword blade. The Desert offered only this miniscule spring and handspan of shade, but it had also provided measure upon measure of barren sand that made them seductive out of all proportion. No shimmer-vision could have done the work as well.

A heat-dazzle was exactly what the Vellanti warriors thought they saw when Maarken's troops appeared suddenly on the opposite side of the spring.

Later, when the little spring and the sand around it was dyed red, Maarken gave Catla the lightning bolt badge taken off the Vellanti leader. It was enameled gold, fine work and very valuable. "Souvenir of how much fun you had—don't try to deny it."

They collected anything else that might be interesting or useful, gathered the horses, left the corpses in the sand for the Desert that had given them the victory, and started for home.

* * *

Neither Andry nor Rusina had any trouble staying awake that night. She had the *dranath* in her blood, keeping her restless and at times jumpy; he had his conjured Fire to maintain, keeping his mind occupied and his body warm.

Long after midnight, as near as Andry could judge, the Vellant'im came back in excellent spirits. Nervous eyes still glanced sideways at the doubled image seated by the fire pit, but not even this could dampen their enthusiasm.

Andry listened, keeping his expression neutral, as they talked among themselves about the journey to be undertaken at dawn. They would go north, find a suitably isolated spot in Grib where a signal fire would be lit, and their ships in Brochwell Bay alerted. The shame of having been left behind would be canceled by the glory of having captured the Lord of Goddess Keep. They intended to present him—the real one of him—to the High Warlord.

Andry mulled that over while the horses were saddled. Absolutely insane even to consider allowing himself to be taken that far—but it was tempting. To meet at last the sorcerer, for sorcerer he must be, responsible for this carnage. To execute him personally with his own people's spells. The stuff of which legends were made.

His lips twisted wry acknowledgment of his own stupidity. What did he think, that he could battle this man as Pol had fought Ruval?

One of the men approached the fire pit. He hesitated, brows bunching above black eyes wary of the Sunrunners. Another strode up beside him and snarled, "*Faradh'im!*" and spat into the flames. Then he hauled Andry up—the first time either of them had been touched by these people—and held a sleek steel knife to Andry's throat.

His pockets were emptied. Then the same was done to Rusina. The parchment of *dranath* was thrown into the fire, where it flared crimson. The rings were distributed among the Vellant'im but not tied into their beards. Instead, they were jammed onto thick fingers—Rusina's not going past the first knuckle—silver and gold gleaming with reflected firelight. Andry's armbands were claimed by the leader, who slipped them on and admired the rich glitter of their gems.

Then a very strange thing happened. A man began rubbing at the finger wearing one of Rusina's rings. He frowned and chafed the gold. Andry glanced at his *devri* and caught

his breath. These people *were* sorcerers—some of them, at least. And in the presence of Rusina's spell, the Sunrunner ring burned.

The man grunted in pain and shook his hand free of the ring, throwing it onto the fire. His gaping companions cried out as flames spat white light the breadth of the cave. Horses squealed, jostling each other as chill Fire from Sunrunner's gold lashed the darkness in the shape of a raging dragon.

"Hurry!" Rusina shouted.

Andry leaped for the horses behind him, yanking the ropes free and grabbing Tibaza's reins. He was in the saddle instantly, his cheek pressed to the pale hide as he urged the stallion forward.

The Vellant'im were rooted to the damp sand by terror. All but one of them. A knife gouged through the flames into Rusina's breast. She staggered, sobbing her agony in tortured gasps. Andry snagged her wrist, trying to drag her up into the saddle. He looked down at her and shuddered. It was not given to most men to see their own eyes in death.

All the light was suddenly gone and the other horses surged past, screaming for their freedom. Tibaza was pulled along with them despite Andry's frantic efforts. Rocks dug into Andry's left leg as it was crushed against the cave wall, tearing bone-deep.

Abruptly he was outside. He pushed himself upright, vaguely startled to find he sprawled on the sand. Tibaza was long gone with the other horses, racing down the beach under a cloud-pale night sky backlit by the moons.

Andry stumbled on his injured leg back toward the cave. Every thought brought an ache, centered in a throbbing at the back of his skull. Bracing himself against the rocks, he conjured a fingerflame with terrible difficulty and sent it into the darkness.

A moan of pain found echo deeper within the cave. Andry followed the little Fire cautiously, and called Rusina's name.

Not that he expected any answer.

By moonsfall he had tied the wrists and ankles of the two men left alive. Rusina lay frail and lifeless near the Fire he'd called to work by. The knife wound that had killed her and the brutal evidence of hooves were hidden beneath his white cloak. He stood gazing at her, swaying a little, telling him-

self he ought to start back for Goddess Keep now, bring people here for the dead and the prisoners, and have someone do something about his leg and the horrendous pain in his head.

But it only got worse as he tried to tell his feet to move, and he supposed he'd better sit down . . . rest for a little while. . . .

Chapter Twenty-two

By means of heroic effort, a safe-conduct through Vellanti lines, and a little horse-stealing, Birioc made excellent time back to Cunaxa. On the way down to Swalekeep he'd come through the Great Veresch Mountains of Princemarch. But on the way back, a token given him by Lord Varek—a tiny silver dragon with enameled green wings—enabled him to cut across the Vere Hills and through the Desert. The only potential danger had been a distant sight of troops riding west to Stronghold. A red-and-orange banner floating on the slight breeze like a flame proclaimed them under the command of Lord Maarken of Whitecliff; Birioc fled to a convenient rocky dune and huddled there until nightfall. It cost him half a day and a bellyful of regret that his escort was too small to dare a raid, but soon, he promised himself. Very soon.

On reaching Cunaxa, he did not go to his father at Castle Pine. He rode straight to his own manor of Catchwater, where his Merida uncles waited. After reporting success, he slept from sundown of one day to noon of the next and rose to find that an army of over three hundred had been assembled almost overnight.

"Riders have gone to the other holdings," said his eldest uncle as Birioc wolfed a meal of cooked grains, venison, and wine. "And to Castle Pine, to empty the armory. Miyon will have no choice but to join us."

"I hope somebody explained to him that I'm to be made his heir—in writing, with all his seals."

Urstra shrugged. "If not at once, then certainly after Tuath is taken. He may suspect that your half-brothers will die of Cunaxan and not Desert steel, but once they are dead, what can he do?"

"You don't understand my father. Now that we're grown, the only hold he has over us is the fact that he hasn't named his heir. He thinks we'll behave ourselves because of it. I may end up being the only one left, but unless he sticks to the law and does it properly, I won't be secure."

"Rohan's law!" Urstra spat. "Who will dare argue with the acclamation you'll receive as the victor of Tuath and Tiglath?"

"My half-sister Meiglan's children at Dragon's Rest, that's who. Or, rather, people on their behalf. And don't tell me it won't matter because Pol will be dead—he's got plenty of powerful kinsmen who'll go to war for them. I want it done legally. I want to be named Miyon's heir."

Urstra shrugged. "Very well. Are you finished? We cannot march until. . . ." He rubbed the scar on his chin meaningfully.

Birioc dressed in the brown and yellow of his mother's people. In front of the Merida warriors assembled he stripped off shirt and tunic and extended his arms straight out to his sides. In one fist was a sword; in the other, a handful of Desert sand. He welcomed the sting of the ritual glass knife and the drip of blood onto his bare chest, and especially the roar of his name that rose from more than three hundred throats.

But what he expected to hear next was not forthcoming. As he mounted a fine Radzyn warhorse to lead his people to victory at Tuath, he cast a dark glance at his uncles. Urstra correctly interpreted the look.

"We'll wait for Miyon's legal choosing—as you desired," he said with a tiny smile. "Then we'll see if the circle fits."

Birioc clamped his teeth shut over a sharp answer and nodded. His own fault, he told himself angrily, that the ancient crown did not rest on his brow today. Rohan's damned laws had affected even Merida ways of thinking.

* * *

Sionell could hear her brother's cold fury even though the words had been filtered through two *faradh'im*. Jahnavi intended to slaughter every last one of the Merida host now riding for Tuath, and if Tallain wanted in on the action he'd better hurry. Jahnavi wouldn't wait for him.

"Will you go, my lord?" the Sunrunner asked after finishing the report.

"Certainly. I wouldn't miss it." Turning to Sionell, he added, "Your little brother inherited your mother's temper."

"He's not so little anymore, Tallain."

"I'm reminded every time we cross swords in the practice yard." He smiled, but his eyes were shadowy. "Vamanis, is there an accurate count of Merida yet?"

"I'll ask, my lord."

While he worked, Tallain drummed his fingers on the wooden balcony railing, intricately carved and painted in Tiglath's blue and yellow. Crystal finials glittered in brilliant sunlight that did not, unfortunately, shine on Stronghold. Haze obscured the keep. He and Jahnavi were on their own, with no chance of advice from Rohan or Chay. But he trusted his instincts and his training at their hands.

"Three hundred, my lord, with half that number setting out from Castle Pine. They can't all be Merida, can they? Lord Walvis wiped out most of them thirty years ago."

"Thirty years is time enough to breed an army. Well, well. Four hundred fifty. Jahnavi's got less than a third of that—but he also has Tuath's walls."

"He won't settle for a siege," Sionell said quietly. "I know him. He'll lead the charge himself."

Tallain nodded. "Downhill, tomorrow morning, with the sun glaring in the enemy's eyes. He knows what he's doing."

"Do you mind if I worry just a little?" she asked tartly.

"As long as it's *just* a little. Vamanis, my compliments to my wife's brother and a promise to be there with my hundred and fifty tomorrow morning."

When the Sunrunner left them, they lingered on the roof, gazing out at their city. Tiglath had prospered under Tallain's rule and that of his late father, Eltanin. Flatboats plied the shallow cove that was the Desert's only northern harbor, enabling Dorval's great merchant ships to anchor out in safe waters while trade goods were brought to them. The Cunaxans paid dearly for the privilege of shipping this way rather than by caravan through the Veresch. With this wealth, Tallain and Sionell had indulged themselves—not with expensive trinkets, but with schools, a scriptorium, an infirmary, and modern drainage and refuse systems. The last were at Sionell's insistence, for she had a sensitive nose.

"I'm glad the Dorvali left yesterday," Tallain said suddenly. "Chadric's restlessness was beginning to worry me."

"Do you think he would have gone with you to fight?"

"I would've had to find some tactful way of preventing him. He still can't accept that there was nothing else he could do except leave Graypearl. Or that Ludhil's only choice was to stay behind."

Sionell looked up in surprise. "You mean he's *ashamed?* That's absurd! Nobody could have stopped them."

"Meath seemed to think *he* could have. Or should have. Or something." Tallain sighed. "The Goddess was good to me when she made me neither Sunrunner nor prince. I like life simple."

"If going to help Jahnavi break Merida heads is your notion of 'simple,' spare me anything complex."

Tallain pulled her to him. "War *is* simple, compared to rule. But being prince or *faradhi*—I don't envy Pol, who's both."

"He's fool enough to thrive on it." She rubbed her cheek against his tunic. "I'll miss you."

"It'll only be a few days. Rohan says he avoids wars because he hates not sleeping in his own bed with his wife. I know what he means."

"And on such selfishness, the fate of princedoms turns! All right then, a few days. Send them back to Cunaxa where they belong."

"No, love," Tallain said gently. "They must die. All of them. And then—orders or no—I'm going to Stronghold with all the troops that can be spared from protecting the north. Rohan's going to need everyone."

Sionell was silent for a moment. "Send Jahnavi. He's my brother and I love him, but he's young and impulsive, as you said. Yours is the cooler head. He can follow orders, but I'd rather trust the defense of the north to you."

"Once the Merida are crushed, regular patrols will suffice here." He gave her a quizzical smile. "Or is it that *you* don't like not sleeping next to *me?*"

"You, who come to bed with frozen feet I'm supposed to warm?"

"It'll only be a few days," he said again, bending to kiss her lips. "A little longer at Stronghold. If Kostas heads east soon to retake the Faolain, they'll be caught between."

"If." She shook off the bleakness and smiled. "Very well,

go save Stronghold single-handed. I promise not to gloat too much. It's unseemly."

* * *

Andry woke in his own bed. How he had come to be there was a total mystery solved only when Valeda crept in, saw he was conscious, and sat beside him on the bed, holding his hand.

"Tibaza came back all sea-wet and sandy. That was three mornings ago. We searched the coastline and found you and Rusiña toward noon. You've been lying here half-dead ever since."

Andry nodded, then regretted it as the movement set up a pounding in his head. "Goddess!" he breathed. "Give me something for this—"

She gave him a cup of drugged wine. He drank, sank back, and shut his eyes.

"We found Oclel, too," she murmured. "He and Rusina burned together last night."

"You should have waited."

"We couldn't. Oclel . . . had already been partially burned, but what remained had been lying in the forest for too long."

The wine threatened to come up again. Andry gulped it back down. He made brief, bitter work of what had happened, and finished with, "What about the Vellant'im?"

"The dead at the cave we gave to the sea. One of the others died this morning. The other is still alive, but—"

"Keep him so," Andry ordered grimly.

Her hand tightened on his. "I'll do my best. You should sleep now, Andry."

"Later. Who knows about this?"

"No one outside these walls."

"See that it stays that way. Bring the prisoner to me for questioning."

"He won't answer. He was trampled by half a dozen horses. Torien tried to get sense out of him, with Jolan translating. It was no use."

"Then all he's good for is executing. Tomorrow, Valeda," he said as the wine started to muddle his tongue. "Tomorrow assemble everyone . . . outside the walls . . . Sunrunners and common."

"Yes, of course. Tomorrow or the next day. Sleep now, my Lord."

* * *

It was a long climb up spiral stairs to the top of the Flametower, but from there one could see halfway across the Long Sand—or at least as far as the small Vellanti encampment halfway to Rivenrock. Kazander found the view breathtaking and said so. Chayla merely shrugged.

"Sometimes I've seen the Sunrise Water from here. You should come up when there's no overcast."

"But only by night," he said, wiping his brow. "We use the fire as a beacon, but I never considered that it turns this room into an oven."

Staring out at the little enclave of tents, sweat trickling down her back from the heat behind her, she was quiet for a time. Kazander respected her silence; for all that he chattered in the most outrageous language most of the time, with her he held his tongue unless he had something important to say.

He and Pol had come back with their souvenirs, Sethric with his, and Lord Maarken with plenty more. But they knew only a little more about the Vellant'im because of them—mainly that some of the older warriors carried little dragons of wood, ceramic, or enameled metal, possibly further tokens of valor or rank. Rohan now had a collection of twenty-seven, all different, all exquisite. The enigmatic beasts stretched their wings on his desk; Chayla had caught him staring at them this morning. As if they could speak to him the way Azhdeen spoke to Pol, she thought. As if they could tell him how to defeat this puzzling enemy.

Chayla watched them go about their business within their outpost: polishing swords, readying the evening meal, exercising their horses—Grandsir Chay's horses, she reminded herself. How long would it be before the main army arrived from Radzyn and Remagev? It was Walvis' opinion that the deadfalls set into the latter had convinced them that it was a place worth thorough investigation, which would take time. The longer the better; once the levies from Tuath and Tiglath arrived, they would have a fighting chance.

The inevitable results of battle reminded her of why she'd wanted to speak with Kazander in the first place. Abruptly,

wanting to get it over with, she said, "Your man Hevlain. I'm sorry, my lord, but there wasn't anything more we could do for him. He died this morning."

His dark head bent for a moment, and then he nodded. "I will send his ashes to our family."

"He was a cousin?"

"My mother's brother's wife's sister's son, and wed to my father's father's sister's granddaughter."

Chayla frowned, trying to puzzle out the relationship. "A cousin," she said at last.

"In your terms, yes. But then, so are you and I, my lady."

She glanced up. "Let me guess—your six-times great-grandfather's half-brother's wife's brother's son married my five-times great-grandmother's sister's granddaughter!"

Kazander's eyes glinted with humor. "Something like that. But we *are* kin, you know. Zehava acknowledged the relationship when my grandfather fought at his side against the Merida. I could even style myself *athri,* though I have no walls to be lord of. My holding is the Desert itself—but perhaps I *do* have walls." His voice changed, became dreamy with thoughts of his home. "My walls are bright wool sewn with silver thread, and at their gates are chimes made of sand-jade so the Desert may speak to us, sing to us, warn us. My keep is made of silk woven of sunlight. Within are lamps that turn darkness to gold and roses, a light soft as dawn."

"I'd like to see all that one day," she said impulsively. "It sounds so free, Kazander—no walls, no responsibilities. . . ."

"I would like you to know these things. The Desert you have never seen or heard, the heritage of our shared blood."

It was suddenly cooler, as if the fire behind her had been gentled by the hand of the breeze that caressed her brow, her lips. She felt herself drifting like a feather on that breeze, although she was positive she had not moved except to close her eyes.

"Look," Kazander said, breaking the spell. "Riders."

She squinted into the haze. "Oh, Goddess—if the Vellant'im see them, they're dead. Come on!"

Their timely warning saved the four men. Sethric led a mounted contingent down from Stronghold to the sand, which discouraged enemy interest in the new arrivals. The young Gribain was disappointed that there was no skirmish,

but Meath—for that was who rode in, filthy and exhausted, with an escort of three Dorvali—thanked him profoundly.

"If you hadn't outnumbered them so handily, they might have risked it. And I'm much too old for that sort of thing. You must be Lord Sethric—I'd heard you were at Remagev, and I recognize the Gribain curls," he added with a tired smile and a glance at the young man's riotous black hair. "I'll express my gratitude more fully later, my lord, but for now I need to see—ah, Sioned, here you are!"

She was enveloped in his embrace and when he let her go, leaned up to kiss him. "Meath! It's good to have you safe. Did Chadric make it to Skybowl all right?"

"As far as I know. If the sky clears tonight I'll have a look." He hugged her to him again. "Goddess blessing to you, too, Sunrunner. There's a lot to tell, but I'm starving and I stink."

He gave her the most important news on their way upstairs. "Tiglath's walls have been fortified and all the levies are assembled. Tallain's just waiting for word from Rohan to be on the march. I left Chadric about fifty measures from Skybowl—he ought to have arrived yesterday at the latest, even considering the trouble some of his people are giving him."

"What trouble? Here's your room—food first, or a bath?"

"Food!" he replied urgently; she laughed and gestured to a servant outside in the hall. Meath continued, "The trouble is that some of the merchants regret the wealth they've lost more than they're grateful for the lives they've still got. Audrite deals with them mostly, but every so often they get to Chadric and it nearly crushes him, that he failed to protect them."

"Idiots. When I can talk to Riyan, I'll tell him to mention that the High Prince is a generous man who sympathizes with their losses. Will that shut them up, do you think?"

"It's worth a try. They're scared, of course, and utterly lost away from the sea. Which I was glad enough to leave behind me."

"I'll just bet. I hope you have clothes in your saddlebags. I don't have anything big enough to fit you." She surveyed him critically. "Or maybe I do. You're thinner."

"Not for long." And he pounced on the tray brought in by a page.

While he ate, Sioned readied his bath. That the High

Princess should be doing this herself rather than having a servant do it held a significance that finally got through to Meath, once his stomach stopped growling. Washing down a meat pasty with a hearty swallow of wine, he stopped eating long enough to ask, "What is it, Sioned?"

"What's what?"

His turn to take stock of her, and what he saw worried him. She, too, was thinner, and her firegold hair was streaked with white. New lines had appeared around her eyes and across her brow; her skin, not as fragile as most redheads', was pallid beneath the Desert's sun-glossing. And her eyes were darker, older with the attempt to hide pain and fear.

He'd last seen her in person four years ago. Though Meath fervently avoided the crossing to Radzyn, Rohan had marked his thirty-fifth year as ruling prince with an elaborate celebration that included as many friends and relations as possible. The gown Sioned wore at the banquet, green and gold sewn with hundreds of tiny crystals that shimmered with her every movement, had been Meath's doing, as had Rohan's dark blue tunic and silvery shirt. He had asked Meath to choose Sioned's silk himself and keep it a secret; she had given him a similar commission in equal secrecy, and he'd had a good laugh when each discovered the other's trick. How beautiful they had been, Sioned sparkling like a sun-misted forest, Rohan her perfect foil—crowned and jeweled and requiring neither, mated in all things, as matched as lovers' clasped hands.

There was little of that regal elegance about her now. It wasn't the clothes—she could look more of a princess in riding leathers than any other woman in full court dress. It was the way she moved, the way she held her shoulders, the lack of her usual swift grace. Meath was afraid he would find Rohan in a similar state. When Sioned stayed silent, he guessed that Rohan was the primary cause of her concern.

"I've known you too long," he said. "Rohan, too. What's bothering you about him?"

She perched on the large bed and hugged a pillow to her chest. "It's not him—or not *just* him. It's Pol. They barely speak to each other."

"Why? They've always thought almost alike on just about everything."

"Not on this. Not when it comes to war."

"Tell me," he said.

"I—"

He cursed under his breath as the page knocked on the door for permission to take the tray. Sioned encouraged Meath to take his time in the bath and send word when he was ready to see Rohan and the others. Then she escaped him. He didn't know if she was sorry or relieved that the opportunity to talk had passed; he did know that it was unlike her to walk up to a thing and then back away. Sioned was a woman who dealt with difficulties by slamming her head against them until they collapsed. He had never seen her frightened of them before.

But in the time it took to tell his news to Rohan as Pol, Chay, Walvis, and Feylin listened, he began to understand why she was afraid. There was a chill in the Summer Room, and it emanated from the High Prince and his heir. Meath was disgusted with them both.

He said as much to Maarken later in the grotto. "Proud, arrogant, stubborn, willful, stone-headed—" He silenced himself with a long pull at a wineskin, and glared at the thin trickle of the waterfall.

"Accurate, if redundant," Maarken commented.

Meath stretched saddle soreness from his legs and scrunched down against a rock dry-furred with moss. "This is the only privacy left at Stronghold, isn't it?"

"Just about—except for a bath. But so many strangers are here who don't know their way around that Hollis was almost surprised in the tub the other day. Stronghold was built to hold an army, but my grandmother changed a lot of it over the years. We've had to pack people in like silk bolts in a crate. Pass the wine."

Meath obliged. "Skybowl won't be much better. At least here there aren't any weeping merchants."

"They'll settle down, once they're assured Rohan will compensate them."

He accepted the wineskin back, drank, and glanced around the grotto. He'd never seen Stronghold in winter, and it was somehow more bleak even than in the heat of high summer. Not until spring snowmelt would the waterfall and Princess Milar's fountain run again, or the mosses plump out pillow-soft, or the poor thirsty roses and grasses and fruit trees awaken.

"Have they been at each other's throats yet?" Meath asked suddenly.

Maarken knew his meaning. "Not publicly. But when it comes to a battle here, I'm afraid it'll all be out in the open. Pol wants to use sorcery the way Andry did. To kill. He never took the oath and won't now. I think he *respects* us for keeping our vows, but he's also contemptuous and a little angry."

"He never knew the discipline of Goddess Keep, as we did. The only discipline he knows is his own. He's a good man, he's got a conscience. But I can understand how hard this has hit him."

"His failure at Radzyn most of all. It rankles that Andry succeeded at Goddess Keep." Maarken sighed. "I wish I knew where it was they parted. They were friends when they were little."

"Does it matter when it happened? The number of years don't count when the jealousy runs that deep. It can happen in an instant and last a lifetime."

Maarken stared up at the cloud-shadowed moons. "That's what scares me. And it can't be like that, Meath. We can't afford it."

"But they both want things their own way."

"Rohan's the only one who can hold them both in check. Andry swore to him, not to Pol, about the *ros'salath*. Not to use it except in defense of Goddess Keep." Maarken paused then shrugged again. "The last few days I've wondered what's holding Rohan together."

"Sioned."

Maarken shook his head. "I've lost count of how many directions she's being pulled in. There's Rohan, and Pol, and her Sunrunner training, and her knowledge of the Star Scroll, and being furious with Andry even while she still cares about him."

"Chay says your mother is the only one of you he'll talk to."

"So far. I think he'd accept Hollis, possibly me, if we ever get some sun again. Goddess! Never in my life have I been so conscious of the sky—or how vulnerable we Sunrunners are." He gestured to the moons that glowed behind the haze. "Look at them. They're up there—I can see them, feel them, almost smell them. But they might as well not exist for all the use they are right now. Always before, you just waited for the next day or the next night, or the one

after. Nothing was so urgent that it couldn't keep. But this—this is maddening."

"Clouds don't last forever."

"Not here. But it's almost winter. The whole Veresch, Goddess Keep, Kierst-Isel, all those places are blocked off most of the season. And Cunaxa—Goddess, I wish I knew what in all Hells was happening in Cunaxa!"

"It'll still be there in a few days, when the sun comes back."

"Yes—but how much of it will have spilled over onto our lands?" He reached for the wine again. "The Vellant'im have some kind of connection with the Merida. We have no idea what it might be. Through sorcery, perhaps. But nobody really knows. It'd be nice to know who it is I'm fighting."

"Would you like a list?"

Maarken snorted. "You mean, add Chiana to it? That's another thing that makes me half insane. We all know damned well she's bedded down with the enemy. Rialt is in Swalekeep and we can't reach him to confirm it. Tilal and Ostvel could march on her from Waes—but you know Rohan. He'll want proof. I'm not so sure Kostas will adhere to the same morals, though, and that might be all for the best. And now I'm talking like Pol—abandoning everything that makes us civilized for the sake of fighting these barbarians *as* barbarians."

"Oh, it's just that you're not drunk enough yet. Have some more wine."

"No, thanks. I'll have to go stick my head into a trough and chew a *pemric* seed before I go up to Hollis." He heaved himself to his feet and tossed the wineskin down to Meath. "Here. Enjoy. It's almost the last of the Syrene gold."

"Go away," Meath said, waving him off. "I was depressed before I got here, and now I'm beginning to wish I'd stayed on Dorval."

Maarken gave him a tired smile and left him. Meath settled back to savor the Syrene vintage in peace when light footsteps crunched the gravel path. Glancing up, he instantly recognized the gleam of fair hair going silver, and nodded thoughtfully to himself. Yes, Rohan was due to be next. He only hoped he could have a night's sleep before Pol's turn came.

"Any of that left?" said the High Prince as he sat lightly on the dry moss.

"Some." Meath gave over the wineskin and conjured a fingerflame to see by. Not that Rohan's face revealed much, except when he was tired, but Meath usually needed all the clues he could get to this man. Friendship only went so far; even Chay complained that Rohan was always at least a half-step ahead of him and rarely waited for him to catch up.

But tonight Rohan was weary indeed, or he wouldn't have been so blunt. "I'm glad you're here, Meath. Nobody else can talk sense into Pol. Maybe you can."

"Maarken's told me. Actually, I'm not surprised that you and Pol disagree. But it's gone too far, hasn't it?"

"Much." Raking one hand back through his hair, Rohan met his gaze and in the flicker of Fire Meath saw anguish in his eyes. "I was outnumbered at Radzyn. I had to fight at Remagev. I lost. So I gave up Remagev too, and trusted it and the Desert to do my work for me."

Meath heard the repetition of *I*—as if there had been no one else there, as if Rohan had fought this war alone.

"Meath, I can't and won't give up Stronghold. It's not just sentiment or stubbornness. It's symbolism—for if Stronghold falls, my power is gone. The power Pol says I'm frightened of using."

Meath blinked. "Frightened? You?"

"Oh, yes." A chill smile touched his lips. "There's much about me my son doesn't understand, but he knows that much. If I lose Stronghold—the High Prince who couldn't even hang onto his own castle? My authority vanishes if Stronghold falls. And after this is over, I'd have to build from the ground up again. I did it once—I don't know that I have patience or strength to do it again. You tell me Tallain has rebuilt the wall his father left in rubble. That was a symbol, too."

"I know," the Sunrunner said quietly. "Walls stronger than mere stone."

"Yes. But the walls I made are useless now. So you see I have to fight and I have to win. There's no other choice."

"And you're tempted to let Pol try the *ros'salath*. The sorcerer's wall."

"Tempted? More than I can say. It's not *my* oath. And

he's pointed out it's not his, either." There was a slight pause. "Would you do it if I ordered it?"

The crisp, brutal simplicity of the question shook him to his bones. All at once he understood Maarken's deepest fear: obey the prince he loved or his Sunrunner vows? Use what he was in defense of his world and thereby betray what he was, or do nothing and watch that world destroyed?

Rohan was smiling again, without bitterness. "I thought as much. Forgive me. I won't ask again, Meath."

"No—Rohan, it's just—I need a little time to think."

"Seductive, isn't it? Forswear yourself, do something wrong to gain a thing you know to be good. I've done it before, and I'm not going to ask it of anyone else. I know how it feels."

"But you'd do it again, wouldn't you?" Meath asked slowly. "Betray what *you* are so that we don't have to."

"If necessary." Rohan plucked a bit of moss, crumbled it between his palms. "That's an interesting word, you know. I must do *necessary* things—and I could, with the power I still have. But it's sliding through my fingers like wind. Like time. I've had hints of it at the *Riall'im*, watching Pol grow into leadership, sitting back and letting him practice being High Prince. He's good at it, Meath—but I'm afraid that there are things in him that will make him good at other kinds of power, too. Roelstra's kind."

"Don't be shadow-fearing like a one-ringed Sunrunner."

"My father enjoyed war. He loved the challenge of it, physical and mental. He was *very* good at it. Maybe it's for the best that Pol shows the same signs. Maybe he's what we need—someone who knows what's necessary and just *does* it."

Meath had never felt so helpless. The ways of princely power were beyond him. He'd witnessed it most of his life and even participated in a few maneuvers, but always as a piece on the board moved by others. He had never understood the movers themselves, never explored their duties and guilts and processes of thought. But now Rohan was telling him things he would have wagered not even Sioned had heard. As if he had answers. As if he could help.

The smile returned—a little wider, apologetic. "And there you sit, wondering, 'Why in the name of the Mother of Dragons is he telling *me* these things?' I'd tell you that, too, if I had any idea." He exhaled a long breath and shrugged

again. "Perhaps because you know most of my secrets, and have none of your own. I trust you because of that, Meath. And it's funny, because it doesn't usually work that way."

Meath nodded. A man who knew one's secrets could be trusted only if one knew his; each would have something to lose. But the usually perceptive High Prince was wrong. Meath did have one secret, kept close ever since the day Sioned returned from the tree circle near Goddess Keep, sixteen years old and newly a woman, with a vision of Fire and Water and her lifemate dazzling her green eyes.

At last Meath said slowly, "You know that in spite of Andrade, in spite of my vows, in spite of my service to Lleyn and then Chadric—in spite of everything else in my life, I am your man and always will be."

"Mine, or Sioned's?"

Meath wore only six rings, but he had practiced his craft for over forty years. The fingerflame held steady, betraying him no more than his face or voice. "Yours, Sioned's, Pol's—it's all one and the same, isn't it?"

"I hope so, my old friend. Goddess help us, I do hope so."

* * *

Miyon of Cunaxa disliked having his only choice presented to him *as* his only choice. It reminded him of the years after his father died of Plague, when he had been prince but his advisers had ruled. It had taken him a very long time, but he had finally rid himself of all of them—some executed by his own hand. The impulse to do the same to the Merida lord who stood in his presence chamber now was almost overpowering.

"So," he said. "I am rousted out of bed at midnight to hear that the Merida are doing what they've been planning to do ever since they bred enough sons to form a respectable army. I note that neither you nor your own sons are at Catchwater, my lord."

"My eldest will be leading the Castle Pine guard—as is his right as its commander. Your grace, our aim is identical to yours. We are fulfilling your ambitions as well as our own. Have they not always been the same?"

"Similar, perhaps. We do have a major difference in who

will rule at Stronghold, but doubtless that can be worked out later." He stretched his lips in a smile.

"Will it matter so much, when all the Desert is ours at last?"

"Oh, little things like that matter a great deal. Little things like who is the ruling prince around here!" He rose from his chair, set on a raised dais, and towered over the Merida, who had the good sense to bend double. Miyon was not fooled, but a narrow thread of satisfaction stitched up his pride. "I trust you won't mind too much if I refuse my official sanction for this war?"

The Merida's head and shoulders snapped up so fast that Miyon wondered why his spine didn't crack. "Your grace—?"

"I've been dealing with Rohan for many years now. His son is my daughter's husband. His grandchildren—" And here he smiled with real enjoyment. "—are *my* grandchildren. Poor innocent darlings, alone with their mother at Dragon's Rest. I believe I'll pay them a visit."

Deprived of the powers of speech, the Merida could only stare. Miyon wondered if they had sent him this imbecile on purpose to irritate him into rash action.

"Yes, to Dragon's Rest," he continued pleasantly, "complaining all the while about my treacherous former allies' unauthorized attacks on the Desert." He warmed to his theme. "Demanding the support of my son-by-marriage in ridding my lands once and for all the Merida vermin." He leaned forward, grinning now. "Depriving Dragon's Rest of half its guard. Protecting my precious granddaughters myself—while the Vellanti army marches in."

The Merida lord's incoherence resolved itself into a long "Ahhh" of enlightenment and a slowly spreading smile.

"I see you understand me. Order my horses and escort. It's a long way to Dragon's Rest."

"Your grace is wise beyond wisdom! Your grace has found the perfect—"

"Yes, yes, I know."

"I am honored to serve your grace." Hesitation, then: "May I humbly ask a boon? Lord Birioc is at this moment proving his worth and valor by leading our people—*your* people—to the walls of Tuath. By tomorrow night, he will be the victor. Although he isn't the eldest of your grace's four fine sons, he is certainly the most clever."

"And he wants to be my heir, just like his brothers. Let

him bring me the Desert, and then he may have the heir's circlet. I'll keep it safe for him, you may count on it." Miyon laughed. "I just hope Rohan lives long enough to see a half-Merida proclaimed a prince!"

Disappointment could not compete with total shock.

"Gentle Goddess, man, don't you think I knew? I inherited you assassins along with my princedom! If his mother wanted to conceal what she was, she shouldn't have had the physician cut the cord with a glass knife. Oh, yes, I heard about that. Pity the sweet girl died before I could execute her for tricking me. But, you know, after I thought about it a while, I decided not to kill Birioc. A Merida son isn't a bad thing to have. It rather binds you to me, doesn't it?"

"Your grace's perceptions—"

"—astound you. Yes, I know that, too. Remember, my lord, very little goes on in my princedom that I *don't* know. And, as we agreed before, it's the little things—like my future heir's bloodlines—that matter. Prepare my escort. I leave at dawn for Dragon's Rest."

The Merida effaced himself and hurried from the chamber. Miyon sank into his chair again and stroked the carved armrests. It would be a bitch of a journey, but he had no choice. He had to get out of Cunaxa, separate himself from the Merida and their plots. Kin to the Vellant'im they might be, through some arcane connection, but he would not count them victorious until both Rohan and Pol were dead and Miyon saw them burned before his own eyes.

The Merida thought him trapped into countenancing the invasion and acknowledging Birioc as his heir. He was just as trapped into this trip to Dragon's Rest. But once there, a gratifying array of options awaited. If the Vellant'im lost, Miyon was covered. If they won, he would deliver Dragon's Rest into their hands. Whichever, he would siphon off some of Pol's troops if he could, to retake Cunaxa for him as a good son-by-marriage ought. Should that fail, Miyon would still be in an excellent position. If Pol won, he would play loyal grandsire to the princesses and share the spoils (specifically, the obliteration of the cursed Merida). If Pol lost, Miyon would have Meiglan and her daughters and their claim to Princemarch under his thumb.

His only difficulty was deciding which he most wanted to lose this war: the Merida, who had been a dead weight around his neck all his reign, or Rohan and Pol. A pretty

problem—and highly amusing to let the Merida think he favored them while he convinced Meiglan he was committed to Pol. He would choose which to betray once the smell of victory was in the wind for one side or the other. He would decide at leisure, safely ensconced at Dragon's Rest.

* * *

Tallain arrived at Tuath Castle before dawn. But it seemed the sun had already risen, and not from the eastern sea. The red-gold glow came from the north. Tuath was in flames.

Only the memory of Sionell's comment about his cooler head kept him from leading a charge over the last rocky hills. His scouts reported grim news: though the castle had not fallen and the gates were still secure, an unheard-of night assault had caught Jahnavi by surprise. Not sleeping —he had been up on the walls, fretting away the time until dawn when he would sweep out of his holding and attack. The battle was over and the Merida commanded the flat plain on three sides of the keep and it wasn't even dawn.

Tallain swung down off his horse—Zadal, a golden Dragon's Rest breed Pol had given him—and paced the stony defile while his troops waited him out. There wasn't much time, and not nearly enough soldiers. The scouts had reported heavy casualties among the Tuathi in defense of their castle. Fully half Jahnavi's warriors lay dead or dying in blood-soaked sand, being stripped of swords and other valuables. The scavenging Merida would be easy enough to slaughter. Tallain was looking forward to it. But if Tuath was well and truly ablaze in this climate that leached water from stone, his main task would not be fighting but rescue. And the Cunaxan regulars would arrive soon.

He sucked in a breath as raucous shouts signaled the start of the Merida celebration. Swinging around on his heel, he strode back to his small army.

"They're congratulating themselves," he said tightly. "Not for long."

One of the women stroked the hilt of her sword thoughtfully. "Begging your pardon, my lord, but aren't there more on the way? I'm all for butchering this herd, but we shouldn't waste our edge."

Before Tallain could answer, a man standing nearby cleared his throat. "Lord Jahnavi may take some persuading to give

us charge of the main battle. The rest of you are too young to recall that time, but I was with Lord Walvis back in 704 and the son is just like the father."

Tallain snorted. "You don't need to tell me about stubborn. I sleep with the daughter."

Bracing laughter greeted this remark. Though Tallain had not intended to be funny, he grinned too. Swinging back up into the saddle, he stroked the sleek sweating neck of his horse and raised one arm high to urge his troops forward. They rode from the defile and around an outcropping of varicolored sandstone, readying themselves to sweep down onto the battlefield like dragons on a flock of sheep. A freshening gust from the north stung smoke into Tallain's eyes and he tightened his hold on the reins as the stallion began to tremble.

"Just a little while," he crooned softly, and an ear tipped in white swiveled back to listen. "Just be patient—"

The wind swept down on Tuath as if a living thing hungry for flames. The firestorm nearly blew the castle apart stone from stone. Tallain heard faraway screams as wooden buildings within the keep exploded into flame. Heat seared his face even at this distance; the roar of fire was unimaginable. Rising twice and thrice the height of a dragon above the walls, sheets of fire were flung toward the sky, ripped by the sudden wind. It was as if the Storm God had exhaled a burning breath, igniting the very stones.

The Merida fled as the gates burst apart and gushed fire. Frenzied animals darted forth; their backs ablaze, there was no escape in running. Horses thundered past, trailing manes and tails of flame like some *faradhi* conjuring. As the wind flared once more, the stench of charred flesh smote Tallain in the face and he nearly vomited.

Nothing could survive that Hell. The Merida who had caused it were out of his reach, galloping to join their Cunaxan fellows still on the march. He wiped his streaming eyes and tasted smoke on his tongue.

"We'll—we'll look for survivors," he managed, and no one dared say the obvious: no one had survived. Tallain led his people slowly across the plain, detailing some to gather corpses for a pyre to honor them.

Tuath burned quickly. By midmorning there was no fuel sufficient to feed those ravening flames, and they wavered down below the line of the walls. By dusk Tallain could

enter the smoking ruin. Leaving his horse outside, he walked through the courtyard, heat rising up through the soles of his boots. He had no way of knowing if beneath the scorched litter of planks and stones were corpses he might recognize. No—he would see no familiar faces here. On the bodies lying free of the rubble there were no faces at all.

He heard a child crying and tore his way through the blackened remains of a stout wooden door, down a stone staircase to a wine cellar. The little girl lay trapped beneath a dead woman, protected by voluminous silk skirts from the smoke that had killed her savior. Tallain freed the child, who wept louder and threw a stranglehold around his neck.

"There may be others still alive," Tallain said to the archers who had come with him. "Those familiar with Tuath can organize the search. But be careful—things are likely to collapse on top of you." He stroked the girl's dark hair, stinking and greasy with smoke. "It's all right, little one. You're safe now."

Back upstairs, he tried to hand her to one of his women soldiers but she would not be budged. Tallain shrugged and let her be. She was no weight at all—and it was a pathetic grace in the midst of this horror to feel her warm, living body against his chest, her soft breath against his neck.

"My lord? We've found them."

Tallain froze. "Alive?"

"Lady Rabisa and the children, yes."

"Jahnavi?" His voice caught on the name.

The man lowered his gaze to the ground.

Tallain pried the little girl's arms from around his neck. She gave a piteous cry and reached for him as he gave her over to the soldier. "I'll come back," he promised absently, "don't be afraid."

The main tower was at the northernmost angle of Tuath. Winds bringing the sudden firestorm had come from that direction, and the flames had been blown away from the tower for the most part. The lower floors and all walls but the northern one were blackened, but the upper chambers were largely untouched. Gusts of fresh hot air off the Desert had kept the smoke away.

Jahnavi lay on his own bed, his wife and two small children keeping watch. He was covered to the neck by a silken quilt stitched in an alternating blue and orange pattern, Tuath's colors, bordered with the blue and white of Remagev

to which he had been heir. The strip of blue silk above his heart was matted to his body by blood. His face was pale and solemn, with a slight frown between his brows, as if trying to understand why he was lying here when there was a battle to be fought. Tallain swallowed hard. Sionell's hair curled back from her brow just that way; had Jahnavi's eyes been open, they would have been the same clear blue as hers.

Tallain knelt beside Rabisa and took her hand. "I'm sorry," he whispered. "Rabisa, I'm so sorry—"

Black-haired and blue-eyed, she was a dainty little thing built along the same lines as Tobin. She gazed down at him dry-eyed, shifting her two-year-old son on her lap. "There's not a mark on him, but for the Merida arrow," she said softly. "I had them save it, to light the fire with. I'm glad you came to honor him, Tallain. He was so fond of you. He admires you so much."

The switch in tenses from past to present unnerved him. Gently he said, "Rabisa, perhaps you'd like to come to Tiglath with me. Sionell will want to see you and the children."

"Thank you, but no," she replied calmly. "I must stay here. He'd want me to. And he'll need me to help him arm when he rides out tomorrow." She slid her son from her lap as if she had forgotten who he was, and went to a nearby chair where someone had left Jahnavi's sword and battle harness.

A hand touched his shoulder. He glanced at it—livid with burns, trembling. Turning, he looked up at Tuath's elderly chief steward. Tears had cut pale pathways through the soot on her cheeks.

"She's been like this since they brought my lord home," the woman whispered. "Sun and shadow."

A north Desert phrase for the shock of any wound. Tallain nodded. "Get her and the children downstairs as soon as you can. The Cunaxans will be here any time now. We've got to hurry."

"Poor hatchlings," she said, gathering Jeren up into her arms. Siona, just four winters old, was staring at Tallain with huge gray eyes—Feylin's eyes, his own son Jahnev's eyes, all smoke and silver.

Riyan, my old friend, he thought as he caressed Siona's cheek in gentle reassurance, *this will be the finish of the*

Merida forever. You and I are going to make Cunaxa run red with blood.

* * *

"Gone?" roared Birioc, and lunged to his feet, nearly toppling his personal physician. "How can they be gone? Is Tuath not in flames?"

"It is," his half-brother Duroth replied shortly. "If you'd rallied your Merida kin instead of counting yourself the victor too soon—"

"Don't lecture me, boy," Birioc warned.

"If you'd kept them in line instead of running away like a coward when that fire hit—"

"If you weren't my brother, I'd show you why the Merida bear that name!"

"A touch of your 'gentle glass,' brother? You're not Father's heir *yet*. And may never be, after this disaster."

"Tuath is mine." He slapped the physician's ministering hands away from his injured leg. "Get out!" he snarled, and the man fled the tent.

"Tuath is burning to foundation stones!" Duroth leaned forward. "And what's more, clever brother, Tallain was here—and got away!"

The sting of the arrow in his leg was forgotten. "He's a dead man."

"A charming sentiment, succinctly expressed," Duroth sneered. "I can't wait to see you storming the walls of Tiglath. How many does Tallain have there? Two hundred? Three?"

"If he commands five thousand, we'll still destroy him!" Birioc calmed himself with an effort. "Besides, *little* brother, those hundreds out there are my own from Castle Pine."

"And what about Riyan, coming from Skybowl? Rohan might be a hunted dragon now, abandoning threatened caves. But the gathering of dragons to come—" He gave a worried shake of the head. "I don't like it, Birioc. You don't corner someone like Rohan."

"He's old and feeble. Whatever courage he had is gone." The half-Merida prince gestured Rohan away with a scornful hand. "He runs instead of fighting. We'll be in Stronghold by winter's end."

"And what about Pol?"

"What about him?" Birioc grinned. "Oh, don't worry—I'll give him a very pretty burning. A courtesy between princes."

Duroth shrugged. "You'd better hope your barbarian kin keep Rohan busy in the south. If Maarken is free to come after you—"

"Me? Don't you mean 'us'? You're in this with me, Duroth, and Zanyr and Ezanto as well. Father might not have chosen among the four of us yet, but when he does—" He bared his teeth in a smile. "Tallain *is* dead. He just doesn't know it yet." *And neither do you, brother mine—you and Miyon's other superfluous sons.*

Chapter Twenty-three

Rohan could feel Sioned watching him as he paced their chambers. He was unable to sit still, even less to lie in bed beside her. He could sense her deciding what tactic to adopt, and though part of him was resentful, most of him wanted her to hurry up about it. Fortunate men had wives who knew how to listen; he had one who knew what to say.

At last she broke her meditative silence. "That first winter we were married, your mother told me I was the best possible wife for you. With me, you *felt* so much that you forgot to *think* so much. She said you'd always been too aware of yourself. No, don't give me that look, Rohan, you know what she meant."

"Perhaps."

"Don't equivocate, either. There's nothing wrong with looking into yourself—just so long as you come back out again."

He stopped pacing. "Sioned . . . what I've tried to be, what I've tried to do with my life . . . those things demand self-knowledge."

"I'm not arguing with that."

"But you're saying I'm getting in too deep?"

"It's possible."

"For your comfort?"

Sioned's reply was serene. "You always come back to me, beloved."

"Then it's Pol again."

"You've hardly spoken to each other since Remagev."

"It seemed the more prudent course."

"He needs you, Rohan. And, quite frankly, you need him."

"To tell me again that I'm a coward? Thank you, no."

"He said that?" Her composure wavered.

"He said many things before he stopped saying anything at all." He began to pace again, caught himself at it, and settled into a chair. "Several of them were rather perceptive. That I internalize conflict, fight it out inside myself, rather than taking the battle to the enemy where Pol feels it belongs."

"He's right, you know," she murmured. "You've always done that. I suppose that's part of what your mother meant."

He considered this for a time, then burst out, "The only real enemy I ever had was Roelstra. The others have been opponents. There's a difference. Enemies require hatred. All I ever felt for everyone but Roelstra was—*contempt*. And annoyance that they take up my time."

"What about the Vellant'im? They frighten me, Rohan. I can't think of them as anything but enemies."

He stared at the silk tapestries on the bedchamber walls—cool blues and greens depicting a forest waterfall and flowers that did not exist. Usually the gentle fantasy delighted him. Tonight it seemed morbidly symbolic of a world that did not exist. The world he'd tried to make.

"Is it me, Sioned? Is it some freak of my character that makes me think that if we can understand them, why they're here, then we can find a way to defeat them that costs the fewest lives? I may be fighting this inside myself—but better my heart blood than my people's."

"That's *my* heart you're ravaging, beloved," she said softly. "The heart that belongs to me. When you bleed, so do I."

"Goddess knows I love you more than my life—I don't mean to hurt you—"

"Come here to me, my love." She held open her arms to him and he lay beside her on the bed, wrapped in her embrace. "I wouldn't change you," she whispered. "I loved you the instant I saw you and I've never stopped. But you're more than my heart and my life, Rohan. You are my honor, my pride, and my lord. If you'd ever allow it, I'd bend my head and my knees to you in front of the whole world. Not because you're High Prince and could command it of me—but because you'd *never* command it." She smoothed his silvering hair. "Do you remember that first *Rialla*, when Roelstra's barge arrived—and everyone was at the dock but you? They'd all bowed or knelt to him—and then you came running up, insolent and innocent all at once—" She chuck-

led softly. "Cami and I laughed ourselves silly. You never did bow to him. He didn't dare command it—you'd already made him look a total fool. He should have known then that he'd never win. Not against you."

He smiled at the memory, youthful satisfaction at his trick stirring even now. "You saw it all?"

"It was worth the rest of that awful *Rialla*, watching you outsmart him. If I hadn't already been in love with you, it would have happened the moment you used those big eyes on him. And I told myself, 'this man is going to be mine.' "

"But he almost won, you know. I got caught up in trying out *his* tactics, *his* way of being a prince. Deliberately creating conflict, making others fight just to watch the show—"

"And you swore never again."

"But Pol isn't like me, Sioned. Perhaps Roelstra might win after all. Or Andrade."

"Never. Pol is ours, Rohan. Not theirs. He'll learn on his own, the way you did—slowly and infuriatingly!—but he *will* learn."

He twisted slightly to look at her. "Even if we have to beat him over the head with it?"

"Even if." She kissed his upturned brow. "Now that I think about it, parts of that *Rialla* weren't so bad. Remember sitting under the bridge steps in the rain?"

"I remember the willow tree better."

"I thought you might."

* * *

Andry suffered Valeda to drape a magnificent white velvet cloak over his shoulders, but refused the jeweled clasp. "Absolutely not. I'm not a prince dressing for a banquet."

"This morning that's exactly what you are," she commented tartly. "Only you're also the feast. They expect to be served up with a powerful protector. You have to look the part."

"And be eaten alive? Thank you, no. I'll meet them as what I am. Lord of Goddess Keep is quite enough."

"As you wish." Shrugging, she slipped the ruby clasp into her pocket.

"Enough!" he snapped.

"I suppose you won't take this, either," Torien said with a rueful smile, twirling a slim wooden cane in his fingers.

"My leg is fine. *I* am fine. Will you two stop? You're not my mother."

"More's the pity," the steward commented. "Her, you'd obey."

Andry wished briefly that pride allowed him the support of the cane on his way downstairs. His muscles were stiff after enforced bedrest, and his left leg was still wrapped tightly. Getting into the saddle was torture. But once mounted and riding with Torien through the main gates, anticipation warmed him.

Andry schooled his expression to impassivity, determined not to show astonishment at the size of the still growing township of tents and lean-to shelters covering the fallow fields. From across Ossetia and Gilad and Grib and even as far away as Meadowlord and Syr the people had come to him—to *him,* not Rohan or Pol—for protection. They were camped nearly to the walls of the keep and merged with the village down the road, braving winter rain and cold to stay here, near him. He wished Andrade could have seen it; he knew Sioned would.

The really remarkable thing was that they kept coming, and asked for nothing, not even food. In leaving their homes they had taken everything they owned, from clothes and cookpots and bedding to their animals—goats, sheep, cattle, plow-elk. Small herds pastured to the south swelled daily. Valeda's latest estimate was that over three thousand people had arrived, and a foray on morning sunlight had shown her a thousand more on their way. Coming to him, to the protection he could give them. They had heard of his defense of Goddess Keep. They trusted in his power. They left their tents now to cheer him, call out blessings on him, welcome him as if he was indeed their rightful prince.

Andry's horse skittered to one side as a gray striped cat slunk past. He calmed the stallion and rode on, picking his way among the tents, looking for one in particular. Torien had spoken yesterday with a merchant from Waes, a dealer in foodstuffs who had become the refugees' leader on the long journey. Andry sought the craft mark in Waesian colors described by his steward, and finally spied a red apple and yellow wheat sheaf. Painted on crates and on wooden signs outside shops or warehouses, a merchant's stencil was as prized a possession as a crafter's hallmark die or a prince's official seal. Most of the Waesian tents had similar mark-

ings, painted on scraps of cloth; a few merchants had actually taken the trouble to save their shop signs as well and tacked them onto rickety poles outside their new homes.

Andry was relieved that someone who understood food supplies had turned up to lead; though these people had asked for nothing from him, it was still his responsibility to see that they were decently sheltered, clothed, and fed. But the obligations of an *athri*, bred into him through generations, could not take precedence over his more essential duties as Lord of Goddess Keep. It was just as well he could delegate the problem to someone else. It would be unseemly and a waste of his time to worry over whether some peasant had enough to eat. Or, worse, to mediate between two farmers claiming the same cow from the herd grazing his pastures, or similar foolishness.

The merchant came from the tent to meet Andry. Black-haired, sturdily made, straight-eyed, and about his own age, she bowed and gestured at a small boy, obviously her son, to hold Andry's horse.

"Please, my Lord, accept what small hospitality I can offer you."

"Thank you, Master Jayachin." Dismounting, he nodded at Torien, who undid the thongs securing his saddlebags. "Perhaps I can add a few comforts to your exile."

"You are most gracious, my Lord." Bowing again, she held aside the tent flap and he entered, trying not to limp. "Please sit down."

He settled on the single cross-legged stool. A quick glance confirmed that Jayachin possessed tidy habits of person and of mind. The dirt floor had been packed down to lessen the dust; blankets enough for three beds were neatly rolled in a corner; and, most telling and most admirable in a merchant, thick account books bound in red leather rested on the upended apple crate that was the only other furniture. Her home, her possessions, her warehouses, her inventory, everything she owned might be forfeit to the war, but once it was all over she could resume her business if she still had the precious records. Andry liked that. It spoke of foresight and stubbornness.

Jayachin saw the direction of his gaze. "I packed my books the moment I heard the order to leave. This won't last forever, my Lord. If I'm to regain my family's fortune, the High Prince will want accurate account of what was lost."

"Lost at his command," Andry murmured. He knew why Waes had been abandoned. "You're a wise woman, Master Jayachin. But young to hold that title."

"I was an only child, my Lord, and not inclined to account books. When I married, my husband took the title and duties with my permission. But he was a thief. I divorced him. For the sake of my son, I learned my father's trade. But then I discovered I enjoyed it, as I had not in my girlhood."

"We all learn as we grow older. You're fortunate to like what you do. And I hope you'll use your skills to the benefit of your fellows here. You'll report to my chief steward, of course. But I expect you to keep order here."

She nodded once. "To that end, my Lord, I have a proposal."

Andry stifled a sigh. Entanglement in these people's concerns was the last thing he wanted. But at least he must listen.

"When someone moves from one princedom to another, for marriage or new opportunity or purchase of land or crafthold, former oaths are canceled and new ones sworn. Those who've come here will return to their homes and holdings. But until then, I think they ought to have an immediate loyalty. To you."

His brows crept up his forehead. "Only the farmers and herders who live in the vicinity are sworn to Goddess Keep. Your people all have other homes."

"That's exactly the point, my Lord. They're not 'mine' and they don't have homes. They have nothing but the soil their shelters are built on—and that belongs to you. If they swear to you, then they'll have a place again in the order of things. When people know their place, they keep to it."

"And by swearing to me, they also swear to you as my . . . *athri*."

"If you choose to think of it that way, my Lord—yes."

That straight, calm gaze met his without the slightest hint of ambition. He nearly grinned. He knew desire for power even when discreetly hidden. He liked that about her, too. As long as she understood *her* place.

"Very well. Arrange it. Tomorrow will do."

"Perfectly, my Lord." Once more she bent her head to him.

"And for you, too—my lady?" He allowed amusement to

tinge his voice as he gave her the new title. "I believe we understand each other."

The corners of her mouth tucked into a demure little smile. "I'm certain of it, my Lord." She hesitated. "Only—there is one more thing."

"Yes?" he asked blandly, suspecting a trap.

"The *Medr'im* who accompanied you here." This least helpless of women gave a helpless little shrug. "Lord Gerwen sees to the High Prince's Writ, as is his duty. . . ."

They *did* understand each other perfectly. "I believe it's time I released him to defend his own lands—don't you?"

"My Lord is wise."

"Incidentally, later today something will happen that I would like you and your people to see," he said.

"Will you send a page for me, my Lord?"

In formal courtesy, as if you were a real athri*? Not likely.* He smiled. "You'll know when to come to the walls. Good day, Master Jayachin."

Outside, Andry swung up into his saddle after thanking the boy who'd held his horse. A servant stood nearby with wrapped cloth bundles from Torien's saddlebags. "What did I give her, anyway?" Andry whispered as Torien mounted.

"Tokens of your appreciation—taze, spices, a silver hairbrush—"

"Good. Jayachin's the type of woman who likes the status shown by small luxuries. When we get back, have the goldsmith design her a badge of office."

They guided their horses through the maze of tents. "She accepted, then."

"Torien, she suggested it all herself." He grinned. "In the humblest and least offensive terms, of course, concealing the fact that she's power-hungry with a yearning to call herself *athri*." He nodded at the folk who'd come to see the Lord of Goddess Keep in person; word had spread through the whole of the encampment by now, and the crowd was even larger. "How's our Vellanti prisoner holding up?"

"Valeda kept her word about keeping him breathing, anyway. It's too bad his jaw was broken and his cheek crushed—he might have told us something."

Andry nodded, idly fingering the little ceramic dragon token inside his tunic pocket. It would have been nice to learn exactly what this meant to the Vellanti, but it wasn't entirely necessary. "He's not a high-ranking warrior, obvi-

ously. I doubt he knows much that's really important. All he really needs to know is how to die."

The sudden bright glaze over the blue eyes warned Torien instantly that someone had touched Andry on sunlight. He grabbed the Lord's reins so his horse would not bolt and waved people back with an impatient hand.

"He speaks with the Goddess," someone breathed, and between one heartbeat and the next the crowd around them doubled. Torien eyed them nervously, but they kept their distance and a reverent silence. Farmers, herders, merchants, crafters, laborers—none of them had ever seen a Sunrunner at work before. Sunrunner magic.

At last Andry blinked and met Torien's gaze. "My mother," he said—and gave a start as a man nearby called out, "He has spoken with the Goddess!"

"Tell us her words, my Lord!"

"Will she protect us? Has she given you a sign?"

Torien met Andry's gaze, sharing his thought. To correct the mistake would be a bigger mistake. Not that these people would believe any explanation. They wanted to believe that he communed with the Goddess.

Andry raised one hand for silence. "She—watches over you all," he said.

Torien hid amusement and admiration. Andry had only spoken the truth—Princess Tobin would certainly keep an eye on things at Goddess Keep—omitting definition of which "she" he referred to.

There were more cheers, more blessings called down upon Andry, but with a different tone. Before, there had been respect. Now there was awe.

They were nearly at the gates before Torien said, "Brilliant, Andry."

"What else could I do?" Then he chuckled. "Can you imagine the look on my mother's face if I told her that in speaking to her, I spoke to the Goddess?"

* * *

Rohan had been awakened by Myrdal shortly after dawn. The ancient autocrat thumped her cane on the carpet and told him to gather his wits.

"Wind has blown the skies clear and the Sunrunners are

already busy. Get up, boy. It's time you gave some orders around here."

"You mean you're abdicating at last?" he asked as he gulped from the cup of hot taze she gave him.

"Impudent hatchling."

He hadn't slept well after Sioned left their bed last night. He suspected that after soothing him the best way she knew how, she had stayed up waiting for a few threads of usable—if forbidden—starshine. If Myrdal was right and the skies were clear, by midday she would be exhausted.

His squires Daniv and Isriam followed close on Myrdal's heels, working with smooth efficiency to get him shaved and garbed and ready for what promised to be a difficult day. The orders Myrdal referred to would span the continent politically and militarily; on his decisions alliances and battles might turn. And the lives—Goddess, the lives he held in his hands.

Isriam was pale with anxiety; today would bring the first word of his family in Einar. Daniv hid his feelings a little better, though he had more to worry about. His father Kostas was marching through Syr. Rohan took both boys with him to the Summer Room, where Feylin was already waiting to take notes. She greeted him around a mouthful of hairpins, testimony to a hasty awakening.

"They're already out there, even Tobin," she said, securing the tag ends of her dark red braids at her nape. "Though how they'll all keep from running into each other, I'll never know."

"Nor I. But Tobin shouldn't be with them."

Feylin shrugged. "*You* try and stop her. Besides, she insists she's the only one Andry will speak to."

"Andry," he said musingly as he sat down.

"Don't start," she warned gently. "Save your worry for when it's needed."

The first Sunrunner to come to them was Relnaya, assigned to scan the northern Desert. He looked directly at Feylin, and as he met her eyes tears welled in his and dripped down his weather-beaten face.

"My lady—my dear lady, the young lord is dead. Jahnavi is dead."

Rohan shut his eyes. In darkness he heard Feylin whisper, "Does—does his father know?"

"Not yet. Lady Rabisa and the children are safe at Tiglath—

but the young lord—ah, my lady, I would I'd lost myself on shadows rather than bring you such words."

Rohan glanced up as Feylin's chair scraped stone. She was dry-eyed and straight-backed, and white as ash. "I must find my husband." She stumbled once on her way to the door. She took Relnaya's arm, the Sunrunner weeping openly now, and helped him from the room.

Rohan stared at his hands. It was a very long time before he heard his squires shift uneasily nearby. He looked up—but behind them was another boy, blue-eyed and dark-haired, face alight with anticipation of a game of dragons. And there were other boys, too—Jahni, for whom Feylin had Named her son; Sorin; Maarken; Tallain and Arlis and Riyan and even Andry. And Pol.

Isriam glanced at Daniv and then said, "We could hear the other reports for you, my lord, and then tell you later what they said."

"If you want to be alone, my lord," Daniv added.

"No. I've heard the worst." He begged the Goddess that it *was* the worst.

The boys—young men, really, at sixteen—exchanged glances again. This time Daniv spoke first. "I never thought—that is, at Radzyn and Remagev, it was so different from what I thought."

"War?" Rohan asked, and the young prince nodded. "In what way?"

"That it would be exciting. It was, at first. Fighting a battle, even as a squire—" Daniv hesitated, searching for words. Rohan recognized that he was indeed nearly a man, that he struggled to define himself. "But I always thought we'd win."

"We haven't lost yet, you know." He loathed himself for the trite lie. This certainly felt like losing.

"We won't lose," Isriam said firmly. "We both know that, my lord. But I think what Daniv's saying is that war isn't what stories make it out to be."

"Proud banners, dragon horns, brave deeds, and glory," he summarized. "They don't write about the dirt and blood and death, do they? Even if they did, no one would believe it. No one but those who've been there."

"The warriors tell stories, my lord," Daniv said, frowning. "But they only talk about the bravery, as you said."

"And leave out the worst of it. Wouldn't you?"

Isriam caught his breath softly. "Remembering it, let alone talking about it, is like reliving it."

"But why don't they *tell* people?" Daniv protested.

"How long has it been since the last major war?" Rohan asked.

"Not counting the battle at Dragon's Rest—" Daniv began.

"—which wasn't really a battle—" Isriam added.

"—it was in 704. When you fought Roelstra."

"When Roelstra *began* a war I had to fight," Rohan corrected, privately wondering why he still needed to make that distinction. What did it matter, anyway? War was war, no matter who started it.

Isriam was struggling now, defining not himself but the past. "Back then, my father was just a little older than I am now. That's a whole generation ago. All these people who grew up not really knowing what war is. . . ."

Daniv picked up the thread. "Just like Isriam and me, thinking it's all riding a fine horse and wearing a sword and glory! Nobody talks about the way it really is, so nobody tries to stop it!"

The other squire nodded vigorously, then made a frustrated gesture with one hand. "But *we* didn't start this, my lord—they did. It's not our fault—it's not that we want to fight. But we have to."

"Like you did, with Roelstra," Daniv added, understanding at last.

Rohan regarded the pair of them, hope stirring even through his grief. "You will make your fathers proud," he murmured. "You will rule your lands with such wisdom—I couldn't be prouder of you if you were my own sons."

Young men became boys again, embarrassed and gratified by praise from the High Prince. They glanced at each other again, and Daniv cleared his throat.

"Thank you, my lord. I should—I should see if any of the other *faradh'im* are waiting outside—"

Rohan nodded. Isriam slid into Feylin's chair and readied pens and parchment. And, as Daniv brought Hollis in, the grim recitals began.

* * *

Sioned hadn't been part of so vast and simultaneous a survey of the continent since Andrade's death. Then, the

Sunrunners gathered around the Lady's pyre had woven a shining net to reach from the Sunrise Water to Kierst-Isel, from Dorval to Snowcoves. They'd sustained each other, lent strength where necessary.

Now each *faradhi* was alone.

They chose the sunniest part of the inner courtyard for more reasons than its access to light; Sioned knew that people must see them at work. The nine *faradh'im*—herself, Meath, Morwenna, Tobin, Tobren, Pol, Maarken, Hollis, and Relnaya—formed a loose circle. They were gently guarded by Pol's squire Dannar, his sister Jeni, Sethric of Grib, and Betheyn, who stood at Tobin's side to support her in case she lost control of her muscles during the work. In truth, there was little to see—just Sunrunners, ranging in age from Meath and Tobin who had each seen more than sixty winters to Tobren's barely twelve, standing relaxed and serene in the middle of the courtyard. But everyone who passed by paused a moment to watch, marvel, and return to assigned tasks feeling unaccountably comforted.

Sioned lost awareness of those around her as she spun sunlight. She didn't hear Relnaya's low moan as he staggered and fled. She didn't see Hollis' quiet departure from the circle a little while later, nor the fire in Tobin's black eyes as she clutched at Beth. Sioned was far away, soaring over the towering snowcaps of the Great Veresch, then south to the Catha Hills, and finally to Goddess Keep.

She sought Donato first. Court Sunrunner at Castle Crag for many years, he had been one of those who had accompanied her to the Desert in 698. Donato, Ostvel, Meath, Hildreth, and Antoun were the only ones left of the friends on that journey. They all still served Sioned in various ways, as if that time had become an unbreakable bond among them.

Donato reported all serene at Castle Crag—but for his resentment that Ostvel had bid him stay. The crippling stiffness in his joints didn't affect him in the saddle, but walking could be torture. Winter at Castle Crag was bad enough, but the wet lowlands of Meadowlord would be the torments of all Hells.

It's not as if Ostvel doesn't walk with a creak in his knees some mornings! he complained to Sioned. *But I shouldn't keep you with my whinings. Let Ostvel know that we're all safe, and getting troops and supplies ready to send down the Faolain whenever he needs them.*

And can collect them safely, Sioned added. *I'll be back this afternoon if the sun holds, and let you and Alasen know what's happening.*

There's something else you can do, if you would. It'd save us a lot of time and trouble if I knew young Andrev's colors.

I'm not sure Tobren can be persuaded to tell me, but I'll try.

After withdrawing from Castle Crag, she glided across Meadowlord and Syr at a great height. She and Meath and Morwenna had staked out the upper reaches of the sun for themselves, leaving the lower sky to those who needed more specific referents along the way. There was no chance that Sioned might mistake a river or a grassy plain; she had been doing this alone and unassisted since her sixteenth year—somewhat in advance of Andrade's permission to do so, and well before she wore the ring that proclaimed her adept at it. "Mind-hungry," Urival had always called her, and suddenly she wished for his steady wisdom.

It was a long search for Kostas and his army between High Kirat and the Catha River. Finally she found them—and nearly gasped. He was marching on Catha Heights. Rain, mud, and cold evidently meant nothing to him. Traitorous Lord Patwin was dead, but his brother and two of his daughters were still within the keep. So was a large contingent of Vellant'im. What in the name of the Storm God did Kostas think he was doing?

Worse, he had no Sunrunner with him. His court *faradhi* was at High Kirat. Sioned knew it was deliberate. Whatever disadvantages he might face through lack of communication, he obviously felt them worth it. Without a Sunrunner, there could be no orders from the High Prince. Kostas had always been more independent in his rule of Syr than his father Davvi had been. The irony was that Tilal was just as autonomous in Ossetia—and didn't have to prove it.

Sioned hesitated, wondering if she could help—and if Kostas would want her to. There were about twenty measures between his army and Catha Heights; she surveyed the land and guessed he would choose to do battle where the road passed through a relatively flat meadow half a measure from the keep. But there was a better place close by, off the main road. It would have to be approached uphill by the enemy, and into tomorrow's morning sun. Sioned didn't know much about military tactics, but she understood rising ground and light.

It took her only a moment. Cold Sunrunner's Fire flared a beacon atop one of the tall pines ringing the meadow. She let it blaze for a while, despite the effort it took at this distance, until she felt sure that Kostas must have seen it and at least sent scouts to investigate. Having done what she could, she drew back across the Faolain, gathered her energies, and then made the long journey to Goddess Keep. On this first clear day in so long, her source there would know to be waiting for her.

* * *

". . . camped tidy as you please around the old Sunrunner keep." Meath grinned. "I think Ludhil's even enjoying himself. And judging by the gold strung from the white ship banner, he's doing rather well."

"Banner?" Hollis asked. "How did he manage that?"

"I think it used to be Iliena's underskirt. There's a flower up in the hills that gives the right shade of blue. But the white ship is flying—and plenty of those little golden beads threaded on silk below it."

Rohan said, "Meath, be sure to contact Riyan at Skybowl, so he can let Chadric know. Is there anything else?"

"Nothing, my lord."

"So," Rohan mused. "Grand Veresch and River Ussh are quiet and unthreatened. Kadar Water, Athmyr, and Medawari are shut up tight. And our cherished princely cousin Velden is sitting on his royal ass at Summer River."

Meath snorted. "Does he think the Vellant'im won't notice him?"

"I've never heard Velden accused of thinking much at all," Hollis observed. She glanced at Rohan, who nodded. "Meath, I'll come with you while you talk to Riyan. Then we can join Maarken and Tobin and Morwenna, and I'll fill you in on everywhere else—since you were too polite to ask."

"Not polite—confused," Meath corrected, smiling. "I'll never understand how you juggle all this, Rohan."

"Believe me, at times I wish I had twelve hands and at least one more brain." He watched them leave, knowing Hollis was right: it was better to say nothing about Jahnavi to the other Sunrunners until their reports were made. Sioned and Pol had yet to arrive in the Summer Room; sheer cowardice to wish Hollis had waited so she could tell them, too.

As he waited for wife or son to appear, he reviewed the information thus far received. Maarken reported that Rohannon prospered at New Raetia, left in complete charge by Arlis, who spent his time pacing the docks at Port Adni in a fury of impatience for some good sailing weather. Fine as today had been, there was another storm roaring down from the northern Dark Water, the kind that funneled through the channel between island and continent and lashed Brochwell Bay to a frenzy. The last one had cost Arlis two ships, their sails and masts shredded by the wind, their crews drowned.

Maarken had also looked in on Zaldivar, and found that Princess Demalia, Arlis' wife, had been safely delivered of their second son. A quick journey back to New Raetia had informed Rohannon, who would get word to the prince. At least there was *some* good news, Rohan told himself.

Except for the Desert, things were not nearly as bad as he'd feared. Tobren, flushed with pride in Andrev and the importance of being the only one who could get news from Waes, said that Tilal, Ostvel, and their armies were occupying the city while sending out raiding parties even more successful than Ludhil's on Dorval. They only awaited the High Prince's orders to march for Swalekeep.

Morwenna had reported that Einar was armed and ready. It had been Tilal's suggestion that Lord Sabriam arrange his troops at strategic points along the coast to guard Princemarch's underbelly. Isriam blew out a soft sigh of relief that his family and city were safe. But Morwenna's survey of Fessenden yielded oddities. Prince Pirro had done absolutely nothing—not even fortified his own keep. Obviously he trusted its distance from the coast to protect him. It irked Morwenna that he wasn't even going through the motions.

"You'd think he'd at least make a show of calling up his troops, and then plead bad weather or something," she grumbled. "Spineless fool!"

Rohan reminded her who Pirro's son Edirne had married: strong-willed, high-strung Arnisaya of Gilad Seahold, whose brother Segelin and his family had been butchered the first day of the war. Rohan hid fury that help from Fessenden depended on the angry persuasions of one person. Still, he knew from personal experience what a stubborn, fiery-tempered female could accomplish. If Arnisaya was half as eloquent as Tobin, all might work out. It annoyed him

further to think that if Segelin hadn't been slaughtered and Seahold demolished, Arnisaya might have cared as little as Pirro for the laws that bound the princedoms in mutual defense. But Morwenna clarified the point.

"I had a little chat with Pirro's Sunrunner—foolish man, never could remember his name, only his colors, and they're unimaginative enough. He says Pirro sees no reason to join the fighting because one princedom hasn't attacked another. No treaty covers this kind of war."

"Hmm. It seems I wrote that one rather badly."

Morwenna's dark eyes narrowed. "How could you have known?"

"I'm High Prince. I'm supposed to know everything." The words held enough self-mockery to fool most people, but not Morwenna. He heard himself add with undisguised bitterness, "Just ask my son."

Daniv and Isriam were in the room, or she would have said more. Shaking her head, she continued, "Firon is even more of a puzzle, my lord. There's no sign of Yarin at Snowcoves. Or his Sunrunner." She paused for effect. "But there's a white-and-yellow flag flying over Balarat."

Rohan sat up straight. "What's Yarin doing there?"

"I'd be pleased to tell you, my lord—if I could find Arpali. She seems to have vanished as surely as Yarin's Sunrunner at Snowcoves."

And Rialt's at Swalekeep. Rohan heard his two squires catch their breath as Pol made his report. When Rohan explained, Pol understood, too—and threw in a wrinkle Rohan hadn't thought of.

"Andry's going to be furious," he said. "If his Sunrunners are being kept out of the light, it may just kick him into this without making conditions."

"It's possible," Rohan conceded. "Did you see anything at Swalekeep?"

"Some activity by the waterfront—flatboats loaded with crates, that sort of thing. I suppose Chiana would say she's getting ready to supply the south."

"Tactfully omitting reference to exactly *whom* in the south." Rohan nodded. "She can say what she pleases—especially if the supplies are 'captured.' "

Daniv shifted uncomfortably. "My lords—forgive me, but even though I don't like her much myself, Princess Chiana is

still my aunt. It is taken so much for granted that she's betraying us?"

A look flickered between Rohan and Pol: Chiana was Pol's aunt as well, and Daniv his cousin not through Kostas but Danladi, another of Roelstra's daughters. The reminder gave Rohan an idea.

"Your family feeling does you credit, Daniv," he said carefully. "But we've dealt with Chiana before. However, you've tweaked my memory, and I thank you." Turning to Pol, he went on, "Princess Naydra is at Swalekeep, isn't she?"

Blue-green eyes lit with comprehension not shared by the squires. "Indeed she is." He changed the subject. "There's good news from Dragon's Rest. Hildreth says everyone is fine, except for poor Lisiel. She's ten days overdue and if Edrel didn't take Laric riding every day to get him out from underfoot, Lisiel would probably divorce him from sheer irritation."

Rohan was glad of the chance to smile. "Let that be a lesson to you," he directed at Isriam and Daniv. "Pregnant wives are like she-dragons. Walk very softly and *maybe* you won't get your eyes clawed out."

Daniv grinned. "You don't need to tell me, my lord. Our Sunrunner at High Kirat threatened to set her husband on Fire if he didn't stop treating her like Fironese crystal."

Isriam's eyes rounded. "She *must* have been joking!"

"You've never met Diantha."

Rohan asked about Meiglan and the twins, wanting to delay talking about Jahnavi. Pol answered easily enough, but sensed something wrong. He seemed about to ask when Sioned stormed into the room, practically breathing fire.

"Do you know what he's done? Do you?" she shouted at Rohan. "If he wasn't the son of his parents, I'd order a march on Goddess Keep myself!"

Daniv and Isriam flinched. Rohan and Pol knew better than to coax her to calm down. Sioned's rages were rarely as spectacular as Tobin's, but this one had his sister beat seven ways to the Far Islands.

Gradually, after venting her fury in hissed curses and a broken glass vase, the story became clear. When she finished, green eyes still spitting sparks, Pol cleared his throat.

"So he's setting up a Sunrunner princedom," he said. "I assume you learned this through your friend at Goddess Keep?"

"No, Andry told me himself! Of *course* I found out in secret! Rohan, how *dare* he do this?"

"Because he thinks he must. Because the opportunity is there, and he's too smart not to seize it." He met Pol's gaze, and for the first time in a long while they were in perfect accord. "Because he sees the salvation of the continent in his own hands."

Pacing, Sioned started in surprise as her boots crunched on shattered glass. She looked down and swore. Isriam came immediately with a parchment page to shovel up the shards, and Sioned strode away from the evidence of her fury.

"What did he tell Tobin?" she asked abruptly.

"Only that people had come seeking safety, and he was providing it." Rohan paused. "She didn't really look around Goddess Keep—just found Andry in his chambers and didn't stay long, believe me. Not after he said that if she hadn't come to relay my permission to use the *ros'salath* when, where, and as he liked, they had nothing to talk about."

"He dared say such a thing to his own mother?"

"A bit more gently than that, I'm sure, but that was the substance."

"Rohan . . . there was something else." She looked anywhere but at him. "On the gates of Goddess Keep."

"Yes?"

"A Vellanti corpse. Nailed to the wood. With his beard gone and the Merida scar showing on his chin—and a sunburst pattern burned into the skin of his chest."

"Oh, Goddess," he whispered.

"There's more. A—a parchment tacked over his head. 'The fate of all who sin against the Goddess' Sunrunners.' " Her fingers twisted around themselves. "Tobren's mother is dead."

"Poor little girl," Pol murmured. Then, squaring his shoulders, "Did your friend tell you anything about it?"

"Andry was out riding with Rusina and Oclel—he's dead, too. Andry escaped capture and caught the Vellanti who'd killed his friends. Nobody outside his inner circle is very clear on the details, except that Andry was wounded and is now better."

"That's too bad," Pol muttered, and handed her a full cup of wine. "Did you get a look at what Kostas is up to?"

She gave a start. "What? Oh, I'm sorry. Daniv, I should

have said something earlier. It's just that Andry's made me so furious—your father is well and safe, and slicing through the Catha Hills like a scythe." She forced a smile and sipped from the wine, and Rohan knew there was much she had not said.

"Thank you, my lady." The young man copied Isriam's exhalation of relief. "Did you look in at High Kirat?"

"No, but I will this afternoon, to give your mother news. If there's anything you'd like me to tell her for you—"

"Just that I'm well."

Sioned's smile was easier. "And doing your duty brilliantly—and you love her. Why don't you and Isriam go get some air? I'm sure your ears must be sore from listening and your hands ready to fall off from all this scribbling."

"Yes, do that," Rohan said. "You've both served me well today. Thank you."

The pair bowed and left, Isriam with the folded parchment of glass shards. Sioned ran one finger along the shelf where the vase had stood.

"I hate losing my temper that way. But the colossal gall of it! First waiting for Tilal to get close enough to witness his work at Goddess Keep, and now his own princedom! What have we done that he hates us so much, Rohan?"

"Not you, Mother," Pol said. "Me." He faced Rohan and asked softly, "*Now* do you understand?"

"I have always understood." Rohan leaned back in his chair, arms folded. "You both do what you must. But I ask you to consider what Andry is making of himself, and if you want to emulate him."

"It's not that simple!"

"Nothing ever is." With a slight sigh, he finished, "You'd better go, too, or we'll end up shouting at each other again. And, frankly, I don't have the strength right now."

Sioned put her cup down very suddenly. "What is it, Rohan? What's wrong?"

Staring at his hands, he told them about Tuath, the Merida, and Jahnavi.

PART FOUR

Chapter Twenty-four

"Jihan! Stop that at once, you'll get filthy!"

But, as usual, her daughter refused to hear her. Meiglan subsided back onto a carved stone bench, frowning as Jihan led the other children in a headlong slide down a grassy, rain-slicked rise. The bare earth at the bottom was soon trampled into a really good mud puddle.

Lisiel, sitting at her side, laughed. "They're in for a good scrubbing later on! One day you must bring Jihan to Balarat so Tirel can show her how to do the same thing in snow."

Meiglan smiled. "I don't think she'll need lessons. Are you sure you should be away from your rooms?" she added with an envious glance at Lisiel's placid bulk.

"Quite sure, thank you. He hasn't kicked all morning—I think he's taking a nap at last!"

"How do you know you'll have a son?"

Lisiel's dark Fironese eyes grew dreamy as she stroked her belly. "I just know."

"I wish—" Meiglan began incautiously, then compressed her lips.

"The Goddess has been so good to you, Meiglan—she won't deny you a son. Don't worry. Have you heard anything else from Pol?"

Shaking her head, she stared at the shorn rose bushes. In the seven days since sunlight had allowed *faradhi* communication, she had repeated Pol's words over and over in her mind, but hadn't been able to imagine him saying them. She couldn't, not when they had been relayed through Hildreth like that. The phrasing wasn't even his. "*You mustn't worry or feel anxious, my lady. Soon he'll be back here at Dragon's Rest. He misses you and the princesses deeply.*" Pol would

have said it differently—but she couldn't frame the words he would use or hear his voice in her head.

Her daughter's voice, however, was loud and clear as she led the children in a game of tag. It was quite a little tribe that scampered through the gardens. Kierun, abandoning the dignity of his position as squire, became Jihan's lieutenant in the pursuit of fun as the offspring of court retainers, from the cook's four-year-old son to the Master of Horse's thirteen-year-old daughter, swarmed the gravel paths and flower beds. The drizzling rains had let up this morning, allowing the children to play in the soggy sunshine. Catallen, the tutor, had been driven half mad by his restless charges, and compassion dictated that Meiglan free him for the day. Fresh air was good for the children after being cooped up inside; it was good for Lisiel, too, whose waiting had become intolerable.

Meiglan knew how that felt. She knew Pol belonged at Stronghold with his parents, that he had responsibilities to them and the Desert and the other princedoms. Awareness of his duties, however, did not lessen the weight of her own. Her servant, Thanys, constantly reminded her that she was a princess and must retain all authority here. She heard regular reports from all quarters of the vast estates. It didn't matter that she understood perhaps four words in ten. It was appearances that counted. As usual.

Edrel and Laric saw to military things, but it was Meiglan's task to make sure the palace was ready for a siege. Having perfected her mimicry of Sioned, Tobin, and Sionell over the years, she did not fear being found out in her ignorance. All she had to do was say "Do everything that needs to be done," and it was done. But if a crisis came, they would look to her for orders that she was terrified would be the wrong ones.

"I admire you so much," Lisiel said suddenly, and Meiglan nearly jumped. "Laric has told me how you're doing everything yourself. I don't think I'd be able to, separated from my husband."

Meiglan said nothing. There was nothing she could say.

"I think if it came to it, I'd do what my sister did," Lisiel went on softly. "She couldn't bear to be without Ludhil. Of course, neither of us knows anything about war, being raised at Snowcoves. You must have seen your father ordering his troops to punish the Merida when they got too ambitious."

Miyon had never dared military action against the Merida; the one skirmish she'd seen preparations for had been to seize the property of a vassal who had irritated him. She had also seen the man executed by her father's own hand.

"I wish I could be more help," Lisiel sighed. "I wish my son would hurry up and be born, so I can be useful to you."

Meiglan nodded wordlessly, and tried to think up something to say. But in the next moment the princess gripped her arm and turned ash-white.

"What's wrong?" she asked—then knew how stupid the question was. Lisiel's long wait was over. Panic clawed her; the only labor she'd ever attended had been her own—and she had been in no state to learn anything but pain.

"Oh!" Lisiel gasped, bending over with one arm wrapped around her belly. "Meiglan—oh, Goddess, find Laric!"

"Kierun!" she cried, hating the high, thin note of fear in her voice. "Kierun!"

A short while later, Lisiel was back in her rooms. Meiglan was seated near the bed, her lute in her lap and music streaming from her fingers. Master Physician Evarin had asked her to play something soothing. She had doubted that any tune would be heard above Lisiel's screams, but not a single sound had come from her yet. Meiglan couldn't decide if the pain was truly nothing, or if the princess was simply prouder and braver than she herself had been. It was different for all women, Thanys had assured her; some suffered terribly, and others barely winced. Pol had not seemed ashamed of her, even though she'd shrieked her throat raw. But after she had lost their sons, he had been too relieved that wife and daughters were safe to have time for any other emotion.

Master Evarin announced himself delighted with Lisiel's progress and Meiglan's music, and sat down to take his ease. Laric, riding the perimeter of the valley with Edrel, had not yet been found. So Meiglan played while Evarin and Norian listened, Thanys and another maid hovered, and Lisiel watched Meiglan's fingers with wide, transfixed eyes.

Meiglan suspected that Evarin's presence was at Andry's order. Appearing at Dragon's Rest eight days after the fall of Radzyn, he had told of outrunning Goddess alone knew how many enemy patrols and was abjectly glad to be safe once more. But she distrusted anything to do with Andry—

though the purpose served by setting a spy where Pol was not could not be explained.

She plucked and strummed automatically, her mind disengaged from the skills of her fingers. Laric and Lisiel had been at Dragon's Rest so long that the chamber bore their personal touches—combs, clothing, cosmetics, purchases from this year's *Rialla* Fair, embroidered pillows Lisiel had stitched while waiting for the birth. But the cradle in the corner was Pol's. Sioned had brought it from Stronghold during Meiglan's first pregnancy. Big enough to hold triplets, it had been draped with Princemarch's violet when Jihan and Rislyn were born. But although she willingly lent it to the Fironese couple, Meiglan had replaced the violet silk with its original pale green. No child not hers would sleep under Princemarch's color—and Firon's black was obviously unsuitable for a nursery. The ruby-eyed dragon spread painted wings on either side of the cradle, as if to protect the infant soon to sleep there. Meiglan longed to see Pol's son and heir snuggled into the velvet coverlet. But the other day a tentative hope had been disappointed again. Eight years since the twins. She heard her lute give forth a plaintive melody that echoed her feelings, and stopped to retune the strings for a lighter song.

The palace physician came, was icily polite to the Sunrunner, and left after making sure all knew his resentment at the stranger's usurpation of his rightful place. Again Meiglan wondered what the *faradhi* was doing here. Perhaps it was as simple as he'd said, and he wanted to be as far from the Vellant'im as possible. Certainly Dragon's Rest was removed from the fighting. The Faolain was a long way away.

But so was Pol.

She was in the middle of a lullaby when Lisiel gave a sudden blurt of pain. The other women started. Evarin glanced at the water clock.

"Right on time," he approved. "Your grace, this child may have been late in making the effort, but now he's got the idea."

"I hope you're right," Lisiel said between her teeth, panting for breath. "I was starting to think he'd changed his mind. Keep playing, Meiglan, please."

She did so, faltering only when candles sprang to life around the room with the onset of dusk. The physician hadn't even moved a finger to light them. By their glow,

Meiglan watched the other woman's pretty face distort—lips drawn back, tilted eyes squeezed shut, brown skin flushed. Had *she* looked like that? she wondered, fascinated and repelled.

Evarin and Thanys suddenly blocked her view. Lisiel gave a single scream, followed the next instant by an affronted wail.

"A fine, big son, your grace," Evarin said. "Over half a silkweight, and healthy—as your own ears can attest! In possession of all fingers, toes, and rather impressive equipment, I might add."

Lisiel laughed wearily. "Takes after his father, like my first son. But his eyes are mine."

Meiglan set down her lute and flexed cramped fingers. Lisiel and the child were transferred from birthing chair to bed, and the servants got to work. Meiglan nearly gagged as bloodied sheets were whisked away. She moved hastily to the bedside and looked at the child: dark-skinned, black-haired, wrinkled, and shrieking.

"Not happy to be out in the bright, chill world, are you?" Lisiel murmured. "It's all right, little prince. You'll like it here, I promise."

Meiglan forced a smile. "He's lovely."

"Isn't he?" was the complacent reply. Then Lisiel glanced up. "But why did Master Evarin think he had to tell *me* how big this baby is?"

Meiglan couldn't help a giggle, and it loosened the spasm of envy.

"Lisi? Damn it, let me by! I want to see my wife! Lisi!"

Laric rushed in trailing a mud-spattered cloak, skidded to a stop, and lost his powers of speech. He stared at his wife and son for a moment, lips moving soundlessly. Lisiel laughed at him. Meiglan bit her lip, trying not to imagine Pol's face in similar circumstances, and fled the room.

Lamps were being lit outside. She hovered at a window to watch the soothing ritual: two servants moving down either side of the water garden in the gathering gloom, lifting lighted wicks to the glass-enclosed lamps. They completed the circle of the inner walk, then turned and worked their way back along the outer arcs to the Princes Hall. Sometimes Pol waited until full dark and then lit all the lamps at once with Sunrunner's Fire. Meiglan delighted in the sudden appearance of bright twin necklets around the fountain. She

didn't like to think too much about the other aspects of his power, but this was a skill she loved.

The torches ringing the fountain were now ablaze, completing the ordinary nighttime illumination. The Princes Hall stayed in shadow but for the thin rows of lights defining its shape. The towers on either side looked as though covered in quilts made of alternate dark and glowing rectangles. At the New Year, at *Riall'im,* on festival days, the whole of Dragon's Rest blazed with colored light like a Sunrunner's thoughts. Tonight there was only the soft golden gleam of ordinary fire. Peaceful enough, but lonely.

Meiglan turned at the sound of footsteps. A tall, lanky figure appeared at the top of the stairs. The candlelit hallway shimmered dizzily around her and she felt all the blood drain from her face and all the strength from her limbs as a familiar voice—knife wrapped in velvet—called her name.

"Meiglan, my sweet flower! My precious treasure! Come give your adoring papa a kiss!"

* * *

Kostas' squires, Rihani of Ossetia and Saumer of Kierst-Isel, were more closely involved in the fighting than either Isriam or Daniv. In fact, Kostas had given each command of fifty mounted soldiers—making sure that a seasoned trooper was there at all times to guide the young princes. They had acquitted themselves well on raids across Syr, but had yet to face a pitched battle. And might not for some time yet: the whoreson Vellant'im refused to come out of Catha Heights for an honest fight.

Kostas was getting angry. By this time he ought to be busy reclaiming the river, but Patwin's betrayal was an offense that could not be overlooked. And if the enemy held onto the castle, they had a base of operations even if Kostas retook the whole length of the Catha River. Having started from High Kirat with an army of five hundred, with minimal losses in the dozen skirmishes along the road, he preferred to gamble on further losses in a decisive battle rather than leave enough of his army to pen the enemy in Catha Heights. Tilal was expecting him, and he did not intend to keep his brother waiting.

The eighth day after a Sunrunner's eerie beacon had guided Kostas to this admirable field—and he thought he

detected his aunt Sioned's elegant touch there—he sent Saumer and Rihani on yet another raid. It angered him further that the land he scoured so methodically was his own, even though it was necessary to strip the surrounding countryside. The Vellant'im had to run out of food sometime and would then be compelled to forage. But sieges took too damned long. Seated within his tent, maps spread out before him, he had again come to the frustrating conclusion that a direct assault on Catha Heights would mean at least two hundred dead.

His senior captain shoved aside the turquoise wool tent flaps, breathlessly announcing, "My lord, you won't believe it—your niece Lady Izaea is riding into camp!"

Izaea, Patwin's eldest daughter, was Kostas' niece through his wife Danladi, half-sister to the long-dead Rabia. Rather impolitic of the captain to mention the blood connection to a family of traitors. Kostas ordered her brought to him and rolled up his maps.

She was a medium-sized, plumpish woman coming up on her twenty-seventh winter, and looked vaguely like her full aunt, Chiana. Kostas did not invite her to sit down; neither did he offer wine or other refreshment. This was not a reception chamber at High Kirat.

"My lord," she began, perfectly composed, "I have been sent to offer terms."

Kostas laughed in her face.

"You'd best listen," she advised coldly. "The offer will not be repeated."

"And what offer is that? To surrender my troops for slaughter?"

"No. To return in peace to High Kirat, so that when the Vellant'im win, as they surely will, you and your family will live."

"Is that what they offered your father in exchange for his treachery?"

She met his gaze levelly and said nothing.

Kostas wanted to know just one more thing. "You like the idea of becoming a princess of Syr, don't you?"

Her answer was demure and damning. "I could not go against my father's wishes, my lord."

"I make you a counteroffer, Izaea. Give me all the information I need on the enemy within your walls, then go back

and at midnight tonight open the postern gates to my soldiers. Do this, and *I* will let *you* live."

Izaea smiled. "They can mire you down here forever, Uncle. And you'll lose. No one will come from Medawari, where Prince Cabar has locked himself in his keep. He will neither help nor hinder either side in this war. But it's no secret from you, surely, that there are more and more Vellanti warriors ready to come destroy you."

"Let them try," said Kostas, shrugging.

Her eyes, brown tinged with green, began to sparkle. "If you care nothing for yourself or young Saumer, Prince Arlis' brother, I feel sure you'll withdraw to keep Rihani safe." After a slight pause, she added, "Princess Gemma's son."

Kostas' face turned to stone.

"And Gemma herself, and her daughter. Did I neglect to mention that? One result of your return to High Kirat will be that Athmyr will be left alone."

Over the years he had learned to care for pale, gentle Danladi. His youthful desire for Gemma had been comprised of one part lust and four parts ambition, and he knew it. Still, the blow to his pride had been a severe one, and even after so long he could not think of his brother's wife without a twinge of uncomfortable emotion kept carefully hidden.

Izaea smiled serenely. "However, if you attack Catha Heights, the order will be given at Athmyr. I've provided very through descriptions so they'll know which women to save for—shall we say—their amusement?"

Any man would have reacted the same way to such threats directed at any woman. He surged to his feet, grasped Izaea's arm, and hauled her outside into the misting rain.

"Assemble the commanders!" he bellowed. Izaea didn't try to shake off his bruising grip; she had succeeded in infuriating him, which had been her goal. She did not yet know what a mistake it had been, or what it would cost her.

The leaders of four major and six minor holdings came running. Titled "commanders" only through courtesy and convenience, for Kostas and his senior captain gave the only orders, they ranged from the middle-aged *athri* of Chalsan Manor to the twenty-three-year-old granddaughter of the ancient crone who ruled Pyrme Landhold. Some of their troops had come with them, and when the crowd swelled to about a hundred men and women, Kostas finally spoke.

"You may not recognize the Lady Izaea—it's difficult to see a daughter of Syr when she wears traitor's clothing. She offers me retreat or destruction. I choose neither! But as Prince of Syr, I *do* choose to judge and sentence her for her betrayal."

Izaea flinched away from him, beginning to understand her danger. Kostas grabbed her around the waist from behind, pinning her arms as well. Holding her immobile to his side, he drew his knife and rested it against her throat. She screamed and twisted her face away.

"Gently—you'll cut yourself," he told her with an almost caressing menace.

"Kill her," someone said.

To Izaea he whispered, "You have made a serious error, my lady. I am not as civilized as some." She cringed again and he chuckled. "Shocking, isn't it?"

"She deserves to die," said another in the crowd.

Kostas nodded. "But I think I'll leave her alive to remind others of what happens to those who listen to treachery."

Deftly, he jerked the knife upward. Izaea shrieked as her left ear was sliced from her skull. Kostas released her and she toppled to the ground, her shrill cries increasing as she saw the blood streaming down her hands. With a flick of his wrist, the knife studded the damp grass beside her.

"Next time," he said softly, "it will be your heart." Turning to his captain, he ordered, "Bind the wound and put her on her horse. And when my squires return, send them to me at once. I've waited long enough to take back what is mine."

* * *

Miyon hated Dragon's Rest as much as he hated Stronghold, and for the same reason: neither belonged to him. His passion to possess the latter was perhaps a whit the more powerful for being of longer duration, but every time he saw the graceful sweep of Pol's palace his guts ground with fury. His iron had helped build Dragon's Rest, iron that Sunrunner witch Sioned had cheated him out of in 719.

But as deeply as he loathed and lusted after both places, Pol's residence had a distinct advantage over Rohan's: there were more secluded places in which to hold a private conversation.

He waited in one such location for Catallen to arrive. The tutor probably had not expected to be summoned so soon, but Miyon needed information before he could select his course of action. The tale he'd told Meiglan last night—fleeing for his life after the Merida had seized command of his army to effect the attack against Tuath—had explained his immediate presence, but there were many things he must know. Catallen had better provide some answers.

The tutor slunk by, glancing nervously around him. Miyon cursed quietly—the man could not have looked more the conspirator if he'd worn a craft sign—and Catallen jumped. After another swift look down the hallway, he slipped into the alcove and sketched a hasty bow.

"Pardon my lateness, your grace—Princess Jihan was slow to learn the day's lesson."

"My granddaughter's education concerns me not at all. Sitting in this closet waiting for you does."

"I'm sorry, your grace. I—"

"Enough. I want to know everything you know, Catallen. Every detail about Dragon's Rest, the Desert, Waes—everything."

"I don't have access to—"

"I didn't send you here to teach history to Pol's children or new songs to Pol's wife! I want information about Pol himself, and I want it now."

Catallen talked for some time, and Miyon did not interrupt him. He learned that Andry had used some bizarre spell at Goddess Keep, and that a considerable village of refugees had sprung up there; that strange things were happening in Firon; that Ludhil was conducting a pathetic little war of his own on Dorval; that Kostas and Arlis had been more successful in their endeavors but that the former was currently frustrated by Catha Heights and the latter by bad weather; that Tilal and Ostvel were cooling their heels in Waes, waiting for Rohan to decide if Swalekeep merited an attack; and that Chiana was universally suspect but that no one had any proof against her.

Miyon also learned that his son Birioc now occupied Tuath Castle and had proclaimed himself its lord. He wondered sardonically what nicety of feeling had prevented the young fool from naming himself Prince of Cunaxa; perhaps one of his Merida uncles had explained Miyon's plans to

him and he had stopped preening himself long enough to understand.

Best of all, he learned that Rohan and Pol were pent up in Stronghold, possibly preparing for a battle. But, knowing Rohan, probably not.

Catallen finished and Miyon sent him on his way. Leaving the alcove some time later, he meandered around the lower gardens in the intermittent sunshine and considered his next moves.

First things first. The Prince and Princess of Firon were in his very hands. The banner of Snowcoves flying over Balarat could mean only one thing: Yarin had decided the time was right for seizing the princedom he thought should have come to him in 719 anyway, rather than to a distant descendant of a long-dead Fironese prince. The *athri*'s discontent had been carefully noted by Miyon some years ago for future use; the time to use the knowledge had come.

But how? He could warn Laric of his brother-by-marriage's treachery, and thereby gain invaluable credit for himself. It had the additional advantage of removing Laric from Dragon's Rest to go save his princedom—taking along with him a sizable contingent of Pol's troops. Pity he couldn't rid himself of Lisiel and her new son at the same time; the brat's squalling had kept him awake all last night.

He could stay quiet about Yarin's ambitions—except in a report to Chiana, who would pass it along to the Vellant'im. He had no need of proving his value to them, however; something else he had in mind would make him their valued ally. Besides, what did the Vellant'im care about the wastes of Firon?

Laric, he decided with a smile, would be going home. If a messenger was sent to Cunaxa now, in twenty-five days or so Yarin could be warned at Balarat to expect his sister's husband. It would take Laric twice that long to get there. With luck, he might even die of cold or avalanche along the way.

Next on Miyon's list was Stronghold. He didn't want it destroyed. He wanted it for himself. But that blue-eyed dragon who held it would continue to do so unless a force vastly outnumbering his own attacked. He'd given up Radzyn and Remagev; Miyon guessed that faced with similar odds, he'd relinquish Stronghold, too. So the objective was to keep Tallain occupied—which Birioc seemed to be doing—

and prevent anyone, mainly Kostas, from coming to Rohan's aid. A little more luck, and not only would Rohan be dead at last, but Meiglan would be a widow. And who would protect her and her young daughters? He grinned again, tore a thin branch off a willow tree that got in his way, and wondered what price to ask for his little treasures from Chiana and Rinhoel.

But before that could happen, Kostas must be stopped. He tagged it mentally for his message to Chiana, and then turned his mind to the more interesting and immediate question: the price he could get for Dragon's Rest itself. The palace was only two days from Stronghold—through a narrow, twisting pass unsuited to the movement of soldiers, true, but Dragon Gap would be the last place from which Rohan would expect the Vellanti army to appear. It would be tricky—handing it over to them without seeming to, preserving his role as innocent victim of circumstances as long as possible—but he felt sure he could do it. With Laric gone and, say, sixty or so of Pol's guard with him as escort, it would be easier to take the valley. Its natural defense of high-walled canyon mouth was formidable, but there had to be a way.

Edrel would have to be dealt with. Miyon turned the problem over in his mind for some time, unaware that he'd left the gardens behind and trudged through open fields until the damp soaked through the thin leather of his boots. But by then he cared nothing for the cold and wet. He had figured out a way to present the Vellant'im with Dragon's Rest on a golden plate.

Seeing that he was nearly at the little cottage Pol had built for Meiglan, he decided to rest and warm himself there. He expected to find comfort, tinder for a fire, and perhaps something to eat or drink.

He did not expect to find saddlebags enough for fifteen horses packed for a journey.

By the time he'd inspected three sets he knew what was going on. Children's clothes, food for a journey, even a map of the route to Stronghold—Miyon reclined in a large cowhide armchair and wondered how in the name of the Storm God he had sired so mortally stupid a daughter.

So she sought escape, did she? Or, knowing her, she sought Pol's pretty face and big strong arms. Well, she would not find him. She must have started planning this

almost the moment he'd arrived last night. It pleased him to think that he could still frighten her so much; she would be easier to control. This desperate bid for freedom and Pol was the best thing he'd learned all day.

He rested a little while, absorbing his surroundings with increasing amazement. Why a prince with so splendid a palace would want to construct something this vulgar—and with his own hands, too—was beyond him. There were two bedchambers and this main room where Meiglan undoubtedly relived her peasant childhood by cooking at the huge hearth. Ludicrous, that a prince wanted to live like the common ruck. But then, Pol's head was stuffed full of strange notions; it was just as well he wouldn't live to inflict them on everyone else as High Prince.

After a time Miyon rose, stretched, and found flint and kindling. He hated having to sacrifice his favorite cloak, but this had to look genuine for Laric's and Edrel's sakes. Meiglan was too thick to guess at once, but Miyon would enlighten her as to exactly what had happened—and why.

He lit a fire in the hearth and made sure it was drawing well—he had to admit that Pol had done a good job setting the chimney. Then he yanked the patterned quilts from the beds and twirled them into long ropes that snaked along the wooden floor from the hearth toward the smaller rooms. A storage chest yielded a jar of cooking grease, congealed in the chill but adequate to his purposes. Smearing it on his cloak, he laid one end to the big quilt and the other in the hearth. Flames guided toward the greasy material caught and burned. Art, he told himself, grinning. Pure art.

Miyon stayed within as long as he could in the gathering smoke. When all the coverlets and the floor beneath them were burning, he stumbled, coughing, out the door.

It was cold outside without his cloak, but knowledge of a task charmingly accomplished warmed him. And as he waved his arms and shouted for help, the blood flowed even more sweetly through his veins.

The first man up the little hill was the winemaster, who had been on his way back from an inspection of his vineyards. Miyon collapsed against the man's chest, keeping a good grip on him so he could neither run for help nor attempt to put out the fire within. By the time others reached the cottage, it was too late. They managed to stop the total destruction Miyon had hoped for, but the place was left only

a hollow shell of wooden beams and chimney. Nearly everything inside was cinders.

"I was chilled by my walk," Miyon explained later from his bed to Meiglan, Edrel, and Norian as Master Evarin mixed a poultice for his smoke-reddened eyes. "The fire I built in the hearth was a little too warm. I dropped off to sleep—and woke up coughing myself half to death. I was sitting too close and my cloak caught." He swallowed wine to ease an admittedly sore throat, and glanced up at Meiglan. "I'm sorry, my treasure, but though they saved the frame and chimney, everything *within* the cottage is gone."

Her stricken expression was seen as shock at the loss of Pol's gift to her; Norian patted her hand in sympathy. Miyon was surprised to find his daughter was smarter than he'd thought, to understand without his explaining it to her in words of one syllable.

Still, just in case, he added, "I know you value what you kept there. But don't let the loss worry you, Meiglan dearest."

"You must lie back now, your grace," the Sunrunner physician said, "and put this on your eyes. I'll mix a draught that will soothe your lungs as well."

"I thank you for your skill, Master Evarin," he said, and coughed. "It won't make me sleep, will it?"

"No, your grace. Not even drowsy."

"Good. I must speak with Prince Laric at once. On my walk—I have a habit of taking long walks alone, they allow me to think in peace—I recalled something he needs to know."

The only walks Miyon was in the habit of taking were from one mistress' bed to another, and Meiglan knew it. She stared at him with velvet brown eyes that had always reminded him of a frightened cow's. Then long lashes lowered and she bit her lip. Miyon pretended a coughing fit to hide laughter, then said, "Lord Edrel, would you be so good as to find Prince Laric for me? This really can't wait."

* * *

Mirsath, his cousin Karanaya, and the Sunrunner Johlarian met in Faolain Lowland's oratory. A simple room off the main hall, it glittered with the treasures of five generations: crystal wedding goblets, silver plate and a delicate container for salt, gold candlesticks, and—the High Prince's gift on

completion of the new keep—a gilt rack to hold vigil candles. Ordinarily these were lit only for a remembrance ritual for royal dead; Mirsath had ordered candles kept burning here until Lowland was free.

No sunshine spilled through the colored glass skylights. The long row of tiny flames at the back of the room provided the only illumination beneath gray-black skies. Mirsath watched Karanaya walk back and forth in front of them, each pass bending the white-gold fires.

"We can forget any help from Kostas," she was saying—another needless repetition of the obvious. In the days since Lord Maarken had summarized the war for Johlarian, they had hoped, beseeched the Goddess, and cursed the Syrene prince for adhering to war's logic rather than Lowland's desperate need.

"We have only ourselves," Karanaya went on, still prowling, fingering the heavy golden chain around her neck. "Rohan can't help. Kostas won't."

"Can't," Mirsath corrected wearily. "We're only two hundred. There are thousands in Syr—"

"We're the gateway to the Desert!"

"In case you hadn't noticed, they're already *in* the Desert," Karanaya snapped.

"But what is it that keeps them here, instead of going around us?" Johlarian asked. "They want Lowland, but what for?"

"Could it be because we're part of the Desert?" Mirsath asked. "They've destroyed every other place they've taken—but not Radzyn or Whitecliff or Remagev. Is it something about castles belonging to Rohan that—"

"There's no sense in that," said his cousin. "They destroyed Riverport and almost leveled Tuath, and they're part of the Desert."

"As much sense as risking your life to grab those pearls that night!" he snarled, out of patience with her.

She clasped both hands over her bodice, where between her breasts rested a tiny silk pouch holding the six iridescent black drops. "The Dragon's Tears were my wedding present," she began furiously, "the only thing I saved from the wreckage, and the only dowry I—"

"Assuming you live long enough to find another husband!"

"My lord, my lady!" Johlarian pleaded.

Mirsath ignored him. "Goddess, if only we could fight

them!" He sank into a spindly fruitwood chair and crossed long legs at the ankles. "All we can do is wait for help. And block their efforts if we can. They've built a dozen bridging ladders, and lost every one of them to Sunrunner's Fire. They've tried diverting the moat—sheer folly at this time of year, with the northern rains swelling the river. They've even poisoned the water, not knowing that we have our own well inside the walls."

"All they have to do is starve us out," Karanaya reminded him.

"But that wouldn't take the hundreds who're camped outside. Fifty or sixty, maybe, to wait for our surrender. Why don't they use their strength and take us? They could. But they don't. Why do they want Lowland?"

The same question was exercising the mind of Princess Tobin at Stronghold. The hardships of travel across the Long Sand had weakened her more than she would admit, but days of rest and recovery in her birthplace had gradually put some strength back into her limbs. Chay no longer shouted at her when she walked downstairs using her canes, although he did scowl horribly when she appeared one morning with just one to support her. Speech was still difficult, and succeeding days of overcast skies nearly drove her mad. But, trapped within her mind for the most part, she had plenty of time to think. And one of the things that puzzled her most was Faolain Lowland.

Tobin had always been a creature of movement. It frustrated her that her body would not respond with its former strength and suppleness to the energy of her mind. As tentative control returned, she took to walking up and down the center of the Great Hall morning and afternoon. Servants dodged nimbly around her, cleaning up after one meal or setting up for the next. Tobin would have gone outside to be out of their way, but courtyard cobbles and gravel garden pathways were difficult for her to negotiate. So across the smooth blue and green tiles of the Great Hall she limped on one good leg, one dragging foot, and her cane.

There must be something they weren't seeing, some connection that had escaped them. Unlike Gilad Seahold and Faolain Riverport and dozens of smaller holdings, Desert castles still stood, for reasons unknown. More to the point, Lowland still stood—and had received an offer of peaceable

surrender, which Radzyn and Remagev had not. What was the value placed on these keeps that kept them intact?

Radzyn was easily explained: a secure base with the only safe harbor on the Desert coast. Remagev was more difficult. It had no strategic significance. Lowland did, but the Vellant'im could have gone around it. They didn't need it militarily. So why—?

She turned at the huge double doors and started back up the central aisle to the high table. Behind it was the immense tapestry, a stylized gold dragon on blue, an emerald set into the ring the crowned beast held. Two chairs—not quite thrones—were directly below it, carved with dragons. It was a powerful setting Rohan had created for himself, lacking only him and Sioned to complete it. No, she corrected, not for himself, but for others. She remembered the night he had been officially acclaimed High Prince, how Sioned had conjured a dragon of Fire to leap through the air and meld into that tapestry. A brilliant piece of dramatic management, flamboyant and effective. Rohan'd shown the same impulse the night of the escape from Remagev, pretending that Pol's dragon had come at his call, playing it for all he was worth. No one could fault her little brother for lack of imagination. . . .

But war was a grimly practical business. War depended on facts. Numbers of troops, directions of march, timing of maneuvers—war was as brutal and direct as the sword that hung near the tapestry, the sword Rohan had not touched for the length of Pol's life.

And yet—Tobin's thoughts whirled and she leaned on her cane, staring at the golden dragon's outspread wings. The Vellant'im had fallen on their faces at sight of a dragon.

Tobin sacrificed pride to haste and snagged a passing servant to help her upstairs. She stammered badly with impatience while telling him she was quite well, merely fatigued, and wished neither husband nor physician to attend her. Alone in her chamber, she settled into a deep armchair and closed her eyes. Her own copy of the book had been offered up to necessity, but she had a very good memory and Sioned had taught her a few Sunrunner tricks for enhancing it. Thoroughly, methodically, she began to review everything Betheyn had read her from Feylin's dragon book.

* * *

Kostas had small use for the gadgets Rohan enjoyed so much. Water clocks were interesting things, no doubt, but the day progressed whether one measured its passing or not; pens that held ink within them rather than needing to be dipped might save time, but the old ones worked just as well. On the twelfth day of Winter, however, Kostas had reason to applaud the High Prince's fascination with innovative devices, and his habit of sharing them with others.

The Fironese who made water clocks also tinkered with other forms of glass. One of the results rested now in Kostas' hands, lent him by Rihani, to whom Rohan had given it at the last *Rialla*. A long, thin tube with clear glass at one end and a lens at the other, it made the faraway loom close enough to touch.

Kostas sat back on his heels amid the trees, gazing once more through the lens at the swollen rush of the Catha River. A flatboat hugged the bank, not daring to venture out into the main current. It rode low in the water, as if wallowing with heavy supplies of grain and meat and other foodstuffs. Thick waterproofs were draped over lumps that could have been crates and barrels. On a thin pennant fluttering from short poles at the stern, the black deer of Meadowlord leaped on a field of light spring green. A nice touch; Saumer's idea. Unhappily, it had been impossible to outfit the men on board with the appropriate tunics. Kostas hoped the flag would be convincing enough, and that none of the soldiers concealed beneath the tarps moved at the wrong moment. The slightest shifting to ease cramped muscles might prove fatal. And Goddess forbid a sneeze.

Taking the lens from his eye, Kostas tucked it in its leather case and crept back into the deeper shelter of the woods. "Only a little while until they reach the docks. Is everything ready?"

Rihani nodded. "Half the army at the roadside field, the other half on the rise Aunt Sioned guided us to."

It could have been any Sunrunner, of course, but Kostas had chosen to attribute the Fire-tipped pine to the High Princess. It heartened the troops—and Kostas had had a feeling, anyway. He passed the lens to his nephew. "Keep watch for me."

"Yes, my lord."

Since sending Izaea back to Catha Heights, Kostas had worked on and rejected plan after plan for taking the keep.

But two days ago a scout had returned with word that three boats were coming downriver. It had been too late to organize a battle, though he'd sent archers to kill as many as possible while the supplies were unloaded and carted up to the castle. But the event had given Kostas an idea. He'd ordered a similar craft made upstream, finding use at last for the six boatwrights from the Faolain who were among his soldiers.

Saumer's notion about the pennant was truly inspired. The other three boats had carried no identification, but that meant little. If Chiana was sending supplies to the enemy, she could advertise it or not; all she needed to claim was that her good intentions had been thwarted by the enemy. But Meadowlord's flag openly displayed might reveal much. Conspiracy with the Vellant'im would mean a peaceable unloading; armed efforts to seize the boat would prove Chiana innocent—perhaps. It could be that along with word of her cooperation had come orders to make everything look good for her sake. Kostas had his doubts about that, but Rihani thought it possible and the boy's mind was a sharp one.

"My lord!" his nephew whispered, drawing his attention, and he scooted forward to the edge of the wood. Taking the lens, he peered through it and nearly yelped in delight. A mere five Vellanti warriors were coming down from the castle to the docks.

"So Chiana is guilty after all," he murmured. "We've just given Tilal the excuse he needs to take Swalekeep!"

"I wish we had a Sunrunner so we could tell him," Rihani said. "But with this sky, a Sunrunner wouldn't be any help anyway. Shall I get a courier ready to leave at once, my lord?"

"We'll wait until we can also send word of a victory." He squinted through the lens once more, waiting, holding his breath as the warriors approached the arriving flatboat. "That's it," he encouraged softly. "Nice and humble, Saumer—you're not a prince but a common boatman, scared half out of your wits by these savages—very good!"

Geography favored them beyond Kostas' hopes. The docks were shielded by a stand of tall trees that provided cooling shade to workers in summer. Anything sailing downriver was seen from the castle long before it reached the docks, but once there it became invisible. He watched gleefully as

Saumer, ragged and rain-soaked like the other two men who had guided the boat, bowed before the bearded enemy. No one at Catha Heights saw when the three Vellant'im who climbed onto the boat had their throats slit, and the other two died on the dock with knives in their guts.

Kostas watched his twenty soldiers conceal the corpses beneath the waterproofs. "Right," he said briskly, casing the lens once more.

"How long before Saumer opens the gates once he's inside?"

"However long it is, we'd better get to our positions." He clasped his nephew's shoulder. "I know you wanted to go with him, but one of you had to take command of the second wing."

"Saumer's a better actor than I am, anyway," Rihani grinned. "Goddess watch over you, my lord."

"And you." But it was not the Goddess he thought of as he returned to his horse and rode to join his main army. It was the Father of Storms, who had dominion over Air and Water. The freshening wind and light rain in his face might be taken as omens of approval—along with sudden thunder above the hills, as if the Storm God laughed in anticipation of a good fight, a fine victory.

Kostas laughed, too, feeling more alive than at any time in his fifty years. He had been born for this—not to preside over law courts or listen to tallies of yearly yield in wheat and cattle and wine. Rohan might deplore the use of swords to settle matters, but not every prince felt the same. And a good thing, too. It was Kostas' kind that was needed now—unafraid of fierce battle, of killing those who dared take what was his. His sword would be wind-swift today, and the blood of his enemies would rain on the land.

* * *

"Madness!" Shaking her head vigorously, Thanys blocked Meiglan's way to the larger of the wardrobes. "You know your father—you can't escape him."

"I *will* leave here and he *won't* stop me!"

"Even if you succeed in leaving, he'll come after you."

"Not if he doesn't know I'm gone until it's too late."

"My lady, what's come over you?" Thanys cried. "You're safe here at Dragon's Rest!"

"If you think that, you're as stupid as my father believes me to be!" She gripped the servant's arms. "I can't stand it here any longer. It was bearable before my father came, but now—I can't stay, I can't!"

"So you'd endanger your children—"

"Goddess help you, don't you see? They'll be safer at Stronghold under siege than here with Miyon! It's not just for me, it's for them!"

It wasn't the exact truth, but Thanys had no need to know that. Meiglan simply could live no longer with her fear and without Pol. She wasn't Gemma or Alasen or Danladi, to hold her keep while her husband was at war. Laric and Edrel would do better without her. In freeing herself from her father, she was freeing them to defend Dragon's Rest—and against him, if necessary.

Miyon's arrival and his destruction of the cottage had pushed her that final step to real panic. All that kept her from tumbling over the precipice was the feverish need to flee to the only safety she had ever known.

Instead of the fifteen she had thought to take, it would be just herself, the girls, and two guards. Instead of ample food and clothing, they would travel only with what they wore and enough for a sketchy meal on the road. Instead of taking the usual two days, they would ride as fast as they could without killing themselves or their horses.

Meiglan had told no one but Laroshin, the guards commander, of her original plan. He had not been happy, but as his liege lady she had given her orders and sworn him to secrecy. She knew that the fire had come as a relief to him, preventing what he considered a rash course of action.

This time only Thanys knew, and she would order Laroshin to have five horses saddled and ready at midnight, after Lisiel formally Named her new son. Meiglan would summon her daughters to her chambers after dinner to hear their lessons as usual. But she would tuck them up in her own bed, and when everything was ready hurry them through the hidden passage to their father's rooms. Pol had long ago shown her the secret stairway there; she hoped she remembered how to open it.

Thanys sighed heavily and got out of Meiglan's way. She busied herself refolding clothes the girls would wear tonight—warm woolen trousers and shirts, with matching dark cloaks—

while Meiglan pulled out similar garments for herself. "My lady . . . I wish you'd reconsider and take me with you."

"I need you to stay and keep my father from this room as long as possible. Tell him—tell him the children and I have caught chills and can't be disturbed. He can't find out I've gone before noon tomorrow."

"He *will* ride after you."

"I've a right to go to my husband!"

"But in secret? In the dead of night? What will Prince Laric and Lord Edrel think? What will I tell *them?*"

"Anything you like!" She tossed clothes onto the bed and rounded on the servant. "I don't care! Don't you understand? This isn't my problem, any of it! I don't know what to do, what to say, how to keep my father from destroying us all if he gets half a chance! I want Pol! I want to be safe and know my children are safe and—and—" Hearing hysteria in her voice, she clapped both hands over her mouth and shook.

Thanys embraced her, rocked her gently back and forth. "There, sweeting, there. You weren't born to this, it's not in your nature to be at war. When you married him, I sang inside. I thought, at last she'll have the life she deserves, all elegance and joy and never an angry word from a husband who'll cherish her. But he left you, and—"

"He had to," Meiglan quavered. "This isn't his fault, Thanys."

"He should be here to protect you, little one. Hush now, hush. Just be brave, and soon you'll be with him again, where you belong."

* * *

The wind up from the southwest strengthened slowly—too slowly for Tobin's temper. She needed sunlight, needed the clouds to blow away from Stronghold and Faolain Lowland. It was noon before the first wisps of sunlight threaded Desert air, but by that time she had summoned Sioned and in a halting, hesitant voice explained her idea.

"But that's *crazy!*" was Sioned's first reaction; her second, "Do you think it'll work?"

"Need sunlight," Tobin reminded her.

"And there's none to be had at the moment, nor likely to

be soon. . . ." Sioned's face changed subtly. "Let me go look something up."

Tobin waited in a storm of restless impotence for Sioned to return. She glared at the sky beyond her window, willing the wind to strength and the sun to burn away lingering haze. The water clock in the corner indicated just noon when Sioned came back, Pol in tow and the translated copy of the Star Scroll in her arm.

"One of you is going to explain this, right?" Pol asked.

Tobin, understanding the fierce, gleeful light in Sioned's green eyes, gave him her half-smile. "Patience," she counseled, blithely ignoring the fact that she herself possessed precious little of that commodity.

"I need a deep, wide bowl, preferably pure metal," Sioned told her son. "And a cup of strong wine." Holding up a small velvet pouch, she finished, "I never have liked the taste of this stuff."

Pol turned pale beneath his tan. "Mother—that's *dranath*."

"Of course it is. I've never done this before and I need all the help I can get. Now, the bowl and wine, please?"

Chapter Twenty-five

The army of Syr paused below Catha Heights, just out of arrowshot. Vellanti warriors jeered insults but wasted no arrows, which Prince Kostas found interesting. He sat his horse and listened, a half-smile on his face.

"They seem to have picked up something of our language," he commented to his captain. "And they're creative with it, I'll give them that."

"It's a new experience for me, my lord, being called the unnatural spawn of the diseased backside of a toad."

"A castrated toad."

"I was trying to be polite, my lord."

Kostes grinned. "Havadi, we'll make a courtier of you yet." He glanced at the sky, where noon sun struggled against clouds. "Does a toad have balls?"

"I've never looked, my lord. But today we'll find out if the Vellant'im do."

The prince nodded, wondering how long it would take Saumer to sneak from the waterside of the castle to the main gates. He fanned his anticipation gently, keeping it controlled but glowing hot enough to burst into flame when he needed it. It was rather like making love: waiting, pacing himself, timing the moment. His wife's delicate fairness and fragile skin came to mind, and another anticipation swelled in him. Perhaps after he'd taken Catha Heights and advanced up the river, he'd ride home and surprise Danladi. High Kirat was only two days from River Run; his troops would need rest by then, and if the roads held clear, he could—

"My lord! Look!"

Kostas did, and laughed. Predictably enough, when the gates swung open there was outcry both within and without

the walls. The Vellant'im bellowed their rage; the army of Syr roared back. Kostas awarded the prize to his own people and gave the signal to attack.

Saumer had done his work perfectly. The chains, ropes, and iron bars holding the gates had been neutralized and they did not close up again. The enemy swarmed out in no order whatsoever. Kostas almost regretted that his battle plan did not call for annihilating them all on the spot.

* * *

Sioned sat back, wiping sweat from her forehead. "Damn! I can't get anything beyond a quiver. I'm doing just what the scroll says, and I can feel the *dranath,* but it's not happening."

"Maybe Karanaya never used it before she gave it to you," Pol suggested, peering into the broad silver bowl of water. A gold thimble glinted at the bottom, intricately carved with flowers. "Or maybe you've used it too much." When Tobin's brow arched eloquently, Pol grinned. "Sorry, Mother. You're as rotten at needlework as you are at cooking."

"Thank you, your gracelessness," she replied, smiling wryly. "You may be right, and this doesn't have enough association with Karanaya to do us any good. But I could swear I feel something. More *dranath* might do it—"

"No," Tobin stated. "Let Pol try."

"What?" They spoke together, staring at her.

"*Diarmadhi.*" She used only the single word not because she could not form any others, but because that was the only one needed. Her gaze flickered back and forth from mother to son, compassionate and inflexible.

It was the first time Tobin had ever acknowledged what he was. Pol felt his breath catch. Most of the time he forgot that Sioned wasn't his birth-mother, forgot that anyone knew about him. But Tobin had been at Feruche the night he was born, and at Skybowl the night he was Named. She had always been there, loving him in spite of what he truly was. No, that wasn't right; what he was didn't matter to her at all.

"It might work," he said at last, with a glance at his mother's wary expression. "A Star Scroll spell ought to be worked by a sorcerer."

Reluctantly, Sioned answered, "Rohan watched Urival do something like this once. And he was *diarmadhi*. I can do the kind of conjuring I used the night Andry became Lord of Goddess Keep, but evidently this is more complicated." She picked up the drug-laced wine cup and set it out of his reach. "But no *dranath*. Urival didn't use any. I don't want you touching the stuff."

"If I can't get anything on first try, I may have to," he warned.

"Let's wait till that egg hatches, shall we? Here, read down to the bottom of the page. It continues on the overleaf."

He read carefully, but part of his mind remembered when his father had shown him the Star Scroll in preparation for his battle by sorcery with Ruval. He knew how to construct the *ros'salath* as well as Andry did—but his cousin had added some twist to the working that made it lethal. Damping the anger always associated with Andry these days, he read through the spell again and handed the scroll back to his mother.

"It's straightforward enough. Don't worry," he said to reassure them—and then recalled that it was not Meiglan he was dealing with. Neither of these women had a timid bone in her body.

Sioned pushed the silver bowl across the table to him. Framing it with his hands, he fixed his gaze on the thimble, concentrating. Urival had shown him several things from the Star Scroll, all minor workings, little more than tricks. For the first time since reading the guidelines for the *ros'salath*, Pol saw how various small sorceries could be woven together—just so—to produce a more powerful spell.

Some of it was familiar. Mental and physical preparation, for instance—so automatic by now that he had to force himself to think about it. Calm the heartbeat and clear the mind, breathe easily and softly, relax outward senses and focus on inward function.

But there were differences, too. Sunrunners lit Fire across Water—but not *in* it. The most disturbing was the recurrence of an image first conjured at Radzyn: his own two hands, palms pressed together but unable to touch. One wore a single moonstone *faradhi* ring that had been Andrade's. The other bore the great amethyst of Princemarch. Two halves, two inheritances, not touching. Some barrier lay between them like a pane of crystal ground to invisible

thinness. Pol tried to press through it, shatter it, curve the fingers around each other. It seemed terribly important that he do so, though he could not have said why. The fingers curled, nails scraping glass with a horrible rasp that made him flinch.

"Pol? What is it? What do you see?"

Sioned's whisper drew him from the troubling image. He opened his eyes, wondering when he'd closed them. "Sorry. It's nothing—just a slight distraction. I'm ready now."

She examined his face narrowly. She didn't believe him—not that he had expected her to. Her nod indicated only that they would discuss it later.

Pol no longer saw the hands, but as at Radzyn the Sunrunner part of him was only a shadow in the background, powerful but subordinate to sorcerer blood. Bending to his task, he called Fire to Water. Tiny misted flames swirled white-gold, staining the silver bowl. Slowly, with gathering intensity, the Fire centered on the thimble. The half of Pol's mind that was *diarmadhi* controlled the light, spread it through the liquid, and a conjuring began to form.

Hazy, infuriatingly indistinct, he could see a woman with dark hair wearing a blue dress. The scroll advised concentration on each detail as it became clear, linking them together to steady the vision. He started with the sweep of hair back from her brow, its twining into a long braid coiled at her nape, the gleam of silver hairpins. Their subtle shine was repeated in the earrings that swung close to her jaw. He solidified those details and others filled in: the curve of her cheek, her lips, nose, eyes, brow. Gold glittered at her neck, drawing his attention, and as the chain took on definite form he could see the pulse beating at her throat, the set of her shoulders, the swell of her breasts where the chain vanished into her bodice.

All at once the vision pulsed with another light, as if stars hung in blackness had acquired iridescent color. Startled, Pol hung onto what he had thus far gained and shied away from that glow. Karanaya wore a thin silver bracelet on one wrist; he focused on that and as she brought a wine cup to her lips, he saw the details of her hand and arm. But when she put the goblet down, the clarity of her physical form was almost obliterated again by the throbbing of that strange light. This time he faced it, more astonished than ever. It was as if a Sunrunner's colors had been captured in a mid-

night sky laced with stars. The glow centered near her heart but did not come from Karanaya herself; its source nestled between her breasts.

Pol rested a moment, checking over the details. Yes, a precise picture of her now, seated at a table with pens, parchment, and inkwell before her, wine cup within reach next to a green ceramic vase of wilting flowers. He could see the graining of the wooden table and the words she had written and the chip in the goblet's foot. Surrounding her was a maze of indistinct shadows, but the dimensions of the room were unimportant. He had completed the first part of the Star Scroll spell; it was time for the essence of the working.

Now his Sunrunner abilities came into play. They were the stronger when it came to communication; he had been trained thoroughly in this and instinct took over, pushing sorcery to one side. Not into the background, as the *faradhi* part of him had been, but as if the two stood separate but equal. Still not touching. He wondered briefly if they ever would, and the bleakness of the thought frightened him.

Karanaya.

No response; he tried again, and this time when he spoke/thought her name, she glanced over her shoulder as if seeking the source of the voice. Alone in the room—as far as she knew—she shrugged and went back to her writing.

Karanaya! She gave a start, glancing around again. *Don't be afraid. It's Pol—not on sunlight, because there isn't any and you can't feel such things. Listen, Karanaya, and don't be afraid.*

Her whole body went rigid. He regretted her terror and the necessity for it, but there was nothing he could do. *Karanaya, listen to me carefully. Princess Tobin believes she knows how to rid you of the Vellant'im. It will take great courage and daring on your part, and Johlarian's help. But I think it can be done.*

Her lips moved—and he heard her voice. Stunned, he missed the sense of the first few words; this had never happened to him before. It wasn't *supposed* to happen. Sunrunners could see on light and, if powerful enough, could use it to conjure at great distances—but not hear.

". . . beg the Goddess in her mercy to take me, I'd rather die than go mad—"

Well, what had he expected, anyway? Of course she thought

that. He would have, too. *You're not going mad. It really is Prince Pol. Look, I'll prove it to you.* He searched through accumulated years to find memory of her. She had never been to Dragon's Rest; he had been to Lowland once and Riverport twice—but she *had* been to Radzyn. *You and your family were at Radzyn when you were about fifteen or sixteen, and one morning we went down to the beach and built a sand castle with Chayla and Rohannon.*

"Gentle Goddess," she whispered. "Your grace—?"

He sighed his relief. *Yes. Thank you for believing me, and I'm sorry I scared you. It was clumsy of me. Karanaya, before I tell you what Tobin's got in mind, I need you to tell me something. What are you wearing around your neck that gives off so many colors?*

* * *

Karanaya slid from her chair, as limp now as she had been stone-stiff an instant earlier. Mirsath, summoned by a page, gathered her up and carried her to her bed.

"There was no answer when I knocked, my lord," the boy stammered. "I came in and—my lady was just staring at nothing!"

"Bring me that wine, quickly."

Karanaya's blank eyes focused slowly on him. She coughed as he poured wine down her throat and turned her face away.

"Stop that. I'm fine." But she shuddered immediately and whispered, "Goddess be thanked for her kindness in not making me a Sunrunner!"

"A—?" Mirsath sat down hard on the bed. "Karanaya, *what happened?*"

"I need a moment to sort it out." She breathed carefully, frowning, then met his gaze again. "It was Prince Pol. He—he was here, Mirsath, right beside me! Or at least his voice was here." Shaking her head, she reached for the wine cup. "Did anybody hear anything? I spoke to him—did I say anything aloud?"

"How should I know? Tell me what his grace said."

"First have somebody find Johlarian. I don't want to repeat myself."

"You'll tell me the whole of it, and *right now*," he commanded.

Her brows rushed together again. "Don't dictate to me, my lord *athri*!"

"*Now*," he repeated.

She glared at him, then took a long swallow of wine. "He said Princess Tobin knows how to save us—using dragons." As his jaw dropped, she smiled grimly. "Satisfied, Cousin?"

* * *

Rihani held his warhorse on a tight rein; the big gelding heard the sounds of approaching battle even more clearly than he. Soon the enemy would burst through what they believed to be the weak flank of the main Syrene army, and be lured up here. Prince Kostas would close off retreat as planned, and the slaughter would begin.

To distract himself from nervousness, Rihani set his mind to the problem of not just repairing the gates at Catha Heights but making them invulnerable to what Saumer had done today. Rihani was mechanically minded —which quality the High Prince encouraged with gifts such as the viewing lens—and since early childhood had been taking things apart to find out how they worked. Mostly he put them back together again. The gates offered a fascinating challenge that occupied his mind but failed to quiet his body. His hands still sweated in riding gauntlets, his guts still fluttered, and his heart alternately raced and thudded in his chest.

He knew he ought to have been thrilled to be out in the field, commanding a wing of the army in a vital battle. In a way, he was. But as the crash and clatter drew nearer and he saw the first flash of steel, he was ashamed to find himself absolutely terrified.

"Hold! Hold!" yelled the *athri* of Chalsan Manor. "Wait until they're close enough to smell!"

All Rihani could smell was his own fear. He was a good enough rider, and the gelding was involved enough in a private war-lust, not to communicate the emotion to his horse. But within moments he would be called upon to be brave and steadfast and a veritable butcher. He could do it, he swore to himself he would do it and no one would guess. He'd managed in skirmishes on the way here. But, Goddess help him, he was so scared that the spit dried up in his mouth.

And then it was happening and he had no time to think or

worry or even breathe with any certainty. The dark bearded men were all around him, and those not hacked to bits by his sword had their chests bashed in by his enraged horse.

Only when the battle was done did he realize he had not fought it as a whole person. It wasn't that his mind detached from his body to watch while his arm swung bright steel and his heels signaled the gelding; he simply was incomplete. Some part of him extinguished like a fingerflame damped by a Sunrunner's thoughts. He had no sense of time or place, being or becoming. Now, as those facets of life returned to him, he heard himself sob once with relief that they *had* returned.

"Rihani? That's it, son, you can dismount now."

He recognized his uncle's voice and tried to obey. One of his legs wasn't working right. He glanced down, bewildered by the red stain on his thigh.

"Didn't even feel it, did you?" Kostas asked, amusement in his voice—and pride. "I'm not surprised, the way you fought. Twenty people have already come to me, telling how you led the charge."

Had he? He didn't remember. Parts of his memory had vanished. Easing down from the saddle, he accepted his uncle's support to a camp stool. A physician approached, and as he worked, Rihani finally started breathing again.

"As soon as you're bandaged, we'll ride into Catha Heights," Kostas was saying. "Saumer sent word that he's found Patwin's daughters and brother—but the one girl, Sangna, was locked up in the guardhouse. I suppose I'll have to spare her—but I want a good look at her first. It could be a trick."

Rihani's shiver of cold coincided precisely with application of a stinging salve to his leg wound. The physician apologized. Rihani shook his head and struggled to keep his teeth from chattering.

"It's not serious, my lord," was the verdict. "The thrust missed the artery and didn't cut too deep into the important muscles. Light exercise will keep it from stiffening into a permanent limp."

Kostas signaled to have the gelding brought around. Rihani stood, tested the leg, and realized the salve had numbed the pain. As he rode at his uncle's side past the scattered corpses, he wished there was something he could smooth across his

mind for the same effect. What he had lost for the length of the battle had indeed returned.

* * *

Karanaya wore a deep blue gown that had belonged to her aunt Michinida. So had the piles of silver and gold chains around her neck, some set with a ruby or emerald or two; matching bracelets that reached nearly to her elbows; and the earrings—large hanging discs of beaten silver set with chips of diamond. She had ever deplored her aunt's flamboyant taste, but had cause to bless it now. Subtlety would be wasted on the Vellant'im; she must shine and dazzle today.

The gown, cut for a mature figure, was huge at the waist and hips. She belted it with a dozen more gold chains. Luckily, she was almost as voluptuous in the bosom as Michinida had been; all she needed to do was pin the neckline down to reveal half her breasts. No, nothing subtle about this performance.

Mirsath gaped at the sight of her. "You look like a jeweler's stall at the *Rialla*."

"Which is precisely the idea," Johlarian reminded him. "Excellent, my lady. I hope there's enough sunlight for the High Princess and Prince Pol to watch."

Karanaya looked them over. "You're not exactly dressed for work in the fields, either," she observed.

Mirsath wore green—velvet tunic, leather trousers, and shimmering silken shirt. Johlarian had chosen the white of Goddess Keep from neck to heels. The Vellant'im would not notice from across the moat that the shirt was too small for him and the tunic too large, and that the cloak had been reversed to show the white wool lining instead of the russet outer fabric.

"We all look ridiculous," she finished. "Me most of all. If this wasn't so desperate, I'd probably laugh in their faces."

"Correctly timed, laughter might be very effective," Johlarian mused.

"Do you know what you're going to say?" Mirsath took her arm and started along the hallway.

"I think so." She grimaced; with every step she rattled and clinked as if she wore full battle armor. "I hope *nobody* watches. I'm going to look such a fool up there."

"Not half as foolish as *they're* going to look with their faces in the mud," Mirsath said fiercely.

The trio drew amazed stares as they crossed the courtyard headed for the gatehouse and presence balcony. Climbing the stairs left Karanaya flushed and out of breath. To calm herself, she trod slowly up and down the inner chamber, rehearsing the main phrases of her speech. Johlarian watched in sympathy; Mirsath, with concern. The whole plan was preposterous. Downright insane.

And it had to work. She reached into the pocket of her gown and clutched the little silk bag of pearls, remembering how she'd snatched the box off the floor where it had dropped from Michinida's dead hands. One of the Dragon's Tears should have hung from her wedding necklet this spring. Instead she was weighted down by all Michinida's finery and all six pearls were clutched in her fist. She thought of her betrothed, and the splintered glass knife quivering in his chest with his faltering breaths. She couldn't completely recall his face, but she could see that knife. And all the blood. The iridescent black teardrop sacrificed today would be the one rightly hers. For him.

"I'm ready," she said to Johlarian.

He glanced out the narrow window and replied, "There's as much sun as there's going to be, my lady. Best you get it done now."

The disc earrings chimed against the chains around her throat as she bent her head for a moment. Straightening, she made herself hear the clatter above her own thundering heartbeat, made it an announcement of her presence. She strode through the door Mirsath held open for her and into a thin shroud of afternoon haze—lit abruptly by twin torches of Sunrunner's Fire in Johlarian's hands.

She needn't have worried about capturing their attention. The sudden apparition of blue, glittering silver, gold, and Fire brought shouts from those assigned to watch the castle; Vellanti warriors were soon leaving their tents to come view the strange scene. Karanaya waited until she had a good-sized crowd across the moat, and then lifted her hands. Bracelets rattled down her arms like the muffled beat of war drums.

"*Azhlel!*" she cried, one of the words Prince Pol had told her to use. She had memorized several more, working her mind around them, but until this moment not her tongue.

They were harsh words, guttural and sharp. "*Azhlel!*" she shouted again. *Dragonwar.*

Tobin's theory was that someone among the enemy had known how to communicate with Patwin. It took a fairly intense vocabulary to arrange the rewards for a betrayal, after all. Once Karanaya had their attention, she could speak in her own language and hope that someone would translate.

A tall, bearded man indistinguishable from the others of his breed pushed through the growing crowd. "You make easy target, my lady!" he called. "Ready to die?"

"*You* should prepare for it, barbarian!" Mirsath yelled, and Johlarian placed a restraining hand on his arm.

Karanaya relaxed slightly, now that she knew her speech would be understood. "Shut up, Mirsath," she hissed, and stepped forward to the balcony rails. "Withdraw now, or be destroyed!"

The man repeated her words to the men around him, and everyone laughed. Though she had expected that, the foolishness of her words put hot blood in her cheeks. She persevered; no matter how outrageous, this had to sound convincing.

"I say again, whoreson—leave now or die!"

"Of what, my lady? Boredom?"

She drew one of the pearls from the silk pouch. "Of the spell cast by a Dragon's Tear!" She panicked for an instant, having lost the other word, then had it. "*Azhketh!*" she called, holding the pearl so its darkness glowed in the sun. "*Azhketh!*"

Pol had told her that Tobin felt they might need some convincing. The princess was mistaken. The word brought a fearful muttering among the crowd. Karanaya blinked in surprise as they began to fall back—slowly, shuffling their feet as if ashamed of their reaction, but moving away from the moat just the same.

"You *do* have them! We searched everywhere—" the tall man gasped out, then realized his error and added, "A lie! A trick!"

He repeated the last part in his own language, but to little effect. Tobin had suggested she claim the pearls had been in her family for centuries, entrusted to them as a defense against those who dared make war on the Desert, and similar nonsense. That part of the plan was obviously use-

less now, but she perceived that things were going even better than anyone could have hoped.

"*Azhketh* that brings *azhlel*!" she taunted. "Will you risk it, barbarian?"

"Give them back! They are not yours, but ours!"

Johlarian gave a violent start. "By Lord Andry's rings," he whispered, "I recognize him now! He was the merchant who sold Lady Michinida the pearls! Look at the way he limps on the left leg! Listen to his voice! It's the same man!"

"Is *this* why they stayed here when they could have moved on to the Desert?" Mirsath asked. "These damned pearls?"

"They're certainly reacting to them," Karanaya said. She spilled all six pearls into her palm. The clouds chose that moment to drift beyond the Faolain, and the teardrops were suddenly brilliant black fire in sunlight. "I have them all! Did you hope to recover them from my dead hands?"

"Give them back, we'll leave you in peace!"

"Return such power to you? Never! I am the vassal of the High Prince, the *Azhrei*, and I know how to use Dragon's Tears! Leave us in peace *now!*" To Johlarian she breathed, "Get ready, Sunrunner."

"At your command, my lady."

"You know nothing!" the man challenged. "None of you understood! *Azhketh'im* mean nothing to you but pretty baubles!"

"So you *will* risk your lives!" Karanaya laughed. Carefully placing all but one pearl back into the pouch, she held the black teardrop up once more. She paused a moment to make sure she had all the words right, then drew in a breath that went to the bottom of her lungs.

"Keth dur azh!" And she flung the dark gleaming pearl down into the moat.

Against all reason and rationality, proving themselves good, honest, superstitious barbarian savages, they ran back even before Johlarian ignited the moat. Sunrunner's Fire circled the castle, leaping up half again the height of the walls, obscuring the view of the chaos below. Yet chaos it was, from the sound of it. Above the roar of flames Karanaya heard cries of terror. There were other shouts, too, from commanders or those made of sterner stuff, unmistakable even in a strange tongue as they ordered warriors to act like it. But all at once even they howled in fear. Dimly, through the writhing white-gold Fire, she saw why.

"Goddess help us," she whispered. "Johlarian—are you doing that?"

"N–no, my lady," he replied in a hushed voice. "It's the High Princess—I can sense her colors—ah, Goddess, it hurts!" He moaned, and Mirsath grabbed him before he could fall.

"Don't stop!" the young lord commanded. "Steady the Fire, damn you!"

An immense, blazing dragon, five times the height of a man, spread wings of red-orange flame just beyond Johlarian's Fire. Head thrown back, it exhaled streaks of light toward the sky. Karanaya knew it to be a conjuring of the High Princess' powerful mind, but even though she felt no awe of Sunrunners she found herself completely understanding the enemy's panic. And if she was frightened, knowing what was happening, they must be mad with horror.

Johlarian held out as long as he could. At last he crumpled to the stone floor, panting for breath. Fire sank into the moat and vanished; the dragon disappeared.

So had the Vellant'im.

* * *

"Someday you must teach me how to do that," Pol remarked as he handed his mother a full wine cup.

With a tired smile, she replied, "One of my more flamboyant talents. Pol, if there's any moonlight to work with later, see if you can find Johlarian and apologize for me. I'm afraid I was a little rough."

"What *happened?*" Tobin snapped in what was almost her old voice, crisp and impatient.

"She scared the spit and piss out of them with a conjured dragon," Pol reported, succinctly if inelegantly. "It was gorgeous! Do you want me to help you to your room, Mother?"

"I'm not decrepit yet, boy. It's just the *dranath*. I'll be all right." She swallowed some wine and sighed. "You didn't find Azhdeen, did you?"

He shook his head. "He's gone back to the Catha Hills with the rest of the dragons. It would've been nice to give them a real one, but yours worked just as well."

"I don't like to think how close we cut it," she mused. "Johlarian's Fire alone might have done it. An appearance

by your dragon would have been better. Maybe our luck is changing, that the sun came out in time for me to work."

Tobin drummed the fingers of her right hand on the table. "Gone for good?"

"Perhaps. I hope they ran like frightened deer all the way to Riverport."

* * *

Catha Heights had not yet been so long in enemy hands that its famous gardens had suffered from anything more destructive than winter. The individual enclaves of rare trees, bushes, and shrubs were richly green with rain that swelled the ponds and leaped in the fountains. Only the flower beds, turned and waiting for spring seed, were brown. Vines scrambled up the walls of a few houses made of reddish brick; the keep itself rose pale yellow and thickly covered on its lower floors with climbing roses. Amid the workshops and storehouses ran narrow cobbled alleys, yet even here trees grew in tubs set at interesting intervals.

Rihani had settled his mind by the time he rode through the gates at his uncle's side. Saumer approached immediately, bowing with as great a flourish as he could muster with one arm in a sling and tight strapping around his ribs.

"I beg to present you with your holding of Catha Heights, my lord," he said, and grinned.

"Accepted," Kostas replied, grinning back. "I think you have one or two other gifts for me as well?"

"Waiting in the square, my lord."

Izaea and her uncle Othreg stood together beneath a tall pine. Sangna, Patwin's middle daughter, had put deliberate distance between them and herself. Rihani saw at once the marks of gyves around her wrists—some of them scabbed, which indicated to him that this was no pose. She had worn iron for some time now. He knew his uncle would execute the other two; he was deeply relieved that Sangna would be spared. There had been enough killing today.

Dismounting, he held Kostas' stallion and when Saumer came to stand beside him whispered, "Shoulder or ribs?"

"Both. And both my own stupid fault—I wrenched it when the balance-weight on the gates lifted. I never even saw who broke my ribs. How about your leg?"

"I don't remember how or when it happened." To Saumer's

startled, disbelieving glance, he defended, "Honestly, I don't remember much of it at all. You'll have to go to someone else for tales of the battle."

"The biggest fight in thirty years, and he doesn't remember! Did your own horse kick you in the head?"

"Not me—just anyone else within reach. Shh—he's about to judge them."

There was no plea and no mercy. Before his assembled army, the few Vellant'im who had been captured, and the frightened castlefolk, Kostas said one simple thing—"Othreg and Izaea of Catha Heights are guilty of treason"—and summarily lopped their heads from their necks with his own sword.

Had there been anything in his stomach, Rihani would have thrown up. Thin, bitter fluid gushed into his mouth; he swallowed it and set his face in stone.

Sangna flinched back against the Syrene trooper holding her up. Kostas wiped his bloodied sword on Izaea's skirts and came toward the terrified woman. "You are evidently blameless, my lady," he said. "But you will understand that by their actions, the rest of your family forfeited this castle. You will be taken back to High Kirat and treated with honor there. Part of the revenue from this place will provide your dowry, should you ever marry. But your line is finished here forever. Is that clear?"

"Perfectly, my lord uncle," she whispered, and swayed to her knees before him. "Thank you for my life."

"You have yourself to thank, Sangna, for not heeding your father's treachery." Kostas gestured her away, and she was taken into the keep. Turning, he addressed the crowd. "For their services today to us and to Syr—and to the High Prince—we have decided to bestow the honor of knighthood on our squires. Prince Rihani of Ossetia, Prince Saumer of Kierst-Isel, come forward."

In shock, the pair approached their prince and knelt. Saumer received the accolade with a proud smile. Rihani, hearing phrases that made him a knight at barely seventeen, could think of nothing but that he was being rewarded for his skill at butchery. Well, why not? After all, he knelt near a pool of blood.

"We have neither salt nor bread nor golden buckle to give you," Kostas said when it was finished. "Those things, and Syr's gift of a coffer encrusted with gems, will have to wait.

But as of this moment, having proven your courage and accomplishments on this fine and glorious day, we acclaim each of you a knight in the service of the High Prince and ourselves, Prince of Syr."

A cheer went up—genuine from the Syrene warriors, pure release of tension from the people of Catha Heights. Some of the former, the captain Havadi in the lead, jostled forward to congratulate the young men. And in the sudden confusion, no one heard Kostas give a grunt of surprise and pain.

Rihani saw his uncle fold to the ground. He saw a bearded man rise from Kostas' side. What he did not see was his own sword—until it was hilt-deep in the Vellanti's guts.

He let the blade go. He knelt in a new pool of blood. He reached for the knife, snatched his hand back. It was made of glass, and had splintered.

"Oh, Goddess—no," he breathed.

"What's wrong with you?" Kostas demanded in a heavy, breathy voice. "It's just a pinprick in the belly. Pull it out."

"I—I can't, my lord. It's a Merida knife."

No one believed it, least of all Kostas. Not until he tried to wrench the glass out himself. He could not move.

Saumer took the prince's lolling head onto his knees. "Rihani got him, my lord," he said, tears thickening his words. "Rihani killed him for you."

"Good. Kill the rest of them, too." He coughed, spat as if the poison had fouled his tongue, and said, "Take me to River Run, where I was born. Reclaim it and burn me there. Swear to uphold my son Daniv as Prince of Syr."

"We swear, my lord," Saumer said for both of them; Rihani could only nod.

Kostas looked at him, his eyes glazing over now. "Take care of your mother," he whispered, his voice going from strength to feebleness in an instant. Rihani didn't understand; his uncle saw it and insisted even more weakly, "Gemma—keep her safe."

"Yes, my lord," he said, for lack of anything else and because it was what the dying man wanted to hear.

Then, quietly, light in his eyes like the last glimpse of sun before night: "My poor Dani."

* * *

Dragon Gap was tough going in daylight at a decent pace. By night, at speed, it was madness. Meiglan's usual mount, a placid little mare with a mouth and disposition like silk, had not prepared her for this great gelding she now bestrode. All she could do was beg the Goddess to keep her on the horse.

Laroshin was in the lead. He knew the trail as well as anyone and better than most. Next came Rislyn and Jihan, then a guard, Meiglan, and finally Kierun. She hadn't planned on bringing the squire along, but it had become necessary when, on entering Pol's chambers through the passage from her own rooms, she had discovered Kierun tidying his lord's clothes for something to do. No use to dissemble; she and the girls were dressed for riding and once Kierun found out where they were bound, his presence was inescapable.

"My lord left strict orders, my lady," he said stubbornly. "I'm to protect you and their graces. I'm coming with you to Stronghold."

Meiglan held the name before her as if the stars had formed it overhead. Stronghold—where Pol was. Where she would be protected and cherished and utterly safe. She bent over the gelding's neck and hung on.

Chapter Twenty-six

Forced to conceal his anger in public, in private Miyon of Cunaxa did not scruple to blister the ears off the hapless tutor. Catallen's initial defenses withered quickly at the onslaught; he trembled and begged forgiveness and was ready to fall on his knees when Miyon ordered him out in disgust.

"Blind and deaf—but not, unfortunately, mute! Shut your mouth, you slug! Kill you? I ought to open your eyes and ears with a hot iron! You had charge of the brats! You should've alerted me when they didn't return to their rooms last night! Get out!"

Miyon stalked from one end of his chamber to the other, seething. Catallen had been a convenient outlet for rage, but ultimately unsatisfying. The fault was his own. He'd badly underestimated the changes in Meiglan since her marriage. Evidently she'd developed some backbone. But there had been such sick terror in her eyes after the cottage burned down . . . perhaps he had frightened her too much. Either way, the mistake was his.

His hostages were gone. He had nothing to offer Chiana and the Vellant'im except Dragon's Rest itself. Moreover, he was stuck here with Laric and Edrel and the whole palace guard, and without Meiglan to bully into giving what orders he desired for his convenience.

Adding to his troubles was the report of the Sunrunner, Hildreth: heavy snow threatened the north in the next few days, making Laric's departure impossible. The prince had believed his story about Yarin—after much persuasion and even more agonizing over the betrayal. Laric's slowness in accepting the tale grossly insulted him. Had Rohan and Pol so poisoned all minds against him that no one believed a

word he said? The fact that he was doubted when telling an obvious truth angered him even more.

Miyon was briefly torn between staying where he was or making for Swalekeep. The latter held attractions. He would be in direct contact with the Vellant'im, planning out the shape of the continent after the wars were done and Rohan and Pol were dead. But at Swalekeep he would be just one more collaborator. Here at least he was senior prince and Pol's father-by-marriage. Too, taking up residence at Swalekeep would be an irrevocable choice of sides. No, he would save that for when he had something to bargain with.

Maybe Pol would do the smart thing and send Meiglan home. Stronghold would soon be under siege in earnest. It was no place for anyone who had a perfectly safe palace only two days' ride away. He began to nourish a certain hope, fed by faith in Pol's protective instinct. Meiglan might come back; Laric would march for Balarat as soon as he could without killing his men or his horses; Edrel was only a younger brother of a ruling *athri*, for all that he had been Pol's squire. With Meiglan to hand once more, Laric gone, and Edrel hopelessly outranked, things would turn Miyon's way again.

He decided he could wait a little while. Not that he had much choice.

* * *

Lord Yarin paused outside his nephew's chambers, arranging his face into properly grave lines. Tirel would be grieving over that damned Sunrunner woman who had taken such a very long time about dying. Yarin had to be sympathetic but firm with the boy.

He hadn't expected the squire to be in attendance, but Idalian's presence altered his plans not at all. He expressed sorrow he did not feel at Arpali's death, then suggested that it might be a good idea for Tirel to remain in his chambers until any threat of contagion was ascertained.

"What did she die of, my lord?" Idalian asked.

"No one knows for certain," he lied smoothly, glad that virulent fevers or wasting sicknesses produced the same kind of drastic loss of weight as that brought by starvation. "But until the physicians are sure it's not catching, they advise me to keep my nephew isolated. I think you should join him,

Idalian—your remaining family would not thank me for risking your life, and you would help make the days go faster for Tirel."

The young man looked uncertainly at the boy, then nodded. "As you wish, my lord. Will you keep Natham isolated, too?"

Yarin searched his face quickly for any signs of suspicion and detected none. "You're kind to worry about him," he replied smoothly. "My son will also be kept apart—but I think he might be allowed to come play with you, Tirel, and share your lessons with your squire. Would you like that?"

"Yes, uncle," he murmured meekly. His wide gray eyes were unreadable—eerie in one so young, but then Tirel had always been a strange child.

"I'll see if I can persude the physicians." Pleased—and reminding himself to order Natham kept to his rooms—he unfolded a thin sheet of parchment and continued, "In this crisis, and because you won't be able to meet with your father's ministers until the danger is past, I've drawn up a document that will ease your mind, Tirel. It gives me certain limited powers to conduct the business of the princedom and see to its defense in these troubled times."

"Do you wish me to sign it, Uncle?" Again that flat, slate-colored stare. It unnerved Yarin for a moment.

"Yes, I do. It would be best."

"Shouldn't you read it first, my lord?" Idalian asked. Then he added too swiftly, "He should become familiar with official documents, Lord Yarin. He'll rule Firon one day."

The lame excuse was mildly amusing, but it warned Yarin that the squire was indeed suspicious. He would be watched. "He should certainly read it—as a matter of fact, I should go through it again myself. These legal minds with their tortured phrasing!"

The parchment was only to reassure the more timorous councillors that what Yarin was doing was perfectly legal. It was, and would be—right up until the time he disinherited Tirel and proclaimed himself rightful Prince of Firon. As should have been done eighteen years ago.

Tirel asked Idalian to read the document aloud. Yarin pretended to listen, thinking instead of the three sets of riders dispatched south to Swalekeep. There had been no news since Arpali had been confined, of course, but Yarin

felt safe in his surmise that Chiana would walk hand-in-glove with anyone who could destroy Pol and put her and Rinhoel in Princemarch. He had taken her measure at several *Riall'im* and knew that her cause was roughly the same as his: to claim a usurped birthright.

He was equally confident that at least one pair of couriers would make it through the winter storms. The message they carried was as much a triumph of vocabulary as the document Idalian recited. It managed to convey Yarin's plots and hopes without actually stating them; it hinted delicately at Chiana's cooperation with the enemy; it guided her toward what he really meant without actually saying it. If read by the wrong people, it would not incriminate him—but the woman for whom it had been written would understand it at once. He might need her help in spring, when the roads would be passable again. By that time he hoped to be in complete control of Firon. But just in case, he had sent a message to Chiana. Besides, she might even do him the favor of killing Laric and Lisiel, or at least putting them in the way of being killed. Whatever happened elsewhere, he believed Chiana would be the new power. The barbarians would win—how could they not, faced with that weakling Rohan and his prating, posturing son? Andry was a worry, but Andry showed scant affection for Rohan or any of his works—including Pol.

"I believe I understand," Tirel said quietly, and again Yarin was amused as the boy played at being a prince. "Idalian, may I have a pen and ink, please?"

Yarin watched him sign, hiding his glee. Whatever he did now would be in Tirel's name, as titular prince while Laric was absent. He was official Regent of Firon. He could rule as he pleased.

"There's a time limit set on this," he said as he waited for the ink to dry. "It's now the thirteenth day of Winter. Soon we should have some sort of word from your father and we can revise the document if necessary. But I think he'll be proud of your maturity, Tirel."

The boy said nothing. Idalian put away pen and ink, avoiding Yarin's eyes. The new regent shrugged to himself and left the room.

"How *could* you!" Idalian hissed as soon as the outer door had closed.

"I couldn't do anything else! What if I refused? He'd lock

me up anyway, and you, too, and probably kill us the way he killed poor Arpali!" Tirel's voice broke and he flung himself onto his bed.

Ashamed of himself, Idalian sat beside the young prince and patted his shoulder awkwardly. "I'm sorry. You did the right thing. I've heard tales of wicked uncles before, but Yarin is a snake!"

"He's worse than a snake," Tirel mumbled into his pillow. "He's so horrible I can't think what to call him."

Idalian had a much larger vocabulary, but didn't contribute any of the choice characterizations Yarin embodied. Instead he told the prince, "At least when they decide it's safe, we'll be able to move about the castle."

"Idalian, I'm scared."

"I know. It shouldn't be too long—you made sure Yarin thinks he's in complete control. He'll get overconfident and make a mistake somewhere."

"I hope he lets me out for my birthday," he said forlornly.

Idalian froze. "What? Say that again."

"My birthday? It's the thirty-fifth."

"And you'll be seven. Glorious great Goddess, Tirel, you're going to be seven!" Idalian picked him up and hugged him.

"Put me down!" He squirmed away. "What are you talking about?"

The young man grinned. "You know how the High Prince keeps changing things? Your father has me read the law books out loud. He says it helps him think and it also teaches me. Well, there's a law that *didn't* get changed last *Rialla*, that goes back to when people used to make children sign apprenticeships and betrothals, that kind of thing. Prince Rohan wanted to raise the age limit. But the crafters couldn't agree on an age, so it didn't get changed. The point," he finished as Tirel made an impatient face, "is that you have to be *ten* to sign anything and have it be legally binding!"

"So Uncle Yarin's document is meaningless?"

"Exactly! Once we're free, we can figure out some way to stop him."

Tirel brightened, tears and panic forgotten. Idalian kept his smile steady and his worries to himself. He knew how feeble the hope was, but the child had to have something to live on.

But the little face took on an adult grimness. "There's

one thing I *will* sign, Idalian, and make it legal. Uncle Yarin's death warrant."

* * *

At New Raetia, Rohannon came back from a morning patrol and was surprised to find Prince Arlis waiting for him.

"I know—you thought me still at Port Adni," said the ruler of Kierst-Isel. "But the ships will stay in harbor for quite some time yet. There's a storm coming—*again*. So I thought I'd spend a few days here."

They climbed the broad, polished stone staircase to what had been Volog's private retreat, a cozy room lined with tapestries. A fire blazed in the huge hearth and a *fenath* stood in one corner. Arlis went to it, stroked a finger over the inlaid wood patterned with birds.

"Nobody in my family has the slightest sense of music," he remarked, plucking a string. The note quivered for a long time. "Except for my aunt Birani. I heard her play when I was a little boy. Aunt Alasen says she lost her music when Obram died—the way Ostvel did, until Alasen brought it back to him." Glancing around the chamber, his Kierstian green eyes filled with sudden pain. "They're all gone now, except Alasen. I can't even feel their presence here anymore."

Rohannon said nothing. A young page peeked in the door and Rohannon motioned him away.

"I love this room almost as much as Grandsir did," Arlis went on softly. "Of them all, it's hardest to believe he's dead. Part of me wants to keep this room just as it is . . . the way they kept Birani's *fenath*. But Rohan told me once that when I became prince of Kierst and Isel, everything would change—everything *must* change. That's what I was trained to do." He smiled bitterly. "I doubt even Rohan in all his wisdom could have guessed that this island that tore itself apart with wars for so long would one day be united by a war."

"United by *you*, your grace," Rohannon said firmly, and Arlis gave him the sharp, assessing look familiar to him from seeing it in Sioned's green eyes.

"You're growing some wisdom of your own, Rohannon," the prince replied, then smiled more easily. "As well as a

handspan in height. I didn't ask you here to listen to me feel sorry for myself. How good are you at Sunrunning?"

"Not very, my lord," he apologized. "My father's been teaching me—but at such a distance, it's hard."

Arlis frowned. "What about the court Sunrunner here? Why isn't she—?"

Rohannon hesitated a long moment, then shrugged and told the truth. "She's very loyal to my Uncle Andry, who says that all Sunrunners must be taught at Goddess Keep."

"Or not at all," Arlis finished in disgust. "Another of his stupid opinions."

"Begging your pardon, my lord, but it's always been that way. Until Pol."

The prince cleared his throat. "Forgive me, Rohannon. My own loyalty to Pol makes me cast Andry in a darker light than he perhaps deserves. And I often forget he's your father's brother. Well, if you can't speak on sunlight yet without someone steadying you, then can you go looking as you like?"

"If the sun's strong enough. I've been keeping track of our patrols when I can, but I'm not practiced enough to do things like guess the weather."

"I have someone else to do that for me. I want to know some very selfish things, Rohannon."

The youth understood at once. "As it happens, my lord, I had a look in at Zaldivar just this morning." He smiled, both at the remembered scene and for the laugh it would give Arlis. "Roric and Hanella were swiping the new baby off with a feather duster, for all the world as if he was a table decoration!"

Laughter belonged in this room. Arlis told him how Roric, two winters Hanella's senior, once asked his nurse why she didn't just send his little sister down to be washed with the rest of the dirty laundry. Rohannon countered with the time he and Chayla had attempted the exploding fish bladder trick that was practically a family tradition by now, having been tried by their father and Pol, and learned, it was hinted, from the redoubtable Lord Chaynal of Radzyn himself.

"My brother had a knack with citrins rather like that—he punctured the rinds with needles and dripped in Goddess alone knew what. He hid them while they fermented, slipped them into his tutor's closets, and after another day or two—" He laughed. "Saumer never did confess to that one."

"I might be able to find him, if there's enough sun over the Catha Hills," Rohannon offered.

"Could you?" Arlis sounded almost wistful, and Rohannon heard the echo of his words about keeping things as they had been.

"I'll try, my lord." He went to windows overlooking a forested cliff, the sea beyond, and the graceful curve of the harbor. The fleet was at Port Adni, a crown holding since Lord Narat's death at Waes this autumn, and it was odd not to see at least fifty ships at the docks. Rohannon opened the window and felt the sun on his face, and carefully wove the brilliant threads of light.

Across Brochwell Bay, so wide that he almost lost sight of land; over the farmlands of Grib and the dark rippling waters of Lake Kadar, white-capped in the wind; a moment's pause to find Athmyr and use it as a directional guide. He wasn't as good at this as he ought to be; he strayed too far south, to the tangled estuaries where the Catha River emptied into the sea. Backtracking upriver, he stopped in shock at Catha Heights.

A pyre was burning outside the walls—the large, tragic kind used in war or pestilence, when dozens were honored at once. Warriors wearing Syrene turquoise and common folk in mourning gray stood watch. What startled Rohannon was that what he at first took for one pyre was in fact five—and that there were so many dead that flames lit last night were still burning at midday.

There must have been a battle. After a moment of panic he realized that the Syrenes had won, or Kostas' people would not be standing guard over the pyres. Rohannon searched for Kostas and his squires, but couldn't find them.

Catching his breath—only figuratively, for his body back at New Raetia did not react—he moved to the castle itself. Relief sparkled through his colors as he recognized the two squires in the main square. Saumer, distinguished by the yellow and scarlet belt that signified his homeland, had one arm in a sling but otherwise looked unharmed. Rihani's leg was tightly bandaged, and his blue eyes looked stunned as he limped forward to consult with Saumer.

Crafters were busy building what looked like another pyre. But this one had carrying poles attached, as if the body was to be taken somewhere else. A woman knelt by one end, her paintbox beside her—and the pot she dipped

into again and again as she decorated the carved handles was filled with Syrene turquoise.

Rohannon felt cold dread darken his own colors. It was confirmed by the turquoise velvet another woman shook out for inspection. Saumer and Rihani both felt the fabric, and then Rihani beckoned someone else over to give the woman a battle flag bearing Syr's silver apple, obviously to be copied in embroidery on the shroud.

Saumer glanced up suddenly, frowning. It seemed that he looked directly into Rohannon's eyes. Traces of Arlis were in that face—the lines of brow and jaw were almost identical—but instead of green his eyes were dark brown, like their father Latham's. All at once it was like seeing the dead prince all over again in his son. But there was something else in that face—or, rather *of* it.

Rohannon glided back to the window of Prince Volog's favorite room.

"My lord, did you know your brother is a Sunrunner?"

* * *

Tallain surveyed what was to have been his troops' rations and couldn't think of a single reason to keep his temper in check. The town baker, whose responsibility it was to provision Tiglath in times of war, was already apoplectic that the loaves had been botched. Tallain now favored him with his blistering views on masters who left such vital work to inexperienced apprentices while he downed a few sociable cups of wine at a nearby inn.

"And Goddess help you if I discover those boys used weeviled flour on your order, thinking no one would notice until we were halfway to Cunaxa! You'll mix the next batch yourself, Master Baker, and use the finest, softest, most expensive Ossetian grind in your barrels—or I'll stoke your ovens with *you!*"

Swinging around in the hot, narrow confines of the bakery, he gestured his cousin forward. "Lady Lyela will supervise your work. By dusk I want the loaves delivered to me, and they'd damned well better be perfect!"

Lyela fixed the man with her large, fine dark eyes, smiling with uncharacteristic fierceness. "He understands you, my lord—doesn't he?" The baker gulped and nodded. Lyela spread her skirts elegantly and sat on a stool near the door.

"I'll just stay here where it's cool, and you carry on as if you were baking for the High Prince's own table."

Seething, Tallain left the shop. No one dared so much as nod respect to him as he stalked back to the residence. Once inside the main doors, he bellowed his wife's name. When she did not reply instantly, he shouted again. "Goddess damn it all—Sionell! Get down here! *Sionell!*"

He should have known better. His lady would not cower like the baker, nor follow orders like Lyela. She gave as good as she got.

"Put a bridle on that foul-mouthed stallion before I make him a gelding!"

Tallain strode to the bottom steps and gripped the carved wooden bouquet of the finial. "You heard me! Move! I won't be gainsaid in my own holding!"

She appeared on the upper landing, hands on hips, sweaty from a day of backbreaking preparations for war. "Take your temper outside and soak it in a horse trough! Drown in it for all I care!"

He took the stairs three at a time. But once within arm's reach of her, his fury drained away. Sionell possessed all the fire usually accompanying a head of red hair, but suddenly all the bright, vivid colors of her seemed—not tarnished, for that could never happen, but as if weariness had faded them beneath the flush of her anger. Tallain stood before her, tongue-tied, abashed, and wondering how he'd been such a fool as to take his frustrations out on her.

She was not so quick to relinquish her wrath. "If you can't speak like a civilized person, then get out of my sight! How dare you come roaring in here?"

"I'm sorry."

She'd flinched at his first shout, wondering what new disaster was upon them. His second had snapped her already overstrained nerves. But hearing those two words reminded her that Tallain was surely unique among men: he never hesitated to admit when he'd been wrong.

She struggled with lingering annoyance, then gave it over with a shrug. If he could be magnanimous, so could she. Besides, now that he wasn't shouting at her, she saw how tired he was and her heart twisted. "I'm sorry, too. What happened?"

"Weeviled flour. Every damned loaf. We can't march out with nothing to eat. What about you?"

"Rabisa hasn't said a word in two days and Siona's sickening for something, I'm not sure what."

"And?" he prompted.

"And what?"

"You're exhausted." Tallain caressed her cheek with one finger.

She didn't particularly want to tell him right now that some of the Dorvali who'd elected to stay at Tiglath had given her a hellish morning with their complaints. Or that the section of wall Tallain had ordered rebuilt would not be finished before he left. She'd worked on it herself after ordering the Dorvali to help or get out, but instead of exhausting her anger in physical labor, she'd only exhausted her body.

She closed her eyes, knowing the action was a mistake. As long as she kept going, she would be *able* to keep going. She suspected it was the same for her husband. But she also knew that he would have no chance to rest once he left Tiglath. So she gave in to weariness and leaned against him. "I'm about to fall over, if you want the truth."

It worked; he drew her along beside him to their chambers and settled her on the bed. Very little effort was required to coax him down across the quilt with her, and that worried her anew. Still, if the provisions weren't ready until this evening, Tallain would have to leave tomorrow instead of this afternoon. She could tell their Sunrunner to tell Riyan the Tiglathi forces would be a little late getting started for the assembly point.

To this end she suggested, "Tallain, why don't you stay the night?"

He laughed so hard that tears came to his eyes. Gasping in enough breath to whoop, "*Mistresses* ask that, not *wives!*", he collapsed and laughed some more. Sionell discovered that a good case of the giggles was a remedy much superior to hauling bricks around. When Tallain showed signs of recovery, she demanded, "And how would *you* know what mistresses ask?" Which set them both off again.

The inevitable had barely gotten started when three children came bounding into the chamber, attracted by sounds of laughter, and swarmed onto their parents' bed. Sionell regarded her brood with pride mixed with exasperation.

Antalya would be eleven on the last day of winter; Jahnev, eldest son and heir, was seven; Meig had turned four that

summer. They were as dissimilar in looks as full siblings could be, as if traits from two preceding generations had been purposely parceled out to make them as unalike as possible. Talya, a redhead like Sionell, resembled the paternal grandmother for whom she had been Named. Jahnev's eyes were the exact shade of Feylin's—gray and luminous as cloudy moonlight—but his features and gold-brown hair had come from Tallain's father, Eltanin. As for Meig—his blond hair and brown eyes were Tallain's, but the shape of his face was already taking on the distinct triangle of Sionell's. It was one of the mysteries of heredity that even though they looked absolutely nothing alike, no one ever mistook them for anything but brothers and sister.

Meig landed on Sionell and gave a battle cry. Talya attacked her sire's ribs; Jahnev paused to take stock of the situation, then grabbed his sister's bare feet to tickle. A brief, chaotic time later, parents subdued offspring and met each other's laughing, rueful eyes over their helplessly giggling prey.

Tallain growled, "Now we can do as we like with these hatchlings—we've got their wings pinned. How about having them for dinner?"

"I don't know any good dragon recipes. Besides, there's not enough meat on their bones," she answered, pretending to take a bite out of Meig.

"Skin them and make saddles from their hides?"

"You wouldn't get even a decent-sized purse out of these runts."

Tallain sighed. "I'm out of ideas. I guess we'll just have to keep them."

They let go and the trio scrambled all over them again, going for revenge. Sionell exclaimed, "Enough! Get off me, you monsters!"—open invitation for husband and children to gang up on her.

Suddenly there was another child in the room. Sionell rolled away from merciless tickling hands to see a pair of big brown eyes in a pale little face. Jeren stood beside the bed, wistful and curious. Sionell's heart turned over and she pushed the others away, holding out her arms to her brother's son.

"Help! Come defend me, Jeren! I'm getting trounced!"

The boy smiled shyly and climbed up. The game was renewed—this time with Tallain stalking the children across

the huge bed from beneath the quilt, to the sounds of much hilarity and shrieking.

The nurse had only to follow the noise to catch up with her charges. She scurried them from the room after a disapproving glance for the Lord of Tiglath. Sionell thought the woman an idiot; Tallain looked delicious, all rumple-haired and flushed with laughter. But as he fell back onto the pillows to catch his breath, his smile faded too quickly.

Sionell was quiet for a time, then made a decision and started hauling off his boots. "Hush," she said when he opened his mouth to protest. "You *are* going to stay the night."

"Yes, but—"

"Bedtime, my lord. I've ordered the sun to set early." She tossed his boots into a far corner.

"And it wouldn't dare refuse you," he answered whimsically. He grasped lightly at one of her braids that had tumbled loose from its pins during the roughhousing. "And neither would I," he murmured. "Bedtime it is. Which means you're going to stay right here and sleep, too."

"I wasn't going anywhere." When he cocked a knowing brow at her, she grimaced. "All right, all right. I was, but now I'm not." Settling against his chest, she closed her eyes.

Tallain's voice was barely tinged with humor as he said, "Shall I bring a Merida back for you?"

Her answer was quite serious. "Yes. Make it an important one. *That's* the hide I want nailed to my wall."

"Then if it pleases you, I will provide a very important Merida for you to kill however you like."

She was about to thank him in all sincerity when it occurred to her that the entire conversation was barbaric. What would flaying a Merida accomplish? Would it bring Jahnavi back? Even if Tallain found the very one who had killed her brother, what good would it do?

Sionell hid her face against her husband's neck in despair. "I *hate* this," she said, her voice quivering.

"It has to be done, you know. The killing. Most people would say that dead is dead, and it doesn't matter how you feel about how the enemy got that way, so long as it's done. I think it *does* matter, Ell. I think it has to matter or there's nothing to difference us from the Merida or the Vellant'im."

"Dead is dead," she repeated softly. "But those of you

who have to do the killing have to live with *how* you did the killing—and why."

"Most people would also say that Rohan corrupted us at a very tender age with his ridiculous ideas." There was a smile in his voice, self-mocking and a little sad.

"Do you feel corrupted?" She didn't wait for his answer. "Neither do I. But I don't feel completely clean, either."

"None of us are, my love. I don't know whether I feel sorrier for those who know it—or those who don't."

* * *

Though Stronghold had been built to house an entire army—two, with a little cramming—it was no disciplined, orderly host that occupied it now. Whole families, toddlers to grandmothers, crowded the keep. The castle wasn't quite ready to burst at the seams, even with the addition of people from Radzyn and Remagev and those who had escaped Whitecliff before its capture. But for anyone used to the sparse population of peacetime, the lack of elbow room jangled the nerves.

Meals in the Great Hall weren't really chaotic—they just seemed that way after years of quiet repasts. Maintaining usual standards of tidiness wasn't impossible, just more difficult. After the first few days, when the servants were simultaneously run ragged and plagued by well-meaning counterparts from other places who didn't understand the way things were done at the High Prince's residence, a routine of sorts was established.

But an army would have been easier to house in good order—and infinitely quieter. Children hurtled through hallways and cried late at night. When they gathered for lessons, their chanted responses could be heard all over the keep. The chatter of crafters and grooms and maids and cooks and Radzyn merchants was constant and maddening.

The only escape from the noise was for the soldiers who rode out every morning on patrol. Maarken went with them gladly—and a little guiltily, at leaving to others the work of keeping Stronghold functional.

As Battle Commander of the Desert, however, it was his duty to go. The forays made him look useful, even if he didn't feel it; at least they got him out of the keep. And one worry was eased by the long days on horseback: his beauties

weren't fretting themselves sick at being confined to a crowded stable. Actually, he mused, horses and people were in roughly the same pass, but the horses were getting better treatment. None but warriors were allowed outside the walls. Everyone else had to make do with a stroll in the gardens.

Maarken chose to ride with Kazander's men today rather than his father's or Rohan's or Walvis'. His mount was a feisty little bay mare who danced and sidled and wanted a run so badly she practically chewed the steel bit to pieces. Kazander noticed, smiling.

"She'd show them her heels at the *Rialla* races, my lord, no doubt of it. A true daughter of her sire, Sevol."

Maarken glanced at him sharply. Sevol was a black Radzyn stallion who had never thrown any but black foals in his whole career at stud. Maarken said so. Kazander grinned.

"Not on *your* mares, my lord," was the unrepentant reply.

Maarken felt his own lips curve in a smile. "You're a sly thief, Kazander, and I ought to reclaim Radzyn stock."

"Thief!" the young man wailed. "The mighty lord wounds me, my heart is bleeding!"

"Save it for my father—Sevol was *his* horse." He tightened the reins a little as they rode into a narrow ravine. Lizards skittered from the path into the shelter of low, sun-baked scrub. There were no birds to take startled wing and no tiny furred creatures to rustle the bushes in warning of approaching riders. The Desert-bred must rely on their own senses and, if the animal was sensitive enough, those of their horses. "Kazander, why don't you just ask when you need a stud? We'd be happy to provide."

The *korrus* considered his answer for some time. Finally he said, "My esteemed sire taught his most unworthy son to respect and honor the dread Lord of Radzyn. How would it look, my lord, if I were to cast aside his teachings and violate generations of understanding between our people?"

"My father would have a lot fewer gray hairs, I can tell you that! When I inherit Radzyn—may it be many years from now—this 'understanding' between us is going to change."

He drew back in shock. "My lord!"

"Yes," Maarken drawled, enjoying himself. "I haven't quite figured out how yet, but I'm not going to let you turn *me* white-haired!"

Kazander looked glum and sighed. "It won't be any fun

anymore!" Then he perked up and gave a sunny smile. "But if my lord makes it more difficult, we will find all the more pleasure in the borrowing! My lord is generous beyond all words to concern himself with our happiness!"

Maarken gave up and laughed, anticipating a delicious battle of wits between himself and this half-mad young man for years to come. Whatever tricks he devised to thwart the Isulk'im, Kazander would puzzle them through and borrow the studs anyway—praising him all the while for providing such excellent sport.

The pair led the way up the ravine, ten of Kazander's men following. They were about five measures from Stronghold now, and after climbing a hill could see the top of the Flametower. Kazander directed his troops to scour the area by threes, himself taking Maarken and a burly youth called Visian with him to the west. It had been many days since any Vellant'im had been found lurking in the hills, but Maarken did not find that reassuring. The ride out of the castle these days seemed to bore the enemy camped down below, which worried him even more. Putting himself in their heads was easy: make a survey of the surrounding terrain and then pretend not to notice scouting parties—while waiting for reinforcements to arrive from elsewhere. But because Maarken was a Sunrunner, he knew things they did not. No one marched from Radzyn or Remagev. In fact, there was no troop movement in the Desert at all, except for Riyan out of Skybowl. He would meet Tallain soon to battle the Merida.

"Is this place sufficient to your needs, my lord?" Kazander asked.

Maarken glanced around. The bare hillcrest, dotted with low scrub and a few water-hoarding herbs, was dreadfully exposed and made the soldier in him nervous. For a Sunrunner, however, it was perfect.

"It's fine, Kazander. You and Visian keep watch. Do you remember what I told you about bringing me back?"

"Gently, firmly, and quickly," Kazander recited. "We will keep you safe, my lord, or die."

"That won't be necessary, but thanks for the thought."

Closing his eyes, he turned his face to the noon sun and listened to the blessed quiet. Ears numbed by Stronghold's multitude regained their usual sensitivity. He heard the silken whisper of dry leaves and grasses, the faint hoofbeats of the

patrols, his own clothes rustling as a breath of wind plucked at them. But it was not his physical hearing that gave him the sound of his son's voice.

Father—thank the Goddess, I found you at last!

He steadied the weaving skillfully. Rohannon barely knew how to do this; the possible reasons for risking a technique he didn't fully understand made Maarken's heart freeze. *Are you all right?*

Me? Oh, yes, of course. Don't worry.

Then what's happened to make you try something you don't really know how to do?

Rohannon hesitated, and then it all burst from him in a rush that Maarken had some difficulty in sorting out. Searching for him at Stronghold and over half the Vere Hills; Prince Arlis' arrival at New Raetia; the excursion to Catha Heights and what he'd seen there; the certainty that Prince Saumer was *faradhi.*

Leave everything to me, Maarken told him briskly, hiding most of his shocked dismay. *And don't try this again without instruction. It's too risky.*

It worked, didn't it?

Maarken replied severely, *You caught me in a fairly tight weaving. Do you have any idea how to disengage from it? I thought not.* Then he relented. *You did well, Rohannon. But don't do it again until you really know how.*

Wait—don't take me back yet! What are you going to do?

Tell Rohan. As he guided his rebellious offspring back to New Raetia, he savored the colors of Rohannon's mind: glowing amethyst, bright diamond, deep garnet, all set in a pattern of elegant clarity. He had always wondered why there was never any family resemblance among *faradh'im*; he might have expected to see parts of himself and Hollis in their son, the way children took after parents in physical ways. Sometimes there was a similarity of color, but not always. Lady Andrade had spent many puzzled years going through genealogies, but there was no pattern to the patterns. Each Sunrunner was unique.

That reminded him of something. *Did you get an idea of Saumer's colors?*

No—sorry. Father, will it be this easy for me someday? It feels like we're flying!

Maarken smiled. *Glad you like it. Learning how is serious business, but the plain truth is that it's fun! And yes, it'll be*

easy for you, too, someday. Have the Sunrunner there teach you.

She's the type who doesn't piss unless Andry gives permission.

Since when does the only son of Andry's only brother need the approval of a court Sunrunner? When Rohannon's colors sparkled with laughter, Maarken joined in ruefully. *Well, all right, I guess I've never been any good at arrogance. I'll have Andry tell her. Will that do?*

I hope so. I want to be able to do this on my own. He paused. *Please let Daniv know how sorry I am about his father.*

Maarken left his son and returned to the Desert. The only explanation he gave Kazander was that all seemed peaceful enough in the hills, but he had received other news he must take back to Stronghold immediately. Visian accompanied him at Kazander's insistence: "The dread Lord of Radzyn would skewer me on my own sword if his most beloved son so much as scuffed the shine on his boots."

Maarken let the mare have her head on the ride back. Visian begged him to slow down through the treacherous ravines, but Maarken ignored him. Two horses racing past the Vellanti camp provided a tempting target; he could feel arrows sighted on his back and kicked the mare to greater speed. At last he was in the crowded courtyard, jumping from the saddle, shouting for the High Prince and his father

But it was Daniv who came forward to conduct him upstairs, and Maarken loathed himself for the silence of sheer cowardice. He didn't want to be the one to tell the boy that his father was dead, and he was now Prince of Syr.

* * *

Rohannon had missed seeing one essential thing at Catha Heights: the pennant of Meadowlord sagging at the stern of the boat. Sioned saw it and drew the right conclusion with the wrong evidence. Unable to find Saumer, and unconvinced that this would be the best time to reveal his Sunrunner gifts anyway, she made a thorough search of the area to get any clues she could about what had happened. The only thing of any worth was that flag. There was no one who could tell her it had been made and placed there by Kostas' order.

Not that it mattered; had she seen the Vellant'im wel-

come the boat's arrival, as Kostas and Rihani had, she would have known her surmise was the correct one. Chiana *was* guilty of collaborating with the enemy. It was just that the evidence was false.

Tobren was given strict instructions about what to say to Andrev—and how to say it. Her only question was who was going to tell Andry about all this. Sioned later expressed her amazement to Rohan that the child experienced no conflict in total loyalty to her father while being proud of the brother who was defying him.

"Be glad of it," he replied. "Once she really thinks it through, or if she gets caught between them, she'll go through all Hells. She loves them both."

Andrev ran through half of Waes to find Tilal and Ostvel, who were meeting with their captains at the inn designated as headquarters for the troops. Those seated around the stoked hearth were surprised that a squire should interrupt so discourteously, but Tilal squelched any rebukes with a simple, "Lord Andrev is also our Sunrunner."

The boy followed Sioned's cautions as relayed through Tobren, telling his lord as gently as possible that Kostas was dead. Tilal sat very still for some moments, then excused himself and strode quickly for the door. Ostvel watched him go, sorrowing more for his friend's loss than for Kostas personally; it had been difficult to be fond of him, although his stern but fair rule had inspired respect. But the death of the Prince of Syr concerned Ostvel more than the death of the man who had held the title.

An examination of Andrev's face told him there was more. Rising, he said to the captains, "We'll finish this at the residence tonight," and led Andrev outside. He frowned up at the graying sky, where clouds were sweeping down from the north. "You cut it close," he observed.

The boy nodded solemnly. "But it was important, my lord. And it's not just Prince Kostas." Andrev made short work of what Sioned had seen as evidence against Chiana.

"So," Ostvel murmured, "we may now attack Swalekeep without compunction. How very convenient." Rousing himself, he finished, "Thank you for your work, Andrev—and for your courage in daring the clouds."

"The Goddess watches over her Sunrunners, my lord."

"I've heard it rumored," he said to himself as the boy ran off. Then he started through the streets, searching for Tilal.

* * *

The little ceremony went smoothly, and Master Jayachin was now an *athri* without the word's actually being used. She was canny enough to decline the title "Lady," which amused Andry. He bet Valeda in private that the woman would subtly encourage use of the title until by midwinter everyone was saying it without thinking twice. Valeda scoffed. "Midwinter? I give it ten days."

It was all highly illegal, of course—or would have been if *athri* had been the term spoken. Only the High Prince could authorize the establishment of a noble title and a new holding. Princes made applications to him and the thing was done in the presence of all the lords of a princedom gathered to acclaim and welcome the new *athri* to their ranks. But there was no wall for Jayachin to be lord of—excepting those surrounding Goddess Keep, or unless one interpreted a split-stick fence as a real wall—and thus the word was inapplicable. But everyone understood what was really going on here, and in truth, it was a perfect solution to Andry's problem. He didn't want his people or his substance involved in this small city growing about Goddess Keep. Now the whole place was Jayachin's responsibility. He was relieved of the burden but had gained even more stature in the people's eyes—for who but a prince could create an *athri*, whether the word was said or not? He was caring for them, honoring one of their own number, allowing them to stay near him where it was safe. The protection of the Goddess had settled around them all, and they were content.

He knew his whole family would be livid at his presumption. He didn't much care. The network of Sunrunners that formed the power base of Goddess Keep—and which Andrade had used ruthlessly—had now been augmented by something that trod on the High Prince's toes. But Andrade had done that, too—though she had never dared establish a holding here, as he had done. Then again, she had never been presented with thousands of refugees on her front lawns, either.

Yes, Rohan and Sioned and all the rest were going to be furious. Doubtless it would anger Tilal most, considering that Ossetia was his princedom. Andry owed him for stealing Andrev away from sheer spite. After a moment's thought, however, he decided Pol's fury would outstrip Tilal's. The

line between their separate powers and influences was growing ever more smudged. Soon it would be obliterated—and then let Pol writhe as he begged Andry and his *devr'im* to turn back the Vellanti invaders.

To this end, he had them practice constructing a *ros'salath*—the non-lethal kind—to encompass the new holding. Torien had tested it, reporting its thinness in spots, as if crocheted wool had stretched and left holes. Not surprising; two of its architects were dead now, and without them the pattern had been disrupted. More drill was needed, more delving into the Star Scroll for refinements of technique—and more *devr'im*. Still unable to get about easily on his wounded leg, Andry spent his mornings in research, his afternoons discussing his findings with Jolan and Torien, and his evenings sounding out potential replacements for Oclel and Rusina.

Their five-year-old daughter, Surida, had taken to trailing Nialdan about the castle. Andry supposed it was because he was tall and broad-shouldered like her dead father. It was a poignant thing to see the little girl trotting gamely along beside the big Sunrunner, who slowed his strides when she was with him and was as tender of her as if she had been his own. Andry, watching them, wondered if Andrev followed Tilal as assiduously, and if the prince matched his steps to those of another man's son.

When there was safe sunlight or moonlight to work with, his Sunrunners brought him word of what transpired elsewhere. He heard with pride of his nephew Rohannon's skillful exercise of authority at New Raetia, and with irritation of the refusal of Grib, Gilad, Fessenden, and Meadowlord to involve themselves directly in the war. The fine points of various treaties grounded them in legality—and he spared a sardonic smile that Rohan had so infected them all with his passion for law that even now they used it to cover their cowardly self-interest. But he also took personal offense. It was his signature and seal as Lord of Goddess Keep that appended some of those documents. In tricking Rohan, they grinned at him, too.

The continuing silence from Balarat was one of his primary concerns. He'd lost one Sunrunner already—the one assigned to Waes, who had accompanied Rialt to Swalekeep and died there of unknown causes. Deniker had seen the last ashes being blown away by a dawn breeze, watched over by Rialt, his family, and a few Waesian notables wear-

ing mourning gray. Conjuring the scene for Andry in Fire, Deniker had been surprised when Andry identified young Princess Palila standing near her cousin Cluthine. It was possible that Chiana had sent the youngest and least important member of her family as a token honor for the dead *faradhi*, but Andry doubted it. The girl's presence therefore remained a puzzle.

As the days wore on and nothing was heard from Arpali in Firon, even when there was enough light, Andry began to fear that perhaps she was dead, too. Strange things had been observed at Balarat: Lord Yarin's flag flying where Laric's standard should be, Lord Yarin's soldiers riding patrol when snowfall permitted, Lord Yarin himself venturing out for a ride on a sunny morning with a retinue who deferred to him as if he was their prince. Andry wondered if Laric knew of this at Dragon's Rest. But even if he was aware that his wife's brother was busily taking over his princedom, what could he do?

More to the point, could Andry do anything about it? Having Laric in his debt would be a very good thing, once this was all over and the inevitable restructuring began. Besides, Firon was rife with *diarmadh'im*; it had been their main place of exile, especially in the forbidding mountains between Firon and Cunaxa. If Laric owed Andry his princedom, Andry would have the chance to find and execute hundreds of sorcerers. They were on the side of the Vellant'im in this war, and along with their Merida henchmen, they deserved to die.

Life would be a fascinating tangle once the war was over. Everyone—prince, *athri*, and commoner—would look to Goddess Keep for the reestablishment of order and stability. And the Goddess would provide.

* * *

Kazander sent word back to Stronghold that he would again spend the night in the hills with several of his men. It was to the High Prince's credit that he had instantly understood Kazander's reasons. Unused to living within any walls but those of his tent beneath the silent stars, the clamor within Rohan's keep set his teeth on edge.

Still, that was only part of it. As he lay back, his head cradled on his saddle, he watched the clouds tease the stars

and thought of Chayla. It was instinct, not mere impulse, that drew him to her—but what would he do if he won her? By the standards of her people she was yet a child; her birth had made her Lady Chayla of Whitecliff; her breeding had made her a *faradhi*. She would not share a tent with other wives. She didn't belong in a tent at all, but in a castle. Isulki blood had been diluted in her. She loved the Desert and understood it as well as anyone whose life did not utterly depend on knowing its every whim, but she didn't hear its songs. Her music was that of stone and wood and silken sheets, and flowers in her hair.

He knew all that. None of it made any difference. He loved her as simply as he breathed.

"*Korrus*," whispered a voice in the darkness.

"My brother," he replied just as softly.

"Someone comes."

Disinterested as the Vellant'im appeared to be, Kazander had not made the mistake of choosing his campsite unwisely. The four men who had elected to stay with him moved with swift silence into positions overlooking the trail. Five horses—no, six—were approaching at a fast trot. By the sound of their hoofbeats they had been ridden at a killing pace for some time. Kazander glanced up at the sky, tasted the air, and decided it was well after midnight. Enemy soldiers coming from the Meadowlord side of the Vere Hills, and in such desperate haste that they had not taken the longer, safer route to the south—he didn't like this at all. With a soft whistle to signal his men, he crouched behind a boulder to wait.

Visian, brother of his youngest wife, had the honor of taking down the first rider. The man roared like an embattled dragonsire, but high above that sound was a woman's piercing scream.

"Hold!" Kazander yelled, leaping down to stand in the center of the road. His men followed, grabbing the reins of winded horses. The woman screamed again. Visian backed away from his victim, who scrambled to his feet and stalked up to Kazander.

"Are you the cause of this outrage?" he demanded. "How dare you lay hands on her grace's escort! You've frightened the princesses half to death!"

"I'm not scared, Laroshin," called a small, light voice,

bubbling with excitement. "And my mother was just startled, weren't you, Mama?"

Kazander identified Pol's wife by the cloud of golden hair for which she was famous. She drooped in the saddle, huddling into a dark cloak, a boy on horseback hovering at her side. He made her a profound reverence in the manner of his people and wondered forlornly if he could charm himself out of this one.

"Your most noble grace, this unworthy fool apologizes from the bottom of his stricken heart. He begs of your highness' benevolence to allow him to escort your grace in safety to Stronghold, where her mighty lord awaits and in his loneliness will weep for joy at seeing—"

"Who the hell are you, and what the hell are you saying?" the one called Laroshin growled.

Kazander bowed to him, too, and similarly craved forgiveness. He almost managed to finish his speech before he was interrupted again—by the child's giggles.

"Oh, just listen to him, Rislyn!"

"Shh! It's not nice to laugh, Jihan!"

Kazander addressed the two little girls. "Your highness' laughter is as sweet water in the Desert."

"Laroshin," quavered their mother, "who *is* this person?"

The boy beside her snorted. "Just what he said, your grace—an idiot."

This was too much for Visian. "Gently," he advised in silken tones. "You speak of the Lord Kazander, *korrus* of the Isulk'im, honored kinsman of the High Prince."

Kazander bowed again. The princess was too exhausted to acknowledge him, but her daughters gave him a pair of regal nods marred only by Jihan's leftover giggles. The other one, Rislyn, hushed her again and spoke quietly to Kazander.

"My lord, please can you take us to Stronghold now? We've been riding since last midnight and we're very tired."

He wanted to ask why they had nearly killed their horses getting away from Dragon's Rest, but that was for Pol to know. One thing was certain: the reasons would bring no one comfort.

"If your grace will permit so humble and worthless an escort—"

"Just get us there, and fast," Laroshin snapped, and then, when Visian gave him a long look, tacked on a "—my lord."

"Yes, please, just let's ride on," the princess said faintly. "Kierun, you take my reins. I'm so tired. . . ."

"I'm not," Jihan stated—and once they were within the castle, proved it by running up to her grandparents' chambers as if it was midday instead of the middle of the night. Pol, roused from bed by all the fuss, was halfway down the stairs when Meiglan tottered in the door, leaning on Kierun.

He stopped cold. "*Meggie?*"

Rohan and Sioned, wrapped in bedrobes and urged along by Jihan, arrived on the upper landing in time to see Meiglan's head lift at the sound of Pol's voice. Her huge dark eyes were set in bruises of sleepless worry, there were dirt smudges on her cheeks, and all that kept her upright was the squire's supporting arm. But when she saw Pol, her tired face lit with a radiance that said home and safety and love and release from all her troubles.

"Meggie—what in all Hells are you *doing* here?"

Rohan winced; Sioned started forward to do battle. Meiglan solved the whole situation by the simple expedient of slipping to the floor in a dead faint.

Chapter Twenty-seven

"Well, *that* was a nice piece of work," Sioned commented to her son over breakfast. "After all that poor child went through to get here, you snarl at her. I trust you've apologized."

"Meggie did a stupid thing, leaving Dragon's Rest where she and the children were safe—"

"I disagree," Rohan told him quietly. "I think it was very clever of her."

Pol set down his cup. "Clever? It was absolute insanity!"

"And you'll thank me to let you manage your own wife, is that it?" Rohan arched a sardonic brow at him. "Before you manage to make her cry by scolding her for doing the only thing she could do, there's something else you ought to know. Jihan had very interesting things to say last night about Grandfather Miyon at Dragon's Rest."

"*What?*"

Sioned rose from the table, her blue bedrobe swirling around her, and began snatching clothes from the closet. "Yes, just think about *that* for a moment."

"In what context?" Pol asked warily. "We know that his Merida bastard has taken over the princedom—naturally he fled."

"Goddess give me patience!" she cried. "After all this time, don't you understand him yet? His son has led his armies against Tuath—and is likely to meet up with Tallain and Riyan any day now." She threw one shirt at Rohan and another onto the bed for herself, giving the impression that if they'd stayed in her hands one more instant she would have shredded them. "Do you think Miyon disapproved? Do you honestly believe that after everything he went through

to gain sole rule of Cunaxa that he'd slink away now, when he's got a chance of grabbing the northern Desert?"

"But he *did* leave," Pol pointed out stubbornly.

"And for where? Dragon's Rest!"

Rohan said, "Meiglan rightly fears her father. And now that she's removed herself and the children, Miyon has nothing to bargain with. No hostages."

"Hos—? No. Impossible. Not even he would dare."

"What would you not do to keep your wife and daughters safe?"

Pol swallowed hard. "So now my palace, instead of my family, is in his hands. What do you suggest I do about it?"

"Nothing."

Sioned paused on her way into the bathroom with an armful of clothes. "Rohan. . . ."

"Oh, come!" he chided. "What does Miyon have now? Dragon's Rest—filled with people loyal to Pol, not to mention his former squire who happens to be married to a princess of Grib, and another prince who's his kinsman. I'm betting our cousin of Cunaxa will be at Swalekeep rather quickly. So you see that Meiglan was *very* clever in escaping—and I must say that my heart warms when I think of the welcome Chiana will give her empty-handed ally."

"So once again you counsel no action at all," Pol said, his voice dangerously soft. "This is my princedom we're speaking of, Father."

Rohan shrugged. "Do as you like. My experience tells me one thing. Obviously you trust yours more. But I do insist that you apologize to your princess. Through her bravery and daring, she's spared you more than you know."

Meiglan heard all this from the antechamber, ashamed to be listening in secret but unable to help it. Flinching when Pol condemned her action, amazed when Rohan and Sioned attributed her flight to cleverness rather than fear, at last she realized that although fear had been her primary motivation, she had indeed recognized the danger from her father.

She crept from the outer room and hurried back down the hallway to her own chambers. Perhaps she wasn't hopelessly inadequate after all—hadn't Rohan called her Pol's princess instead of just his wife? Pride, pleasure, and sudden confidence flushed through her, and so when Pol appeared a little while later in her room, she told him the whole tale

without fearing his reaction. She had done the right thing; Rohan and Sioned had said so. And Pol—his initial anger had only been that she had risked herself and the children. He said as much when he apologized, and then praised her cleverness. It was only later that she remembered how seldom anyone in the High Prince's circle complimented anyone else on their intelligence; everyone was *expected* to have wits, and to use them.

* * *

Jihan had slain the dragon—as usual. Remarkable, the way she moved in for the kill, her blue eyes glittering and her sword held defensively close to her body, the way squires were taught. She planted a bare foot on the fallen dragon and laughed aloud, waving her sword in the air.

The dragon suddenly came to life. A hand closed around her ankle and toppled her. Jihan shrieked and fought for possession of her sword, but the dragon tossed it away and grappled with her on the carpet. Rislyn came to her rescue, grabbing up the sword and attacking the roaring dragon. At last they had defeated the beast, and stood on his back yelling their triumph at the top of their lungs.

"Jihan! Rislyn! You should be in bed! Stop all this noise at once!"

The dragon peeked out from under his woolen wing. "I'm afraid you're too late, Meiglan. They've done me in right and proper, and now I expect they'll make necklets of my teeth and talons. Poor dragon!"

Meiglan gave a little gasp of surprise. "Your grace!"

Rohan shook off his granddaughters, snatched up one under each arm, and groaned to his feet. "Goddess, what do you feed these two? It's only the first of Autumn since I've seen them and already they've grown half a silkweight!" He shook the giggling pair, set them on their feet, and discarded the cloak with a flourish. "Your dragon has had enough for one night. He's not as young as he used to be!"

"No, Grandsir—again!" Jihan demanded.

"Please?" seconded Rislyn.

"Your mama says it's bedtime, and so it is. Whup, wait a moment—hands and faces washed? Jihan, don't rub the dirt off on your clean nightgown! Rislyn, I will allow you *one* glass of water, and then get to bed."

"And a story," she suggested slyly, big green eyes dancing.

After a glance at Meiglan, who nodded and smiled, he said, "Very well. A story. No, don't tell me—you want one about dragons."

He told them one of the less bloodthirsty tales about a village maiden who outsmarted a dragon by dazzling him with a handful of jewels, although where a peasant girl would get such things or why a dragon would react so to them was beyond him, and the story never elucidated. Unfortunately, Rohan was very good at telling stories; the twins were wide awake and begging for more by the time he finished, and he cast a guilty look at their mother. Meiglan tried to suppress a smile, failed, and moved in to exert some parental discipline.

"You may have another story tomorrow, if you're good and ask Grandsir politely. *And* do your lessons well. But it's long past time you were asleep."

"Lessons?" Jihan wailed. "But we're at Stronghold, we never have lessons at Stronghold!"

"This time you do."

She kissed them and stood back while Rohan tucked in the sheets and then had the breath hugged out of him, which necessitated a retucking. At last the adults left the room, nodding to the maidservant on duty in the outer chamber.

"It's wise of you to establish a routine for them as quickly as possible," Rohan commented.

"It's not wisdom, my lord. It's certainty of what Jihan would get up to, running around here without six eyes on her at all times."

He grinned. "I saw poor Kierun and Dannar chasing after her today. Rather wicked of Pol to assign them guard duty." He slipped an arm around her waist and walked her to the door of her rooms. "I think perhaps it's time you got some sleep, too. That was a hard ride, my dear. You still look tired."

"I slept most of today, my lord."

Her blush told him that not all of her time in bed had been spent in slumber, but Meiglan was not a girl one teased about such things. "Just the same, why don't you have a good long bath? I'll have taze and cakes sent up."

"That would be lovely, my lord," she sighed.

After nine years, Rohan had given up trying to get her to

call him by his name. It was enough that he no longer frightened her—though he'd never understood what she found so awesome about him. He kissed her cheek lightly and bade her good night, and started down the hall.

"My lord?"

He turned and saw fear in her wide, soft brown eyes. "What is it, Meiglan?"

"Will there be battle?"

"I hope not." Then, because she needed more reassurance than that, he added with a smile, "That's the beauty of Stronghold. It's the Desert they'll be fighting, not us. Don't worry, Meggie."

"I won't, my lord. Good night."

He considered going down to the kitchens himself to order Meiglan's taze, then decided against it and snagged a passing servant. "Nothing elaborate—but she didn't eat much tonight."

"At once, my lord. And the High Princess said that if anyone saw you, to tell you she'd be waiting for you in the Summer Room."

"Mmm. Tell the High Princess—" *That no one can find me.* "—that I'll join her in a little while."

"Very good, my lord."

Sioned would not think it "very good," but she would also understand that he needed some time to himself. But where could he be alone in his overpopulated castle? He watched the servant pause to replace a faltering torch in a wall sconce, and as light blazed anew turned resolutely for the stairs.

The fire in the Flametower had been built up at sunset, as always. Someone would come at dawn to replenish it for the day. It had been thus for a very long time now. He'd lit these flames himself from a torch carried back from his father's funeral pyre.

The day Zehava died, his fire was allowed to burn out. Rohan's mother and sister had cleansed this room with their own hands. Incredibly, Andrade had helped them. That same day, Rohan had killed his first, last, and only dragon, the one that had killed his father. That day, too, he had seen Sioned for the first time. And the next morning, just after dawn, he had climbed the spiral stairs to find fresh kindling stacked and waiting. His fire had burned here for nearly forty years.

He walked slowly around the outer edge of the room, close to the windows, remembering. He'd come here often as a little boy, needing a high, light-filled place to be alone—or needing only to gaze out at the land he loved. In this room he had seen Sioned's face for the first time, conjured in Fire by Andrade. From here he had watched princes arrive at his command in 705, come to acknowledge him as High Prince. He smiled suddenly—over on the floor was an inkstain from a bottle spilled by Chay during that wild dragon-counting of 719.

But foremost in his mind was the single morning of his life when no fire had burned here at all. The day after his father's death; the day of the battle with the dragon. Lack of sleep, the panic of Tobin's joining with the *faradh'im*, and the exhaustion of that long walk back from the pyre had made his grip on the torch shaky at best. It had suddenly felt much too heavy, and he'd had an irrational fear that he would drop it or its flame would die. That morning the floor, walls, and ceiling had been scrubbed to gleaming whiteness. The window arches had been cleaned of soot accumulated during his father's long reign, and the sleeping dragons carved at the point of each window had seemed ready to stir to life, lift their wings, and fly.

The dragons were black again. He ran a finger over the wall, felt the gritty residue of his own long fire. Sighing, he wiped his fingertip on his trousers and wedged himself into one of the windows, spine against the stone. Out beyond Stronghold was the Desert; where he sat, the night breeze met the fire's heat and the scents were oddly the same, fierce and wild. He closed his eyes and breathed of his princedom.

I am afraid.

Always better to admit it than to pretend otherwise. Lately his actions—or lack of them, Pol would say—had felt . . . not *wrong*, but as if there was something out of balance. Radzyn had been a disaster. That the keep still stood was no work of his. Remagev had been no better. He knew the Desert would not betray him, would do his killing for him. But the Long Sand required time, and though Sunrunners had reported no immediate march on Stronghold yet, he could feel Vellanti footfalls like the thud of his own heart.

What have I done wrong? Where am I failing, that my people die and my lands are beneath enemy boots? That the

failure was his was a thing he never questioned. He was High Prince. That made it his fault.

Yet through all of it—and even because of some of it—there was Pol. The Goddess' recompense for finally learning not to play people like chess pieces? Pol's existence wasn't simple chance. Rohan didn't believe in chance.

Neither did he believe in flying against the storm. You waited it out, or died with shredded wings. Any hatchling dragon knew that. His own wings were a little battered. His own fault; he should have learned sooner.

In his youth, in the first rush of arrogant determination, he had sought to mold people and events to his own ends. Not because it amused him; not because he enjoyed the flex of power. He *knew* his ways were better. He had faith in himself and his goals. But there had been no patience, no understanding. And greater than his belief in the rightness of what he wanted was his belief in his own cleverness.

He'd played princesses off against each other, kept everyone guessing, pretended to be a callow idiot. He'd bought off the Merida one year and crushed them in battle the next. He'd thought he could control events—and ended up at their mercy.

Roelstra's hunger for his death had increased tenfold after Rohan had made a fool of him. Ianthe's vengeance had been for pride's sake, too, as well as power's. The Merida had become even more poisonous, reasoning that if they could not regain the Desert, they would gain Cunaxa through Miyon and come to power as lawful princes. The *diarmadh'im* had been able to murder Andrade because Rohan had not murdered the pretender to Princemarch at once, as he should have. They had nearly murdered Pol because Rohan had waited too long.

Yet he had come to believe that things happened as they were meant to, for reasons he might or might not understand. Events played out until there was only one correct, necessary action. When all had come down to the pretender's life or Maarken's, the knives had been in Rohan's fingers before he even had to think about them. By the time they were embedded in the pretender's throat, the time for thought had passed. In Pol's battle against his own half-brother, Rohan's interference would have been utterly wrong. Pol had to prove himself *to* himself—and to everyone who had ever doubted him.

Rohan supposed that in many ways he had ruthlessly used challenges to Pol's claim in order to strengthen that claim. Using people was nothing new to him—but only to do for him what their own natures led them to do anyway. At least he didn't manipulate people, didn't bend souls awry to his own ends. That had been the lesson of his first *Rialla*, when he'd ended up loathing himself and nearly losing Sioned. He'd learned to use the strengths and selfishnesses of other princes to gain what he wanted. He justified himself with what Chay had told him years ago: *"You have the courage of your dreams—when most of us don't even know* how *to dream."* He told himself he was teaching the others how—ah, but only when their dreams coincided with his.

He'd explained himself to Pol as best he knew how—but Pol's instincts were different. The irony was that the usual complaint of younger generation to elder, the complaint he'd had about his own father—*"You don't understand me!"* —was in this case turned on its tail. Rohan understood Pol perfectly. It was the son who did not comprehend the father.

I've done what I thought was right. I was put into this place and decided better me than someone who doesn't know himself for the barbarian he is. It was a supreme arrogance—but I could do none other. I've ruled by laws and broken only a few of them—for which I've paid dearly in my own heart blood.

But Pol saw patience as indecision, and waiting as cowardice.

Rohan felt salt sweat sting his eyes, tasted it on his lips. A sudden gust through the window dried the moisture on his face and neck to chill pinpricks, while the fire burned hotter in response to the wind. When brightness flared against his closed eyelids, he turned his face to the night. Strongly as his fire might blaze now, one day it would go out. Pol's would replace it. Pol, who was impatience and quickness and action and three kinds of power personified.

A creature of instinct. Thus far, gut reactions had served him reasonably well. He was alive—quite an accomplishment, considering some of the events in a life not half over. But instinct was not enough. Any savage could lash out at a threat to survival; any animal preserved its own life at almost any cost.

Rohan believed with all his soul that to act on sheer instinct without knowledge was folly. It was the mark of the

barbarian, the triumph of belly over brain. Yet to know and act, but not to understand the consequences, could be worse. One must wait for alternatives to develop, then choose which action to take. Sometimes there was only one, and life resolved itself into the simplest possible choices. Sometimes there were many, and he had to trust himself to pick the right one. Or at least the one he could live with.

Pol saw his ways as an invitation for events to force him into a corner. For all the sobering experience of learning his Sunrunner and sorcerer powers, Pol still didn't understand that power of any kind was to be used as little as possible. There were two reasons for that. The first was outward perception: when others saw that there was no other choice, they were unthreatened by power when it was finally used. The second was a far graver reason. The more one used power, the more one wished to use it—until it ended by using the user.

Look at Andry—setting himself up as a prince, thinking that he's the one making the decisions. His power is doing it for him. He understands even less than Pol.

It was their peculiar tragedy that in standing as rival to Pol, Andry would be Pol's most stringent lesson.

As Roelstra was mine. He, too, was trapped by his power—by what he could *do as opposed to what he* should *do. He began a war simply because he* could. *Power wasn't his tool, it was his master.* He hoped for Tobin's sake, and Chay's and Maarken's—and especially Andry's—that Pol would learn that without the Lord of Goddess Keep as disastrous example.

And yet . . . if Pol wasn't already aware of it, Rohan had failed. He was High Prince, responsible for what the next High Prince would be and do and become. What manner of light would shine when Pol's fire burned here?

He must trust the past to protect the future, trust Pol's training and experiences and nature. But this future was unlike anything Rohan and Sioned had envisioned. He stared out at the Desert night, telling himself that he could hardly be blamed for failing Pol simply because he was not prescient.

When the torches appeared in the Desert, hundreds of them like fatal golden flowers converging on Stronghold from west and south and east, he nodded quietly, unsurprised. This, at least, he had expected. This choice had been coming for a long time now. He was done with waiting and

with patience. Now he would fight because he must, use power because he must.

Picking his way through the maze of sleepers on the floor of the Great Hall, he awakened no one—not even when he lifted his long-unused sword from its place on the wall near the dragon tapestry. It felt curiously light, as if all the blood that had weighted it down years ago had sheened away.

* * *

By morning everyone knew that the Vellanti army was camped outside in daunting numbers. From Faolain Lowland and Radzyn and Remagev they'd come, now under the single flag of the lightning bolt, more than two thousand of them.

"They can attack and keep on attacking," Hollis said worriedly, but Chay wore a tight grin.

"And spend themselves against the walls until there aren't any of them left. Why do you think they called this place 'Stronghold'?"

Maarken nodded. "Judging by the preliminary count, I estimate five to seven days before they're down to a force we can defeat in pitched battle."

"I don't know that I care to wait that long," Rohan commented mildly, earning himself a stare from his son.

Meath exchanged a glance with Sioned and murmured, "It's when the dragon's roar is softest that he's most dangerous."

"Noticed that through the years, have you?" she replied. "My lord," she went on, addressing him not as his wife and princess but as his Sunrunner, "tell us the when and the how, and we'll be ready."

Rohan nodded. "Maarken, as Battle Commander, you are excused from their working. Sioned, you'll have Meath, Hollis, Morwenna, and Relnaya to work with. Pol, what part you take in this is up to you."

"Whatever you wish, your grace," said the next High Prince.

Rohan inclined his head in acknowledgment—both of his son's submission to his will and of the circumstances that had prompted it. "Maarken, I'll expect plans of attack and defense by this evening, taking into account all the means at our disposal."

"Rather formidable means," Chay observed.

"Yes," Rohan said. "We won't be using their fear of dragons against them—at least, not as our primary weapon, as at Lowland. I don't want these people fleeing for their lives. I don't want them to survive and try again."

Maarken nodded his understanding and agreement.

"I have only two requests," he continued. "First, that you give Walvis and Daniv commands of their own, but place someone cool-headed with each. Grief breeds the need for vengeance, but I don't want either of them endangered by that need. Second, that you treat my other squire, Isriam, as yours."

"My squires, too," Pol put in. "Jihan has plagued Kierun long enough, and he and Dannar will be more use to you than to me right now."

"Accepted with thanks," Maarken told them with a slight bow. "I'll make this room my headquarters, if that's all right."

"Perfectly." Rohan stood, paused to study their faces. "It's always been one of my principles that I should never do myself what someone else can do for me better and faster." He let a smile touch his mouth. "Therefore, I leave you to do all the work while I go take my ease on this splendid morning."

When the door of the Summer Room shut behind him, Chay snorted derisively. "Listening to him, you'd think any idiot could be High Prince."

"Many idiots have," Meath remarked.

"As if all it took was a group of admittedly brilliant people to advise him," Chay went on. "As if he's not going to examine everything we present to him tonight with one of those lenses of his—and then make every single decision himself."

Sioned chuckled. "Tell me something new. Hollis, if Dannar's still out in the hall, would you have him bring Myrdal here, please? There's more than one way into and out of Stronghold—and she's the only one who knows them all."

* * *

Rohan frowned slightly at his granddaughter. "I thought you liked having lunch by the grotto. What's wrong? Why aren't you eating?"

"It smells like goats," Jihan said, pointing to the cheese.

"Hardly surprising, as it's goat cheese. Try some." He cut a slice off the crumbly round—served on a gold plate because Rislyn liked the glitter of pretty things—and extended it to Jihan.

Her nose wrinkled. "No, thank you."

"Then have some fruit."

"I don't like that kind, Grandsir."

"At least drink your milk."

"It smells like goats, too."

He sighed. "The goat is a noble animal and I'm sure the ones who contributed to our meal would be highly insulted that a princess scorns them. Drink your milk."

"No."

"Jihan, you've got to eat something."

She glanced over her shoulder at Rislyn, who had finished her meal and sat on a rock near the little pond, tossing pebbles and singing to herself. Jihan said, "I want to go play now, Grandsir."

"Eat some fruit first."

"I don't want any."

He put a marsh apple on the blanket in front of her. "Eat some fruit," he repeated.

Her jaw set and her brows rushed together. He fixed her with a stern gaze, feeling slightly ridiculous. Here he was, a High Prince who had stared down powerful men and women all his life, locked in a battle of wills with a seven-year-old.

"Don't try to outstubborn me, hatchling," he said at last. "I've got more than fifty winters on you."

Narrowed blue eyes regarded him in resentful silence for a long moment. Then she picked up the apple and bit into it sulkily.

"Thank you," he said, feeling a terrible urge to laugh.

"Welcome," she muttered.

"You can go play now if you like," he offered when she finished.

"I don't want to. I want to ride my horse but nobody will let me, except in the courtyard and that's no fun. Why can't I go out in the Desert, Grandsir?"

"Because—" He hesitated, then decided that this hatchling was capable of hearing the truth. "Because there are some nasty people out there who'd jump on you like a dragon on a lamb."

"Oh, I could ride away fast enough so they wouldn't catch me—just like we rode away from Grandsir Miyon."

"I don't think you could outride these people, Jihan."

"I bet I could," she challenged.

He knew brewing mischief when he saw it. "Kneel," he commanded. She blinked. "I'm the High Prince, and you've been ordered to kneel."

She was so startled that she did as told.

"Now, on your honor as a princess, swear your oath to me."

"My oath?"

"Yes. Promise to obey the High Prince in all things."

She gulped. "I—I promise, Grandsir."

"Not Grandsir. Your grace."

"I promise, your grace," she whispered.

"I accept your promise, Princess Jihan. And the first order you will obey is not to ride out into the Desert." He softened his expression with a smile. "The second is to go play with your sister."

But she made no move. "Am I your *athri* now, Grandsir?"

"I suppose you are."

"But I don't have a holding."

Good point; she was a sharp little beastie, no doubt about it. Feeling suddenly whimsical, he said, "*Athri* means 'wall lord.' Your name means 'noble rose.' Well, I give you those walls over there, covered in roses—which is appropriate to your name. Jihan, *athri* of Rosewall."

She bounced, delight shining in her face. "And I get a ring, too, don't I? Like your other *athr'im*? And what about Rislyn?"

He got to his feet. "Wait here. I'll be right back."

He returned to find Rislyn wide-eyed at the prospect of being made an *athri* of the High Prince. He repeated the little ceremony with her, naming her Rislyn of Willow Tree. In Sioned's collection of gifting jewelry he'd found two rings that would fit the girls, and gave the emerald to Rislyn and the ruby to Jihan.

"Grandsir. . . ." Rislyn gazed in awe at the sparkle of her new ring. "Does this mean that part of Stronghold is ours now?"

"It always was, heartling. All of it. Now it's just a little more official." He was amused and oddly touched that his impulse was so very serious to them. Much too serious for

being seven years old. He made them a low bow and they bent heads and knees to him in return—and then he had them. Grown-up solemnity dissolved in giggles as he swept them up in his arms and threatened to dunk them in the grotto pool.

* * *

Meath slouched low in his chair, elbows propped on its arms and fingertips pressed together in front of his face. His forefingers stroked the bridge of his nose with the same steady rhythm as the water dripping through the clock in the corner. Even Sioned had forgotten his existence as she proposed and argued and doubted and approved ideas. Meath didn't really know why he was here at all, but didn't mind. This conference gave him the chance to study anew people long familiar to him. People he loved.

Chay had similarly withdrawn, but not into the half-ghostly oblivion Meath had achieved. He still injected the occasional comment, though in general seemed content to let his son lead the discussion. No, not merely content, Meath corrected himself: proud—and for good reason. A leader Maarken certainly was. The leader Chay, Rohan, Lleyn, Chadric, and Meath himself had taught him to be. There was a certain sadness in his having to become Battle Commander at all—but his easy confidence in himself and in those around him fulfilled all their hopes. Meath remembered a young squire at Graypearl, and smiled.

Another former squire sat opposite Meath, another boy he'd guarded and schooled and watched grow from child to man. Pol was on speaking terms with his father again, Goddess be thanked, but the circumstances of it were bittersweet at best. They were so different; though they wanted the same things, believed in the same things, they approached these goals from sometimes opposing directions. He hoped Pol would grow into Rohan's wisdom with time. Yet events had made Pol question that wisdom—and not in the way he questioned Maarken about tactics, to clarify and understand. He *doubted* his father, a thing Meath comprehended in no way whatsoever. His own trust in Rohan had never wavered since the day he'd given it, the day he'd watched a prince walk with a Sunrunner across the sand and return to

their horses trying to hide how the Goddess had stunned them with each other.

His gaze strayed to that Sunrunner now. The years had paled her hair to make a finer frame for those green eyes, but the flush of color in her cheeks made the crescent scar whiter by contrast. Pol had a similar scar in almost the same place. Meath knew how both had come about. He had seen Sioned stumbling across the Desert with her bleeding cheek forgotten as she held another woman's child in her arms; he had seen Pol staggering under the attack of another sorcerer's conjuring. He wondered if Pol, looking into a mirror, saw it as the warning Sioned did: that power was a terrible thing to possess. That Fire—called to raze a castle or blaze across the Long Sand—could scar more than the skin.

Meath was taken from his thoughts as Relnaya came around the table, filling their cups with cool wine. Sitting straighter, he wrapped his hands around his brimming goblet—blue Fironese crystal, one of a set of Goddess knew how many dozen—and saw old Myrdal's eyes on him. He had the uncomfortable sensation that she knew every thought in his head. Andrade used to do that same thing with that same look; he knew it wasn't a product of age, because he was living his own sixty-fifth winter and *he* couldn't do that.

"So we're agreed on most things," Myrdal said, her voice as whispery-brittle as the hands resting flat on the table before her. "Maarken, perhaps you'd care to go over it one last time."

"Just to clear up a few points," Morwenna added.

Meath watched Pol glance rapidly at all of them, thinking that one thing he hadn't inherited from Rohan was that uncanny ability to draw everyone's immediate attention without effort. That wasn't an acquisition of age, either; the first time he'd seen it, Rohan had been barely twenty-one.

"I have something to say first." Pol sat forward, fingers laced in front of him. "It has to do with what will be required of the Sunrunners."

Here it comes, Meath thought, his gaze flickering to Sioned. She met his eyes, then stared for a moment at the great emerald on her hand. He understood the message: she was Rohan's, not Andrade's.

"Those of you who were trained at Goddess Keep face a difficult choice. Maarken glossed over it because it wasn't the time to talk about it. But we have to discuss it now. Will

you be breaking your vow not to use your gifts to kill? Indirectly, yes. You'll be enabling the soldiers to kill more easily." He looked each—Hollis, Morwenna, Sioned, Relnaya, and Meath—in the eye and finished quietly, "If any of you has a problem with this, please say so now."

Sioned spoke first. "What we plan is something I've done before. All of you know it. When my lord fought Roelstra. . . ." She gave a soft sigh. "Lady Andrade never said anything, never censured me for it. That was to be expected. It was her dream of a Sunrunner High Prince that I was protecting. But even if she had attempted to punish me, if she'd said a single word—I wouldn't have listened.

"There's precedent in the Star Scroll," she went on. "Lady Merisel recorded several instances of what we plan to do. But it was used as a protection for those who observed from the outside a battle by sorcery. Not for this. It's a pretty question, and rightly saved for the last, as Pol says.

"But there's something else." Sioned looked down at her hands again. "I've killed, using my gifts. Most of you know that. For those of you who don't—"

"Mother, this isn't necessary," Pol urged.

"I think it is. It's been many years—but I have never stopped feeling the weight of those deaths. It could be argued that . . . what I did . . . was the only possible choice to make each time. I believe this to be true. But while I don't regret what I did, I also know why I did it." Her head lifted. "I had no thought in my head for Goddess Keep, or its laws, or my oath, or anything else. I did what I did for my husband and my prince. The commitment was easy, but with hard consequences. Any of you who feel unable to make that same kind of commitment will not be blamed. I understand your conflict only too well."

Meath repressed a sigh of relief that she hadn't felt the need to confess her kills in specifics. He thought of the Firestorm she'd created at Feruche and all those who died there, knowing it was in her mind and Pol's, too—though they had no notion that he knew what had happened that night.

Morwenna cleared her throat. "I have this to say. The rule we'll really be breaking is one none of us swore: Lady Merisel and Lord Gerik's rule about not using the gifts *in battle*. This was the original vow. I've seen it in the scrolls. We're vulnerable to iron while conjuring—and a battlefield

is a blizzard of arrows and swords, any one of which could kill us. It was a wise rule—prompted by sheer self-preservation. All the best rules are." Her dark Fironese eyes glittered with irony, then with humor. "But I made my commitment, too—not as long ago as Sioned, and not for her reasons, though one has only to look at the High Prince to—"

"Mind your shameless tongue, Morwenna," Meath interrupted with a smile. "We all know what duty you most preferred at Goddess Keep!"

She laughed aloud, not even bothering to blush. "I was damned good at it, too, and I miss it!" She sobered. "I have a qualm or two about this. No *faradhi* with a conscience could not. Especially no *faradhi* trained by Lady Andrade. But—and forgive me, Chay, Maarken—I broke with Lord Andry a long time ago."

Pol nodded. Meath noted that he avoided looking at either uncle or cousin. He was startled to find those blue-green eyes regarding him instead. "Meath?"

"What's asked of me, I'll do," he replied simply, hoping he wouldn't be required to elaborate.

He was not. Pol turned to Hollis, who bit her lip, hesitated a long moment, and finally nodded.

"There are too many lives in the balance," she whispered.

"I know how difficult this is for you," Pol told her gently. "Thank you."

Relnaya was the only one left. Fair hair long since bleached white-blond by the Desert sun was raked back by nervous fingers. At last he burst out, "I know nothing of consequences or balance or qualms, my lord. All I can see is Jahnavi lying dead. He gave his life—my oath means nothing compared to that."

Meath realized suddenly that this was the first breaking of Goddess Keep's hold by sworn Sunrunners in a group. It saddened him but he knew there was no alternative. What he found fascinating was that Pol had been wise enough not to mention that Andry himself had broken the vow, and quite spectacularly—surely a powerful argument in favor of doing the same thing without worrying about it. Too, both Pol and Sioned were powerful enough to draw on the other Sunrunners' gifts and do this with or without their permission. And everybody knew it.

Myrdal tapped one finger on the table. "If you're quite finished," she said, evidencing scant patience for the ethical

wranglings of the *faradh'im*, "then I'll hear Maarken repeat this grand plan in some sort of order. Make it good, child. I'm the *least* critical audience you'll face with it. A few more lines up on that infernal device over there—" She waved a hand at the water clock. "—and you'll have to sell all this to the Dragon."

* * *

After the others were gone, Maarken and Pol bent over the map of Stronghold and environs one last time.

"It'll work," Pol said.

"It had better." Leaning back in his chair, Maarken regarded him musingly. "You can't conceive of its not working, can you? Is it lack of imagination or simply confidence in yourself?"

"In you," Pol smiled.

"But not in him."

No need for further identification. Shrugging, Pol emptied a wine pitcher into his cup and slouched back to drink.

"You have no idea why he's done what he's done," Maarken went on. "You think he's failed. I tell you now, Pol, it's *we* who've failed *him*."

"What are you talking about?"

"He trusts in his Sunrunners, his soldiers, and his Desert. Is it his fault that none have lived up to his faith in them?"

Pol was silent for a long while. Then, very slowly: "I know this about him—that he'll preserve his people's lives at any cost, including his own pride. That's why he ran. Why he didn't fight. But now he must—and don't think I can't see how it eats at him. But being High Prince means making hard choices."

"Sometimes it means not choosing at all."

"Oh, he's taught you well, hasn't he? Maarken, leadership is decisions and risks. An effective leader knows which to take."

"And *successful* leadership is knowing which to avoid."

"I can never make you understand."

"Pol, I understand you perfectly. Your problem is you've never been really hurt. You've never known the kind of pain that goes to your heart and makes you think you're going to die of it. And you've never said to yourself, 'I'm *not* going to die.' All that's ever happened to you is you've

been wounded enough to make you angry. All you've ever said in response is 'I'm going to *win*.' "

"I *will* win." Pol finished his wine and stood. "And I'm going to take all the rest of you with me."

Maarken's brows arched. "I was wrong. Not confidence —arrogance."

"Don't confuse me with your brother."

"In many ways, you're just like him. Neither of you has any room in his head for thoughts of failure. Neither of you believes that anyone or anything could harm what's yours. Gentle Goddess, Pol, up until Meiglan and the girls arrived, I heard you mention them four times! It wasn't your faith in Dragon's Rest that kept you from worrying—it's your damned arrogance. Nothing would dare threaten your possessions. Andry doesn't think I know it, but he lost a girl he loved from just such blindness."

"And who did I learn it from? My father—who still can't believe that his Sunrunners and his soldiers and his Desert haven't won this war for him!" He began to pace, circling the wide table with short, angry strides. "Oh, he lets me play at being High Prince—leading the little dance we princes do at the *Rialla* to arrange other people's lives—only because *he's* there to make sure I do it right. Has it ever occurred to you that he doesn't really trust me?"

"Pol!' Maarken sat up straight, gripping the arms of his chair.

"Sorry to shock you," he replied, not sounding it in the least. "But don't you see? He's made a system that can survive just about anyone—even a very bad High Prince."

"That's insane."

"Maarken, you're my kinsman and my friend and I love you dearly, but you don't see beyond Whitecliff and Radzyn. Look at those who held Princemarch before me. Goddess, what a collection! Even if I turn out reasonably well, what about my sons and grandsons?"

"All right, then, what if he *has* created something that will work despite who's running it? Something that will outlast all of us—" He stopped, gaze narrowing. "That's it, isn't it? You can't stand that you'll have to fit yourself into what he made. You think everything ought to conform to *you*."

"If that's how you want to see it, go ahead," Pol responded coldly.

"I really do understand you now," the older man said quietly. "Some people think they can make room in time for themselves—strangle all the clocks and stop the sun in the sky so they can fulfill their visions. Andrade was like that. So is Andry. So are you. But that's not how it works, Pol. Time itself makes the room, the space—and for good or ill, somebody fills it. And you're eager to fill a place still occupied."

"You're where your own father used to be, *Battle Commander*."

Maarken rose slowly to his feet. "Yes. I am. And the prince I serve is waiting to hear about a battle that's going to tear his heart out."

Pol took a few steps toward him. "I didn't mean that—Maarken, I'm tired and angry—"

"I know what you meant." He sighed his own exhaustion. "I'm sorry, too. But this doesn't hurt you the way it does him. You're not watching your life's work being destroyed." He shook his head. "You won't be the same kind of High Prince he is. You're different men, with different work to do. But until the same kind of pain shows in your eyes, you're not going to understand what it is to be High Prince at all."

Chapter Twenty-eight

At midnight a contingent of Desert warriors filed silently out the grotto passage. They waited behind a northern outcropping of the Vere Hills, calming their restive horses and trying to repress their own fierce anticipation. Radzyn and Remagev had been fought for and lost; Stronghold would be different.

The day broke clear and free of haze, for which grace the Sunrunners thanked the Goddess. They would be able to work with sunlight today, not be forced to the sorcery all had learned but none felt comfortable with.

At dawn, while the Vellant'im were still arming themselves, Kazander's men rode full tilt in an insane charge from the tunnel, bellowing Isulki war cries and "*Azhrei!*" Angling for the right flank, they sliced off a section of the startled enemy host. Instantly the hidden troops swept down to attack the isolated Vellant'im, some to engage them, the rest to form an adamant circle around the fighting.

And then a very odd thing happened. Within the protective ring of Desert warriors, springing up between them and the concentrated battle, was cast a thin bright circle of Fire, like a huge and empty crown. It rose, arcing dragon-high, then curved inward to meet in a graceful goldfire dome.

Inside it, Desert warriors grinned—and slaughtered the stupefied Vellant'im.

Outside it, Desert warriors laughed—and protected the *faradhi* weaving from enemy iron.

Maarken thundered down from Stronghold with the main Desert force to engage the bulk of the Vellant'im in more traditional battle. Kazander again carved off a manageable portion; another squadron, this one secreted by night slightly

to the south, rushed forward to attack while the Sunrunners constructed another sunfire dome.

It was gorgeous work, and Tobin was half-mad with wanting to see it for herself.

She had fought in the last battle at Stronghold, tucked in a canyon niche with a bow and full quiver, happily picking off Merida warriors. This time age and infirmity condemned her to the safety of the keep. She strongly suspected husband and brother of making deliberately certain she couldn't even vent her frustration in curses; Tobren, Meiglan, and the twins were with her, and the face she presented to the four innocents had to be a serene and confident one.

It might not have been so infuriating if she'd been able to go Sunrunning. But the ground floor room faced west; sunlight wouldn't touch it before noon. At least Betheyn took pity on her; at mid-morning she slipped away from her duties as physician's assistant to whisper a report.

"It's a little like butchering a stag," Betheyn murmured as she fussed with a tray of taze and fruit, her excuse for coming in to inform Tobin of the battle's progress. "Lord Kazander makes the main cut and the others do the finer carving."

"Armies move to the right," Tobin observed, low-voiced, keeping one eye on the children's game and the other on Meiglan. She'd heard of a battle in which that instinctive shift to protect the sword arm had ended by reversing the opposing armies' positions entirely.

"Maarken took that into account. Prince Daniv and Commander Laroshin will charge soon from the tunnel to the enemy's right flank, to drive them back toward the main battle. The High Prince doesn't want any of them to get away."

Tobin grunted her approval.

"Lord Walvis has killed nearly sixty so far," Beth went on. "Nobody's ever seen anything like it."

"Chay?" she asked, knowing that her idiot lord had assigned himself the duty of keeping Walvis alive.

"Trying to equal Lord Walvis." Beth smiled reassurance. "With Lord Kazander's brother-by-marriage stuck to him like sap on a pine."

"Hmph. Old fool." Tobin wished the sun would hurry its journey across the sky so she could see things for herself. Damn Chay and damn Rohan, caging her with three prattling children and that timid little doe Pol had married.

After Beth bowed to Meiglan and left the room, she reapplied herself to her pretense of reading a book. Conversing with Meiglan was always a trial. She was a sweet girl—but in Tobin's lexicon that equated with "colossally boring." She knew she intimidated Meiglan at the best of times, though she had never figured out why. Now her halting speech and the tension of the day made her totally unequal to sustaining even the most rudimentary talk. So she took refuge in a book, lest Meiglan think she required other entertainment and try to engage her in conversation.

The water clock dripped liquid time. The refreshment was served and consumed. The children tired of one game and began another. Meiglan sat in pallid silence, stitching methodically at a tapestry pillow. Tobin strained her ears for the sound of battle., but heard nothing.

* * *

A hell of a good fight, Chay reflected, but if he didn't rest soon he'd return to Stronghold across his saddle rather than in it. He fought his way to his guards captain, gave over command to him, told Visian to go find Kazander and make himself useful, and declined assistance out of the fray.

"No, my dear," he grinned at the young woman who had volunteered to be his escort. "You'll have much more fun without me!"

Fun? he asked himself suddenly as he left the battle and its heat behind him. *That's a thought for a* young *man, not an old fool like you.* But the instincts of war, honed many years ago, had kept him alive. That was their purpose: to preserve his life while his enemies found death at his sword.

Chay glanced back over his shoulder as he rode up the approach to the tunnel, skirting litters bearing the wounded. Maarken's plan was working, as far as he could tell. It would be slow and many would die, but they'd win.

He scowled suddenly, uncomfortable with the aftermath of a battle fever that felt different from previous wars. Not as clean or light-headed giddy—just sad. When he was the young Battle Commander of the Desert, presiding with Zehava over victory banquets, he'd lifted his wine cup with fierce satisfaction to announcements of how many Merida had died. He turned in his saddle, glancing briefly back at the field. But he didn't really see the hundreds of Vellanti

corpses. What Chay saw instead was the courage and determination of his own people. Sudden as a sword stroke, he knew that this time he would raise his glass to the living. The offering desired by the Goddess was not enemy deaths, but that people could triumph over fear in defense of what they loved.

"My lord! Are you hurt?"

He had ridden right through the tunnel to the outer courtyard without even knowing it. Looking down at Kierun's frantic face near his stirrup, he shook his head and smiled. "No. But I have a hellish thirst, and the need to ease my ancient bones."

He swung down off his horse, finding that last comment truer than he'd thought. Another thing about cooling blood after a fight: a young man stretched young muscles and grinned, but an old man was stiff and sore for days. Repressing a wince, he accepted a clay pitcher of water from Kierun, poured half of it down his throat, then dumped the rest over his head to clear the sweat from his hair and face.

"Where's my wife?" he asked suddenly, adding to himself, *She'd better be exactly where I left her.*

"I don't know, my lord. Shall I find her for you?"

"If that stubborn little bitch sneaked out, I'll—" He grinned at the squire's shocked expression. "Never mind, Kierun. I'll go find her myself."

* * *

It was Jeni's turn next to bring news, with the excuse of gathering used dishes. Typical of Meiglan, Tobin thought, not to find this unusual, that someone came to serve her needs even with a battle raging outside. A kinder part of her chided the sharpness; Meiglan wasn't meant for this kind of day.

"Lord Walvis took a leg wound and is out of the fighting," the girl whispered. "Lady Feylin is binding it now—and I don't think she'd be scolding him half so much if it was serious. And Prince Rohan wrenched his shoulder again, so he's returned as well."

"Too old for such nonsense anyway," Tobin muttered.

"Not according to their men, my lady." Jeni hesitated. "I've had the oddest feeling. It doesn't make any sense. It's as if somebody's touching me, but *not* touching me."

"In sunlight?"

Gray eyes the color of smoke-stained pearls went wide. "How did you know?"

Alasen's daughter—and Ostvel's, Tobin thought. It would take too long to explain. "Stay in shade," she ordered, her good hand gripping the girl's arm for emphasis. "Sioned . . . is powerful."

Tobren noticed their conversation and asked, "Can't we go see what's happening? I could help with the wounded or—"

Shaking her head, Jeni told her, "I'm sorry. I know it must be dreadful to be cooped up in here, but believe me, you'd get trampled outside in the courtyard. I'd better get back now."

The child looked rebellious, then shrugged. Tobin watched Jeni leave, then said to her granddaughter, "My eyes are tired. Read to me, please?"

That kept her occupied and out of mischief while Tobin closed her eyes, pretending to listen. She remembered the first time she'd been caught up in a *faradhi* working—the night of her father's ritual. Sunrunners had spread moonlight over the whole continent; she had gone with them, untrained as she was, and only Sioned had been able to bring her back whole. There had been other times when power had entangled her, but clearest in her mind was Sioned's first attempt at what she and the other Sunrunners were doing right now. She felt again her initial fright, then absolute trust, then the outpouring of everything she was in response to Sioned's need. There had been thin starlight and strange, distorted impressions of a fiery translucent dome, and a ringing like a gigantic silver bell. She learned later that the sound had come from a knife hitting Sioned's starfire weaving.

A knife. Worked metal. Steel. Specifically, iron ore smelted with other metals to make it strong, rustproof, gleaming. Iron that poisoned Sunrunners, that had slashed into the *ros'salath* Pol had tried to use as protection at Radzyn, that had disrupted his work with sharp pain.

There had been no such hurt that night. The knife had clanged harmlessly against Sioned's woven dome. Tobin heard it again in memory, clear and fine. She remembered Sioned's overpowering will, the raw force that was Pol, the

other Sunrunners caught up in the working—Andrade, Urival, Pandsala—

Pol. Urival. Pandsala. *Diarmadh'im* who were resistant to iron, though not immune to its effects.

There had been no effects that night.

Her mind seemed to ignite. She ruthlessly ordered the rush of thought into coherence. Pandsala had been pure *diarmadhi*. Not a hint of sickness ever came to her when crossing water. Urival had been a half-breed, possessing both kinds of power. So did Pol. In theory, they had inherited the sorcerers' resistance to iron. But Pandsala, the purebred, had died of a steel knife in her leg—no! She'd died of poison, Merida poison—not iron. The knife might have hurt, but it hadn't killed her. Nine years ago, Mireva, who had raised Ianthe's other sons, had projected a conjuring at a distance of fifty measures with steel wires piercing her flesh. Whatever pain there had been, it hadn't crippled her.

Yet that night of Roelstra's death there had been no pain when iron struck the weaving of starfire.

Had Pandsala, caught in Sioned's power, been their protection? Not by herself, Tobin guessed, recalling the others who had been there. Urival had lent added strength; Pol, day-old infant though he'd been, had provided the last link. The Star Scroll specified workings of three—and those three *diarmadh'im* had been part of Sioned's weaving.

She had only two of them to bolster her work today, Pol and Morwenna—both of whom were also Sunrunners, with a Sunrunner's fatal vulnerability to iron. Maarken was protecting them as best he could, by using part of the army to keep steel from their woven dome. But if there could be a third sorcerer involved in the working, would they be completely protected from any assault by iron?

The presence of Riyan or his wife Ruala—both of *diarmadhi* blood—would have proved Tobin's idea one way or the other. But he was leading his troops to meet Tallain against the Merida, and she was far away at Skybowl. Still—Sioned had amassed the powers of Sunrunners and sorcerers hundreds of measures away on the night of Roelstra's death. Jeni had sensed the pull of power today; could Sioned expand her range, draw in Ruala, and gain virtual omnipotence?

"Tobren!" she interrupted, and her namesake started with surprise. "Find Rohan. Bring him here."

"But I don't know where he is, Granddam."

Meiglan looked up from her sewing. "What is it, your highness?"

Nothing you'd understand, she thought impatiently. "I—I want—f-find—" Speech chose exactly the wrong time to desert her. She slammed her cane down on a nearby footstool, incoherent with frustration. Damn the sun for not moving more quickly, for trapping her.

Jihan abandoned the game she was playing with her sister. "What do you need, Aunt Tobin?"

"She wants me to find the High Prince," Tobren said, puzzled and alarmed by her grandmother's urgency.

"I'll do it!" Jihan leaped to her feet. And before Tobin could work a protest around her tongue, she had raced from the room.

Into the sunlight.

"Jihan!" she cried. "Meiglan, st–stop her!'

There was no mistaking the panic in her voice. Meiglan's huge eyes were dark smudges in her blanched face. Rislyn, just as pale, called her sister's name and ran after her. Tobren followed at her heels.

Tobin dug her cane into the rug, staggering to her feet. "No—" she moaned, aware that all three of them were now in danger because of her.

* * *

Morwenna had never suspected what she was until, on the long journey to Stronghold in 724, Urival had explained it to her. The shock had been eased by his revelation that he was another such as she, with Sunrunner and sorcerer blood both. "We are uniquely qualified to teach Pol," he'd said over a campfire on the shores of Lake Kadar. His explanation of how Rohan's heir had come to possess *diarmadhi* blood, and thus why they must be especially painstaking in his education, had left her thunderstruck. They had never spoken of it again—and, indeed, she had never revealed to anyone that she knew. But as Sioned wove the six Sunrunners together, Pol felt familiar and the *faradh'im* felt strange, and it was like learning about herself and him all over again.

She saw a hand wearing the ring of Princemarch extend toward her, and laced her fingers easily with his. It was more difficult to clasp the other hand held out to her, the

one wearing Sunrunner's rings as her own did. The strength of her shared grip with Pol was astonishing; the touch of Relnaya's fingers was barely discernible.

The images had been suggested by Pol during their long discussion of this technique. Sioned had listened, shrugged her shoulders, and told them that if it helped, they could visualize anything they liked—just so long as their power was accessible to her without hindrance. Relnaya had been taken aback by the whole operation, having only five rings and not being accustomed to Sioned's ways. But she was a Sunrunner and High Princess; he obeyed. Morwenna consciously tightened her grasp on his hand to bring him more deeply into the working, so that he would continue to obey. She didn't fear a wavering of loyalty—but Sioned in full flight, as it were, could be awesome.

At her direction, they hovered in readiness and waited for Kazander to carve off a section of Vellanti troops. It was an outrageous thing to be so peripherally aware of oneself, to merge one's colors into a gleaming wholeness, nearly blind but for what Sioned chose to see, and subordinate in all things to her strength. Morwenna's own awe of the woman had source in her youth; she had been a Sunrunner of two rings and seventeen winters when Sioned was summoned to the Desert to marry a prince. An astounding thing, never before done—Morwenna had known Sioned was skilled, but Andrade's choice of her had staggering implications. Now that Morwenna had lived at Stronghold for a dozen years, reverence had been tempered by fondness and shared purpose. But when Sioned functioned solely as a *faradhi*, Morwenna could only offer in all humility her own gifts for her use. Not even Andrade had inspired that.

Yet there was a portion of her that Sioned could not use to its fullest. It allowed her, after a time, to see with her own eyes. She watched the battle within the gleaming shell of sunfire, and the fierce struggle going on without to keep Vellanti swords and arrows from getting within reach. She felt it when some got through, and the pain startled her, but it wasn't the rending agony she'd been led to believe. Meath had described what it had been like to get hit by a steel arrowhead while conjuring—but the metal had been in his flesh, not in a structure woven of his mind. Morwenna felt the shock, gritted her teeth the way one did during a muscle

spasm or an attack of joint stiffness, and went on with her work.

The dome shifted to encase another small and deadly battle. There was relief from the sting of iron for a time, but as Morwenna watched the outer conflict she saw a group of Vellant'im break free and hurtle toward their besieged comrades. Young Prince Daniv's troops pursued, their swords like silver feathers fluttering on the wind, running scarlet. They would not intercept the enemy in time. Without knowing quite what or how she did it, Morwenna repositioned herself directly in the path of the oncoming warriors. She sensed startled outrage and imperious command from Sioned, and ignored her.

When the steel struck, Morwenna cried out, a silent howl of agony. But she held firm, she must hold her part of the weaving steady, she must spare the vulnerable Sunrunners from shattering by iron. She understood Meath's experience now, for it was as if those swords slashed her body to ribbons. Her mind began to fragment, her colors to grow dim and brittle.

And then the pain eased, subsided entirely. It was several moments before she could see again, yet she knew what she'd find. Daniv had pounced on the Vellant'im, and they had more urgent use now for their swords.

The sun felt stronger as the day wore on toward noon—that was Morwenna's only clue to time. She felt little weariness, thanks to the *dranath* she and Meath had taken in wine at dawn—secretly, and wary of Sioned's finding out. Maarken's tactic worked over and over, and now that Morwenna knew how to protect the other Sunrunners, she loosened the *diarmadhi* part of herself from the weaving and concentrated on defense. The stab of iron was at times a mere pinprick, at times hideous, but she endured.

There was an abrupt shift in Sioned's tactics, a reordering of her stance. Morwenna and the others were drawn in tighter—not in terms of their powers, but in the working's physical distance from Stronghold. The change told Morwenna that Maarken had begun the maneuver designed to drive the Vellant'im up the canyon toward the keep. Out of range of iron, she relaxed, almost drifting as the pain vanished entirely. Sioned had comprehended by this time what she'd been doing, and positioned her and Pol accordingly—smack in the middle of the road leading to Stronghold. Morwenna

sensed an apology circle quietly through the weary Sunrunners, and smiled. Sioned would use them until they dropped—but she asked nothing of them she didn't demand of herself. The difference, perhaps, between her and Andrade.

* * *

Maarken had spent the morning fighting two battles: one against the swords wielded by Vellanti warriors, and the other against the sunlight wielded by Sioned. She had warned him that he might be caught up in the weaving if he wasn't careful. Pol had shared a trick or two for keeping other Sunrunners away—without saying how he'd learned them, but there was only one Sunrunner Pol could possibly wish to avoid at all costs. Maarken figured if such things worked on his powerful little brother, then they would keep him from being snared by this working.

But he hadn't counted on Sioned's ability to take power wherever it presented itself. There'd been many frenzied moments when the force of her mind sought his while he was in the middle of defending himself against enemy attack. Rohan would have characterized it in his mild, amused way as being one Hell of a confusing morning.

Even so, it was all going pretty much as planned. Sometimes the Vellant'im broke through a protective ring of Desert troops and assaulted the weaving, but that never lasted long. Three and then five and then eight lumps of dead enemy warriors scattered the sandy plain. Maarken rejoiced in the decrease of their numbers and ordered his culminating stroke.

Harassing the rear guard to maneuver an enemy army to a desired location was a tactic hoary with age. Splitting one's main force so the advancing troops had somewhere to go was slightly less ancient. But Maarken had an advantage in the structure of the castle behind him. He planned to herd the Vellant'im into the canyon where archers could pick them off even as his soldiers closed in behind them to cut off their escape. Much the same thing had been done at Dragon's Rest nine years before. The river course leading into the valley provided a like bottleneck.

He'd felt fairly confident that the wooden frames with their stone-throwing arms would not be used. The actual walls of the castle were out of range, for one thing—and for

another, the Vellant'im had destroyed no Desert keeps and he very much doubted they'd start with Stronghold. Yet as he guided his careful plan to fruition, he glimpsed one of the machines being cranked into readiness.

For a moment his jaw sagged open against the chinstrap of his helm. What were they doing? The flow of the battle was now such that any stones directed at the Desert army would also rain down on Vellanti warriors.

Maarken shrugged at enemy insanity and returned his attention to the fray. He hoped Sioned would know that it was time. The opening moves were well underway when the tug he'd been fighting was suddenly gone. He staggered mentally, as if he'd been straining to hold up a stone wall that simply wasn't there anymore. The shock nearly overbalanced him physically and he missed his stroke at a man with what seemed like a hundred gold beads decorating the thick black hairs of his beard.

A Radzyn veteran parried the Vellanti's eager thrust toward Maarken's vitals. Gasping out thanks, he reined his warhorse around and fought his way to the rise of a sand dune, where he could be relatively safe from harm. There, despite all cautions to the contrary, he wove the few rays of sunlight that penetrated the roiling dust of battle and surveyed the field.

There was no more protective dome leaping to encase group after group for slaughter. He'd suspected as much, and blessed Sioned for recognizing that it was time for the final push. Confidence bubbled up in him—he knew such elation was dangerous, but couldn't help its escape from his throat in a sharp, satisfied laugh. He had succeeded in conbining all Stronghold's resources—Sunrunners, warriors, and military lore learned from a sire who had been the finest commander of his generation. Quickly he unthreaded himself from sunlight and shook a defiant fist at the enemy, still laughing.

The Isulk'im, hidden from the rest of the battle by clouds of dust, were busy portioning off yet another section of the enemy, herding them like sheep toward troops commanded by Sethric of Grib and young Isriam of Einar. But this time there would be no shielding enclosure of light to trap the combatants and cut off outside aid. Maarken spurred his horse down the rise and caught up with them, bellowing Kazander's name.

The *korrus* instantly wheeled his own horse around and galloped to Maarken's side. He was breathing hard, his teeth gleaming in a wide grin below his mustache. "Great and valiant lord!" he greeted Maarken. "A thousand thanks for this perfect day!"

"Glad you're enjoying yourself," Maarken responded. "But it's time to regroup. You remember your part?"

"It is engraved upon my soul, mighty lord, in letters aglow with Sunrunner's Fire."

"Then get to it." When Kazander grinned widely with excitement, Maarken couldn't help laughing a bit in reply. He was actually growing fond of his verbal embroidery. "Have a care to yourself, you madman!" he yelled after him.

As Maarken rode back to the main battle, he sobered on seeing how many Vellant'im were still left. He missed the effervescent confidence, but knew it could only have hindered him. This had to work—it *would* work. But so many were going to die at his command. He drew in a long breath.

"And now," he murmured to himself, "we find out if I'm even half as smart as my mother says I am."

* * *

Chay strode through the outer courtyard, catching a fleeting glimpse of Chayla's bright head. People hurried purposefully about, anxious but not frightened. Rohan's influence, he thought approvingly. The man could calm a flight of raging dragons.

The inner ward was less populated. He had not far to look before he found his wife's slight figure, standing in the sunshine near the circle of *faradh'im*. Chay scowled, ready to march up and carry her back to her rooms if she even looked at him in a way he didn't like.

But then he saw Jihan. She stood motionless on the cobbles, her little face gone blank and blind. Jeni was over by the wall, her expression just as vacant, her bleeding fingers dug into the mortar between stones. Tobren and Rislyn huddled next to Myrdal, who was holding them up with an arm around each.

Chay stopped dead. He knew what the look on those faces meant. His first instinct was to grab the children away,

shake them out of it. But that might send them into a shock so deep they would never recover. *Goddess help her, what has Sioned done?*

He approached Myrdal, who looked at him with bleak eyes. "We can only wait," the old woman whispered. "She'll use what she needs of them, and then weave them back together. She forgets her own power."

He took his granddaughter carefully from Myrdal's frail arms. The blue of the child's eyes had been nearly swallowed by their black centers. She looked just as Tobin had on the night of Zehava's burning, when she'd been snared by Sioned's hungry, powerful mind.

Chapter Twenty-nine

Rohan sat a horse to one side of the tunnel entrance, watching as much as he could of the battle's progress. He absently massaged his left arm until the ache faded to numbness and went away altogether. If only that damned Vellanti warrior hadn't swung to one side, making Rohan lurch to compensate, he might have a right hand good for something besides rubbing his other arm. At least the shoulder hadn't been wrenched out of the socket, as Chayla had originally feared. But it was useless just the same.

He followed the four divisions of his army with comprehension, but could not have anticipated them without having studied Maarken's battle plan. Tactics had never been his strong point. He knew the basics, but had always relied on Chay to provide detail and inspiration. Maarken was proving just as adept at arranging the deadly dance of battle—in some ways it really was reminiscent of the pivots, whirls, approaches, and retreats of one of those court balls Meiglan had established at the *Rialla*. Only one did not leave one's partner with a kiss on the hand, but a sword through the guts.

All at once he realized that he didn't understand what was going on out there. Maarken's careful template no longer fit. He urged his mount forward a little, searching the field. The little circle of white-hot battle that had jumped over the plain all morning no longer existed. Piles of corpses indicated where Sioned had directed the working—but no new skirmish was enclosed.

Good Goddess—so soon? he thought, remembering Maarken's plan. "Sting them from behind—and don't let them regroup. Kazander and Sethric will drive them forward. Our main force will split down the middle to accommodate them.

We'll funnel them toward the canyon, and hit them from both sides at once. The Sunrunners will establish a screen halfway up the canyon. We have to keep pushing them forward, cramming them in, making them panic."

The indicated spot for Sioned's weaving was only a little way ahead of him. Rohan's halfling gift responded to its proximity like the pricking of a cat's whiskers. But he was no more use to her than to Maarken. All his power as High Prince, of his wealth in dragon gold, of his education and spirit and insight, and he was no use to anyone right now.

When a group of bearded warriors broke through at a gallop and headed straight for him, Rohan didn't even move. His nervous mare lifted her front hooves tentatively, scraping them against the stony ground, but he held her fast. *Let them come,* he thought—*let them come. I have my Sioned as my sword and shield.*

They caught sight of him, and after his performance at Remagev they knew him even without the circlet on his brow. "*Kir'rei!*" one of them thundered, and it took him a moment to translate that into *High Prince*.

An archer braced in one of the canyon niches behind him yelled out a warning. He heard the cry echo back for a troop to protect him from the onslaught. Rohan smiled and shook his head. It was a curious experience, to sit calmly on a horse while a score of enemy warriors thundered toward him, desperate for his blood. Even more strange to watch them slam into an invisible wall. Most bizarre of all was this feeling of omnipotence, knowing he was wrapped in the power of his wife's mind and nothing could touch him.

* * *

When the first new and unexpected colors hovered outside the weaving, Morwenna barely noticed. But then a second presence was snagged into the pattern, and a third and even a fourth, and Sioned used them. Morwenna sensed the surge in strength lent by young, untrained, highly gifted minds. That so many Sunrunners could be threaded together so easily more than justified Andrade's faith in her.

But then Morwenna recognized that *sameness* she'd felt in Pol. Two of the newcomers were pure Sunrunner. Another was like herself and Pol, a half-breed. But the last was *diarmadhi* to the bone: rich colors, dark and lustrous, garnet

and emerald and onyx and amethyst, all edged in opaque black. These colors, this power, remained outside Sioned's grasp. It was by independent choice that a small hand wearing a delicate ruby ring reached up, rested atop Pol and Morwenna's joined hands. There was innocent wonder and a bright laughing delight in this marvel as the colors stitched themselves throughout the weaving with instinctive, frightening skill—and shaded every strand with a silvery sorcerer's glow.

* * *

The quiver of light on the far edges of Rohan's perceptions flared and then nearly vanished. Something replaced it that kept the enemy from him just as effectively, but which he could not sense at all.

He turned at the sound of clattering hooves. Ten mounted soldiers stormed through the tunnel behind him. "No!" he shouted. "Get back!"

Dannar reined in beside him, green eyes as big as two-crown coins as he saw the Vellant'im thrust themselves against that barrier and fall back stunned. "My lord? What in all Hells—" He gulped. The thought *Sunrunner magic*—was written all over his face. "My lord—please come back within!"

"Ah, no. I'm a very effective lure."

"At least let us stay to protect you!"

"Back up the canyon, if you must," he conceded, "but out of their sight. I'm the one they want. Let them come after me."

"No, my lord, please—"

"Enough, Dannar!"

The boy gave him a last agonized glance, then led his troop back up the canyon. Rohan stayed where he was, calming the skittish mare, and tried not to think what it meant when he could no longer sense a Sunrunner weaving.

* * *

Walvis had found comfort for his son's death in the deaths of the enemy. As he worked, as assiduous in weaving a fabric of blood on the sand as the *faradh'im* were in threading light across the sky, he chanted softly to himself.

"This one for Jahnavi's first year. This for his second. This for his third—" and so on until he had accounted for each of his dead son's twenty-six winters. Then he had started over. He'd reached six for the third time when he was wounded badly enough to be hauled out of the fighting. But once his wife had bound his leg he escaped her and remounted, intending to finish the tally and at least two more before the day was through. He just hoped there would be enough Vellant'im left.

He was at twenty-five and looking around for the gold-speckled beard that would complete the third recital when his eye caught on a structure being raised from a nearby dune. The great wooden frames that had flung destruction at Remagev had finally been brought into play.

Sunrunner's Fire had not touched the awful things at Remagev. But Walvis swore to himself that if those ropes resisted his sword, he'd put gold beads in his own beard and join the Vellanti army. Shouting at Visian, who was glued even more tightly to his side now that Chay was back at Stronghold, he wordlessly pointed his sword at the wooden tower.

Visian put fingers between his teeth and gave a piercing whistle that brought ten Isulk'im to him in a matter of moments. "This abomination offends the eyes of Remagev's noble lord. Destroy it."

They surged forward at Walvis' command. But the enemy knew how to defend as well as attack; the wooden arm drew back and let fly the contents of its hand before it was hacked to bits.

But this time it was not stones the arms threw. It was steel. Knife blades broken from hafts and otherwise useless, arrow tips split off wooden shafts—the Vellant'im knew the Sunrunner weakness. Walvis plunged his own steel into five more breasts and swung around, squinting into the storm of dust.

* * *

Iron struck the weaving with ferocious suddenness. Morwenna had readied herself in anticipation, but the death-metal cut into her in a thousand places and agony robbed her of reason.

Then she felt children scream.

Their pain was intense and terrifying, and their panic shot through the weave like wildfire. Sioned's control turned rigid in response. The children struggled like caged hawks, their undisciplined powers more potent than any trained Sunrunner defense. In the next instant Sioned must have realized her mistake, for the spun colors relaxed as if a loom's tension had been undone. Morwenna thought it might work—but then the weaving began to unravel.

Morwenna snatched her hand from Pol's. She groped for the children, constructing her own fabric of *diarmadhi* light around them. As she had protected the other Sunrunners, so now she strove to blanket the children. But Relnaya still had hold of her other hand—the *faradhi* part of her, locked by Sioned's strength into the faltering dome.

She had spread herself too thin. She realized it at once, but there was nothing she could do. The pull in opposite directions, Sunrunner and sorcerer, was ripping her apart. She could do one, but not both. She could shield the children or she could take the entire weaving herself, trusting her *diarmadhi* heritage to give Sioned time to stitch everyone back together.

She must choose. She could feel herself shredding at the edges, ragged threads falling away. Calling on the *dranath* in her blood, she made a grab for Pol's fingers once more and firmly placed that other small hand in his. Screams raced through the weaving as she withdrew her sorcerer strength—and left the Sunrunner part of her behind.

* * *

It had felt so familiar, weaving the protection of light around her lord. But *too* familiar was this frantic reworking of chaotic color into recognizable, unique patterns. Tobin first—then Meath—so familiar to sort swiftly through bright threads—a stray, slightly mad thought crossed her mind that this must have been the way the world had been formed, when the two deities sat down to decide that these elements should make a tree, and these others a fish, and these a drop of water, until everything had its own uniqueness. Had they ever changed their minds? Had they ever reconsidered the horse, taken its wings back and given them instead to dragons? What if she gave Hollis' graceful garnet faceting to Meath, replacing it with his complex topaz angles and arcs?

She was dangerously near madness. Sanity reasserted itself with angry impatience, rock-solid practicality ruthlessly quenching wild whimsy. She was the only one who could do this thing. But she had never done it before with children whose terror made the work doubly urgent. It was that critical need for swiftness that brought her back to reality—Sunrunner reality, which the ungifted might easily mistake for a kind of madness.

The children slipped through her fingers like fine, trembling silk filaments. She tried to be gentle, but their fear was more dangerous to them than her power. At last she clamped down on them with all her strength. First Tobren and Jeni, who were Sunrunners only; then Rislyn, with more difficulty because of her *diarmadhi* blood. Jihan was infuriatingly elusive. She tugged Sioned along with her by the thin glittering light that connected them. Now that there was no more pain, she was determined to explore this new world. The sorcerer in her was strong enough to take Sioned with her.

Sensing Pol nearby, Sioned cried out soundlessly to him. It was he who brought Jihan back—coaxing, cajoling, finally tricking her with a skein of even more brilliant color that attracted the child's curiosity. Sioned finally felt herself whole again, no longer woven into the pattern of Jihan. She let go of the sunlight and collapsed to her knees on the courtyard stones.

Eventually she had the strength to look up. Pol clasped his sorcerer child to his chest, his face still stricken with fear even though she was safe in his arms. Rislyn was weeping quietly in Hollis' embrace. Chay knelt, clutching his wife to one shoulder and his granddaughter to the other, eyes closed in silent thanksgiving. The castlefolk clustered at a respectful distance—no, Sioned amended, a *frightened* distance. She could hardly blame them.

At her side crouched Meath, waiting for her to notice him. When she did, he gestured wordlessly to the two still forms crumpled nearby.

"Morwenna?" she whispered. "I thought she'd done it herself—separated herself and Relnaya from the rest of us."

"I tried to reach them," Meath said, low-voiced. "I couldn't. And don't you try," he added tersely. "She's gone, Sioned. They both are."

"No." She made it to her feet and he helped her over to where they lay. "They're still breathing—"

The tall Sunrunner shook his head. "She's functioning on *diarmadhi* instinct now. We can't touch her, not that way. Relnaya didn't have the strength or the skill to free himself."

"We can do it for him—for both of them—"

"No, I tell you! There's no pattern to either of them anymore—except the pattern of that dome outside."

She wove sunlight just the same, trying to connect to them. She caught her breath in horror. Meath was right: both Sunrunners were no longer really there. Only the weaving existed. Despite Relnaya's Sunrunner presence within it—helplessly trapped—Morwenna had woven it of sorcery. Nothing in the Star Scroll could help Sioned. "Oh, Goddess," she whispered, "what have I done?"

Meath shook her arm emphatically. "You couldn't have known she'd do this. Who'd believe that she *could?*" He knelt where Morwenna lay senseless and almost lifeless on the ground. She was barely breathing now. "The nearest thing it compares to is being shadow-lost. Except—except there are no shadows."

Sioned made a choking sound.

He looked up at her with a strange intensity in his blue-gray eyes. "I'm guessing that the work will last as long as they do."

"But we can't leave them like this," she breathed. "There's something of them alive still, Meath—not just the gifts, something of *them.*"

"There's nothing we can do to bring them back."

When she understood what he meant, she gasped.

"It has to be done, Sioned. They might live until evening."

"No—"

"Would *you* want to live even one moment this way?" he asked harshly.

He made two painless, efficient strokes with a gleaming knife. There wasn't even much blood from the two heart wounds.

Sioned turned away. So once again someone else had done her killing for her. Kept the final guilt from her. She could no more look at Meath now than she had been able to look at Ostvel then. But Ianthe's had been a death she actively desired. Morwenna and Relnaya—their deaths were her responsibility. Her failure. Her shame.

Rohan—she must find Rohan. She glanced around wildly, dizziness sweeping her. Myrdal came forward, and Meath,

to hold her up as she swayed. But it was no use; she fought the encompassing blackness and lost.

* * *

Rohan had seen the Vellanti warriors hack at the weaving—*Whose weaving?* he thought, battling panic—and finally fall back in defeat. He had smiled slightly as others tried to the same effect. Archers positioned down the canyon picked off the enemy at leisure. Maarken was ready to close the two halves of his army around the troops obligingly herded into his grasp by Kazander and Sethric and Daniv and Isriam.

But then a rain of small, glittering steel objects impacted on the invisible wall and shattered it. Rohan raised both arms to shield his head, was pummeled by broken knives and shards of swords. Someone behind him screamed. It echoed off the sandstone walls in a sudden, terrible silence.

Rohan swung the mare around and galloped through the tunnel, past Dannar and his stunned troops. "Close the gates!" he roared. "Now!"

The outer ward swarmed with people—servants on hasty errands, litter-carriers with the wounded, those who were injured but able to walk swaying a path toward the barracks infirmary. Rohan stood in his stirrups, frantic for sight of Sioned. But it was Pol's sun-bleached head he saw coming from the inner courtyard, and he shouted his son's name.

Pol ran for him and grabbed the mare's reins as Rohan dismounted. "Mother's all right," he said at once. "But the children were caught in it and—I don't know how she separated all of us. All," he repeated grimly, "except Morwenna and Relnaya. They're dead."

Rohan swallowed convulsively. "The children?"

"Scared half to death, but they'll be all right. The weaving collapsed. I can't do any more good as a Sunrunner, so I'm going out to help Maarken. He's going to need everybody."

Rohan's fingers tightened convulsively around his son's arm. "Pol—" he began. He knew how close he himself had just come to death. It made him even more aware of Pol's danger. But if he ordered Pol back to safety, the rift between them would open wide and he was afraid they'd never be able to close it again. Besides, what could he do? Physically restrain him? And fundamental honesty forced him to admit that were he still young enough, strong enough, he

would do exactly what Pol was going to do. So he swallowed what he'd been about to say and managed a fleeting smile. Then he turned and shouted for Kierun.

It was the work of a few moments for the boy to find battle harness to fit Pol. Rohan gave him his own sword.

"Thirty years and more didn't even take the edge off it," he said as Kierun fastened the belt around Pol's waist. "I found that out earlier this morning."

Then he heard what he'd said and it took a lifetime of self-discipline to conceal his despair. Yet somehow Pol saw right through him, and compassion shadowed the blue-green eyes. Not a complete understanding, not a sharing of his emotion, but—it was enough.

Pol enveloped him in a quick, hard embrace. "Don't tell Meggie about this—she'll have my teeth for shirt buttons."

"She'll have to fight your mother for the privilege. Goddess keep you safe, my son."

And then Pol was jumping onto the Radzyn-bred mare and racing from the courtyard. Rohan looked down at the young squire. Big eyes in a sweaty, dirt-stained face yearned to follow Pol into battle.

"Kierun," he said, "take me to the High Princess at once."

Startled from whatever visions of excitement and glory had galloped away with Pol, Kierun blinked. "My lord? Oh—this way, my lord. Last time I looked, she'd woken up."

From what? he asked himself bleakly, but knew he'd find out soon enough.

* * *

The worry in Meath's eyes alerted Rohan before Sioned even spoke. Her voice was quiet, if a little too quick, betraying her tension. He heard a brief explanation of what had happened to the Sunrunners—and especially to Morwenna and Relnaya, whose bodies had been removed to the barracks. A large chamber therein was serving as a death room. And there were too many inside it.

"Hollis took Tobin and the children inside," Meath told him, standing well away from Sioned—farther than a friend's distance, much farther than even a stranger's. "Chayla was out of the sunlight. I don't know that she even felt anything. So she's all right."

"And you?" Rohan asked. When the big Sunrunner shrugged, Rohan went on, "Then will you follow the battle for me? Maarken has things in hand, but. . . ."

"Of course, my lord." He removed himself from their presence and went to stand in a corner of the courtyard, sunlight gleaming on his upturned face.

"Sioned?" Rohan took her arm. "What is it?"

"Nothing."

He met her gaze steadily, waiting her out.

After a moment she gestured impatiently. "Very well, then—everything. Lady Merisel was right. Andrade was right. No matter how we try to work around it, justify it—the gifts can kill. And not just when and if we intend them to."

"This wasn't your fault."

"You weren't there," she retorted brutally.

"Forgive me for presuming I understand Sunrunner ways," he snapped, the tone deliberate. "Or the one I've lived with for forty years."

Annoyance flickered in her eyes. "I'll never forgive you for knowing me better than I know myself."

He left it at that. "I need Chay. Where is he?"

"With Tobin, I suppose. Rohan, what's going on out there? Are we winning?"

"They may outnumber us, but we've got Maarken."

"And Pol. Oh, don't try for surprise, you've never done it with a straight face. You're not wearing your sword and there's only one person you'd give it to."

His turn to be irritated at being understood so well. "Come on, I want to find Chay and—"

"Rohan!" Meath's hoarse cry swung them around as one. "Riders coming up from Rivenrock—"

"Sweet Goddess, not more of them!" Sioned cried.

The big Sunrunner shook his head. "No, no—only a few dozen. But under a lightning-bolt banner—*crowned*. And beneath it a man *without* a beard."

Rohen's breath hissed between his teeth. "So. Their warlord at last. I've been wondering when I'd meet him."

"Warlord?" Meath echoed sharply.

"Of course. The man who needs no tokens of his kills or his power." He turned to Sioned. "Find Maarken. Tell him I don't care how he does it, but Pol must be seen to lead the charge." He held her stricken gaze with his own. "I'd do it

myself, but it must be Pol. They must look to him now, not me."

"Rohan—"

"I'm no warrior, Sioned. I've failed."

"No!"

"But I have a son whose very nature won't *allow* him to fail. Not in this. Not in battle like this. Find Maarken. Hurry, beloved." He started away, unable to bear the sight of her anguish.

"My lord?" Meath had caught up to him in two long-legged strides, a hand on his arm. "I'll keep watch if that's your order, but—isn't there anything else I can do?"

"Stay with her," he murmured, low enough so Sioned wouldn't hear. "Just—stay with her."

* * *

Myrdal saw Chay's broad shoulders sag, his proud head bending to his chest. "No," he breathed. "Ah, Goddess, not again. This will break him."

"He's not as brittle as all that," the old woman retorted, hoping it was true. "He can't afford to be."

"He'll fight for Stronghold until his last breath."

"It must be done," Myrdal insisted, rapping her cane on the tiles. "If I'm wrong, and the castle holds as it's done countless times, it won't matter."

"All right, then," he said, defeated. "Show me."

Betheyn came forward from the silent shadows of the Great Hall. "I've broken the seal. It must be at least a hundred years old."

"More," said the old woman, and did not elaborate. She leaned on Chay's arm as they walked the length of the blue-and-green tiled floor. Its crystalline sheen was gone, worn by the hundreds who had been housed here—folly to wax and buff the tiles during a siege in any case. The one place no one ever walked was to the raised dais, where the high table rested, and the carved chairs, and above them the empty place near the dragon tapestry where Rohan's sword had hung unused so long.

There was an anteroom between the Great Hall and the kitchens, a place for squires and servants to organize the presentation of courses during a banquet. Beth struggled to

pull aside a heavy tapestry from one wall, a floor-to-ceiling depiction of a forest scene.

"Don't bother, child," Myrdal said. "Chay, tear it down."

He did so. The fabric ripped and the thick iron rod holding it came loose from the wall. Beth ducked out of the way and all three of them coughed as dust rose from the crumpled hanging.

There was indeed a seal—a huge circle of plaster as large as a cartwheel. Half of it lay propped against the wall. The other ragged half remained. It had been incised with a few words in the old language that Chay couldn't read, and there lingered traces of blue and yellow paint.

"It's said that sorcerers put this seal here, with a spell woven into it so none could break it." Myrdal snorted. "You aren't by any chance secretly *diarmadhi*, are you, Betheyn?"

"So there's a seal," Chay said impatiently. "What was it there to protect?"

"Put your shoulder to that stone—third in, fifth up—and find out."

Dust-thickened air clogged his lungs. He was aching and bathed in sweat by the time the stone finally moved. With it, creaking on ancient mechanisms, went half the wall. Revealed was a passage that descended at a steep slant into absolute darkness.

"It's almost like the one at Remagev," Beth said. "Only bigger."

"And more complicated. The passages go on for a full five measures into the hills."

Betheyn jumped and gave a little shriek as a family of mice scurried past her feet.

Myrdal continued, "The main one comes out near the road to the Court of the Storm God. Or so my mother led me to believe."

"*Passages?* More than one?" Chay asked, shaken.

"I'm not sure where some of them lead," she answered almost casually. "But the main one is marked."

"Or so your mother led you to believe," he said sourly. "Wonderful." He wiped his hands on his trousers. "Beth, we're going to need a lot of torches. And a Sunrunner in front of us. Let's get busy."

* * *

Pol yanked his father's sword from the nape of an enemy neck and glanced around again, trying to find Maarken. His cousin's banner suddenly sprang up on a little sandy knoll, and Pol made for the spot with a single-minded will, leaving five corpses and three severed sword arms behind him.

Maarken turned as the familiar voice yelled his name. Pol reined in so hard beside him that the mare danced back on her hind legs. Knowing what Maarken needed to hear, he reported that Hollis, Chayla and the others were well—only a partial lie.

"But there's no working—it's gone. We're on our own."

"Goddess damn these whoresons! Pol, take the Second—the Radzyn and Remagev regulars my father and Walvis were commanding. Swing them around and attack the left flank. Daniv and Laroshin are doing the same on the right. Hurry!"

"Yes, my lord," he responded automatically, and galloped off.

"So that is how one commands a prince," Kazander mused at Maarken's side. Then he saluted and rode down the rise, howling *"Azhrei!"*

Maarken directed his attention back to the main battle. He longed to be in there with his people, but the collapse of his basic strategy demanded that he separate himself and, as his father would have said, use his imagination.

It was not imagination that gave him the sight of a banner the size of a bedsheet riding on a pole like a naked pine trunk. It was the same lightning-bolt design of the troops they'd battled all day—but its sheer size and its telltale crown signaled that someone special accompanied it. He had the sudden unshakable conviction that beneath that tremendous flag rode the real architect of all this slaughter.

And between that person and the rest of the Vellanti army, exactly where Maarken had told him to be, was Pol.

He flinched with the impact of Sioned's mind. The techniques of resistance—the mere thought of resistance—never even occurred to him.

Rohan says their warlord has come to lead them—and that Pol must lead us. *Do as you think best, but make sure he's seen. Make sure, Maarken.*

And then she was gone. He understood what Rohan meant—Pol was the prince here, not he—but what in the name of the Goddess could he do? If the Vellant'im rallied

further, as they had begun to do in earnest with the sight of that banner, the Desert host would go on fighting, would blunt their swords hacking at enemy bones and retrieve arrows from corpses to take aim once more. Would follow Pol as they had always followed Rohan.

But the sky was already paling with sunset, and the glow of the Flametower was brighter, and soon the winter night would darken the battlefield. Could they set the sands ablaze as Pol had years ago, and struggle on until—

Until what?

He couldn't plan anything without knowing what was going on. He wove sunlight and saw Sethric and Kazander and Daniv and even Walvis—and who had let him back on a horse, anyway?

But mostly he saw Pol. His cousin didn't need to be told to rally soldiers to his side. He had created a place for himself—pushed time aside, claimed room enough for what he believed must be done. It was the place Rohan had once occupied. But it wasn't enough.

Sudden shattering pain in his right arm. Leather and steel battle harness digging into Maarken as he slumped in the saddle. Sword dropping from his aching right hand. Agony more fierce than Sunrunner's Fire—

Surcease.

* * *

"Come on, all of you. There's nothing down there that will eat you! Just follow each other—it's simple. Sheep can do this. Take your candle and mind you don't bump your head!"

Myrdal felt the tray of candles grow lighter in her hands, and interrupted her urgings to call for another supply. Jeni brought them and told her that in a few moments the more seriously wounded would be brought across the courtyard.

"You handle this, child," Myrdal said, pushing herself from the wall and picking up her cane again to support her. For a moment she watched the girl calmly hand out candles to each person entering the passage. Jeni had them moving with instant efficiency. She smiled reassuringly, encouraged in a soft voice—and lit each candle herself with Sunrunner's Fire. Myrdal blinked, wondering when she'd learned this—and who had taught her. But then she shrugged off the

irrelevancy. Camigwen's namesake was worthy of her, she told herself with uncharacteristic sentiment, then cleared her throat and limped back into the Great Hall.

Most of Stronghold's augmented population was out on the battlefield. The able-bodied had already gone down the tunnel; only the wounded who must be carried remained. Soon someone was going to have to ride down and tell Maarken to send groups of his soldiers back to follow through the passage. Myrdal was not sanguine about their following orders.

Meiglan and her daughters sat in one of the window embrasures, all three of them stormy-eyed. But it wasn't Jihan who was refusing to budge; it was Rislyn.

"No. I won't leave Papa and Grandsir," she was saying as Myrdal approached.

"What's all this, then?" She was furious with Meiglan for not managing her children better. She didn't have time for this.

Meiglan must have seen the angry disapproval in her eyes. Her spine straightened and her gentle eyes flashed. But the access of energy was brief; she wilted back against the stones and looked an appeal at the old woman, who repressed a sigh.

A fine time for Rislyn to turn stubborn. She was still white-faced and strained after her ordeal; Jihan was eager for another adventure. Lacking time to coax Rislyn to obedience, she decided the three of them would be close enough to escape here in the Great Hall. But she had to lay the foundation for an order that would be heeded.

So she said, "You know that Lady Betheyn went first and took your cousin Tobren with her to call Fire so everyone could see." The girls nodded. "Well, the younger you are, the more powerful your magic in the maze. Yes, that's what's down there—a magical maze that not even your grandfather has ever seen. Your mother will need you to guide her—but she's rightly waiting for your father and the High Prince and High Princess. When they come, any of them, you have to be ready to take them through. Will you do that?"

"Somebody will have to teach us how to call Fire—we don't know how," Jihan said shrewdly, perking up at the notion of learning this Sunrunner skill.

Meiglan said firmly, "Papa or his mother will do that for you."

"Yes," Myrdal said, grateful that she'd gotten them past that sticky point. "But you have to be ready, and not delay. They're counting on you."

After due consideration, Rislyn nodded. "But not until *they* leave. You see, Grandsir made us his *athr'im* here." She displayed her little emerald ring of office. Jihan thrust her hand forward too, for her ruby to be admired.

At last Myrdal understood Rislyn's balkiness. "That's a very great honor. But it also means you must serve him and obey him." The girls nodded, and she exchanged a relieved glance with Meiglan before hobbling past the line of castlefolk into the courtyard.

She ran down her mental list of those who must be persuaded to leave Stronghold. Hollis, Chayla, Jeni, and Feylin would accompany the wounded; she anticipated no trouble there. Well, Hollis perhaps, but Myrdal intended to use Chayla's safety as surety for Hollis' cooperation. There was nothing she could do about Rohan and Sioned. But she spied her next target over by the stables. Tobin was directing grooms and pages to lead the few horses left within the keep—mares in heavy foal, colts and fillies too young to be ridden—toward the gardens. They would be taken out by the grotto exit. Myrdal shook her head in wonder that even without reliable speech, the princess managed to make herself understood. She started over to where Tobin sat neatly on the edge of a trough, marshaling her arguments.

Chay beat her to it. Striding up to his wife, he picked her up and carried her to the Great Hall—protesting vehemently all the way, of course—with young Kierun following to escort Tobin through the passage. Myrdal grunted her satisfaction and turned her attention elsewhere.

The wounded were taken across the courtyard, scores of them carried on litters or helped by more ambulatory companions. Myrdal saw Dannar run up to Feylin, question her, and head for the gardens with something she gave him from her coffer of medicines. Myrdal caught her attention, waving her over.

"What did the boy want?"

"Pain killer. That old wound in Rohan's shoulder took a hell of a beating this morning."

The last she'd seen him, he'd been rubbing his left arm,

not his right. "Get up front and send Beth back to close the passage. The rest of us will leave by the grotto."

Feylin glanced around. "Remagev was difficult enough," she murmured. "I never thought I'd see this."

"This is *my* doing, not Rohan's."

"I'd like to hear you convince him of that." She strode away, calling for one of the pages to carry her medical case.

With the departure of the wounded, the inner ward was eerily quiet and empty. Myrdal shivered. Only once before had Stronghold felt so hollow, during that long summer and autumn when Sioned had paced the silent stones and waited for Ianthe to give birth at Feruche. Then, they'd only been marking time before everyone returned. Myrdal wondered if there would be a Stronghold to return to.

Zehava would never have left the castle he'd killed thousands to possess; the home Milar had civilized and made gracious; the place where his children had been conceived and born. Would he blame Rohan for failure? Was his spirit now cursing his only son?

Myrdal glanced up at the sky. *The responsibility was mine, as you charged me in his childhood: keep him safe,* she said to the tall, black-haired ghost of her kinsman. *He did everything possible. Could you have done more? Could anyone?*

There was no answer—not that she had expected one.

* * *

Maarken became aware of Isriam's strong arm keeping him upright—more or less—in his saddle. The young man held an arrow in his other hand, its tip coated in blood.

"What in all Hells—?" he managed, sick and dizzy but no longer in pain. The he realized that the blood was his, and what Isriam had done by tugging that arrow from his flesh. Shaken, he gripped the young man's shoulder. "Thank you. More than you can know." Confusion glimmered in the brown eyes; Maarken didn't have time to enlighten him. The sight of Pol fighting at the rear of the Vellanti army while that huge banner advanced on him flared in his memory, and he said swiftly, "Take fifty warriors and go to Pol's aid. Hurry."

Isriam's jaw set in fury. He threw down the arrow and spurred his horse, shouting, "To me, for Prince Pol!" as he went. Maarken glanced briefly at the bleeding hole in his

sword arm and swore luridly. His wrist had been giving him trouble since noon, wrapped in supporting bandages though it was. Now he was unable to fight at all. Yet he had to lead his main force back to Stronghold, defend its gates, make a path for his army to safety within.

And then? A siege such as had not been known since his grandfather had surrounded Stronghold, trapping the Merida within, starved them out, and slaughtered them as they emerged under a flag of truce. Zehava had avoided blame for this gross dishonor by claiming he had been at dinner, hadn't seen the flag, and overzealous warriors had acted without his approval. Maarken had always known what a lie that was—for Zehava's troops had been very careful to keep the chief Merida lord alive. His name, scrawled unsteadily at the bottom of the parchment, had given the title to the Treaty of Linse. He'd lived long enough to sign in High Prince Roelstra's presence, then succumbed to an "accident" on the way to exile in Cunaxa.

Maarken saw the same thing happening again—only this time it would be his family and his people caged within Stronghold. There would be no surrender. Aid was many hundreds of measures away, across a Meadowlord given over to the enemy and a Syr whose ruling prince was dead. The northern Desert was under siege from the Merida and the whole Cunaxan army. Everyone within Stronghold would die before help came. All the warriors of Radzyn and Remagev and Stronghold itself would be pent up, useless but for brief and meaningless skirmishes against the overwhelming host outside.

He made the only decision possible, understanding at last Rohan's until now incomprehensible theory about how and when to act.

* * *

"He's pulling half his own forces and the whole right flank away," Meath said incredulously. "What does he think he's doing? Trying to make them follow him into the Desert?"

Chay shook his head. "He knows that if he's locked up in here, he'll never get out. His best bet is to save enough of his army to lift a siege later on. He's leaving enough to defend Stronghold until our people get back in and the gates can be closed. It's exactly what I'd do," he added.

Sioned nodded numbly. Meath's back-and-forth Sunrunning had drawn a horrifying picture of what was going on out there. Myrdal had just informed her that all the castlefolk and all the wounded were now fleeing through the passage, carrying with them everything they could. Some of it was useful—food, clothing, blankets; some of it frivolous, compared to lives—books, precious objects, jewels. Betheyn had come back to report that Feylin had gone ahead to lead. Sethric, the Remagev youths, and nearly fifty other mounted soldiers had left through the grotto; they would meet up with the others to protect against Vellanti ambush. Walvis was fighting his way up the canyon now toward the tunnel. Once his troops were through, the gates would be shut tight and he would follow Sethric. By nightfall there would be nothing and no one left in Stronghold to make it needful of defending—except that it was *Stronghold.*

Chay lifted Sioned's face gently with a finger at her cheek. "It's over," he murmured. "For now, it's over."

She knew what he wanted. "I can't."

"You must."

A flinch crossed her face as the first of Walvis' soldiers clattered through the inner ward, bloodied and exhausted. She raked her hands back through her hair that had long since come loose of its pins and braids. "He won't leave, don't you understand that?"

"Then neither will I."

"Nor I," Meath seconded. Myrdal nodded her agreement.

Sioned turned away in defeat. "Meath, tell Maarken what we're . . . tell him," she said shakily, unable to speak the words. "Get Meiglan and the children out of here, Myrdal. And Dannar. You follow them, Meath. No arguments."

"Yes, my lady," he responded.

"Chay," she began, but then a terrible despairing cry went up in the outer courtyard. A moment later a single flame soared across the sky, long and bright and almost floating. It was followed by another and then another.

"The gate's been breached!" Chay exclaimed. "Goddess help us, there's no more time!"

* * *

Maarken swayed once more under the impact of a powerful *faradhi* mind. For the instants it took Meath to commu-

nicate the frantic message, he saw nothing but the older Sunrunner's blazing colors. When Meath left him, he found he'd had sense enough to fling his arms around his stallion's sweaty neck to keep himself in the saddle.

Straightening, he cut to the outside of the riders thundering their way across the Desert and reined in. The work of a single thought allowed him to see the enemy that had forced their way up to the gatehouse along with Walvis' last troops. But their fiery arrows could only destroy the empty shell that was Stronghold. Tears stung his eyes. He tasted salt and blood and the Desert itself on his lips.

Isriam had fought his way to Pol—and Pol was no fool. The left flank of Rohan's army was now heading into the Desert, archers clinging to mounted troops, almost every horse carrying a double load. They could make no real speed that way. But the hundreds gathered now beneath that lightning banner showed no interest in the chase. They were marching with awful resolve for the keep now open to them.

He turned to Stronghold once again. Flames shot on enemy arrows sprouted in both inner and outer courtyards; the gatehouse was ablaze from the inside. But they were careful to direct their arrows away from the main keep. Radzyn, Whitecliff, Remagev—even Faolain Lowland, that they could have destroyed instead of trying to capture—what was it the Desert possessed that these barbarians wanted so much?

Coming back to himself, he cast one last agonized glance at the great castle with his own eyes, then swung his stallion around and galloped away.

* * *

Someone said she'd heard he was in the Great Hall, helping the wounded enter the passage. Someone else thought he'd been seen near the grotto, urging balky horses through. A servant, carrying Sioned's casket of jewels and cursing for not remembering them earlier, said he'd been upstairs but that had been some time ago.

She found him in the dimness near the stream that meandered out from the grotto pool. He lay on his back on the brittle yellow grass, and his face and hands were wet, as if

he'd bent to cup water to his cheeks before starting back to the grotto.

She sank to her knees beside him. His skin was still warm beneath the cool droplets of water. His eyes were open, reflecting the Desert sky. There was no blood, no wound, no pain on his features. All age was smoothed away. She stroked silver-blond hair, fine as silk over his brow. Traced the proud line of his jaw from ear to cleft chin. Brushed a fingertip along the sensitive curve of his mouth.

Her head tilted back and her lips parted and her lungs filled and she gave a single howl of anguish that shattered her very bones.

Chay turned back from the grotto path and ran. He saw Sioned; then he saw Rohan. A strangled cry of grief and denial clogged in his throat and he stumbled to his knees at his prince's side, tears running down his face.

Still blood, cold bones, lifeless flesh. He had known Rohan almost all his days and now there would be no more days. Looking on that serene face, he saw his own youth. Gone.

He closed Rohan's eyes, feeling the lashes soft and thick against his fingertips. He gently slid the topaz-and-emerald ring off Rohan's finger. For Pol. The High Prince. Then he reached across the body and put one hand on Sioned's huddled shoulder.

"Come, heartling," he murmured. He heard the sounds of battle out in the courtyard. He said her name, and again, and still she bent over Rohan, unknowing and uncaring.

"Sioned! For the love of him, we've got to—"

"No," she said, quite clearly. "No."

He smelled smoke and glanced up at the keep. But the plumes rose from the gatehouse and the outbuildings; the Vellant'im wanted Stronghold intact, too, just like every castle in Rohan's princedom.

Pol's princedom now.

"Come away, Sioned. We must."

She had placed her hands on his chest, feeling for a heartbeat that was no longer there. Chay took her wrists, pulled her roughly to her feet. Her green eyes were wild, tearless, glaring at him as she struggled against his strength. He caught her close, holding her head to his shoulder.

"He's gone. He doesn't need us now. Pol does. Sioned, don't fight me—"

" 'For the love of him—' " she echoed suddenly in a

queer, high-pitched voice. And she broke away, swooped down like a hawk, slipped Rohan's belt-knife from its sheath. Chay cried out in horror—but the knife sliced only through her loose, heavy hair. She hacked it off in short, sharp strokes and it spread over Rohan's chest, gold and red and silver gleaming in the last sunlight.

Ablaze with Sunrunner's Fire.

She spun around, threw back her head, raised both hands toward the Flametower. Fire overflowed its pointed windows. It spilled white-hot down walls, streamed across roofs, flooded every room and hallway and stair. Beyond the garden wall flames leaped in the shadowy courtyard. And people began to scream.

Chay staggered back from the Fire consuming Rohan. He grabbed Sioned in his arms and ran for the grotto. Flames flowed across dry grass. Fire and Water became one, the stream and pool and even the thin trickling waterfall ablaze.

He carried her through the narrow gap in the rock wall, barely ahead of the flames. Then somebody took her from him, put her on one horse and pushed him onto another, and they were riding for their lives while behind them, all through the night, all Stronghold burned as a funeral pyre.

Index of Characters

ALASEN of Kierst (696-). m719 Ostvel. Mother of Camigwen, Milar, Dannar.

ALLEYN of Dorval (724-). Daughter of Ludhil and Iliena.

ANDREV of Goddess Keep (724-). Andry's son by Othanel.

ANDRY of Radzyn Keep (699-). Lord of Goddess Keep 719-. Squire at High Kirat 711-713. Father of Andrev, Tobren, Chayly, Joscev, Merisel.

ARLIS (710-). Prince of Isel 727- (regency to 730). Squire at Stronghold 722; knighted 730. m730 Demalia. Father of Roric, Hanella.

ARPALI (704-). Court Sunrunner at Tiglath 725-727; Balarat 730-.

AUDRAN of Dorval (728-). Son of Ludhil and Iliena.

AUDRITE of Sandeia (670-). m692 Chadric. Mother of Ludhil, Laric.

AURAR of Catha Heights (715-). Daughter of Patwin and Rabia. Fostered at Swalekeep 732-.

BETHEYN (707-). At Radzyn 731-.

BIRIOC of Catchwater (716-). Miyon's bastard son. Trained at Remagev 735-36. Half-brother of Meiglan, Ezanto, Zanyr, Duroth.

BRENLIS (718-). Mother of Andry's daughter Merisel. Fostered briefly at Stronghold 730.

CAMIGWEN of Castle Crag (720-). Daughter of Ostvel and Alasen. Fostered at Stronghold 734-.

CATALLEN. Bard, tutor, and Miyon's spy at Dragon's Rest.

CHADRIC (664-). Prince of Dorval 720-. m692 Audrite. Father of Ludhil, Laric. Squire at Stronghold 677; knighted 683.

CHAYLA of Whitecliff (722-). Daughter of Maarken and Hollis. Fostered at Remagev 736-.

CHAYNAL (668-). Lord of Radzyn Keep 689-. m690 Tobin. Father of Maarken, Jahni, Andry, Sorin. Battle Commander of the Desert 695-.

CHIANA (698-). Roelstra's daughter. m719 Halian. Mother of Rinhoel, Palila.

CLUTHINE (695-). Halian's niece; Isaura's sister.

DANIV of Syr (721-). Son of Kostas and Danladi. Squire at Stronghold 734-.

DANNAR of Castle Crag (726-). Son of Ostvel and Alasen. Squire at Dragon's Rest 737-.

DENIKER (705-). *Devri*. m735 Ulwis.

DONATO (671-). Court Sunrunner at Castle Crag 720-.

DRAZA (709-). Lord of Grand Veresch 732-.

DUROTH (718-). Miyon's bastard son.

EDREL of River Ussh (715-). Squire at Dragon's Rest 727; knighted 735. m737 Norian of Grib. Brother of Kerluthan, Paveol.

EVARIN (716-). Physicians School in Gilad 733-735; Goddess Keep 735; Master Physician 736.

FEYLIN (684-). m706 Walvis. Mother of Sionell, Jahnavi.

GEMMA of Syr (694-). Princess of Ossetia 722-. Fostered at High Kirat 704-719. m719 Tilal. Mother of Rihani, Sioneva, Sorin.

HALIAN (680-). Prince of Meadowlord 722-. m719 Chiana. Father of Rinhoel, Palila.

HEVATIA of Isel (682-). m707 Latham. Mother of Arlis, Saumer, Alathiel.

HOLLIS (691-). m719 Maarken. Mother of Chayla, Rohannon.

IDALIAN of Faolain Riverport (718-). Son of Baisath and Michinida. Fostered at Balarat 732-.

ILIENA of Snowcoves (697-). m721 Ludhil. Mother of Alleyn, Audran. Sister of Lisiel, Yarin.

ISRIAM of Einar (721-). Son of Sabriam and Isaura. Squire at Stronghold 734-.

IZAEA of Catha Heights (711-). Daughter of Patwin and Rabia.

JAHNAVI of Remagev (711-). Lord of Tuath Castle 734-. m732 Rabisa. Fostered at Skybowl 722; knighted 730. Father of Siona, Jeren.
JAYACHIN (702-). Waesian merchant.
JIHAN of Princemarch (730-). Daughter of Pol and Meiglan.
JOHLARIAN. Court Sunrunner at Faolain Lowland.
JOLAN (702-). *Devri*. m722 Torien.

KARANAYA of Faolain Lowland (711-). Cousin of Mirsath and Idalian.
KAZANDER (711-). *Korrus* (battle leader) of Isulk'im. Trained at Remagev 728-729.
KERLUTHAN (706-). Lord of River Ussh 729-. Brother of Edrel, Paveol.
KIERUN of Lower Pyrme (725-). Son of Allun and Kiera of Einar. Squire at Dragon's Rest 737-.
KOLYA (696-). Lord of Kadar Water 701-. Father of Malyander.
KOSTAS (687-). Prince of Syr 724-. m720 Danladi, daughter of Roelstra. Squire at Kadar Water 700; knighted 708. Brother of Tilal. Father of Daniv, Aladra.

LARIC of Dorval (698-). Prince of Firon 719-. m721 Lisiel. Squire at High Kirat 710; knighted 718. Father of Tirel.
LATHAM of Kierst (683-). Regent of Isel 727-730. m707 Hevatia. Father of Arlis, Saumer, Alathiel.
LISIEL of Snowcoves (699-). m721 Laric. Mother of Tirel.
LUDHIL of Dorval (694-). m721 Iliena. Squire at Fessada 705; knighted 714. Father of Alleyn, Audran.
LYELA of Waes (709-). Tallain's cousin. Resident at Tiglath 720-.

MAARKEN of Radzyn Keep (693-). Lord of Whitecliff 719-. Squire at Graypearl 702; knighted 712. m719 Hollis. Father of Chayla, Rohannon.
MALYANDER of Kadar Water (725-). Son of Kolya. Squire at Athmyr 737-.
MEATH (673-). Court Sunrunner at Graypearl 698-.
MEIGLAN of Gracine Manor (710-). Miyon's bastard daughter. m728 Pol. Mother of Jihan, Rislyn.
MEVITA (714-). m731 Rialt. Mother of Polev.
MICHINIDA (688-). m708 Baisath of Faolain Riverport. Mother of Mirsath, Idalian.

MIRSATH of Faolain Riverport (716-). Son of Baisath and Michinida. Squire at High Kirat 728; knighted 736.
MIYON (689-). Prince of Cunaxa 701-. Father of Ezanto, Zanyr, Birioc, Duroth, Meiglan.
MORWENNA (680-). At Stronghold 724-.
MYRDAL (645-). Commander of Stronghold guard 675-703. Rohan's bastard cousin.

NAYDRA of Princemarch (673-). Roelstra's daughter. m705 Narat of Port Adni.
NIALDAN (703-). *Devri.*

OCLEL (705-). *Devri.* m727 Rusina. Father of Surida.
OSTVEL (673-). Lord of Castle Crag 719-. m (1) 698 Camigwen; (2) 719 Alasen. Father of Riyan; Camigwen, Milar, Dannar.

PALILA of Meadowlord (723-). Daughter of Chiana and Halian.
PATWIN (691-). Lord of Catha Heights 701-. m709 Rabia, daughter of Roelstra. Father of Izaea, Sangna, Aurar.
POL (704-). Ruler of Princemarch 726-. m728 Meiglan. Squire at Graypearl 716; knighted 726. Rohan's bastard son by Ianthe of Princemarch. Father of Jihan, Rislyn.

RABISA of Tuath Castle (712-). m732 Jahnavi. Mother of Siona, Jeren.
RELNAYA (675-). Court Sunrunner at Remagev 724-.
RIALT (701-). Chamberlain at Dragon's Rest 726-730; Regent of Waes 730-. m (2) 731 Mevita. Father of Mistrin, Tessalar; Polev.
RIHANI of Ossetia (720-). Son of Tilal and Gemma. Squire at High Kirat 732-.
RINHOEL of Meadowlord (720-). Son of Chiana and Halian.
RISLYN of Princemarch (730-). Daughter of Pol and Meiglan.
RIYAN (699-). Lord of Skybowl 719-; Lord of Feruche 728-; Lord of Elktrap Manor 730-. Son of Camigwen and Ostvel. Squire at Swalekeep 711-713, 717-719; knighted 719. Goddess Keep 713-717. m728 Ruala. Father of Maara.
ROHAN (677-). Prince of the Desert 698-; High Prince 705-. Squire at Remagev 690; knighted 695. m698 Sioned. Father of Pol.
ROHANNON of Whitecliff (722-). Son of Maarken and Hollis. Squire at New Raetia/Zaldivar 735-.

RUSINA (708-). *Devri.* m727 Oclel. Mother of Andry's daughter Tobren; Surida.

SAUMER of Kierst-Isel (720-). Son of Latham and Hevatia. Squire at High Kirat 734-.
SEGELIN (702-). Lord of Gilad Seahold. m732 Paveol of River Ussh. Father of Edrelin.
SETHRIC of Grib (717-). Velden's nephew. Remagev 736-.
SIONED of River Run (677-). Goddess Keep 689-698. m698 Rohan. Princess of the Desert 698-; High Princess 705-.
SIONELL of Remagev (708-). m726 Tallain. Daughter of Walvis and Feylin. Mother of Antalya, Jahnev, Meig.

TALLAIN (700-). Lord of Tiglath 724-. m726 Sionell. Squire at Stronghold 713; knighted 721. Father of Antalya, Jahnev, Meig.
TESSALAR (723-). Daughter of Rialt. Fostered at New Raetia 737-.
THANYS (683-). Meiglan's servant.
TILAL of River Run (692-). Prince of Ossetia 724-. m719 Gemma. Squire at Stronghold 702; knighted 712. Father of Rihani, Sioneva, Sorin.
TIREL of Firon (730-). Son of Laric and Lisiel.
TOBIN of the Desert (671-). m690 Chaynal. Mother of Maarken, Jahni, Sorin, Andry.
TOBREN of Goddess Keep (725-). Andry's daughter by Rusina. Fostered at Whitecliff 737-.
TORIEN (697-). *Devri.* m722 Jolan. Chief Steward of Goddess Keep 723-.

ULWIS (711-). *Devri.* m735 Deniker.

VALEDA (700-). *Devri.* Mother of Andry's daughter Chayly.
VELDEN (683-). Prince of Grib 701-. Father of Elsen, Norian.
VOLOG (659-). Prince of Kierst 692-. Father of Latham, Birani, Alasen, Volnaya. Sioned's cousin.

WALVIS (685-). Lord of Remagev 714-. m706 Feylin. Squire at Stronghold 697; knighted 703. Father of Sionell, Jahnavi.

YARIN of Snowcoves (690-). m725 Vallaina. Father of Natham.

Genealogy

(as of 737)

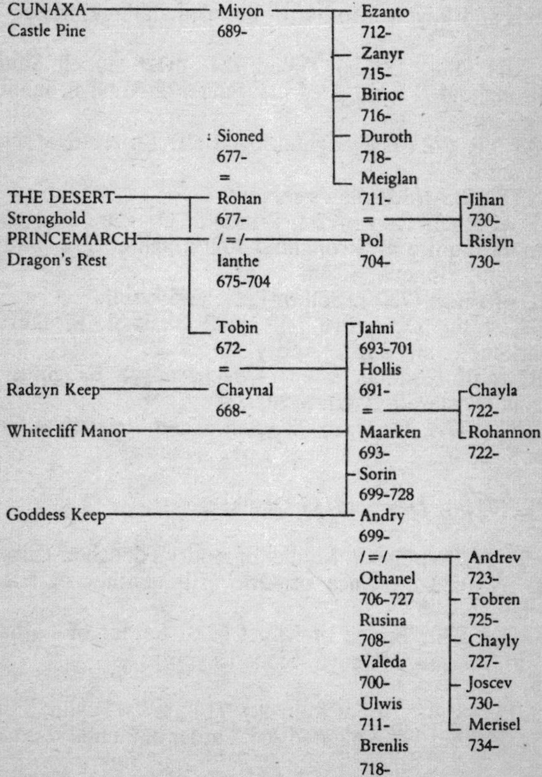

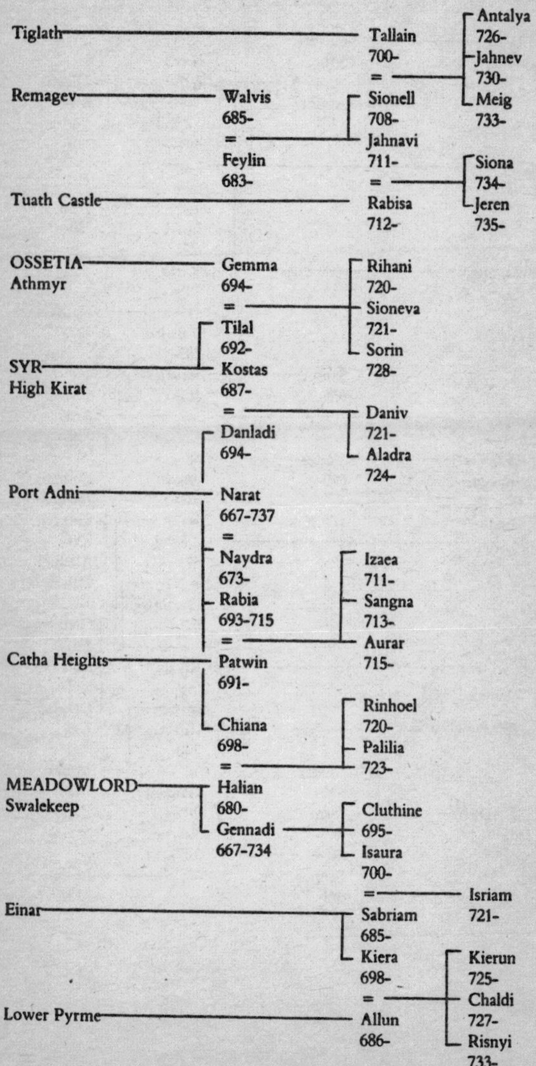

Tiglath
Tallain
700-
Antalya
726-
Jahnev
730-
Meig
733-
Remagev
Walvis
685-
Sionell
708-
Jahnavi
711-
Feylin
683-
Siona
734-
Jeren
735-
Tuath Castle
Rabisa
712-
OSSETIA
Athmyr
Gemma
694-
Rihani
720-
Sioneva
721-
Sorin
728-
Tilal
692-
SYR
High Kirat
Kostas
687-
Daniv
721-
Aladra
724-
Danladi
694-
Port Adni
Narat
667-737
Naydra
673-
Rabia
693-715
Izaea
711-
Sangna
713-
Aurar
715-
Catha Heights
Patwin
691-
Chiana
698-
Rinhoel
720-
Palilia
723-
MEADOWLORD
Swalekeep
Halian
680-
Gennadi
667-734
Cluthine
695-
Isaura
700-
Isriam
721-
Einar
Sabriam
685-
Kiera
698-
Kierun
725-
Chaldi
727-
Risnyi
733-
Lower Pyrme
Allun
686-

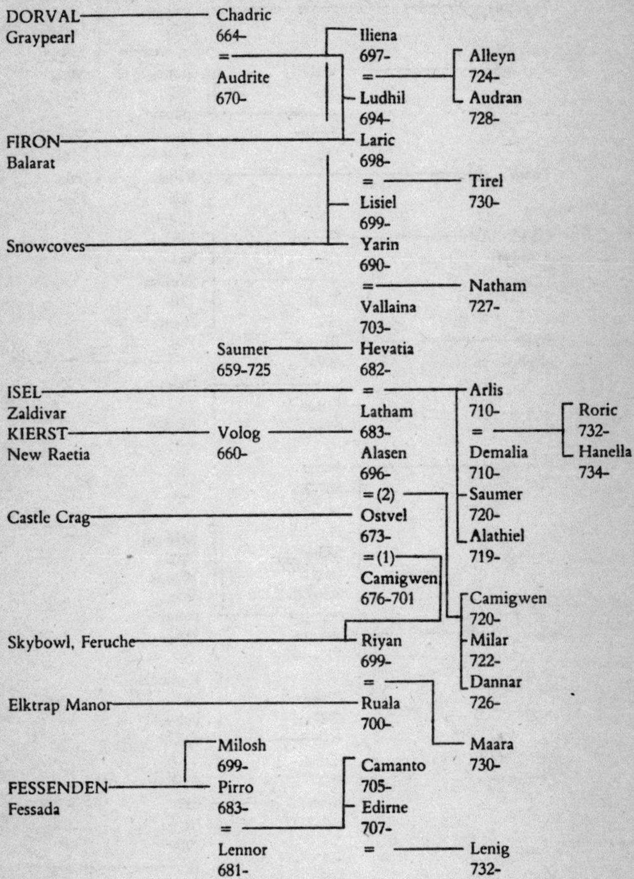
DORVAL
Graypearl
Chadric
664-
=
Audrite
670-
Iliena
697-
=
Ludhil
694-
Alleyn
724-
Audran
728-
FIRON
Balarat
Laric
698-
=
Lisiel
699-
Tirel
730-
Snowcoves
Yarin
690-
=
Vallaina
703-
Natham
727-
Saumer
659-725
Hevatia
682-
ISEL
Zaldivar
=
Latham
683-
Arlis
710-
=
Demalia
710-
Roric
732-
Hanella
734-
KIERST
New Raetia
Volog
660-
Alasen
696-
=(2)
Saumer
720-
Alathiel
719-
Castle Crag
Ostvel
673-
=(1)
Camigwen
676-701
Camigwen
720-
Milar
722-
Dannar
726-
Skybowl, Feruche
Riyan
699-
=
Elktrap Manor
Ruala
700-
Maara
730-
Milosh
699-
FESSENDEN
Fessada
Pirro
683-
=
Lennor
681-
Camanto
705-
Edirne
707-
=
Lenig
732-

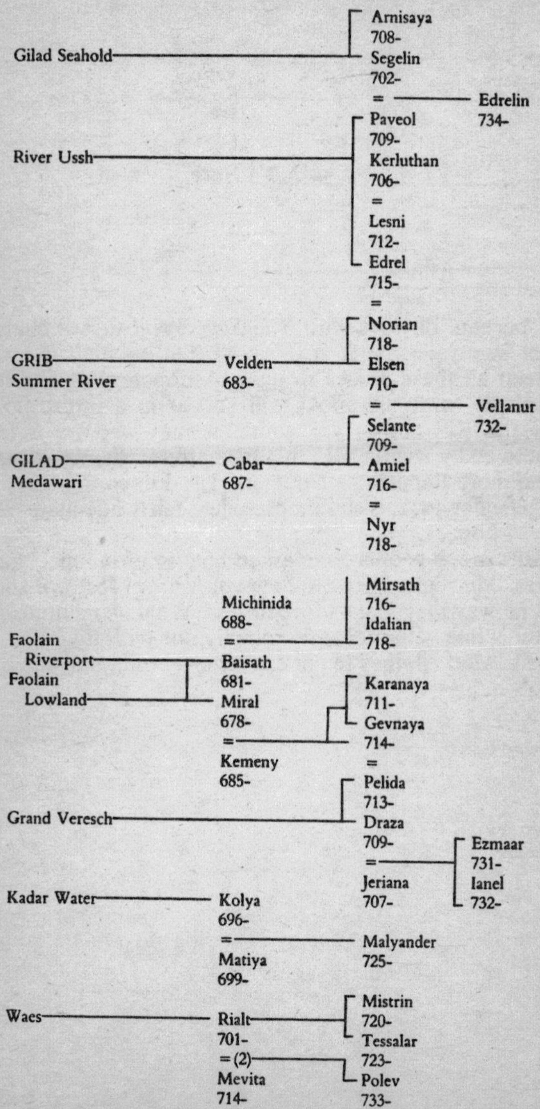
Gilad Seahold
Arnisaya
708-
Segelin
702-
=
Edrelin
734-
Paveol
709-
River Ussh
Kerluthan
706-
=
Lesni
712-
Edrel
715-
=
Norian
718-
GRIB
Summer River
Velden
683-
Elsen
710-
=
Vellanur
732-
Selante
709-
GILAD
Medawari
Cabar
687-
Amiel
716-
=
Nyr
718-
Mirsath
716-
Michinida
688-
Idalian
718-
Faolain
Riverport
=
Baisath
681-
Faolain
Lowland
Miral
678-
=
Kemeny
685-
Karanaya
711-
Gevnaya
714-
=
Pelida
713-
Grand Veresch
Draza
709-
=
Jeriana
707-
Ezmaar
731-
Ianel
732-
Kadar Water
Kolya
696-
=
Matiya
699-
Malyander
725-
Waes
Rialt
701-
= (2)
Mevita
714-
Mistrin
720-
Tessalar
723-
Polev
733-

Author's Note

It became obvious with *The Star Scroll* that a character index was necessary if anybody—including me—was going to keep all these names straight. A directory of absolutely everybody in all six books will appear in a future volume (and the way things are going, it may *become* a future volume all by itself!). But this time around the list is limited to the more important characters. Used in conjunction with the genealogies, this should provide a fairly adequate Who's Who. I hope.

Quite a few people have asked how to pronounce various names. My reply: Any-old-how you want. Most are spoken just the way they look. More or less. Whatever sounds good to you is fine with me, and probably fine with the characters as well. After all, they're not exactly in a position to complain.

SAVE THE DRAGONS!

The hunt is up, the enemy is on the move, but it's not too late for you to join High Prince Rohan in his desperate battle to save the dragons. So order your very own "Save the Dragons" T-shirt now (in dragon green, orange, and black on a white background) and rally to the cause.

Certain to become a classic, these T-shirts are available for a limited time only—so order today!

SAVE THE DRAGONS T-SHIRT

Penguin USA
C/O Tyme
250 Hudson Street • New York, NY 10014

Please send me _____ **STRONGHOLD** "Save the Dragons" T-shirt(s) at $6.95 ($10.95 in Canada) plus $1.50 per order to cover mailing costs. I enclose ☐ check, ☐ money order (no C.O.D.'s or cash; please make check payable to Penguin USA.)

Name___________________________________

Address_________________________________

City____________________________________

State_______________________Zip__________

large ☐ extra large ☐ (check one)

Please allow 4-6 weeks for delivery. Offer subject to withdrawal without notice—valid while supplies last.

DAW Books, Inc. BB 991